PENGUI
CLASSIC

Satyajit Ray was born on 2 May 1921 in Calcutta. After graduating from Presidency College, Calcutta, in 1940, he studied art at Rabindranath Tagore's university, Shantiniketan. By 1943, Ray was back in Calcutta and had joined an advertising firm as a visualizer. He also started designing covers and illustrating books brought out by Signet Press. A deep interest in films led to his establishing the Calcutta Film Society in 1947. During a six-month trip to Europe, in 1950, Ray became a member of the London Film Club and managed to see ninety-nine films in only four-and-a-half months.

In 1955, after overcoming innumerable difficulties, Satyajit Ray completed his first film, *Pather Panchali*, with financial assistance from the West Bengal government. The film was an award-winner at the Cannes Film Festival and established Ray as a director of international stature. Together with *Aparajito* (The Unvanquished, 1956) and *Apur Sansar* (The World of Apu, 1959), it forms the Apu trilogy and perhaps constitutes Ray's finest work. Ray's other films include *Jalsaghar* (The Music Room, 1958), *Charulata* (1964), *Aranyer Din Ratri* (Days and Nights in the Forest, 1970), *Shatranj Ke Khilari* (The Chess Players, 1977), *Ghare Baire* (The Home and the World, 1984), *Ganashatru* (Enemy of the People, 1989), *Shakha Proshakha* (Branches of a Tree, 1990), and *Agantuk* (The Stranger, 1991). Ray also made several documentaries, including one on Tagore. In 1987, he made the documentary *Sukumar Ray*, to commemorate the birth centenary of his father, perhaps Bengal's most famous writer of nonsense verse and children's books. Satyajit Ray won numerous awards for his films. Both the British Federation of Film Societies and the Moscow Film Festival Committee named him one of the greatest directors of the second half of the twentieth century. In 1992, he was awarded the Oscar for Lifetime Achievement by the Academy of Motion Picture Arts and Science and, in the same year, was also honoured with the Bharat Ratna.

Apart from being a film-maker, Satyajit Ray was a writer of repute. In 1961, he revived the children's magazine, *Sandesh*, which his grandfather, Upendrakishore Ray, had started and to which his father used to contribute frequently. Satyajit Ray contributed numerous poems, stories and essays to *Sandesh*, and also published several books in Bengali, most of which became best-sellers. In 1978, Oxford University awarded him its D.Litt degree.

Satyajit Ray died in Calcutta in April 1992.

Gopa Majumdar has translated several works from Bengali to English, the most notable of these being Ashapurna Debi's *Subarnalata*, Taslima Nasrin's *My Girlhood*, and Bibhutibhushan Bandyopadhyay's *Aparajito*, for which she won the Sahitya Akademi Award in 2001. She has translated several volumes of Satyajit Ray's short stories, a number of Professor Shonku stories and all of the Feluda stories for Penguin Books India. She is currently translating Ray's cinematic writings for Penguin.

SATYAJIT RAY
CLASSIC FELUDA 2

TRANSLATED FROM THE BENGALI BY
GOPA MAJUMDAR

PENGUIN BOOKS

PENGUIN BOOKS
Published by the Penguin Group
Penguin Books India Pvt. Ltd, 11 Community Centre, Panchsheel Park, New Delhi 110 017, India
Penguin Group (USA) Inc., 375 Hudson Street, New York, New York 10014, USA
Penguin Group (Canada), 90 Eglinton Avenue East, Suite 700, Toronto, Ontario, M4P 2Y3, Canada (a division of Pearson Penguin Canada Inc.)
Penguin Books Ltd, 80 Strand, London WC2R 0RL, England
Penguin Ireland, 25 St Stephen's Green, Dublin 2, Ireland (a division of Penguin Books Ltd)
Penguin Group (Australia), 707 Collins Street, Melbourne, Victoria 3008, Australia (a division of Pearson Australia Group Pty Ltd)
Penguin Group (NZ), 67 Apollo Drive, Rosedale, Auckland 0632, New Zealand (a division of Pearson New Zealand Ltd)
Penguin Group (South Africa) (Pty) Ltd, Block D, Rosebank Office Park, 181 Jan Smuts Avenue, Parktown North, Johannesburg 2193, South Africa

Penguin Books Ltd, Registered Offices: 80 Strand, London WC2R 0RL, England

First published by Penguin Books India 2000
This edition published 2013

10 9 8 7 6 5 4 3 2 1

ISBN 9780143420354

Typeset in Sabon by Mantra Virtual Services, New Delhi
Printed at Replika Press Pvt. Ltd, India

CONTENTS

AUTHOR'S NOTE

I have been an avid reader of crime fiction for a very long time. I read all the Sherlock Holmes stories while still at school. When I revived the children's magazine *Sandesh* which my grandfather launched seventy-five years ago, I started writing stories for it. The first Feluda story—a long-short—appeared in 1965. Felu is the nickname of Pradosh Mitter, private investigator. The story was told in the first person by Felu's Waston—his fourteen-year-old cousin Tapesh. The suffix 'da' (short for 'dada') means an elder brother.

Although the Feluda stories were written for the largely teenaged readers of *Sandesh,* I found they were being read by their parents as well. Soon longer stories followed—novelettes—taking place in a variety of picturesque settings. A third character was introduced early on: Lalmohan Ganguli, writer of cheap, popular thrillers. He serves as a foil to Felu and provides dollops of humour.

When I wrote my first Feluda story, I scarcely imagined he would prove so popular that I would be forced to write a Feluda novel every year. To write a whodunit while keeping in mind a young readership is not an easy task, because the stories have to be kept 'clean'. No illicit love, no *crime passionel,* and only a modicum of violence. I hope adult readers will bear this in mind when reading these stories.

Calcutta
February 1988

Satyajit Ray

FOREWORD

My husband was always deeply interested in science fiction stories. It was not surprising, therefore, when he decided to write them for his children's magazine *Sandesh*.

One day, he told me that he wanted to experiment with stories other than the science fiction ones.

'What other kind?' I asked, although I knew the answer instinctively, since both of us were avid readers of detective stories. He didn't have to tell me, so he smiled and said ruefully, 'But there's a big snag . . .' I looked inquiringly at him. 'The magazine is meant for children and adolescents, which means I shall have to avoid sex and violence—the backbone of crime thrillers . . . you do realize the difficulty, don't you?'

I did, indeed. Still, I told him to go ahead and give it a try—I had so much faith in him!

He did. And that's how 'Feluda' was born and became an instant hit. Story after story came out, and they all met with resounding success. When they were published in book form, they became best-sellers. It was really amazing!

After finishing each story, he would throw up his hands and say, 'I have run out of plots. How can one possibly go on writing detective stories without even a hint of sex and hardly any violence to speak of?'

I couldn't agree with him more, but at the same time, I knew he would never give up and was bound to succeed at his endeavour. That is exactly what he did. He never stopped and went on writing till the end of his days. That was my husband, Satyajit Ray, who surmounted all difficulties and came out on top!

Calcutta
October 1995

Bijoya Ray

INTRODUCTION

One of my earliest recollections of childhood is of struggling to get two thick bound volumes from my father's bookshelf, with a view to using them as walls for my dolls' house. To my complete bewilderment, when my father saw what I had done, he told me to put them back instantly. Why? They were only books, after all. 'No,' he explained, handling the two volumes with the same tenderness that he normally reserved for me, 'these are not just books. They are bound issues of *Sandesh*, a magazine we used to read as children. You don't get it any more.' Neither of us knew then that *Sandesh* would reappear only a few years later, revived and brought to life by none other than Satyajit Ray, the grandson of its original founder, Upendrakishore.

That Satyajit Ray was a film-maker was something I, and many other children of my generation, came to know only when we were older. At least, we had heard he made films which seemed to throw all the grown-ups into raptures, but to us he was simply the man who had opened a door to endless fun and joy, in the pages of a magazine that was exclusively for us. This was in 1961.

In 1965, *Sandesh* began to publish a new story (*Danger in Darjeeling*) about two cousins on holiday in Darjeeling. The older one of these was Feluda, whose real name was Pradosh C. Mitter. The younger one, who narrated the story, was called Tapesh; but Feluda affectionately called him Topshe. They happened to meet an amiable old gentleman called Rajen Babu who had started to receive mysterious threats. Feluda, who had read a great many crime stories and was a very clever man (Topshe told us), soon discovered who the culprit was.

It was a relatively short and simple tale, serialized in three or four instalments. Yet, it created such a stir among the young readers of *Sandesh* that the creator of Feluda felt obliged to produce another story with the same characters, this time set in Lucknow (*The Emperor's Ring*), in 1966. Feluda's character took a more definite shape in this story. Not only was he a man with acute powers of observation and a razor-sharp brain, we learnt, but he also possessed a deep and thorough knowledge of virtually every subject under the sun, ranging from history to hypnotism. He was good at cricket, knew at least a hundred indoor games, a number of card tricks, and could write with both hands. The entries he made into his personal notebook were in Greek.

After *The Emperor's Ring*, there was no looking back: Feluda simply went from strength to strength. Over the next three years, *Kailash Chowdhury's Jewel* and *The Anubis Mystery*, the first two Feluda stories set in Calcutta, appeared, followed by another travel adventure, *Trouble in Gangtok*. Over the next two decades, Ray would write at least one Feluda story every year. Between 1965 and 1992, thirty-four Feluda stories appeared. *The Magical Mystery*, the last in the series, was published posthumously in 1995-96.

In 1970, Feluda made his first appearance in the *Desh* magazine, which was unquestionably a magazine for adults. This surprised many, but it was really evidence of Feluda's popularity amongst young and old alike. Between 1970 and 1992, nineteen Feluda stories appeared in the annual Puja issue of *Desh* (the others were published in *Sandesh*, except for one which appeared in *Anandamela*, another children's magazine). Pouncing upon the copy of *Desh* as soon as it arrived, after having artfully fended off every other taker in the house, became as much a part of the Puja festivities as wearing new clothes or going to the temple.

A year later, Ray introduced a new character. Lalmohan Ganguli (alias Jatayu), a writer of cheap popular thrillers, who made his debut in *The Golden Fortress*. Simple, gullible, friendly and either ignorant of or mistaken about most things in life, he proved to be a perfect foil to Feluda, and a means of providing what Ray called 'dollops of humour'. The following year (1972) readers were presented with *A Mysterious Case*, where Jatayu made an encore appearance. After this, he remained with the two cousins throughout, becoming very soon an important member of the team and winning the affection of millions. It is, in fact, impossible now to think of Feluda without thinking of Jatayu. Interestingly, the two films Ray made based on Feluda stories *(The Golden Fortress* in 1974, and *The Elephant God* in 1978) both featured Lalmohan Babu, as did the television film *Kissa Kathmandu Ka* (based on *The Criminals of Kathmandu*) made by Sandip Ray a few years later.

Ray had often spoken of his interest in crime fiction. He had read all the Sherlock Holmes stories before leaving school. It was therefore no surprise that he should start writing crime stories himself. But why did the arrival of Feluda make such a tremendous impact on his readers? After all, it wasn't as though there had never been other detectives in children's fiction in Bengal. The reason was, in fact, a simple one. In spite of all his accomplishments, Feluda did not emerge as a larger-than-life superman whom one would venerate and admire from afar, but never get close to. On the contrary, Topshe's charming narration described him as so utterly normal and human that it was not difficult at all to see him almost as a member of one's own family. A genius he might well be, but his behaviour was exactly what one might expect from an older cousin. He teased Topshe endlessly and bullied him often, but his love and concern for his young Watson was never in doubt. Every child who read *Sandesh* could see himself—or, for that matter, herself—in Topshe. Herein lay Ray's greatest strength. Feluda came, saw and conquered chiefly because each case was seen and presented through the eyes of an adolescent. Ray's language was simple, lucid, warm and direct, without ever becoming boring or patronizing, even when Feluda corrected a mistake Topshe made, or gave him new information. Added to this were his graphic descriptions of the various places Feluda and Topshe visited. Sometimes it was difficult to tell whether one was watching a film or reading a book, so well were all relevant details captured in just a few succinct words, regardless of whether the action was taking place in a small village in Bengal, a monastery in Sikkim, or the streets of Hong Kong.

It would be wrong to think, however, that it was smooth sailing at all times. Feluda and his team, like most celebrities, had to pay the price of fame. It was their popularity among adults that began to cause problems. Naturally, the expectations of adults were different. They wanted 'spice' in the stories and would probably not have objected to subjects such as illicit love or *crime passionnel*. Feluda's creator, on the other hand, could never allow himself to forget that he wrote primarily for children and, as such, was obliged to keep the stories 'clean'. Clearly, letters from critical or disappointed readers became such a sore point that Feluda spoke openly about it in *The Mystery of Nayan*, the last novel published during Ray's lifetime. 'Don't forget Topshe writes my stories mainly for adolescents,' Feluda says in the opening chapter. 'The problem is that these stories are read by the children's parents, uncles, aunts and everyone else. Each reader at every level has his own peculiar demand. How on earth is he to satisfy each one of them?'

The readers were suitably chastened. And Feluda's popularity rose even higher. In 1990, when he turned twenty-five, an ardent admirer in Delhi went to the extent of designing a special card to mark the occasion. Ray is said to have been both amazed and greatly amused by the display of such deep devotion.

By this time, Feluda had already stepped out of Bengal. In 1988, the first collection of Feluda stories appeared in English translation (*The Adventures of Feluda*, translated by Chitrita Banerji). This was followed by my translations of the remaining Feluda stories, which appeared in *The Emperor's Ring: The Further Adventures of Feluda* (1993), *The Mystery of the Elephant God: More Adventures of Feluda* (1994), *Feluda's Last Case and Other Stories* (1995), *The House of Death and Other Feluda Stories* (1997), *The Royal Bengal Mystery and Other Feluda Stories* (1997) and *The Mystery of the Pink Pearl: The Final Feluda Stories* (1998). *The Magical Mystery* was published in Indigo, a collection of Ray's short stories, in 2000.

Initially, Ray was hesitant to allow the Feluda stories to be translated as he was unsure about the response of non-Bengali readers. However, the two films he had made as well as the television series made by his son had evoked an interest from other communities. When he did finally give his consent, it was only to discover that he need not have worried at all. The Three Musketeers, comprising Pradosh C. Mitter, Private Investigator, and his two assistants, were received with as much enthusiasm elsewhere in India as they had been in Bengal.

Translating the Feluda stories has been a deeply fulfilling experience for me. Those who have read the originals will, no doubt, notice the changes I have had to make in order to present the stories before a wider readership, but I hope they will agree that these have not affected the main plot in any way.

This definitive edition contains, in two volumes, all the Feluda stories that Ray completed. Included are new translations (by me) of *The Golden Fortress, The Bandits of Bombay, The Secret of the Cemetery* and *The Mysterious Tenant*. For the first time, they are arranged in chronological order, and one can note Feluda's development from a totally unknown amateur detective to a famous professional private investigator. Those who have read them before may be pleased to find them all together in an omnibus edition. To those who haven't, one hopes it will give an excellent opportunity to get acquainted with a legend in Bengal, and catch a glimpse of the brilliant mind of its creator.

London *Gopa Majumdar*
May 2004

CHRONOLOGY OF THE FELUDA STORIES

No	Name of story	Bengali title	Published	Written in
1	Danger in Darjeeling	Feludar Goendagiri	Sandesh	1965-66
2	The Emperor's Ring	Badshahi Aangti	Sandesh	1966-67
3	Kailash Chowdhury's Jewel	Kailash Chowdhury'r Pathar	Sandesh	1967
4	The Anubis Mystery	Sheyal-Debota Rahasya	Sandesh	1970
5	Trouble in Gangtok	Gangtokey Gandogol	Desh	1970
6	The Golden Fortress	Sonar Kella	Desh	1971
7	Incident on the Kalka Mail	Baksho Rahasya	Desh	1972
8	A Killer in Kailash	Kailashey Kelenkari	Desh	1973
9	The Key	Samaddarer Chabi	Sandesh	1973
10	The Royal Bengal Mystery	Royal Bengal Rahasya	Desh	1974
11	The Locked Chest	Ghurghutiyar Ghatona	Sandesh	1975
12	The Mystery of the Elephant God	Joy Baba Felunath	Desh	1975
13	The Bandits of Bombay	Bombaiyer Bombetey	Desh	1976
14	The Mystery of the Walking Dead	Gosaipur Sargaram	Sandesh	1976
15	The Secret of the Cemetery	Gorosthaney Sabdhan	Desh	1977
16	The Curse of the Goddess	Chhinnamastar Abhishaap	Desh	1978
17	The House of Death	Hatyapuri	Sandesh	1979
18	The Mysterious Tenant	Golokdham Rahasya	Sandesh	1980
19	The Criminals of Kathmandu	Joto Kando Kathmandutey	Desh	1980

No	Name of story	Bengali title	Published	Written in
20	Napoleon's Letter	Napoleoner Chitthi	Sandesh	1981
21	Tintoretto's Jesus	Tintorettor Jishu	Desh	1982
22	The Disappearance of Ambar Sen	Ambar Sen Antardhan Rahasya	Anandamela	1983
23	The Gold Coins of Jehangir	Jahangirer Swarnamudra	Sandesh	1983
24	Crime in Kedarnath	Ebar Kando Kedarnathey	Desh	1984
25	The Acharya Murder Case	Bospukurey Khunkharapi	Sandesh	1985
26	Murder in the Mountains	Darjeeling Jamjamat	Sandesh	1986
27	The Magical Mystery	Indrajal Rahasya	Sandesh, 1995-96	1987
28	The Case of the Apsara Theatre	Apsara Theatre'r Mamla	Sandesh	1987
29	Peril in Paradise	Bhuswargya Bhayankar	Desh	1987
30	Shakuntala's Necklace	Shakuntalar Kontthohar	Desh	1988
31	Feluda in London	Londoney Feluda	Desh	1989
32	The Mystery of the Pink Pearl	Golapi Mukta Rahasya	Sandesh	1989
33	Dr Munshi's Diary	Dr Munshir Diary	Sandesh	1990
34	The Mystery of Nayan	Nayan Rahasya	Desh	1990
35	Robertson's Ruby	Robertsoner Ruby	Desh, 1992	1990

The House of Death

DUNGRU'S STORY

Dungru laid his instrument on the grass that was still wet with the morning dew, and began singing. He had a pretty good voice. The song he was now singing was one he had heard only once before. Yet, he had picked it up, almost without making an effort. It was a song a beggar usually sang just outside Hanuman Phatak. But he played an instrument, too. Shyam Gurung, the local greengrocer, had an instrument like that. Dungru had borrowed it for the day, but had already realized playing it wasn't half as easy as singing. Who knew running a bow over a few strings could be so difficult?

Dungru's voice rose. There was a maize field in front of him, in which a couple of buffaloes and three goats were roaming freely. There was no one else in sight. Behind him was a very steep hill. Just under it, not far from the mound on which he sat, stood an almond tree. The little house in the distance with a tiled roof was where he lived. His father owned this maize field. There were other hills and several mountain peaks dimly visible through the morning mist. One of these, called 'Machhipuchh' because it was shaped like a fish tail, had started to turn pink.

Dungru began the second line of the song, but had to break off abruptly. A strange rumble in the hill behind him made him spring to his feet and jump to one side. In the next instant, a large boulder rolled down the hill and went past him, crushing his instrument and missing him by inches.

Dungru could hardly believe his luck. But before his heartbeat could get back to normal, something else happened: something much more unexpected and far worse than a rolling boulder. But, like the boulder, it came crashing down the hill, struck against the almond tree and fell to the ground, together with several broken branches. What on earth was that? He gaped, his mouth hanging open. Good heavens, it was a man! Not just any man, but a well-dressed babu, probably from a big city. There was blood on his head, his face and chin. One of his legs was folded under him at a very odd angle. Was he dead? No. Dungru saw him move his head.

Then he remembered the others. There was a group of men camping out near the spring across the main road. Dungru had often stared in amazement at the colour of their hair and their beards. No one that he knew in his own village had hair like that. And certainly no one had a beard. But if anyone could help this man, it had to be those men. They knew Dungru. They had bought maize from him and given him money, almost every day.

Dungru began running.

'Hi, Joe, come here quickly!' shouted one of them on seeing Dungru.

'Why, what's up?'

Dungru stood panting. He couldn't speak their language. In fact, he was too breathless to speak at all. So he just rolled his eyes and stuck his tongue out. Then he pointed at the hill. The man caught on immediately.

'OK. Jeep. Go . . . Jeep!'

Their jeep had all the colours of a rainbow. Dungru had never seen a vehicle like that. He jumped into it. Joe, Mark, Dennis and Bruce joined him.

'Jesus Christ!' one of them exclaimed softly when Dungru took them to the exact spot where the injured man still lay on the ground. All of them bent over him. Mark, who had left studying medicine in Minnesota, checked his pulse. Then they picked him up and placed him carefully in the jeep.

The nearest hospital was in Kathmandu, thirty-three kilometres from here.

ONE

There was something special about Feluda's palm. The line called 'headline' that's supposed to indicate one's intelligence, was exceptionally long and clear. Feluda did not believe in palmistry, but had read up on the subject. Lalmohan Babu, who believed in it wholeheartedly, had once asked Feluda to show him his palm. Feluda had obliged with a grin, but Lalmohan Babu had failed to share his amusement. He had inspected the headline, then said, 'Amazing, amazing!' After this, he had opened his own palm, looked at it and sighed deeply. I had had to try very hard not to laugh.

One of my uncles could read palms. I had heard him make reasonably accurate statements about one's past and make predictions for the future that often turned out to be true. Some people, I was told, could look at a person's face and tell him about his future, But I didn't know it was possible to place one's little finger in the middle of a person's forehead and reveal what the future had in store for him. I saw this being done only when we visited Puri.

Incessant power shedding and a temperature of 110°F had driven us out of Calcutta. The power crisis had got so bad that Lalmohan Babu's latest novel could not be printed in April. He was most annoyed at this, particularly as it was his first crime thriller with a touch of the supernatural. As a matter of fact, it was Feluda who had given him the idea. 'Ghosts and spooks go very well with flickering candlelight.' Lalmohan Babu had taken this seriously and written *Frankenstein in Frankfurt*. When he learnt it could not be published as scheduled, he came straight to our house and said, 'We cannot go on living in this city. Besides, you've heard of the skylab, haven't you?'

There was really no reason to assume the skylab would come crashing down on Calcutta, but Lalmohan Babu kept saying that a large portion of it might, since the entire city of Calcutta appeared to have caught the 'evil eye'.

Feluda is normally extremely adaptable. I have seen him remain perfectly unperturbed even under the most trying circumstances. If he had to spend a whole night at a railway station and the waiting room happened to be full, he'd quite happily stretch out on the platform. But there was one thing he couldn't do without: reading in bed for a few hours before going to sleep. Weeks and weeks of power cuts had deprived him of this one luxury he allowed himself to indulge in. This had made him rather cross. He had tried practising card tricks, written limericks, and tried many other things to amuse himself. Long periods of darkness, I had hoped, would result in more crime. But sadly, no interesting cases had come his way. He was, in short, utterly bored.

This was perhaps the reason why he appeared to agree with Lalmohan Babu and said, 'Really, the City of Joy has been causing us a lot of grief, hasn't it? I can put up with the physical discomfort, but constant disturbances at work, having to give up reading at night, not even being able to think because of mosquitoes . . . these are very difficult to live with.'

'Orissa, I hear, has got excess power,' Lalmohan Babu observed.

This led to a discussion about Orissa, Puri, the sea beach in Puri and the hotel called Neelachal that had recently opened there, and was owned by Lalmohan Babu's landlord's classmate.

Unfortunately, it turned out that we couldn't get reservations before mid-June. 'Never mind, we'll go in June,' said Feluda.

Eventually, we left on 21 June by the Puri Express. It was decided that Lalmohan Babu's driver would take his car and get to Puri by road a day later. We might have gone by car ourselves, but Lalmohan Babu had a sudden attack of nerves at the last minute and said, 'Suppose there's a storm or something on the way? Suppose we get stranded?'

But he agreed having our own car was a good idea, since we intended visiting a few other places. Hence the two different travel arrangements.

Our journey was uneventful, except for the fourth passenger in our four-berth compartment. He was the only exciting thing that happened. First we saw him fit a cigarette into a holder that seemed to be made of gold. Then he took out a gold-plated lighter ('At least three thousand rupees,' Feluda whispered) to light it. His cigarette case was also golden, as were his cuff links, the frames of his glasses and the three rings he wore. While climbing down from the upper berth, one of his feet accidentally brushed against Lalmohan Babu's shoulder. He gave an embarrassed smile at this and said, 'Sorry.' One of his teeth, we all noted, flashed as he opened his mouth. When he got off at Puri with us and disappeared with a coolie and his luggage, Lalmohan Babu sighed.

'We didn't even get to know the man's name. Have you ever seen so much gold on a man, Tapesh?' he asked.

'There was a very easy way to find out his name, Lalmohan Babu,' Feluda replied. 'Didn't you see the reservation list at Howrah? That man is called M.L. Hingorani.'

TWO

'This is a six-star hotel,' Lalmohan Babu declared, nodding with approval after checking in at Neelachal.

'No hotel can claim to be five-star unless it has a swimming pool; and five-star is the maximum rating a hotel can get. Can you spot a swimming pool anywhere, Lalmohan Babu? Or are you counting the sea as this hotel's very own, private pool? If so, your rating is fully justified.'

We went in to have lunch, after which Lalmohan Babu continued the argument with fresh vigour. 'What lovely food, Felu Babu! Their cook is absolutely brilliant. I had no idea koftas made of green banana could be so delicious. Besides, see how clean everything is, such beautiful carpets and furnishings, and a totally uninterrupted power supply, not to mention the sea breeze . . . why shouldn't I call it a six-star hotel?'

Feluda laughed in agreement. What might happen to the hotel in a few years was impossible to tell, but right now it was certainly in very good condition. Feluda and I were sharing a double room. Lalmohan Babu had the next room, which he was sharing with a businessman from Calcutta. We had briefly met Shyamlal Barik, the manager. He had promised to come and have a chat with us in the evening.

The hotel was really very close to the sea. The sandy beach was only a minute's walk from the main gate. The last time I visited Puri, I was only five years old. Feluda had come here many times, but, to our surprise, we learnt that this was Lalmohan Babu's first visit.

'What's there to be so surprised about?' he asked, a little annoyed. There are so many things in Calcutta I haven't yet seen. Would you believe it, there's that famous Jain temple only three miles from my house, but I have never been there!' Now, standing before the sea, he suddenly remembered a poem written by his favourite poet, Baikuntha Mallik. 'When I was twelve,' he told me, 'I recited this poem in a competition and won a prize. Listen to it carefully, Tapesh, and note how beautiful even modern free verse can be:

In these roaring waves,
I hear the call of infinity;
when on these sandy beaches,
stand I, so eagerly,
on one leg.'

'One leg? Why one leg?' Feluda sounded puzzled. 'Was the poet identifying himself with a crane? That must be it, for it would be quite difficult for a man to stand on one leg on the sand, hour after hour, in this strong wind. But never mind your poet. Look at the sand over there. See those prints? Do you think that might have any significance?'

The footprints had come from the east, and made their way to the western side. A smaller mark by the side of these indicated a stick. Lalmohan Babu stared at these for a few seconds and said, 'Well, shoes and perhaps a walking stick . . . that much is clear, but what special significance could it have?'

'Topshe, what do you think?'

'Usually, people hold a stick in their right hand. These marks are on the left.'

Feluda thumped my shoulder. 'Good! The man is probably left-handed.'

There weren't many people about. Three small Nulia children were busy collecting crabs and seashells. There were other hotels a little way ahead, where no doubt we'd find many more visitors. Just as we began walking in that direction, someone called, 'Mr Ganguli!'

We turned to find it was Mr Srinivas Som, Lalmohan Babu's plump and cheerful roommate. We had already met him. He owned a saree shop in Calcutta.

'Aren't you coming?' he asked Lalmohan Babu. 'He said to be there by six o'clock sharp.'

Lalmohan Babu gave Feluda a sidelong glance. 'I didn't tell you, Felu Babu,' he said hesitantly, 'because I thought you might not be interested.'

'Didn't tell me what?'

'Er . . . Mr Som told me about a man who lives here. He has an extraordinary power. He can place a finger on the forehead and talk about one's future.'

'Whose forehead?'

'The person who goes to him, naturally.'

'You mean he can actually read what's written in one's destiny?'

'Yes, supposedly.'

'Very well. I have no wish to have my future read, but let's all go and see where he lives.'

Mr Som led the way. We followed him, walking towards the east, past a colony of Nulias and groups of visitors, and up a sandy slope. Then we saw an abandoned house, partially submerged in the sand. Mr Som walked past it, but stopped before another house only a few yards away. This house had three storeys and was obviously in a far better condition. The astrologer, it turned out, occupied two rooms on the ground floor. There was a big gate. On one side was written, 'Sagarika'. A marble slab on the other side said, 'D.G. Sen'. It was an old-fashioned house, but whoever had had it built had good taste. There was a garden, a portion of which was visible from the gate.

'The owner lives on the second floor,' said Mr Som. 'Ah, here we are . . . this is Laxman Bhattacharya's room.'

There were nearly a dozen people waiting outside on the veranda. No doubt they were all Mr Bhattacharya's clients. Lalmohan Babu said, 'Jai Guru!' and walked in with Mr Som. We came away.

'What did your forehead reveal?' asked Feluda about an hour later, as Lalmohan Babu swept into our room in great excitement.

'Incredible, extraordinary, absolutely uncanny!' Lalmohan Babu replied. 'He told me everything about my past—whooping cough at the age of seven, an accident when I was eighteen, which left me with a dislocated kneecap, then the publication of my first novel, my spectacular popularity, and he even told my how many editions my next book will have.'

'And the skylab? Did he tell you whether or not it's going to fall on your head?'

'You can joke all you like, Felu Babu, but I think you ought to visit him. In fact, I insist that you do. He seemed to know about you. He said I was very lucky to have a good friend, and even gave your description!'

'What about my profession? Did he say anything about that?'

'He said my friend was very hard-working, and intelligent, with a great interest in many subjects, and had remarkable powers of observation. Is that close enough for you?'

'May I come in?' said a voice at the door.

We turned to find the manager, Shyamlal Barik, waiting to come in with a small box of paan in his hand. Feluda invited him in, and he opened his box at once. Our room was filled with the sweet smell of paan-masala. 'Have one,' he offered. Then, looking at our faces, he laughed. 'Don't worry, there's no tobacco in any of these,' he assured us. We helped ourselves. Feluda lit a Charminar.

'Tell me, Mr Barik, what is D.G. Sen's full name?' he asked.

'I've only just been to his house, and it never occurred to me to ask!' exclaimed Lalmohan Babu.

Shyamlal Barik smiled. 'The truth is, Mr Mitter, that I don't know his full name. I doubt if anyone does. Everyone calls him D.G. Sen. Some even call him DG Babu.'

'Doesn't he go out much?'

'He used to. Last year, he went to Bhutan or Sikkim or some such place. He returned about six months ago. We've hardly ever seen him since he came back.'

'Do you know why he suddenly turned into a recluse?'

Shyamlal Barik shook his head. 'Did he build that house?' Feluda went on.

'No. It was built by his father. You may have heard of him. Do you know about Sen Perfumers?'

'Yes, yes. But they've gone out of business, haven't they? S.N. Sen's Sensational Essences. Is that what you mean?'

'Yes. DG is S.N. Sen's son. Their business was doing very well. They had three houses in Calcutta, one here in Puri. and one in Madhupur. But, sadly, no one took any interest in the business when S.N. Sen died. He had two sons. DG is the younger of the two, I think. S.N. Sen had left a will, dividing all his property between his sons. DG got this house. He may have had a job at one time—I don't think he ever bothered about the family business—but now he's retired and his sole interest is art.'

'Art?' Feluda suddenly seemed to recall something. 'Is he the one who has a collection of ancient manuscripts and scrolls?'

My Uncle Sidhu had a few scrolls. Some of them were more than three hundred years old. Scrolls and manuscripts written before the advent of the printing press were called *puthi*. Feluda had once explained this to me. A long time ago, people used to write on the bark of a tree. Then they began to write on palm leaves and, finally, on paper. Uncle Sidhu had often lamented the fact that people had forgotten these manuscripts were an important part of our art and cultural heritage.

Shyamlal Barik nodded. 'Yes, those old manuscripts are his only passion in life. Many people come—even from abroad—to take a look at his collection.'

'Doesn't he have any children?'

'A son and daughter-in-law used to visit him occasionally, but I haven't seen them for ages. D.G. Sen himself came to live here only three years ago. He's a widower. He lives on the top floor. The ground floor has been rented out to an astrologer; and the rooms on the first floor are let out to tourists during the tourist season. At the moment, a retired judge and his wife are staying there.'

'I see.' Feluda stubbed out his cigarette.

'Would you like to meet him?' Mr Barik asked. 'He's a peculiar man, doesn't normally agree to meet outsiders. But if you have an interest in manuscripts . . .'

'I do,' Feluda interrupted him, 'but if I simply say I have an interest, that won't do, will it? I must do my homework before I meet someone who has a profound knowledge of old manuscripts.'

'That's no problem,' Mr Barik assured us. 'I'll take you to Satish Kanungo's house. It's just five minutes from here. He's a retired professor. There's probably no subject on earth he doesn't know about. You can have a chat with him, and do your homework.'

THREE

The next morning, by the time I got up, Feluda had already called Professor Kanungo and gone over to his house. This surprised me, since I had no idea he was in such a hurry to meet the professor. My plans were different. I had wanted to spend the morning bathing in the sea. Feluda might have accompanied me. I asked Lalmohan Babu, but he said, 'Look Tapesh, at your age, I used to swim a lot. My butterfly-stroke often earned me applause from onlookers. But a small Calcutta swimming pool is not the same thing as the Bay of Bengal, surely you can see that? Besides, the sea in Puri is extremely treacherous. Had it been the sea in Bombay, I wouldn't have hesitated.'

He was right. It had rained the night before and was still cloudy and kind of oppressive. So we decided to wait until Feluda got back. 'Let's go and have a walk on the beach,' Lalmohan Babu suggested. I agreed, and we left soon after a breakfast of toast and eggs. Lalmohan Babu seemed to be in a very good mood, possibly as a result of what Laxman Bhattacharya had told him.

The beach was totally empty. A few boats were out in the sea, but there was no sign of the Nulia children. A couple of crows were flying about, going near the water as the waves receded, then flitting quickly away as they came surging back again.

We walked on. A few minutes later, Lalmohan Babu stopped suddenly. 'I have heard of people sunbathing on a beach,' he observed, 'but do they also cloud-bathe?' I could see what he meant. A man was lying on his back about fifty yards away, at a spot where the beach ended and a slope began. There was a bush on one side. Had the man chosen to lie down a little to the left, he would have been hidden from sight.

'Seems a bit odd, doesn't it?' Lalmohan Babu whispered. I said nothing, but went forward to have closer look. Why was the man lying here? It certainly did not seem right.

Even from ten feet away, he looked as though he was sleeping. But as we went a few steps further, we realized with a shock that he was dead. His eyes were open, and around his head was a pool of blood; or, at least, it had been a pool hours ago, now it was a dark patch on the sand.

The man had thick curly hair, thick eyebrows, a heavy moustache and a clear complexion. He was wearing a grey cotton jacket, white trousers and a blue striped shirt. There were shoes on his feet, but no socks. On one of his little fingers he wore a ring with a blue stone. His nails were long and dirty. The front pocket of his jacket was crammed with papers. I was sorely tempted to take them out and go through them quickly, just to find out who the man was. But Lalmohan Babu said, 'Don't touch anything.' There was actually no need to say this, for I knew from experience what one should or should not do in a case like this.

'We are the first to . . . to . . . discover, I think?' Lalmohan Babu asked, trying very hard to appear cool and nonchalant. But I could tell his mouth had gone dry. 'Yes, I think so, too,' I replied, feeling rather shaken myself. 'Well, we must report it.'

'Yes, yes, of course.'

We hurried back to the hotel to find that Feluda had returned.

'Judging by the fact that you forgot to wipe your feet before coming in and spread a few hundred grams of sand all over the floor, I assume you are greatly perturbed about something,' Feluda announced, looking at Lalmohan Babu. I spoke hastily before Lalmohan Babu could get the chance to exaggerate what we had seen. Feluda heard me in silence, then rang the police to explain in a few succinct words what had happened. Then he turned to me and asked just one question: 'Did you see a weapon anywhere near the body? A pistol or something?'

'No, Feluda.'

'But I'm absolutely certain the fellow isn't a Bengali,' Lalmohan Babu said firmly.

'Why do you say that?'

'Those eyebrows. They were joined. Bengalis don't have joined eyebrows. Nor do they have such a strong, firm jaw as this man. I shouldn't be surprised if he turns out to be from Bundelkhand.'

Feluda, in the meantime, had made an appointment with D.G. Sen. His secretary had asked him to call at 8.30 a.m. and not take more than fifteen minutes of Mr Sen's time. We left almost immediately.

On our way to Mr Sen's house, we noticed a small crowd near the dead body. It hadn't taken long for word to spread. This was no doubt a most unusual event. The police were already there. One of the officers spotted Feluda and stepped forward with a smile and an outstretched arm.

'Inspector Mahapatra!' Feluda exclaimed, shaking his hand warmly. 'We met over a case in Rourkela, didn't we?'

'Yes, I recognized you at once. Are you here on holiday?'

'Yes, that's the general idea. Who is the deceased?'

'No one from this area. His name is Rupchand Singh.'

'How did you find out?'

'There was a driving licence.'

'Where from?'

'Nepal!'

A gentleman wearing glasses made his way through the crowd, pushing the police photographer to one side. 'I saw the man yesterday. He was at a tea stall in Swargadwar Road. I was buying paan at the next stall. He asked me for a light, and then lit a cigarette.'

'How did he die?' Feluda asked Mr Mahapatra.

'Shot dead, I think. But we haven't yet found the weapon. This was tucked inside the driving licence. You may wish to take a look.' Feluda was handed a visiting card. Printed on one side was the name and address of a tailor's shop in Kathmandu. On the other side was written, in an unformed hand, the following words: A.K. Sarkar, 14 Meher Ali Road, Calcutta.

'Do let me know if you hear of anything interesting. We're staying at the Neelachal,' Feluda said.

We walked on, and soon arrived at D.G. Sen's house. Last evening, it had appeared impressive, even inviting. But now, under an overcast sky, it looked dark and forbidding.

A young man was standing outside the gate. He was probably a servant. On seeing us arrive, he came forward and said, 'Mitter Babu?'

'I am Mitter Babu,' Feluda replied.

'Please come with me.'

A cobbled path ran towards the garden. But, in order to get to the second floor, it was necessary to go to the rear of the house where there was a separate entrance. A few steps down the passage,

Lalmohan Babu suddenly sprang back with a stifled exclamation. It turned out that his eyes had fallen on a long strip of paper. 'I th-thought it was a s-snake!' he exclaimed.

The servant left us at the bottom of the stairs. We saw another man coming down. 'Mr Mitter?' he asked with a smile, 'This way, please.' He looked about thirty-five, although his hairline had started to recede.

'I am Nishith Bose,' he said on the way up, 'I work here as Durga Babu's secretary.'

'Durga Babu?'

'Durga Gati Sen. Everyone calls him D.G. Sen.'

There was a room on the right where the stairs ended. It was probably the secretary's, for I caught sight of a typewriter on a small table. On the left was a small corridor and two more rooms. Beyond this was a terrace. It was on the terrace that D.G. Sen was waiting for us.

A portion of the terrace was occupied by a greenhouse in which there were a few orchids. Mr Sen was sitting in a cane chair in the middle of the terrace. He appeared to be about sixty. Lalmohan Babu said afterwards, 'Personality with a capital P.' He was right. Mr Sen's complexion was very fair, his eyes were sharp, and he had a French beard. His broad shoulders indicated that once he must have been a regular visitor to a gym. But he didn't rise as we approached him. 'Namaskar,' he said from his chair. I found this odd, but the reason became clear as my eyes fell on his feet. His left foot was peeping out of his blue trousers. The whole foot was covered by a bandage.

Three chairs had been placed on the terrace. We took these and returned his greeting. 'We're very grateful to you,' Feluda told him, 'for allowing us to barge in like this. When I heard about your collection, I couldn't resist the temptation to come and see it.'

'I've had this interest for many years,' Mr Sen replied. His eyes held a faraway look. His voice was deep. It seemed to match his personality.

'My uncle—Siddheswar Bose—has a small collection of old manuscripts. I think you went to his house once, to look at what he had.'

'Yes, that's possible. I used to travel pretty widely in search of scrolls.'

'Is everything in your collection written in Bengali?'

'No, there are other languages. The best of the lot is in Sanskrit.'

'When was it written?'

'Twelfth century.'

This was followed by a short pause. There was no point in asking him to show us anything. He'd do so only if he felt like it.

'Lokenath!' Mr Sen called. Lokenath was probably the name of the servant, but why was he calling him?

Mr Bose appeared instead of Lokenath. Had he perhaps been standing behind the door? 'Lokenath's gone out, sir. Can I help?' he asked.

Mr Sen stretched out an arm. Mr Bose caught his hand and helped him get to his feet. 'Please follow me,' Mr Sen said to us. We trooped back to the corridor, and went into one of the two bedrooms. It was a large room, with a huge four-poster bed in it. Next to the bed was a Kashmiri table, on which stood a lamp, two medicine bottles and a glass. There was also a desk, a chair and lined against the wall, two Godrej safes.

'Open it,' Mr Sen commanded, looking at his secretary. Mr Bose fished out a bunch of keys from under a pillow and opened one of the safes.

I could see four shelves, each one of which was stacked with narrow, long packets, covered by red silk. A brief glance told me there were at least fifty of them. 'The other safe has a few more, but the really valuable—'

The really valuable one came out of a drawer in the first one. I noticed there was one more packet in the same drawer. Mr Bose untied the ribbon that held the piece of silk, revealing an eight-hundred-year-old scroll, held between two thin cylindrical pieces of wood.

'This one's called *Ashtadashasahasrika Pragya Paramita,*' said Mr Sen. 'There's one more, just as old, called *Kalpasutra.*'

The wooden cylinders were painted beautifully. Neither the colour of the paint, nor the intricate designs had dimmed with the passage of time. The manuscript itself had been written on a palm leaf. I could never have believed anyone's handwriting could be so beautiful.

'Where did you get this?' Feluda asked.

'Dharamshala.'

'Does that mean it came from Tibet, with the Dalai Lama?'

'Yes.'

Mr Sen took the scroll back from Feluda and passed it to Mr Bose. He tied it up again with the piece of silk and put it back in the safe.

'Were you sent here by your uncle?'

I was startled by the abruptness with which the question was asked. Feluda remained unruffled. 'No, sir,' he replied calmly.

'I am not a businessman, and I certainly don't wish to sell any of these. All I can do is show people what I've got, if anyone is interested.'

'My uncle could not afford to buy what you just showed me,' Feluda laughed. 'But then, I have no idea how much something like this might cost.'

'You couldn't possibly put a price on it. It's invaluable.'

'But there are people who'd quite happily pass these on to outsiders, aren't there? Aren't ancient manuscripts from India being sold to foreigners?'

'Yes, I am aware of that. Those who do this are criminals—confound them!'

'Doesn't your son share your interest?'

Mr Sen did not reply immediately. He seemed to grow a little preoccupied. Then he said, staring at the table, 'My son? I don't know him.'

'Sir, Mr Mitter's a famous detective, sir!' Mr Bose piped up, somewhat unnecessarily. D.G. Sen promptly brought his gaze back to focus it directly on Feluda. 'So what?' he barked, 'why should that make any difference? Have I killed anyone?'

Mr Barik had warned us about this. D.G. Sen really was a most peculiar man. But the next words he spoke made no sense at all.

'No detective could bring back what is lost. He who can do anything is still trying; closed doors are opening now, one by one. There's no need for a detective.'

None of us dared ask what he meant by this. In any case, our time was up. So we turned to go. 'I'll see you out,' Mr Bose said a little urgently. Feluda thanked Mr Sen once more, and we all said goodbye. Then we began climbing down the stairs.

'What's the matter with his foot?' Feluda asked Mr Bose.

'Gout,' he replied. 'He used to be very healthy and fit, even a few months ago. But, over the last three months, he's been in a lot of pain and discomfort.'

'I noticed two bottles in his room. Were they for his gout?'

'Yes. One of them is to help him sleep. Laxman Babu gave it to him.'

'Who, the astrologer?' Lalmohan Babu asked in surprise.

'Yes, he knows many more things beside astrology, including ayurveda, as well as conventional medicine.'

'You don't say!'

'Oh yes. I've even heard him talk of old manuscripts when he's with Mr Sen.'

'What an extraordinary man!' Lalmohan Babu said admiringly.

Feluda remained silent.

FOUR

Lalmohan Babu wanted Feluda to meet Laxman Bhattacharya. But the astrologer was out and his room was locked. We came out of Sagarika and began walking back to our hotel. The beach was quite crowded by this time, for the clouds had dispersed and the sun had come out. There was a hotel on our right, not far from the beach. 'That's the Railway Hotel,' Feluda said. 'Most of these people are staying there.' We made our way through the crowd and moved away. Suddenly, someone called out: 'Mr Mitter!'

A tall gentleman was standing alone, away from groups of bathers, and smiling at Feluda. He must have spent quite a few days on the beach, for when he removed his sunglasses, I could see a pale mark running from his eyes to his ears. The rest of his skin was deeply tanned.

He came walking towards us. He was nearly as tall as Feluda and quite good-looking. He had a beard and a neatly trimmed moustache.

'I have heard of you,' he said. 'Are you already working on a case?'

'Why do you ask?'

'There's been a murder, I gather. So I thought you might be making enquiries.' Feluda laughed. 'No. I haven't been asked to investigate, so I couldn't make enquiries even if I wanted to.'

'You're staying at the Neelachal, aren't you?'

'Yes.'

'Er . . .' he seemed to be hesitating.

'Have you been appointed as guard?' Feluda asked. I had noticed it, too. The man was clutching three golden rings in his hand. He gave an embarrassed smile.

'It's such a bore . . . but you're right. These belong to a guest in my hotel. I met him only yesterday. This morning, he said he wanted to have a swim in the sea, but was afraid these might come off. So he asked me to hang on to them until he came out of the water. I wish I hadn't agreed.'

Before any of us could say anything, the owner of the rings arrived, dripping wet and accompanied by a Nulia. We recognized him instantly. It was our 'golden' fellow passenger, Mr M.L. Hingorani. He saw Feluda and shouted, 'Good morning!' Then he took his rings back, and said 'Thank you' to the gentleman, adding that out of all the beaches he had seen in Goa, Miami, Acapulco and Nice, there was none like the beach in Puri.

We said goodbye to him and began walking again, this time accompanied by the bearded gentleman.

'I don't think I got your name—?' Feluda began politely.

'No, I didn't tell you my name, chiefly because I thought it might not mean anything to you. There is a special area in which I've made a small contribution, but not many would know about it. I am called Bilas Majumdar.'

Feluda frowned and looked at the man. 'Have you anything to do with mountains?' he asked.

'My God, your knowledge . . . !'

'No, no,' Feluda interrupted him, 'there's nothing extraordinary about this. It's just that I thought I had seen your name somewhere recently, in a journal or something. There was a mention of mountains in that report.'

'You're right. I joined the institute in Darjeeling to learn mountaineering. I am actually a wildlife photographer. I was supposed to go with a Japanese team to take photos of a snow leopard. You're probably aware that snow leopards can be found in the high altitudes of the Himalayas. Many have seen this animal, but there are virtually no photographs.'

We reached our hotel without further conversation. Lalmohan Babu kept casting admiring glances at Bilas Majumdar. Feluda ordered tea as soon as we got to our room. Mr Majumdar sat down and took out a photograph from his pocket.

'See if you can recognize this man,' he said to Feluda.

It was a postcard-size photograph. A man wearing a cap was holding a strange animal, and several others were looking at them both. The man Mr Majumdar was pointing at was someone we had just met.

'Yes, we left his house only a few minutes ago,' Feluda said. 'It's not easy to recognize him in that photo, since he's now got a beard.'

Mr Majumdar took the photo back. 'That's all I needed to know,' he said, 'I saw his name-plate outside his gate, but couldn't be sure if it was the same D.G. Sen.'

'That animal looks like a pangolin,' Feluda remarked.

Yes! Now I could remember having read about it. It was a species of anteater. It looked as though it was wearing a suit of armour.

'You're right, it is a pangolin. It's found in Nepal. That photo was taken outside a hotel in Kathmandu. D.G. Sen and I were both staying there.'

'When was this?'

'Last October. I had gone to meet that Japanese team. Some of my photos had been published in Japanese journals. When this team contacted me, I was naturally very excited. But, in the end, I couldn't go with them.'

'Why? Why?' Lalmohan Babu asked, sounding concerned. A mention of snow leopards had clearly made him smell an adventure.

'I had an accident. I was so badly injured that I had to spend three months in hospital.'

'Did your hurt your left leg?' Feluda asked.

'I broke the shin bone in my left leg. Why, is that obvious from the way I walk?'

'No. But yesterday, we saw some footprints on the sand, and the mark left by a walking stick on the left side of these prints. So I thought whoever had come walking was either left-handed, or his left leg was injured. You, I can see, do not use a stick.'

'Sometimes I do. Walking on the sand can often be difficult. But I am only thirty-nine, you see. I don't feel like walking about with a stick in my hand all the time, like an old man.'

'Then it must have been someone else.'

'Perhaps. But I can tell you one thing. Breaking a shin bone was not my only injury. I had rolled down the side of a hill—nearly five hundred feet. A local farmer's son saw me fall on top of a tree—in fact, that's what saved my life—and informed a group of hippies. They took me to a hospital. I had seven broken ribs. Even my collar-bone was broken. There were injuries on my face, my chin was crushed. Eventually, I grew a beard simply to cover the marks on my chin. I lay unconscious for two days. When I came to, I could remember nothing, not even my name. Someone found my name and address in my diary and informed my family in Calcutta. A nephew came to see me. I couldn't recognize him. Then, gradually, my memory returned. Now, after a lot of treatment, I can remember most things, but not what happened just before the accident. For instance, my meeting with D.G. Sen was recorded in my diary, but it was only two days ago that I finally remembered what he looked like.'

'Can you remember why Mr Sen had gone to Kathmandu? Was it anything to do with ancient manuscripts?'

'Manuscripts? Well, I don't know . . . what do these manuscripts look like?'

'Long, thin and flat. About the size of a carton of cigarettes. They're usually covered by red silk.'

Mr Majumdar said nothing. His eyes were resting on a table lamp; he appeared to be lost in thought. All of us looked at him without saying a word. After a long time, he raised his eyes. 'I suppose I ought to tell you everything,' he said. 'The hotel in Kathmandu where Mr Sen and I stayed was called Vikram Hotel. It was a rather strange place. There were a few rooms with identical locks. You could use the key meant for one room to open the door of another, something which in a hotel one wouldn't expect at all. One day, purely by accident, I happened to unlock the room next to mine, thinking it was my own. It was, in fact, D.G. Sen's room. At first, I was surprised to find other people in what I thought was my own room, but soon I realized my mistake. So I quickly said "sorry" and came away, but not before I had seen something. D.G. Sen was sitting on the bed, and two strangers were sitting in chairs. One of them was taking out a thin, long packet from a cardboard box. As far as I can recall, it was red, though I couldn't tell you whether it was silk or not.'

'I see. What happened next?'

'Nothing. I mean, I can remember nothing. My mind's gone totally blank. The next thing I can remember is waking up in hospital.'

'Hey!' Lalmohan Babu exclaimed suddenly, 'Why don't you go to the astrologer? He'll tell you everything, remind you of every detail.'

'Who are you talking about?'

'Laxman Bhattacharya the Great. He's a tenant on the ground

floor of Mr Sen's house. I can make an appointment for you, if you like. Just try it out, it can't do any harm.'

'Well . . . that's an idea, anyway. Thanks.' Mr Majumdar seemed quite taken with the idea.

'All he'll do,' Lalmohan Babu continued, encouraged, 'is place his little finger on that mole in the middle of your forehead, and then he'll be able to see it all: your past, present and future.'

I hadn't noticed it before, but now I saw a small mole on Mr Majumdar's forehead. It looked almost as though he was wearing a bindi.

'Does your astrologer allow visitors?' Feluda asked.

'Sure. You mean you and Tapesh would like to go as observers? No problem, sir. I'll tell him.'

'Very well. Please see if he's free at six o'clock this evening.'

Lalmohan Babu nodded happily, then told Mr Majumdar that the astrologer's fee was five rupees and seventy-five paise. Mr Majumdar started to laugh, but stopped when Feluda pointed out it wasn't a figure to be laughed at. 'Just think. If he gets even ten visitors every day, that gives him a monthly income of nearly two thousand rupees. That's not bad, is it?'

It was clear to me that although Feluda had no wish to have his future read, he was quite curious about the return of Mr Majumdar's memory.

FIVE

We decided to go to the famous temple of Jagannath in the evening before our meeting with Mr Bhattacharya. I was more interested in looking at the chariot. I had learnt from Feluda that every year, the old wooden chariot of Jagannath was broken methodically and a new one built in its place. Toys were made with the broken pieces of wood from the old one and sold in the market.

Feluda was not speaking much. Perhaps he was thinking of all the new people we had met and what they had said to us. There was one little thing that I felt I had to say to him.

'Have you noticed, Feluda,' I said, 'how everything seems to be related to Nepal? The man who got murdered was from Nepal, Bilas Majumdar went to Kathmandu, and so did D.G. Sen . . .'

'So? You think that has a special significance?'

'Well, yes, I mean . . .'

'There is no reason to assume anything of the kind. It's most probably no more than a coincidence.'

'OK, if you say so.'

Having seen the famous chariot, we were roaming around in the huge street market in front of the temple, looking at tiny statues and wheels of Konark being carved out of stone, when suddenly we bumped into Inspector Mahapatra. It took me a few seconds to recognize him, for he had had a haircut. One look at his new, freshly cropped hair reminded me of an uncle who always used to fall asleep the minute he sat in a barber's chair. When he woke up, the barber would show him his handiwork, which would invariably result in a violent argument. Inspector Mahapatra seemed to be a man who had a lot in common with my uncle.

'Hello, Inspector!' Feluda greeted him. 'Any progress? Did you manage to contact Mr Sarkar of Meher Ali Road?'

'We received some information this afternoon,' the Inspector replied. 'Fourteen Meher Ali Road is a block of apartments. There are eight apartments. Mr Sarkar lives in number three. His flat's been locked for a week. Apparently, he goes out of town quite frequently.'

'Do you know where he's gone this time?'

'Puri.'

'Really? Who told you that?'

'The occupant in flat number 4. He's supposed to be here on holiday.'

'Did you get a description?'

'Yes, but it doesn't really mean anything. Medium height, clean-shaven, age between thirty-five and forty.'

'What does he do?'

'He calls himself a travelling salesman. No one seems to know what he sells. He took that flat a year ago.'

'And Rupchand Singh?'

'He arrived in Puri yesterday, and checked in at a hotel near the bus stand. He didn't even pay his bill. Last night, he had tried making a call from his hotel, but the phone was out of order. So he went to a chemist across the road and used their phone. The chemist saw him, but didn't hear what he said on the phone as he was busy serving his customers. Rupchand left the hotel at eleven, but did not return. We found a suitcase in his room with a few clothes in it. They were good clothes, well-made and expensive.'

'That's not surprising. A driver these days earns pretty well. So I don't think Rupchand found it too difficult to be able to afford a few good things in life.'

Inspector Mahapatra left soon after this. We made our way to the Railway Hotel, where Mr Majumdar was waiting for us. We reached there at a quarter to six. The hotel had obviously been built during the British times. It had been renovated, but there was, even today, an old-fashioned air about it. In the large front garden, guests were drinking tea under garden umbrellas. Mr Majumdar rose from a table and came forward to meet us, with a brief 'Excuse me' to his companions.

'OK, let's go and find out what's in store,' he remarked.

Lalmohan Babu was our guide today. His whole demeanour had changed. When we reached Sagarika, he walked straight up the cobbled path and climbed on to the veranda, knocking the front door smartly. When no one appeared, he looked around just a little uncertainly, then pulled himself together and shouted 'Koi hai?' with a ring of such authority in his voice that we all looked at him in surprise. A side door opened instantly.

'Welcome!' said Laxman Bhattacharya. He was wearing a silk lungi and a fine cotton embroidered kurta. There was nothing remarkable in his appearance, except a thin moustache that drooped down, nearly touching the edge of his chin.

Lalmohan Babu began introductions, but was interrupted. 'Please come in,' Mr Bhattacharya invited, 'we can get to know each other when we're comfortably seated.'

We went into his sitting room, most of which was occupied by a large divan. This was probably where he worked. We took the chairs and stools that were strewn about. Apart from these, the room had no furniture. There was a built-in cupboard, the lower shelves of which were visible. Papers and wooden boxes had been crammed into them. There also appeared to be a few jars and bottles.

'Could you please sit here?' Mr Bhattacharya looked at Bilas Majumdar and pointed at the divan.

Mr Majumdar rose and took his place. Lalmohan Babu quickly introduced us. 'This is the friend I told you about,' he said, indicating Feluda, 'and the gentleman here is a famous wil—' he stopped, biting his lip. I knew he was about to say 'wildlife photographer', but had had the sense to check himself.

Feluda said hurriedly, 'I hope you don't mind two extra people in the room?'

'No, not at all. The only thing I do mind is being asked to perform on a stage. Many people have asked me to do that, as if I were a magician. Why, only this other—' Laxman Bhattacharya stopped speaking. I glanced at him quickly to find him staring at Bilas Majumdar. 'How very strange! You have a mole on the very spot where gods and goddesses have a third eye. Do you know what there is in the human body under that spot?'

'The pineal gland?' Feluda asked.

'Exactly. The most mysterious portion of the brain; or at least that's what western scientists say. Some thinkers in India are of the opinion that, thousands of years ago, most creatures, including man, had three eyes. In the course of time, the third eye disappeared and became the pineal gland. There is a reptile called Taratua in New Guinea that's still got this third eye.'

Feluda asked, 'When you lay a finger in the middle of one's forehead, is it simply to establish contact with the pineal gland?'

'Yes, you could say that,' Mr Bhattacharya replied. 'Mind you, when I first started, I hadn't even heard of this gland. I was only twelve at the time. One Sunday, an uncle happened to get a headache. "If you press my head," he said, "I'll give you money to buy ice-cream." So I began pressing his temples, and then he told me to rub his forehead. As I began running my finger on his forehead, pressing it gently, a strange thing happened. Scenes began to flash before my eyes—as though I was watching a film. I could see my uncle as a small boy, going to school; then as a young man, shouting "Vande Mataram" and being arrested by the police; then I saw him getting married, saw his wife's death, and even his own death. There he was before my eyes, lying with his eyes closed, surrounded by many other members of our family. Then the scenes disappeared as suddenly as they had appeared. I did not say anything to anyone, as I could hardly believe it myself. But when he did actually die and everything I had seen turned out to be true—well, then I realized somehow I had acquired a special power, and . . .' his voice trailed away.

I looked at the others. Lalmohan Babu was gaping at Laxman Bhattacharya, round-eyed with wonder. Bilas Majumdar was looking straight at the astrologer, his face expressionless.

'I hear you have some knowledge about medicine, and I can see evidence of that in this room,' Feluda remarked. 'What do you call yourself? A doctor, or an astrologer?'

'Well, I did not actually learn astrology. To tell you the truth, my knowledge of stars and planets is quite limited. If I have the power to see a person's past and future, it is a God-given power. I myself have nothing to do with it. But ayurveda is something I have studied, as well as conventional medicine. So if you asked me what my profession was, I'd say I was a doctor. Anyway, Mr Majumdar, could you please come forward a little?'

Mr Majumdar slid forward on the divan, and sat cross-legged. The astrologer turned and dipped the little finger of his right hand into a little bowl, then wiped it with a spotless white handkerchief. I hadn't noticed the bowl before, nor could I tell what it contained. Whatever it was, it seemed to give Mr Bhattacharya sufficient encouragement to start his job. He closed his eyes, stretched his hand and placed his little finger on the mole on Mr Majumdar's forehead in a single, precise movement. After this, the next couple of minutes passed in silence. Nobody spoke. All I could hear was the ticking of a clock and the roaring waves outside.

'Thirty-three . . . nineteen thirty-three . . .' Mr Bhattacharya suddenly started speaking. 'Born under the sign of Libra . . . the first child. Tonsils removed at the age of eight—a scholarship—and a gold medal when leaving school—physics—a graduate at nineteen—started earning at twenty-three—a job—no, no, freelance—photography—struggle, I can see a lot of struggle—but great endurance and determination—love of animals—mountains—skill in climbing mountains—not married—travels a lot—not afraid to take risks . . .' he stopped.

Feluda was staring steadily at an ashtray. Lalmohan Babu was sitting straight, his hands clenched in excitement. My own heart was beating fast. Bilas Majumdar's face was still devoid of expression, but his eyes were fixed on the astrologer's face. Not for a single second had he removed them.

'Seventy-eight . . . seventy-eight . . .' the astrologer resumed speaking. Beads of perspiration stood out on his forehead. His breath came fast; he was obviously finding it difficult to speak.

'. . . Forest—there's a forest—the Himalayas—acci—acci—no, it's not.' He fell silent again, but only for a few seconds. Then he opened his eyes, and took his finger away. 'You,' he said, looking directly at Mr Majumdar, 'should not be alive today. Not after what happened.

But you've been spared. God saved your life.'

'You mean it, was not an accident?' Mr Majumdar's voice sounded choked. Laxman Bhattacharya shook his head, and helped himself to a paan. 'No,' he said, stuffing it into his mouth, 'as far as I could see, someone had pushed you deliberately down that hill. The chances of survival were practically nil. It's nothing short of a miracle that you didn't die on the spot.'

'But who pushed him?' Lalmohan Babu asked impatiently.

'Sorry,' Laxman Bhattacharya shook his head again, 'I couldn't tell you that. I did not see who pushed him. If I were to describe the person, or give you a name, it would be a total lie. And I would be punished for lying. No, I cannot tell you what I did not see.'

'Give me your hand, sir,' said Bilas Majumdar, offering his own. A second later, the photographer and the astrologer were seen giving each other a warm handshake.

We left soon afterwards.

SIX

'What will you call this? Five-star, or six-star?' Feluda asked, looking at Lalmohan Babu.

We were having dinner at the Railway Hotel, at Mr Majumdar's invitation. 'I am very grateful to you,' he had said as soon as we had come out of Sagarika. 'Had it not been for you, I would not even have heard Laxman Bhattacharya's name. What he told me helped clarify a lot of doubts. In fact, I can even remember some of the details of what happened after that night when I walked into Mr Sen's room. So I'd be delighted if you could join me for dinner at my hotel.'

'I had no idea food in a railway hotel could be so good,' Lalmohan Babu freely admitted. 'I had assumed it would be as tasteless as what is served on trains. Now I know better, thanks to you.'

Bilas Majumdar smiled. 'Please have the souffle.'

'What? Soup plate? But I have already had the soup!'

'No, no. Souffle, not soup plate. It's the dessert.'

'Oh. Oh, I see.'

Mr Majumdar told us about the return of his memory while we all helped ourselves to the dessert.

'I was naturally embarrassed to have walked into someone else's room, but what I saw did not make me suspicious at all. Mr Sen was going to Pokhra the next day. He invited me to join him. The Japanese team I was waiting for was not expected for another three days. I had plenty of time, so I agreed. Pokhra is about two hundred kilometres from Kathmandu. We had to drive through a forest. Mr Sen asked the driver to stop there, to look for wild orchids. I got down with him, thinking even if we didn't find any flowers, I might get to see a few birds. I remember taking my camera with me. He went off in one direction to look for orchids. I went in another to look for birds. We decided to return to the car in an hour. I started to walk with my eyes on the trees, scanning every branch to see if I could find a bird. Suddenly, out of the blue, I felt a blow on my head, and everything went black.'

He stopped. We had already heard what followed next.

'You're still not sure about who had struck that blow?' Feluda asked.

'No, not at all. But I do know this: the car was parked on the main road, about a kilometre away, and I hadn't seen a single soul in that forest.'

'If the culprit was Mr Sen, you have no real evidence to prove it, have you?'

'No, I am afraid not.'

Lalmohan Babu seemed a bit restless, as though there was something on his mind. Now he decided to get it off his chest.

'Look,' he said, 'why don't you go and meet Durga Gati Sen? If he really is the man who tried to kill you, surely he'll think he's seeing a ghost? And surely that will give him away?'

'You're right. I thought of doing that. But there is a problem. You see, when he met me, I didn't have a beard. So he might not recognize me. Not instantly, anyway.'

We chatted for a few minutes before taking our leave. Mr Majumdar came up to the main gate to see us off. We set out, to discover that the sky was now totally clear and the moon had come out. Feluda had a small, powerful torch in his pocket, but the moonlight was so good that there was no need to use it.

We crossed over to the other side and began walking on the paved road that ran by the side of the sea. 'Tell me frankly, Felu Babu,' Lalmohan Babu said a few minutes later, 'what did you think of Laxman Bhattacharya? Isn't he incredible?'

'Incredible he might be, Lalmohan Babu. But what knowledge he has is not good enough. If Bilas Majumdar has to find out who had tried to kill him, he must come to me. It's Felu Mitter's brain that's required to discover the truth, not somebody's supernatural power.'

'You mean you're going to investigate?' Lalmohan Babu asked, his eyes glinting with excitement. Feluda opened his mouth to make a reply, but stopped as our eyes fell on a man, walking briskly towards us, staring at the ground and muttering to himself. It was Mr Hingorani.

He stopped short as he saw us. Then he shook a finger at Feluda and said, 'You Bengalis are very stubborn, very stubborn!' He sounded decidedly put out.

'Why?' Feluda smiled. 'What have we done to make you so annoyed?'

'That man refused. I offered him twenty-five thousand, and he still said no.'

'What! You mean there's actually someone in this world who could resist such profound temptation?'

'The fellow's mad. I had heard of his collection of manuscripts, so I made an appointment to go and see him. I said, "Show me your most valuable piece." So he opened a safe and brought out a piece going back to the twelfth century. An extraordinary object. God knows if it was stolen from somewhere. Last year, three old manuscripts were stolen from the palace museum in Bhatgaon. Two of them were recovered, but the third is still missing. It was one written by Pragya Paramita. So what I just saw might well have been the stolen one.'

'Where is Bhatgaon?' Lalmohan Babu asked. I had not heard of it either.

'Ten kilometres from Kathmandu. It's a very old town, used to be known as Bhaktapur.'

'But if it was stolen, he wouldn't have shown it to you, would he? And, as far as I know, there are plenty of manuscripts written by Pragya Paramita that are still in existence,' Feluda remarked.

'I know, I know,' Mr Hingorani said impatiently. 'He said he bought it in Dharamshala, and it came to India with the Dalai Lama. Do you know how much he paid for it? Five hundred. And I offered him twenty-five thousand. Just imagine!'

'Does that mean your visit to Puri is going to be a total waste of time?'

'No. I do not give up easily. Mr Sen does not know this Mahesh

Hingorani. He showed me another manuscript of the fifteenth century. I'm here for a couple of days. Let's see what happens. I don't usually take no for an answer. Well, good night to you all.'

Mr Hingorani went towards his hotel.

'It sounds a little suspicious, doesn't it?' Lalmohan Babu asked.

'What does?'

'This business of not wanting to sell something for twenty-five thousand rupees, when all he had bought it for was five hundred.'

'Why? Do you find it impossible to believe that a man can be totally devoid of greed? Did you know Uncle Sidhu refused to sell a manuscript from his own collection to Durga Gati Sen?'

'Why, Mr Sen didn't mention this!'

'That is what strikes me as most suspicious. He visited Uncle Sidhu only a year ago.'

Mr Sen was not just peculiar, but also rather mysterious, I thought. And if what Bilas Majumdar had said was true . . .

'But then,' Feluda continued, 'it isn't just Mr Sen my suspicion's fallen on. Take your astrologer, for instance. The three-eyed reptile he told us about is called Tuatara, not Taratua; and it's not found in New Guinea, but New Zealand. Now, it's all right for Jatayu to make such mistakes. But if Laxman Bhattacharya's aim in life is to impress people with information like that, he really must learn to be more accurate. Then there's Nishith Bose. He has the awful habit of eavesdropping. He said Mr Sen suffers from gout. Those medicines in his room weren't for gout at all.'

'What were they for?'

'One of them was released only last year. I read about it in *Time* magazine. I can't quite recall what it's for, but it's certainly not for gout.'

'There's one other thing,' I put in, 'Mr Sen seemed amazingly preoccupied, didn't he? What's on his mind, I wonder? Besides, why did he say he didn't know his son?'

'No idea. I find it puzzling, too.'

'If it is true that he did try to kill Bilas Majumdar,' Lalmohan Babu said slowly, 'that could be a reason for his being so preoccupied. Maybe he is deeply worried. Maybe—'

He stopped. So did we. All of us stood staring at the ground.

There were footprints on the sand and, on the left, marks made by a walking stick. They were fresh marks, made in the last few hours.

Bilas Majumdar, who was likely to use a walking stick, had

returned straight to his hotel from Laxman Bhattacharya's house to wait for us. He could not have come walking this way.

Who, then, had left these footprints?

Who else walked about on the beaches of Puri with a stick in his left hand?

SEVEN

Lalmohan Babu's car arrived the following morning just as we were planning to go out after breakfast. His driver told us he had got held up in Balasore for nearly four hours because of torrential rain, othewise he'd have reached Puri much sooner.

The Neelachal being full, we had booked a room for the driver at the New Hotel, which was not far. He left the car in the car park of our hotel, and went off to find his own room. We told him we might go to Bhubaneshwar later, weather permitting.

Feluda wanted to go to the station to buy a copy of the *Statesman*. He wasn't satisfied with the Bengali newspaper the hotel provided. Walking to the station took us about half an hour. By the time we got there, it was eight forty-five. The Jagannath Express from Calcutta had arrived at seven. The Puri Express was late by an hour, but it was expected any minute. I love going to railway stations, and to watch how a quiet and peaceful place can come to life and hum with activity when a train arrives.

Lalmohan Babu found a bookstall. 'Do you have books by the famous writer, Jatayu?' he asked. There was, in fact, no need to do this since I could see at least three of his books displayed quite prominently. Feluda bought his newspaper and began leafing through some of the books. At this moment, we heard a voice. 'Has the latest *Mystery Magazine* arrived yet?' it asked. I turned to find Nishith Bose. He hadn't seen us at first, but when he did, he grinned from ear to ear. 'Just imagine, here I am buying the *Mystery Magazine*, when a detective is standing right next to me!' he exclaimed.

'How is your boss?' Feluda asked.

'Under great stress. People turn up without making an appointment, and then beg me to arrange a meeting. Who knew so many people were interested in old manuscripts?'

'Why, who else came visiting?'

'I don't know his name. He had a beard and he wore dark glasses. He said there was no point in giving his name, since Mr Sen wouldn't recognize it, but he knew someone who had some manuscripts to sell. So I went and informed Mr Sen, and he said all right, bring him up to the terrace. I showed him in, then went to my room to type a few letters. In less than three minutes, I heard Mr Sen calling my name. I ran to see what the matter was, and found him looking pale and greatly distressed, almost as though he was about to have a heart attack. All he could say to me was, "Take this man away, at once!" So I took him down the stairs immediately. He had the nerve to say before going, "I think you employer's heart isn't all that strong. Get him to see a doctor." Imagine!'

'How is he now?'

'Better, much better.' Mr Bose glanced at the clock and gave a start. 'Good heavens, I had no idea it was already so late. I must go now. You're going to be here for a few days, aren't you? I'll tell you everything one day. I have a lot to tell. Goodbye!'

The Puri Express had arrived while we were talking. The guard now blew his whistle and it began pulling out of the platform. Mr Bose disappeared in the crowd.

Feluda had selected a book from the stall and paid for it. I glanced over his shoulder and saw that it was called *A Guide to Nepal.* On our way back to the hotel, he said, 'I think it might be a good idea for you and Lalmohan Babu to go to Bhubaneshwar today. Something tells me I ought to remain here. I don't think anything drastic is going to happen very soon, but there's something in the air . . . I just don't like it. Besides, I need to sort a few things out. I must make a phone call to Kathmandu. Let's straighten all the facts out before they get too muddled.'

I was quite familiar with this mood Feluda was in. He would now withdraw himself totally and stop talking altogether. He would go back to his room and lie flat on his back, staring at the ceiling. When he did this, I had noticed in the past, sometimes he stared into space for three or four minutes without blinking even once. Lalmohan Babu and I usually left him alone at a time like this or spoke in whispers. Going to Bhubaneshwar would be much better, I thought, than just hanging around waiting for Feluda to break his silence. I nodded at Lalmohan Babu, to indicate that we should leave as soon as possible.

We reached our hotel to find Mr Majumdar coming out of it.

'I'm so glad I've caught you!' he exclaimed. 'If you returned even a minute later, I'd have missed you.'

'Let's go upstairs.'

Mr Majumdar came into our room and sat down, wiping his face. 'You took my advice, didn't you?' Lalmohan Babu asked with a big smile.

'Yes. Mr Sen reacted exactly as you'd said he might. He jumped as though he'd seen a ghost. Amazing, isn't it, how he could recognize me despite this thick beard?'

'There is something very special in your face, Mr Majumdar, that your beard cannot hide,' Feluda pointed out.

'What?'

'Your third eye. It isn't easy to forget.'

'Yes, you're right. I forgot all about it. Anyway, something rather strange happened today. When I saw Mr Sen, I found a man who has aged dramatically in these few months. Why, he looks at least ten years older than what he had seemed in Kathmandu. I felt sorry for him. Yes, truly I did. Now I can put the whole thing behind me. If Mr Sen did try to kill me, I think he has paid for it already.'

'Good,' said Feluda, 'I am glad to hear this, for you couldn't have got very far without concrete evidence, anyway.'

Mr Majumdar rose. 'What are your plans now?' he asked.

'These two are going to Bhubaneshwar today. I'll stay on here.'

'I think I'll leave Puri tomorrow. I haven't yet seen the forests of Orissa. I'll try and meet you again before I go.'

By the time we could leave, it was twelve-thirty. But it was a fine day, and the roads were good. Lalmohan Babu's driver drove at 80 kmph, which enabled us to reach Bhubaneshwar in exactly forty-two minutes. We went, first of all, to the temple called Raja Rani. A few years ago, the head of a yakshi carved on the wall of this temple had been stolen. Feluda had had to exercise all his brain power to get it back. It sent a shiver of excitement down my spine to see it back where it belonged.

There were dozens of other temples to be seen—Lingaraj, Kedar Gauri, Mukteshwar, Brahmeshwar and Bhaskareshwar, among others. Lalmohan Babu insisted on seeing each one because, he said, one of his school teachers—a very gifted man called Baikuntha Mallik—had written a poem on Bhubaneshwar that haunted him even today. Disregarding the presence of at least forty other tourists (many of them from abroad), he recited this poem for me in the temple of Mukteshwar:

On its walls
        does Bhubaneshwar
tell the story of
        each sculptor.

Like Michaelangelo
        and Da Vinci,
all unsung heroes
        of our own country.

'It doesn't rhyme very well, does it?' I couldn't help saying, 'I mean, "Bhubaneshwar" hardly goes with "sculptor", and how can you rhyme "Da Vinci" with "country"?'

'Free verse, my boy, it's free verse!' Lalmohan Babu replied airily. 'It doesn't have to rhyme.'

We returned to Puri around seven in the evening. Bhubaneshwar was a nice place, neat and tidy, but I liked Puri much better because of the sea. Our manager, Shyamlal Barik, called out to us as we climbed the front veranda of the Neelachal.

'Mr Ganguli, there's a message for you!'

We went quickly to his room.

'Mr Mitter went out ten minutes ago. He told you to wait in your room.

'Why? What's happened?'

'There was a call from the police station. Mr D.G. Sen's house has been burgled. A very valuable manuscript has been stolen.'

How very strange! Feluda said only this morning he thought something might happen. Who knew it would happen so soon?

EIGHT

A shower and a cup of tea refreshed me physically, but I felt too restless to sit still. Feluda had now officially begun his investigation. Puri, like so many other places we had gone to on holiday, had given us a mystery to work on. Knowing Feluda's calibre and his past performance, I was sure we would not go back disappointed.

But, I wondered, would Feluda get paid for his pains? After all, no one had actually hired him in this case. Not that it mattered. If the case was challenging enough and if he got the chance to exercise his brain, Feluda did not really care about money.

'Who do you suspect, Tapesh?' asked Lalmohan Babu. Unable to remain in his own room, he had joined me in mine and was pacing up and down, holding his hands behind him.

I said, 'Well, Nishith Bose had free access to the manuscripts, so he ought to be the prime suspect. But for that reason alone, I don't think he did it. Then there's Mr Hingorani. Didn't he say he wouldn't give up easily? And there's Bilas Majumdar. He might have stolen it to settle old scores. Maybe he couldn't bring himself to forgive and forget, after all. But Laxman Bhat—'

'No, no, no!' Lalmohan Babu interrupted, protesting violently, 'Don't drag Laxman Bhattacharya into this, please. He couldn't possibly be involved in theft. Why should he even dream of it? Just think of his special power!'

'Well then, what are your own views on this?' I asked him.

'I think the most important man is missing from your list.'

'Who?'

'Mr Sen himself.'

'What! Why should he steal his own property?'

'No, I'm not saying he stole anything. I mean, not this time. That manuscript was stolen, anyway, as Mr Hingorani said. So Mr Sen has sold it to him, for twenty-five thousand; and he's saying it's been stolen, to remove suspicion from himself. Don't you see, now if anyone asks for that particular manuscript, he has a valid reason for saying he hasn't got it?'

Could this be true? It seemed "a bit far-fetched, but . . . I could think no further, for a room boy arrived at this moment and said there was a phone call for us. It had to be Feluda. I ran downstairs and took the call.

'Yes?'

'Did Mr Barik give you my message?' asked Feluda's voice.

'Yes. But have you been able to work anything out?'

'Mr Bose has disappeared.'

'Really? Who informed the police?'

'I'll tell you everything when I get back, in half an hour. How was Bhubaneshwar?'

'Fine. We—' I couldn't finish. Feluda had put the phone down.

I returned to my room and told Lalmohan Babu what Feluda had just said. He scratched his head and said, 'I would like to visit the scene of the crime, but I don't think your cousin would like that.'

We waited for another hour, but Feluda did not return. I began to feel rather uneasy. A little later, I ordered a fresh pot of tea, just to kill time. Then I did something Feluda had told me many times not to do. In my present state of mind, I simply could not help it. I opened his notebook and read the few entries he had made:

Diabid—gout—snake?—what will return?—why doesn't he know his son?—blackmail?—who?—why?—who walks with a stick?—

None of this made any sense. We waited for another twenty minutes, then our patience ran out. Lalmohan Babu and I left the hotel to look for Feluda. If he was going to return from Sagarika, we thought, he would probably take the road that ran by the sea. We turned right as we came out of the hotel.

As we began walking, it struck me once more how different the sea looked in the dark. The waves roared with the same intensity as they did during the day, but now they looked kind of eerie. It was the phosphorous in the water that did it. How else could I have watched them lashing the shore even under a cloudy sky? In the far distance, the sky looked a shade brighter, possibly because of the lights from the city. The rows of flickering lights by the beach meant there was a colony of Nulias. Lalmohan Babu had a torch, but there was no need to use it. My feet kept sinking in the sand. Lalmohan Babu was wearing tennis shoes, but I had chappals on my feet. Suddenly, one of these struck against something. I stumbled and fell flat on my face. I must have cried out, for Lalmohan Babu turned quickly with 'Why, Tapesh, whatever—' A second later, he went through the same motions and joined me on the ground. 'Help! Help!' he cried hoarsely.

'Lalmohan Babu,' I whispered, 'I can feel something under my tummy . . . I think it's a body, I can feel its legs!'

'Oh, my God!' Lalmohan Babu managed to struggle to his feet, pulling me up with him. Then he switched his torch on, only to discover it wasn't working.

He turned it upside down and began hitting the rear end in the hope of getting the batteries to work. At this moment, a human figure slowly sat up on the sand. I felt, rather than saw, it move.

'Give me your hand!' it said.

Feluda! Oh God, was it Feluda? Yes, it was.

I offered him my right hand. Feluda grabbed it and stood up, swaying from side to side. Luckily, Lalmohan Babu got the torch to work. He shone it briefly on Feluda's face, holding it in an unsteady hand. Feluda raised a hand and touched his head, wincing in pain. When he brought his hand down, we could see, even in the dim light from the torch, that it was smeared with blood.

'D-did they c-crack open your sk-skull?' Lalmohan Babu stammered. Feluda ignored him. I had never seen him look so totally dazed.

'What happened? I can't imagine how—' he broke off, taking out a small torch from his own pocket. In its better and steadier light, we saw a series of footprints going from where he had fallen towards the high bank, where the sandy stretch ended.

We followed the footprints right up to the bank. Whoever it was had climbed over it and disappeared, but not without difficulty. There were clumps of uprooted grass strewn about, to prove that climbing had not been an easy task. There was nothing else in sight, not even a small Nulia hut.

Feluda turned back to return to the hotel. We followed him.

'How long did you lie on the ground?' Lalmohan Babu asked, his voice still sounding strange. Feluda shone the torch on his watch and replied, 'About half an hour, I should think.'

'Shouldn't you see a doctor? That wound on your head may need to be stitched.'

'No,' Feluda said slowly. 'It is true that I received a blow on my head. But there is no injury, no open wound.'

'No? Then how did all that blood—?'

Lalmohan Babu's half-spoken words hung in the air.

Feluda made no reply.

NINE

Feluda placed an ice-pack on his head as soon as we reached our hotel. In half an hour, the swelling began to subside. None of us had any idea who might have hurt him. He was returning from Sagarika, Feluda said, when someone had flashed a powerful torch straight into his eyes, blinding him momentarily, and then knocked him unconscious. When he rang Mahapatra at the police station and reported the matter, Mahapatra said, 'You must take great care, Mr

Mitter. There are a lot of desperate characters about. Why don't you stop your own investigation and let us handle this? Wouldn't that be safer?'

'If you had suggested this before I was attacked, I might have agreed. Now, Inspector, it is too late.'

When we came back to our room after dinner, it was nearly eleven. Rather unexpectedly, our manager, Mr Barik, turned up, accompanied by another gentleman. 'He has been waiting for you for half an hour. I didn't want to disturb you while you were eating,' he said and returned to his room.

'I have heard of you,' thc other man said to Feluda. 'In fact, having read about some of your past cases, I even know who your companions are. My name is Mahim Sen.'

Feluda frowned. 'That means—?'

'D.G. Sen is my father.'

None of us could think of saying anything for a moment. Mahim Sen went on, 'I came by car this afternoon. My company owns a guest house here. That's where I am staying.'

'Didn't you meet your father?'

'I rang him as soon as I got here. His secretary answered, and said after checking with my father that he did not wish to speak to me.'

'Why not?'

'I have no idea.'

'When I met your father recently, I got the impression that he wasn't very pleased with you. Can you tell me why?'

Mahim Sen did not reply immediately. He took out a packet of Rothmans from his pocket, and extracted a cigarette. He then lit it, inhaled and said, 'Look, I was never close to my father. I took no interest in his passion for manuscripts—I simply don't have the eye for art and antiques. I live in Calcutta and work for a private company. Sometimes I have to go abroad on business tours. But despite all this, I used to be on fairly good terms with my father. If I wrote to him, he always replied to my letters. I visited him twice with my family after he moved to Puri, and spent a few weeks on the first floor of his house. He was—and perhaps still is—extremely fond of my eight-year-old son. But his behaviour on this occasion just doesn't make any sense to me. I can hardly believe that a strong man like him has gone senile at the age of sixty-two. I do not even know if a third person is responsible for this. So when I heard you were in town, I thought I'd come and see you.'

'How long has your father had this secretary?'

'About four years. I saw him when I came in '76.'

'What kind of a man do you think he is?'

'That's difficult to say, I hardly knew him. All I can say is that he may be good at keeping papers and files in order and typing letters, but I'm sure my father couldn't talk to him as he would to a friend.'

'Well then, you ought to know this: a most valuable manuscript in your father's collection has been stolen, and his secretary has vanished.'

Mahim Sen's jaw fell open.

'What! Did you actually go there?'

'Yes.'

'How did you find my father?'

'In a state of shock, naturally. Apparently, he has recently started to sleep in the afternoon, and he takes something to help him sleep. Today, an American was supposed to meet him at half past six. Nishith Bose had made this appointment. But, he wasn't there to take this visitor up to meet your father. A servant met him downstairs and accompanied him. Normally, Mr Sen gets up by four o'clock, but today he slept till six. Anyway, he was up when this American arrived and said he wanted to take a look at the oldest manuscript. Your father then opened the safe in which it was kept, but discovered that, wrapped in red silk, were masses of white strips of paper. These were placed between two small wooden bars, so it was impossible to tell without unwrapping the packet that the real manuscript had gone. When he realized his most precious possession had been stolen, your father became so distressed that eventually the American visitor informed the police.'

'Does that mean it was Nishith Bose who—?'

'That's what it looks like. I met him this morning at the railway station. Now it seems he had gone to buy a ticket. The police made enquiries at the station, but by then, the Puri Express and other trains to Calcutta had left. They're still trying to trace him.'

Feluda stopped speaking. None of us knew what to say. Such a lot had happened in the last few hours—it made my head reel.

'Did you know your father had gone to Nepal last year?' Feluda asked.

'If he went after August, I wouldn't know, for I was abroad for seven months, starting from August. Father used to travel quite a lot to look for manuscripts. Why, what happened in Nepal?'

Feluda said nothing in reply, but asked another question instead. 'Are you aware that your father's got gout?'

Mahim Sen looked completely taken aback.

'Gout? My father's got gout? What are you saying, Mr Mitter?'

'Why, is that so difficult to believe?'

'Yes, it is. I saw Father last May. He used to go for long, brisk walks on the beach. He's always been careful with his diet, never drank or smoked, or done anything that might damage his health. In fact, he's always been rather proud of his good health. If what you're telling me is true, it's as amazing as it's tragic.'

'Could that be a reason for his present state of mind?'

'Yes, certainly. I don't think he could ever accept himself as an invalid.'

'Well, I am going to be here for a few days. Let's see what I can do. I must confess a lot of things are not clear to me,' Feluda said.

Mahim Sen rose. 'I came here to discuss a few things related to our old family business. I have to stay on until Father agrees to see me.'

He said goodbye after this, and left. We chatted for a while, then decided to go to bed. It was nearly midnight.

Lalmohan Babu stopped near the door and turned back. 'Felu Babu,' he said, 'I've just remembered something. You were supposed to ring Kathmandu, weren't you?'

'Yes, I was; and I did. I spoke to one Dr Bhargav in Veer Hospital, and asked him if anyone called Bilas Majumdar had been brought to this hospital last October with serious injuries.'

'What did he say?'

'He confirmed everything Mr Majumdar had told us. There was a broken shin bone, a fractured collarbone, broken ribs and an injured chin.'

'Didn't you believe Mr Majumdar's story?'

'Checking and re-checking facts is an essential part of an investigator's job. Surely you're aware of that, Lalmohan Babu? Doesn't your own hero, Prakhar Rudra, do the same?'

'Y-yes, yes, of course . . .' Lalmohan Babu muttered and quickly left the room. I lay down, listening to the waves outside. I knew there was a similar turmoil in Feluda's mind. One thought must be chasing another, exactly like the restless waves of the sea, but he appeared calm, collected and at peace. When the Nulias went into deep water in their fishing boats, past the breakers near the shore, perhaps that was what they got to see: a serene and tranquil sea.

'What is that, Feluda?' I asked, suddenly noticing a brown, square object Feluda had taken out of his pocket. A closer glance told me it was a wallet.

Feluda opened it and took out a few ten-rupee notes. Then he put them back and said absently, 'I found it in a drawer in Nishith Bose's room. He took his suitcase and his bedding, but left his wallet behind. Strange!'

TEN

I opened my eyes the next morning to find Feluda doing yoga. This meant the sun wasn't yet up. He had been awake when I went to sleep the previous night, and had worked in the light of a table lamp until quite late. How he had managed to get up at the crack of dawn was a mystery.

A slight noise from the veranda made me glance in that direction. To my amazement, I saw Lalmohan Babu standing there, just outside his room, idly putting his favourite red-and-white Signal toothpaste on his toothbrush. Obviously, like us, he was too worked up to sleep peacefully.

Feluda finished his yoga and said, 'I'll have a cup of tea now, and then go out.'

'Where to?'

'Nowhere in particular. Just out. I need to clear my brain. Sometimes looking at something enormous and colossal helps get things into perspective. I must stand before the sea and watch the sun rise. It may act like a tonic.'

By the time we finished our tea, many other guests in the hotel were awake, including Mr Barik.

Feluda went to see him before going out.

'Will you book another call to Nepal, please? Here's the number,' he said, 'and if Mahapatra calls, please tell him to leave a message. And—oh—are there good doctors here?'

'How many would you like? Of course we have good doctors here, Mr Mitter, you haven't come to a little village!'

'No, no, I know I haven't. But you see, I need a young and efficient doctor. Not someone doddering with age.'

'That's not a problem. Go to Utkal Chemist in Grand Road after ten o'clock. You'll find Dr Senapati in his chamber.'

Lalmohan Babu and I decided to go out with Feluda. The beach was deserted except for a few Nulias. The eastern sky glowed red. Grey clouds floated about, their edges a pale pink. The sea was blue-black; only the tops of the waves that crashed on the shore were a bright white.

The three Nulia children we had seen on the first day were back on the beach, looking for crabs.

'The only minus point of this beautiful beach is those crabs,' Lalmohan Babu remarked, wrinkling his nose in disgust.

'What's your name?' Feluda asked one of the boys. He had a red scarf wound around his head.

'Ramai,' he replied, grinning.

We walked on. Lalmohan Babu suddenly turned poetic. 'Look at the sea . . . so wide, so big, so . . . so liberating . . . it's hard to imagine there's been bloodshed in a place like this!'

'Hm . . . blunt instrument . . .' Feluda said absently. I knew murder weapons were usually of three kinds: fire arms such as revolvers or pistols; sharp instruments like knives and daggers; or blunt instruments such as heavy rods or sticks. Feluda was clearly thinking of the attack on him last night. Thank God it was nothing serious.

'Footprints . . . look!' Feluda exclaimed suddenly. I looked where he was pointing, and saw fresh marks: footprints, accompanied by the now familiar mark left by a walking stick.

'Bilas Majumdar! He must be an early riser,' Lalmohan Babu observed. 'Do you really think so? Look at that person over there,' Feluda said, pointing at a figure in the distance. 'Do you think he looks like Bilas Majumdar?'

It was not difficult to tell, even from a distance, that the man who was walking with a stick in his left hand, was not Mr Majumdar at all.

'You're right. It's someone else. Why, it's the Sensational Sen!' Lalmohan Babu shouted.

'Correct. It's Durga Gati Sen.'

'But how come he's walking? What about his gout?'

'That's what I'd like to know. Perhaps Laxman Bhattacharya's medicines can bring about miraculous recoveries, who knows?'

We resumed walking, each of us feeling puzzled. How many mysteries would we finally end up with?

The Railway Hotel emerged as we took a left turn. On our right I could see a few Nulias and three foreigners clad in swimming trunks.

One of them saw Feluda and raised a hand in greeting. Feluda waved back, explaining quickly that it was the same American who had informed the police from Mr Sen's house.

We walked on. There was Mr Hingorani, walking swiftly, with a towel flung over his shoulder. He was frowning darkly, looking most displeased. He didn't even glance at us. Feluda left the beach and began climbing up a slope. Something told me he was making his way to Sagarika. Had his brain cleared? Was he beginning to see the light? Before I could ask him anything, however, another voice piped up from somewhere. 'Good morning!' it said.

Laxman Bhattacharya was standing before us, wearing a lungi tucked in at the waist, a towel on his shoulder and a neem twig in his hand.

'Good morning. Where were you yesterday evening?' Feluda asked.

'Yesterday evening? Oh, I had gone to listen to some keertan. There's a group in Mangalghat Road. They sing quite well. I go there every now and then.'

'You weren't home when I went looking for you. What time did you leave the house?'

'I can get away only after six. That's when I went.'

'I thought you might be able to shed some light on this theft in Mr Sen's house, since you live in it yourself. It's possible to see the side lane from your room, isn't it?'

'Yes. In fact, I saw Nishith Bose leave with his luggage through that lane. This did not surprise me at the time, for he was expected to leave for Calcutta, anyway.'

'Really? Why?'

'His mother was seriously ill. He received a telegram the other day.'

'Did you see this telegram?'

'Yes, so did Mr Sen.'

'Why, he didn't say anything about it!' Feluda sounded surprised.

'Well . . . now, what can I say? You've seen for yourself the state he's in. He's destined to suffer. Who can change what's ordained?'

'Have you examined Mr Sen's future as well?' Lalmohan Babu asked anxiously.

'There are very few people in this town who haven't come to me. But do you know what the problem is? I cannot always tell people what I see. I open my mouth if I see symptoms of an illness. But how is it possible to say to someone things like: you'll one day commit a murder, or you'll go to prison, or you'll be hanged? No one will ever want to come to me if I told them such unpleasant things. So I have to choose my words very carefully because people wish to hear only good things.'

Mr Bhattacharya went off in the direction of the sea. We moved on towards Sagarika. It looked beautiful in the early morning sun.

'The house of death,' Lalmohan Babu said suddenly.

'How can you say that?' Feluda protested. 'You might call it the house of theft, but there hasn't been a death in this house.'

'No, no. I don't mean Sagarika,' Lalmohan Babu explained hastily. 'I mean this other house that looks like it might collapse any minute.'

We had seen this house before, but hadn't really noticed it in any detail. Sagarika was about thirty yards away from it. Now I looked at it carefully, and found myself agreeing with Lalmohan Babu. As it is, an old and crumbling building with damp, dank walls isn't a very pleasant sight. This building, in addition to all that, had sunk into the sand. Nearly six feet from the bottom was buried in the sand. This gave it a rather spooky air. I felt my flesh creep to look at it in broad daylight. What must it look like at night?

Instead of walking past it, Feluda walked into it today. The pillars of the front gate were still standing upright. There was a cracked and dirty marble slab that said 'Bhujanga Niwas'. If the house kept sinking, it wouldn't be long before the slab was submerged in sand. Beyond the gate there must once have been a small garden. A series of steps then led to a veranda. Only the top two steps were visible; others had disappeared in the sand. The railing around the veranda had worn away. It was surprising that the roof had not caved in. The room behind the veranda must have been a drawing room.

'It doesn't look totally abandoned,' Feluda remarked. I saw immediately why he had said that, for, on the dusty floor of the veranda, were footprints.

'And there are matchsticks, Feluda!' I said. There were three matchsticks lying by a pillar.

'Yes, I guess if you tried to light a cigarette standing here in this strong wind, you'd be bound to waste a few,' Feluda replied.

We walked in through the gate. I was bursting with curiosity to go and find out what was inside the house. The door to the drawing room was open, rattling in the wind. Feluda inspected the prints on the floor. They were not very clear, for a fresh layer of sand had already settled over them. But there was no doubt that someone wearing shoes had walked on this veranda pretty recently.

Another thing became visible as Feluda removed some of the sand with his foot—a dark stain, which to me looked like paan juice. Lalmohan Babu, however, quickly stepped back and declared it had to be blood. Then he muttered something about it being time for breakfast. This clearly meant he had no wish to go into the house and would much rather go back to the hotel. I felt my own heart beating faster, partly in excitement and partly in fear. Only Feluda remained completely unperturbed. 'I think we ought to visit your house of death,' he announced, pushing the door gently. It swung open with a loud creak.

A musty, slightly foul smell wafted out immediately. Perhaps there were bats inside. It was totally dark in the room. If there were windows, they were obviously shut, and we ourselves were blocking the light coming in through the open door. Feluda crossed the threshold and stepped in. I followed him a second later. Only Lalmohan Babu hesitated outside. 'All clear?' he asked after a while in a voice that sounded unnaturally loud.

'Oh yes. And things will no doubt soon become even clearer. Come and see what's inside,' Feluda invited. By now my eyes had got a little focused in the dark, and I had seen what Feluda was referring to. There was a small trunk and bedding, wrapped carelessly in a durrie. Both had been dumped in a corner.

'The police are wasting their time,' Feluda said slowly. 'Nishith Bose has not gone to Calcutta.'

'Well then, where is he?' Lalmohan Babu asked, surprised. He had finally joined us in the room.

Feluda did not reply.

'Hmm. Very interesting,' he muttered, staring at something else. I followed his gaze. In another corner was a small heap, consisting of long, narrow pieces of wood and reams and reams of cheap yellow paper, tied with strings.

'Any idea what this might mean?' Feluda asked.

'Those pieces of wood . . . why, they look like the wood used for manuscripts!' Lalmohan Babu exclaimed. 'And . . . oh!' He seemed bereft of speech.

'It seems Nishith Bose had started a regular factory,' I said slowly, 'for making fake manuscripts. I guess all he had to do was chop bits of wood down to the right size, then place bits of paper between them, and wrap the whole thing up in red silk. It would certainly have looked like an ancient manuscript.'

'Exactly,' said Feluda. 'It is my belief that many of Mr Sen's manuscripts are fake. What he had bought was genuine, of course, but since then someone has removed the original piece and replaced it with plain paper. The real stuff has been sold to people like Hingorani.'

'Oh, ho, ho, ho!' Lalmohan Babu suddenly found his tongue. 'Remember that strip of paper I saw on our first visit to Mr Sen's house? The one I thought was a snake? That must have been a piece of paper used for making dummies of real manuscripts.'

'Undoubtedly,' Feluda said firmly.

We were standing in the middle of the room. There were two side doors, one on our right and the other on our left. Presumably, they led to other rooms. Through the open front door—through which we had walked a few minutes ago—a strong sea breeze blew in with considerable force. The door to our right opened unexpectedly, making a loud noise that sounded almost like a gunshot. What followed next froze my blood. Even now, my heart trembles as I write about it.

Lalmohan Babu was the first to look through the open door. He made a strange noise in his throat, his eyes began popping out, and he'd probably have fainted; but Feluda leapt forward and caught him before he could sink to the floor. In speechless horror, I stared at the figure that lay on the floor in the next room. It was a man. No, it was the dead body of a man; and even I could tell he had lain there, dead, for quite some time, although his eyes were still open. I had no difficulty in recognizing him.

It was D.G. Sen's secretary, Nishith Bose.

ELEVEN

Feluda had to miss breakfast that day.

Once Lalmohan Babu had recovered somewhat, we went to the Railway Hotel as it was closer and rang the police from there. Then we returned to our own hotel.

Feluda left us soon afterwards. 'I have a few things to do, particularly in the Nulia colony, so I've got to go,' he said. He had already told us—even without touching the body—that Mr Bose had been killed with a blunt instrument, though there was no sign of the weapon. Who knew when Lalmohan Babu had called the broken old Bhujanga Niwas the 'House of Death', he was actually speaking the truth?

There was, however, a piece of good news. D.G. Sen and his son appeared to have got back together. While coming out of Bhujanga Niwas, I happened to glance at Sagarika and saw both father and son on the roof. Mahim Sen gave us a cheerful wave, so presumably all was well. How this sudden change in their relationship had occurred, I could not tell. It was most mystifying.

Feluda returned at a quarter to eleven. I suddenly remembered he had booked a call to Nepal. 'Did your call come through?' I asked.

'Yes, I just finished speaking.'

'Did you call Kathmandu?'

'No, Patan. It's an old town near Kathmandu, on the other side of the river Bagmati.'

'Felu Babu,' Lalmohan Babu squeaked, 'I can't get over the shock. Look, I am still shivering.'

'Do stop, Lalmohan Babu. At least, save some of it for tonight.'

'Why—what is happening tonight?'

'Tonight,' Feluda replied calmly, 'we'll have to stand—not on one leg, mind you—but stand still and wait.'

'Where?'

'You'll see.'

'Why? What for?'

'You'll learn, by and by.'

Lalmohan Babu opened his mouth once more, then shut it, looking crestfallen. But then, like me, he wasn't unfamiliar with the kind of mood Feluda was in. One could ask him a thousand questions, but he wouldn't give a straight answer.

'Dr Senapati is quite a smart young doctor,' Feluda said, changing the subject.

'Why, have you been to his clinic already?' I asked.

'Yes. He has been treating Mr D.G. Sen. He went to America last April. It was he who brought that medicine.'

'Diapid?' The name had got stuck in my memory for some reason.

'Since you ask, I can tell you'll never need to use it yourself,' Feluda laughed. God knows what this cryptic remark meant. I didn't dare ask.

Inspector Mahapatra rang an hour later. The police surgeon had finished his examination. According to him, Nishith Bose had been killed between 6 and 8 p.m. last evening, with a blunt instrument. There was still no sign of the weapon. But the police had found traces of blood under the sand below the veranda. Presumably, the murder took place near the front gate. Mr Bose's body was then dragged inside.

A sudden idea flashed through my mind, but I chose not to say anything to Feluda. Could it be possible that whoever killed Mr Bose had attacked Feluda, using the same instrument? Perhaps that was why there was blood on his head, even without an open wound?

At around half past twelve, I began to feel hungry. Lalmohan Babu, too, started to comment on the heavenly smell emanating from the kitchen. But, at this moment, Bilas Majumdar turned up.

'Would you like to go?' he asked without any preamble.

'Where to?' Feluda asked, busily scribbling something in his notebook.

'A place called Keonjhargarh, in an airconditioned limousine supplied by the tourist department. There's room for six. But I found only one other person to go with me, an American called Steadman. He's a wildlife enthusiast as well. You'll find it interesting, I'm sure, if you come with us.'

'When are you leaving?'

'Straight after lunch.'

'No, thank you. I'm afraid I've got some work this afternoon. In fact, if you could stay back for a few hours, I might be able to show you a sample of the wildlife in Puri!'

'No, Mr Mitter, thank you very much.' Mr Majumdar smiled and left.

A minute later, we heard a heavy American car start. Then it turned around and sped towards the north.

When was the last time I had been under such tense excitement? I couldn't remember.

We had dinner at nine that evening. An hour later, Feluda announced it was time to go. 'You'll have to be suitably dressed,' he told me. 'Don't wear kurta-pajamas, and don't wear white. I don't need to tell you what you must wear to hide in the dark, do I?'

No, there was no need to do that, I thought, my mind going back to our experience in the graveyard in Park Street.

'My instincts tell me something is going to happen tonight,' Feluda added, 'but there is no guarantee that it will. So prepare yourselves for possible disappointment.'

I looked at the sky as we went out, and saw that there were no stars. Lalmohan Babu, who had formed a habit of looking up at the sky every now and then (not in search of stars or the moon, but for signs of the skylab), quickly raised his head and said, 'Had the wind been blowing in a different direction, the pieces might have fallen into the sea. Now . . . anything can happen.'

Although Bhujanga Niwas was surrounded by sand, the actual beach was about fifty yards away from it. There were a few makeshift shelters where the beach started, presumably for the guests in the Railway Hotel who came to bathe in the sea. Large reed mats had been fixed over bamboo poles to create these shelters. Feluda stopped beside one of these. Behind us was the sea, still roaring loudly, but now hardly visible in the dark. If anyone went walking past our shelter, we'd be able to see his figure, but we might not recognize him. There was no chance of being seen ourselves. Feluda could not have chosen a better spot in which to hide. It was still not clear why we were hiding, and I knew he wouldn't tell me even if I asked. Annoyed with his habit of keeping things to himself, Lalmohan Babu had once said to him, 'You, Felu Babu, should make suspense films. People would die holding their breath. Much better than even Hotchkick, that would be!'

I could see Mr Sen's house from where we were standing. The light in his room on the second floor was still on. A light on the first floor had just gone out. Only one window on the ground floor was visible over the compound wall. A light was on, so perhaps Laxman Bhattacharya was still awake.

We were all sitting on the sand under the shelter, in absolute silence. Speaking would have been difficult, in any case, because of the noisy waves. By now my eyes had got used to the darkness and I could see a few things. On my left was Lalmohan Babu. The few remaining strands of hair around his bald head were blowing hard in the strong wind, rising like tufts of grass. Feluda sat on my right. I saw him raise his left hand and peer at his wrist. Then he slipped his hand into his shoulder bag and took out an object—his Japanese binoculars.

He placed it to his eyes. I knew what he was looking at. D.G. Sen was standing near his open window. After a few moments, he moved aside and picked something up with his right hand.

What was it?

Oh, a glass tumbler. What was he drinking from it?

The light on the ground floor had gone out. Now Mr Sen switched off his own light. Immediately, the darkness around us seemed to grow more dense. However, I could still vaguely see my companions, especially if they made a movement.

Lalmohan Babu took out his torch from his pocket. I quickly leant over and whispered in his ear: 'Don't switch it on!' In reply, he turned his head and muttered: 'This is a blunt instrument. It may come in handy, even if I don't switch it on.' He moved his head away; and, at this moment, I saw something that made my heart fly into my mouth. On our right, about ten yards away, was another shelter. A man was standing next to it. God knows when he had appeared. Lalmohan Babu had seen him, too. He dropped the torch in astonishment.

And Feluda?

He hadn't seen him. He was looking straight at Sagarika. I forced myself to look in the same direction, and spotted instantly what Feluda had already seen.

A man was walking out of Sagarika. Was he going to come towards us? No. He made his way to the broken and abandoned Bhujanga Niwas. He slowed down as he got closer to the building, then stopped near one of the pillars. What was he going to do?

It became clear in the next instant. A second man appeared from behind the house and joined the first. There were now two male figures standing before the gate. It was impossible to tell if they spoke to each other, but they separated in a few seconds and started to walk in different directions. The one who had come from Sagarika was making his way back—!

On no! Lalmohan Babu had jabbed at his torch carelessly and switched it on by accident. Feluda snatched it from his hand and threw it down on the sand. But, in the same instant, someone fired a gun. A bullet came and hit one of the bamboo poles of our shelter, making an ear-splitting noise and missing Lalmohan Babu's neck by a few inches.

'Get the other one!' hissed Feluda and shot up like a rocket to chase the second man. To my own surprise, I discovered that those few words from Feluda were enough to make me forget fear. I jumped to my feet without a word and began sprinting towards the first man.

It did not take me long to catch up with him. I threw myself at his legs, a bit like a rugby player doing a 'flying tackle', and managed to grab them both. The man tripped and fell flat on his face. I lost no time climbing on to his back. Then I looked around for Feluda.

Two silhouettes were standing at a slight distance, facing each other. I saw one of them raise a hand and aim for the other's chin. A second later, the second figure was knocked down on the ground. I even heard the faint thud as he fell.

In the meantime, Lalmohan Babu had joined me and was dancing around with his blunt instrument in his hand, waiting for a suitable opportunity to strike the figure wriggling under me. However, another soft thud soon told me that, in his excitement, he had dropped his weapon on the sand once more.

'Bring him over here!' Feluda shouted.

This time, Lalmohan Babu was of real help. He took one leg, and I caught the other. Together, we dragged the man to join Feluda. Feluda was standing with one foot on the chest of his opponent, and the other on his right hand. The revolver this hand had held a few moments ago was lying nearby.

'Until today, you had no injury on your chin. But after this, I think there will be a permanent mark,' Feluda declared solemnly, shining his pocket torch on the man.

The word 'wildlife' suddenly flashed through my mind. Pinned down by his feet, staring back at Feluda, his eyes wild with anger, was Bilas Majumdar. His left hand was still curled around an object wrapped in red silk. Another manuscript! Feluda bent down and snatched it away. Then he turned and shone his torch on our prisoner. 'What is your third eye telling you, Laxman Babu?' Feluda asked, 'Did you know what was written in your own destiny?'

Suddenly, several shadows emerged from the darkness. Who on earth were these people?

'Hello, Mr Mahapatra,' Feluda greeted one of them, 'I'm going to hand these two culprits over to you, but I haven't yet finished. I'd like us all to go and sit in the living room of Bhujanga Niwas. These two men must come with us.'

Four constables stepped forward and grabbed Bilas Majumdar and Laxman Bhattacharya. 'Mahim Babu, are you there?' Feluda called.

'Oh yes. Here I am!' Mahim Sen raised a hand. With a start, I realized he was the man we had first seen standing near a shelter. 'I think Father's about to join us. Look, there he is, with a torch,' he added, pointing.

'We've made seating arrangements in the front room of that building,' said Mr Mahapatra, pointing at Bhujanga Niwas. 'There will be room for all, don't worry.'

'Why, it's just fine outside, why not—?' began Lalmohan Babu, but I don't think anyone heard him, for everyone had already started walking towards Bhujanga Niwas.

TWELVE

'Come in, Mr Sen, we're all waiting for you,' Feluda opened the door. Mahim Sen came in with his father. Three lanterns had been lit in the room, the police had clearly worked quite hard at cleaning and dusting. It looked a different room altogether.

Father and son took two chairs.

'Here's your *Kalpasutra,*' said Feluda, offering him the manuscript he had just recovered from Bilas Majumdar. Mr Sen looked visibly relieved as he took it, but asked with considerable anxiety, 'What about the other one?'

'I am coming to that. You'll have to bear with me. I hope you didn't take a sleeping pill today?'

'No, no, of course not. That's what led to this disaster. God knows what he put in my glass of water yesterday!' Mr Sen glared at Laxman Bhattacharya.

'What I fail to understand is why you went to this humbug in the first place. Didn't you know there were other much better doctors in town?'

'I did, Mr Mitter. But he came to me himself, and everyone else said he was very good. So I thought I should give him a chance. Besides, he said he knew of old manuscripts and scrolls . . . he could get me a few . . .'

'That's your biggest weakness, isn't it? And he took full advantage of it. Anyway, I hope the Diapid has worked? That's supposed to be the best among modern drugs to bring back lost memory.'

'It's worked like a charm!' Mr Sen exclaimed. 'My memory is coming back to me, exactly as if one door is being opened after another. Thank God Dr Senapati came to me himself and gave me that medicine. You see, I had even forgotten that it was he who used to treat me before!'

'Well then, tell me, Mr Sen, can you recognize this gentleman?' Feluda flashed his torch on Bilas Majumdar. Mr Sen stared at him for a few seconds, then said slowly, 'Yes, I could recognize him yesterday from the look in his eyes and his voice. But still, I wasn't sure.'

'Can you remember his name?'

'Certainly. But he may have changed it here.'

'Is his name Sarkar?'

'Yes, that's right. Mr Sarkar. I never learnt his first name.'

'Liar!' Mr Majumdar screamed. 'Do you want to see my passport?'

'No, we don't,' Feluda's voice was ice-cold. 'A criminal like you may well have a fake passport. That won't mean anything at all. What's in it, anyway? It describes you as Bilas Majumdar, right? And states that you have a distinguishing mark on your forehead, a mole? OK. Now watch this.'

Feluda strode over to Mr Majumdar and took out his handkerchief from his pocket. Then, without any warning whatsoever, he struck at his forehead with the handkerchief still in his hand. This made the false mole slip out and hit the dark floor.

'You made a lot of enquiries about Bilas Majumdar, didn't you?' Feluda went on. 'You knew he had gone to take photos of a snow leopard, and then he had had an accident. You even knew which hospital he had been taken to, the nature of his injuries and that he had been kept in the same hospital until last month. But a tiny news item escaped your notice. I had read it, but hadn't paid much attention at the time. Yesterday, Dr Bhargav of Veer Hospital in Kathmandu confirmed what I vaguely remembered having read. Bilas Majumdar's most serious injury was to the brain. He died three weeks ago.'

Even in the dim light from the lanterns, I could see the man had turned white as a sheet. 'Listen, Mr Sarkar,' Feluda said, 'your profession is something that no passport will ever reveal. You are a smuggler. Perhaps you don't always steal things yourself, but you certainly help in transferring smuggled goods. In Kathmandu, you had come upon the scroll stolen from the palace museum in Bhatgaon. Mr Sen will tell you the rest.'

The look in D.G. Sen's eyes was cold and hard as steel. He said, 'This man and I happened to be staying in the same hotel in Kathmandu. One day, I unlocked his door by mistake, and found two other men in his room. One of them was in the process of handing him an object wrapped in red silk. I realized immediately that it was a manuscript. But all I could do at that moment was apologize and come away. God knows what happened to me that night. When I woke up, I found myself in a hospital. Every memory prior to this incident was gone from my mind. But people were very kind. They found my address from the hotel, and eventually managed to inform my family. Nishith went and brought me back. I had to spend three and a half months in hospital.'

'I think I can fill the gaps in your memory. If I get anything wrong, perhaps Mr Sarkar will correct me?' Feluda said coolly. 'You were obviously given something that made you unconscious. You were then taken by car outside the main city, into the mountains and dropped from a height of five hundred feet. Mr Sarkar was convinced you were dead. However, nine months later, when he came to Puri to transfer the stolen scroll, he saw your nameplate and began to get suspicious. It is my belief that the occupant of your ground floor, Mr Laxman Bhattacharya, supplied him with all the necessary information regarding your present condition. Am I right?'

Laxman Bhattacharya, who had not uttered a single word so far, burst into speech at this. 'What are you saying, sir? I supplied all the information to him? Why, I saw him for the first time when you brought him to my place!'

'Really?' Feluda walked across to stand directly before Laxman Bhattacharya. 'Well then, Mr Astrologer, tell me this: when we took him to your place, you asked him to sit on the divan immediately, and told us to take the chairs. How did you know he was Bilas Majumdar, and not me? Who told you that?'

Laxman Bhattacharya could not make a reply. He seemed to shrink into himself with just that one question from Feluda.

Feluda continued. 'I think the idea of stealing manuscripts first occurred to Mr Sarkar when he heard about Mr Sen's loss of memory, and when Laxman Bhattacharya offered to help him. He knew he could easily find a buyer for an old and valuable scroll, since Mr Hingorani was in the same hotel. But three major difficulties suddenly arose to complicate matters. Firstly, a totally undesirable character followed Mr Sarkar all the way to Puri. It was Rupchand Singh. He really gave you a lot of trouble, didn't he? I mean, it's easy enough to bribe the driver of a car that takes an unconscious man to the top of a hill to kill him. But what happens if this driver is not happy with what he has paid? What if he's greedy and starts blackmailing you to get more? What can anyone do under such circumstances, tell me, but kill the blackmailer?'

'Lies, lies, lies!' Mr Sarkar cried desperately.

'Suppose, Mr Sarkar, I could prove that the bullet that killed Rupchand Singh had come from your own revolver? This same revolver you had tried to use on us a little while ago? What then?'

Mr Sarkar sank back instantly. I could see that his whole body was bathed in sweat. I was sweating, too, but that was simply in breathless excitement. Lalmohan Babu, sitting next to me, was looking as though he was watching a fencing match. It was true, of course, that Feluda's words were as sharp as a sword; and the game wasn't over yet.

'Rupchand Singh was victim number one,' Feluda continued. 'Now let's look at the second problem Mr Sarkar had to tackle. It was my own arrival in Puri. Mr Sarkar realized he could do nothing without somehow pulling the wool over my eyes. So he decided to pass himself off as Bilas Majumdar. I must say initially he succeeded very well in this task. Not only that, he even managed to shift his own blame on to an old man who had lost his memory. It was this initial success that made him a bit reckless. His plan was quite simple. If he could get hold of a manuscript, he'd sell it to Hingorani. There was no way he could get it from its rightful owner, for Mr Sen wasn't even remotely interested in money, and the old manuscripts to him were perhaps more precious to him than his own life. So the stuff had to be stolen from the safe. How would he do that? Very simple. The job would be done by Laxman Bhattacharya, because he had been doing it for quite sometime. When he did it before, he had obviously pocketed the whole amount himself. In this particular case, he agreed to share with Mr Sarkar the money Hingorani offered, since it was a fairly large sum. But they had to consider one other person. It was Mr Sen's secretary, Nishith Bose.'

Feluda paused. Then he walked over to Mr Bhattacharya once more and asked, 'Didn't you say something about going to a keertan?'

Laxman Bhattacharya tried to appear nonchalant. 'So I did,' he said. 'Why, you think I lied?'

'No. You didn't lie about the keertan. It is true that a group of singers get together every Monday for a session of keertan. But you have never gone there. I checked. However, there was one person who used to go there regularly. It was Nishith Bose. He used to be absent from his duties every Monday from five to six-thirty in the evening. A servant used to be around at that time to take care of visitors. He was bribed last Monday, after Mr Bose left the house. You, Mr Bhattacharya, tampered with Mr Sen's glass of water, got him to take a heavy dose of your sleeping pills, and then entered his room at five-thirty. Then you took the key from under his pillow, opened the safe and removed one of the most precious manuscripts, in order to hand it over to Mr Sarkar. You had arranged to meet him on the veranda of this house. You arrived here first, and spent some time waiting for your accomplice. Your footprints, your used matchsticks and the paan juice you spat out on the floor, all gave you away. But something totally unexpected happened while you were waiting, didn't it, Mr Bhattacharya?'

Laxman Bhattacharya made no attempt to speak. He was trembling violently, as—with the only exception of Mr Sarkar—everyone in the room was staring at him. I felt my body go rigid with tension.

Feluda started speaking again.

'An American was supposed to visit Mr Sen at half-past six that evening. So Nishith Bose returned at six, which was much earlier than usual. Perhaps he started to get suspicious when he found his employer still asleep. He must then have opened the safe and discovered the theft. You were not at home. This must have made him even more suspicious. So he came out of the house, saw your footprints on the sand, and followed you to Bhujanga Niwas. When you realized you had been caught red-handed, what could you do but finish Mr Bose instantly? You had a blunt instrument in your hand, didn't you? So you used it to kill Mr Bose, then removed his body and returned to Sagarika to fetch his suitcase and bedding. Just as all seemed to be well, you saw that there were blood stains on your weapon. So you left once more to throw it into the sea, but who did you run into on your way to the beach? It was me. You struck my head with the same weapon, and then dropped it in the water. Tell me, is any of this incorrect?'

Feluda stopped, although he must have known Laxman

Bhattacharya was totally incapable of making a reply. But the brief pause helped in emphasizing his next question. It shot through the air like a bullet.

'In spite of all this, Mr Bhattacharya, could you get what you wanted?'

Silence. Feluda answered his own question. 'No. Hingorani didn't get that scroll, nor did Mr Sarkar. That was why you found it necessary to steal the second most valuable manuscript tonight. By this time, you had told everyone the story about Mr Bose's mother's illness which accounted for his absence. But can you tell these people now why you failed to get the first manuscript? No? Very well, I'll tell them, for I don't think you could explain the details of such an extraordinary occurrence. Even I was fooled at first. I've solved a number of difficult cases, but this one was truly amazing. I knew the instrument used was a blunt one, but how was I to know it was the scroll itself? Yes, the stolen scroll, written by Pragya Paramita in the twelfth century. How was I to know that that was the only thing Laxman Bhattacharya had in his hand to strike a person with? I couldn't figure it out, despite being hit by the same wooden bars. The scroll was bloodstained. Some of that blood got smeared on my own head. Naturally, you could not pass it on to either Sarkar or Hingorani.'

'Oh no, oh no, oh no!' cried D.G. Sen, covering his face with his hands. 'My manuscript! My most precious, my very—'

'Listen, Mr Sen,' Feluda turned to him. 'Did you know that the sea doesn't always accept what's offered to it? In fact, sometimes, it returns an offering almost immediately?'

Feluda slipped a hand into his shoulder bag and, almost like a magician, brought out a manuscript covered in red silk.

'Here is your *Ashtadashasahasrika Pragya Paramita*. The silk wrapper is quite unharmed. The wooden bars have been damaged, but the actual writing is more or less unspoilt. Not much water could seep in through layers of wood and cloth.'

'But. . . but . . . where did you get it, Felu Babu?' Lalmohan Babu gasped.

'You saw that piece of red silk this morning,' Feluda replied. 'That little Nulia boy called Ramai was wearing it round his head. It made me think. That's why I went to the Nulia colony and retrieved it. Ramai had found the scroll stuck in the wet sand near the edge of the water. He took the silk wrapper, but the manuscript was kept safe in his house. I had to pay ten rupees to get it. Mr Mahapatra, will you please get Sarkar's wallet and give me ten rupees from it?'

I had no idea the sea looked so much more enormous from the terrace of Mr Sen's house. I stood near the railing, marvelling at the sight.

Last night, after the police had left with the two culprits, Mr Sen had invited us for morning coffee. Mahim Sen had spent the night with his father, since Nishith Bose was dead and the servant had run away. On hearing this, Feluda offered immediately to speak to Shyamlal Barik of our hotel and arrange for a new servant. The cook brought us coffee on the terrace.

By this time, Mr Sen had handed a cheque to Feluda. The amount on it was so handsome that it made up for all the weeks Feluda had spent at home before coming to Puri. Initially, Feluda had refused to accept it, but when Mr Sen began to insist, he had to take it. Lalmohan Babu said to him later, 'If you didn't take that cheque, Felu babu, I would have hit you with a blunt instrument. Why do you turn all modest and humble when you're offered payment? I find it most annoying!'

'Do you know, Mr Sen,' said Feluda, sipping his coffee, 'what baffled me the most? It was your gout.'

Mr Sen raised his eyebrows. 'Why? What's so baffling about that? Can't an old man get gout?'

'Yes, but you go for long walks on the beach, don't you? I saw your footprints on the sand but, like an idiot, thought they were Majumdar's—I mean, Sarkar's. But yesterday, I realized it was you.'

'So what did that prove? Gout is extremely painful, but the pain does sometimes subside, you know.'

'I'm sure it does. But your footprints tell a different story, Mr Sen. I didn't raise this last night because I thought you wanted to keep it a secret. The trouble is, you see, it isn't always possible to keep secrets from an investigator. The stick you use is pretty significant, isn't it? Besides, your shoes aren't both of the same size. I noticed that.'

Mr Sen sat in silence, looking straight at Feluda. Feluda resumed speaking. 'The Veer Hospital in Kathmandu confirmed the news about Bilas Majumdar's accident. But no one else had been brought there with similar injuries. Then I looked at my guide book and realized that there was another hospital called Shanta Bhavan in

Patan, which is near Kathmandu. I rang them, and was told that one Durga Gati Sen had been brought there with severe injuries in October last year. He remained there until early January. They even gave me the details of those injuries.'

The expression on Mr Sen's face changed. He sighed after a short pause, and said, 'Nishith knew I didn't want anyone to learn about what had happened. If I had visitors in the morning, he always dressed my foot with a fresh bandage and told them I had gout. Today, Mahim has done this job. I certainly did not want this fact publicized, Mr Mitter. What happened to me was no less tragic than losing an ancient and valuable manuscript. But since you have already guessed the truth . . .'

He raised his trousers to expose his left leg.

To my complete amazement, I saw that the dressing finished three inches above his ankle. Beyond that was an artificial leg, made of wood and plastic!

The Mysterious Tenant

ONE

'Who was Jayadrath?'

'Duryodhan's sister, Duhshala's husband.'

'And Jarasandh?'

'King of Magadh.'

'Dhrishtadyumna?'

'Draupadi's brother.'

'Arjun and Yudhisthir both owned conch shells. What were they called?'

'Arjun's was called Devdatt, and Yudhisthir's was Anantavijay.'

'Which missile causes such confusion in the enemy camp that they start killing their own men?'

'Twashtra.'

'Very good.'

Thank goodness. I had passed that little test. Of late, the Ramayan and Mahabharat had become staple reading for Feluda. I, too, had joined him and was thoroughly enjoying reading them. There was story, after story, after story. A new word has come into use these days—unputdownable. If you pick up a book to read, you cannot put it down till you've finished it. The Ramayan and the Mahabharat are like that—quite unputdownable.

Feluda was reading the Mahabharat in Bengali, written by Kaliprasanna Sinha. Mine was a simplified version meant for youngsters. Lalmohan Babu says he can recite large chunks of the Bengali Ramayan by heart. His grandmother used to read aloud from it when he was a child, so he still remembers quite a lot of it. We haven't got the Bengali version in our house, but I think I'll get a copy and test Lalmohan Babu's memory one day. At the moment he is busy writing a new novel, so he hasn't been visiting us all that frequently.

Feluda had to stop reading and glance at the front door, for someone had rung the bell. Feluda had returned only last Friday after solving a murder case in Hijli. He was in a relaxed mood, which was probably why he didn't seem too keen to get up and find out who was at the door. As a matter of fact, he does not even need more than one case every month. His needs are so few that he can manage perfectly well on the fees he is paid for each case. Lalmohan Babu calls his lifestyle 'totally unostentatious'. But he always finds it difficult to pronounce that word and ends up saying 'unossenshus.'

Feluda therefore found a tongue-twister for him and told him to practise saying it several times, so that his tongue would stop getting stuck on long and difficult words. 'Pick up these sixty-six thistle sticks' was what he had suggested. Lalmohan Babu tried saying it once, and stumbled four times!

I have often heard Feluda say, 'When a new character appears in your tale, you must describe his looks and clothes in some detail. If you don't, your reader may imagine certain things on his own, which will probably not fit whatever you say later on.' So here's a description of the man who entered our living room: his height was probably 5'9", age around fifty; the hair around his ears had turned grey; there was a mole on his chin, and he was wearing a grey safari suit. From the way he cleared his throat as he stepped into the room, he appeared to be feeling a little uneasy; and judging by the way his hand rose and covered his mouth when he cleared his throat, he was somewhat westernized in his behaviour.

'Sorry I couldn't ring you and make an appointment,' he said. 'All the roads are dug up in our area, so the phone lines are dead.'

Feluda nodded. We all knew about the dug up roads in Calcutta, and the effects they had had on the city.

'My name is Subir Datta,' our visitor went on. His voice was good enough for him to have been a television newsreader. 'Er . . . *you* are the private inves-?'

'Yes.'

'I am here to talk about my brother.'

Feluda looked on in silence. The Mahabharat was lying closed on his lap, but he had placed a finger in it to mark his page.

'But I must tell you something about myself. I am a sales executive in Corbett & Norris. You know Dinesh Choudhury in Camac Street, don't you? We were in college together.'

Dinesh Choudhury was one of Feluda's clients.

'I see,' said Feluda. Mr Datta began talking about his brother.

'My brother was a biochemist. He had once made quite a name for himself, not here but in America. He was studying viruses, in the University of Michigan. His name is Nihar Datta. One day, there was an explosion in his laboratory. He was badly injured, and for a while it looked as if he wouldn't survive. But a doctor in a local hospital saved his life. What he couldn't save were his eyes.'

'Your brother became blind?'

'Yes. He then returned home. At the time of the accident, he was married to an American woman. She left him after a while. He did not marry again.'

'So it means his research remained incomplete?'

'Yes. That depressed him so much that for six months, he did not speak to anyone. We thought he was having a nervous breakdown. But, gradually, he recovered and became normal again.'

'How is he now?'

'He is still interested in science. That much is clear. He has employed a young man—something like a secretary, you might say—who was a student of biochemistry. One of his tasks is to read aloud from scientific journals. On the whole, though, my brother isn't entirely helpless. In the evenings, he goes up to the roof for a stroll, all by himself. All he has to guide him is his stick. Sometimes, he even goes out of the house and walks up to the main crossing. Inside the house, he is quite independent. He doesn't need any help to go from one room to another.'

'Does he have an income?'

'He had written a book on biochemistry before he left America. He still gets royalties from its sale, so he has an income.'

'What went wrong?'

'Sorry?'

'I mean, what happened that made you come to me?'

'Yes, I am coming to that.'

Subir Datta took out a cigar from his pocket, lit it, and blew out quite a lot of smoke.

'Last night, a thief stole into my brother's room,' he said.

'What makes you think it was a thief?' Feluda lifted the Mahabharat off his lap and put it on a table, as he asked that question.

'My brother had no idea what had happened. He has a servant, but that fellow isn't all that bright. His secretary arrived at nine, and saw the state the room was in. It was he who realized what had happened. Both drawers of my brother's desk were half-open; some papers were scattered on the floor, everything on the desk was in disarray. And there were scratches around the keyhole on his Godrej safe. It was obvious that someone had tried to open it.'

'Tell me, has any other house in your area been burgled recently?'

'Yes. One of our neighbours was burgled. He lives only two houses away. A couple of policemen now come on regular rounds and keep an eye on the whole neighbourhood. We live in Ballygunj Park. Our house is nearly eighty years old. My grandfather built it. We were once zamindars in Bangladesh. My grandfather moved to Calcutta in 1890, and began making chemical instruments. We had a large shop in College Street. My father ran the family business for some years. Then our business folded up, about thirty years ago.'

'How many people live in your house?'

'Very few, compared to the number we had before. My parents are no more. My wife died in 1975. Both my daughters are married, and my elder son is in Germany. Only three of us live in that house now—my brother, my younger son and myself. There are two servants and a cook. We live on the first floor. The ground floor has been divided into two flats. Both are let out.'

'Who are your tenants?'

'In the first flat, there's Mr Dastur. He has his own business—electrical goods. In the other flat, that faces the rear of the house, there's Mr Sukhwani. He has an antiques shop in Lindsay Street.'

'Didn't the burglar try breaking into their flats? They sound reasonably well off!'

'Yes, they have both got money. Sukhwani's rooms are full of expensive things, so he locks them at night. But Dastur says he feels suffocated in a locked room, so he keeps his bedroom unlocked.'

'Why did the thief go to your brother's room? I mean, what might have interested him? Do you have any idea?'

'Look, all his research papers are kept in the safe. They are unquestionably most valuable, even though his research was never completed. But then, an ordinary thief would not understand their value. I think his aim was to steal whatever cash he could find. A blind man makes an easy target, as you can imagine.'

'Yes. Since your brother is blind, I assume he doesn't have a bank account? I mean, signing cheques would be . . . ?'

'You're right. Whatever royalty he earns is made out in my name, and deposited in my account. If my brother needs any money, I write a cheque and take it out. All his money is kept in the same safe. At a guess, I'd say that it has about thirty thousand rupees in it right now.'

'Where do you keep the key?'

'As far as I know, it is kept under my brother's pillow. My main anxiety is because he cannot see. He sleeps with his bedroom door open. His servant—he's called Koumudi—sleeps on the floor, just outside the threshold. He's supposed to get up if my brother calls him during the night. But if a thief is reckless enough, and if Koumudi doesn't wake up, then my brother is quite vulnerable. There's no way he can defend himself. Yet he refuses to inform the police. He has no faith in them—says they are all corrupt, and all they'd ever do is harass everyone, but never catch the culprit. So I told him about you, and he agreed that talking to you was a better idea. If you could come to our house, perhaps you could advise on what we might do to prevent such a thing. In fact, you might even be able to see if it was an inside job, or . . .'

'Inside job?' Feluda and I both pricked up our ears.

Mr Datta flicked the ash from his cigar into an ashtray, and lowered his voice as much as he could. 'Look, Mr Mitter, I believe in plain speaking. Besides, I realize it's not going to help you if I am not totally honest. To start with, I like neither of our tenants. Sukhwani came about three years ago. I'm no expert myself, but I've heard from others who know about art and antiques that Sukhwani is a shady character. The police have got their eye on him.'

'And the other tenant?'

'Dastur took that flat only four months ago. My elder son used to live in it before that. He's now moved permanently to Germany. He works in an engineering firm in Dusseldorf, and has married a German woman. It's not as if I've heard anything bad about Dastur. It's just that he is amazingly quiet and withdrawn. That alone is a bit suspicious. And then there is . . . er . . .'

Mr Datta stopped. When he spoke again, he hung his head and kept his eyes fixed on the ashtray. '. . . there's Shankar, my younger son. He's completely beyond redemption.' He fell silent again.

'How old is he?' Feluda asked.

'Twenty-three. He had his birthday last month, though I didn't get to see him that day.'

'What does he do?'

'Drugs, gambling, mugging, burglary . . . just name it. The police have arrested him three times. Every time, I have had to go and get him released. Our family is quite well known. So I still have a certain amount of influence . . . but God knows how long it's going to last.'

'Was Shankar at home the night you were burgled?'

'He came in to have his dinner, though that's something he doesn't do every day. I did not see him after dinner.'

Before Mr Datta left, it was agreed that Feluda and I would go to Ballygunj Park that evening. It could not really be described as a 'case', but I could tell that Feluda was intrigued by the story of a scientist blinded by an explosion. He was probably thinking of Dhritarashtra, the blind king in the Mahabharat.

*

It took Uncle Sidhu just three and a half minutes to find a press cutting that reported an explosion in a laboratory in the University of Michigan, which made the rising biochemist, Nihar Ranjan Datta, lose his sight. The cutting was pasted in Uncle Sidhu's scrapbook number 22. Mind you, he spent two minutes out of those three and a half in telling Feluda off, for not having visited him for a long time. Uncle Sidhu is not a relative, but is closer to us than any relative could ever be. If Feluda needs information about any past event, he goes to Uncle Sidhu instead of the National Library. His work gets done far more quickly, and with good cheer.

Uncle Sidhu frowned as soon as Feluda raised the subject. 'Nihar Datta? The fellow who was working on viruses? Lost his vision after an accident?'

Good heavens, what a fantastic memory he had! No wonder Feluda called him Mr Photographic Memory. If he read or heard anything interesting, it was always immediately and permanently printed on his brain.

'. . . but he wasn't alone in the laboratory, was he?' Uncle Sidhu ended with a query.

This was news to us.

'What do you mean—not alone?' Feluda asked.

'What I mean,' Uncle Sidhu moved to his bookshelf and lifted a scrapbook, 'is that he had a partner. Here . . . look!'

He read out the news item in question from his scrapbook. It had happened in 1962. Another Indian biochemist called Suprakash Choudhury was working with Nihar Datta as his assistant. He was not harmed in any way when the accident took place as he was at the opposite end of the room. If Nihar Datta escaped certain death, it was because of Choudhury's efforts. It was he who put the fire out and arranged for Mr Datta to be taken to hospital.

'So what happened to this Choudhury?'

'No idea. I couldn't give you that information. I would have known if something important had happened to him and was reported in the press. *I* don't go out of my way to make enquiries about people.

Why should I? How many people enquire about *me*, eh? But one thing is for sure. Had Choudhury done some really significant work in his field, I would certainly have heard about it.'

TWO

7/1 Ballygunj Park stood with clear and visible signs of age and decay. Naturally, if its owners had had the means to remove those signs, they would have done so. It could only mean that the Dattas were not doing all that well financially.

If there was a garden, it was possibly at the back. The front of the house had a circular grassy patch, in the middle of which stood a disused fountain. Gravelled paths ran from the grassy patch to the porch. A marble plaque on the front gate said, Golok Lodge. That appeared to intrigue Feluda. Subir Datta explained that his grandfather was called Golok Bihari Datta. It was he who had had the house built.

Inside, Golok Lodge still bore signs of its past elegance. Three steps from the porch led to a marble landing. A marble staircase to its left went to the first floor. Through an open door in front of me, I could see a corridor which ran alongside the two flats which were let. To the left of this corridor was a huge hall, which the Dattas had retained. At one time, lively parties had been held in it.

We were taken to the living room upstairs, which was directly above the hall. Hanging from the ceiling was a chandelier, wrapped in a cloth. Its main stem had several branches, but clearly it was never going to be lit again. On one of the walls hung a huge mirror set in a gilded frame. Subir Datta told us it had come from Belgium. There was a thick carpet on the floor, but it was so badly worn in many places that, through those gaps, the marble floor was exposed. It was chequered, like a black and white chessboard.

Mr Datta switched on a lamp, which dispelled some of the darkness. As we were about to sit down, we heard a noise in the passage outside. Tap, tap, tap, tap!

It was a combination of a pair of slippers and a stick.

The sound stopped just outside the threshold, then the owner of the stick entered the room. We remained standing.

'I heard some new voices. So these are our visitors?'

The man had a deep, mellow voice that seemed to go very well with his height, which must have been around six feet. All his hair was white and a little dishevelled. He was wearing a fine cotton kurta and silk pyjamas. His eyes were hidden behind dark glasses. The explosion had affected not just his eyes, but also other parts of his face. Even in the dim light of the lamp, we could see that clearly.

Subir Datta went forward to help his brother. 'Sit down, Dada.'

'Yes. Ask our guests to sit down first.'

'Namaskar,' said Feluda. 'My name is Prodosh Mitter. On my left is my cousin, Topesh.'

'Namaskar!' I said gently. It would have been a bit pointless to raise my hands since Nihar Datta could not see me.

'Mr Mitter is possibly as tall as myself, and his cousin is five feet seven inches, or may be seven and a half?'

'I am five seven,' I said quickly, silently applauding Nihar Datta for his accurate guesses.

'Please sit down, both of you,' Nihar Datta sat down himself, without taking any assistance from his brother.

'Have you ordered tea?'

'Yes, I have,' replied Subir Datta.

Feluda got straight down to business, as was his wont. 'When you were doing your research, you had a partner, didn't you?'

Subir Datta moved restlessly in his chair, which implied that he knew about the partner, and was perhaps feeling a little awkward for not having told us.

'No, I wouldn't call him a partner,' said Nihar Datta. 'He was my assistant, Suprakash Choudhury. He had been a student in America, but he could not have got much further without my help.'

'Do you know where he is, or what he's doing now?'

'No.'

'Didn't he stay in touch with you after the accident?'

'No. He lacked concentration. Biochemistry wasn't his only interest in life—he had various other distractions.'

'What caused the explosion? Negligence?'

'I was never negligent, or careless. Not consciously.'

The tea arrived. The atmosphere in the room had turned sombre. I cast a sidelong glance at Subir Datta. He, too, seemed a little tense. Feluda was looking straight at Nihar Datta's dark glasses.

There were samosas and sweets to go with the tea. I picked up a plate. Feluda did not appear interested in the food at all. He lit a

Charminar and said, 'So your research remained incomplete? I mean, no one else did anything after—?'

'If anyone had done any useful work in that subject, I would certainly have heard about it.'

'Do you happen to know for sure that Suprakash did not do any further research afterwards?'

'Look, all I know is that there is no way he could have proceeded without my notes. The notes related to the last stages of my research were kept safely in my own personal locker. No one from outside could have had access to them. All those papers came back to India with me, and I have now got them. If I could complete my research, Mr Mitter, I know one thing for sure. It wouldn't have been difficult to win the Nobel Prize. Treatment for cancer would have been revolutionized!'

Feluda picked up his cup. By that time, I had already sipped the tea and realized that it was of such high quality that even Feluda—who was always fussy about his tea—was going to be satisfied with it. But I didn't get the chance to see his face when he took his first sip.

The light suddenly went out. Loadshedding.

'Over the last few days, we've been having a power cut about this time in the evenings,' said Subir Datta, leaving his chair. 'Koumudi!'

Outside, it was not yet completely dark. Subir Datta went out to look for their servant.

'A power cut?' asked Nihar Datta. Then he sighed and added, 'It makes no difference to me!'

At this moment, a grandfather clock suddenly started striking, startling everyone. It was six o'clock.

Subir Datta returned, followed by Koumudi, who was carrying a candle. Once it was placed on the centre table, every face became visible again. Two yellow points began glowing on Nihar Datta's dark glasses: the flame on the candle.

Feluda sipped his tea and looked once more at Nihar Datta. 'Suppose your notes fell into the hands of some other biochemist, would he gain a lot?'

'If you think the Nobel Prize is a gain, then yes, most certainly he would gain a lot.'

'Do you think the burglar came looking particularly for your notes in your room?'

'No, I have no reason to believe that.'

'I have one more question. Who else knows about your notes?'

'There are plenty of people in scientific circles who might be able to guess—or assume—that I have such notes. The people in this house know about their existence. And so does my secretary, Ranajit.'

'When you say the people in this house . . . do you mean your tenants as well?'

'I have no idea how much they know. Both are businessmen. Papers related to scientific research should not be of any interest to them. But then, these days, everything under the sun can be bought and sold, can't it? So why not a scientist's research data? Not every scientist is a paragon of virtue, is he?'

Nihar Datta rose. So did we.

'May I see your room?' Feluda asked.

Nihar Datta stopped at the threshold. 'Yes, certainly. Subir will take you. I must go up to the roof now, for my evening walk.'

All four of us went out into the passage outside. It was much darker than before. Candles flickered in various rooms that lined the passage. Nihar Datta went towards the staircase, tapping his stick. I heard him mutter under his breath, 'I've counted the steps. Seventeen steps from here, turn left, and there's the staircase. Seven plus eight. . . fifteen steps to climb, and then there's the roof. Call me if you need me . . .!'

THREE

Nihar Datta's bedroom turned out to be large. An old-fashioned bed took up quite a lot of room on one side. A small, round table stood by the bed. On it was a glass of water covered with a lid, and about ten tablets sealed in aluminium foil. Perhaps they were sleeping pills.

Next to the table was a window. An easy chair was placed before it. Clearly, the chair had been in use for a long time, for its backrest had developed a dark patch. It could be that Nihar Datta spent much of his time resting in that chair.

In addition to this furniture, there was a desk with a flickering candle on it; a steel chair faced the desk, which had writing material on it, a rack to store letters, an old typewriter, and a pile of scientific journals.

A steel Godrej safe stood by the desk, to the left of the door.

Feluda ran his eye quickly over the whole room before taking out a mini torch from his pocket to examine the keyhole on the safe. 'Yes, someone did try very hard to open it. It's full of scratches.' Then he moved to the table and picked up the tablets. 'Soneril . . . yes, I thought as much! If Mr Datta wasn't used to taking a strong sleeping pill every night, he would have woken up.'

Koumudi was hovering near the door. Feluda turned to him. 'How come *you* didn't wake up, either? Is this how you guard your babu?'

Koumudi hung his head. 'I'm afraid he's a heavy sleeper,' Subir Datta informed us. 'When he's asleep, I have to call him at least three times before he wakes up.'

There were footsteps outside. A man of about thirty entered the room. He was slim, wore glasses and had wavy hair. Mr Datta introduced us. He turned out to be Nihar Datta's secretary, Ranajit Banerjee.

'Who won?'

Feluda's unexpected question was meant for Mr Banerjee. He was so taken aback by it that he could only stare. Feluda laughed. 'I can see the counterfoil of your ticket in your shirt pocket. Besides, your face looks sunburnt, so it's not really that difficult to guess that you went to watch a major League game!'

Mr Banerjee smiled in return. 'East Bengal,' he replied. Mr Datta was also smiling, with a mixture of surprise and appreciation.

'How long have you been working here?'

'Four years.'

'Has Mr Nihar Datta ever spoken about the explosion?'

'I asked him, but he did not say very much. But sometimes, even without realizing it, he talks of the terrible damage caused by his loss of vision.'

'Does he speak of anything else?'

Mr Banerjee thought for a moment. 'There's one thing I've heard him say. He says that if he's still alive, it is because a job remains unfinished. I haven't dared ask him what it is. Perhaps he still hopes to finish his research.'

'But obviously he can't do it himself. Maybe he thinks he can get someone else to work for him. Could that be it?'

'Perhaps.'

'What are your working hours?'

'I come at nine, and leave at six. Today, I wanted to leave early to see the game. Mr Datta raised no objection. But if I leave the house during the day, I normally drop by in the evening. In case he has . . .'

'Where is the key to that safe kept?' Feluda interrupted him.

'Under that pillow.'

Feluda lifted the pillow and picked up a key ring. Five keys were hanging from it. He chose the right one and opened the safe.

'Where's the money?'

'In that drawer,' Mr Banerjee pointed at a drawer. Feluda pulled it open.

'Wh-wh-what!'

Mr Banerjee gasped in horror. Even in the dim candlelight, I could see that he had gone visibly pale.

Inside the drawer was a rolled up parchment, which turned out to be a horoscope; and in an old wooden Kashmiri box, there were some old letters. Nothing else.

'How . . . how is it possible?' Mr Banerjee could barely whisper. 'Three bundles of hundred-rupee notes . . . about thirty-three thousand rupees . . .'

'The research papers? Were they in this other drawer?'

Mr Banerjee nodded. Feluda opened it. The second drawer was completely empty.

Tap, tap, tap, tap! Nihar Datta was coming down the stairs.

'There was a long envelope . . . with a seal from the University of Michigan . . . it had all the notes . . .!' Mr Banerjee's throat had clearly gone quite dry.

'Was the money here this morning? And the research papers?'

'Yes, I saw it myself,' Subir Datta told us. 'The numbers on all the hundred-rupee notes have been noted down. My brother has always insisted on that.'

Feluda's face looked grim. 'It means that the money and the papers were stolen in the last fifteen minutes—soon after the power cut began, when we were sitting in your living room.'

Nihar Datta entered the room. It was clear from his face that he had heard everything. We stepped out of his way as he went and sat on his easy chair. 'Just imagine!' he said with a sigh. 'The thief walked away with his loot from under the detective's nose!'

We left him and went out to the corridor. 'Is there another staircase anywhere, apart from the one we used?' Feluda asked Subir Datta.

'Yes. There's a staircase at the back, which the cleaners use.'

'Do you have a power cut at the same time every day?'

'Over the last ten days or so, yes, we've been having a power cut every evening, from six to ten o'clock. Some people have started to set their watch by it!'

I tried to think if a similar thing had happened before in Feluda's career as a detective. Not a single instance came to mind.

'Has either of your tenants returned?' Feluda asked as we reached the top of the stairs.

'We can find out. They normally return about this time.'

Opposite that landing on the ground floor was the door to Mr Dastur's flat. The door was closed and it wasn't difficult to see that the room behind it was in complete darkness.

'We have to go to the rear of the house to find Sukhwani,' said Subir Datta.

We walked down a path that ran alongside a garden to reach Sukhwani's flat. There was a fluorescent light on in his front room, the kind that is operated by a battery.

He heard our footsteps and emerged on the veranda. He could see Feluda's torchlight, but naturally could not see the people behind it. Mr Datta spoke, 'May we come in for a minute?'

Mr Sukhwani's expression underwent a rapid change as he recognized his landlord's voice. 'Certainly, certainly!'

When he heard Feluda's name and learnt the purpose of our visit, he grew quite agitated. 'You see, Mr Mitter, my room is full of valuable things. Any mention of theft and burglary gives me a heart attack! So you can imagine how I felt when I heard this morning about the attempted burglary upstairs!'

Honestly, I could not have imagined that a room could be crammed with so many valuable objects. There were at least thirty statuettes made of stone, brass and bronze, many of them of either Buddha or various forms of Shiv. Apart from those, there were pictures, books, old maps, pots and vases, shields and swords, spittoons, hookahs and containers for *ittar.* Feluda told me later, 'If only I had the money, Topshe! I'd have bought at least the books and those prints!'

Mr Sukhwani had returned ten minutes before the power cut, he said.

'Did anyone come this side in those ten minutes? I can see that the second staircase going up is right behind your flat. Did you hear any noise from that side?'

Mr Sukhwani had heard nothing, as he had gone straight into his bathroom. 'Besides, how could I have seen anyone in the dark? By the way, do you really think an outsider did it?'

'Why do you ask?'

'Have you spoken to Mr Dastur?' Mr Sukhwani's tone implied that if we spoke to Mr Dastur, we would see immediately that if anyone should be under suspicion, it was Dastur.

Before Feluda could say anything, Mr Sukhwani added, 'He is a most peculiar character. I know I should not speak like this about my neighbour, but I've been watching him for some time. Before I actually met him, all I could hear through his window was the sound of his snoring. I bet that sound reached the first floor!'

From the way a smile hovered on Subir Datta's lips, Sukhwani's remark was not an exaggeration.

'Then, one morning, he came to borrow my typewriter. That's when I first met him. I tell you, I didn't at all like the greedy way in which he was looking at everything in this room! Out of simple curiosity, I asked him what he did for a living. So he said he sold electrical goods. If that's the case, why doesn't he get himself a battery light and a fan, when we have power cuts every day? The whole business is highly suspicious.'

Mr Sukhwani stopped. We took the opportunity to rise. Before we left, Feluda said, 'If you notice anything odd, please inform Mr Datta. It will help us in our work.'

As we began walking down the same path to go back to the front of the house, we heard a taxi toot its horn outside. Then we saw a man on the gravelled path, making his way to the porch. Even in the dim light, I could see that he was of medium height and rather plump. He was wearing a brown suit, and had a neatly trimmed, salt-and-pepper French beard. In his hand was a briefcase, possibly new.

He turned towards us. 'Good evening!' Subir Datta greeted him. The man looked taken aback. Perhaps he wasn't used to hearing 'Good morning!' and 'Good evening!' from other people in the building. But he returned the greeting.

'Good evening, Mr Datta!'

His voice was extraordinarily squeaky. He turned to go, but Feluda whispered, 'Stop him!' Subir Datta obeyed instantly. 'Er . . . Mr Dastur!'

Mr Dastur stopped. We strode forward to join him. When Mr Datta explained what had happened, he appeared perfectly amazed. 'You mean all that happened in just a few minutes? Your brother must be terribly upset!' he exclaimed.

Feluda had once told me that, sometimes, if a person is profoundly moved or shaken, his voice can change so much that it may well be impossible to recognize it. When Mr Dastur spoke those words, with a mixture of surprise and fear, I noticed that the squeakiness in his voice disappeared completely. It sounded as if a totally different person had spoken.

'When you arrived, did you see anyone go out of this building?' Feluda asked him.

'Why, no!' Mr Dastur replied. 'But then, I could easily have missed seeing him in the dark. Thank God I don't have anything valuable in my flat!'

'Who's there?' asked a voice from the landing on the first floor. It was Nihar Datta. We were standing on the front steps near the porch. Now we went back into the house and looked up. Even in the dark, Nihar Datta's glasses were shining.

'It's me, Mr Datta!' Mr Dastur responded. 'Your brother just told me about your loss. My commiserations!'

The dark glasses moved away. In a few seconds, so did the sound of his slippers and his stick.

'Won't you come in?' Mr Dastur invited us. 'After a hard day's work, it is very nice to have some company.'

Feluda raised no objection. I could see why. It is a detective's first job to get to know the people in a house where a crime has been committed.

After Mr Sukhwani's room, the barrenness of Dastur's was really striking. The only pieces of furniture were a sofa, two couches, a writing desk and a bookshelf. There was a small, low table placed in front of the sofa, on which stood a candle. Feluda flicked his lighter on and lit it. The room became brighter, but there was nothing else in it, except a calendar on the wall.

Mr Dastur had disappeared inside, possibly to call his servant. When he returned, Feluda offered him a cigarette. 'No, thanks,' Mr Dastur said. 'I gave up smoking three years ago, for fear of getting cancer.'

'I assume you don't mind others smoking in your house? In fact, I can see a half-finished cigarette in your ashtray.' Feluda picked it up. 'My own brand!' he added. I, too, had learnt to recognize Charminars, even from a distance.

'You know,' said Mr Dastur, 'I have thought many times of getting myself an emergency light and fan, like Sukhwani. But then, when I think that ninety per cent of the population in Calcutta has to suffer in the dark and the heat, I start feeling most depressed. So I. . .'

'You sell electrical goods, don't you?' Feluda asked.

'Electrical?'

'Mr Sukhwani told us.'

'Sukhwani frequently talks rubbish. My business is to do with electronics, not electricals. I started it about a year ago.'

'By yourself?'

'No, I have a partner—a friend. I am from Bombay, though I spent several years abroad. I used to work for a computer manufacturing firm in Germany. Then my friend wrote to me, asking me to join him here. He's put up the money, I'm providing the technical expertise.'

'When did you arrive in Calcutta?'

'Last November. I stayed with my friend for three months. Then I heard about this flat, and moved here.'

A servant entered the room with cold drinks. Thums-Up. Mr Dastur had already learnt that Feluda was a detective. He now lowered his voice as he went on speaking, 'Mr Mitter, it is true that I don't have anything valuable in my flat. But there's something I feel I ought to tell you about my neighbour. He is not a simple and straightforward man. His flat is a place for all kinds of fishy and shady activities, I can tell you!'

'How do you know?'

'My bathroom is next to his, you see. There is a door between the two. It remains locked, but if I put my ear to it, I can hear conversations from his bedroom.'

Feluda cleared his throat. 'Eavesdropping is hardly an honest and straightforward activity, Mr Dastur!'

Mr Dastur remained perfectly unmoved. 'I would not have eavesdropped. I mean, not normally. But, one day, one of my letters was delivered at his flat by mistake. Do you know what he did? He steamed it open, then stuck it back with glue. When I realized what he'd done, I couldn't help doing something naughty in return. Look, I don't like making trouble. But if Sukhwani is going to harass me, I am not going to spare him, either.'

We thanked Mr Dastur for the cold drinks, and left.

Feluda stopped at the front gate to ask the chowkidar if he had seen anyone go in or come out of the house in the last half an hour. The chowkidar said he had seen no one except Sukhwani and Dastur. That did not surprise us. 7/1 Ballygunj Park had a compound wall that surrounded the house. The house directly behind 7/1 was empty, and had been so over the past few months. Any able-bodied thief could have jumped over the wall without being seen; but all of us secretly thought it was done by someone from within the house. Or someone who lived in the house had hired an outsider for the job. No one knew anything for sure.

Since we didn't have a car, Subir Datta offered to drop us back, but Feluda assured him we could quite easily walk to the main road and get a taxi.

'Informing the police might not be such a bad idea, you know,' Feluda said suddenly. It was a totally unexpected remark. Even Mr Datta looked taken aback. 'Why do you say that?' he asked.

'No matter what your brother thinks of the police, they have the means to track down thieves and burglars. A private investigator cannot do that. Besides, the amount of money stolen isn't that small, is it? You said the numbers on the notes were written down somewhere. So, if you told the police, they would probably find their job relatively simple.'

Subir Datta said, 'Since J asked you to come here, and there *has* been an unfortunate occurrence, I cannot even think of asking you to leave the case. Even if I inform the police, I'd like you to work alongside them. If you do that, my brother and I will both feel much more reassured. But . . . to tell you the truth . . . I can tell who the thief is, even without any help from anyone.'

'Do you mean your son?'

Subir Datta sighed and nodded. 'It couldn't possibly be anyone but Shankar. He knows the lights go off in this area at six o'clock. He's an agile young man. Scaling that wall would not have been a problem for him. Using those back stairs, going up to his uncle's room and opening that safe . . . all this would be child's play!'

'But what would he do with his uncle's research papers? Does he know a lot of people in scientific circles?'

'He doesn't have to. He can blackmail my brother. Get him to pay for the return of his papers. Shankar knows very well how much those papers mean to his uncle.'

So much had happened in such a short time—my head was reeling. I had no idea, when we left Mr Datta's house, that much more was in store. But, before I describe what happened later that day, I ought to mention the conversation I had with Feluda when we got home.

After dinner, I went to his room to find him lying flat on his back, chewing a paan and smoking a Charminar. I went and sat on his bed, and finally asked the question that had bothered me ever since we'd left the Dattas' house.

'Why did you want to leave this case, Feluda?'

Feluda blew out two perfect smoke rings, and said, 'There's a reason, dear Topshe, there's a reason!'

'But you told us what that reason was. The police can catch a thief more easily, especially if he's got a lot of money.'

'You are convinced that it was Subir Datta's son who stole the money?'

'Who else could it be? It's obvious that someone from the family was responsible. Mr Dastur wasn't there at all. And I can't believe Sukhwani could have stolen the stuff and continued to sit at home, as if nothing had happened. Ranajit Banerjee arrived after the theft. Apart from these people, there are only the servants . . .!'

'But—suppose—my client himself is responsible?'

I stared at Feluda in surprise.

'Subir Datta?'

'Try to think of everything that happened just before we realized there had been a theft,'

I shut my eyes and cast my mind back. There we were, sitting in the living room. The tea was brought in. We began drinking it. Feluda was holding his cup. The lights went out. And then. . .

Suddenly, I remembered something that made my heart give a lurch.

'Subir Datta left the room as soon as the lights went out, to call his servant!'

'Right. How do you think I'm going to look if it turns out that my own client had gone and opened the safe? It is not entirely impossible, you know. After all, we do not know a great deal about him, do we? Yes, he did call the servant, there's no doubt about that. However, supposing he has lost a lot of money speculating on the stock market, or at the races, or gambling, and has run up a huge debt, then would you be surprised to learn that it was he who took the money?'

'But . . . but . . . he came to you himself! *He* asked you to investigate the case!'

'Yes. If he is a high-class criminal—one of the really clever ones—then his coming to me is not in the least surprising. That is exactly the kind of thing he *would* do.'

After this, there was really no more left to be said.

Feluda picked up his copy of the Mahabharat and switched on his reading lamp. I rose and left his room.

I heard the sound as soon as I got to our living room. A scooter. No, not just one scooter. There was more than one. They shattered the silence of the whole area, and appeared to stop right in front of our house.

A second later, someone rang our doorbell.

*

Although we did get visitors at odd hours, no one ever came on a scooter. It might not be safe to open the door at once. So I returned to Feluda's room and lifted his curtain to take a quick peep. Feluda had put his book away, and was already on his feet. 'Wait,' he said. It meant that he wanted to open the door himself.

When he did, a young man swept into the room. I could see, in a matter of seconds, that he was evil incarnate. He did not find it necessary to sit down. Slamming the door behind him and leaning against it, Subir Datta's son, Shankar Datta, stared at Feluda with glazed eyes, and began a harangue. Each word sounded like a whiplash.

'Look here, Mister, I don't know what my father told you about me, but I can guess. All I can tell you is that no one can do anything to me, even if they employ a snoopy sleuth. I'm here to warn you. I am not alone, see? We have an entire gang. If you try acting smart, you'll regret it. Oh yes, sir, you'll be sorry you were ever born!'

Having finished his speech, Shankar Datta made an exit, which was as dramatic as his entrance. Then we heard three scooters roar into life and leave, the entire neighbourhood reverberating under the racket.

Until that moment, Feluda remained still. He could stay perfectly calm even when someone stood there flinging insults at him. He really has extraordinary control over his nerves. I have heard him say that he who can keep rising anger firmly under control must have far greater will power than someone who has a furious outburst.

However, when Shankar left, Feluda moved quickly even before the sound of the scooters had faded away. In a flash, he had put on his kurta and grabbed his wallet. 'Come on, Topshe. A taxi. . .!'

Within three minutes, we were in Southern Avenue, flagging down a taxi. The scooters had gone towards the north. That much I knew.

'Try Lansdowne Road,' Feluda said to the driver as we got in. The main road was dug up, so it was highly likely that the scooters would go down Lansdowne Road.

It was a quarter to eleven. Southern Avenue was almost completely empty. Our driver was a Bengali, a local man. We had seen him before. 'Do you wish to follow someone, sir?' he asked.

'Three scooters,' Feluda said in a low voice.

Our hunch was right. We saw the three scooters near the Elgin Road crossing. Shankar was on one, and the other two had two riders on each. None of us had to be told that they were all hardened criminals. Our taxi began tailing them.

We passed Lower Circular Road and Camac Street. Upon reaching Park Street, they turned left. They were driving in a zigzag fashion, possibly because each of them was in a good mood, without a care in the world. Feluda was hiding in the dark depths of the taxi, trying to avoid the streetlight that came in through the windows. I could not tell what he was thinking.

The scooters went down Mirza Ghalib Street, and then turned left again. Marquis Street. The road was narrow here, the lights were dim, and every house was dark. Feluda told the driver to reduce the speed and increase the distance between the scooters and our taxi, in case those men became suspicious.

A little later, after taking two more turns, the scooters stopped before a building.

'Drive on, don't stop,' Feluda said.

As we passed the building, I realized it was not an ordinary house, but a hotel. It was called The New Corinthian Lodge. New? The building was at least a hundred years old.

Feluda's mission was accomplished. All he had wanted to do was to see where the gang was based.

By the time we returned home, it was eleven-forty. The meter on the taxi read nineteen rupees and seventy-five paisa.

The following morning, Uncle Sidhu turned up most unexpectedly. I knew that he went out for a walk every morning, but that was always in the direction of the lake. If he had come to our house instead, there had to be a special reason.

'That scrapbook was too heavy to carry, so I simply copied out the press cutting,' he told us. 'Look, here it talks about an S. Choudhury, and he's a biochemist. But I've no idea if it's Suprakash.'

'When was it reported?'

'1971. The police raided a pharmaceutical company in Mexico, and arrested a Bengali biochemist. He went to jail. He was said to be selling spurious drugs, which were causing terrible diseases. That is all the report says. Since I was thinking only of the name "Suprakash", I didn't immediately connect that name with this report. But whether it's the same . . . ?'

'Yes, it's the same person,' Feluda replied gravely.

Uncle Sidhu rose to take his leave. His barber was expected at home—it was time for his regular haircut. He thumped Feluda's back, grabbed my ear and gave it an affectionate twist, tucked his dhoti in at the waist, and stepped out.

Feluda began scribbling in his notebook. I went and stood by his side. There were three questions listed on a page:

1. Why were there so many scratches around the keyhole on the safe?
2. 'Who's there'? What does it mean?
3. What is the 'unfinished job'?

The questions made me think, too.

Last evening, I had seen the scratches around the keyhole when Feluda had shone his torch on it. Yes, they *were* rather suspicious. Such marks would not have been left there unless someone had scuffed the steel surface really hard. Was Nihar Datta such a heavy sleeper that even the sound of so much scraping did not wake him?

The second question was not immediately clear to me. Then I remembered Nihar Datta calling out from the landing when he heard Mr Dastur's voice. What I could not understand was why Feluda should find anything suspicious in Nihar Datta saying, 'Who's there?'

It was Nihar Datta who had talked about an unfinished job. At least, that was what Ranajit Banerjee had told us. I had assumed that was a reference to his incomplete research. Didn't Feluda believe that?

Feluda was about to scribble some more, when the telephone rang. He reached out and picked up the receiver.

'Hello.'

There was a pause. Then he said, 'Hmm . . . hmm . . . yes, I'll be there straightaway.'

He replaced the receiver and grabbed a hanger in his wardrobe, from which were hanging a shirt and a pair of trousers. Feluda yanked those off and said to me, 'Get ready at once. There's been a murder in Golok Lodge.'

My heart flew into my mouth.

'Who?'

'Mr Dastur.'

As soon as we entered Ballygunj Park, I could see a police van parked outside 7/1, and a knot of people. Luckily, it was a quiet and genteel locality, or there would have been many more onlookers.

There is no one in Calcutta Police who does not know Feluda. We found Inspector Bakshi as we walked into Golok Lodge. He came forward with a smile on his face. 'Ah. So here you are! Could you smell the murder, even from your house?'

Feluda offered his lopsided smile. 'I met Subir Datta recently. He rang me, so I came. I will not interfere with your work—I promise. How was he murdered?'

'Blow on the head. Not one, but three—while he was asleep. The body is about to be removed for a post-mortem. Dr Sarkar has seen it already. It happened between two and three o'clock last night.'

'Did you learn anything about the victim?'

'Suspicious character. Seems he was on the point of leaving. Had started to pack his suitcase!'

'Was any money stolen?'

'I don't think so. There's a wallet on the bedside table, with about three hundred rupees in it. Perhaps he didn't keep a lot of cash in the house. But we can't find his bank passbook, or cheque book, or anything. A gold watch was lying by his pillow. Mind you, we haven't yet made a thorough search. We'll do that now. But, from what we've found so far, we've learnt nothing about the real man.'

By this time, we had been joined by Subir Datta. He looked at Bakshi and said, 'Sukhwani is making a lot of fuss. He says he has a most important appointment in Dalhousie Square. But I've told him no one can leave the house until the police have finished asking questions.'

'Yes, you did the right thing. But then, we'll question everyone, even you.'

Bakshi smiled as he spoke. Subir Datta nodded to indicate that he was aware of the situation. 'The fewer questions you ask my brother, the better,' he pointed out.

'Naturally,' said Bakshi.

'May I see the room?' Feluda asked.

'Certainly.'

Bakshi went forward with Feluda, followed by me. Just before stepping into Dastur's living room, Feluda turned to Mr Datta and said, 'By the way, your son came to my house yesterday.'

'When?' Mr Datta sounded quite taken aback.

Feluda explained quickly. 'Did he return home last night?'

'Even if he did, I didn't hear him come in,' Mr Datta replied. 'I haven't seen him this morning.'

'At least now we know where your son and his friends are to be found. That hotel has a bad reputation. It's been raided twice,' Inspector Bakshi informed us.

The room looked entirely different. The previous night, it had been totally dark. This morning, bright sunlight was streaming in through the windows and falling on the sofa and the floor. To my surprise, I saw that the old stub of a Charminar was still lying in the ashtray. Two constables were posted in the room; and the photographer, having finished his work, was in the process of packing away his equipment.

The murder had taken place in the bedroom. Feluda and Bakshi went in. I went up to the threshold and caught a glimpse of the corpse, covered with a white sheet. A constable was searching the room. On the floor, a suitcase was lying open, with a few clothes folded and packed in it. Beside the suitcase stood Dastur's new briefcase which I'd seen him carrying the previous day.

I returned to the living room and spent the next three minutes simply staring at the furniture. I knew I must not touch anything. Besides, the two constables were both gaping at me.

'Come on, Topshe!'

Feluda had emerged from the bedroom.

'Are you going to be here for some time?' Bakshi asked.

'Yes, I'll go and see the old Mr Datta. Let me know if you find anything interesting.'

Subir Datta was waiting upstairs. He took us to his brother's room.

Nihar Datta was reclining in his easy chair. He was wearing his dark glasses, and his stick was lying on his bed. So far, I had seen that stick clutched in his hand, so I had not realized that it had a silver handle. A design was carved on it, and in its centre, were the letters G B D. The stick must have once belonged to his grandfather, Golok Bihari Datta.

On being told of our arrival, he raised his head slightly and said, 'Yes, I heard their footsteps. Sound and touch . . . only these two things have helped me survive for twenty years. And I have memories . . . thoughts of what might have been. Some say it was just my misfortune. *I* know it had nothing to do with fate or fortune. You asked me that day, Mr Mitter, whether the explosion was a result of negligence. Today, I am prepared to tell you frankly that the whole thing was planned, just to destroy my work. Jealousy can make some people stoop incredibly low. As a detective, I am sure you can appreciate that.'

Mr Datta stopped. Feluda said, 'You mean you think Suprakash Choudhury was responsible for the explosion?'

'No Bengali could have a greater enemy than a fellow Bengali. You can believe that, can't you?'

Feluda was staring steadily at the dark glasses. Nihar Datta appeared to be waiting for an answer.

'Have you ever mentioned this to anyone else, in the same way?'

'No, never. When I woke up in hospital, this was the first thing that came to my mind. But I did not say anything. What good would it have done? The damage was done, anyway. Even if the culprit responsible was punished, I would not have got my sight back, or completed my research.'

'But how did it help Suprakash Choudhury? Did he think he could steal your papers, finish the research alone and make a name for himself?'

'Yes, that's what he must have thought. But he was wrong. I've already told you, Mr Mitter. There was no way he could have got anywhere without my help.'

We were sitting on the bed. Feluda was deep in thought. Ranajit

Banerjee had come into the room, and was standing by the table. Subir Datta had left the room, possibly to attend to something.

'I'm not sure about the money,' said Feluda. 'Perhaps the police will find it easier to recover it. But what I can't accept is that all those valuable papers should be stolen while I was present in this house! I will do my utmost to get those back.'

'You may do exactly as you please.'

We left soon after this. The police were still interviewing everyone. Bakshi promised to call Feluda and tell him of their findings.

'Don't forget to tell me about the New Corinthian Lodge!' Feluda reminded him.

*

We returned home at half past ten. Feluda spent the rest of the morning pacing in his room, stopping occasionally, sitting or lying down, frowning, shaking his head, muttering to himself, and sighing from time to time. Obviously, various questions, doubts and suspicions were chasing one another in his mind. Then, suddenly, he turned to me and said, 'Can you remember the general layout of the ground floor in Golok Lodge?'

I thought for a moment and said, 'Yes, I think so.'

'How would one go from Sukhwani's flat to Dastur's?'

I thought again. 'As far as I can remember, the passage that runs past both flats towards the inner part of the house has a door in its centre. It probably stays locked. But if it was opened, one could easily slip through that door and go from one flat to another.'

'Right. As things stand, if Sukhwani had wanted to visit Dastur, he'd have had to go round the garden, walk down the passage between the compound wall and the house, and come straight to the front door to gain entry.'

'But what about the collapsible gate at the front of the house? Would that be open in the middle of the night?'

'No, of course not.'

Then he began pacing again, muttering under his breath, 'X Y Z . . . X Y Z . . . X is the research, Y is the money, and Z is murder. What we need to find out is whether these three are tied together by the same thread, or whether they are separate.'

While he was still muttering, I couldn't help saying, 'Feluda, do you know what I think? I think Suprakash Choudhury disguised himself as Dastur and came to live in Nihar Datta's house.'

To my surprise, Feluda did not dismiss the idea. On the contrary, he patted my back and said, 'Such an idea has already occurred to me, but I have to say you aren't far behind in getting brainwaves. If Dastur was Suprakash in disguise, then presumably he was there only to steal the research papers. But the question is, if he stole the envelope, where did it go? Besides, how could he have stolen it himself? He'd never been to the first floor!'

I had an answer to that. Really, I *had* become quite clever. 'Why should Dastur have to go anywhere? Suppose he was in league with Shankar? Shankar could have stolen that envelope, passed it to Dastur, and been paid for it!'

'Excellent!' said Feluda. 'At last, you have become a worthy assistant of mine. But it still doesn't explain the murder.'

'Ranajit Banerjee could have figured our that Dastur and Suprakash were the same. Mr Banerjee knows Mr Datta's history, and has enormous respect for him. So, is it not possible that he should want to kill the man who destroyed Mr Datta's entire career as a scientist?'

Feluda shook his head. 'No. Murder isn't such a simple business, Topshe. Banerjee's motive could not be strong enough. It's a great pity that the police haven't yet found anything suspicious in Dastur's room. He was obviously a most cautious man.'

'You know what I feel, Feluda?'

Feluda stopped pacing and looked at me. I said, 'If *you* had searched the room instead of the police, you would have found various clues.'

'Ah. You think so?'

I couldn't ever imagine Feluda losing confidence in himself. But the way he said, 'You think so?', that was what the words seemed to imply. What he said next made my heart sink further.

'I doubt if even Einstein's brain could have functioned in this heat and so many power cuts.'

Inspector Bakshi rang us around two o'clock. They had found a secret compartment in the heel of a shoe belonging to Dastur. It was crammed with American dollars and German marks, worth about seventeen thousand rupees. However, they had found no papers or documents that might help identify the man. No new electronics shop could be located that knew of Dastur; nor had his friend been traced. There were virtually no letters in the flat. The only personal letter they found had been written from Argentina. It simply proved that Dastur had spent some time in South America.

The second piece of news that Bakshi gave us was that they had shown Shankar's photo to the manager of New Corinthian Lodge. The manager had recognized him, and told the police that Shankar and his friends had hired a room in his hotel and spent the previous night drinking and playing cards. They paid their bill in the morning and left. According to Bakshi, it was 'only a matter of minutes' before Shankar was arrested.

Feluda heard what Bakshi had to say, put the phone down and said, 'If Shankar Datta had used some of the stolen money to settle his hotel bill, that really would have been most convenient. But anyway, at least it proves he could not have killed Dastur. He has an alibi.'

I had learnt the meaning of the word 'alibi' some time ago. But at first I couldn't figure out how to explain it to those who might not know it. When I asked Feluda, he just said, 'Write what it says in the dictionary.' So an alibi is 'a plea that accused was elsewhere when the crime was committed'. In other words, Shankar could very easily say, 'When the murder took place, I was in a hotel playing cards with my friends!'

Even after Bakshi's telephone call, Feluda continued to be restless. At around three, I saw that he had changed and was dressed to go out. He had to get some information, he said. It was half past four by the time he returned. I read the Mahabharat during that time, and nearly finished it.

I was reading the bit where, on their final journey, the Pandavas begin falling one by one—and Arjun was just about to fall—when the phone rang suddenly. I answered it. It was Subir Datta, asking for Feluda. Feluda picked up the extension in his own room. I placed my ear to the phone in the living room and heard the whole conversation.

'Hello.'

'Mr Mitter?'

'Yes?'

'The sealed envelope with my brother's research papers has been found.'

'In Mr Dastur's room?'

'Yes, that's right. It was stuck with some Sellotape to the underside of the bed. But one side came unstuck and it was left dangling. Our servant, Bhagirath, found it.'

'Does your brother know about it?'

'Yes. But he seems very depressed—he's not really interested in anything at all. He did not leave his chair today, even once. I have asked our family physician to take a look at him.'

'Any news about your son?'

'Yes. The entire gang has been arrested near G T Road.'

'And the stolen money?'

'No, that wasn't found. Perhaps they kept it safe somewhere else. But Shankar is denying the whole thing—says he had nothing to do with the theft.'

'What do the police say about the murder?'

'They suspect Sukhwani. Besides, they've found a new clue. There was a crumpled piece of paper outside Dastur's window.'

'Did it say anything?'

'It was just a one-line warning: *you know what excessive curiosity can do*.'

'What does Sukhwani have to say about all this?'

'He's denying everything. It's true that one can't get to Dastur's flat from his, but a hired killer could easily have climbed up to the first floor, then gone down the stairs and killed Dastur.'

'Hmm . . . all right, I'll go over to your house.'

Feluda replaced the receiver. Then I heard him mutter to himself: 'X is the same as Y. Now we need to find out about Z.' A second later, he called out to me, 'Destination Golok Lodge. Get ready, Topshe!'

FOUR

'Leaving, are you?'

Ranajit Banerjee was walking towards the front gate as we arrived at Golok Lodge. A constable was posted outside, so obviously the police were keeping their eye on the house.

'Yes,' Mr Banerjee replied. 'Mr Datta told me I would not be required today.'

'How is he?'

'The doctor's seen him. He said so much has happened lately that Mr Datta is in a state of shock. His blood pressure is fluctuating.'

'Is he talking to people?'

'Oh yes, yes!' Mr Banerjee said reassuringly.

'I'd like to look at the envelope found in Dastur's room. Could you please come back to the house, unless you're in a tearing hurry? Is that envelope now back in the safe?'

'Yes.'

'I won't keep you long—promise! I don't suppose I'll visit this house again.'

'But . . . the envelope is sealed!' Mr Banerjee said a little uncertainly.

'I just want to hold it in my hand,' Feluda replied.

Mr Banerjee raised no further objection.

The house was dark, as on previous days. The power supply would not be resumed till ten o'clock. Now it was only a quarter past six. Kerosene lamps burned on the passage on the first floor, and on the landing. But they did nothing to dispel the gloom in nooks and corners.

Mr Banerjee showed us into the living room and went to inform Subir Datta. Before he left the room, he told us that if Nihar Datta objected to taking the envelope out, it could not be shown to anyone.

'That goes without saying,' Feluda told him.

Subir Datta looked quite tired. He had spent all day keeping press reporters at bay, he said. 'The only good thing is that this entire business has made everyone think of my brother again. People had almost forgotten his name!'

Mr Banerjee returned a minute later, carrying a long white envelope. 'Mr Datta didn't mind . . . because I mentioned your name. He would not have allowed anyone else to look at his papers.'

'Amazing!' exclaimed Feluda, peering closely at the envelope under a kerosene lamp. To me, it appeared an ordinary long envelope. There was a red seal on one side; and on the other, on the bottom left hand corner, were the words 'Department of Biochemistry, University of Michigan, Michigan, USA'. What was so amazing about that? Mr Datta and Mr Banerjee were seated on the sofa in the dimly lit room. Perhaps they were feeling just as puzzled.

Feluda returned to his chair, still staring at the envelope. Then he ignored the other two men completely, and began talking only to me. He sounded like a schoolteacher. As a matter of fact, he had used the same tone many times in the past, to enlighten me on various subjects.

'You see, Topshe, English typefaces are an extraordinary business.

Bengali has ten or twelve different typefaces; English has two thousand. Once I had to read up on this subject while investigating a case. Each typeface belongs to a particular group, and each group has a particular name. For instance, this typeface here is called Garramond,' Feluda pointed at the printed words on the envelope. Then he continued, 'Garramond came into being in the sixteenth century in France. Then it began to be used everywhere in the world. Countries like England, Germany, Switzerland and America didn't just use this typeface but, in their own factories, made the mould required to use it. Even India has started doing that now. The funny thing is, if you look very carefully, you will always find a subtle difference between Garramond used in one country and another. The formation of certain letters usually gives away this difference. For example, the letters on this envelope should have been American Garramond. But they have turned into Indian Garramond. In fact, you may even call it Calcutta Garramond!'

The silence in the room became charged with tension. Feluda's eyes were now fixed on Ranajit Banerjee's face. I had seen pictures of waxworks of famous people in Madame Tussaud's in London. Every feature looked amazingly lifelike, except the eyes. Only the glass eyes were an indication that those figures were lifeless. Ranajit Banerjee was alive, but his eyes were unseeing. They looked very much like the eyes of those wax figures.

'Please don't mind, Mr Banerjee, I feel obliged to open this envelope!'

Ranajit Banerjee raised his right hand as if he wanted to stop Feluda, but let it fall almost immediately.

With a sharp, rasping noise, Feluda's fingers tore open one side of the envelope. Then the same fingers took out a sheaf of ruled foolscap paper. Yes, the sheets were ruled—but that was all. There was no writing on them. Each sheet was blank.

The glassy eyes were now closed; Ranajit Banerjee's head was bent, his elbows were placed on his knees, and his face was buried in his hands.

'Mr Banerjee,' Feluda said grimly, 'You said yesterday something about a thief breaking in. That was a lie, wasn't it?'

Mr Banerjee could not speak. All he could do was make a sound that was more like a groan than anything else. Feluda continued to speak: 'You just had to create the impression that there had been a burglar the previous night, because you were getting ready to steal everything yourself and had to make sure that no suspicion should fall on you. Then yesterday afternoon, when you saw your chance, you opened the safe and removed thirty-three thousand rupees and Nihar Datta's research notes. I don't think this printed envelope was ready yesterday. You had it printed last night. Why, may I ask?'

Ranajit Banerjee finally raised his face and looked at Feluda. When he spoke, his voice sounded choked. 'Yesterday, when Mr Datta heard Dastur's voice, he knew it was Suprakash Choudhury. He said to me, "The fellow has become greedy again, after twenty years. *He* must have removed my papers." So I. . .'.

'I see. So you thought this was your chance to pin the theft on Dastur. When the police left, it was you who fixed the envelope with Sellotape to the underside of Dastur's bed, am I right? But you made sure that it could be seen if someone bent low enough.'

Mr Banerjee let out a wail. 'Forgive me, please forgive me! I swear I will return everything tomorrow—both the money and the papers. I . . . simply . . . I simply couldn't stop myself . . . the temptation was just too much.'

'Yes, you shall certainly return everything, or I'll have to hand you over to the police.'

'Yes, I appreciate that. But may I please make a request? Please don't tell the old Mr Datta anything about this. He is very fond of me. I don't think he could withstand the shock.'

'Very well. Nihar Datta will learn nothing, I promise you. But you were such a brilliant student . . . why did you have to do such a thing?'

Ranajit Banerjee looked blankly at Feluda.

'I went to meet your professor—Professor Bagchi. You see, I began to have doubts about you when I saw those scratch marks around the keyhole on the safe. No thief would be so careless, especially when someone was actually sleeping in the room, and a servant was just outside the door. Anyway, Professor Bagchi told me what a bright future you had. If you had taken your final exams, he thought you would have obtained a first class degree. Why did you abandon your studies and suddenly take the job of a secretary here? Was it to try and find a short cut to a Nobel Prize? Is that what tempted you?'

A mixture of fear, shame and remorse made Ranajit Banerjee completely speechless. I could see that, like me, Feluda was feeling most sorry for the man.

'You may go home now, but you must return at once with the money and the papers. We cannot wait until tomorrow. If you wait a moment, I will arrange for one of the constables to go with you. It wouldn't be wise to travel with such a lot of cash.'

Ranajit Banerjee nodded, like an obedient child.

In spite of what Subir Datta had told us about his son, the news that he was not the thief must have come as a major relief. At least, that was what the look on his face and his voice implied.

'Will you go and see my brother?' he asked.

'Certainly,' Feluda replied. 'That's really why I am here.'

We followed Subir Datta into his brother's room.

'So you're here?' Nihar Datta asked, still reclining in his chair.

'Yes, sir. Your research papers have been found, I hear. You must be feeling quite relieved?'

'They no longer mean anything to me,' Mr Datta's voice sounded low and dispirited. I had no idea a man could grow so pale in just one day. Even the day before, he had appeared quite strong.

'Perhaps not. But they are still of great value to us, to many scientists in this world,' said Feluda.

'If you say so.'

'I would like to ask you just one more question. After that, I promise I won't bother you again.'

A thin, wan smile appeared on Nihar Datta's lips. 'Bother me? No, Mr Mitter, no one can possibly bother me now.'

'Well then, here's my question. Yesterday, I had seen ten sleeping pills on your table. There are still ten of them lying there. Does that mean you did not take a pill last night?'

'No, I didn't. But tonight, I shall'

'Thank you. We will now take our leave.'

'Wait!'

Nihar Datta offered Feluda his right hand. Feluda grasped it. The two shook hands most warmly. 'You will understand. You have a special vision,' Mr Datta said.

*

Feluda seemed quiet and withdrawn even after we got home. But I wasn't prepared to be kept in the dark any longer. 'You have to tell me everything!' I said. 'Don't just beat about the bush.'

In reply to my question, Feluda suddenly made a reference to the Ramayan. This was his way of adding further suspense—I could never tell why he did that.

'Six days after Dasharath sent Ram into exile, he remembered that, as a young prince, he had committed a crime. That was the reason why he was suffering so much in his old age. Can you remember what that crime was?'

It was some time since I'd last read the Ramayan, but I could remember that particular story.

'A blind sage lived in a forest. His son was filling his pitcher from a river one night. Dasharath heard that noise from a distance, and thought it was an elephant drinking water. He shot one of his special arrows that could hit the source of any sound. The arrow found its target and killed the young boy.'

'Good. Dasharath had the power to reach a target simply going by the sound it made, even if it was dark and he couldn't see anything. Nihar Datta could do the same.'

'Nihar Datta?' I nearly fell off my chair.

'Yes, sir. He did not take the sleeping pill because he knew he would have to stay awake and alert during the night. When everyone else went to sleep, he walked down the stairs barefoot and went to Dastur—or, if you like, Suprakash's room. His nephew used that room at one time. So he knew its layout. In his hand was a weapon—a stout stick with a solid silver handle. He went close to the bed and struck, not once but three times!'

'But . . . but . . .' I felt totally confused. What on earth was Feluda talking about? Mr Datta was blind, for heaven's sake!

'Don't you remember something?' Feluda sounded a little impatient. 'What did Sukhwani say about Dastur?'

It came back to me in a flash. 'Dastur used to snore very loudly!'

'Exactly. That means Nihar Datta could make out where on his pillow Dastur's head was resting, whether or not he had turned on his side—everything. For someone with ears as sharp as Mr Datta's, no other detail was necessary. If one blow wasn't enough, three certainly were.'

After a few moments of stunned silence, I said slowly, 'Was *that* the unfinished business? Revenge?'

'Yes. A desire for revenge can produce enormous energy, even if a person is blind. It was this desire that had kept him alive so far.

Now he is very close to death . . . and no one can touch him, not even the law.'

*

Nihar Ranjan Datta lived for another seventeen days. Just before he died, he made a will and left all his research papers and savings to his trusted and talented secretary, Ranajit Banerjee.

The Criminals of Kathmandu

ONE

'Nowhere in this country,' said Lalmohan Babu—alias Jatayu—in an admiring tone, 'will you find a market like our New Market!'

Feluda and I were in full agreement. Some time ago, there had been talk of pulling it down to build a modern multi-storey supermarket in its place. This had seriously upset Feluda.

'Don't they realize,' I had heard him fume, 'that if New Market is destroyed, it would mean the destruction of the very spirit of Calcutta? If they do go ahead, I hope the citizens will not hesitate to take to the streets in protest!' Luckily, the proposal was dropped.

We were now standing opposite New Market, having just seen *Ape and Superape* at the Globe. Lalmohan Babu needed batteries for his torch and a refill for his ball-point pen. Feluda wanted a packet of daalmut from Kalimuddi's shop. Besides, Lalmohan Babu wanted to go around the whole market to inspect its nooks and crannies. 'Only yesterday, you see, I got the most wonderful idea for a ghost story that can take place right here in the market!' he told me.

We stepped into the traffic to cross the road, making our way carefully through endless private cars and taxis. Lalmohan Babu began to give me the details of his plot. 'There is this man, you see, a retired judge. One day, he comes to this market in the evening and discovers, a few hours later, that he can't get out! All shops are closed, all lights have been switched off, and he just can't find an exit. Every dark corridor is empty, except for an old antiques shop in a small, narrow alley. There is only a flickering light in this shop. This man runs towards the shop, in the hope of finding help. Just as he reaches it, an arm comes out of the darkness. It is the arm of a skeleton, a dagger clutched in its hand, dripping with blood. It is the skeleton of a murderer, on whom the judge had once passed a death sentence. He has come back to take his revenge. The judge starts running blindly through the dark corridors, but it's no use. No matter how fast he runs or where he goes, he can still see the skeleton's arm, getting closer. . . and closer.'

Not bad, I thought quietly to myself; an idea like this certainly had possibilities, although I was sure he'd have to appeal to Feluda for help, if only to produce a plausible explanation for the retired judge getting locked in.

We had, by now, come into the market. In front of us was a shop selling electrical goods. Lalmohan Babu could buy his batteries there and a refill for his pen from the shop opposite.

The owner of Dey Electricals knew Feluda. He greeted us with a smile. We were followed almost immediately by another man—about forty years of age, medium height, a receding hairline, wearing a white bush-shirt and black trousers. In his hand was a plastic bag.

'You're Mr Mitter, aren't you?' he asked.

'Yes, that's right.'

'A man in that book shop over there pointed you out. "The famous investigator, Pradosh Mitter," he said. It was really strange because I have been thinking of you for the last couple of days.'

'Really? Why?'

The man cleared his throat. Was he feeling nervous for some reason? 'I'll explain later if you allow me to call on you,' he said. 'Will you be home tomorrow?'

'Yes, but only after 5 p.m.'

'Very well. May I please have your address?' He took out a notebook and a fountain pen from his pocket, and handed them over to Feluda. Feluda wrote down our address and returned the notebook and pen to the gentleman. 'Sorry,' he said, looking ruefully at Feluda's finger, which was slightly smeared with violet ink. His pen was obviously leaking. 'My name is Batra,' he added.

Lalmohan Babu had gone to buy a refill. He returned just as Mr Batra left. 'Have you found yourself a client already?' he asked. Feluda smiled, but did not say anything. The three of us came out, and began walking in the direction of the daalmut shop. Lalmohan Babu took out a red notebook and began scribbling in it. This meant, inevitably, that he got left behind each time he stopped to make a note. Then he had to rush forward to catch up with us. Feluda was walking in silence, looking straight ahead, but I knew his eyes and ears were taking in every detail.

The market was very crowded today, possibly because Puja was just round the corner. Lalmohan Babu said something about the crowd. I only caught the word 'cosmopolitan', but couldn't ask him to repeat what he had said, for we had arrived at Kalimuddi's shop. 'Salaam, Babu,' he said and began making up a packet for us. He knew what we wanted. I loved watching the way he mixed all the masala, shaking the packet gently. Its contents, I knew, would taste heavenly.

He finished in a few moments and passed the packet to me. Feluda put his hand into his pocket to take out his wallet, and turned into a statue. What on earth was the matter? What was he staring at? Had his wallet been stolen?

It took me a moment to realize what it was. Feluda's wallet was quite safe, but he was still staring at the man who had just walked past us, glancing once in our direction without the slightest sign of recognition. He looked exactly like Mr Batra.

'Twins,' whispered Lalmohan Babu.

I felt inclined to agree with him. Only an identical twin could bear such a startling resemblance. The only difference was that this man was wearing a dark blue shirt. And, of course, he didn't seem to know Feluda at all,

'There's nothing to feel so amazed about, really,' Feluda remarked. 'So what if Mr Batra has a twin? Dozens of people do!'

'No, sir,' said Lalmohan Babu most emphatically, 'if a mountain doesn't have a snow-capped peak, I don't call that a mountain at all.'

He was sitting in our living room the next evening, talking idly about going to a hill station for a holiday. There was an atlas lying on the coffee table. Lalmohan Babu stretched out a hand towards it, possibly to find the map of India, but withdrew it as the bell rang.

Srinath answered the door and, a minute later, Mr Batra walked in. Srinath followed, only a few moments later, with a cup of tea.

'Do you have a twin?' Lalmohan Babu asked as soon as Mr Batra was seated. His eyebrows shot up immediately, and his mouth fell open.

'How . . . how did you . . . ?'

'Let me explain,' Feluda said. 'We saw your twin soon after we met you yesterday in New Market.'

'Mr Mitter!' Mr Batra cried, bringing his fist down on the arm of his chair in excitement. 'I am the only child of my parents. I have no brother or sister.'

'Well, then—?'

'That is precisely why I've come to see you. It started a week ago, in Kathmandu. I work in a travel agency there called Sun Travels. I am their PRO. There is a good restaurant near my office where I have lunch every day. Last Monday, when I went there, the waiter said he was surprised to see me, for hadn't I already eaten my lunch?

A couple of other people also said they had seen me eating only half an hour ago. Just imagine, Mr Mitter! It took me some time to convince them that the man they had seen wasn't me. Then the waiter said he had felt a little suspicious since this other man had a full lunch with rice and curry and everything, whereas I normally have a few sandwiches and a cup of coffee.' Mr Batra paused to take a sip from his cup. Then he continued, 'I arrived in Calcutta the day before yesterday, which was a Sunday. My work is such that I have to travel to Calcutta, Delhi and Bombay quite often. Anyway, yesterday, I was walking out of the hotel—I'm staying at the Grand—to buy some aspirin, when I heard someone say, "Mr Batra, can you come here for a minute?" It turned out to be a salesman from the hotel's gift shop. I went in, and he showed me a hundred rupee note.' "This is a fake," he said, "there's no water mark on it. Please change it, sir." At first, I could only stare at him. You see, I hadn't been to that shop at all. But the salesman assured me that I—or someone who looked like me—had bought a kukri from them and given them that fake note!'

'Kukri? You mean a Nepali knife?' Lalmohan Babu asked.

'Yes. Why should I buy a Nepali knife here in Calcutta, tell me? I live in Nepal, for heaven's sake! I could buy a kukri any day at half the price.'

'Did you have to change the note?'

'Oh yes. I tried telling them I wasn't the same man, but they began to give me such strange looks that I . . .'

'Hm.'

'What am I to do, Mr Mitter?'

Feluda flicked the ash from his Charminar into an ashtray and said, 'I can understand how you must feel.'

'I am getting into a state of panic, Mr Mitter. God knows what this man will do next.'

'Yes, it's an awkward situation,' said Feluda slowly. 'I might have found it difficult to believe your story if I hadn't seen your look-alike myself. But even so, Mr Batra, I must confess I'm at a loss to see how I can help you.'

Mr Batra nodded, looking profoundly miserable. 'Yes, I know there's nothing for you to do—yet,' he said. 'My problem is that I am going back to Kathmandu tomorrow. What if this man follows me there? It's obvious he's trying to harass me deliberately. So far it's cost me only a hundred rupees, but who knows what he might do next? What if—?'

'Look,' Feluda interrupted gently, 'at this point of time I really cannot help you. Go straight to the police if you're harassed again in Kathmandu. What a man like this needs is a sound thrashing, and the police can hand it out much better than anyone else. But let us hope it won't come to that.'

'Yes, I certainly hope so,' said Mr Batra, rising to his feet. 'Anyway, at least this gave me the chance to meet you. I had heard such a lot about you from Sarweshwar Sahai.'

Sarweshwar Sahai was an old client.

'Goodbye, Mr Batra. Good luck!'

'Thank you, I may well need it. Goodbye!'

Lalmohan Babu was the first to speak after Mr Batra had gone.

'Strange!' he said. 'Kathmandu is a hill station! Why didn't I think of it before? Just because it's in a foreign country?'

TWO

What happened the next day marked the real beginning of this story. But before I talk about it, I must mention the telephone call Feluda received a few hours after Mr Batra's departure.

Lalmohan Babu left at 7 p.m. 'It looks as though it's going to rain,' he said, looking out of the window. 'I had better be going today. Tell you what, Tapesh, I'll come back tomorrow. You see, I've thought some more about that new plot. I'd like to discuss it with you.'

It began to pour at around eight. The phone call came at 8.45. Feluda took it on the extension in his room. I heard the conversation on the main telephone in the living room.

'Mr Pradosh Mitter?' asked a deep, rather refined voice.

'Speaking.'

'You're the private investigator?'

'Yes.'

'Namaskar. My name is Anikendra Som. I'm calling from the Central Hotel.'

'Yes?'

'I need to meet you personally. When can I—?'

'Is it urgent?'

'Yes, very. It's raining so heavily it might be difficult to go out tonight, but I'd be grateful if you could find some time tomorrow morning. I've travelled to Calcutta expressly to meet you. I think you'll be interested in the reason.'

'I don't suppose you could explain a bit further on the telephone?'

'No, I'm sorry.'

'All right. How about nine o'clock tomorrow?'

'That's fine. Thank you.'

Mr Som rang off. Two clients in one evening, I thought to myself. At this rate, Feluda would soon have a queue outside our front door!

I had recently decided to follow Feluda's example and started to do yoga in the morning. We were both ready for the day by 8 a.m. Lalmohan Babu rang at half-past eight.

'I'm on my way to your house,' he said. 'I'll stop on the way at New Market to look at a green jerkin I saw the other day. I need to find out its price.' He had clearly started making preparations for going to a hill station.

More than an hour later, we were still waiting in the living room, but there was no sign of Mr Som. At 9.45, Feluda glanced at his watch and shook his head irritably. I could tell he was about to comment bitterly on Mr Som's sense of punctuality. But the telephone rang before he could utter a word.

'Why do I find your phone number in the diary of a murder victim?' boomed a familiar voice. It was Inspector Mahim Dattagupta, in charge of the Jorasanko police station.

Feluda frowned. 'Who's been murdered?'

'Come to Central Avenue, Central Hotel. Room number 23. All will be revealed.'

'Is it Anikendra Som?'

'Did you know him?'

'No, I was supposed to meet him this morning. How did he die?'

'Stabbed.'

'When?'

'Early this morning. I'll give you the details when you get here. I arrived about twenty minutes ago.'

'I'll try to get there in half an hour,' said Feluda.

Lalmohan Babu walked in five minutes later, but did not get the chance to sit down. 'Murder,' said Feluda briefly, pushing him out of the house. Then he threw him into the back seat of his Ambassador, got in beside him and said to Lalmohan Babu's driver, Haripada, 'Central Hotel. Quickly.'

I got in the front with a swift glance at Lalmohan Babu's face. Shock and bewilderment were writ large, but he knew Feluda wouldn't tell him anything even if he asked.

Haripada drove as fast as the traffic let him. Inspector Dattagupta filled us in when we arrived. Apparently, Anikendra Som had checked in on Sunday evening. The hotel register showed he lived in Kanpur. He was supposed to check out tomorrow. At 5 a.m. this morning, a man came and asked for him. On being given his room number, the man went up, using the stairs, not the lift. He was seen leaving the hotel fifteen minutes later. The hotel staff who had seen him described him as a man of medium height, clean shaven, clad in a blue bush-shirt and grey trousers. The chowkidar said he had a taxi waiting.

Mr Som had ordered breakfast at 8 a.m. A waiter arrived on the dot, but when there was no response to his loud knocking, he opened the door with a duplicate key. He found Mr Som's body sprawled on the floor, stabbed in the chest with a kukri. The knife had not been removed.

In due course, the police arrived and searched the room. All they found was a small VIP suitcase with a few clothes in it, and a pair of boots. There was no sign of a wallet or money or any other valuables. Presumably, the killer had removed everything. Feluda went in to have a look at the body. 'A good looking man,' he told us afterwards, 'couldn't have been more than thirty.'

According to the receptionist, Mr Som had spent most of his time outside the hotel the day before. He had returned an hour before it started raining. Since the rooms did not have telephones, he had used the telephone directory at the reception desk to look up a number. Then he had written it down in his notebook and used the telephone at the reception counter to make a call.

The police found the notebook with Feluda's number in it. It was lying on the floor between the bed and the bedside table. Only the first three pages had been written on. There were disjointed sentences, apparently written at random.

'What do you make of this?' Feluda asked, showing me the scribbles.

'Well, it looks as though a rather shaky hand wrote these words. The word "den", in particular, is almost illegible.'

'Perhaps the man was under terrible mental strain,' remarked Lalmohan Babu.

'Maybe. Or he may have been travelling at enormous speed. I think those words were written in an aeroplane, and as he was writing the word "den", the plane dropped into an air pocket.'

'Yes, you must be right!' exclaimed Lalmohan Babu. 'Awful things, air pockets. I remember on our way to Bombay, I had just taken a sip from my cup of coffee when there was such a mighty bump that I choked and spluttered . . . God, it was awful!'

Feluda wrote the words down in his own notebook and returned Mr Som's to the inspector.

'I will inform his people in Kanpur,' said Mahim Babu, 'the body will have to be identified.'

'I believe there is an evening flight from Delhi that comes via Kanpur. You can check if the passenger list last Sunday had Mr Som's name on it. But I think he had recently been to a hilly area.'

'Why, what makes you say that?'

'Did you notice those heavy boots in that corner? One of them has a piece of fern stuck on its heel. It couldn't have come from a place on the plains.'

'Yes, you're probably right. I'll keep you informed, Mr Mitter, especially if we find any fingerprints on the kukri.'

'There's one other thing. Please check with the gift shop in the Grand Hotel if the kukri was sold by them.'

On our way back, Feluda showed us the words he had found in Mr Som's notebook:

1. Is it only LSD?
2. Ask CP about methods and past cases.
3. Den—is it here or there?
4. Find out about AB.
5. Ring up PCM, DDC.

The last sentence was followed by Feluda's number.

'Is it something to do with foreign exchange?' asked Lalmohan Babu.

'Why do you say that?'

'Well, LSD . . . I mean, it looks like an L, but could it be pound-shillings-pence?'

Feluda clicked his tongue in mock annoyance. 'Do stop thinking of money all the time,' he admonished. 'This LSD refers to the drug, Lysergic Acid Diethylamide. The whole world knows about it. The human brain contains a chemical called serotonin, which helps the brain function normally. LSD, I believe, reduces the level of this chemical. The brain then acts abnormally, causing hallucinations. For instance, if you took a dose of the drug now and looked out of the window, you wouldn't see the traffic or the crowds. Green meadows and rippling rivers may greet your eyes instead.'

'Really? Is it possible to buy this stuff?'

'Yes, it most certainly is; but not, obviously, at your local pharmacy. It is sold secretly. If you went to the hotel behind the Globe cinema where a lot of hippies stay, you might be lucky enough to get a sugar cube.'

'Sugar cube?'

'Yes. Just one grain of LSD in a sugar cube is quite enough. It would have the strength of—to borrow your own phrase—five thousand horse power! But, mind you, hallucinations caused by this drug needn't necessarily be beautiful. I have heard of a case where a man climbed to the roof of a multi-storey building and threw himself over, thinking all the while that he was simply going down a flight of stairs.'

'My God! You mean—?'

'Yes. Instant death.'

'How terrible!'

THREE

Two days after the murder, Inspector Dattagupta rang Feluda. He had a lot to say.

Anikendra Som, it turned out, used to teach at the Kanpur IIT. He had no family there, but the police had located a brother in Calcutta, who had identified the body. Apparently, Mr Som was a loner. He was barely in touch with his relations, although his brother agreed that he had always been a brave and honest man.

Secondly, there were no fingerprints on the kukri. But it was possible to tell from the way it had been used that the murderer was left-handed. The shop in the Grand Hotel had confirmed that the weapon had indeed been sold by them, to one Mr Batra. He was staying in the hotel and had left for Kathmandu by the nine o'clock flight the same morning Mr Som was killed.

Finally, Anikendra Som's name could not be found on the list of passengers on the flight from Kanpur. However, the police had checked the passenger lists of all other flights that came in on Sunday, and discovered that Mr Som's name featured on the Kathmandu-Calcutta flight. It had reached Dum Dum at 5.30 p.m.

Mahim Babu finished by saying, 'Since the culprit seems to have escaped to Nepal, there's nothing we can do from here. The case will have to be passed on to the CID (homicide), and the Home Department. Once the Home Department gives the go-ahead, the government of Nepal can be requested to help with enquiries. If they agree, a man from the CID will travel to Kathmandu.'

Feluda said only one thing before replacing the receiver, 'Best of luck!'

Feluda sank into silence after this and, for the next couple of days, said virtually nothing. But I could tell that he was thinking deeply and trying to work something out, from the way he paced in his room, cracking his knuckles absentmindedly, and occasionally throwing himself on his bed, only to stare at the ceiling.

On the second day, Lalmohan Babu arrived in the evening and stayed for nearly two hours, but Feluda did not utter a single word. In the end, Lalmohan Babu told me what he had come to say.

'You know what, Tapesh,' he began, 'I've just been to see a palmist. His name is Moulinath Bhattacharya. An amazing man. He doesn't just read palms, but also does his own research. And his theories are fantastic. According to him, monkeys, like human beings, have lines on their palms and it is possible to read them. So he spoke to the curator of the local zoo and actually went into the cage of a chimpanzee. Apparently, it was a very well-mannered and well-trained animal. Mouli Babu took ten minutes to look carefully at his palms, but he didn't seem to mind at all. Only, as Mouli Babu turned to go, the chimp stretched out a hand and pulled his trousers down. But that might have been an accident, don't you think? Anyway, Mouli Babu says this animal will live until August 1983. I've noted the date down in my diary. Thrilling, isn't it?'

'Yes,' I said, 'if his prediction comes true, it will be remarkable. But what did he tell you about yourself?'

'Oh, something very interesting. Five years ago, another palmist had told me I'd never travel abroad. Mouli Babu said I would, most definitely.'

As things turned out, Lalmohan Babu was not disappointed. Feluda broke his silence the next day, saying over breakfast, 'Do you know what my heart's been telling me, Topshe? It keeps saying all roads lead to Nepal. And some of them are long and winding. So I think it's time for Felu Mitter to pay a visit to Kathmandu.'

It took us three days to make all the arrangements. The three of us were booked on an Indian Airlines flight. Our travel agent also made hotel reservations in Kathmandu.

'Do you think Batra number two has returned to Kathmandu?' I asked Feluda one day.

'Possibly. You heard what Mahim Babu said. If a criminal manages to escape to another country, he can be quite safe until the two governments come to an agreement. And that can take ages. Criminals in the USA try to cross the border into Mexico. It's the same story between India and Nepal.'

Lalmohan Babu turned up the day before we were to leave to say that he had seen the 'fake' Mr Batra near Lenin Sarani, having a glass of lassi.

Feluda's eyes narrowed.

'Was he holding the glass in his left hand?' he asked.

'Eh heh—I didn't notice that!'

'In that case, your statement has no value at all.'

The officer who checked us in at the airport happened to know Feluda. 'I'll give you seats on the right,' he said. 'You'll get a good view.'

But I had no idea just how good the view could be. Within ten minutes of leaving Calcutta, I could see Kanchenjunga glittering on our right—a sight as rare as it was breathtaking. This was followed by glimpses of several other famous peaks, each of which, I knew, held an irresistible attraction for adventurous mountaineers.

We were still looking out of the window, transfixed, when an air hostess stopped by Feluda's seat and said, 'Captain Mukherjee, the pilot, would like to see you in the cockpit.' Feluda unfastened his seat belt and stood up. 'Can my friends go too, when I get back?' he asked.

The air hostess smiled. 'Why don't all of you come with me?' she said.

The cockpit was too small for us all to get inside, but what I saw from the top of Feluda's shoulder was enough to make me give an involuntary gasp. Lalmohan Babu was peering from the other side.

He later described his feeling' as one of 'speechless, breathless, enchanting, captivating wonder'.

A row of peaks formed a wall in the distance. The closer we got, the bigger they seemed. The co-pilot laid aside the paperback he had been reading and began to point these peaks out to us. After Kanchenjunga came Makalu, and a little later, we saw Mount Everest. Then came Gourishankar, Annapurna and Dhaulagiri.

We returned to our seats in five minutes. In less than half an hour, I could sense that the plane was losing height. I looked out of the window again and saw a thick green carpet spread below. This must be the famous Terai. The Kathmandu valley lay behind this.

At this point, we disappeared into a grey mist and the plane started bumping up and down. Luckily, the mist cleared only a few minutes later, the plane steadied itself, and we caught our first glimpse of a beautiful valley, bathed in sunlight.

'One doesn't have to be told this is a foreign country!' exclaimed Lalmohan Babu, swallowing hard.

True. I had never seen anything like this in India. There were trees and rivers and rice fields and houses—but, somehow, everything seemed different.

'Look at those little houses,' said Feluda. 'They're made of bricks, with roofs thatched with straw. They were built by the Chinese.'

'And what are those? Temples?'

'Yes, Buddhist temples.'

I now noticed the shadow of our plane on the ground. Suddenly, it began to grow larger and larger, until it seemed to shoot up in the air and disappear. We had landed at Tribhuvan airport.

FOUR

We had been warned that customs officials in Nepal were very strict. Apparently, every single passenger was required to have all his baggage examined.

Lalmohan Babu, I noticed, was looking somewhat uneasy. This surprised me since I knew none of us was carrying anything suspicious. On being questioned, he said, 'I brought a little *aam papad* in a tiffin box. Suppose they object?'

They didn't. Lalmohan Babu relaxed, turned towards the exit, and froze. I followed his gaze and saw why. One of the two Batras was standing near the door, talking to a tall, white man with a beard.

It turned out to be the real Mr Batra. His face broke into a smile as he caught sight of Feluda. He said 'Excuse me' to his companion and came forward to greet us.

'Welcome to Kathmandu!' he said.

'I felt I had to come,' Feluda explained.

'Very good, very good.' Mr Batra shook our hands. 'I don't think that other man followed me back here. There hasn't been any problem in the last few days. How long are you here for?'

'About a week.'

'Where are you staying?'

'Hotel Lumbini.'

'It's a new hotel, and quite good. If you want to go sightseeing, I can make all the arrangements for you. My office is only five minutes from your hotel.'

'Thank you. By the way, do you get Indian newspapers here? Did you see this?' Feluda took out a cutting from the *Statesman* and handed it to Mr Batra. It was a report on the murder of Mr Som. Mr Batra read it quickly, then looked up, his eyes filled with apprehension.

'What that report does not say,' Feluda told him, 'is that a man called Batra bought that Nepali kukri from the shop in the Grand Hotel. The police had this verified.'

'Oh my God!' Mr Batra went very pale.

'You didn't know Anikendra Som, did you?'

'No, never heard of him.'

'He travelled on the same plane as you.'

'From Kathmandu? Nepal Airlines?'

'Yes.'

'Then maybe I'd have recognized him if I saw him, although—mind you—there were a hundred and thirty passengers on that flight.'

'Yes. Anyway, try and stay away from Calcutta for the moment,' Feluda said lightly.

'But why should anyone try to harass me like this, Mr Mitter?' Mr Batra wailed.

'Well, I can think of a good reason,' Feluda said slowly. 'If a criminal discovers that he has a look-alike, isn't it natural for him to try and frame the other man, so that he himself can get away scot free?'

'All right, but this is no ordinary crime, Mr Mitter. We're talking of murder!'

'I am convinced, Mr Batra, that the killer will return to Kathmandu. Anikendra Som had gone to Calcutta to seek my help. I do not know what he wanted me to do, but I won't rest in peace until I've caught the man who murdered him. So if you, or anyone you know, sees this man who looks like you, I hope you'll let me know immediately.'

'Oh yes, certainly. I have to go out of town tomorrow, but I'll contact you the day after.'

We came out of the airport and got into a taxi. It was a Japanese Datsun, one of the many that could be seen on the clean, broad, beautiful roads of Kathmandu. Eucalyptus trees stood in neat rows by the sides of these roads. We passed a large park with a stadium in it. There were huge buildings everywhere, many of which had once been palaces owned by the Ranas. Some among them were Hindu and Buddhist temples, their spires towering over everything else.

It was easy to see from the way Lalmohan Babu was rubbing his hands that he was already quite impressed by what he had seen in this foreign land. When Feluda told him that the king of Nepal was the only Hindu king in the world, and that Lumbini, where Lord Buddha was born, was in Nepal, his mouth parted and formed a silent 'O'.

Our taxi drove down Kanti Path and passed through a large and elaborately carved gate. A right turn brought us into New Road. Hotel Lumbini, together with many other hotels and rest houses, stood on one side of this road. Our taxi drew up near its front door.

The first man we met as we were checking in turned out to be a Bengali. He rose from a sofa and came forward to greet us.

'Did you come by the Indian Airlines flight?' he addressed Lalmohan Babu.

'Yes.'

'Is this your first visit to Nepal?'

'Yes. We're on holiday,' Lalmohan Babu replied with a sidelong glance at Feluda.

'You must visit Pokhara, if you can.'

This time, Feluda spoke.

'Do you live here?' he asked. A bell boy, in the meantime, had taken our luggage upstairs. We were given two adjacent rooms on the second floor, numbers 226 and 227.

'I am from Calcutta. I've come on a holiday with my family. My friend here lives in Kathmandu.'

I noticed for the first time that another elderly gentleman was sitting on the sofa. His skin was very fair, and his hair totally white. He was distinguished looking. He now rose and joined us.

'His family has lived here for three hundred years,' the first gentleman told us.

'What!'

'Yes, you must get him to tell you his story.'

'Well, if you don't mind, why don't you come up to our room and join us for a cup of tea?' said Feluda. 'I am interested in Bengalis living in Nepal . . . for a specific reason, you see.'

I knew exactly what he meant. I also knew that Feluda didn't normally invite people up to his room so soon after being introduced to them.

Feluda and I had been given a double room. All of us trooped into it, and Feluda rang room service for tea. Our guests formally introduced themselves. The gentleman from Calcutta was called Mr Bhowmik. The other gentleman was Mr Harinath Chakravarty. Over a cup of tea, he related the history of his family.

Nearly three hundred years ago, Nepal had been struck by a severe drought. The Mallyas were then the rulers. King Jagatjit Mallya invited a tantrik from Bengal, to see if his magical powers could bring rain. This tantrik was Harinath's ancestor, Jairam Chakravarty. Jairam did some special puja, as a result of which it rained in the Kathmandu valley for eleven continuous days. After this, Jagatjit Mallya could not allow him to go back. He gave him land to live on, and made sure that Jairam and his family lived in comfort.

When the Mallyas were ousted by the Ranas, Jairam continued to be looked after, for the Ranas were orthodox Hindus. Until two generations ago, the men of the Chakravarty family lived as priests of the royal household. An uncle of Harinath was still a priest in the temple of Pashupatinath. It was his father who was the first in the family to go to Calcutta for higher studies. He returned to work as a private tutor for the Ranas. Harinath himself did the same. He went to Calcutta to study English literature. When he came back to Nepal, the Ranas appointed him as private tutor. But, over a period of time, the Ranas lost their power. When, eventually, a college opened in Kathmandu in the name of Raja Tribhuvan, Harinath joined it as a professor of English.

'My sons, of course,' said Harinath Babu, bringing his tale to an end, 'were not even remotely interested in priesthood. The older, Niladri, used to work as a trainer in the mountaineering institute.'

'Used to? I mean—?'

'He died in a climbing accident in 1976.'

'I'm sorry. What about your other children?'

'I had another son, Himadri. He worked as a helicopter pilot. Took tourists to look at the Terai and the famous Himalayan peaks. I . . . I lost him, too. Only three weeks ago.'

'Air crash?'

Harinath Babu shook his head sadly. 'No. That would have made sense. What really happened was weird. He had taken a friend to look at a monastery. When he returned, he found a small injury on his hand. He had no idea how he had got it, but his friend thought it might have been caused by barbed wire. Himadri tried to shrug it off, but his friend insisted on calling a doctor to give him an anti-tetanus shot.'

'What happened then?'

Harinath Babu shook his head again. 'Nothing. The shot didn't help. He got tetanus and died.'

'Perhaps by the time he was given the shot, it was already too late?'

'No, I don't think so. According to the friend, he cut his hand in the evening. The shot was given the following morning. But he began to have convulsions soon after that. We lost him the same day.'

'The doctor who was called . . . was he your own?'

'No, but I know him. It was Dr Divakar. He has quite a large practice. It seems to have grown since our family physician, Dr Mukherjee, died. Dr Divakar is now a fairly wealthy man.'

Mr Bhowmik spoke suddenly. 'Never mind about the doctor,' he said. 'It is the drug that must be questioned. It's not unusual at all these days, is it, for a patient to die because of a spurious drug? They put water in ampoules, talcum powder in capsules, or powdered chalk, or just plain dust. Surely you've heard of this before?'

Harinath Babu gave a wan smile. 'Yes. But what could I do? I had to accept the situation. My son was dead. That was that.'

The two gentleman rose to leave.

'I am afraid I have wasted a lot of your time,' said Harinath Babu.

'Not at all,' Feluda replied. 'There is only one thing I'd like to ask.'

'Yes?'

'Is it possible to meet your son's friend?'

'No, I'm afraid not. He was staying at our house. He had been profoundly shocked by Himadri's death. I tried to comfort him by saying it was destiny, no one was to blame. But this seemed to upset him even more. He stopped speaking to me. Then, a week after my son's death, he left our house without a word. I do not know where he went. But he's bound to come back sooner or later, for we've still got most of his things.'

'What is his name?'

'Anikendra Som. We call him Anik.'

FIVE

Half an hour later, we had had a shower and were down at the hotel's restaurant, Nirvana, to have lunch. I had not expected things to move quite so quickly so soon after our arrival. Mr Som's murder in Calcutta, Himadri Chakravarty's death in Kathmandu, the fake Mr Batra—all these were undoubtedly linked together. Had Mr Som wanted Feluda to investigate the death of his friend ? Did he really die because he was injected with a spurious drug?

A waiter arrived to take our order. Lalmohan Babu peered at the menu and asked, 'What is mo-mo?'

'It's meat balls in sauce, sir,' the waiter replied.

'It's a Tibetan dish,' Feluda told him. 'Try it, Lalmohan Babu. When you go back to Calcutta, you can tell your friends you ate the same thing as the Dalai Lama.'

'OK, one mo-mo for me, please.'

The waiter finished taking our order and left. Lalmohan Babu now produced a light green card.

'A man at the counter handed this to me,' he said, 'but, for the life of me, I can't figure out what to do with it. I can recognize the word "casino", but what's all this? Jackpot, pontoon, roulette, blackjack... and, look, it says its value is five dollars. What does it mean?'

Feluda explained, 'There is a very famous hotel here, which has a big casino for gambling. Those words that you read out are names of various types of gambling. Gambling in public isn't permitted in our country, so you won't find a casino in any Indian hotel. What you can do with that card is show it at the casino and try your hand at any game. You can spend up to five dollars without paying anything from your own pocket.'

'Hey, that sounds interesting! Why don't we . . .?'

'I don't mind!' I said.

'Yes. How can a horse resist a carrot if it dangles right before its nose? What do you say, Felu Babu?'

'Horse? You may well feel like an ass when you've finished. But then, if you're lucky enough, who knows what might happen?'

We decided to spend an evening at the casino. Our hotel would arrange transport, at no extra cost.

Our food arrived. 'Delicious!' said Lalmohan Babu, tasting his mo-mo. 'I must get the recipe from somewhere. I have an excellent cook back home who, I'm sure, could make it for me. Six months of consuming this stuff and one is bound to start looking distinguished.'

We went out after lunch. 'Let's go to Darbar Square,' said Feluda. 'That is where the main police station is. I must go there. The two of you can look around, then meet me somewhere.'

Darbar Square startled us all. It reminded me of a chessboard, when a game is well under way. Just as the board is littered with chessmen in various positions, the square was strewn with palaces, temples, statues and pillars. Amidst these, hundreds of people went about their business, and traffic flowed endlessly. In a distant way, it was a bit like Varanasi. But in Varanasi, all famous temples were hidden in narrow lanes. Here, the roads were so much wider. The old royal palace had a huge open space in front of it. It must have held a vast number of people when the king used to stand on a balcony to grant an audience.

Feluda consulted a map. 'If you go straight, you'll soon find the statue of Kaal Bhairav. I'll meet you there in half an hour.' He strode away.

Lalmohan Babu and I began walking. I was struck by the amazing carvings on the wooden doors, windows and even roofs of old buildings. I had heard Nepal was famous for its woodwork. Now I could see why. There were a few Hindu temples, built in a style similar to those in India. And there were pagodas, built in several layers, each layer getting narrower as one moved to the top.

However, Darbar Square wasn't just a place for religion. There was a large market, spread all over. Every imaginable object from vegetables to garments was being sold on pavements, corridors and stairs. Lalmohan Babu and I stopped at a small stall selling rather attractive Nepali caps. He brought out his little red notebook again.

I found a nice cap for myself, and had just started bargaining over its price, when Lalmohan Babu nudged me. 'Tapesh!' he whispered. I turned around and found him staring at something, transfixed.

A few yards away stood one of the two Batras. He was in the process of lighting a cigarette. Then he walked away, without looking at us.

'Have you ever seen your cousin use a lighter with his left hand?'

'No.'

'This man did.'

'Yes, I saw him. Then he put it in his left pocket.'

'Should we follow him?'

'Do you think he saw you?'

'No.'

'OK, let's go.'

We didn't have to meet Feluda for another twenty minutes. The two of us leapt forward.

There was a temple in front of us. The man seemed to have disappeared in the crowd. But we saw him again once we had left the temple behind us. He was going into a lane. We followed, keeping a distance of about twenty yards between us.

There were small shops and restaurants on both sides of the lane. Many had 'Pie Shop' written on their signboards. I could smell food everywhere. A group of hippies came strolling by. As they walked past us, the smell of food was momentarily drowned by that of *ganja*, sweat and unwashed clothes.

'Oh no!' said Lalmohan Babu. The man had gone into a shop to our right.

What should we do now? Should we wait for him to come out? What if he took a long time? We had only fifteen minutes to spare.

'Let's go into the shop,' I said. 'He doesn't know us. We're quite safe.'

'Yes, you're right.'

We stepped in. It was a shop selling Tibetan handicrafts. There was a counter facing the front door. Behind it was another open door, leading to a dark room. The second Mr Batra must have slipped into this room, for he has nowhere to be seen. 'Yes?' said a voice. I now noticed a Tibetan lady standing behind the counter, smiling politely. By her side sat an old man with a withered and wrinkled face. He appeared to be dozing.

Obviously, we had to pretend we had come in to buy something. There were certainly plenty of things to choose from—masks, *tankhas*, prayer wheels, brassware, statues.

'I like mo-mo,' Lalmohan Babu declared, for no apparent reason.

'I am sorry, sir, but that's something you'll get in a restaurant, not here,' the lady replied.

'No, no, no,' Lalmohan Babu shook his head vigorously. 'I don't want to eat it.'

The lady raised her light eyebrows. 'I thought you just said you liked it!'

'No. Yes, I mean—not now. What I want now—I mean—'

I raised a hand to stop him. 'Do you have a Tibetan cookbook?' I asked, knowing very well they didn't.

'Sorry,' said the lady.

We said 'Thank you' quickly and came out. There was nothing to do now but go tamely back the way we had come, and find the statue of Kaal Bhairav. We stopped on the way briefly to buy a couple of Nepali caps.

What a horrifying statue it was! It gave me the creeps in broad daylight. Heaven knew how people felt if they saw it at night.

Feluda arrived five minutes later. The main entrance to the police station was right opposite the statue. We were both dying to tell him about our little adventure, but I was curious to learn why he had gone to the police station in the first place. 'I just met the OC, Mr Rajgurung. He said they'd cooperate in every way if the Nepal government officially agreed to help. He seemed a very nice man.'

'That man is here, Felu Babu,' Lalmohan Babu blurted out. I explained fully.

'Are you sure you saw him light his cigarette with his left hand?'

'Yes. We both saw him!'

'Very good,' said Feluda. 'We must inform Mr Batra tomorrow. Look, why don't you carry on? I must go back to the hotel right now to make a few phone calls.'

Something told me Feluda was not going to do much sightseeing in Kathmandu.

SIX

A right turn from the main crossing outside our hotel led to Shukra Path, which ran straight on to join a shopping complex. A large covered area stood packed with rows of small departmental stores. Each one of them sold imported stuff, ranging from clothes, watches, tape recorders, radios and calculators, to writing material, sweets and chocolates.

'I feel like howling!' Lalmohan Babu proclaimed, standing outside one of these shops.

'Why?'

'All these shops, dear boy, just look at all those goodies! They are not meant for people like us, are they? I'm sure all these shops are patronized by people like . . . like . . . John D. Rockefeller, or superstars from Bombay, perhaps?'

In the end, however, he succumbed to temptation and bought two metres of light orange Japanese terrywool. 'I need new trousers,' he told me. The shop offered to have them tailored by 4 p.m. the next evening.

'That colour would be most apt for the Land of the Lamas, wouldn't you say?' he asked, emerging from the shop, looking immensely pleased. I didn't want to cast a damper, but felt obliged to point out that Nepal could hardly be called the Land of the Lamas, since eighty per cent of the population was Hindu.

We came back to the hotel to find Feluda scribbling in his notebook. 'Sit down,' he said. 'I've called a doctor.'

Doctor? Was he unwell?

We promptly sat on the sofa, fixing anxious eyes on him. Feluda took a couple of minutes to finish writing. Then he pushed aside the notebook and explained, 'I've called Dr Divakar, the same doctor who had given the tetanus injection to Himadri Chakravarty. He normally sees patients at the Star Dispensary on Dharma Path. I will, of course, have to pay him his fee, but that cannot be helped. I'd much rather talk to him here.'

'Drugs and medicines seem to play an important role in this investigation,' Lalmohan Babu observed.

'Not just important, Lalmohan Babu,' Feluda said. 'I believe in this whole sad business, they play a crucial role.'

'What about that surgical acid Mr Som's notebook mentioned? Is it—'

'Lysergic Acid, not surgical. But then—'

Feluda picked up his notebook again, frowning. 'The term LSD can mean something else. It occurred to me only a few minutes ago. You see, LSD could also stand for Life Saving Drugs, such as anti-tetanus serum, or things like penicillin, teramycin, streptomycin, drugs to fight TB and heart problems. I think,' Feluda glanced at his notebook, 'where it says "find out about AB", it's referring to these drugs. AB could mean antibiotics. Mr Som was clearly trying to find out more about these. "Ring up PCM, DDC"—well, PCM is Pradosh Chandra Mitter, and DDC is probably the Directorate of Drug Control. It's likely that Mr Som had a sample of a drug that he wanted people at Drug Control to test. It's amazing how methodically he was working. With a brain like that, he could have been a sleuth himself!'

'Didn't the letters "CP" feature somewhere?'

'That's easy. It stands for Calcutta Police. Here, it says "Ask CP about methods and past cases."'

'That would mean you've decoded everything—'

The door bell rang. I opened the door.

The man who walked in startled me somewhat, for I had never seen a doctor so impeccably dressed. His suit must have been made by the best tailor in Kathmandu. He wore glasses with gold frames. The watch on his wrist was obviously imported, and expensive. A gift from a grateful patient, perhaps?

Since Feluda was sitting on the bed, the doctor assumed he was the patient. He walked over to him and asked, 'What's wrong?' I offered him a chair. Feluda had risen, but at the doctor's question, sat down again. Then he took out an envelope from under his pillow and held it out. 'Here you are,' he said. Dr Divakar looked quite taken aback.

'What is this?'

'This contains your fee. And this is my visiting card.'

Dr Divakar sat down, looking curiously at Feluda's card.

'I realize I have some explaining to do,' Feluda went on, 'and I apologize for dragging you out like this. Allow me to tell you first of all that I am here to investigate a murder. It happened in Calcutta, but I have reason to believe the killer is in Kathmandu. I am trying to gather as much information as I can. I believe you can help me.'

Dr Divakar's brows were knitted in a frown. 'Who was murdered?' he asked.

'I'm coming to that. Please let me verify something first. Was it you who gave an anti-tetanus shot to Harinath Chakravarty's son, Himadri?'

'Yes, that's right.'

'Did the injection come from your own stock?'

'Yes, from my dispensary.'

'But it did not work, did it?'

'No, but surely you don't think I am responsi—'

'No, no, Dr Divakar, nobody's blaming you, or trying to establish who was responsible. After all, a case like this is, by no means, unique. Most people accept it quietly. Harinath Babu did the same. What I want to know is whether you, as a doctor, have any ideas or theories about the reason behind Himadri's death.'

'There may well be more than one reason,' Dr Divakar replied. 'Firstly, Himadri couldn't tell me for sure when he had cut his hand. His friend thought it was about sixteen hours before they came to me. Now, if his friend was wrong and it was twenty-six hours instead of sixteen, then by the time that shot was given it was too late. Secondly, no one knew whether he had ever taken a preventive. If he had, the injection might have worked. His father seemed to think he had, but Himadri wasn't sure. Harinath Babu might have been mistaken. After the death of his wife and the other son, his memory, I have noticed, fails him at times.'

'All right. But did Himadri's friend take an ampoule from your dispensary after he died?'

'Yes.'

'Anti-tetanus?'

'Yes.'

'How do you know that? Did he speak to you?'

'No, he didn't just speak to me. He threatened me, Mr Mitter. He said it was my fault that Himadri died.'

'It is this friend of Himadri's who has been killed.'

'What!'

'Yes. His name was Anikendra Som.'

Dr Divakar stared. Feluda went on, 'He took that ampoule to Calcutta to have it analysed. He must've been convinced that its contents were not genuine. But I don't think he got the chance to contact a laboratory. He wanted me to help him get to the bottom of this business.'

'No drug that came from my dispensary could be spurious,' said Dr Divakar firmly.

'How can you be so sure? Do you examine every ampoule before you give an injection?'

The doctor's face turned red. 'How is that possible, Mr Mitter? When a patient needs immediate attention in an emergency case, how can I waste time getting all my drugs tested?'

'Where do you get your medicines from?'

'From wholesalers. Each batch has a number, a date of expiry—'

'Don't you know these can be faked? Those involved in this racket have secret dealings with printers who print those labels. Numbers, dates, even names of well-known foreign pharmaceutical firms can be locally printed. Surely, you're not unaware of this?'

Dr Divakar looked as though he couldn't find a suitable reply.

'Listen, doctor,' Feluda said, his tone milder now, 'I give you my word no one will come to know of this. But I would like you to have an ampoule of your anti-tetanus injection tested. Then let me know what the lab says in its report. We haven't much time, as you know.'

Dr Divakar rose slowly and began walking towards the door. 'Tomorrow I have an urgent case to attend to. I shall contact you the day after,' he said.

'Thank you very much. Your help will be much appreciated.'

There was no doubt that we had got involved in a most complex affair. The more I saw, the more I began to respect Mr Som. Feluda would not allow his killer to escape, no matter who he was.

'Let's go for a walk,' said Feluda after dinner. I began to feel vaguely suspicious about his intent as he started walking in the direction of Darbar Square. My suspicions were confirmed when he stopped before the old royal palace and said, 'All right, then. Which lane was it?'

Darbar Square looked quite different at night. Bells pealed in temples, from somewhere came the strains of a Hindi song, and tourists and cycle rickshaws made walking difficult. We had to push our way through to find the right lane.

'The hippies would call it a pig alley,' remarked Feluda. We walked past the pie shops and finally found the shop selling handicrafts.

It was still open. A couple of customers were standing before the counter. The same lady stood behind it. The old man had gone.

Feluda ran his eyes over the building from outside. It had two floors. The shop was on the ground floor. There were two windows on the first floor facing the lane. Both were closed, but through a crack we could see a faint light.

Another narrow lane ran on the other side of the shop. A few yards down this lane stood a building with three storeys, with 'Heaven's Gate Lodge' written on its front door. Its appearance evoked no heavenly images, but it was clearly a hotel, situated rather conveniently near the Tibetan shop. We pushed open the door and went in.

'How much do you charge for rooms here?' Feluda asked.

'Ten for a single. Fifteen for a double,' replied the man sitting behind the reception desk. He was busy tapping at a calculator.

'Are any rooms available?'

'How many do you need?'

'A single and a double, please, preferably on the first floor. But we'd like to have a look first, if you don't mind.'

The receptionist rang a bell without a word. A Nepali bearer appeared. The gentleman handed him a key and motioned us on. He was obviously a man of few words.

We followed the bearer up a flight of stairs and down a long passage. He stopped before the last door on the right and unlocked it. We stepped into the room. One look at the window told me that our mission was successful. Through it we could see a portion of a room above the Tibetan store.

By the time Lalmohan Babu had inspected the room, tested the light switches, checked on the number of blankets and done everything possible to convince the bearer that we had indeed come to book the room, Feluda and I had seen what there was to see.

The old man from the shop was sitting in the dimly lit room. We could see only his head and shoulders. There was a pile of cardboard boxes behind him. His hands were busy either taking something out of the boxes, or packing something in them.

There was another man in the room, though all we got to see was his shadow. He was leaning over the old Tibetan, watching him work.

Suddenly, my heart skipped a beat.

The shadow took out a packet of cigarettes from its pocket, and placed a cigarette between its lips. Then it took out another object.

It was a lighter.

The shadow now lit the lighter.

With its left hand.

SEVEN

'You two can do some more sightseeing today,' said Feluda, the next morning after breakfast. 'Try and see Swayambhu, Pashupatinath and Patan. That should be enough for a day. Let's go to Sun Travels. They should be able to arrange a car.'

We bumped into Mr Batra the minute we stepped out of the hotel. This must be telepathy, I thought. He smiled as he greeted us. But his face grew grave almost instantly.

'That man is back here,' he told us. 'A colleague of mine saw him yesterday, coming out of a jeweller's shop on New Road.'

'Did your colleague think you had returned unexpectedly from Pokhara?'

Mr Batra smiled again. 'No, and I'll tell you why. You see, my "twin" appears to be rather partial to bright colours. Yesterday he was wearing a shocking pink pullover and green shirt. People who know me well would never mistake him for me. But anyway, I went to the police and told them about it. I happen to know a sub-inspector.'

'What did he say?'

'I feel much reassured by what he said. Apparently, the police already know about this man. They think he's involved in smuggling, but is being protected by someone rich and influential. So the police can't actually do anything until he makes a false move.'

'Didn't you tell him about the inconvenience he has caused you? He did buy that kukri in your name, you know.'

'Yes, yes. I asked the sub-inspector if this man could commit a crime, and then get me framed. Do you know what the sub-inspector did? He burst out laughing. He said, "Please Mr Batra, don't think the Nepal Police are so stupid!"'

'Well, that's that, then. Surely now you're feeling a lot better?'

'Well, yes". I am much relieved, I must admit. And I think you should also relax a little. Why should you spend your entire stay in Kathmandu simply chasing a criminal? Tell you what, why don't you spend a day at the new forest bungalow our company has just built in the Rapti valley, in the Terai? It's a really wonderful spot. I need only a few hours' notice to get a car to pick you up. In fact, if I happen to be free, I can join you myself. What do you say?'

The very mention of the Terai made my heart jump for joy. Lalmohan Babu's eyes were shining, too. 'Let's see how it goes,' said Feluda noncommittally. Thank goodness he didn't reject the idea outright. Mr Batra said 'Goodbye' and left.

'Why didn't you tell him about what we saw in that pig alley?' Lalmohan Babu asked curiously.

'Because,' Feluda replied, 'it is not my wont to divulge every detail of my investigation to all and sundry. And certainly not to someone I have met only briefly.'

'I see. I understand. Felu Babu, I have learnt,' said Jatayu, chastened.

On the way back to our room, we ran into Mr Bhowmik on the stairs. 'Can you recognize this?' he asked, holding up a medicine bottle. 'Benadryl Expectorant' said its label. It was a familiar enough sight—I was given the same red syrup at home every time I had a cough.

'Yes, I can certainly recognize the bottle, but the colour of the syrup seems a little different, doesn't it?' asked Feluda.

'Oh, can you see a difference in the colour? Then you are exceptionally observant. I noticed a difference in the smell.' He unscrewed the cap and offered the bottle to Feluda, who sniffed a couple of times and said, 'Yes, there is a subtle difference. You must have a very sensitive nose!'

'Yes, I do! And you know what I am going to do? I'll take this bottle right back to the chemist, and ask for my money back. I mean it. Didn't I tell you virtually every medicine these days is adulterated? Why, I've even heard they put chalk in baby food! Even innocent babies aren't going to be spared!'

We had told Mr Batra that Lalmohan Babu and I needed a car for the day. A Japanese Toyota arrived at nine. When we left a few minutes later, Feluda was poring over the telephone directory. 'Just noting down the addresses of the local chemists,' he said.

Only a place like Kathmandu could have both Swayambhunath, a Buddhist stupa and Pashupatinath, a Hindu temple.

Lalmohan Babu left the Pasupati temple with a brief, 'Tapesh, you can look at the view' and disappeared inside the temple. When he came out, his forehead was smeared with sandalwood paste. He had clearly been blessed by the priest.

The temple was made chiefly of wood. Its doors and the spire were plated with gold and silver. The first thing one saw on coming though the main gate was a huge statue of Nandi, also covered in gold. A walk down a courtyard brought the river Bagmati into view. The mountains stood on the other side of the river.

The way to Swayambhu was through a road that wound up a hill like a snake. Our car stopped before a flight of stairs. We'd have to climb these and walk the rest of the way, we were told.

There were little stalls near the stairs, selling Tibetan goods. Lalmohan Babu suddenly seemed quite keen on buying a prayer wheel. It wasn't really a wheel—a small box was attached to one end of a stick. A chain hung from the box, with a little ball fixed at its tip. If one twirled the stick, the whole contraption moved round and round.

These prayer wheels were made of wood, copper, brass and ivory. Lalmohan Babu wanted a wooden one, but it turned out that it was too expensive. All prices had been fixed, no doubt, with rich American tourists in mind. With a sigh, Lalmohan Babu came away.

The stupa was built on top of the mountain two thousand years ago. What was most striking about it was a pillar that stood below it. Several pairs of eyes were painted on it, making it seem as though they had witnessed, for years and years, every event that occurred in the Kathmandu valley; but every secret was safe with them. They would never speak out.

The flat open area on which the stupa stood was packed with people and monkeys. 'Damn these animals! One of them just poked me!' I heard Lalmohan Babu exclaim. We didn't, of course, know then that it wasn't a monkey. But I shall come to that later.

The real incident took place in Patan, which was on the other side of the Bagmati, three miles from Kathmandu. Our car had to pass through a huge gate to enter the town. We stopped at a shop to buy a couple of American Coca-Cola cans, and then made our way to the local Darbar Square. I will not go into lengthy descriptions of what we saw. Feluda, as a matter of fact, warned me not to get carried away. 'When you write about our adventure in Nepal,' he told me when we returned home, 'make sure it doesn't read like a tourist guide.'

Suffice it to say that the temples, stupas, palaces, exquisite wooden carvings and a statue of the King atop a golden pillar were so spectacular that Lalmohan Babu kept breaking into exclamations every three minutes. 'Incredible!' he would say, 'Incomparable! Unbelievable! Inimitable! Fascinating! Unforgettable!' God knows how long he'd have continued if we were not distracted by a certain event.

We had left Darbar Square and turned right to find ourselves in yet another market called Mangal Bazar. It was full of handicrafts and other knick-knacks from both Nepal and Tibet. We went through the stalls, looking at their wares. Lalmohan Babu began inspecting prayer wheels once more. He picked up a few, but rejected them saying, 'The carving on these isn't good enough.' Things here were considerably cheaper than at Swayambhu.

About five minutes later, we noticed an old house where the market ended. A tempo was standing in front of it, being loaded with goods. This area was quiet, being some distance away from the hubbub of the main market.

As we got closer, we realized that what was being loaded on the tempo was nothing but what Lalmohan Babu had spent all day trying to buy—stacks and stacks of prayer wheels.

'This must be a factory,' Lalmohan Babu observed, looking at the house. 'I think this is where the stuff is made, and sent to Kathmandu. Which means . . . they might sell them cheaper here. Shall I go in and ask?'

'Yes, that's a good idea.'

But we were to be disappointed. The man supervising the loading shook his head and said, 'No, these are not for sale. These were made for a special order. You'll have to go back to the main market.'

'Oh no! Just my l—' Lalmohan Babu stopped abruptly, staring at a figure that was walking up the lane.

It was a Tibetan man. We recognized him instantly. He was still wearing the same yellow cap and the long red coat. One of his eyes was smaller than the other. This was our dozy old friend from the Tibetan shop in that pig alley. He stopped and went into the house through a side entrance. Or, at least, we couldn't see him any more. The door through which he appeared to have passed wasn't directly visible from where we were standing. If we took a few steps down the lane on the left, we might be able to see things better.

Suddenly, it became imperative to find out where that man had got to.

We turned into the lane on our left and proceeded to walk, as casually as we could. Only a few seconds later, we saw a door, made of solid wood and very delicately carved. It was locked from the inside. The Tibetan must have slipped in through this door and locked it behind him. But how could we be sure?

There was not a soul in sight. But someone was playing an instrument at the back of the house. We turned again to walk around the house. This time, we found its back door. It was much smaller in size, and had been left ajar. A Nepali beggar sat opposite the door, playing a sarinda. A rusted tin lay by his side. Our appearance did not disturb him at all. He continued to play a slow and rather mournful Nepali tune. His eyes were half-closed.

Lalmohan Babu dropped a few coins into the tin and asked under his breath, 'Shall we go in?'

'Yes, why not?'

'What if we're seen? What if someone asks us what we're doing inside?'

'Well, we can simply say we're tourists, and were curious to see the inside of an old house!'

'All right. Let's go.'

A quick look around showed that there was still no one about on the street. The beggar went on playing, unperturbed. We stepped in through the back door.

There was a passage. A portion of a courtyard could be seen where the passage ended. A strange, rhythmic noise came from beyond the courtyard. Were there rooms on the other side? We tiptoed our way down the passage.

Here was a door on our left. It opened at a slight touch. The room it led to was dark. Should we—?

Oh God, there were footsteps! Someone was coming from the opposite end. The sound of footsteps began to get louder. Very soon, we were going to be discovered. There was a sudden tightness in my throat. If this person coming down the passage asked us who we were, I knew I couldn't speak.

The beggar outside was now playing a different tune. It was a faster one and much more cheerful. But there was no time to think. I caught Lalmohan Babu's hand and pulled him into the dark room on our left, and quietly shut the door. The footsteps went past the door and out of the house.

The beggar had stopped playing. We could hear voices. Clearly, whoever just walked out of the house was talking to him.

I looked around helplessly. A shaft of light was coming in through a skylight. I could now spot a few things in the room. There was a string bed, a large copper bowl and a few clothes hanging from a rack. On my right was another door, leading to another room. An odd instinct made me slip into this second room, dragging Lalmohan Babu with me.

Pieces of wood and cardboard boxes filled the room. Besides these were a few statues, wooden frames and, lying in a corner, three prayer wheels. Behind this room was a veranda. The courtyard lay on the other side. That strange noise had stopped. A different noise now made my heart jump into my mouth. The footsteps were coming back. The man was obviously looking for us.

I heard him walk down the passage, then retrace his steps and stop outside the first room we had walked into. In a matter of seconds, he had walked across and opened the door of the room we were hiding in. I saw him cross the threshold and hesitate for a moment before his eyes fell on us.

The room being almost totally dark, I could not see his face at all. But I knew what I must do. Without another thought, I sprang up and attacked the man, trying to pin him against the wall. But I couldn't. He was much taller than I, and heavier. He shook me off, then grabbed me by the lapel of my jacket and picked me up straight off the floor. He would probably then have tossed me aside, but Lalmohan Babu stepped in at this point and caught his arms, trying to shake them free.

The man proved to be a good deal stronger than we had thought. With one mighty push of his elbow, he made Lalmohan Babu spin and fall on a pile of cardboard boxes. I placed my own hands under his chin and tilted his head back as far as I could. But I could sense it wasn't really going to make much difference for the man was still holding me high, and would, any minute—

Clang!

Suddenly, the hands holding me went limp. I dropped to my feet, on solid ground.

Our adversary was lying on the floor, knocked unconscious by a blow on his head. Lalmohan Babu was standing by my side, staring dumbly at the wooden prayer wheel he was still holding in his hand.

Ten seconds later, we were out on the street, walking as fast as our feet would take us.

The prayer wheel was resting peacefully in Lalmohan Babu's bag.

EIGHT

Before coming to Nepal, Feluda and I had often talked about our past adventures and wondered what had become of those villains Feluda had exposed. Bonobihari Sarkar of Lucknow, Mandar Bose in Jaisalmer, Mr Gore of Bombay, Maganlal Meghraj of Benaras—had they been adequately punished and had they learnt their lesson? Or were they still out there somewhere, spinning more webs of crime? After all, they all had enormous cunning. Why, some of them had so nearly managed to get away!

Little did we know that here in Kathmandu we were going to find one of these figures so unexpectedly.

When we returned from Patan in the late afternoon, after having stopped for lunch at a restaurant (sadly for Lalmohan Babu, their menu did not include mo-mo), Feluda was lying on his bed, reading a book called *Black Market Medicine*. One look at us made him raise an eyebrow.

'What's the matter with you? Where have you been?' he asked.

We told him. Feluda heard us out, throwing in a few rapid questions every now and then, and added, 'Well done!'

It was nice to be praised, but I knew what we had done was a big step for all of us. Something fishy was going on in that house. I had no doubt about that.

'If I could, I would give you a special reward for bravery',' Feluda went on, 'but let's have a look at your weapon, Lalmohan Babu!'

Lalmohan Babu took out the prayer wheel from his shoulder bag.

'Have you checked if it's got the prayer in it?'

'Prayer? What prayer?'

'*Om Manipadmey Hoom*. It's a Tibetan prayer. These words are either written or printed a thousand times on a piece of paper, which is then placed inside the wheel.'

'Really? How would they put it in?'

'The top of that little box with the chain should unscrew like a cap. You should find a piece of paper in it.'

Lalmohan Babu twisted the top of the box. It came off quite easily. He peered inside and said, 'No, sir, no sign of a prayer.'

'Nothing at all?'

Lalmohan Babu moved closer to the window where the light was better and looked again. 'No—wait a minute! There is something. It's glistening in the light.'

'Let's see.'

Feluda took the prayer wheel from Lalmohan Babu and had a good look into the box, holding it under a table lamp. Then he turned it over. A few pieces of glass slipped out.

'Look at that large piece, Feluda. It must have been a glass pipe or something.'

'No, not a glass pipe. It was an ampoule. Someone must have broken it accidentally, so they cast the whole thing aside.'

'Does that mean these prayer wheels are used to despatch spurious medicines?'

'Yes, that is entirely likely. What they probably do is fill these wheels with ampoules or capsules, and store them in packing cases in that house in the pig alley. From there they go to wholesalers, who pass them on to pharmacies and chemists. Tell me, did the packing cases you saw today being loaded on the tempo look like the ones we saw in that other house?'

'Identical,' Lalmohan Babu replied.

'I see,' Feluda frowned. 'The second Mr Batra must be in charge of supplies. And if they're operating on a large scale, they're probably sending some of this stuff across to India. God knows how many people in UP and Bihar are being treated with these spurious drugs. Even if someone suspects something, they won't do anything about it. We've grown so accustomed to turning a blind eye to all malpractices!'

Feluda rose from the bed and began pacing restlessly. Lalmohan Babu sat twirling the prayer wheel. So far, he had nearly always been just an onlooker in all our adventures. Today, he was out on the stage himself. I looked at my watch. It was nearly 4 p.m.

'Lalmohan Babu,' I said, 'isn't it time to go and collect your trousers?'

'Hey, that's right! I had forgotten all about them.' He sprang to his feet, adding, 'We are going to the casino tonight, aren't we? I'm getting the trousers made solely for that purpose, you see.'

Feluda stopped pacing. Then he shook his head vigorously, as if to drive away all unpleasant thoughts, and said, 'Good idea! Today we have earned ourselves a visit to the casino. Yes, we'll spend an hour there after dinner.'

We left at 8.30, in a bus arranged by our hotel.

It soon became clear that the casino was away from the main city. We drove for about fifteen minutes before our bus went up a hill, passed through a gate, drove past a lawn and a swimming pool and finally stopped at the entrance to the casino. Feluda had already told us that the casino was part of a large hotel. When we got out of the bus, I realized that the casino stood separately; one didn't actually have to go into the main hotel to get to it.

Lalmohan Babu seemed determined to behave exactly the way he had seen people behave in western films. He was dressed for the part, too. New trousers made here in Kathmandu, a light green jerkin from New Market in Calcutta, and a Nepali cap added a certain polish to his appearance.

He strode in, saying 'Hel-lo!' to the two gentlemen who sat near the entrance to check the five-dollar card our hotel had given us. They looked up, startled. But by then Lalmohan Babu had walked on, studying his card carefully. A few seconds later, he nearly ran into a Japanese lady who was coming up a flight of stairs. He skipped aside just in time, with a brilliant smile and a 'Hex-hex-cuse me-hee!' I had to look away quickly to stop myself from laughing. Inside the main casino, however, his confident air vanished. I caught him looking at Feluda appealingly.

'Take another look at your card,' said Feluda. 'You'll find five coupons for five different games. I suggest you first try your hand at jackpot, it's the simplest. If you tear off one of those coupons and hand it in at that counter, they'll give you the equivalent of one dollar in Nepali rupees. I think you'll get about eleven rupees. That means you get eleven chances at the jackpot. If you run out of money but still wish to go on, you'll have to pay out of your own pocket. I don't need to remind you of what happens to people who don't know when to stop. Just think of Yudhisthir in the *Mahabharata*!'

After collecting our money from the counter, Lalmohan Babu and I made our way to the nearest jackpot machine. Feluda walked into the next room, which was bigger and had roulette, pontoon and blackjack as well as jackpot.

'It's all quite simple, really,' I said to Lalmohan Babu. 'Look, here's a slot machine. All you need to do is put a coin into this slot, just as you'd do in a weighing machine, and pull this handle on the right. The machine will do the rest.'

'What does that mean?'

'If you win, more coins will come out of the machine. If you lose, then obviously nothing happens. The machine just swallows your money.'

'I see. Shall I—?'

'Yes, go on!'

'Ah well, here goes . . .!'

A whirring noise told us the money had gone to the right place. A light came on instantly and a sign said, 'Coin accepted'.

'All right. Now pull this handle. Pull it hard.'

Lalmohan Babu yanked with all his might. Behind a small square window on the machine were three pictures: a yellow fruit, a red fruit and a bell. As the handle was turned, the machine began whirring again and the pictures started to change. Five seconds later, they stopped with a click and showed a different combination—two yellow fruits and a blue flower.

In the next instant, two coins slipped out of the machine. 'Look, look!' Lalmohan Babu cried. 'Does that mean I won?'

'Yes, certainly. You've now got two rupees. If you're lucky enough, you might insert a rupee and get a hundred in return. Here's a chart that tells you how much each combination will fetch. All right?'

'Ok-kay!'

I found another machine for myself. There were at least another ten machines in this smaller room. A man was sitting in a corner with small plastic bowls which could be used to keep our coins in. I got two from him and gave one to Lalmohan Babu.

Very soon, we were both totally engrossed in our game. I lost all track of time. All that seemed to matter was pulling the handle of the machines and then waiting with bated breath. This must be my lucky day, I thought, watching the little bowl fill with coins. Despite Feluda's warning, I wanted to go on playing. Out of the corner of my eye, I saw Lalmohan Babu walk over to the counter and change his coins for bank notes. He was winning, too.

At this moment, however, Feluda turned up, accompanied by a young lady.

'We'll take a break,' he said, the perfect spoilsport.

'Why, sir?' asked Lalmohan Babu, annoyed at being interrupted.

'We're wanted in 433.'

'What?'

The young lady explained quickly, 'A friend of yours is staying here in room 433. He's sent a special request for you to go and meet him.'

'Who is this friend?' Lalmohan Babu was still looking cross.

'He didn't tell me his name, but said you knew him very well.'

'Let's go and meet him,' said Feluda. 'I feel quite curious. Besides, we can come back here in ten minutes.'

Rather reluctantly, Lalmohan Babu and I turned to go. The lady came with us up to the lift, then said 'namaskar' and left. She must have been an employee of the hotel.

Room 433 turned out to be the last room at the end of a long corridor. Feluda rang the bell. 'Come in!' said a gruff voice. The door had been left unlocked. Feluda pushed it open and went in. Lalmohan Babu and I followed.

Only one lamp was on in the huge living room. Someone was sitting on a sofa at the far end, but we couldn't see his face clearly as the lamp was directly behind him. Opposite him was a video showing some American film. After a few seconds of silence, the man spoke. 'Come in, Mr Mitter!' he said. 'Come on in, Uncle!'

My head began to reel, and my knees suddenly turned to jelly.

I knew this voice well. We all did. It belonged to a man we had met in the holiest of holy places—Varanasi; and Feluda had freely admitted that this man had been the toughest among all the criminals he had ever had to deal with.

Maganlal Meghraj.

What was this dangerous crook doing in Kathmandu?

NINE

'Do sit down,' Maganlal invited, switching the video off. Lalmohan Babu and I sat down on a settee, Feluda took a chair.

'Well, Mr Mitter?'

Feluda said nothing. Like me, he was looking straight at Maganlal. He hadn't changed much in these few years. He was still wearing a dhoti and a sherwani. The latter had clearly been made by an expert tailor. What had changed, of course, were his surroundings. A dark and dingy house in a narrow alley in Benaras was a far cry indeed from this luxurious suite in a five star hotel.

'This time, I hope, you are on a real holiday, Mr Mitter?' Maganlal asked.

'No, Maganlalji, not really,' Feluda said pleasantly. 'Some people are just not destined to have a holiday without having to mix business with pleasure. I am one of them.'

'What business have you got here, Mr Mitter?' Maganlal picked up a telephone. 'Tea or coffee? You can get the best quality Darjeeling tea here.'

'In that case, let's have tea.'

Maganlal rang room service, ordered tea for all of us and turned to Feluda again. 'You are a big hero in India, Mr Mitter. But Nepal is a foreign country. Do you know many people here?'

'Well, I seem to have found at least one person I know!'

Maganlal smiled wryly. His eyes did not move from Feluda's face.

'Are you surprised to find me here?'

'Yes, I am, a little,' Feluda lit a Charminar. 'Not to find you outside the prison—I realize you have all the right connections to have organized an early release—but to see you outside Benaras.'

'Why? Benaras is a holy place, and so is Kathmandu. We have Baba Vishwanath there, and here's Pashupatinath. My karma, you see, is related to places of dharma! What do you say, Uncle?'

'He heh!' Lalmohan Babu tried to laugh. I could see he had gone visibly pale. All the horrors of Arjun's knife-throwing must have come rushing back.

'You talk of your karma, Maganlalji,' said Feluda casually. 'Would that by any chance involve drugs and medicines?'

A cold shiver ran down my spine. How could Feluda be so reckless?

'Drugs? Medicines? What are you talking about?' Maganlal sounded perfectly taken aback.

'If you have nothing to do with them, then do you mind telling me what you're doing here?'

'No, not at all. But we must have a fair exchange.'

'All right. You go first.'

'It's all very simple, Mr Mitter. I am an art dealer—you know I like statues and paintings, don't you? Many houses in Nepal are crammed with such stuff. My job is to collect them.'

Feluda remained silent. I could hear Lalmohan Babu breathing heavily.

'Now you tell me about yourself.'

'I don't think you've been entirely honest with me,' Feluda replied, 'but I am going to be quite frank. I am here to investigate a murder.'

'Murder?'

'Yes.'

'You mean the murder of Mr Som?'

I gaped. Lalmohan Babu drew in his breath sharply. Only Feluda's face remained expressionless. 'Yes, that's right, Maganlalji,' he said coolly. 'Mr Anikendra Som.'

A waiter came in with the tea. He placed the tray on a table in front of Maganlal.

'It is my belief,' Feluda continued when the waiter had gone, 'that Mr Som had started to cause some concern to a certain individual. So he had to be removed from the scene.'

Maganlal began pouring. 'One or two?' he asked me, holding the sugar pot. It was filled with sugar cubes.

'One, please,' I replied. Maganlal dropped a cube in my cup and passed it to me. Then he turned to Lalmohan Babu, who was eyeing the cubes with open suspicion. I knew he was thinking of hippies and LSD.

'What about you. Uncle.' Two? Three?'

'N-no, no.'

'No sugar at all?'

'No, th-thank you.'

I looked at him in surprise. We all knew he had a sweet tooth.

'You amaze me, Uncle,' Maganlal said with a slight smile. 'Why are you saying no?'

This time, Lalmohan Babu gave me a sidelong glance and said, 'OK. One, please.' Perhaps the fact that I had accepted a cube gave him courage. Feluda, too, was given one. He went on speaking, 'I think Mr Som had unearthed an illegal racket. He had gone to Calcutta to make further enquiries, and to meet me. He was killed before he could do so. Since you appear to know about the murder, naturally one would wish to know if you are involved in any way in this case.'

Maganlal stared at Feluda for a few moments, his eyes narrowed, his lips contorted in a twisted smile. Lalmohan Babu and I sipped our tea. It really was the very best Darjeeling tea anyone could get.

'Jagdeesh!' Maganlal shouted suddenly. I couldn't help but start. A door behind Maganlal opened and a man came into the room silently. Lalmohan Babu put his cup down on the table with a clatter.

The man called Jagdeesh standing behind Maganlal was the second Mr Batra. There were very slight differences in his appearance which were apparent only because we could watch him, for the first time, at close quarters. His eyes were lighter than our Mr

Batra's, his hair was greyer, and—most important of all—the look in his eyes held not even a glimmer of warmth.

'Do you know this man?' asked Maganlal.

'We haven't met him, but we know him by sight.'

'Then listen carefully, Mr Private Investigator. Do not harass Jagdeesh. I know you have been trying to track him down ever since you arrived. I will not tolerate your interference, Mr Mitter. Jagdeesh is my right-hand man.'

'Even though he is left-handed?'

Feluda was still speaking lightly. Before Maganlal could say anything, he asked another question. 'Are you aware that there is a gentleman who looks almost exactly like your Jagdeesh?'

Maganlal frowned darkly. 'Yes, Mr Mitter. I know that. If this other man is a friend of yours, tell him to take care. He must think before he acts. You have seen the cremation ground near the temple of Pashupatinath, haven't you, Uncle? You went there today, didn't you?' Without a word, Lalmohan Babu finished his tea in one long gulp and replaced the cup carefully on the table. His hand trembled slightly.

'If Batra thinks he can commit a crime and try to get Jagdeesh blamed for it, then within two days Batra's body will be cremated in that ground. Go tell your friend, Mr Mitter!'

'Very well, I shall pass on your message.'

Feluda, too, finished his tea and rose. 'We must take our leave now, Maganlalji. Thank you for the tea. It really was very good.'

Maganlal made no comment. Nor did he move from his seat. He simply reached for the remote control and switched the video on again.

TEN

We returned to our hotel soon after our meeting with Maganlal. None of us had any idea that there was more in store.

We found Harinath Chakravarty waiting for us in the lounge. This surprised us all. What was he doing here so late at night? It was past eleven.

'Let's go up to our room,' Feluda said. Harinath Babu joined us without a word. He was clearly anxious about something.

'What is the matter, Mr Chakravarty?' asked Feluda when we

were all seated in our room.

Harinath Babu took a few seconds to collect his thoughts. Then he said slowly, 'When Himadri left us so suddenly, I couldn't think straight. Besides, it didn't seem worthwhile to talk about such matters when nothing would bring him back.'

'What are you talking about?

'About three years ago,' Harinath Babu replied after a pause, 'Himadri had exposed a gang who were smuggling things like *ganja* and *charas*. I told you, didn't I, that he often took his helicopter both to the north and south of Nepal? He discovered the den of these smugglers in the north and informed the police. The whole gang was caught.'

'Are you telling us, that just before his death, he had come upon something involving another gang?'

'He didn't tell me anything. But a few days before he died, I saw him discuss something rather animatedly with his friend. I told him not to meddle in these things. These criminals can be totally merciless. But he only laughed and told me not to worry.'

'I believe, Mr Mitter, my son would have died, anyway. If an attack of tetanus did not kill him, these crooks would have taken his life somehow.'

'Why are you saying this?'

Harinath Babu took out a piece of paper and handed it to Feluda. It had something scribbled on it in red ink.

'We found this in his trouser pocket after he died.'

'Is it written in Nepali?'

'Yes. It says, "You have gone too far".'

Feluda returned the piece of paper to Harinath Babu and smiled wryly.

'The biggest irony is that one who was on the verge of exposing a drug racket had to die of a spurious drug himself.'

'Do you really believe the injection he was given wasn't genuine?' Harinath Babu asked.

'Yes. Hopefully, by tomorrow, we shall know for sure. You see, I've asked Dr Divakar to have a sample analysed.'

'I see. Well, that is all I came to tell you. I hope it helps in some way,' said Harinath Babu and stood up.

'It certainly does. I am now much clearer in my mind about what I'm looking for. Thank you, Mr Chakravarty.'

Harinath Babu left. Lalmohan Babu, too, said, 'Good night' and went to his room.

I went straight to bed after this. What a day it had been!

I must have fallen asleep immediately, but was woken a little later by the doorbell. A quick glance at my watch told me it was a quarter past twelve. Who on earth could it be at this hour? I got out of bed and opened the door. Then my mouth fell open.

It was Lalmohan Babu. In his left hand he held a scrap of paper. In his right was the prayer wheel. His lips were parted in a smile that could only be described as beatific.

'Hoom! Hoom! Hoom!' he said, coming into the room, turning the prayer wheel. I took the piece of paper from his hand and saw what was written on it in English. 'You have been warned,' it said. It was written with the same red ink as the warning in Nepali we had just seen.

Feluda was sitting up on his bed. I passed the paper on to him and asked Lalmohan Babu, 'Where did you find it?'

He patted the right pocket of his jacket. He had been wearing the same jacket in the morning. I remembered him saying a monkey had pulled at his clothes.

'Om-m-m-m!' said Lalmohan Babu, sitting down on a chair. The smile hadn't left his face. I looked at Feluda. He was staring at Lalmohan Babu, looking concerned. 'LSD,' he whispered as he caught my eye.

That sugar cube!

Maganlal had made tea for all of us. Since Feluda and I were still sane, he had obviously tampered only with Lalmohan Babu's tea, just to make a fool of him. What a swine he was!

Lalmohan Babu had stopped smiling. For some unknown reason, he was now looking decidedly displeased. 'Take off your skull!' he said sternly to Feluda. 'I said take it off, you old scallywag!'

'Maganlal—you scoundrel!' said Feluda under his breath.

Lalmohan Babu turned his eyes to the glass of water on the bedside table, and frowned. Then, slowly, his eyes widened in amazement and he began smiling again.

'Ooooh!' he said appreciatively. 'Just look at those colours! Vibgyor! Look, Tapesh, have you ever seen such shades, such hues?

Vibgyor? Could he actually see a rainbow in that glass of water?

'It's vibrating! Have you ever seen colour vibrate?'

Then he fell silent. I began to feel sleepy again and nodded off. But I woke with a start almost instantly as I heard him shout, 'Mice!'

He was sitting ramrod straight, staring at the floor.

'Mice!' he said again. 'Terramyce, tetramyce, subamyce, chloromyce . . . compromise . . . there they are, wriggling on the floor . . . don't play the fool with me, I tell you!'

He jumped up and began stamping his foot on the carpet, as if that was the only way he could get rid of the mice. Then he began hopping all over the room, still stamping his foot constantly. I hoped fervently the room below ours was empty.

'Finished! Ah, at last! All ticks finished!'

He sat down again. How had the mice turned into ticks?

'Antibioticks! Killed them all, I did. Ha!'

Now his eyes drooped. Perhaps the sudden burst of activity had tired him out. 'Om-m-m-m!' he said softly, looking very pleased with himself. 'Om-m-m-m-mo-mo-mo!'

I couldn't keep my eyes open any longer. When I opened them, sunlight was streaming in through an open window. Feluda had already had his bath, shaved and seemed ready to go out. He finished talking to someone on the phone and replaced the receiver when he saw I was awake.

'Get up, Topshe, we have lots to do. Mr Batra must be told he's not as safe as we had thought.'

'Who were you calling."

'The police. They gave me some good news. The two governments have agreed to carry out a joint investigation.'

'That's splendid!'

'Yes. But I made another call, and that worried me.'

'What happened?'

'I rang Dr Divakar. Apparently, he received an urgent call early this morning and left. I don't like this at all.'

'Why?'

'I have a feeling the gang we're after found out I had asked him to get a sample tested. But I could be wrong. I'll call him again a little later. If I can't get him on the phone, I'll go straight to his dispensary.'

'Er . . . . where is Lalmohan Babu?'

'He left an hour ago, looking as though he had attained *moksha*. But he was quite calm, no problem there. The whole effect of the drug will take about eight hours to wear off.'

'Were you up all night?'

'Yes, someone had to keep an eye on him.'

'Is he normal now?'

'Almost. Just before going he told me one-third of my brain was made of solid stuff, the remainder was water. God knows what he meant.'

ELEVEN

It took me half an hour to get ready. Feluda had already gone down. I found him waiting for me by the reception, pacing anxiously.

'Dr Divakar hasn't returned to his house,' he told me. 'I rang him again. His family doesn't know where he's gone.'

'And Batra?'

'I couldn't get through. I'll try once more, then I'll go over to his office. We need a car, anyway.'

Lalmohan Babu came down in less than five minutes, looking absolutely normal. But a few things he said implied the effects of LSD hadn't quite worn off. There was a large Nepali mask hanging on the wall near the reception. He stroked it gently and asked, 'What is the name of the palace in England?'

'Buckingham Palace?'

'Yes, bat it's nothing compared to this.'

'Compared to what?'

'This hotel. Hotel Lumumba.'

'Lumbini.'

'All right. Lumbini. He was born here, wasn't he?'

'Who?'

'Gautam Buddha.'

'Not in this hotel!'

'Why, you mean to say they didn't have hotels before Christ?'

Luckily, this weird conversation could not continue for long, for Feluda turned up soon after and said we had to finish our breakfast quickly and go to Sun Travels, for he still couldn't get them on the phone.

We decided to just have a cup of coffee for breakfast. Something told me today was going to be another eventful day.

It took us only five minutes to walk down to Sun Travels. Their office was obviously new, and very smartly furnished. Mr Pradhan, Batra's secretary, ushered us into Batra's room; and then dropped a bombshell.

'Mr Batra has gone out, I'm afraid,' he said. 'A very important person rang him this morning, you see. He wanted to see our new bungalow in the Rapti valley. So Mr Batra had to go with him. But he did tell me you might need a car. I can arrange one quite easily.'

'Thank you. But could you please tell us who this important person was?'

'Certainly. It was Mr Meghraj. He's staying at the Oberoi. A very important art dealer.'

Lalmohan Babu clutched my hand. The very mention of Meghraj's name had brought him to his senses. But Mr Batra? Who could have known he would fall into Maganlal's trap so soon?

'How long does it take to get to your bungalow?' Feluda asked.

'You will need to go via Hetaora—that's 150 km. You might wish to stop for lunch in Hetaora. Our bungalow is new, you see, so the kitchen isn't ready yet. Turn right as you come out of Hetaora and go along the river for three kilometres. You'll find our bungalow there, in the middle of the jungle. It's a beautiful spot.'

'I see. Could you have a car pick us up from the hotel in half an hour?'

'Very well, sir. No problem!'

'You two go back to the hotel and wait for me. I have to go to Darbar Square. I won't be long,' Feluda said as we came out of Sun Travels.

The car arrived in twenty minutes. Feluda took twenty-five. 'Had to go to Freak Street,' he explained.

'Where is that?'

'Not very far. That's where most hippies stay.'

In five minutes, we were on our way to Hetaora. Feluda had his notebook open and was studying its entries, frowning deeply. Lalmohan Babu had been restored to his normal self, although I noticed he had a strangely tranquil air, suggesting he was totally at peace with the world. Looking at the scenery, he made only one comment: 'I had double vision yesterday. Now I can see only one of everything.'

Feluda looked up at this and said with a slightly preoccupied air, 'That is true. But then, so is its reverse.'

I found this remark extremely mystifying.

We had climbed four thousand feet from Kathmandu. Snow-capped peaks were clearly in view. Soon, it became necessary to take out woollen mufflers, and drink the hot coffee we had brought in a flask.

Half an hour later, we began climbing down, making our way to the Shivalik hills. The Rapti valley and the town of Hetaora were not far.

'Topshe, do you know Batra's first name?' Feluda asked suddenly, closing his notebook.

'No. He never told us, did he?'

'He didn't. But you should have noticed the name-plate on his desk. It's Anantlal Batra.'

When we reached Hetaora, it was nearly 2 p.m. None of us felt hungry, so we didn't stop for lunch. 'What is food at a moment like this?' asked Lalmohan Babu. 'It is nothing!'

The driver drove on, turning right from the highway. I could now see the river Rapti gushing through the trees. The road we were on was lined with tall trees on both sides. I couldn't get over the fact that we were actually passing through the famous Terai, which was well-known for its vicious wild animals. I had read such a lot about it! After the sepoy mutiny in 1857; Nana Saheb was supposed to have taken refuge in its leafy depths, together with all his men.

We took another right turn, which brought us to a dirt road. A few minutes later, we saw the bungalow. A large area had been cleared to build it. It had a sizeable compound. Our car passed through the gate and went up a cobbled driveway. Then it stopped just before the front door.

I realized how quiet the place was as soon as our driver switched off the engine. He then got out and moved towards the garage. I could see another car parked there. We too got out of the car and went into the house. The front door was open.

'Come in, Mr Mitter!'

It wasn't difficult to recognize the deep voice of Maganlal Meghraj. We walked into the living room. There were two settees. The floor was covered by a Tibetan carpet. A radio stood on a small table on one side, and on a shelf were a few books and magazines.

Maganlal was sitting on one of the settees, eating puri-sabzi from a tiffin carrier. A servant stood waiting with a towel and a bowl of water. There was no one else in the room.

'I knew you'd come,' he said, wiping his hands. By this time, we were all seated. 'I also know why you've come,' Maganlal went on, 'but I am going to win this round. You can't have it your way each time, can you?' Feluda did not speak.

'I haven't forgotten the humiliation you caused me in Benaras, Mr Mitter. I am going to pay you back.'

I could hear a funny thudding noise coming from one of the rooms to our right. God knows what was causing it.

'Where is Mr Batra?' asked Feluda calmly, ignoring Maganlal's threat.

Maganlal clicked his tongue. 'Very sorry, Mr Mitter. I told you Jagdeesh was my right hand. One needs only one right hand, doesn't one? I saw no reason to have two.'

'You did not answer my question. Where is he?'

'Batra is still alive. He'll be safe during the day. But who knows what might happen at night? There is a law against destroying wild-life. But tell me, have you ever heard of a law protecting a man from hungry wild animals?'

'Why did you leave Kathmandu, Maganlalji? Do you know what's happening there today?'

'You tell me.'

'Your factory in Patan and warehouse in Kathmandu are both being ransacked by the police.'

Maganlal burst into laughter. His massive body swayed from side to side. 'What kind of a fool do you take me for, Mr Mitter? The police will find nothing, absolutely nothing! The warehouse in the pig alley is empty, and all that is now being made in Patan are handicrafts. Perfectly genuine handicrafts. I have brought all my stuff with me, Mr Mitter. Didn't you see lorries going to India through Hetaora? They carry timber; and some of them, Mr Mitter, carry what I wish to have hidden in the timber. Yes, that is how I send fake drugs to India. Mind you, most of my work is done in India by Indians. Labels, capsules, ampoules, phials—they all come from India. The rest is done here, for Nepalis work harder—and better—than Indians.'

Maganlal stopped. I could hear crickets outside, making a racket. But what was that noise—?

Jagdeesh lifted a colourful embroidered curtain and came in, a revolver in his left hand. He stood mutely, pointing it at Feluda.

'Get up!' Maganlal ordered. We rose slowly.

'Raise your hands.' We did.

'Ganga! Kesri!'

Two other men came in and began to search us. One of them found Feluda's revolver and handed it to Maganlal.

The thudding noise seemed to have grown louder and more insistent. Maganlal looked faintly annoyed and said, 'I am sorry, Mr Mitter, but I had to get hold of another friend of yours. He was trying to get our drugs analysed and create more problems for us. So naturally he had to be stopped.'

'Will you feed him to the animals, too?'

'No, no, Mr Mitter.' Maganlal grinned. 'I can use him to my own advantage. It's very useful to have a doctor to turn to. My heart—'

Before he could finish speaking, a number of things happened all at once. The two men called Ganga and Kesri had left the room. Now they came back carrying thick ropes. At this moment, a car drew up outside. Jagdeesh promptly removed the safety catch of his revolver; but Feluda was too quick for him. He leapt up in the air and kicked the revolver out of Jagdeesh's hand. But somehow the gun went off. A bullet shot out and hit the ceiling fan, making it spin.

In these few seconds, as if by magic, a large number of men had appeared out of nowhere. I couldn't recognize any of them, but could tell that they were all policemen in plain clothes from both India and Nepal. One of them grabbed Jagdeesh and pinned him against the wall.

Maganlal was on his feet, glaring with smouldering eyes. 'Don't touch me! Don't you dare!' he hissed.

'We'll deal with you in a minute, Maganlalji,' Feluda said, 'but first, let me get something settled.' He turned to Jagdeesh. 'I couldn't see your fingers properly because you were holding that gun,' said Feluda, 'but now . . . yes, I can see that two of your fingers have got ink on them. Are you still using that same old pen that leaks, Mr Batra?'

'Shut up, Mr Mitter!' shouted Maganlal. 'Just shut up! Jagdeesh is my—'

'Not Jagdeesh. Batra—Anantlal Batra—is your right hand. There is no Jagdeesh; nor is there a second Mr Batra. It's the same man. I'm sure the police can make him remove his contact lenses. There is something he doesn't yet know. His house was searched this morning after he left. The police found a lot of counterfeit money, which—no doubt—used to be produced in your factory in Patan.'

An officer from the Nepal Police brought out a large bundle of hundred-rupee notes. Batra went white.

'You made one false move in Calcutta, Mr Batra,' Feluda told him. 'In trying to establish that there were two Batras, you bought a kukri at the gift shop in your hotel and gave them a fake note. But you could not take it back, since later you had to pretend to be totally innocent. So the shop passed it on to the police. The number on it was the same as the number on all the notes they found in your house.'

Batra looked as though he wanted to sink through the floor. But Maganlal had not given up.

'I warn you, Mr Mitter—' he began.

'You're talking too much!' Feluda interrupted him. 'I must do something to keep you quiet. Topshe, get the man!'

I was quite willing to do this, but noticed, to my surprise, that Lalmohan Babu seemed much more keen to grab Maganlal and push him down on the sofa. He wriggled a lot, but the two of us held him back.

Feluda, in the meantime, had taken out two objects from his pocket. One of them was a sugar cube. This explained why he had gone to Freak Street. He forced it into Maganlal's mouth and made him swallow it.

The second object was a roll of cellotape. Feluda tore a portion of it and sealed Maganlal's mouth with it.

Finally, he put his hand inside his jacket pocket and brought out something that looked like a cigarette case. He handed it to one of the police officers and said, 'I had switched on this mini cassette recorder the minute we stepped into this room. You will get a lot of information from it, given by Mr Meghraj himself.'

TWELVE

'I believe Batra came into contact with Maganlal through his job as a PRO,' said Feluda.

We were sitting at a restaurant, on our way back to Kathmandu, having coffee and sandwiches. With us were Dr Divakar, Inspector Sharma of the Nepal Police and Inspector Joardar from Calcutta. We had found Dr Divakar in one of the rooms in the bungalow. His hands and feet were tied, and he had been gagged. But that had not stopped him from stamping his feet, making that thudding noise we had heard.

According to what Dr Divakar told the police this morning, Batra had called at his house and picked him up, saying there was an emergency case needing his attention. He had then collected Maganlal and the two men had forced him to go to the bungalow with them.

Maganlal and his men were now back in Kathmandu, all under arrest. I was dying to know how he'd react to the LSD, but knew I'd have to wait until tomorrow to find out.

Feluda was still speaking. 'Maganlal knew an educated, intelligent man like Batra would be very useful to him. So he got him to join his gang. When he came to know Anikendra Som was making enquiries, he realized Som had to be got out of the way. He chose Batra for this task. Batra took the same plane from Kathmandu as Som, and managed to get talking with him, although he later denied this. We found one sentence in Mr Som's notebook that said, "Find out about AB". I had thought at first that meant antibiotics, but the minute I learnt Batra's first name was Anantlal, I realized Som was referring to him. It could be that something Batra said made him suspicious.'

Feluda paused to take a sip from his cup, and continued, 'It now looks as though Mr Som had mentioned to Batra that he was going to meet me. Batra knew who I was. So he could guess that should Som get killed, I would be asked to make an investigation. He didn't know then that we would run into each other purely by accident. But when we did, the idea of creating a "double" occurred to him immediately. I have to admit it was a very clever idea. He happened to have bought a blue shirt just before he met me, which, in fact, he was still carrying in a plastic bag. Soon after we parted, he must have gone into a shop for readymade garments and changed into the blue shirt in one of their fitting rooms. Then he deliberately walked past us, pretending never to have seen me in his life. The next day, he staged a little drama in the gift shop, and came to my house in the evening to convince me of the existence of this "double". The day after that, he left his hotel very early in the morning in a taxi, went to Mr Som's hotel at five and killed him. Then he went to the airport and caught his flight to Kathmandu at nine o'clock. He left the kukri behind to make me think that the murderer was the "fake" Mr Batra.'

'When did you first begin to have doubts?' asked Inspector Joardar.

'Well, you see, when I first met him, he got me to write down my address in his notebook. This was necessary, since he would have had to use his left hand if he wrote it himself. Now, that would have spoilt things, for he was then trying to establish that it was the other Batra who was left-handed. But I noticed something odd about the nib of his fountain pen. If a left-handed person uses a fountain pen, he holds it at a certain angle and the nib gets worn. A right-handed person then finds it difficult to write with the same pen. I felt the same difficulty, but paid no attention at the time. When I saw that the murderer of Mr Som was left-handed, my suspicions were roused and I felt I should probe into the matter a bit further in Kathmandu. But I did not know then that it was a case of two murders, not one.'

'Two murders?' Lalmohan Babu couldn't hide his amazement. We all stared. Which was the second murder? What was Feluda talking about?

But Feluda said nothing. Finally, Dr Divakar broke the silence.

'He's right,' he said. 'I did get a sample of anti-tetanus serum from my dispensary and had it tested. It turned out to be just plain water. I was going to call on Mr Mitter and tell him personally, but I never got the chance. Those who deal with spurious drugs certainly deserve to be called murderers. I agree with Mr Mitter.'

'But, Dr Divakar, I am not talking of spurious drugs,' said Feluda.

This time, even the doctor looked startled. 'Then what are you talking about?' he asked.

'I'll explain that in a minute. Before that I wish to mention something else. Three years ago, Himadri Chakravarty had exposed a gang of criminals. His father told us he was working on catching another group meddling with medicines and drugs. If he succeeded, Maganlal and his men would have been in deep trouble. So obviously Maganlal had a strong motive for getting him out of the way.'

'But how?'

'That was fairly simple. Maganlal got a doctor to help him.'

'A doctor?' Dr Divakar frowned.

'Yes.'

'Who? Which doctor do you mean?'

'A doctor who has suddenly come into a lot of money. He's now got a new house and a new car. He wears an expensive watch, glasses with golden frames . . .'

'What utter nonsense are you—?'

'—A doctor who looks at a mere scratch and gives an anti-tetanus shot, although he knows it is totally unnecessary. Do you think, Dr Divakar, that I didn't see through your clever ploy? All that business of getting yourself tied up and gagged was just an act, wasn't it? You are a member of Maganlal's team, aren't you? Just like Batra?'

Dr Divakar was actually trembling with rage. 'How is it possible, Mr Mitter, to kill with plain water?' he shouted.

'Not plain water, doctor. But it is easy enough to kill with poison. You used strychnine, didn't you? The symptoms Himadri showed once the injection had been given were very similar to symptoms of tetanus. Inspector Joardar, am I right?'

The inspector nodded gravely.

'Yes,' he said, 'strychnine causes convulsions and other symptoms not very different from tetanus.'

Dr Divakar had risen to his feet. The inspector's words made him sink back into the chair, then roll off it and slip to the floor, his face hidden in his hands.

Our story ended here. But three things happened later which I ought to add.

One—the sugar cube Maganlal was made to swallow caused him much discomfort. He was reported to have scratched the walls of his cell like a cat for three hours continuously. Then he mistook a floorcloth for a plate of rubri, and chewed it to shreds.

Two—Feluda was given a cash reward by the government of Nepal for unearthing not just those who were producing spurious drugs, but also those involved in making counterfeit money. The amount given was not insubstantial—we had a fair bit left over even after meeting all our expenses.

Three—Lalmohan Babu urged me, more than once, to call our adventure in Kathmandu 'Om Manipadmey Hoomicide'. When I told him that would be going a bit overboard, he said 'Hoommmm!' and sat twirling his prayer wheel, looking positively put out.

Napoleon's Letter

ONE

'Are you Feluda?'

The question wafted up from somewhere near Feluda's waist.

A little boy of about six was standing next to Feluda, tilting his head to look up at him. Only a few days ago, one of the local dailies had published an interview with Feluda, with a photograph that showed him sitting with a Charminar in his hand. As a result, people now recognized him nearly everywhere, almost as if he was a film star. Today, we were at the Hobby Centre at the corner of Park Street and Russell Street. It sold many interesting things, apart from toys and goldfish. Our Uncle Sidhu was soon going to turn seventy. Feluda had decided to come to the Hobby Centre to look for a good chess set for him.

Feluda placed a hand gently on the boy's head. 'Yes, that's right,' he said.

'Can you catch the thief who took my bird?' said the boy, sounding as though he was throwing him a challenge. Before Feluda could reply, a gentleman of about the same age as Feluda walked over to us quickly, carrying a longish object wrapped in brown paper. He looked both pleased and slightly embarrassed.

'Tell Feluda your own name,' he said to the boy.

'Aniruddha Haldar,' the boy declared solemnly.

'One of your many young admirers,' the gentleman laughed. 'His mother has read out to him all the stories about your adventures.'

'What's this about a bird?'

'Oh, that's nothing. He said he wanted to keep a bird, so I bought him a chandana. Someone took it out of its cage the day it arrived.'

'There's just one feather left,' Aniruddha told us.

'Really?'

'Yes. It was there in the cage when I went to bed, but was gone in the morning. Great mystery?'

'Yes, that's what it looks like, doesn't it? Can't Aniruddha Haldar shed any light on the mystery?'

'Why, I am not a detective! I'm only in the second standard in school.'

The child's father intervened. 'Come along now, Anu, we have to go to New Market. What you might do is ask Feluda to come to our house.'

Anu looked very pleased at this, and shyly repeated his father's invitation. 'My name is Amitabh Haldar,' the gentleman said, offering his card. Feluda took it and looked at it briefly. 'I see you live in Barasat,' he remarked.

'Yes. You may have heard of my father, Parvaticharan Haldar.'

'Oh yes. I've even read some of his articles. He's got a large collection of antiques, hasn't he?'

'That's right. He used to be a barrister, but now he's retired. His chief passion in life is collecting ancient artefacts. He's travelled very widely, all over the world, to add to his collection. I think you'll enjoy seeing some of it—he's got an ancient gramophone, a chessboard from Mughal times, Warren Hastings's snuff box, Napoleon's letter . . . you know, things like that. Our house itself is quite interesting, it's a hundred and fifty years old. If you're free one day, I mean on a Sunday or something . . . ? You just need to give me a ring—no, I'll ring you myself. Your number will be in the directory, won't it?'

'Yes, but here you are,' Feluda handed him one of his own cards. It was then decided that we would visit Mr Haldar later in the month. Going to Barasat wouldn't be a problem, since Lalmohan Babu's car was always at our disposal. He wasn't with us today, but I knew he'd love to go with us. Of late, he had been in a particularly good mood, since a giant Jatayu omnibus had come out only recently, containing ten of his best novels. It was apparently 'selling like hot kachauris', even at twenty-five rupees.

We returned home. I noticed much later that Feluda was looking a little depressed. When I asked him what was wrong, he said, 'It's that young admirer of mine. I can't forget what he told me.'

'You mean about that chandana?'

'Have you ever heard of a bird being stolen out of its cage?'

'No, I can't say I have. But does it really strike you as a big mystery?'

'Well, it's not the kind of thing that happens every day. A chandana is not a bird of paradise. No one would wish to steal it for its beauty. Why, then, did it disappear?

'Of course, it could be that someone had forgotten to shut the door properly, and it was really no more than negligence . . .' His voice trailed away.

'There's no way to find out, is there?'

'Of course there is. All we have to do is go there and ask a few questions. As far as I can make out, no one took the matter seriously.

But obviously that little boy is upset, or he wouldn't have told me straightaway. I wish I could go.'

'Where is the problem with that? Mr Haldar invited us, didn't he?'

'Yes, but that may well have been simply out of politeness, just because he happened to run into us. He may have already forgotten all about it. After all, we didn't fix a date or anything. It wouldn't matter, and normally I wouldn't care, but . . . it was something a small child asked me to do, so I feel I shouldn't ignore it.'

Mr Haldar rang in less than a week, on a Saturday morning. I transferred the call to Feluda's extension, and heard the whole conversation from the main phone in the living room.

'Mr Mitter?' said Mr Haldar.

'Yes, how are you?'

'Fine, but my son is driving me crazy. When are you coming to our house?'

'Did the bird come back?'

'No. I don't think there's any chance of getting it back.'

'What if your son assumes I've come just to retrieve his chandana? When he realizes I cannot help him, isn't he going to be very disappointed?'

'No, no, don't worry about that. He'll be thrilled if you spend some time with him. Actually, I'd like you to meet my father. I am free today. Are you doing anything special?'

'No. Will it be all right if we reach your house by ten o'clock?'

'Certainly. See you later then. Goodbye.'

We were expecting Lalmohan Babu to join us shortly. He turned up at our house, every Saturday and Sunday, at nine o'clock. Naturally, the traffic being what it is, he couldn't always arrive on the dot, but seldom did he keep us waiting for more than ten minutes. Today, he walked in at five past nine.

'This is really nice,' he said, seating himself in an easy chair. 'I do enjoy the winter, when I'm under no pressure to go on writing. Only a couple of months ago, just before Durga Puja, I thought I'd go mad meeting my publisher's deadlines! Now I don't even feel like looking at a pen and paper.'

He certainly was in a good mood, for he had brought a large packet of hot, crisp kachauris. 'Are hot kachauris still selling well?' Feluda asked with a smile.

'Oh, more than ever. If you saw the queue outside Mohan's sweetshop in Bagbazar, you might mistake it for a cinema showing a superhit Hindi film. Now if you just taste one of these, you'll realize how appropriate the comparison is.'

We took the kachauris and a flask of water with us. Lalmohan Babu had not heard of Pravaticharan Haldar, but was most impressed to hear that in his collection he had a letter written by Napoleon. 'When I was in school, Napoleon used to be my hero,' he informed us. 'Great man, Bonaparte.' He repeated this last remark three times, pronouncing 'Bonaparte' as 'Bonaparty'. I caught Feluda trying to hide a smile, but he said nothing.

The traffic got better only after we reached VIP Road. By the time we got to Barasat, it was nearly half past ten. The home of the Haldars was on the main road, but because it was surrounded by large trees, it wasn't easy to see it. One had to pass through the main gate and go up a cobbled drive before the main house became visible. There was no doubt that it had been built during British times, but it had obviously been very well maintained. At least, the walls on the front portion looked clean and freshly painted. There was a pond on one side, around which stood tall supari trees.

Amitabh Haldar was waiting for us in the living room. Feluda introduced Lalmohan Babu. 'I'm afraid I have read none of your novels, but my wife has devoured each one of them,' he said to Jatayu. Then he took us upstairs, where his father liked to keep his collection. The stairs, I noticed, were made of marble.

'Before you meet my father, please say hello to my son,' Mr Haldar requested. 'Baba has a visitor right now. He prefers having visitors in the morning.'

'I'm surprised people come and disturb him even here!'

'Most of his callers are other collectors. They come frequently to exchange notes, with offers to buy or sell. Recently, Baba had advertised for a secretary. Today he's interviewing candidates.'

'Doesn't he have a secretary at the moment?'

'He does, but he is leaving next week. Apparently, he's got a much better offer in Delhi. It's a pity, for he was quite good in his work. Baba appears to be rather unlucky in the matter of secretaries. He's had four in the last ten years. One of them died of meningitis, the second one suddenly decided to renounce the world and join Sai Baba's ashram. The man who's talking to Baba right now was, in fact, his third secretary. He had been sacked seven years ago.'

'Why?'

'He was a good worker, but extremely superstitious. Baba use to get furious with him at times. Once, he went to Egypt and acquired an Egyptian statue made of jade. On his return to Calcutta, Baba happened to fall ill . . . Sadhan Babu told him in all seriousness that the statue was of a goddess, and her curse had fallen on Baba. This annoyed my father so much that he sacked him the same day.'

'Well, if the same Sadhan Babu has returned with the hope that he might get his old job back, I must say he is very optimistic; and your father must have a very forgiving nature, if he decides to take him back.'

'The thing is, you see, Baba felt quite bad after Sadhan Babu left. He didn't have any money, nor did Baba write him a recommendation.'

There was a veranda on the first floor where the stairs ended, across which was a sitting room and Parvaticharan's study. Behind these were bedrooms belonging to various members of the household. Feluda's little client was standing in front of his room. We were about to go and join him, when the sound of footsteps made us look toward the sitting room. We saw a man wearing a blue jacket and carrying a briefcase come out of there and march down the stairs.

'That was Baba's ex-secretary. He didn't seem very happy, did he?' remarked Mr Haldar.

'This is the cage my bird was in,' Aniruddha said as soon as we reached him.

'Yes, that's what I came to look at,' Feluda replied.

An empty cage was hanging from a hook over the railing on the veranda. It looked brand new. Maybe it had been bought together with the bird. Feluda went to inspect it. Its door was still open.

'Are any of your servants allergic to birds?'

Mr Haldar laughed at Feluda's question. 'No, not that I know of. All our servants are old, we've had them for twenty years or more. Besides, we used to have a couple of grey parrots once. Baba himself had bought them. They remained with us for many years. Then they died.'

'Have you seen this?' Feluda frowned, holding the cage and turning it around.

'Seen what?' Mr Haldar took the cage from Feluda. Lalmohan Babu and I walked over to get a closer look. Feluda pointed at a red stain on the door of the cage.

'I see what you mean. Could it be—?'

'Yes. It's blood.'

'The Chandana Murder Case?' Lalmohan Babu exclaimed.

'Well, it's impossible to say whether the blood is that of a bird or a man without doing a chemical analysis. But it's obvious the bird did not fly out simply because the door was open. Someone deliberately took it out, and there was a struggle. Where did you buy it?'

'New Market,' said Aniruddha immediately.

'Yes, we got it from Tinkori Babu's shop. It's a very well known pet shop. Many of my friends have bought birds from him.'

'Come and look at my toys. I've got a new machine-gun,' Aniruddha tugged at Feluda's sleeve.

'Later, Anu,' his father stopped him. 'I promise you I'll bring these people back to your room before they go. Then you can show them all your toys, and they can meet your mother, and have a cup of tea. Right now, I think I ought to take them to meet your Dadu.'

We turned and made our way to Parvaticharan's study.

But we were not destined to meet him. Lalmohan Babu told me afterwards about the effect of receiving an enormous shock. 'Sometimes, it is impossible to overcome it, even if you try all your life!' he said. After what happened in Mr Haldar's house a few seconds later, I found myself in full agreement.

We had to pass through the sitting room to get to the study. The whole room was packed with curios. But we ignored these for the moment, and went towards the communicating door that let to the study. Amitabh Haldar lifted the curtain, and said, 'Please come in'. However, before any of us could take another step, he shouted, 'Baba!' in a choked voice and would probably have fallen, if Feluda hadn't rushed forward to grab his arms. A second later, Lalmohan Babu and I entered the room.

Parvaticharan was sitting in a revolving chair behind a massive mahogany table. His head was tilted back, his lifeless eyes stared straight at the ceiling, his arms hung loosely by his sides.

Feluda ran across to take his pulse. Then he said to me, 'Go quickly and see if you can find that man called Sadhan. Ask the chowkidar. Go out and search the main road if need be.'

Lalmohan Babu and I began sprinting towards the staircase. In my heart I knew the chances of finding the man were virtually nil. He had left the house at least ten minutes ago.

On our way down, we nearly collided with another gentleman. We learnt later that he was Parvaticharan's present secretary,

Hrishikesh Datta. There was no time then to ask for or offer explanations.

We found no one outside the house, or on the main road. What was most surprising was that the chowkidar assured us no one had stepped out of the gate in the last ten minutes. He knew there would be visitors this morning, he said, and was therefore being extra vigilant. He couldn't possibly have made a mistake.

'Let's search the whole compound. There's a garden behind the house, I think. Perhaps that's where he's hiding?' Lalmohan Babu said. This sounded like a good idea, so we combed the whole place. We looked behind bushes, we searched the rose garden, went behind the supari trees near the pond, checked the compound wall to see if there was any evidence of someone having scaled it—but still we found nothing. The wall was nearly eight feet high. Scaling it in a hurry would have been pretty difficult, anyway.

In the end, we had to give up and admit defeat.

Sadhan Babu had gone—vanished into thin air.

TWO

Parvaticharan had been struck on the head with a heavy instrument. The Haldars' family physician said his death must have been instantaneous. He wasn't in very good health, apparently. His blood pressure often fluctuated and his heart wasn't in good condition either.

The police arrived soon afterwards. The inspector in charge of the case turned out to be Inspector Hajra, who knew Feluda. Unlike some other police officers, he did not look down upon private investigators. He seemed to like and respect Feluda a great deal. 'We'll make all the usual enquiries, and let you know if we find anything useful,' he offered.

'Thank you. Have you formed any idea regarding the weapon?'

'No, there's nothing in the room that might have been used, is there? The murderer must have taken it with him.'

'Paperweight.'

'What? You think it was a paperweight?'

'Come with me.'

We followed Feluda and Inspector Hajra into the study. Feluda pointed at a portion on Parvaticharan's desk. There was a thin layer of dust on the green felt that covered its surface. In one corner, there was a circular mark, free of dust. It wasn't immediately noticeable, unless one looked carefully.

'I checked with Amitabh Haldar,' Feluda said. 'He said there used to be a large and heavy Victorian glass paperweight in that corner. Well, it's missing now.'

'Well done, Mr Mitter.'

'But what about the chief suspect? Did he really vanish into thin air?' Feluda asked as he came out of the study.

'We have his name and a good description. It shouldn't take us long to find him. Besides, he had applied for a job here, hadn't he? So we can easily get his address. No, my own suspicion is that the chowkidar isn't telling us the truth. Maybe he had left his seat for a few moments, and that's when the culprit slipped out. But then, who is the real culprit, anyway? Didn't the victim see a visitor before Sadhan Babu turned up? This other person is just as likely to have killed him.'

'How can you say that? If the old Mr Haldar was already dead when Sadhan Babu walked into the room, surely he'd have raised an alarm?'

'You have seen the room, haven't you? Doesn't it look like a curio shop? Assuming that Sadhan Babu is dishonest and a crook, what do you think he'd do if he walked in there and found the owner dead? Wouldn't he simply help himself to whatever he could and disappear with it?'

Feluda turned to Parvaticharan's present secretary, Hrishikesh Datta. We had been introduced by this time. He said he had gone out to the post office just before ten o'clock to send a couple of cables abroad. On his return, he had found us rushing down the stairs. 'If something valuable was missing from that room, would you be able to tell us what it was?' Feluda asked him.

'Yes, probably. I have a good idea of what is displayed outside. Mr Haldar had once given me a list of things he kept locked away in a glass case. Maybe he took some of those things out to show Pestonji. Pestonji came at nine-thirty.'

'Did they know each other?'

'Oh, yes. Pestonji is also a collector. They had known each other for more than ten years. He used to come occasionally to look at a certain letter Mr Haldar had here.'

'Napoleon's letter?'

'Yes.'

'Was Mr Haldar thinking of selling it?'

'Certainly not. Pestonji was very keen to buy it, but Mr Haldar used to get a kick out of refusing his offer. But then, it wasn't just Pestonji he refused. Once an American offered twenty thousand dollars. All Mr Haldar did was shake his head. After much persuasion, the American eventually lost his temper and began using foul language, but even so Mr Haldar remained totally unmoved. In fact, I think he quite enjoyed having the power to disappoint a prospective buyer. Today, Pestonji seemed to have got rather cross with him. I heard him raise his voice.'

'Where was this famous letter kept?'

'In an Alkathene envelope.'

'Then it's probably still safe. I saw an Alkathene envelope on his desk, and there was a folded piece of paper in it.'

'Good. That certainly is a relief.'

There was no way to check immediately if the letter was there, for the police were still working in the room. The police surgeon had just arrived, and was examining the body.

'What beats me completely is that I returned about the same time Sadhan Babu left. Why didn't I see him anywhere?'

'What time did you go out of the house?'

'Exactly at five minutes to ten. It takes five minutes to reach the post office. I wanted to send those cables as soon as the post office opened.'

'That should not have taken you more than a few minutes. Why were you so late coming back?'

'I was looking around in the local shops for a new strap for my watch. It suddenly became loose. It's so annoying, I can't tell you. I'm having to wear the watch on my right wrist. You see, my left wrist is thinner than my right. So I get this problem frequently. But none of the shops had what I was looking for. Now I think I'll have to try in New Market.'

I had already noticed he was wearing his watch on his right wrist.

'Do you live here?' Feluda asked. Amitabh Haldar was busy with his family and was naturally very upset by what had happened, so Feluda was trying to get as much information from Hrishikesh Datta as he could.

'Yes. I have a room on the ground floor. Since I had no family, Mr

Haldar told me I could stay in the same house. God knows they have plenty of rooms. I believe Sadhan Babu used to live here as well.'

'But you were going to leave this job, weren't you? Weren't you happy working here?'

'I was getting thoroughly bored. Mr Haldar was a good employer, I have nothing against him personally. But opportunities for a promotion or anything like that were non-existent here, so obviously I grabbed the first good offer that came along.'

By this time, we had met another gentleman in addition to Hrishikesh Datta. It was Amitabh Haldar's younger brother, Achintya. There had been no time to talk to him properly. He was being questioned by the police at this moment, since he was in the house at the time of the murder. Feluda continued talking to Mr Datta.

'What does Achintya Haldar do?'

'He's in the theatre.'

'Theatre? You mean professional theatre?'

All of us were considerably taken aback. Hrishikesh Datta took his time before making a reply. 'It's a family matter,' he said finally. 'Really, I shouldn't be talking about it, for it's none of my business at all. But if Achintya has joined the theatre, I think it's because he was unhappy with his family. Old Mr Haldar had four sons. Only Achintya amongst them was not sent abroad to study. Sometimes, the youngest in a large family gets neglected. Perhaps that's what happened in this case. At least, that's the impression I've got from what little he's told me. His father had found him a job, but he gave it up quite soon. For a while, I believe he was happy working for the local dramatics club, but now he's trying to get work from a theatre company in Calcutta. I think it's called Nobo Rangamanch. He's played the lead role in a couple of plays. Even yesterday, I saw him learning his lines.'

Inspector Hajra emerged from an inner room, followed by Achintya Haldar, who came out looking morose and depressed. He left without even looking at us.

'The murder took place between ten and ten-thirty,' the inspector told us. 'Pestonji arrived at nine-thirty, and stayed until about five past ten. Sadhan Dastidar came at ten-fifteen, and left at ten-thirty. A passage runs straight from Achintya's room to his father's study. He could have gone to his father between five past ten, and ten-fifteen, although he maintains he was in his room all morning, learning his lines. The only time he left it was at ten-thirty, and that was because little Anu called him to his room to show him his new toy machine-gun. At this time, he had no idea his father was dead. Anyway, all three had a likely motive to kill Parvaticharan. Pestonji was his rival, Sadhan Dastidar might want revenge, and Achintya didn't get on with his father. That's how it stands at present. Could you come back with me, Mr Datta, and tell us if you think there's anything missing?'

All of us went back to the study. Mr Datta ran his eyes quickly over the whole room. Parvaticharan must have been fond of mechanical gadgets, for in the drawing room downstairs I had noticed a cylindrical gramophone, and here in his study was an ancient magic lantern. Besides these were statuettes, plates, inkstands, pens, old firearms, pictures, maps and books. Mr Datta took out a key from a drawer, opened a glass case and examined its contents. Then he opened a few more wooden boxes, and pulled out more drawers, each of which was stashed with similar objects. Finally, he heaved a sigh of relief and said he didn't think anything had been stolen.

'What about that envelope with Napoleon's letter in it?' Feluda pointed out.

'But it looks as though the letter's still in there, quite intact!'

'Yes, but there's no harm in checking, is there?'

Mr Haldar shook his head, and opened the envelope. My heart missed a beat as he pulled the paper out. An old letter could never look so clean and white.

'Oh my God!' Mr Datta screamed. 'This is only a sheet torn from Mr Haldar's letter pad!'

Napoleon's letter had gone.

THREE

We spent another half an hour in Mr Haldar's house. Feluda examined the compound carefully. He went into the garden with us, checked the compound wall to see if parts of it were broken, and finally ended up near the pond. His eyes were on the ground, looking for footprints. The ground being dry, I didn't think he'd find any prints; but even so, something seemed to attract his attention, and he stopped. I glanced at him quickly, to find him staring at a tiny flowering plant. Something heavy had crushed it, and it had happened obviously in the last few hours. Feluda examined the ground around the plant, then stood looking at the pond. It was not used by the Haldars, so most of it was covered by weed and water hyacinth. Only a small portion looked as if it had been disturbed, for the thick growth of weed had parted to reveal the water underneath.

Could it be that something had been thrown into the water? Feluda made no comment on this, so I didn't venture to say anything either. We turned to go back to the house.

'I thought I saw a chandana in the garden,' Lalmohan Babu confided as we began walking, 'it flew from a guava tree and disappeared into another.'

'Why didn't you tell us immediately?' Feluda sounded cross.

'Well . . . because I wasn't sure. It might well have been an ordinary green parrot. It's not easy to tell the difference, is it? But this bird can talk.'

'What, you heard it say something?'

'Yes. You two were at the far end, inspecting the ground. I had just seen a scorpion and jumped aside, when this bird flew over my head and said something. I mean, I heard these words, looked up and found it was a bird that had spoken them.'

'Oh? And what did it say?'

'It said, "fake hair, babu; fake hair, babu"!'

Feluda gave him a level look. 'The bird said, "fake hair"? What a rude bird! Casting aspersions on the absence of hair on your head?'

'See, that's why I didn't tell you anything!' Lalmohan Babu returned, sounding peeved. 'I knew you wouldn't believe me, and make fun of me instead.'

We said nothing more, since neither of us could really take it seriously.

But the fact remained that in spite of the murder and the theft, Feluda continued to be intrigued by the disappearance of the bird. Two days after the murder, on the following Monday, he said to me, 'A man gets murdered, and an old valuable letter gets stolen—now, unfortunate it may be, extraordinary it is not. But why should a small chandana vanish from its cage? I just cannot figure it out!'

Amitabh Haldar had called us the day before. Feluda had told him he didn't think there was any reason for him to go back to their house, especially as the police were making their own enquiries. Lalmohan Babu had given us a ring a few minutes ago, to say that he would drop by to find out about the latest developments, although he didn't normally visit us on Mondays.

'Feluda,' I said, 'we didn't find out whose blood it was on the cage, did we?'

'Well, I don't really think a chemical analysis is necessary. Those stains were left there by a man, I am sure of it. Whoever had tried to take the bird out by force would have been injured. I mean, the bird would naturally have thought it was being attacked, wouldn't it? So it would have used its claws and its beak to defend itself, and most certainly it would have left its mark on the hand of its attacker.'

'Did you notice any such mark on anyone in Mr Haldar's house?'

'No. I looked at everyone very closely, including all the servants, but I found nothing. It would have been a fresh injury, it should have shown on someone. To be honest, I cannot focus my attention on anything else—I keep thinking of that bird!'

'Didn't you make a list of people who had had the opportunity to kill?'

'Yes, the opportunity as well as the motive.'

Feluda's notebook was lying next to him on the sofa. He picked it up and opened it. 'Sadhan Dastidar. Our suspect number one. Everything we've learnt about him is pretty straightforward. The mystery lies in his disappearance. The only likely explanation is that he bribed the chowkidar adequately, and the chowkidar is lying through his teeth. If that is the case, I'm sure the police can handle that. They have means of dealing with liars.

'Pestonji—suspect number two. He is seventy years old. It doesn't seem likely that an old man would commit a crime that requires physical strength. Parvaticharan had been struck with a great deal of force. But then, age doesn't always affect one's strength. We cannot make a final decision about Pestonji without actually seeing him.

'Achintya Haldar—the third suspect. He wasn't fond of his father, but did he really dislike him so much that he'd want to kill him? We don't know that for certain. All I can say is that if he could get hold of that letter written by Napoleon and sell it, that might make him rich. At a guess, Pestonji would buy it readily. I'm sure Achintya knew that. The fourth . . .'

I interrupted him, 'You mean there is a fourth suspect?'

'Not exactly a suspect, but we need to know what exactly he was doing that morning. I am talking of our friend, Amitabh Haldar. In his statement to the police, he said he came down to the drawing room at nine o'clock to ring me, then went straight to the garden to tend to his flowers. He stayed there until ten o'clock, then left the garden and went to a side veranda on the ground floor. A servant brought him a cup of tea here. According to Amitabh Haldar, this is where he was sitting when he heard us arrive. He went back upstairs together with us.

'The last person to be considered is Hrishikesh Datta. He left the house at five to ten. The chowkidar remembers seeing him go out, but cannot recall having seen him return. I don't think the chowkidar makes a very reliable witness. He's faithful, but he's old. He's been with the Haldar family for over forty years. So perhaps his memory isn't as sharp as it used to be. We don't know if Mr Datta really did spend all that time looking for a strap for his watch. But even if he lied about that, I'm not sure that he had a suitable opportunity. His motive is also questionable. Why should he want to kill his employer, unless it was simply to be able to steal that letter and sell it elsewhere?'

Feluda shut his notebook.

'I suppose all the servants are above suspicion?' I asked.

'They are all old and trusted. One of the bearers called Mukundo had brought coffee for Parvaticharan and Pestonji just before ten. Apparently, Parvaticharan used to have a cup of coffee after nine. The other members of the household are Amitabh Haldar's wife, Aniruddha, Parvaticharan's mother who's more than eighty years old, a mali and his son, a driver and the chowkidar. Achintya Haldar isn't married.'

Feluda stopped speaking, and lit a Charminar. The phone rang the same instant. It was Inspector Hajra.

'Good morning,' said Feluda, 'what's the latest?'

'We found the address Sadhan Dastidar had given.'

'Very good.'

'Very bad, because no one by that name has ever lived there.'

'Really?'

'Yes. So we're back to square one. This Dastidar appears to be quite a cunning crook.'

'What about Hrishikesh Datta? Did you check his alibi?'

'He did go to the post office and sent those telegrams. But no one in the local stationery shops can actually remember having seen him. So we can't be sure, one way or the other.'

'And Pestonji?'

'A most bad-tempered man. Terribly wealthy. I believe his family has lived in Calcutta for a hundred and fifty years. He appears pretty well-preserved for his age, but suffers from arthritis. He cannot raise his right hand even up to his shoulder. Every morning, he goes to a clinic in Lord Sinha Road for physiotherapy. This is true, I checked with the clinic.'

'In that case, I guess all we can do is try and find Sadhan Dastidar.'

'Oh we'll find him, don't worry. I think he's hiding somewhere in Barasat. The envelope his application came in had a mark from the Barasat post office.'

'I see. This is most interesting.'

'By the way, a thief broke into that little boy's room.'

'What? Again?'

'What do you mean, again?'

Inspector Hajra didn't know about the missing chandana. Feluda decided not to enlighten him. 'No, I mean there's been a theft already. That letter's gone. And now someone steals into the boy's room?' he said hurriedly.

'Yes, but nothing was taken.'

'How did the boy realize there was someone in his room?'

'He heard a noise. I went to his room this morning. He sleeps alone in the room next to his parents'. I must say he's a brave lad, for instead of feeling scared, he shouted, "Who's there?" and so the thief ran away. I asked him how come he didn't feel scared, and he said it was because he had been sleeping with his machine-gun under his pillow ever since he heard about his grandfather's death.'

Lalmohan Babu arrived at ten. 'Why are you looking so grim, Felu Babu?' he asked anxiously. 'Haven't you seen the light yet?'

'No, I'm afraid not. What am I to do if a new mystery comes up every day?'

'A new mystery?'

'A thief broke into Aniruddha's room last night.'

'What! This thief is mad. He's already got Napoleon's letter, hasn't he? What was he expecting to get in a little boy's room?'

'I don't know. Do you have any ideas?'

'Who, me? Heh heh, Felu Babu, how do you suppose my brain's going to work when yours has failed? But I'll tell you one thing. This business of the stolen bird keeps haunting me. I think a thorough investigation is needed. I'm prepared to do this for you. You see, I used to visit Tinkori Babu's shop in New Market pretty frequently in the past.'

'Why, you never mentioned this before!'

'No, but I used to be quite fond of birds myself. I had a mynah that could speak. I taught it a line from Shakespeare.'

'Shakespeare? Good heavens! That was rather ambitious, wasn't it? Wouldn't nursery rhymes have been simpler?'

Lalmohan Babu ignored this jibe, and turned to me. 'What do you say, Tapesh, to a trip to New Market?'

'If you leave right way, I can meet you there in an hour,' Feluda said.

'Where?'

'Right in the centre of the market, where there's that cannon. There's a lot that I have to do today; and then we're eating out, don't forget.'

I hadn't forgotten. We ate out once every week.

Lalmohan Babu and I left in his car almost immediately.

Tinkori Babu's shop was packed with birds of an amazing variety. But he failed to recognize Lalmohan Babu. This was not surprising as he had not visited the shop since 1968. However, this seemed to distress him so much that, in the end, I had to do all the talking.

'Have you sold a chandana in the last ten days, to someone in Barasat?' I asked.

'I don't know about Barasat, but yes, I've sold a couple of chandanas in the last ten days. One of them went to a film company. They wanted to hire it just for a day, but I told them the days of hiring birds for a day's shooting were gone. If they had to have a bird in a cage, they'd have to buy it. And if they didn't know what to do with it afterwards, they could always give it to their heroine!'

'What about the other one? How did it come to your shop?'

'Why, what's it to you? Why are you asking so many questions?' Tinkori Babu sounded openly suspicious.

'That bird has disappeared from its cage under mysterious circumstances,' Lalmohan Babu joined the conversation. 'We have got to find it.'

'Well then, put an advertisement in the papers.'

'Yes, we might do that. But if you could tell us how you had found it . . .'

'No, I'm going to tell you no such thing. Just write an ad, and send it in.'

'Did that bird talk?'

'Yes, but don't ask me what it could say. I have seventeen talking birds in my shop. Some say "Good morning", some say "I'm hungry", other say "Jai Guru", or "Hare Krishna". It's impossible to remember what a particular bird's been taught to say.'

We thanked Tinkori Babu and came out of the shop. There was half an hour left before our appointment with Feluda. Lalmohan Babu spent that time buying a nailcutter and some toothpaste, and looking at shoes in Chinese shops. Then we made our way to the cannon that stands in the very heart of New Market. Feluda arrived a couple of minutes later.

'Where are we going now?' Lalmohan Babu demanded.

'Did you know the Parsis have been living in Calcutta for two hundred years?'

'What! You mean right from the time of Siraj-ud-daula? No, I certainly did not know that.'

'We are going to visit an ancient Parsi household today. Their address is . . .' Feluda took out a notebook from his pocket and consulted it, ' . . .133/2 Bowbazar Street.'

FOUR

I was not sure that 133/2 Boubazar was really more than a hundred and fifty years old. But most undoubtedly it was the oldest house in Calcutta I had ever stepped into. The entrance was through an archway between two shops on the main road. There was a narrow passage beyond the archway, which led to a flight of wooden stairs. We climbed these up to the second floor, and turned right, to find ourselves facing a door with a brass name-plate on it. 'R.D. Pestonji', it said.

Feluda rang the bell. A bearer opened the door almost instantly. Feluda handed him one of his cards. He disappeared to inform his master. In about three minutes, he was back. 'You may come in, but Mr Pestonji cannot give you more than five minutes of his time,' he said.

Feluda agreed. We followed the bearer into the drawing room.

It was a large room, but dark and stuffy. I could dimly see the figure of a man sitting on a sofa, a bottle and a glass resting on a low table before him. As we got closer, I could see him more clearly. His skin was pale, and his nose hooked like a parrot's. His wide forehead was covered with freckles. Hazel eyes stared at us through the golden frames of his glasses. When he spoke, his voice sounded harsh.

'But you are not one man, you are a crowd!' he complained.

Feluda apologized for our presence, and explained quickly that he was the one who would do the talking. Mr Pestonji could ignore us completely. This seemed to mollify the old man.

'Well, what do you want?' he asked.

'I believe you knew Parvaticharan Haldar.'

'My God, not again!' Mr Pestonji exclaimed, his tone indicating both horror and disapproval. Feluda raised a reassuring hand.

'I am not from the police. Please don't worry on that score, sir. It so happens that I was there when Mr Haldar's body was found. I therefore got involved in this case purely by chance. All I want to know from you is what you really think about the stolen letter.'

Pestonji was quite for a few seconds. Then he said, 'Have you seen that letter?'

'No, sir. How could I? Mr Haldar was dead by the time I reached his house, and the letter had gone.'

'But surely you have read about Napoleon?'

'Yes, a little.'

I began to wish Feluda wouldn't be so modest. He had spent the last two days reading as much as he could about Napoleon's life, as well as art and antiques. Uncle Sidhu had lent him a lot of books.

'Then you must know about his exile in St Helena.'

'Yes.'

'When was he exiled?'

'In 1815.'

Pestonji smiled faintly, as though he was impressed by Feluda's answers.

'This letter that Parvati had in his collection was written in 1814. Napoleon was not allowed to write to anyone during the six years of his exile in St Helena. This would mean that that letter was among the very last Napoleon wrote before he died. It's not known to whom it was addressed. The salutation simply said "mon cher ami"—my dear friend. But the contents of the letter and his language showed that even after he had lost everything, he was still fully prepared to stand by his beliefs. His spirit had remained unbroken. That is why that letter is so precious. Parvati had bought it for a song from some drunken fool in Zurich. It was going to come to me, for a mere twenty thousand rupees. Just imagine!'

'How?' Feluda's voice echoed the surprise we all felt. 'You mean Mr Haldar had agreed to sell that letter to you for that paltry sum?'

'Oh no, no. Parvati didn't agree to sell it. He was a most determined fellow. I used to respect him for it.'

'Well then?'

Pestonji poured himself a drink. Then he said, 'Can I offer you anything? Tea? Coffee? Beer?'

'No, thank you. We ought to be leaving soon.'

'All right,' Pestonji took a sip from his glass, 'I'll tell you what happened. I didn't tell the police because the way they showered me with questions, my blood pressure shot up dangerously. I'm prepared to tell you, for you look like a gentleman. Yesterday, I received an anonymous phone call. Someone asked me straightaway if I would buy that letter for twenty thousand. I said yes, and told him to come here with it in the evening. He then said he wouldn't come himself, but would send someone else. I must pay this man, and if I tried to inform the police, I'd end up just like Parvati Haldar.'

'Did anyone come?' we asked in unison.

'No. Nobody came.'

There seemed to be no point in asking anything more. We rose to take our leave. Suddenly, Feluda's eyes fell on a vase kept on a high shelf. 'Would that be a Ming vase?' he asked.

Pestonji smiled more openly, casting him a look of appreciation. 'You do seem to know about these things. Good, very good. Yes, that's a Ming vase. Absolutely exquisite.'

'Could I . . .?'

'Of course, of course. You cannot see the details unless you hold it in your hand.'

Pestonji got up, and stretched an arm towards the shelf. The next instant, he let it drop, wincing in pain.

'Ouch!'

'Why, what's the matter?' Feluda asked anxiously.

'Old age. That's what's the matter. It's arthritis. I cannot raise my arm even up to my shoulder.'

'Oh, I'm so sorry.' Feluda himself took the vase down, inspected it briefly, then said 'Superb!' before putting it back.

'I had to check if what I had heard about his arthritis was true,' he told us when we were out in the street.

'Ah. I did wonder why you were so keen on looking at that vase.

Honestly, Felu Babu, what a clever man you are! Anyway, where are we going now?'

'Cornwallis Street. It's quite far from here, I'm afraid.'

'So what? Yes, yes, petrol is expensive, but then so is everything else. Just don't worry about it.'

From Bowbazar Street, we made our way to the new theatre, Nobo Rangamanch, in Cornwallis Street. The proprietor was called Abhilash Poddar. He called us to his office as soon as Feluda sent his card in.

'Do come in, Mr Mitter. I am honoured by your visit. How may I serve you?'

Mr Poddar was plump and dark. A gold watch graced his left wrist, his lips were bright red. He had just stuffed a paan into his mouth. The whole room reeked with the scent of attar. Somehow, his appearance seemed to match the slightly theatrical way in which he spoke.

Feluda introduced Lalmohan Babu as the 'great thriller writer'.

'Really?' Mr Poddar turned his gaze on Jatayu.

'Yes. A Hindi film was made from one of my stories. *The Buccaneer of Bombay.*'

'Why don't you send a copy of your giant omnibus to Poddar?' Feluda suggested.

'Sure, I'd love to see your book, Mr Ganguli. Mind you, I'm not much of a reader myself. I pay people to read stuff for me, and then they let me know what they think. Anyway, what brings you here?'

'I need some information regarding one of your leading men.'

'Our leading men? Who do you mean? Manas Banerjee?'

'No. Achintya Haldar.'

'Achintya? I don't think . . . no, wait, wait. I do remember now. A young man by that name has been trying to get a good role. His appearance is all right, but his voice isn't suitable for the stage. He might do better in films. I've told him so, for all I could offer him was a small role, and that, too, was a long time ago. But in fact, he has offered me money for the lead role in my latest play.'

'What! He has offered you money?'

'There's nothing to feel so surprised about. It's quite common in this line.'

'But did you agree?'

'No, of course not. Ours is a new company, Mr Mitter, we cannot afford to get into shady dealings. I told him there was no question of my accepting his proposal. Now, what would you like to have? A cold drink, or . . .?'

'No, nothing, thanks. Thank you for your time.'

We got up and left. It was nearly one-thirty. I was feeling quite hungry.

Luckily, Feluda didn't suggest going anywhere else. We went straight to our favourite restaurant. After the food had been ordered, Feluda made a draft of the advertisement we had decided to put in regarding the missing chandana. Feluda knew a few people in the press. The ad would come out tomorrow, or at the latest by the day after. It said: 'If anyone sold a chandana to Tinkori Babu in New Market, could he/they please contract P.C. Mitter at the following address . . .'

Feluda helped himself to some biriyani. Then he cracked open a bone to get at the marrow inside, and said, 'If we keep getting one new mystery after another, heaven knows where all this will finally end.'

'Another new mystery? Wait, wait, let me guess, Felu Babu, you're talking of this man who offered to bring Pestonji the stolen letter, aren't you, and you can't figure out why he didn't come?'

'Right. All it can mean is that the man was hoping to get hold of the letter, but couldn't.'

'That means the man who rang Pestonji was not the actual thief, but someone else.'

'Yes, that's what it looks like.'

'Good heavens, now we'll have to look for one more criminal!' Lalmohan Babu stopped chewing for a minute.

'Feluda,' I began, 'there's something I've been meaning to ask you.'

'Yes?'

'If you hit someone on the head with a heavy paperweight, you are certainly likely to hurt him; but is there any guarantee that the man will die?'

'Good question. The answer to that is simple. There is no guarantee at all. But, in this case, whoever struck Parvaticharan must have been pretty sure about his death.'

'Or . . . maybe . . . he thought he'd just knock him unconscious. Perhaps he didn't think the man would die.'

'Yes, that's a possibility. I didn't know the food here would act as a brain tonic, Topshe! But even so, we're not really getting anywhere, are we? Whether the killer had actually wanted to kill or not is not the issue. The point is, where did he go? How did he vanish? It almost seems like magic.'

That same evening, we learnt the answer to this question. It came in a rather dramatic manner.

At around four-thirty, Inspector Hajra rang to tell us that they still hadn't found Sadhan Dastidar. Lalmohan Babu stayed on at our house. At seven-thirty, we were chatting over a cup of coffee, when suddenly the doorbell rang. This startled all of us, since it was unusual for anyone to call at this hour on a winter evening. I opened the door, to find Hrishikesh Datta standing outside.

'Do forgive me,' he said, stepping into the room. 'I know this is hardly a suitable time for a visit, and I should have called. But the telephone has been in constant use since Mr Haldar's death, I just couldn't find a free moment . . .'

'Never mind all that. You appear greatly disturbed. Please sit down, try to relax and tell us what's happened.'

Srinath appeared with a fresh cup of coffee. He no longer waited to be told. The sound of a new voice was enough to warn him. Feluda passed the cup to Mr Datta.

He took a long sip and began talking. 'You didn't see my room the other day, did you? Well, I can tell you it takes a lot of courage to live in that room. I am the only one living in the ground floor. All the other bedrooms are upstairs. The servants have their own quarters behind the main house. Even after all this time, I feel slightly uneasy being entirely on my own, specially at night. Anyway, last night, I returned to my room after dinner at around half past ten. I shut the door, pulled down the mosquito-net and was about to go to bed, when someone knocked on my door. This was most unusual, for nobody in that house bothers with knocking. If people want to see me, they simply stand outside the door and call out my name. So my suspicions were aroused at once. I said, "Who is it?", but no one answered. A little later, there was another knock. At first I thought I wouldn't open the door; but then I realized whoever it was might continue to knock, and that would be even worse. So I went and opened it, telling myself to be brave. A man came in quickly, and shut the door behind him. I didn't see his face immediately, but a second later he turned to face me.

He had a thick beard, so there was no problem in recognizing him. Before I could say a single word, he began talking. In his hand he held a huge knife. He kept that pointed at me until he had finished.'

Lalmohan Babu gasped. Even I felt goose pimples breaking out on my arms.

'What did Sadhan Dastidar tell you?' Feluda asked calmly.

'Something terrible. You see, he obviously knows quite a lot about what is in Mr Haldar's collection. He said there was a golden snuff box studded with emeralds. It used to belong to Bahadur Shah Zafar. He had found a buyer for it, so I would have to get it for him. He said he'd wait for me near the broken indigo factory, not far from the house. There's a lake there, called Madhumurali Deeghi. I should get the snuff box and meet him there at eleven tonight. He told me to stand under a particular tree.'

'And what would be your reward? Would he share his profits with you?'

'Forget it. He wouldn't share a penny. His only intention was to frighten me into doing what he wanted. He said going to the police would mean death. He'd kill me, just as he killed Mr Haldar.' Mr Datta's voice shook slightly as he spoke.

Feluda frowned. 'Don't you have a night watchman at the gate?' he asked.

'Sure. I think he jumped over the wall to get in.'

'How did he know which room you were in?'

'That was easy. Sadhu Dastidar used to live in the same room.'

'Sadhu? Is that his pet name?'

'I don't know but Mr Haldar used to refer to him by that name.'

'What did you tell him?'

'I said I couldn't do it. The police were coming to the house every day, and keeping a careful eye on things. So how could I possibly steal anything? He said that shouldn't be a problem at all. Since I was Mr Haldar's secretary, I could easily get into his room by saying I needed to look at some papers, or something. He wasn't going to listen to my excuses, he said, and then he left. I know you'll now get cross with me, and say I should have gone to the police, or at least informed Amitabh Haldar. But can't you see how frightened I was? I mean, my life was at stake! So I decided to come to you, Mr Mitter. I don't think Sadhu knows about your involvement in the case. You are my only hope. Please save me!'

'You didn't get that snuff box, did you?'

'No, no, certainly not.'

'I see. So are you suggesting that we should all go wherever he's asked you to meet him?'

'Yes. Don't you think it's a golden opportunity to catch him red-handed? You could go a little early and hide somewhere. I would go at eleven, and then . . . well, I guess you'd know what to do if you saw him.'

'You don't think going to the police might be a good idea?'

'No, no, no. Please don't do that. You must go alone, or with your friend and your cousin here, if you like, but please don't even mention the police. He'll kill me, I tell you! In fact, you ought to be armed yourself. Sadhu Dastidar is a dangerous man.'

'Go on, Felu Babu, say yes,' Lalmohan Babu said without a moment's hesitation. 'If the dacoits of Rajasthan couldn't frighten us, what chance does this man have? None at all!'

'I'll show you the place. It's about four miles from the station.'

Feluda agreed. Mr Datta finished his coffee, and stood up.

'Thank you, Mr Mitter. Will you please meet me at ten o'clock tonight?'

'All right. Where should we meet you?'

'If you go past our house, a couple of furlongs later you'll find a crossing where three roads meet. There is a sweet shop on one side. That is where I'll be waiting for you.'

FIVE

Although the traffic was not likely to be heavy at that time of night, we left a little before nine, giving ourselves more than an hour to reach Barasat. We had our dinner before leaving, which felt slightly strange because none of us was used to eating so early. 'If we start to feel peckish a little later,' Lalmohan Babu observed, 'we can always go to that sweet shop where Mr Datta is meeting us. I'm sure they'll have kachauris and aloo-sabzi.'

Lalmohan Babu's driver was greatly excited on being told why we were returning to Barasat. Luckily for us, he was a great admirer of Feluda, and quite fond of watching action-packed Hindi films. Any other driver would have been cross at being told to drive out of town late at night. But Lalmohan Babu's driver, Haripada, seemed to get new life in his tired limbs when Feluda explained the situation.

When we reached VIP Road, Lalmohan Babu decided to burst into song. 'Everyone has gone to the wood, on this moonlight night . . .' he began, but one look from Feluda stopped him immediately. The sky was totally dark. There was no sign of the moon. But it was a clear night. Perhaps the faint light from the stars would be of some use. In accordance to Feluda's instructions, I was wearing a dark shirt; and Lalmohan Babu had put on Feluda's raincoat over his light yellow pullover. Although it wasn't possible to see it in the car, I knew that when he got out, one of his pockets would hang heavy under its load. He had borrowed the iron rod of Srinath's hand-grinder and stuffed it into his pocket. Feluda, too, was armed, but not with an iron rod. In his jacket pocket lay his Colt revolver.

We reached the crossing just before ten. Mr Datta was standing in front of a paan stall next to the sweet shop. Haripada stopped the car. Mr Datta got in swiftly, and said, 'Please take the next right turn.' Only a few minutes later, the number of houses grew appreciably less. The streetlights disappeared. I realized we had left the town of Barasat behind us and were in the country.

'The first indigo factory was built in Barasat,' Mr Datta told us. 'If you ever come this way in daylight, you'll be able to see broken old houses in which the British owners of these factories used to live.'

We drove in silence for another twenty minutes. Then, suddenly, Mr Datta said, 'Here we are. Stop the car.'

Our car came to a halt. All of us trooped out.

'Please tell your driver to wait here with the car. I'll show you where Sadhu Dastidar has asked me to meet him. Then your car can take me home, and come back here. I'll make my own way to the right place just before eleven.'

Lalmohan Babu gave some money to his driver, and said, 'Get yourself something to eat after you've dropped Mr Datta. It may well be quite late by the time we get back home.'

We began walking through a field. Five minutes later, we found ourselves in what appeared to be a wood.

'Madhumurali Deeghi is behind all these trees. But we have to go over there,' Mr Datta pointed at the trees. We began walking again. It was too dark to see anything clearly, but I could make out the outlines of broken structures. This place wasn't really a wood. It had probably been a part of private grounds that belonged to some rich owner of an indigo factory. Years of neglect had turned it into a jungle. A large house must have stood here once. Part's of its front veranda were still standing upright. Thank goodness it was winter, or we might have had to deal with snakes.

'It's probably quite safe at this moment to use a torch,' Feluda remarked.

'Yes, I don't think right now it would matter.'

Feluda switched on his small pocket torch. We made our way towards the rubble of the derelict building, trying not to stumble or fall into potholes.

'There it is, look!' Mr Datta pointed at a tree. 'That's a sheora tree. That's where Sadhu Dastidar asked me to wait.'

Feluda shone his torch briefly on the tree, then switched it off.

'Perhaps I should go now,' Mr Datta said.

'Yes. We'll see you in . . . let's see . . . about forty-five minutes?'

'OK.'

Mr Datta made an about turn and disappeared in the direction from which we had come. A minute later, we couldn't even hear his footsteps.

'Here's some Odomos,' Feluda said, taking out a tube from his pocket, 'you may find it useful.'

'Oh, thank you, Felu Babu. Malaria is on the rise again, isn't it?'

All of us applied Odomos on our hands, faces and necks, and prepared ourselves for a long wait. We didn't have to stand, for there were small piles of bricks strewn about everywhere that could be used as chairs or stools. Conversations had to be carried out in whispers, but after the first few minutes, we fell silent. By now my eyes had got used to the dark, and I could see that there was a wide variety of trees, including mango, banyan and peepal. There were bamboo groves as well. From the far distance came the faint noises of rickshaw horns, trains, barking dogs—I could even hear a transistor being played somewhere. Feluda's watch had a luminous dial, so he could see the time even in the dark.

It seemed to be getting colder by the minute. Lalmohan Babu hadn't brought his cap, and his handkerchief was white, so all he could do to protect his head was cover it with his hands. After a long period of silence, we heard him say something under his breath. 'What did you say?' Feluda whispered.

'N-nothing,' he whispered back. 'It's just that I suddenly remembered old fairy tales. Don't spooks and ghosts live in sheora trees?'

'Yes, particularly female ones. They slip down the tree and attack you. Have you ever seen a sheora tree before? I haven't.'

The stars in the sky were changing their positions. The one that was right over a coconut tree even a few minutes ago was now practically hidden behind it. I raised my eyes to the sky to see if I could see a familiar constellation. At this precise moment, there was a noise, quite distinct from all the other noises my ears were getting used to. Footsteps. There could be no mistake.

It was not yet eleven o'clock. Only a couple of minutes ago, Feluda had looked at his watch and said, 'Ten forty-five.' All of us sat still like statues.

The sound of footsteps was coming from the path—if it could be called a path—that led to the tree. We had taken the same path half an hour ago. It wasn't possible to hear the sound unless I strained my ears. The racket the crickets were making in the bamboo groves was pretty loud, but the noise of the traffic on the main road had gone.

A few seconds later, a figure emerged from the shadows. It was walking toward the sheora tree, slowly reducing its speed as it got closer. We were only a few yards away, partially hidden by a broken wall. Who was this man approaching us? Was it Sadhan Dastidar? There was no way to tell.

'Mr Datta!' the man called softly. He had stopped walking. I could feel Feluda standing next to me, his body tense, and ready to spring into action.

The man took a few steps forward. 'Mr Datta!' he called again.

Lalmohan Babu moved slightly, raising his right elbow. He was digging into his pocket to get his weapon.

The man was now only a few feet away. 'Mr Dat—!' He couldn't finish. Feluda leapt up, and landed on him. I was about to do the same, when something happened to halt me in my tracks.

Two other men sprang forward and fell on top of Feluda. This was so completely unexpected that for a few moments, I could only stand and stare foolishly. But years of experience had taught me not to lose my nerve easily. I could see that Feluda had hit one of the men, and he was moving in my direction, swaying slightly. It took me only a couple of seconds to pull myself together, grab him and sock him on the jaw. He fell down on the grass without uttering a single sound. I began to feel quite jubilant.

But . . . but . . . what was this? Loads of other men were creeping out from behind the trees and other parts of the broken building. One of them caught my arms and pinned them behind my back. Two more went and attacked Feluda. I could hear him struggle, but he was totally helpless to do anything, except try to kick at my adversary.

What was Lalmohan Babu doing? Where was he?

There was no time to look, for just as I thought of him, I felt a severe blow on my chin. In the same instant, my knees buckled under me and, quietly, I slipped into oblivion.

'Are you all right?' asked a familiar voice.

Feluda was the first person I could see when I came round.

'There's nothing to worry about I, too, had been knocked out for ten minutes,' he added.

Now I could see the others in the room. There was Amitabh Haldar, and a lady next to him—his wife most probably—and Lalmohan Babu, Mr Datta, and standing near the door was Achintya Haldar. I had not seen this room before.

I sat up slowly. Apart from an aching chin, there didn't appear to be any other problem. Feluda had been hit on his right eye. The area around it had already started to turn black. I had seen black-eyes only in films so far.

'Only Jatayu managed to remain totally unharmed,' Feluda told me.

'Oh? How? What did he do?'

'It was that iron rod,' Lalmohan Babu explained. 'I tell you, Tapesh, there is no weapon on earth that can match that rod from a hand-grinder. All I did was hold it over my head and whirl it around like a helicopter. Not a single hooligan could come near me.'

'Who were those hooligans?'

'Hired goondas.'

'I knew the man was dangerous,' Mr Datta shook his head with profound regret, 'but I never though he would go this far. Can you imagine the shock I got when I returned to the spot? One of you was lying flat on the ground, the second was lying on his stomach, and the third was sitting, looking completely dazed! The culprit and his team had disappeared without a trace.'

Feluda filled me in quickly. When Mr Datta arrived, he and Lalmohan Babu carried me back to the car. Luckily, Amitabh Haldar was still awake when they brought me to the house. He and his wife had made arrangements for me to rest in one of their guest rooms on the ground floor. It was a large and comfortable room, with an attached bathroom. Mr Haldar insisted that we spend the night in his house. I didn't mind, although none of us had brought extra clothes.

'If only you had told us, Mr Datta! I would have informed the police, and then none of this would have happened,' Mr Haldar said severely.

'I know, I know. I am so sorry, sir. I wish I hadn't allowed myself to be so utterly terrorized, but . . .' Mr Datta's voice trailed away. I couldn't really blame the man. Who would have the courage to go to the police after being threatened like that?

Mrs Haldar finished making all the arrangements for our stay. 'I have read all your books, and greatly enjoyed them. But with one disaster after another, there's been no chance to talk to you properly,' she said to Lalmohan Babu.

'I must speak to your son tomorrow, before I go,' Feluda said. 'If a thief got into their room, not many young boys would be able to show the courage he has shown.'

About an hour later, as we were getting ready to go to bed, Feluda suddenly made a remark that surprised us.

'I had no idea a sock on the jaw could also work like a brain tonic,' he observed.

'What do you mean?'

'I have finally been able to figure out how Sadhu Dastidar could vanish like that.'

'You don't say, Felu Babu!'

'A very cunning man, I have to admit. But the man he's up against is no less clever, or crafty.'

He refused to say any more.

SIX

Feluda got up early to meet Aniruddha before he left for school. The little boy told us in great detail how he had chased the thief away. He certainly had a lively imagination. Had he perhaps imagined the whole thing, I wondered.

'You haven't shown me the gun you were going to attack the thief with,' Feluda said to him. 'I mean the one you showed your uncle Achintya.'

Aniruddha found his machine-gun and gave it to Feluda. 'It

breathes fire,' he said solemnly. The gun was made of red plastic. It made a noise like a real machine-gun when the trigger was pulled, and bright sparks came out of the barrel. Feluda examined it carefully, then returned it to Anu.

'A beautiful weapon,' he said. 'Now let's see if something can be done, so your sleep doesn't get disturbed.'

'You mean you'll catch the thief?'

'Catching thieves is a detective's business, isn't it?'

'I guess. What about my chandana? Will you catch whoever took it?'

'I'm trying very hard to catch him, but it's not easy.'

'Is it most terribly difficult?'

'Yes, most terribly difficult.'

'A huge, big mystery?'

'You're right. It is a huge, big mystery.'

'But you found blood on its cage!'

'Yes, that is my only clue.'

'What is a clue?'

'It's something that helps a detective to catch thieves.'

Lalmohan Babu suddenly interrupted this conversation. 'Tell me, Anu,' he said, 'did you hear this bird talk?'

'Yes, I did. I was in my room, and the bird was in its cage. I heard it say something.'

'What did it say?'

'It said, "deck chair, dadu", "deck chair, dadu". It said it twice. I ran out of my room, but it didn't speak at all after that.'

Lalmohan Babu grinned. I had to admit 'deck chair, dadu' didn't sound very different from 'fake hair, babu', especially if it was said quickly.

'Is there anyone in your house who might be able to catch a bird?' Feluda asked Amitabh Haldar.

'Yes, our mali's son Shankar has caught a couple of birds in the past. He's very quick on his feet.'

'Tell him to watch out for your chandana. I'm now pretty sure it's still somewhere in your garden at the back.'

We left for home soon after this. I had already seen in the local daily that Feluda's advertisement had come out. But none of us could anticipate how quickly we'd get a result.

Around twelve the same day, a young man of about twenty-five turned up at our house. Judging by his hairstyle and the jeans he was wearing, he was a man keen on following the current fashion. Feluda asked him to sit down, but he shook his head.

'No, I haven't got time to sit down. I am on my way to an interview,' he said. 'I came only because I saw your advertisement about a bird.'

'I see, was it yours?'

'No. It used to belong to my grandfather. He died last month. He was very fond of this bird, and used to look after it himself. Since my mother's not very well and my father's far too busy, and I couldn't be bothered at all, we decided to sell it.'

'How long did it stay with your family?'

'Nearly ten years.'

'Did it talk?'

'Yes, my grandfather had taught it a few words. He had a rather weird sense of humour. The bird learnt to say some strange words.'

'How do you mean?'

'I mean, what it used to say was very different from the usual "Radhe Shyam" or '"Hare Krishna". My grandfather used to play chess every day. He taught the bird to say "checkmate". He also played bridge. If he could figure out that his opponent had got a good hand, he used to warn his partner. The words he spoke were a kind of code that his partner understood. The bird had picked it up, because he used to say it so often. Then the bird began to say it, too.'

'What were these words?'

'Take care, Sadhu.'

'What? Why Sadhu?'

'I don't know. I told you, it was a code between him and his partner.'

'I see. Very well. Thank you very much indeed. You've been extremely helpful.'

'Would there be anything else—?'

'No, nothing else, thank you.'

'OK. Er . . . I didn't realize from the address it was your house.'

'That isn't surprising.'

'I'm very glad to have met you. I mean, it isn't every day that one meets someone famous . . . ha ha!'

After the young man had gone, Feluda told me he was not to be disturbed and disappeared into his room. He emerged five hours later to have a cup of tea. Then he rang Inspector Hajra.

'What are you doing tomorrow?' he asked.

'Nothing special. Why?'

'Could you reach Mr Haldar's house by nine o'clock tomorrow morning? I think I've managed to solve the mystery. You must come fully prepared.'

Lalmohan Babu was given more or less the same message. We would take a taxi to reach his house by eight-thirty. Then we'd go to Barasat in his car.

'Why, what's the matter? More mysteries?' he asked.

'No, Lalmohan Babu. Every mystery's cleared up!'

Amitabh Haldar was the last one to be informed.

'I'm planning to hold a meeting in your house tomorrow morning,' Feluda told him.

'A meeting?'

'Yes. I want all male members of your household to attend it. Inspector Hajra will also be present.'

'What time did you have in mind?'

'Nine. This may delay your other work, but believe me, it's urgent.'

'All right. But when you say male members, do you mean Anu should be included?'

'Oh, no, no. He, in fact, should not be present. I meant only the adults.'

We reached Mr Haldar's house to find that the inspector and his men had already arrived. Lalmohan Babu and I were both feeling very excited. Heaven knew what Feluda was going to reveal, and who would turn out to be the culprit. 'I am not even trying to think,' Lalmohan Babu whispered to me. 'I just can't, and I totally fail to see how your cousin could not only have worked everything out, but remain so calm about it!'

Everyone had gathered in the large drawing room on the ground floor. Mr Datta greeted us as we entered. 'I am so glad I'll soon be leaving for Delhi,' he confided. 'I am going crazy without any real work to do!'

We hadn't yet had the chance to speak to Achintya Haldar properly. He came over and asked Feluda, 'How long will this take? I am very busy with a new role. It's a long and difficult one, and the play starts tomorrow. I can't afford to spend a lot of time on anything else.'

'This won't take more than half an hour, I promise.'

Achintya Babu went away, muttering under his breath. A bearer had served coffee to everyone. Feluda finished his, and stood up. He was wearing dark glasses to cover his black eye. It made him look smarter than ever. Everyone in the room fell silent as he began speaking.

'When I came here at Amitabh Haldar's invitation, I had no idea I would get involved in a murder case. What was most puzzling about Parvaticharan's murder was, of course, the disappearance of Sadhan Dastidar. He was in Parvaticharan's study from ten-fifteen to ten-thirty. At ten-thirty, we saw him coming out of the sitting room upstairs and then going down the stairs. Five minutes later, when we went to the study after a chat with little Anu, we found Parvaticharan dead. We looked for Mr Dastidar everywhere, but he was nowhere to be seen. The chowkidar insisted he hadn't seen him go out. He wasn't hiding in the garden. The compound wall was too high to jump over, especially with a briefcase in one hand. We—'

Achintya Babu interrupted Feluda. 'Why are you forgetting the man who visited my father before Mr Dastidar arrived?'

'Pestonji? He couldn't have used the force with which your father was struck. He's an old man, Mr Haldar, and he suffers from arthritis. He cannot even raise his right arm properly. We have to rule him out. But there was a third person who might have gone to your father's room before Sadhan Dastidar's arrival.'

'Who?'

'You.'

Achintya Haldar sprang to his feet. 'You m-mean I . . . I would try to k-kill . . .?'

'No. I am not saying that you actually tried to kill your own father. I am merely saying that you had the opportunity to do so.'

'Oh. Thank God for that.'

'Anyway,' Feluda continued, 'there were two likely explanations for Dastidar's disappearance. One, the chowkidar was lying. Two, he did not leave the premises at all, in which case the chowkidar was obviously telling the truth.'

'You mean he might have been hiding somewhere inside the house? In the attic, or some unused room?' Hrishikesh Datta asked.

'No,' Amitabh Haldar protested, 'I don't think he could have gone up to the attic without being seen; and except for the drawing room, the store and Mr Datta's bedroom, every other room on the ground floor is locked. How could he have got into any of those?'

'Well, he certainly wasn't hiding in my room, I can tell you that!'

Mr Datta said emphatically. 'In fact, I wasn't home when he arrived.'

'Well, Mr Datta, we checked with the post office. They confirmed that you had gone there at ten o'clock and sent two telegrams. Then you—'

'Then I went to look for a strap for my watch.'

'Yes, so you told us. Unfortunately, no one in the local shops can remember having seen you.'

'So what? What are you saying, Mr Mitter? Is your entire investigation dependent on what busy shop assistants can remember about their customers?'

'No. I saw no reason to pay a lot of attention to what the shop assistants had to say. Equally, I didn't think there was any reason to assume that you were telling us the truth.'

'Why? Why would I tell lies?'

'Because you yourself might have gone into Parvaticharan's study at ten-fifteen.'

'Have you gone mad? Didn't you just say you had seen Sadhan Dastidar coming out of the sitting room upstairs? And now you're suggesting I was there at the same time?'

'Yes. Suppose Mr Dastidar did not come at all? Suppose it was you who went in his place?'

This remark was followed by pindrop silence. Mr Datta seemed bereft of speech. My head started reeling. What on earth was Feluda talking about?

Suddenly, Mr Datta burst out laughing.

'You are joking Mr Mitter, aren't you? I mean, are you implying that Parvaticharan was either totally insane, or completely senile? If I went in wearing a beard, wouldn't he have recognized me?'

'No. How could he, Mr Datta? You took off your glasses, you put on a false beard and a moustache, and you changed your clothes. Parvaticharan was sitting in his room, expecting to see a man he hadn't seen for seven years. Why shouldn't he think you were that same man? Because you *were* the same man, weren't you? What is the difference between Sadhan Dastidar and Hrishikesh Datta, tell me? How was Parvaticharan to know that his new secretary was really his old one in disguise? As Sadhan Dastidar, you did have a real beard. You shaved it off. Dastidar didn't wear glasses, but you decided Hrishikesh Datta should. And you waited all this while to settle old scores. You could never forget the humiliation of being fired, could you?'

The expression on Mr Datta's face had changed completely. His lips trembled, but he couldn't speak. Two constables went and stood by his side. But Feluda had not finished.

'You used the heavy paperweight to kill your employer. Then you thrust in into a pocket of your jacket, and threw it into the pond. After that, it took you only a couple of minutes to discard your disguise and come out once more as Hrishikesh Datta. Am I right?'

Mr Datta said nothing. I could see that the collar of his shirt was drenched with perspiration, even in December.

'There's one more thing. Do the words "Take care, Sadhu" mean anything to you? Didn't you hear these words recently from a bird, the same chandana that went missing? Superstitious as you are, didn't you think the bird knew about your plan and was warning you? And isn't that why you took it out of its cage and released it outside? But it fought back, didn't it, and left its mark on your arm?'

This time, Hrishikesh Datta found his tongue. 'Absurd!' he exclaimed, jumping up from his chair in excitement. 'That's utterly ridiculous. Where did it hurt me? Can you see a mark anywhere on my arms?'

'Inspector Hajra, will you please tell one of your men to take off his wristwatch from his right arm?'

Mr Datta did his best to stop him, but one of the constables undid the clasp of his watch and it slipped off easily. Even from a distance I could see an inch-long scratch, which he had safely hidden under the strap of his watch.

'I . . . didn't mean to kill him. You must believe me, you must!' Mr Datta's voice was barely audible. His whole body shook.

'I do. Your idea of revenge wasn't murder. Nevertheless, he died. All you had wanted to do was steal that letter Napoleon wrote, knowing how precious it was to Parvaticharan. You knew Pestonji was prepared to buy it. So you—'

'No, no, it wasn't me. I didn't do it!' Mr Datta shouted desperately.

'Please let me finish. I do know the whole story, I assure you. You were not alone in this, were you? You took that letter, went to your room to change your make-up, and then passed it on to your accomplice. But knowing that the police were bound to search the house, your accomplice hid it quickly, in what he thought was a perfectly safe place. Isn't that so, Achintya Babu?'

The last question shot out like a bullet. But Achintya Haldar, it turned out, was made of sterner stuff than we had expected. He remained perfectly unperturbed, and stared back at Feluda with a smile on his lips.

'Pray continue, Mr Mitter,' he said sarcastically, 'do tell us more.'

'You went to your nephew's room a little after half past ten, didn't you?'

'Yes, I did. So what? He wanted me to see his new toy. Surely there was nothing wrong with that?'

'No. But I'm sure your are aware that a thief broke into your nephew's room shortly after the murder. He didn't get what he was looking for. Are you going to deny that you were that thief, and you had stolen into little Anu's room in the hope of retrieving that letter because you had hidden it in there? I know it was you who rang Pestonji and offered to bring him the stolen letter. But you didn't find it, so nobody turned up in Pestonji's house.'

'Now, isn't that strange? If I had hidden that letter myself, why couldn't I find it?'

'The reason is simple, Mr Haldar. The object into which you had thrust that letter was resting under Anu's pillow. Here it is.'

Feluda stretched a hand towards Inspector Hajra, who silently passed him the red toy machine-gun Anu had been bought only the other day. Feluda slipped a finger into its nozzle and brought out a rolled piece of paper—Napoleon's letter.

The smile slowly faded from Achintya Haldar's lips.

'Was it you who had supplied Mr Datta's costume and make-up?' Feluda asked casually. 'How were you going to split the money? Fifty-fifty?'

The mail's son, Shankar, succeeded pretty quickly in catching the chandana and restoring it to its little owner. Anu, however, gave full credit for its recovery to Feluda.

Amitabh Haldar said Feluda was welcome to choose anything from his father's collection as his reward. But Feluda shook his head. 'No, Mr Haldar. I was not appointed to unravel this mystery, was I? My involvement was purely by accident, and I happened to have come here only because your son had invited me. How can I expect a six-year-old child to pay me a fee?'

Two days later, Lalmohan Babu arrived at our place, looking

'Sir,' he declared solemnly, looking straight at Feluda, 'in view of your incredible intelligence and devastating powers of detection, I do hereby bestow an honorary title on you—ABCD.'

'ABCD? What's that?'

'Asia's Best Crime Detector.'

Tintoretto's Jesus

ONE

On Tuesday, 28 September 1982, a taxi drew up in front of the house of the Niyogis in Baikunthapur. The Niyogis had once been the zamindars in the area.

The durwan at the gate came forward, just as a middle-aged man got out of the taxi. He was of medium height. His cheeks were covered by a heavy stubble and his hair looked decidedly dishevelled. He wore a dark blue suit and tinted glasses.

The driver took out a brown suitcase from the boot and put it down on the pavement.

'Niyogi sahib?' asked the durwan.

The man nodded. The durwan picked up the suitcase.

'Please come in,' he said. 'Babu has been waiting for you for some time.'

The present owner of the house, Soumyasekhar Niyogi, was reclining in an easy chair on the veranda. He nodded as the newcomer approached him and indicated a chair nearby. Soumyasekhar was nearly seventy. He was fairly well-preserved for his age, except that failing eyesight had necessitated wearing glasses with thick lenses.

'Rudrasekhar?' he asked.

The newcomer took out a passport from his pocket and held it open for inspection. Soumyasekhar looked at it briefly and smiled.

'Awful, isn't it?' he said. 'You are my first cousin, and yet you have to show me your passport to prove it. But it's easy enough to see that you're a Niyogi.'

The other man looked faintly amused. 'Never mind,' Soumyasekhar continued, 'I hope you got the letter I sent you after you wrote to me from Rome. What surprised us was that you didn't get in touch all these years. Uncle left home in 1955, twenty-seven years ago. When he returned without you, we assumed there was a problem and you didn't get on with each other. Uncle never talked about it, and we didn't ask him anything, either. All we knew was that he had a son in Rome. Well, you've come now—I take it—to talk about the property?'

'Yes.'

'I wrote to you, didn't I, that the last time I received a postcard from your father was ten years ago? So, in the eyes of the law, he is no more. Have you spoken to a lawyer about this?'

'Yes.'

'Very well. You can stay here for as long as you like, and look at everything we've got. You'll find Uncle's studio upstairs. His paintings, and canvases and colours are all still there, just as he had left them. We didn't touch anything. Then there are the bank passbooks. You'll need to see those, obviously. It may well take six months for all formalities to be completed. I hope you can stay that long?'

'Yes.'

'You may have to travel to Calcutta from time to time. You've got a taxi, haven't you?'

'Yes.'

'We'll arrange for your driver to stay here. No problem!'

'Gra . . . thanks!'

Rudrasekhar had started to say 'Grazie' in Italian, then changed his mind. 'By the way, you wouldn't mind eating Indian food every day, would you? I hear London has an Indian restaurant virtually at every street corner. What's it like in Rome?'

'There are a few.'

'Well, that should help. I can only offer . . . why, Jagadish, what's the matter?'

An old servant stood near the door. There were tears in his eyes.

'Thumri . . . huzoor, Thumri is dead.'

'What! Dead?'

'Yes.'

'Why, Bhikhu just took her for a walk, didn't he?'

'Yes, but that was a long time ago. When neither of them returned when they should have, I went to look for them. I found Thumri's body in the woods. Bhikhu has run away, huzoor.'

'I . . . don't . . . believe . . . this!'

Soumyasekhar had always been interested in music. One of his two fox terriers was called Kajri. The other was Thumri. Kajri had died a natural death a couple of years ago. Thumri was eleven. Until a few hours ago, she was alive and in perfect health.

Rudrasekhar rose quietly to his feet. The older man was clearly deeply distressed. He didn't want to disturb him. It was time to find out where his room was.

TWO

Our car passed through the heavy traffic in Shibpur and turned onto the national highway. It felt like going into a new world.

When I say 'our' car, I really mean Jatayu's car. Lalmohan Ganguli—alias Jatayu—the very successful writer of blood-curdling thrillers, owned this green Ambassador. But he was perfectly happy to let us use it whenever we wanted. 'My car, sir,' he had once said to Feluda, 'is equal to yours. What I mean is, it's your right—that is, it is a privilege for me to offer you the use of my car, considering all you've done for me.'

'What have I done for you, Lalmohan Babu?'

'Why, you've—you've opened such a lot of new doors for me! And it's brought me renewed vigour and a totally different outlook. Just think of the many places I've now travelled to—Delhi, Bombay, Jaisalmer, Benaras, Simla, Nepal. Could I have done it without your help? No, sir! I had only heard of the saying "Travel broadens the mind". Now I know what it means.'

This time, however, we were not going to travel very far. Mecheda was only a few miles from Calcutta. But according to Lalmohan Babu, living in Calcutta was no different from living in the black hole. So if one could get away even for a single day, it gave one a new lease of life.

Why, one might wonder, were we going to Mecheda, of all places? The reason was simple. We were going there to meet the numerologist, Bhabesh Chandra Bhattacharya. Lalmohan Babu had read about him—and his powers—nearly three months ago. Now he was determined to meet him in person.

Mr Bhattacharya, apparently, could use his knowledge of numbers to make amazing and accurate predictions. Hundreds of people were queueing up outside his house in Mecheda to seek his advice. Lalmohan Babu wanted to join the queue, for his last book had not sold quite as well as he had hoped. 'There must have been something wrong with the title of the novel,' he mused.

'I don't think so, Lalmohan Babu,' Feluda told him. 'All that happened was that you got carried away. Your hero gets hit by seven bullets, but even after that he's alive and well. Now, that is a bit hard to swallow, isn't it? I mean, even for the readers of your adventure series?'

'What are you saying, Felu Babu?' Jatayu sounded indignant. 'My hero Prakhar Rudra isn't an ordinary man, and my readers know it. He's a super-super-super man of extraordinary—'

'All right, all right, we believe you!'

This time, Feluda had declared himself perfectly happy with the plot of his latest novel. But Lalmohan Babu was not going to take any risks.

'I must consult this numerologist,' he said. Hence our visit to Mecheda.

We had left Calcutta at 7.30 this morning and hoped to reach Mecheda by half-past nine. By 1.30 p.m., we planned to be back home.

There wasn't much traffic on the highway, and we drove at 80 km per hour. Soon, we passed Kolaghat. Mecheda wasn't far from here. A couple of minutes later, we saw a strange car by the side of the road, its owner standing helplessly by its side. Our arrival made him jump and wave madly. Our car screeched to a halt.

'A most unfortunate business,' the gentleman said, wiping his face with a large handkerchief. 'One of the tyre's gone, but I think I left the jack in my other car.'

'Don't worry,' Lalmohan Babu reassured him, 'my driver will sort things out. Have a look, Haripada.'

Haripada took out a jack and passed it to the other man, who began working on the flat tyre immediately.

'How old is your car?' Feluda asked.

'It's a 1936 model. Armstrong Siddeley.'

'Does it often give you trouble on a long run?'

'No, never. I join the vintage car rally every year. Er . . . are you going far?'

'Only up to Mecheda. We don't expect to spend more than half an hour there.'

'Well then, why don't you come to my house from there? Turn left as you get out of Mecheda. I live just eight kilometres away, in Baikunthapur.'

'Baikunthapur?'

'Yes, that's where my parents live in our ancestral home. I live in Calcutta, but I'm visiting them at the moment. Our house is two hundred years old—I'm sure you'll enjoy a short visit. You could have lunch with us, and return to Calcutta in the evening. Do say yes. I'd like to show you how very grateful I am for your help.'

Feluda frowned. 'Baikunthapur . . . I have seen that name recently somewhere.'

'Yes, you may have read Bhudev Singh's article in the *Illustrated Weekly*.'

'Oh, yes. Now I remember. It was published about six weeks ago.'

'Yes, although I must confess I haven't read the article myself. Someone told me about it.'

'It's about someone from the Niyogi family in Baikunthapur. He was an artist, who went to Rome.'

'My great-uncle, Chandrasekhar,' the gentleman smiled. 'I am a Niyogi, too. My name is Nobo Kumar.'

'I see. I am Pradosh Mitter, and this is Lalmohan Ganguli. Here's my cousin Tapesh.'

Nobo Kumar raised his eyebrows. 'Pradosh Mitter? The investigator?' he asked.

'Yes.'

'Oh, then you've got to come to our house! Why, you're a famous man! Besides, to tell you the truth, I had already thought of contacting you.'

'Why?'

'There's been a murder. You may laugh at this, for the victim was not a man but a dog.'

'What! When did this happen?'

'Last Tuesday. It was a fox terrier. My father was very fond of it.'

'Why do you say it was a murder?'

'A servant took the dog out for a walk. Neither of them returned. The dog's body was found in the woods. It looked as though it was poisoned. Biscuit crumbs lay everywhere.'

'How very strange! Have you any idea who—?'

'No. The dog was eleven years old. It wouldn't have lived for long, anyway. That's why the whole business strikes me as extremely mysterious. Anyway, I don't expect you to carry out an investigation. I'd simply be grateful for a visit. I could show you where Chandrasekhar painted. His studio was left untouched.'

'All right,' said Feluda. 'I must admit that article made me curious about the Niyogi family. We'll be there, say around eleven?'

'OK. You'll find a petrol pump soon after you leave Mecheda. They'll be able to tell you how to get to Baikunthapur.'

Mr Niyogi returned the jack to Haripada, and we drove off.

'So many interesting people have lived in our time, but we don't often get to know about them,' Feluda remarked. 'Chandrasekhar Niyogi left the country at the age of twenty-four. He went to an academy in Rome to study art, and married an Italian girl. He came back home years later after his wife died. He became quite well known as a painter of portraits. Various wealthy people—including maharajahs of a few princely states—commissioned him to paint their portraits. One of these maharajahs got to know him quite well. It was he who wrote that article. Chandrasekhar eventually left home in his old age and is said to have become a sanyasi.'

'Yes, most interesting,' said Lalmohan Babu, 'but I can't get something out of my mind. Have you ever heard of a dog being murdered?'

'No, I've got to admit I haven't.'

'In that case, Felu Babu, I would urge you to get on with it. If you solved this mystery for Nobo Kumar Niyogi, I can assure you you won't be disappointed. A man who can afford to maintain three vintage cars must be absolutely loaded. Just think about it!'

THREE

We had made an appointment with Bhabesh Bhattacharya, so it was relatively easy to meet him. He might have been a school teacher—wearing thick glasses, a loose shirt, a cotton chadar draped over his shoulders. He was sitting very straight before a small desk, on top of which lay a few finely sharpened pencils and a fat, bound ledger.

'Lalmohan Gangopadhyaya?' he asked, glancing at the postcard Lalmohan Babu had sent him.

'Yes.'

'Age?' Lalmohan Babu told him.

'Date of birth?'

'Sixteenth August.'

'Hm. Leo. All right, what can I do for you?'

'Well . . . I am a writer, you see. I have thought of three names for my next novel, but I can't decide which would be the best.'

'What are these names?'

'*Hullabaloo in Honolulu, Hell in Honolulu,* and *The Honolulu Holocaust.*'

'Hm. Please wait.'

Mr Bhattacharya wrote the names down in his ledger and began making some calculations. Then he said, 'Your name adds up to twenty-one. Your date of birth and the month you were born in gives us six. Both can be divided by three. I suggest you use the third title. When is your book coming out?'

'The first of January.'

'No, make it the third. Anything to do with the book must be divisible by three.'

'I see. And . . . er . . . how will it . . . I mean . . . ?'

'Don't worry. It'll sell well.'

Lalmohan Babu smiled, paid a hundred rupees and came out with us.

'A bit expensive, wasn't he?' I asked.

'Maybe. But I don't mind. I'm positive this book's going to be a hit. Oh, I can't tell you how relieved I feel!'

'Does that mean you'll come back to Mecheda every time you write a book?'

'Why not? It would only mean two visits every year. When there is a guarantee of success . . .' I said nothing more.

We got into the car once more and set off for Baikunthapur. It took us twenty minutes to reach the home of the Niyogis. 'Niyogi Palace', said a marble slab at the gate.

That the house was old was easy enough to see. One portion of it looked as though it had recently been repaired and restored. Perhaps that was where the family lived. A long drive lined with palms ended in a large portico. Nobo Kumar came out, beaming.

'Welcome!' he said. 'I'm so glad you came. I was afraid you might change your mind. Do come in. This way—'

We were taken to the first floor. 'I've told my father about you. He'll be very pleased to meet you,' Nobo Kumar informed us.

'Who else lives in this house?' Feluda asked idly.

'Only my parents. My mother suffers from asthma, you see. The country air suits her much better. Then there is Bankim Babu. He used to be Baba's secretary. Now he's become a kind of manager. Besides these people, there are a few servants, that's all. I visit occasionally. I was going to come with my family a few days later, for Puja. But a guest arrived, so I came earlier than the others. My uncle from Rome—Chandrasekhar's son—is visiting, you see. I thought Baba might need my help.'

'Were you in touch with your uncle all these years? I mean, after

Chandrasekhar left home?'

'No. This is his first visit. I think he's here to sort out his share in our property.'

'Did Chandrasekhar die?'

'We don't know. We haven't heard from him—or of him—for years and years. So I assume the law would regard him as dead.'

'Did he live here when he returned from Rome?'

'Yes.'

'Why didn't he live in Calcutta?'

'That would not have made any difference. He had to travel a lot. His clients were spread all over the country. It didn't really matter where he lived.'

'Do you remember having seen him?'

'I was six when he left. All I can remember is his affection for me.'

We were ushered into the living room. A beautiful, huge chandelier hung from the ceiling. I had never seen anything like it before. On one of the walls was a life-size portrait of a bearded man. He wore an achkan; a sword hung at his waist; on his head was a turban from which glittered pearls and rubies. The portrait dominated the whole room.

'My great-grandfather, Anant Nath Niyogi,' explained Nobo Kumar. 'Chandrasekhar painted it soon after he got back from Italy. By that time Anant Nath had forgiven him for having left the country and married an Italian woman.'

'Why,' I had to ask, 'does it say "S. Niyogi" at the bottom? His name was Chandrasekhar, wasn't it?'

'Yes. But people in Italy called him Sandro. So he used "S" in his signature.'

There were other smaller paintings by S. Niyogi in the room. Each bore evidence of the painter's skill. He had undoubtedly been blessed with a rare gift.

A bearer came in with glasses of sherbet. Feluda picked one up, and said, 'That article said something rather interesting about your great-uncle's private collection of paintings. Apparently, he had a painting by a world famous artist, but he had told Bhudev Singh, the writer, not to mention it to anyone since no one would believe him if he did. Do you happen to know anything about it?'

'There is a painting, yes. Everyone in our family knows about it. It's a painting of Jesus Christ. But I couldn't tell you if the artist was world famous or not. You can see it for yourself when you go to the studio. That is where it has always hung.'

'Bhudev Singh himself must know whose work it is.'

'Yes, I'm sure he does. He and Chandrasekhar were very close friends.'

'Doesn't your uncle know anything about it? After all, he's Chandrasekhar's son, isn't he?'

Nobo Kumar shook his head. 'He didn't get on very well with his father, from what I gather. Besides, he doesn't seem interested in art at all.'

'That means no one from your family would have any idea about the real value of the painting?'

'Yes, that's right. My father's interest lies in music. He wouldn't know any more about paintings and artists than I would. And the same applies to my brother, Nondo Kumar.'

'Why, does he have a lot to do with music as well?'

'No, his passion was acting. You see, we have a travel agency in Calcutta. Our father wanted Nondo and me to be partners. Everything was fine, until 1975 when Nondo left suddenly for Bombay. Apparently, he knew somebody from Hindi films who got him a few roles. He's been living in Bombay since then.'

'Is he successful?'

'I don't think so. I remember seeing his pictures in film magazines soon after he left, but nothing recently.'

'Are you in regular touch?'

'No, not at all. All I know is that he lives in a flat on Napean Sea Road. I think the building's called "Sea View". I redirect his mail occasionally, that's all.'

We finished our drink and went down to meet Nobo Kumar's father. He was sitting on an easy chair on a large veranda, holding a paperback very close to his eyes. Nobo Kumar introduced us.

'Have you told him about Thumri?' the old gentleman asked.

'Yes, Baba,' Nobo Kumar replied with a slightly embarrassed air, 'but Mr Mitter and the others are simply paying us a visit, they're not here on business.'

Soumyasekhar frowned. 'I cannot see why you aren't taking the matter seriously. Is it just because Thumri was a dog? Don't you think a heartless killer like that should be punished? Not only did he kill a poor, defenceless animal, but he also threatened my servant. I am sure of it, or he wouldn't have run away. The whole business strikes me as decidedly fishy, and I'm sure any detective worth his salt would find it a challenge. What do you say, Mr Mitter?'

'You are absolutely right,' Feluda replied.

'Good. I am glad to hear it, and shall feel gladder if you can actually catch the culprit. Oh, by the way,' he turned to his son, 'have you met Robin Babu?'

'Robin Babu? Who is he?' Nobo Kumar sounded surprised.

'He is a journalist. Quite young. He wrote to me about coming here to do research on Chandrasekhar. He's got a fellowship or a grant or something, to write Chandrasekhar's biography. Well, he turned up a couple of days ago, and has already collected a lot of material. He might even go to Italy. He talks to me every morning for about an hour, and records everything. A smart young man. I like him.'

'Where is he now?'

'In his room, I expect. I gave him one of the bedrooms on the ground floor. He'll be around for another ten days, I think. He works very hard.'

'I had no idea you had two guests to look after!'

'Well, to tell you the truth, neither requires any real looking after. I hardly ever get to see my cousin from Rome; and when I do, he speaks very little. I've never seen anyone quite so taciturn.'

'Has he talked about his father at all?'

'No. When Chandrasekhar returned to India, his son was in his late teens. The relationship between father and son was not a happy one, it seems. I think Rudra avoids talking to me because he thinks I might ask awkward questions. It is strange, isn't it, that I do not know my own first cousin? He had to show me his passport to prove his identity!'

'Was it an Indian passport?'

'Yes, I think so.'

'You did look properly, Baba, didn't you?'

'Yes, of course. But I needn't have bothered. You only have to look at him to see the family resemblance.'

'He's arrived only to claim his share in the property, hasn't he?' Feluda remarked.

'Yes, and there shouldn't be any problem in his getting what is rightfully his. He didn't even know that his father left home a second time. I told him when he wrote to me from Rome that there had been no news of his father for ten years. That was when he decided to come.'

'Does he appear to know anything at all about that famous painting Chandrasekhar brought with him?' Feluda was clearly still curious.

'No. Rudrasekhar is an engineer. He knows nothing of art. But . . . someone else is interested in that painting.'

'Who?' Nobo Kumar looked up.

'A man called Somani. Bankim would have his details. He was acting on behalf of someone from Europe—or was it America?—who had, apparently, offered a lakh for the painting. Somani was prepared to pay me twenty-five thousand right away. If the buyer was satisfied it wasn't a fake, he'd pay me the balance, he said.'

'When did this happen?'

'A couple of weeks ago, before Rudra's arrival. I told Somani he d have to wait until Rudra got here, as he was the rightful owner. I could not sell it.'

'Did Somani come back?' Feluda asked.

'Oh yes. A most persistent man. He talked to Rudra this time.'.

'Do you know what was said?'

'No. All I can tell you is that if Rudra wants to sell any of his father's belongings, he has every right to do so.'

'Yes, but surely not before all legal formalities have been completed?'

'No, he'll certainly have to wait until then.'

We met the other guests at lunch. Robin Babu looked vaguely familiar. Perhaps I had seen his photo in some journal. He was clean-shaven, and of medium height. He had very bright eyes.

'Oh, I've discovered such a lot of curious facts about Chandrasekhar,' he told us. 'There is a wooden case in his studio, packed with the most interesting stuff.'

'Rudrasekhar's presence must be an additional help, I'm sure?' said Feluda. 'He can tell you about Chandrasekhar's life in Italy.'

'I haven't yet talked to him since he has been so busy himself. I am, at the moment, trying to find out what happened after Chandrasekhar returned home.'

I looked at Rudrasekhar. He said, 'Hm,' and no more.

In the evening, we set off for a walk with Nobo Kumar, to look at some local old, beautiful terracotta temples. But we were only halfway there, walking through a large field, when a storm broke out. We tried running back to the house, but it started to rain even before we reached the front gate. Lightning ripped the sky, and we could hear frequent thunder. By the time we stepped into the house, we were all drenched. Great sheets of water were cascading down from the heavens.

'I have never,' Lalmohan Babu declared, 'seen it rain like this. Isn't there something dramatic about it?'

He was right. Having lived in a city all my life, I hadn't seen such torrential rain out in the open, either. It soon became clear that the rain was not going to stop in a hurry. And that meant we could not return to Calcutta.

Nobo Kumar wasn't the least bit put out. 'These sudden storms and heavy rain are not unusual,' he told us. 'All it means is that you must spend the night here.'

'But . . .' Feluda began. Nobo Kumar cut him short, 'It's not a problem at all, believe me. We have at least ten spare bedrooms in this house, all fully furnished. And I could even lend you some clothes. Don't worry about a thing!'

We were given two adjoining rooms on the ground floor. Both rooms were huge, with matching furniture. Lalmohan Babu climbed onto his massive bed and said, 'Aaah . . . this reminds me of that tale in which a common man becomes an emperor for a day. *Arabian Nights,* isn't it?'

I wasn't sure, but I could see what he meant. The white marble dishes in which lunch was served were fit for a king, I had thought. At night, the marble dishes disappeared. We were served dinner on plates made of pure silver.

'We didn't get to see Chandrasekhar's studio,' said Feluda over dinner. 'I'll take you there tomorrow morning,' Nobo Kumar replied. 'It's directly above your room.'

The rain stopped just as we were getting ready to go to bed. I looked out of the window. A few stars were peeping out from torn shreds of clouds. There was something eerie about the silence outside. Our room faced the garden. A number of fireflies buzzed outside, and from somewhere came the faint sound of a transistor radio.

Lalmohan Babu rose at half-past ten and went to his room. There was a communicating door between his room and ours, which he thought was 'convenient'.

It was through this door that he slipped in in the middle of the night and woke Feluda. I woke only a few seconds later.

'What's the matter?' Feluda was asking when I opened my eyes, 'So late—'

'Sh-h-h-h! Listen carefully!'

We both pricked our ears.

Tap, tap, tap, tap, tap.

The noise was coming from above. There was someone walking upstairs. At one point, I thought I heard a click. The noise subsided in about three minutes, and silence fell once more.

Sandro Niyogi's studio was above our room, Nobo Kumar had said. Was someone in there?

'You two wait here,' Feluda whispered, 'I'll be right back.' He went out, barefoot. Lalmohan Babu and I sat on the bed, holding our breath until he came back in five minutes. It felt like five hours. Somewhere, a clock struck two.

'Did you see anyone?' asked Lalmohan Babu.

'Yes. I saw him come down the stairs.'

'Who was it?'

'The journalist. Robin Babu.'

FOUR

The next morning, Feluda said nothing about the previous night's experience. All he asked Nobo Kumar over breakfast was, 'Doesn't the studio stay locked?'

'Yes, normally it does. But we've had to keep it unlocked lately. Robin Babu works in there. Rudrasekhar, too, visits the studio occasionally. So we don't bother with locking it any more. Baba has got the key.'

He took us to the studio after breakfast. It was on the second floor. The wall facing north was made almost entirely of glass, since the light from that end was supposed to be the best for an artist to paint by.

There were stacks of paintings on the floor. Stretched white canvases were scattered in a corner, together with paints, brushes and palettes. An easel stood by the window. It looked as though the artist had stepped out only for a minute.

'Everything he used appears to have been brought from abroad,'

Feluda remarked, testing some of the paints and a bottle of linseed oil, 'and they are still in reasonably good condition. Rudrasekhar could make a lot of money simply by selling these. Any Indian artist would jump at the chance to buy such good quality stuff.'

A number of portraits hung at the far end. Nobo Kumar pointed at one of these and said, 'That's Chandrasekhar's self-portrait.'

A handsome man with sharp features stared from the canvas, dressed in western clothes. Long, black hair rippled down to his shoulders. He had a beard and a moustache, very neatly trimmed.

'Yes, that is the picture that was published with the article,' said Feluda.

'You may be right,' Nobo Kumar replied. 'Baba told me Bhudev Singh's son had come down for a day to take pictures for his father's article.'

'Where is that famous painting?'

'This way.' Nobo Kumar took us to the far corner.

The painting of Jesus hung from a golden frame. There was a crown of thorns on his head. His eyes held a faraway look. One hand was placed across his chest. A halo encircled his head and, beyond it, were trees and hills and a river. The sky could be glimpsed behind the hills. It appeared to be overcast and held a hint of lightning. The whole effect was most impressive.

We stared at the painting for a whole minute. None of us knew anything about it—not even the artist's name—and yet, it seemed to have a mysterious captivating power.

'Do you think you could give us a copy of your family tree?' Feluda asked as we came out of the studio and made our way downstairs. 'Starting with Anant Nath Niyogi,' he added, 'and preferably with all important dates related to Chandrasekhar.'

'That's easy. I'll tell Bankim Babu. He's a most efficient man. He'll get it ready in ten minutes.' This struck me as a very good idea. I was getting quite confused trying to remember how the various Niyogis were related to one another. A family tree was the best answer.

'And . . . one more thing,' Feluda said. 'Could Bankim Babu also give me Mr Somani's address, if he's got it?'

'Yes, of course.'

Bankim Babu turned out to be a middle-aged man, jovial and intelligent. A family tree was no problem, he said, for he had already had one made for Robin Babu. He produced a copy immediately, together with the business card Mr Somani had left. It said: 'Hiralal

Somani, 23 Lotus Towers, Amir Ali Avenue, Calcutta'.

Bankim Babu handed it over to Feluda, and stood silently. I saw him open his mouth to speak, then he shut it again.

'What is on your mind, Bankim Babu?' Feluda smiled.

'I have heard about you. Er . . . you are an investigator, aren't you?'

'Yes.'

'Will you come back here again?'

'Certainly, if need be. Why do you ask?'

'No, nothing. I mean, that's fine. There was a . . . never mind, I'll talk to you later.' He moved away.

'I wonder what that was all about,' I said, somewhat mystified.

Feluda grinned. 'I think,' he said, 'Bankim Babu wanted my autograph, but felt too embarrassed to ask.'

It was now time to leave. 'Thank you very much for everything,' Feluda said to Nobo Kumar as we got into our car, 'What I've seen in your house is really most interesting. You wouldn't mind, would you, if I made a few enquiries elsewhere?'

'No, no, not at all.'

'I'd like to meet Bhudev Singh of Bhagwangarh. He should be able to tell us how much that Jesus is worth.'

'All right, go ahead and see Bhudev Singh, anytime you want. I have no objection whatsoever.'

'Thank you. And, Mr Niyogi, your father, I think, is quite right. Do not ignore the matter of your dog's death. I can smell the most complex mystery in the whole case.'

'You're right, I found it incredibly cruel.'

Nobo Kumar and Feluda exchanged cards. 'Goodbye,' he said, waving from the front door, 'give me a ring, if you like, or come over any time. And please let me know what Bhudev Singh tells you!'

'I didn't even know there was a place called Bhagwangarh,' said Lalmohan Babu on our way back to Calcutta.

'I believe it's in Madhya Pradesh, but I'm not sure,' Feluda replied. 'I'll have to check with Pushpak Travels.'

'I haven't seen much of MP,' Lalmohan Babu observed.

'I don't think you'll get to see much this time. All I intend doing is meeting Bhudev Singh and getting a few facts straight. We mustn't neglect Baikunthapur for long.'

'Why? What's so special about Baikunthapur?'

'Did you look at Rudrasekhar's feet?'

'Why, no!'

'Did you notice the way Robin Babu ate?'

'No, of course not. Why should—?'

'Besides, I'd like to know what the man was doing in the studio at 2 a.m., what was it that Bankim Babu really wanted to say, why did their dog get killed . . . there are a lot of questions that need to be answered, Lalmohan Babu.'

'If one has a good watchdog,' I ventured to say, 'burglars might wish to get rid of it before breaking into a house.'

'Good point. But the dog was killed on 28 September, and today is 5 October. There has been no burglary in all this time. Besides, I don't think an eleven-year-old fox terrier could be all that good as a watchdog.'

'I have only one regret,' Lalmohan Babu sighed.

'What is that?'

'I know so little about art.'

'Don't let that worry you. All you need to know at the present moment is that if an unknown painting by a famous artist from the past was put up for sale, it could quite easily fetch a couple of lakhs, or much more.'

'Really?'

'Yes, really.'

'You mean the Niyogis have had something so valuable for years and years, and no one is aware of it?'

'Yes, that is exactly what I am saying; and that is why we need to go to Bhagwangarh.'

FIVE

Bhagwangarh did indeed turn out to be in Madhya Pradesh. 'You will have to go to Nagpur,' said our travel agent, 'and take a meter gauge train to Chhindwara. Bhagwangarh is 45 km to the west of Chhindwara.'

Feluda promptly sent a telegram to Rajah Bhudev Singh, explaining why he wanted to meet him. The Rajah's reply arrived the next day. We were most welcome, he said. If we could let him know the date and time of our arrival, he would send a car to meet us at

Chhindwara.

Feluda rang the travel agent again. 'If you're in a hurry to get there,' said Mr Chakravarty of Pushpak Travels, 'there is a flight to Nagpur tomorrow morning. It leaves at 6.30 a.m. and reaches Nagpur at 8.15. You could catch a train to Chhindwara at 10.30, and get there by 5 p.m.'

'That sounds fine, but how do we get back?'

'Well, you could spend the whole day in Bhagwangarh the day after tomorrow, and catch an overnight train from Chhindwara. It will bring you to Nagpur at 5 a.m. the following morning. The Nagpur-Calcutta flight is at 8 a.m. You could be back in Calcutta by half-past ten.'

Feluda told Mr Chakravarty to go ahead with the bookings and sent another telegram to Bhudev Singh.

'Since we are free all day today,' he said, 'let's go and meet Mr Somani.' Somani was available, as it turned out, and willing to meet us in the evening at 5.30 p.m.

We turned up on the dot at his flat in Lotus Towers, Amir Ali Avenue. A bearer showed us into his living room. A quick look around told us the man liked collecting a variety of things, many of which were obviously expensive. But there was no discernible order in the way they were displayed. Each object seemed to have been dumped anyhow.

We were kept waiting for ten minutes. Then Mr Somani wafted into the room, which was filled immediately with the smell of cologne. He had clearly been in the shower when we arrived. He was dressed in white trousers and a white kurta. Light Kolhapuri chappals were on his feet. There were touches of grey in his carefully brushed hair, though the thin moustache he sported was completely black.

He offered cigarettes to Lalmohan Babu and Feluda, then lit one himself and said, 'Yes, gentlemen, how can I help you?'

'We need some information,' Feluda began.

'Yes?'

'You went to Baikunthapur recently, didn't you?'

'Yes, I did.'

'To buy a painting?'

'Yes.'

'But the owner refused to sell, is that right?'

'Yes.'

'Could you tell me how you got to know about the painting?'

Mr Somani seemed to stiffen at this question. He gave Feluda a look that simply said, 'That's none of your business'. But he replied civilly enough.

'I did not get to know about it at all. Someone else did. I went at his request.'

'I see.'

'Why, can you get that painting for me? But it must be genuine. If it turns out to be a piece of forgery, you won't get a paisa.'

'How would you tell if it's genuine or not?'

'The buyer would know. He has been buying paintings for the last thirty-five years. He knows his business, believe me.'

'Is he a foreigner?'

Mr Somani continued to stare steadily at Feluda through a haze of smoke. His jaw set at the last question but, a second later, he gave a slight smile and said, 'Why should I divulge this information, tell me? Do you really take me to be a fool?'

'All right.'

Feluda was about to rise, but Mr Somani went on speaking. 'If you can get me that painting, I'll give you a commission.'

'I'm glad to hear that.'

'Ten thousand in cash.'

'And then you'll sell it for ten lakhs?'

This time, Mr Somani did not reply. But his gaze did not waver.

'Why should I come to you, Mr Somani, if I could lay my hands on that painting? I'd go straight to the buyer!' said Feluda.

'Yes, certainly; but only if you knew where to go.'

'I'd find my way, if I had to . . . Well, Mr Somani, thank you for your time. We shall now leave you in peace.'

All of us got to our feet and began moving towards the front door.

'Goodbye, Mr Pradosh Mitter!' hissed Mr Somani, his tone implying that he was quite familiar with both Feluda's name and profession.

'Isn't there a certain carnivorous plant,' Lalmohan Babu asked when we were outside, 'that looks rather harmless and attractive, but swallows all insects that go near it?'

'Yes, there certainly is.'

'This man was a bit like that, wasn't he?'

Feluda rang Baikunthapur as soon as we got home. But Nobo Kumar said all was well, there had been no new development. Why was Feluda so anxious?

I didn't get a chance to ask since Lalmohan Babu had, by this time, happily settled down on a settee in our living room, and brought out a book from his bag. He placed it on the centre table with a loud thump. *History of All Western Art*, said its title.

'What is that, Lalmohan Babu?' Feluda asked with a smile.

'A very useful book, I tell you! I decided not to let myself feel left out, you see. When you start talking to Bhudev Singh about art and artists, now I'll be able to take part in the conversation.'

'I see. Well, you needn't read the whole book. Just read the chapter on the Renaissance.'

'Renaissance . . . yes, here it is. Er . . . what does it mean exactly?'

'The fifteenth and sixteenth centuries. Nearly two hundred years of rebirth and reawakening in Italy. That's what the word means.'

'Why rebirth?'

'Because during this time there was a return to the ideology of the ancient culture of Greece and Rome. This had been suppressed in the Middle Ages. That is why it's called rebirth. It began in Italy, but soon spread to other parts of Europe; and it wasn't confined just to art and painting. A great many famous writers, musicians, scientists and politicians lived during this period—Copernicus, Galileo, Shakespeare, Da Vinci, Raphael, Michelangelo. A lot of new discoveries and innovations were made, including the printing press, which made education and communication a lot simpler.'

'Do you think that painting of Jesus was done by a Renaissance artist?'

'Yes, that's quite likely. It was certainly not painted before that period. If you look at paintings done in the Middle Ages, you'll see that all figures and objects have a stiff, lifeless quality about them. Later, in the Renaissance period, they become much more natural and lifelike.'

'This book mentions . . . my God, such a lot of names! . . . Botticelli . . . Giotto . . . Mantegna . . .'

'Yes, and you'll find at least thirty other names in Italy alone!'

'And to think a painting by one of these is hanging on a wall in Mr Niyogi's house! Just imagine!'

After dinner that night, Feluda took out the Niyogi family tree, and began studying it carefully. I peered over his shoulder. It looked like this:

Anant Nath Niyogi (1862-1941)

Suryasekhar (1888-1948) Chandrasekhar (1890-?)

Soumyasekhar (1913-) Rudrasekhar (1920-)

Nobo Kumar (1941-) Nondo Kumar (1944-) ?

There was another piece of paper. It said:

Chandrasekhar Niyogi
Born in Baikunthapur 1890
Graduation from Presidency College 1912
Travelled to Rome to study art in the Academy of Fine Arts 1914
Married Carla Cassini 1917
Birth of son, Rudrasekhar 1920
Carla died 1937
Returned to India 1938
Left home 1955
Present whereabouts unknown.

SIX

We left as scheduled the next day. By the time we reached Chhindwara, it was almost 6 p.m. A Mr Nagpal was waiting for us at the station in an old Chevrolet. He greeted us with a warm smile. We left immediately, and by a quarter to seven, we were in Bhagwangarh.

'I will show you to your rooms,' said Mr Nagpal. 'The Rajah will meet you at 7.30. I'll come and pick you up.'

Our rooms turned out to be as large and luxurious as any in a five-star hotel. 'Good heavens!' Lalmohan Babu exclaimed. 'My room here is five times the size of my bedroom back home. It's a pity we haven't got the time, or I'd have had a good, long soak in the bathtub.'

Mr Nagpal arrived exactly on time and took us to meet our host. Bhudev Singh was seated on a cane chair in a covered veranda. He had a quiet dignity about him, and looked younger than his age.

Feluda introduced us. Bhudev Singh smiled and invited us to sit down. I could smell Hasnuhana as I took a chair, which meant that there was a garden behind the veranda, but I could see nothing in the dark.

The conversation that followed turned out to be most interesting. True to his word, Lalmohan Babu did his best to make a contribution. It went thus:

Bhudev: How did you find my article?

Feluda: Very informative. Chandrasekhar would have remained unknown to us if it hadn't been for you.

Bhudev: The thing is, you see, we don't often give our artists the credit they deserve. So I thought I'd try and do something worthwhile before I died—after all, I am nearly eighty—and let people know what a very gifted artist Chandra was. I sent my son to Baikunthapur, and he got me a photo of his self-portrait.

Feluda: When did you first meet him?

Bhudev: Here, it's all noted in this diary. Let me see . . . yes, he came here to do my portrait on 5 December 1942. I had heard of him from the Nawab of Bhopal. Chandra had already done his portrait. He really had a wonderful skill.

Lalmohan: Oh, wonderful!

Feluda: Your article said he married an Italian woman. Do you know anything about her?

Lalmohan: Anything?

Bhudev: Chandra joined the Academy of Fine Arts in Rome. That was where he met Carla Cassini. She came from an aristocratic family. Her father was Count Alberto Cassini. Chandra and Carla fell in love, and she introduced him to her father. What many people didn't know was that Chandra had a fairly good knowledge of ayurvedic medicine, and he had carried a number of special herbs from here. As it turned out, Carla's father suffered from gout. Chandra's medicines worked on him like magic. It was not difficult after this for him to marry her. They got married in 1917. The Count's wedding gift to them was a painting.

Feluda: That famous painting of Jesus?

Lalmohan: Renaissance?

Bhudev: Yes, but how much do you know about it?

Feluda: Nothing at all. We've seen it, that's all. We think it was painted by a Renaissance artist.

Lalmohan: (muttering under his breath) Bottici . . . Davincelli . . .

Bhudev: Yes, you're right. But it was no ordinary artist. It was probably the best known artist in the last phase of the Renaissance—Tintoretto.

Lalmohan: Ooooooh!!

Feluda: Tintoretto? But isn't it true that there aren't too many paintings done wholly by Tintoretto?

Bhudev: Yes. Most known paintings were begun by him, and finished by others who worked in his studio or workshop. Many artists of those times worked like that. But this particular painting bears every evidence of Tintoretto's style. Chandra showed it to me. It had been with the Cassini family since the sixteenth century.

Feluda: That would make it totally invaluable, wouldn't it?

Bhudev: That's right. If the Niyogis decided to sell it, it's difficult to say how much they might get. Twenty-five lakhs, perhaps. May be even more.

Lalmohan: (drawing his breath in sharply) Aaaaaahh!!

Bhudev: That is why I didn't mention the painter's name in my article.

Feluda: Even so, someone went to Baikunthapur to make enquiries.

Bhudev: Who? Was it Krikorian?

Feluda: Why, no! Nobody by that name.

Bhudev: He is an Armenian. He had come to me. Walter Krikorian. Stinking rich. Has a business in Hong Kong and is a collector of paintings. Said he had an original Rembrandt as well as originals by Turner and Fragonard. He had heard of a Bosch that I happen to have, bought by my grandfather. He wanted to buy it from me. I didn't sell, of course. Then he said he had read my article. He was bragging so much that when he began to ask me about the painting in Baikunthapur, I couldn't resist showing off . So I told him the painter's name. He nearly fell off his chair. I said to him, 'Sorry, Mister, but you cannot buy that picture, either. Indians value their pride of possession far more than money. The Niyogis are fairly wealthy, anyway. You couldn't tempt them.' He then said he would get hold of that painting by hook or by crook. 'I'll go there myself,' he said. So I thought . . . but perhaps he had to go back to Hong Kong on business. He has an agent—

Feluda: Hiralal Somani?

Bhudev: Yes, yes.

Feluda: He's the one who went to Mr Niyogi's house.

Bhudev: He's a very cunning man. They must handle him with care.

Feluda: But that painting now belongs to Chandrasekhar's son. He's in Baikunthapur at this moment.

Bhudev: What! Chandra's son has come back to India? I didn't know this!

Feluda: We saw him.

Bhudev: I see. Well, he can, of course, claim his father's property. But I don't like the idea, Mr Mitter.

Feluda: Why?

Bhudev: I know about Chandra's son, and how much pain he caused his father. Chandra never mentioned it to his family, but he told me. His son had become a follower of Mussolini. He was at the height of his power then. Most Italians worshipped him. But certain intellectuals—writers, artists and musicians—fiercely opposed his ideas. Chandra was one of them. When his own son went and joined Mussolini's party, he was deeply distressed. Carla had died of cancer only a year earlier. After a while, he just could not take it any more and came back home. He refused to stay in touch with his son. And now the same son is in his house! What is he like? He should be around sixty.

Feluda: Yes, he's sixty-two. He seems quite strong and agile. Doesn't talk much.

Bhudev: Possibly because he's too ashamed to speak of himself. Perhaps he's realized how disappointed his father was with him—so much so that, in the end, he left his home, his career, everything. We used to have arguments about this. I kept telling Chandra he mustn't give up and turn his back on life, his talent was far too great to be wasted. But he did not listen to me.

Feluda: Did he stay in touch?

Bhudev: Yes, he used to write to me occasionally. But I haven't heard from him for a long time now.

Feluda: Do you remember when he last wrote to you?

Bhudev: Wait, I should have it somewhere . . . ah, here it is. A postcard from Hrishikesh, written in September 1977.

Feluda: Nineteen seventy-seven? That's only five years ago! That means—legally speaking—he's still alive!

Bhudev: Yes, of course. I say, that had never occurred to me!

Feluda: Rudrasekhar, therefore, cannot claim his father's property. At least, not yet.

The next day, Bhudev Singh showed us everything worth seeing in Bhagwangarh—the Bhawani temple, Laxmi Narayan Gardens, ruins of the old city, and even a herd of deer in a forest.

In the evening, he arranged to have us driven straight to Nagpur. Mr Nagpal turned up as we were leaving, and handed a piece of paper to Feluda. It bore the Armenian's name and address.

Bhudev Singh brushed aside our thanks for his wonderful hospitality. 'Mr Mitter,' he said, laying a hand on Feluda's shoulder, 'please see that the Tintoretto does not fall into the wrong hands.'

We reached home at around 11 a.m. the next day. The phone rang almost immediately as we stepped in. It was Nobo Kumar calling from Baikunthapur.

'Come here at once,' he said urgently, 'we've got problems.'

SEVEN

We left in half an hour.

'Do you think that painting's been stolen?' Lalmohan Babu enquired.

'Yes, that is what I am afraid of.'

'I wasn't really all that interested in the painting before. But now, having read that book and talked to the Rajah, I feel sort of personally involved with Tontiretto.'

Feluda was frowning, so deep in thought that he didn't even try to correct Lalmohan Babu.

This time, Lalmohan Babu's driver drove faster and we reached Baikunthapur in a couple of hours.

A few new people had arrived in the Niyogi household—Nobo Kumar's wife and two children.

But two people were missing. One of them was Rudrasekhar, who had left for Calcutta very early that morning.

The other was Bankim Babu.

He had been murdered.

Someone had struck him on his head with a heavy object. Death must have been instantaneous. His body was found by a servant in the studio. The police surgeon had placed the time of death between 3 and 5 a.m.

'I rang you first,' said Nobo Kumar, 'but you appeared to be out. So I had to inform the police.'

'You did right,' Feluda said. 'But tell me, is the picture still here?'

'That's what's so strange. Mind you, it's easy enough to see who the killer might be. I had found his behaviour extremely suspicious right from the start. He was clearly in need of money, but to go through the legal system would have taken at least six months, so I guess . . .'

'No. It would have taken much longer. I learnt from Bhudev Singh he had heard from Chandrasekhar only five years ago.'

'Really? Well, in that case, his son has no legal rights at all.'

'That wouldn't stop him from stealing, would it?'

'But that's the whole point! He didn't steal the picture. It's still hanging in the same spot.'

'That is most peculiar,' Feluda had to admit. 'What do the police say?'

'They are still asking questions. The main thing now is to catch our departed guest. Last night, I was here with my family, my parents, Robin Babu and our servants. I didn't see Rudrasekhar at dinner.'

'I am curious about Robin Babu.'

'He seems all right. He normally works in his room until two in the morning. Our bearer brings him his morning tea at eight. Rudrasekhar used to get up at the same time. But today, while Robin Babu was still in his room, Rudrasekhar had gone. He left at six-thirty, apparently. With him went his artist.'

'What artist?'

'An artist arrived the day you left, at Rudrasekhar's invitation, to assess the value of everything in the studio. I suspect he wanted to sell the whole lot.'

'I assume he didn't speak to you before he left?'

'No, not a word to me or anyone else. Our chowkidar saw him leave. At first I thought he had just gone up to speak to his lawyers. But now I'm sure he's not going to come back.'

'May I see his room?'

'Certainly. It's through here.'

We were sitting in a room on the ground floor. A door on our right opened into a room that had been given to Rudrasekhar. It looked like something straight out of a film, set in the nineteenth century. The bed and the stands for hanging a mosquito net, the writing desk and the dressing table were all old, the likes of which would be difficult to find nowadays.

'This room was originally my grandfather, Suryasekhar Niyogi's,' Nobo Kumar informed us. 'In his old age, he couldn't climb stairs at all. So he stayed on the ground floor permanently.'

'The bed hasn't been made yet,' Feluda observed.

'The morning's been so chaotic! I bet the maid who usually makes beds simply forgot her duties.'

'I wouldn't blame her. Who's got the next room?'

'That is . . . was . . . Bankim Babu's.'

There was a communicating door between the two rooms, but it appeared to be locked. We trooped out and entered the other room through another door. This room looked much more lived in. Clothes hung from a rack, under which were some shoes and chappals. A table stood in a corner, piled high with books, papers, writing material and a Remington typewriter. A few framed photos hung on the wall. No one had bothered to make the bed in this room, either.

Feluda suddenly strode forward and stood by the bed. Then he slipped his hand under the mosquito net and lifted the pillow. A small blue travelling alarm clock lay under it.

'Hey, I used to do this when I was in school,' Lalmohan Babu said casually. 'I used to set the alarm very early in the morning, particularly before my exams, and place it under my pillow, so it didn't wake others.'

'Hm,' said Feluda, looking at the clock. 'Bankim Babu set the alarm at 3.30 a.m.'

'Half-past three? That early?' Nobo Kumar sounded amazed.

'Yes, and that was when he probably went to the studio. I believe he was suspicious of something. He tried to tell me about it the last time I was here, but then seemed to change his mind.'

Nobo Kumar offered to take us to the studio where the murder had taken place. Before we could move, however, his children burst into the room and grabbed Lalmohan Babu's hands. 'Are you the famous Jatayu? Hey, we've read all your books!' they exclaimed. 'Come on, tell us a story!'

They dragged him back to the front room. Lalmohan Babu couldn't help feeling flattered. He smiled and beamed, forgetting for the moment the rather sombre atmosphere in the house. But, as it turned out, he wasn't quite as good at telling stories as he was at writing them. We left him there, struggling to get a few sentences together before the children interrupted with, 'No, no, no! That's from *The Sahara Shivers*!' or, 'We know that one. It's in *The Vampire of Vancouver*!'

Nobo Kumar took Feluda and me to the studio on the second floor.

Feluda stepped in, but stopped short, staring at a small table kept in the centre of the room.

'Wasn't there a bronze statue on this one?' he asked. 'The figure of a man on horseback?'

'Yes, you're right.' Inspector Mondol took it away to check it for fingerprints. He seemed to think that was what had been used to kill Bankim Babu.'

'I see.'

The three of us walked slowly towards the painting of Jesus. It seemed to have a special glow today. Had it been cleaned?

Feluda strode right up to the picture and peered at it closely for a few moments. Then he asked a totally absurd question.

'Did they have green flies in Italy during the Renaissance?'

'Green flies in Italy? What on earth do you mean?'

'Yes, the little green flies that buzz around lamps, especially after heavy rain. That's what I mean, Mr Niyogi. Did they exist in Venice in the sixteenth century?'

'I wouldn't know about Venice. But we've certainly had them here in Baikunthapur. Why, even yesterday—'

'In that case, two questions come to mind. How come two little insects are stuck in the totally dry paint of an ancient painting, and second, why did they get into a room which was supposed to be in total darkness all through the night? I mean every night?'

'Oh my God! What are you saying, Mr Mitter?'

'This is not the original painting. In the original, the face of Jesus did not have two small flies stuck on it; nor were the colours so bright. This painting is a copy; very cleverly done, no doubt, but a copy, nevertheless. It must have been painted at night, by candlelight, which explains why the insects came in and got stuck in the wet paint.'

Nobo Kumar's face went white.

'Where is the original?' he whispered.

'It's been removed. Possibly only this morning. And it's not difficult to guess who took it, is it?'

EIGHT

'Good afternoon, Mr Niyogi.'

'Good afternoon.'

Rudrasekhar came forward and took a chair opposite Mr Somani. A large, modern office desk lay between them. The room was air-conditioned, blocking out all noise from outside. An electronic clock on a shelf showed the time mutely.

Hiralal Somani spoke again. 'Have you got the painting?'

Instead of giving him a straight answer, Rudrasekhar asked another question. 'You wish to buy it for someone else, don't you?'

Hiralal did not reply. Rudrasekhar continued, 'I have come to collect the name and address of the actual buyer.'

Hiralal's eyes remained fixed on Rudrasekhar's face. 'I shall ask you once more, Mr Niyogi,' he said coldly. 'Have you got the painting?'

'I am not obliged to tell you that.'

'Then I am not obliged, either, to give you the information you want.'

'Think again, Mr Somani!'

Rudrasekhar leapt to his feet. In his hand was a revolver, aimed at Somani. 'Tell me, Mr Somani,' his breath came in short gasps, 'I need to know. I want to contact the buyer. Today.'

Somani quickly leant forward, pressing with his right knee a white button fixed under the desk. A door behind Rudrasekhar opened immediately and two men slipped in.

Before he knew it, one of them had grabbed Rudrasekhar's right arm and taken the revolver from him. The other caught his left hand and twisted it behind his back.

'It's no use, Mr Niyogi. You know you can't escape. These two men will go with you and bring the painting from your hotel. I hope you won't be foolish enough to resist.'

Twenty minutes later, a taxi drew up outside a hotel on Sadar Street. Rudrasekhar, accompanied by the two men, emerged from it and walked in. It seemed as though he was merely taking a couple of friends to his room. One of them had his hand in his pocket, but no one could have guessed he was clutching a revolver.

They went into Room 19. The gun came out. Rudrasekhar realized there was absolutely nothing he could do. With a sigh, he opened a suitcase lying on the bed, and brought out a thin, flat board wrapped in a newspaper.

The man whose hands were free snatched it from him and unwrapped it quickly. The tranquil face of Jesus gazed at him. The man wrapped the painting again. Then, with calm deliberate movements, he took out a silk handkerchief from his pocket and tied it around Rudrasekhar's mouth. A second later, Rudrasekhar was lying flat on the floor, knocked unconscious. The two men tied him up with a nylon rope and left. All of this took less than five minutes.

It took them another fifteen minutes to get the packet to Somani. He glanced briefly at the painting, and handed it back to one of the men. 'Pack this properly,' he said. Then he turned to the other.

'I have to send an urgent cable. Go to the Park Street post office immediately and send it now,' he instructed, quickly writing on a sheet of paper. It said:

Mr Walter Krikorian
Krikorian Enterprises
14 Hennessey Street
Hong Kong

ARRIVING SATURDAY NINTH OCT.
—SOMANI

NINE

Inspector Mondol came in the evening—a slim, brisk and efficient man. He had heard of Feluda, as it turned out.

'You solved the case of that double murder in Kharagpur, didn't you? In 1978?' he asked.

I remembered the case well. A goonda had been hired to kill one of a pair of identical twins. He didn't want to take any risks, so he killed both. Feluda's name became quite well known after he solved this case.

'Yes,' Feluda replied. 'What do you think of the present case?'

'It's difficult to say. The chief suspect has run away, as you know. There is no doubt that he did it, but I am still doubtful about his motive.'

'Are you aware that the man walked away with a most valuable object?'

'What! Why, no one mentioned this before!'

'Well, Mr Niyogi realized it after you had gone. Er . . . I had something to do with this discovery.'

'I can believe that. What was it?'

'A painting. It was in the studio. Perhaps Bankim Babu caught the man in the act.'

'Yes, that would certainly give him a strong motive.'

'Have you questioned the journalist?'

'Yes, of course. To tell you the truth, I find it distinctly odd that two virtual strangers were staying in the same house as guests. But Robin Babu seemed perfectly straightforward. Besides, we found some fingerprints on that bronze statue. They didn't match his.'

'Did you try and trace Rudrasekhar's taxi? WBT 4122?'

'That's terrific, you've got quite a memory! Yes, we did find the taxi. It took Rudrasekhar from here to a hotel in Sadar Street. But he wasn't there. We're making enquiries at other hotels, but so far we haven't had any luck. If he wants to sell what he stole, he's most likely to do that in Calcutta, isn't he?'

'No, one can't be too sure about that.'

'Why not? You mean he may leave the city?'

'He may even leave the country.'

'You don't say—'

'I think there's a flight to Hong Kong today.'

'Hong Kong? It will become a case for Interpol if he goes to Hong

Kong. I couldn't do a thing if he left the country!'

'I'm not absolutely sure that that is where he's gone. But even if you cannot do anything to help, I've got to at least try and catch him.'

'You will go to Hong Kong?' Nobo Kumar failed to hide his surprise.

'I have to make a few enquiries first. Then I shall decide.'

'Well, if you do decide to go, let me know. I know a Bengali businessman there. Purnendu Pal. He and I were at college together. He runs a shop for Indian handicrafts. I believe he's doing quite well.'

'All right. I'll take his address from you.'

'I'll get him to come and meet you at the airport. If necessary, you can even stay at his flat.'

Inspector Mondol rose. 'Good luck!' he said. 'I'll keep you posted.'

He left. We returned to our room.

'Good,' said Lalmohan Babu, 'we'll get to use our passports at last!'

Two years ago, an Arab was murdered in Bombay. Feluda had been called in by his friend, Inspector Patwardhan. It had begun to look as though we would have to go to Abu Dhabi for investigations. So we got our passports made and were all set to go, when word came that the culprit had given himself up.

Lalmohan Babu had been sorely disappointed. 'We were so close to going abroad, Tapesh Bhai!' he had lamented. 'We've been to Kathmandu, I know, and of course Nepal is a foreign country. But to travel somewhere with your passport is . . . something, isn't it?'

That 'something' might happen this time. Looking excited, Lalmohan Babu began to make some observations on the crime rate in Hong Kong, but was interrupted by the sound of a small cough just outside the door.

'May I come in?' asked the voice of the journalist, Robin Chowdhury.

'Yes, please do,' said Feluda.

Robin Babu walked in. Once again, he made me think I had seen him somewhere before. But, for the life of me, I couldn't remember where it might have been.

'Have a seat,' Feluda offered him a chair.

'I believe you are an investigator?' he asked as he sat down.

'Yes, that's my profession.'

'The job of a biographer can sometimes be almost like a detective's. New pieces of information, like fresh clues, often shed a different light on events.'

'Why, did you discover something new about Chandrasekhar?'

'You see, I had taken two cases from the studio. Both were filled with letters, legal documents, old bills and catalogues. But, amongst these, I found this press cutting. Look!'

He held out a piece of an old and yellow newspaper. A few lines on it had been highlighted. This is what is said:

> La moglie Vittoria con il figlio Rajsekhar annunciano con profondo dolore la scomparsa del loro Rudrasekhar Niyogi.
>
> Roma, Juli 27, 1955

'Why, this is written in Italian!' Feluda exclaimed.

'Yes, but I consulted a dictionary and worked out what it meant. What it's saying is, "Wife Vittoria and son, Rajsekhar, announce with deep regret the loss of Rudrasekhar Niyogi."'

'You mean it's an announcement of his death?' Feluda frowned.

'What! Rudrasekhar dead?' Lalmohan Babu jumped up in surprise.

'So it seems. And he died in 1955. This also tells us he had married and had a son called Rajsekhar.'

'My God! What a villain that other man must be! I did have my suspicions, but never thought we'd find such irrefutable evidence. When did you find this?'

'Only this afternoon.'

'What a pity! If only you'd found it earlier . . .'

'Yes, I know. He did behave strangely, didn't he? Each time I asked him a question, he either didn't answer at all, or gave me the wrong answer. So I had actually stopped trying to get him to talk.'

'Anyway, please keep this to yourself for the moment. We've got to find the man. You've been a real help. Thank you very much.'

Robin Babu smiled and went out. Yes, he had given us a new lead. But . . . why did I still feel uncomfortable about him? And why did his shirt have bloodstains on one side?

I had to mention this to Feluda. Lalmohan Babu, too, had noticed the stains. 'Highly suspicious!' he proclaimed.

Feluda looked grave. All he said was, 'Yes, I saw it, too.'

We left Baikunthapur at around 7 p.m. Nobo Kumar did something totally unexpected just before we left. He thrust a white envelope into Feluda's hands and said, 'Please take this, especially if you go to Hong Kong. Treat this as an advance payment. After all, you are doing this for our family. One mustn't forget that.'

'Thank you so much.'

'I'll cable Purnendu tomorrow. If you do decide to go, just send a telegram to this address. He'll take care of everything.' Nobo Kumar handed a piece of paper to Feluda.

The envelope contained a cheque for five thousand rupees.

'How will you go about tracking down the impostor?' Lalmohan Babu asked in the car.

'It's going to be most difficult, especially if he's left the country.'

'How do we find out if he has?'

'We can't, for he'll obviously travel under a different name and a different passport. The one he had shown Nobo Kumar's father was undoubtedly a false one. It must have been easy to deceive an old man with bad eyesight.'

'What do we do then?'

'Well, as far as I can see, Mr Fake would have to contact Somani to get the name and address of the Armenian buyer. From what I've seen and heard of Somani, he'd never pass on the details to another soul. I think he'd try and get the painting somehow from Rudrasekhar and go to Hong Kong himself.'

'In that case we have to look for Somani's name on flights to Hong Kong!'

'Yes, our going would depend on whether or not we find his name on a passenger list.'

Lalmohan Babu quickly raised his eyes heavenward. I could tell he was sending up a silent prayer for a visit abroad.

'I say,' he said after a while, 'do you think we might have to learn Chinese?'

'Chinese? Are you aware how many letters there are in the Chinese alphabet?'

'No. How many?'

'Ten thousand. You could never speak the language unless you had plastic surgery done to your tongue.'

'Oh. I see.'

Feluda got to work the next morning. Only Air-India and Thai Airways ran flights to Hong Kong from Calcutta. The Air-India flight went every Tuesday; Thai Airways ran three flights a week—on Wednesdays, Fridays and Saturdays—but only up to Bangkok. One had to transfer to another aircraft to get to Hong Kong.

Today being Saturday, Feluda rang Thai Airways. They looked up their passenger list in five minutes.

Hiralal Somani had left for Hong Kong that morning.

The earliest flight we could take was on Tuesday, by which time Somani would undoubtedly have passed on the painting to the Armenian.

Was there any point in our following him?

We looked at each other in silence. Then Lalmohan Babu took out a small notebook and a pen from his pocket and began scribbling in it. I looked on in puzzlement and Feluda with an amused smile, until he finished and looked up. 'One hundred and fifty-six,' he said, putting away his notebook. 'Add one plus five plus six. That's twelve. Add two plus one. That's three. Well, it's all settled. Tintoretto's name adds up to three. I mean, if you substitute the letters with numbers.'

'What are you talking about?' I asked, even more mystified.

'Numerology, dear boy. "T" is the twentieth letter in the alphabet, "i" is the ninth . . . and so on. If you add it all up, you get 156, which finally gives you three. Now, if that is the case and I am going to be with you—considering the number three is supposed to bring me luck—our mission has got to be successful!'

'Bravo, Lalmohan Babu!' Feluda slapped him on the back. 'I did think a visit to Hong Kong was important, but I could never have found enough justification for it, the way you just did!'

TEN

We were booked to travel to Hong Kong by Air-India flight number 316. We had flown before in Boeing 707s and 737s. This was the first time we would travel in a jumbo jet.

As we got into the aircraft, it seemed impossible to see how such a huge plane would actually lift itself off the ground.

'Good God! Such a lot of people!' Lalmohan Babu exclaimed, looking around. 'All these passengers in the economy class alone would fill the Netaji Indoor Stadium!'

This struck me as an exaggeration, but certainly there were enough people to fill the balcony of a medium-sized cinema hall.

Feluda had already cabled Purnendu Pal. We were scheduled to reach Hong Kong the next morning at 7.45 a.m.

It was normal practice with Feluda to get some reading done about any new place he was going to visit. He had gone to a bookshop yesterday and bought a book on Hong Kong. I had leafed through it briefly, but what I saw in the glossy photos was enough to convince me that there could be few cities as lively and colourful as Hong Kong. Lalmohan Babu was bursting with excitement, but appeared to know very little about what to expect.

'Will we get to see the Wall of China?' he asked innocently.

'The Wall of China,' Feluda had to explain, 'is in the People's Republic of China, near Peking. Hong Kong is at least a thousand miles from Peking.'

Our plane took off on time. I noticed how smoothly it flew, especially since the weather outside was good. It reached Bangkok at midnight; but passengers to Hong Kong weren't allowed to get off the plane. So I promptly went back to sleep.

When I woke in the morning, I saw that we were flying over the sea. Gradually, little islands in the water became visible, standing out like the backs of giant turtles. As the plane began losing height, these grew larger and larger, and I realized many of them were really the tops of mountains submerged in water.

Soon, we were flying over real mountains. There were white dots among the green foliage on the mountains which, later, turned out to be massive highrise buildings, all built close to the hills. They glittered in the sun.

I had heard that landing an aeroplane at the Hong Kong airport called for special skill. The runway seemed to be stretched out on the water. Even a slight mistake could result in either a loud splash in the sea or a big crash in the mountains.

Luckily, neither of these things happened. The plane landed where it was supposed to, and then stopped before a terminal building. Two chutes on wheels came out and fitted perfectly with the two main exits of the plane. We could, therefore, walk through these and go straight into the terminal without having to go down a flight of stairs. Lalmohan Babu was completely round-eyed. 'This isn't exclusive to Hong Kong, Lalmohan Babu,' Feluda told him. 'All major airports in the world have this system.'

Since we did not have much luggage, it did not take us long to clear customs. We were out in less than half an hour. Just outside customs was a large group of people. One of them was holding a large board with 'P. Mitter' written on it. This must be Purnendu Pal. He was about the same age as Nobo Kumar—a man in his early forties, smart and well-dressed. Nobo Kumar had been right in saying his friend was doing well.

'Welcome to Hong Kong!' he said, leading us to his car. It was a dark blue German Opel. Feluda got in beside him, Lalmohan Babu and I climbed in at the back. 'The airport,' Mr Pal said, starting his car, 'is in Kowloon. I live and work in Hong Kong. So we have to cross the bay to get there.'

'We're really sorry to trouble you like this,' Feluda began. Mr Pal raised a hand to stop him.

'It's no trouble at all, I assure you. You can't imagine how happy it makes me feel to meet fellow Bengalis. There are quite a number of Indians in Hong Kong, but not too many people from Bengal.'

'Our hotel booking—?'

'Yes, I've arranged that. But let us first go to my flat. You are a detective, I believe?'

'Yes.'

'Are you here on business?'

'Yes. It shouldn't take more than a day. We intend taking the Air-India flight back to Calcutta tomorrow evening.'

'What exactly are you looking for, may I ask?'

'An Armenian. You see, a most valuable painting was stolen from Nobo Kumar's house and brought here. We suspect a man called Hiralal Somani has brought it here and will pass it on to a wealthy Armenian. It will sell for—I think—more than a million rupees.'

'What!'

'We have to recover that painting.'

'My goodness, this sounds like something out of a film! But where does this Armenian live?'

'I have his office address.'

'I see. Is Somani from Calcutta?'

'Yes. He arrived in Hong Kong last Saturday. Chances are, he's already sold that painting to the Armenian.'

'But that's terrible! What are you going to do?'

'All we can do is meet the buyer and explain the situation to him. He must be made to realize that it's not safe for him to have a stolen object in his possession.'

'Hm,' said Mr Pal, looking concerned.

Lalmohan Babu, too, was looking thoughtful.

'What's the matter?' I whispered.

'Can . . . can one say Hong Kong is like England?'

'No, how can you do that? England is in the West. This is the Far East.'

Feluda's sharp ears did not miss our conversation. 'Don't worry, Lalmohan Babu,' he said without turning his head. 'Tell your friends back home that Hong Kong is also known as the London of the East. I'm sure they'll be sufficiently impressed.'

'London of the East? Oh good. London . . . of the East . . . ah, very nice indeed . . . '

As he continued to mutter, our car suddenly slipped into a large tunnel. There were rows of lights on both sides, spreading an orangish glow inside. Mr Pal said we were passing through an under-water tunnel, and would emerge in the city of Hong Kong.

'Such a beautiful city, but why does its name sound like whooping cough?' asked Lalmohan Babu.

'Do you know what Hong Kong means?' Mr Pal said.

'Perfumed port,' Feluda replied. He must have learnt this from that book he bought yesterday.

A few minutes later, we came out of the tunnel. The entire port, with its vast collection of ships and boats of all shapes and sizes, lay on one side. Behind it was Kowloon, which we had just left.

On our left were endless skyscrapers. Some were offices, others hotels. Each had shops on its ground floor, stacked from floor to ceiling with the most tempting objects. I came to realize later that the whole city was like a colossal departmental store. There was apparently nothing that you couldn't get in Hong Kong.

A little later, we turned left and joined a high street. I had never seen anything like it before. A stream of humanity flowed down the pavement. The street was filled with buses, taxis, private cars and double-decker trams. Both sides of the street were lined with shops. Their signboards hung so closely together that it was difficult to see the sky. Since Chinese is written vertically, all the signboards hung in a vertical line.

Our car moved slowly in the traffic, giving us the chance to take in everything. I had seen crowded streets in Calcutta enough times, but everyone there moved slowly, as if they had all the time in the world.

Here, each person was in a hurry, trying to move as quickly as possible. Most of them were Chinese. But there were also a number of people from the West. From the way they carried their cameras, casting curious glances about them, it was easy to tell they were tourists.

At last, we came out of the high street and found ourselves in a relatively quiet area, on a street called Patterson Street. This was where Mr Pal lived, in a flat in a tall building with thirty-two floors. His flat was on the seventh.

As we were getting out, a black car shot past us and disappeared round the corner. I saw Feluda stiffen. That car had been behind us for some time, but could it actually have been following us deliberately? There was nothing we could do, anyway. So we followed Mr Pal in.

'Make yourselves comfortable,' Mr Pal said, ushering us into his living room. 'My wife and children are away—I took them back to Calcutta only a few weeks ago to attend a nephew's wedding—so please forgive me if there are lapses in my duties as host. What would you like to drink?'

'I think tea would be best, thank you.'

'You wouldn't mind tea bags, would you?'

'No, of course not.'

Mr Pal left to make the tea. Lalmohan Babu moved to the window to look at the view. There was a television in the room and a video player. Stacks of video cassettes, most of them of Hindi films, stood on a shelf. A small table beside these was littered with film magazines. Feluda picked up a few of these and began leafing through them. I seized this opportunity to ask him, 'Who was in the car, Feluda?'

'The man we're after.'

'What! Somani?'

'Yes.'

'How did he learn about our arrival?'

'Very simple. He did exactly what we had done—checked the passenger list. He must have been at the airport and followed us from there.'

Lalmohan Babu came back from the window. 'If he's already sold the painting, why should he still be interested in us?' he asked.

'That's what I'd like to know!' Feluda said.

Mr Pal came in with the tea. He set the tray down, saw what

Feluda was reading and laughed. 'What are you doing with those ancient magazines?'

'Oh, just glancing at them. Look, would you mind if I kept this issue of *Screen World?* It's a year old.'

'No, not at all. I never look at them myself. It's my wife who's passionately interested in Hindi films.'

'Thank you. Topshe, go and put this magazine in my bag. Mr Pal. when do offices open here?'

'They should be open in about ten minutes. You want to ring your Armenian friend, don't you? Do you have his number?'

'Yes,' Feluda took out his notebook, 'it's 5311686.'

'Hm. It's a Hong Kong number. Where's his office?'

'Hennessey Street. Number 14.'

'OK. I think you'll get him soon after ten.'

'Thanks. Tell me, which hotel are we booked in?'

'Pearl Hotel. Less than ten minutes if you go by car. But why are you in such a hurry to get to your hotel? Why don't you have lunch with me? There's a very good Cantonese restaurant just down the road. If your mission is successful today, tomorrow I shall take you to a restaurant in Kowloon and introduce you to something I bet you have never had before!'

'What is that?' Lalmohan Babu asked, sounding a little apprehensive. 'I've heard the Chinese eat cockroaches.'

'And many other things, Lalmohan Babu,' Feluda told him. 'Shark fins, monkey brains, and even dog flesh, at times.'

'No, what you'll taste is quite different, I mean fried snake,' said Mr Pal with a grin.

'S-s-s-nake?' Lalmohan Babu gasped.

'Yes. You can get snake soup, snake meat, fried snake, everything.'

'How does it taste?'

'Delicious. You must try it.'

'Ah . . . very well,' Lalmohan Babu replied, with a marked lack of enthusiasm.

Feluda rose. 'If you don't mind, Mr Pal, may I use your phone?'

'Yes, of course.'

Feluda dialled Krikorian's number.

'May I speak to Mr Krikorian?. . . Went out of town? When?. . . Last Friday?And he'll be back this evening? Thank you.'

Feluda replaced the receiver and looked at us.

'It can only mean,' said Mr Pal slowly, 'that Somani has still got the painting.'

'Yes, so it would seem. Now I am really glad we came.'

ELEVEN

We had lunch at Yung Ki restaurant. The food was heavenly.

'You needn't check into your hotel before three,' Mr Pal said. 'If you want to do any shopping, I suggest you do it now, although you may well have a little time tomorrow. Your flight isn't till 10 p.m., is it?'

'That's right. Yes, I would like to look at a few shops,' Feluda admitted.

'Let me take you to Lee Brothers. I know them well. You'll get good quality stuff, and at a reasonable price.'

Lalmohan Babu wanted to buy a pocket calculator. 'It might come in handy,' he said to me as an aside, 'to calculate the royalty from all my books.' He found what he wanted—a calculator so small and so flat that I failed to figure out where the battery went in. I bought a few rolls of film for Feluda's Pentax; and Feluda bought a mini Sony audio cassette recorder. 'From now on,' he told me, 'remember to switch this on when a new client visits us. It will make life a lot easier if we can record conversations.'

We returned to Mr Pal's flat at three. He couldn't take us to the hotel himself since he had to go to his shop. 'That's all right, Mr Pal,' Feluda said to him. 'You have already done so much for us. We'll take a taxi, don't worry.'

'All right. But do let me know how you get on. I'll be thinking of you!'

We came out of the building and found a taxi waiting just outside the front gate. Taxis in Hong Kong looked different. Instead of black and yellow, they were red and silver.

'Pearl Hotel,' said Feluda. The driver nodded and started the car.

Lalmohan Babu seemed unusually subdued. When I asked him why, he said it was because his mental horizon had spread enormously in a short span of time. 'If it spreads any further, I don't think I could cope!'

'What do you mean?'

'I had only seen Chinese workmen and Chinese shoemakers in

Calcutta. I would never have believed they could build a city like this if I hadn't seen it with my own eyes!'

Mr Pal had told us that the hotel was less than ten minutes from his flat. But our chauffeur kept driving for much longer than that. It was most puzzling. Feluda frowned, then raised his voice and said, 'We said Pearl Hotel!'

'Yes,' said the driver without turning his head. He was wearing dark glasses, so I couldn't see his eyes. Surely he had heard us right the first time? And surely there couldn't be more than one hotel by the same name?

The taxi passed through a number of small lanes and finally, after about twenty minutes, stopped at a street corner. There was no doubt that this was an area where only the Chinese lived, far removed from the cosmopolitan atmosphere of the high streets. The buildings were tall and narrow, and terribly congested. Heaven knew if the sun ever went in through those small windows. There were only a few small shops that bore no resemblance to the tempting departmental stores we had seen earlier. All of them had signboards written in Chinese, so there was no way of telling what the shops sold.

'Where is Pearl Hotel?' Feluda asked. The driver raised a hand to indicate that we'd have to go into the lane on our right. I looked at the meter. What it showed in Hong Kong dollars amounted to a hundred rupees. But there was nothing we could do except pay up.

Having done this, we picked up our luggage and turned to go. Even without looking at Lalmohan Babu, I could tell that he had turned visibly pale. Everything he had heard about the crime rate in Hong Kong must have been flashing through his mind.

We turned right. The lane was narrow and dark. But before anything else registered, shadows leapt out of the darkness and surrounded us. In the next instant, I felt a blow on my head and passed out.

When I came round, I found myself lying on the floor of a dingy room. Feluda was sitting on a wooden packing crate, smoking a Charminar. There was a funny smell in the room that made me want to close my eyes again and go to sleep. I learnt later that it was the smell of opium. Apparently, the British used to produce opium in India and sell it to the Chinese. This made the British rich, and the

Chinese got hooked.

Lalmohan Babu was still unconscious, but was beginning to stir. Our luggage had disappeared. There were four or five packing crates in the room, a cane chair that lay tilted to one side, and a Chinese calendar. Through a tiny window fairly high on the wall came a faint shaft of light, which meant that there was still some daylight left outside.

There were two doors, one on my right and the other in front of me. Both were closed. The only sound to be heard was the chirping of a bird. The Chinese, I had noticed elsewhere, were fond of keeping birds in cages.

'Wake up, Lalmohan Babu!' Feluda said. 'How long will you sleep?'

Lalmohan Babu opened his eyes and winced in pain. 'My God! What a horrific experience!' he exclaimed, sitting up with some difficulty. 'Where on earth are we?'

'In the massacre chamber,' Feluda replied calmly. 'It's just like one of your stories, isn't it?'

'My stories? Ho!'

Perhaps the act of saying 'Ho!' brought on a fresh twinge of pain, for he made a face. Then he lowered his voice slightly and said, 'What just happened to us beats anything I've ever written. I'll give up writing altogether, I swear. Enough is enough.'

'What! You mean you'll never write again?'

'No, never.'

'All right. Your statement has just been recorded, remember. You can't go back on your word.'

Feluda's mini cassette recorder was placed beside him. He pressed the replay button to show Lalmohan Babu his words had truly been taped.

'Somani is behind this, isn't he?' Lalmohan Babu asked.

'Undoubtedly. Let's just hope we get our bags back. They took the revolver. But I managed to save this recorder.'

'Are both those doors locked?'

'The front door is. The side one opens into a bathroom.'

'No chance of escaping through there, I suppose?'

'None. There is a window, but it's far too small.'

'Was that taxi driver planted by Somani?'

'Yes, probably.'

'But how could he be sure we'd take that same taxi? We could have taken another, or just walked!'

'If we did, I'm sure Somani would have made some other arrangement for us. It's no use talking about what might have happened, Lalmohan Babu.'

Lalmohan Babu sighed and lay down again. A minute later, I heard him humming under his breath. How could he sing at a moment like this? I strained my ears and caught the words: 'O Lord, my time has come/Take me ashore to the other world.' Did he really think he was about to die?

'What are you thinking of, Lalmohan Babu?' Feluda asked, raising an eyebrow.

'Strange . . . it's all so strange. I had no idea one could have a dream even after being knocked unconscious. Do you know what I saw? A number of monkeys were being sold, and a man was beating a drum and saying, "Perfumed monkeys from the Renaissance—two dollars each—all from the Renaissance—"'

There were footsteps outside. Someone was coming up a flight of stairs. The footsteps got louder and eventually stopped outside the front door. A key turned in the lock, and the door swung open.

A man in a dark suit came in, followed by two others. All were Indians. The first man turned out to be Hiralal Somani. His mouth was spread in a sly, insolent smile.

'Hello, Mr Mitter! How are you?'

'Just as you'd except me to be.'

'Don't worry, sir. I haven't imprisoned you for life. I'll let you go the minute my job is done.'

'I fail to see why you removed our luggage.'

'That was a mistake. Kanhaiya! Kanhaiya!'

One of the two men had disappeared somewhere. Now he came back. The other was standing behind Somani with a gun in his hand.

'Bring the luggage back,' Somani instructed the man called Kanhaiya. Then he turned to Feluda and added, 'I'm afraid you'll have to miss your dinner tonight. You can start eating again from tomorrow.'

Kanhaiya brought our bags and threw them into the room.

'Don't try and be difficult, Mr Mitter,' Somani warned. 'Radheshyam here has your revolver. He knows how to shoot, and will not hesitate to pull the trigger if need be. Besides, remember that this is Hong Kong, not Calcutta. No one knows you here. I shall leave you now, and come back tomorrow morning. I'll set you free then. Good night!'

The faint light coming in through the window had virtually gone. There was a broken lampshade in the room, but no bulb in it.

Hiralal left. Kanhaiya went to the door to close it.

'Kanhaiya! Kanhaiya!' Hiralal called from somewhere.

'Ji, huzoor,' said Kanhaiya and went out.

Radheshyam now turned to the door to finish what Kanhaiya had started to do and, in that instant, events suddenly took a different turn.

Feluda's shoulder bag was lying on the floor near his feet. He picked it up and threw it at the door with all his strength. It hit the back of Radheshyam's head. Before he could do anything, Feluda sprang to his feet and threw himself on Radheshyam. The revolver fell from his hand.

I lost no time in jumping up and joining Feluda. It took me only a second to pick up the revolver and aim it at Radheshyam. I had used airguns as a child. There was no question of missing at point blank range.

Radheshyam, however, was still struggling to get out of Feluda's grasp. It wasn't easy to hold him down for he was a tall and hefty fellow. Out of the corner of my eye I saw that Lalmohan Babu had picked up one of the packing crates and was dancing around the room, looking for a suitable opportunity to hit Radheshyam with it.

Such an opportunity came only a few seconds later. A corner of the crate struck Radheshyam's head, causing him to fall flat on his face with a groan. He then lay there, motionless. I noticed blood oozing out of his head. Feluda took the gun from me and quickly turned around to face the figure of Kanhaiya, who had returned to the room. Kanhaiya raised his hands without a word, clearly realizing the tables had turned.

'Take the bags outside,' Feluda said. Lalmohan Babu and I carried our luggage out of the room.

Radheshyam was still lying where he had fallen. One blow from Feluda now made Kanhaiya join his mate on the floor. By the time the men came round, we'd be totally out of danger.

There were stairs outside leading to the main exit of the building. Luckily, no one seemed to be about. We made our escape as swiftly as we could, and stepped out into the street.

There were neon signs everywhere. It seemed as though each one of the ten thousand letters in the Chinese alphabet was staring at us.

But this wasn't the main road. There were no trams or buses running on it. All it had were taxis, private cars and loads of people.

We got into the third empty taxi that sailed by. I asked Feluda as soon as we got in, 'When Somani's voice shouted for Kanhaiya, it was really your tape recorder doing a replay, wasn't it?'

'Yes, that's right. I had switched it on the moment Somani opened the door. Then I switched it off after I heard him call out to Kanhaiya. Something told me it might prove handy; and it did!'

'You're really brilliant!' said Lalmohan Babu with a great deal of feeling.

'Thank you, Lalmohan Babu, and your assistance is much appreciated.'

It took us ten minutes and seven dollars to get to the real Pearl Hotel. Feluda rang Mr Pal as soon as we had checked in.

'I was beginning to get worried,' said Mr Pal. 'I rang you at the hotel several times, but they said you hadn't arrived at all. What happened?'

'I'll tell you later. Can you come to the hotel right away?'

'Of course. I've got news for you, too.'

Mr Pal arrived in a few minutes. Feluda quickly explained what had happened. 'Oh, I'm proud of you!' Mr Pal said. 'Now let me tell you what I've learnt. I found Krikorian's home address in the telephone book. I have also discovered where Hiralal's staying.'

'How?'

'There are five other Somanis here. I began calling them one by one. It turned out that Hiralal is Keshav Somani's cousin. Keshav has a fabrics shop in Kowloon. That's where he lives, and Hiralal is staying with him. Krikorian is coming back this evening, isn't he? Hiralal will obviously attempt to transfer the painting to him today. I've posted Wong Soo outside Hiralal's house. Wong Soo works with me. A most capable and reliable young man. He was told to ring me if he saw a car leave Somani's house.'

'Where does Krikorian live?'

'Victoria Hill. A rather posh area, closer from here than it is from Kowloon. So if we left soon after Hiralal, we would get there before him. In fact, you could stop him on the way.'

Feluda shook Mr Pal's hand. 'That's absolutely wonderful. But did Wong Soo call you?'

'Yes. Just as I was leaving. He saw a man come out of the house carrying a thin, flat parcel. This man then got into a car and left.'

We shot out in Mr Pal's car in three minutes, and began going up a hill. The road was full of curves and bends and the higher we rose, the better it was to see the city of Hong Kong spread below us. Lalmohan Babu gaped at its million lights, the cars, the highrise buildings, the sea, and kept muttering under his breath, 'Dreamland, dreamland!'

Ten minutes later, Mr Pal said, 'This is the right area, but we'll have to look for the right house.' There were beautiful old houses everywhere, surrounded by well-kept lawns and gardens. The British had clearly made these houses for themselves to live in comfort. In time, some of them had changed hands.

It did not take us long to find Krikorian's house. There was a black car parked in its portico, which we recognized instantly. It was the same car that had followed us from the airport. It belonged to Hiralal Somani. He had obviously beaten us to it.

Mr Pal parked his car a little way ahead under a tree, and said, 'Now we must find a spot from where we can keep an eye on that house.'

We got out of the car and walked back to stand opposite Krikorian's house. There were shrubs and bushes dotted about. It wasn't difficult to find a suitable spot. But we did not have to wait for long. Only a minute or so later, the front door of Krikorian's house opened. A shaft of light streamed out and, in it, we saw Somani come out. He glanced back once, said 'Good night' to someone, and got into his car. We saw it move away and disappear round the corner, its engine purring smoothly.

'What will you do now?' Mr Pal whispered.

'Go in and talk to Mr Krikorian,' Feluda replied.

We stepped out of the dark and walked in through the gate of Krikorian's house. But before we would reach the portico, a most peculiar thing happened.

The front door opened again, and an old man—possibly in his seventies—rushed out and began running as fast as he could towards the gate. In his hands was Tintoretto's Jesus, with a new, shining golden frame around it. The presence of four strange people on his driveway did not seem to bother him at all. He looked around wildly, then slapped his forehead and started to yell. 'Scoundrel! Swindler! Son of a bitch!'

Then he turned to us, a crazed look in his eyes, and said, 'He just sold me a fake, and I paid fifty thousand dollars for it!' He did not find it necessary to question who we were and what we were doing at his house.

'Are you talking about this painting by Tintoretto?' Feluda asked gently. The old man exploded. 'Tintoretto?' he said, panting. 'Tintoretto my foot! Come with me, I'll show you.'

He walked with amazing swiftness back to the portico. We followed him quietly. 'Look!' he said, holding the painting up in the bright light that came through the open front door. 'Can you see them? Three green flies. All sticking to the paint. These stupid creatures had made life miserable for me in my room in the hotel in Calcutta. And now I find not one, not two, but three of them in this painting! And that idiot had the nerve to tell me it was genuine. He fooled me because it's a damn good copy. But I didn't pay all that money for a fake!'

'You're quite right,' said Feluda soothingly. 'These flies did not exist in Italy four hundred years ago. They obviously got in there pretty recently.'

Mr Krikorian's white face had turned red. 'That dirty double-crossing swine! I don't even know where he's staying!'

'I do,' Mr Pal said quietly.

'You do?' The Armenian turned to him eagerly, now hope in his eyes.

'Yes. He's staying in Kowloon. I have the address.'

'Good. I'll get hold of him, and skin him alive!' Then a sudden thought seemed to occur to him. He turned back to Feluda and asked, 'Who are you?'

'We knew Somani's-painting wasn't genuine. So we came to warn you. But he got here first,' Feluda replied calmly, lying through his teeth.

'But . . .' Mr Pal said suddenly, 'it's not too late. We could catch him now, before he gets home. We could follow him in my car. He couldn't have got very far.'

Mr Krikorian's eyes took on a new glint. 'Let's go,' he said briefly.

We had been unable to drive very fast on our way here because we had to climb up a hill. Now, on our way down, Mr Pal told us to hold on tight and drove as though the devil was after him. But this did not last for very long.

We saw Somani's car only five minutes later. He had finished his business, a cheque for fifty thousand dollars was warming his pocket, so naturally he was in no hurry to get anywhere. Mr Pal caught up with his car and began blowing his horn. Somani moved to one side to let him pass. Mr Pal overtook him, went ahead and then parked diagonally across the road, blocking the way completely. Thankfully, there was no other car coming from either direction.

I saw Somani get out of his car with a puzzled air. In the same instant, Mr Krikorian leapt out of ours, still clutching the painting. Feluda followed quickly.

'Excuse me,' he said, taking the painting from Mr Krikorian. The old man let go, looking somewhat bemused.

Feluda walked straight up to Somani, carrying the painting. Then, without the slightest warning, he raised his hands and brought the painting down on Somani's head with a resounding crash. Somani's head pierced through the canvas and the frame hung round his throat like a necklace. He simply stared, wide-eyed and speechless.

'Mr Krikorian, you will now get your cheque back,' Feluda said coldly, his revolver in his hand.

Hiralal Somani continued to look dazed, but seemed to have caught the general drift. With a trembling hand, he took out a cheque from the front pocket of his jacket. Mr Krikorian swooped upon him and snatched it from his hand.

'Please, Hiralalji,' said Feluda before returning to the car, 'do not hold me responsible for this unexpected stroke of misfortune. This was brought about by three green flies.'

Somani's jaw fell open. We drove off.

TWELVE

What I found most amazing was that the second painting sold to Krikorian also turned out to be a fake. But Feluda did not comment on it at all.

Lalmohan Babu raised a different point. 'Felu Babu,' he said, 'how can you be so sure that green flies did not exist in Italy in the sixteenth century? Why, I have heard water hyacinth did not originate in our own country. It was brought by a lady from Europe!'

Feluda gave his lopsided grin, but said nothing.

Mr Pal came to the airport the next day to see us off. Feluda had bought him a beautiful silk tie as a token of thanks. Mr Pal laughed.

'I have never had so much excitement in a single day!' he told us. 'But it's a pity I couldn't take you to Kowloon to try fried snake. You must visit me again, and stay a little while longer.'

To tell the truth, I didn't want to leave Hong Kong so soon, but knew that Feluda's ruling principle in life was 'duty first'. He would never allow himself to be lured by the bright lights of Hong Kong before he had solved the mystery of the fake painting, the murder of Bankim Babu and the poisoned dog in Baikunthapur.

We left Hong Kong on Wednesday night, and reached Calcutta the next morning. 'Today is going to be a day of rest,' Feluda said to Lalmohan Babu. 'Tomorrow, Topshe and I will arrive at your house around eight o'clock. Then we'll all go to Baikunthapur. All right?'

'OK, sir. No problem.'

On our way back, Feluda stopped at the Park Street post office, saying he had to send an urgent telegram. He did not reveal who it would go to.

After this, he sank into complete silence. I knew this mood well. It was like the lull before a storm, though I had no idea when the storm would break. I tried to work things out for myself, but nothing made sense. In any case, our experience in Hong Kong had thrown me into total confusion. Everytime I closed my eyes, I could only see the long Chinese signboards hanging over my head. It was impossible to think straight.

The next day, by the time we reached Mr Niyogi's house, it was nearly 11 a.m. Nobo Kumar was waiting for us. He began to ask anxious questions about our visit to Hong Kong, but Feluda shook his head.

'No, our mission wasn't entirely successful, I'm afraid. We couldn't get the original painting,' he said, adding, 'The one we did find turned out to be another case of forgery.'

'What! How is that possible, Mr Mitter? Two copies of the same painting? Well then, where did the original go?'

'Let's go into your living room upstairs. We can talk more comfortably there.'

'Oh yes, of course. I'm sorry.'

We walked into the living room, to find Inspector Mondol sitting on a sofa, sipping a glass of lemonade.

'Well, well!' he grinned. 'Had any luck in Hong Kong, Mr Mitter?'

'If you're referring to the stolen painting, the answer is no. We didn't find it. But in other respects, yes, we got a few things straightened out.'

'I see. What about the murderer?'

'He may give himself up.'

'Really?'

Feluda did not sit down. Glasses of lemonade arrived for us. He picked one up and took a sip. Then he brought out his blue notebook. The rest of us sat on sofas and chairs, facing him.

'Allow me to begin at the beginning,' Feluda said, 'On Tuesday, 28 September, two events occurred in Baikunthapur. Someone poisoned Mr Niyogi's fox terrier, Thumri; and Chandrasekhar's son Rudrasekhar arrived here. This made me wonder if there was a connection between the two. Who would kill an old dog, and why, I asked myself. When I thought about it, I found two possible explanations. In fact, Topshe mentioned the first one. Anyone with the intention of burgling the house would have a motive for killing the dog. But nothing was stolen immediately. The theft of the painting took place long after Thumri was killed. Therefore, I had to consider the second option. If someone known to the family—and the dog—wanted to return incognito, in disguise, not wanting to be recognized, he would certainly wish to remove the dog before he arrived because if the dog showed signs of recognition, it would arouse suspicion at once.

'This led me to wonder if the new arrival—Rudrasekhar—wasn't someone known to you. His behaviour was certainly odd. He hardly ever opened his mouth, wore tinted glasses, and spent most of his time either outside the house or in his room. Who was he? He was supposed to have arrived straight from Italy, and yet on his feet were shoes from Bata. Yes, he had presented his passport to your father, but he is old and his eyesight weak. In any case, he was too embarrassed to scrutinize it closely or call someone else for help. It was, therefore, not too difficult to get by with a false passport.

'However, if the passport was not genuine, then how did he hope to get Rudrasekhar's share of the property? I mean, lawyers and other people who deal with such matters aren't fools, and they would most certainly have made extensive enquiries. The chances of deceiving them were really pretty dim.

'Why, then, was this man here? There could be only one reason. He wanted to lay his hands on the most valuable painting in this house. Thanks to Bhudev Singh's article, hundreds of people now knew about it.

'What this man didn't know, and what we learnt only recently from an old press cutting, was that the real Rudrasekhar died in Rome twenty-six years ago.'

'What!' Nobo Kumar shrieked.

'Yes, Mr Niyogi. I am very grateful to Robin Babu for pointing this out to me.'

'Then . . . then who was that man who came here?'

Feluda took out a piece of paper from his pocket. It was a page torn out of a magazine.

'I came upon this magazine in Hong Kong, entirely by accident. Please take a look at this picture, Mr Niyogi. It's a scene from a film called *Mombasa.* Some of it was shot in Africa. The villain was played by the bearded man in this picture. Look at it carefully, please. Can you recognize him?'

Nobo Kumar peered at the page. 'Ah, here's Rudrasekhar!' he said.

'Read the actor's name in the caption.'

Nobo Kumar peered more closely and gave a violent start.

'My God! It's Nondo!'

'Yes, Mr Niyogi. He is your brother. He wore almost identical make-up when he came here. I suspect the beard was his own, but he wore a wig to cover his hair. He got someone else to write a letter to your father from Rome. That shouldn't have been too difficult, anyway.'

Nobo Kumar looked deeply distressed. He shook his head and sighed. 'Nondo was always far too reckless,' he muttered.

Feluda continued to speak. 'If the original painting disappeared suddenly, it would have caused an enormous stir. So Mr Nondo Kumar hit upon a rather ingenious idea. He got an artist to come here and make a copy. It was this copy that he placed on the wall, and took the one already hanging there. For some reason, Bankim Babu had started to suspect something. So he set the alarm of his clock for 3.30 the morning Rudrasekhar—I mean Nondo Kumar—disappeared. Perhaps Bankim Babu actually caught him in the act of removing the painting. That was the reason he had to die.'

There was pindrop silence in the room when Feluda stopped speaking. He glanced around briefly and went on, 'There was one man who could have exposed Nondo Kumar. But he didn't, possibly because he was too embarrassed. Isn't that right?'

All of us turned to find that someone had come into the room silently during Feluda's speech and was sitting quietly in a corner.

It was the journalist, Robin Chowdhury.

'Is that true?' Nobo Kumar asked him. 'Did you know Rudrasekhar was an impostor?'

Robin Babu smiled, looking at Feluda. 'You began the whole story; now you finish it!' he said.

'I might. But I still don't have answers to all the questions. You'll have to help me.'

'Very well. Go ahead with your questions.'

'First, you told us you had to consult a dictionary to work out the meaning of that Italian press cutting. That was a lie, wasn't it?'

'Yes, I lied.'

'Second, that red spot on your shirt, which we all thought was blood, was red oil paint, wasn't it?'

Yes.

'Where did you learn to paint?'

'In Switzerland. My mother took me to Zurich soon after my father died. She was a qualified nurse. So she began working in a hospital in Zurich. I was then thirteen. I began attending art classes after school. Then, later, I went to Paris. I decided to write Chandrasekhar's biography a couple of years ago. I went to Rome and Venice, and met members of the Cassini family. That's where I learnt about the Tintoretto painting.'

'What it really means is that you, too, made a copy of it.'

'Yes, that's right.'

'And it was this second copy that Nondo Kumar took, thinking it was the original, and it eventually reached Hiralal Somani?'

'Yes.'

'What I want to know is,' Nobo Kumar interrupted impatiently, 'where is the original?'

'I have got it,' replied Robin Chowdhury.

'Why? Why have you kept it?'

'Because if I didn't, it would now be in Hong Kong. I began to suspect soon after I arrived that the fake Rudrasekhar was planning to remove it. So I made a copy and put away the original.'

'You did want to take the original, though, didn't you?' Feluda asked.

'Yes, but not for myself. I wanted to take it to a museum in

Europe. Any museum there would jump at the chance to add it to their collection.'

'What do you mean?' Nobo Kumar rose to his feet, both excited and outraged. 'Who are you to take away our painting? It belongs to our family!'

'Yes, of course, Mr Niyogi, you are absolutely right,' Feluda reassured him. 'But, you see, Robin Babu here is one of your family, too!'

'What? Is this a joke?'

'Not at all. I have reason to believe that he is actually Rudrasekhar's son and Chandrasekhar's grandson. His real name is Rajsekhar Niyogi. His passport, I am sure, bears the same name.'

'I never thought I'd ever have to show my passport,' Robin Babu laughed. 'I did not want anyone to know who I was and make a fuss over me. All I wanted to do was collect research material on Chandrasekhar, and take that painting since I had a claim on it. Yes, it did mean deception, but I thought things might be easier if I did not turn up as a long-lost member of the family. How was I to know so many unexpected things would happen, or that I would run into someone with such a remarkable power of detection as Mr Mitter? All I can now do is offer my apologies and hope you will forgive me for what I did.'

'There's just one little thing I'd like to point out,' Feluda put in. 'You see, Bhudev Singh told me that the last time he heard from your grandfather was five years ago. So, strictly speaking, you don't really have a claim on Tintoretto's Jesus. However, I don't think anyone will object to your taking it since you will appreciate its value the most and will know what to do to have it properly preserved.'

'Yes, I quite agree,' said Nobo Kumar, still looking amazed. 'But you'll have to tell me, Mr Mitter, how did you work this one out? What made you think Robin Babu was my cousin? I . . . to me, it's like . . . well, magic!'

'It was relatively simple. There was something odd about him. He didn't fit in, somehow. For instance, I noticed at the first meal we had together that he didn't seem to know the right order in which different dishes should be eaten. No Bengali would need to be told that *shukto* must be eaten before anything else. But he seemed to hesitate. He began eating the daal, then he ate the fish, and came to the bitter *shukto* last of all. He was obviously a man who had spent a long time living abroad. But that wasn't really what made me stumble on the truth. It was this—'

Feluda broke off, and walked over to Chandrasekhar's portrait of his father, Anant Nath Niyogi. He placed his hands over Anant Nath's beard and moustache. Immediately, it seemed as though it was Robin Babu's face that was staring out of the canvas.

Lalmohan Babu started clapping, and it finally dawned upon me why Robin Babu had seemed familiar.

But there was one more surprise in store.

A bearer had been standing at the door for some time, holding a telegram. He now passed it to Nobo Kumar. He read it quickly, and grew round-eyed again. 'Why, it's from Nondo in Bombay!' he exclaimed. 'He says he's going to arrive in Calcutta by the evening flight today! I don't see—'

'Er . . .' Feluda said, looking, for the first time, vaguely uncomfortable, 'I'm afraid that's my doing, Mr Niyogi. I took the liberty of sending him a telegram yesterday, under your name, saying that he must come immediately because your father was critically ill. I hope you'll forgive me for doing this without consulting you, but I thought you and Inspector Mondol here might wish to see him and sort a few things out . . . ?'

'No, I can't!' said Feluda.

'Why not?' Nobo Kumar asked, looking annoyed.

'I cannot take any more money from you because—look, didn't my investigations reveal that your own brother was the culprit?'

'So what? I asked you to investigate, didn't I? Why would anyone hold you responsible for the results you produced? You only did your job! I am telling you, Mr Mitter, I consider it my duty to pay you your full fees, and if you don't accept it, I am going to be most displeased. Surely you wouldn't want that?'

His own brother might be a criminal, but the cousin Nobo Kumar had acquired proved to be a gem. There was no doubt in anyone's mind that Tintoretto's Jesus had gone to the right person. In a few weeks, it would grace the wall of some famous European museum.

Nobo Kumar persuaded us to spend an extra day in Baikunthapur. On our way back, we stopped in Mecheda at Lalmohan Babu's request, to consult Bhabesh Bhattacharya once more.

It was imperative, said Lalmohan Babu, to find out if he might call his next novel *Hoodwinked in Hong Kong!*

The Disappearance of Ambar Sen

ONE

'From now on, Felu Babu,' Lalmohan Babu declared, 'you needn't bother about correcting mistakes in my books.'

Feluda was sitting in his favourite sofa, busy twisting and turning a pyramid-shaped Rubik's cube. 'Really?' he asked, without raising his eyes.

'Yes, sir. I happened to meet a gentleman yesterday, in our park. His name is Mrityunjay Som, and he's just moved to our neighbourhood. We spoke for nearly half an hour. He's a great scholar.'

'A scholar?'

'Yes. A double MA from Herbert University, or some such thing.'

'For heaven's sake, Lalmohan Babu,' this time Feluda had to look up, 'it isn't Herbert. What you mean is Harvard.'

'OK. Harvard.'

'How do you know that? Was he speaking with an American accent?'

'Well no, but he does speak in English most of the time. A very learned man, no doubt about that. He's actually from Behrampore, but he's moved to Calcutta to do some research for a book he's writing. Even his appearance is most impressive . . . I mean, he has a distinct personality. A French beard, glasses with golden frames, smart clothes. I gave him a copy of my book, *The Fearsome Foe*. He pointed out thirty-four mistakes, but said it made very enjoyable reading.'

'Well then, your problems are over. You don't have to drive all the way to my house every day. Think of the money you'll save on petrol.'

'Yes, but the thing is, you see . . .'

We never got to hear what the thing was, for Lalmohan Babu was interrupted at this point by the arrival of Feluda's client, Ambar Sen. We were expecting him at nine o'clock. Our door bell rang just as the clock struck nine.

Mr Sen was in his mid-forties, clean-shaven, wearing glasses set in thick frames. A jamavar shawl was wrapped round his shoulders. Feluda had taken me to a museum one day and shown me just how many different types of Kashmiri shawls there could be.

Mr Sen took a chair opposite Feluda's and came straight to the point.

'You're a busy man, Mr Mitter, and so am I. So let's not waste any time. But before I tell you anything further, take a look at this.' He took out a piece of paper from his pocket and offered it to Feluda. It had been crumpled into a ball, then smoothed out again. Written on it in large red letters were these words:

You destroyed me. Now you will pay for it, in just seven days.
Don't think you can get away with it this time.

Feluda turned the paper over, and asked, 'How did you find it?'

'My study is on the ground floor. Last night, someone threw it into the room through an open window. My bearer, Laxman, found it this morning and brought it to me.'

'Does your study overlook the street?'

'No. There's a garden outside the study which is surrounded by a compound wall. But I suppose anyone could have climbed over it.'

'What's this about destroying someone?'

Mr Sen shook his head. 'Look, Mr Mitter, I am a simple man. I run a business, although most of the work is handled by my brother. I have various other interests and hobbies which keep me busy. I cannot recall ever having harmed anyone—not consciously, anyway; and even if I did, it could certainly not have been so bad as to merit a threat like that. I cannot make head or tail of it.'

Feluda frowned, and thought for a minute. Then he said, 'Well, it could of course be some sort of a practical joke. Perhaps there's a group of young boys in your area?'

'I live in Palm Avenue. There is a slum not all that far from my house. There may well be young men living there who might do such a thing for a laugh. Who knows?'

'Don't they harass you for a donation before Durga Puja?'

'Yes, but we have always paid our share without a fuss.'

Srinath came in with the tea at this moment, so Feluda had to stop asking questions. I heard Lalmohan Babu mutter under his breath. 'Revenge, revenge!' he said.

Feluda took this opportunity to introduce us to Mr Sen.

'I see, so you are the famous Jatayu?'

'Heh, heh!'

Mr Sen took a long sip from his cup with great relish. 'Actually,' he said, 'I came to know about you, Mr Mitter, only after reading some of Tapesh's stories. That's why I thought I'd come to you first.'

'Have you told the police?'

'My brother told me to go to the police, but I happen to be a bit unorthodox in these matters, you see. I don't like doing what everyone else would do. Besides, I don't think at this moment there is anything to feel seriously concerned about. I came to you really because I wanted to meet you. Everyone in our family knows about you.'

'Who else is there in your family?'

'I live with my younger brother, Ambuj. I am a bachelor, but Ambuj is married. He has three children—two sons and a daughter. His sons are grown up now, they don't live here. His daughter is about ten. Then there is my mother—my father's no more—and a distant cousin who has lived with us since he was a child. Apart from these family members, there are three bearers, a cook, a maid, a mali, a chowkidar and a driver. We live at 5/1 Palm Avenue. My father was the well-known heart specialist, Anath Sen.'

Feluda nodded, but seemed reluctant to say anything more. Mr Sen obviously sensed this, for he quickly added, 'All I wanted to do was just tell you what had happened. You may be right, perhaps the whole thing is no more than a joke. But what strikes me as odd is that normally it is the rich and the famous who become targets for such jokes. I am neither, so . . .' he shrugged.

'Well, Mr Sen, you must see that if this is only an empty threat, there is nothing I can do. May I please keep this piece of paper?'

'Of course.'

Coming to see Feluda just because he had received a weird note did seem to be something of an overreaction. However, the phone call from Palm Avenue that came the following morning made the whole thing take a totally different turn. I took the call in our living room and transferred it to Feluda's extension. Then I picked up the receiver again and heard the whole conversation.

'Hello, is that Mr Mitter?'

'Yes.'

'My name is Ambuj Sen. Did my brother see you yesterday regarding an anonymous letter?'

'Yes.'

'Well, he's missing.'

'What do you mean?'

'What I just said. My brother went out in our car early this morning. This was nothing unusual, for he does this every day. He takes the car to the river, then he gets out and walks a couple of miles before getting back home. Today . . . today he did not return.'

'What!'

'The driver waited for a whole hour, then searched for him everywhere. But he was nowhere to be found, so finally the driver came back.'

'Have you informed the police?'

'No. There's a problem, you see. Our mother is eighty years old, and not in very good health. I haven't yet told her about my brother's disappearance. But if the police were told they'd naturally come round to make enquiries, and then I wouldn't be able to keep anything from her. She'd get extremely upset. So I'd request you to handle this case yourself. We've all got every faith in you. And of course we'll pay you your fee.'

'OK, I'll be right over. Is that all right with you?'

'Certainly. You know our address, don't you?'

'Five by one, Palm Avenue?'

'Yes, that's right.'

TWO

Mr Sen's house turned out to be a sprawling building, somewhat old fashioned in style, with a front porch. There was a small garden in front of the house. A splash of green behind it suggested a tennis court. A slab of marble on the gate still bore Ambar Sen's father's name, which was followed by a lot of letters from the alphabet and commas and full stops. The last word was (Edin.), by which I assumed he had gone to Scotland to study medicine.

The man who came out to meet us as our taxi drew up under the porch bore a general resemblance to Ambar Sen, but unlike him, was short, stout and dark. He gave us a smile, but it faded quickly. Ambuj Sen was clearly worried.

'Please come in,' he said.

We walked across a landing with a marble floor, and went into the living room. Here, too, the floor was made of marble. On it lay a beautiful carpet; there was also a lot of expensive furniture. The sofa I sat on was so soft that it sank by about six inches under my weight.

'Runa, come here,' called Ambuj Babu. I noticed a small girl in a frock standing near a door, staring at us in open amazement. She came in and stood by her father.

'Do you know who this is?' Ambuj asked her.

'Yes, it's Feluda,' she said softly.

'And who is this?'

'Topshe.'

'Oh, so you know both of them?'

'Where is Jatayu?' asked Runa, sounding somewhat disappointed.

'He couldn't come with us today, but I'll bring him here another day, I promise!' Feluda told her.

'She has read every story he has written,' Ambuj Babu informed us.

'Do you think you can find my uncle?' Runa asked, looking straight at Feluda.

'I'll try; and if you can find me a clue, so much the better.'

'A clue?'

'Yes. Do you know what that means?'

'Yes.'

'Well then, have you got any that might help us find your uncle quickly?'

'Why should I give you a clue? You're the detective. Finding clues is your job!'

'True. You are a very clever girl. What is your real name, Runa?'

'Jharna.'

Feluda turned to Ambuj Babu. 'I need your help in certain matters, Mr Sen, without which I cannot proceed at all.'

'I'll do whatever is required.'

'I need to talk to every member of your family. I met your brother for just a few minutes. That was not sufficient to get to know him. I also need to go into his study and go through some of his papers. I hope you wouldn't mind?'

'No, of course not.'

'Then I shall have to see the spot where your brother used to go for his morning walk.'

'No problem. Our driver, Bilash, can take you there.'

By this time, Feluda had risen and was pacing, his eyes fixed on three large bookshelves.

'Whose books are those?'

'Dada's.'

'He appears interested in a lot of subjects, even criminology!'

'Yes, he's studied that subject, too.'

'. . . Science, cookery, history, collecting coins, drama . . .'

'Drama is something of a passion for Dada. He builds a stage every year during Durga Puja and gets us to take part in the plays he directs. Nearly every member of our family has taken some role or the other in his plays, including Runa.'

I looked at the little girl. She was still gaping at Feluda.

'I see. May I please see his study?'

'Yes, certainly. Please come with me.'

A passage ran outside the living room, leading to the study which was in the rear portion of the house. Sunlight poured through an open window in the room, making it look bright and inviting. There was a desk and a revolving chair, and an easy chair by the window. Two more chairs stood on one side, presumably for visitors. Behind the desk was a shelf, a cabinet and a Godrej safe. A grey jacket hung from a folding bracket fixed on the wall next to the safe.

Ambar Sen clearly believed in order, for his papers, pen-holder, pincushion, paperweight, paper-knife, telephone and various other objects were placed very neatly on his desk. The only thing that struck me as odd was a desk calendar. The date on it had not been changed for three days. When Feluda pointed this out, Ambuj Babu said, 'Yes, that's strange. Normally, Dada wouldn't forget to change the date, but he had been rather preoccupied the last few days.'

Fussy as he was, Feluda changed the date himself from Saturday, the second to Tuesday, the fifth.

'May I open the drawers?' he asked, pointing at the desk.

'Please go ahead.'

Feluda opened all three drawers and rummaged through their contents. A piece of paper he found in the top drawer appeared to intrigue him, for he took it out and examined it closely.

'Did your brother usually get his glasses made by Himalaya Opticals?'

'Yes.'

'This is a new cash memo. He had new glasses made only a week ago. Is that right?'

'No!' cried a childish voice. We turned to find that Runa had followed us quietly.

'How do you know that, Runa?' Feluda asked.

'Uncle would have shown me his new glasses. He didn't.'

Ambuj Sen smiled. 'We didn't always get to know Dada's plans or his activities.'

Feluda closed the drawers and we came out of Ambar Sen's study.

'I believe a cousin of yours lives in this house. Is that right?' Feluda asked when we were back in the living room.

'Samaresh? Oh yes. He was brought up here.'

'Could I speak to him, please?'

Ambuj Sen sent for Samaresh Babu. He turned out to be a man in his mid-thirties, with pockmarks on his face. He wore glasses with very thick frames. He came and stood somewhat stiffly at a little distance.

'Please sit down,' said Feluda.

Samaresh Babu took a chair, still looking uncomfortable.

'What is your full name?'

'Samaresh Mallik.'

'How long have you spent in this house?'

'About twenty-five years.'

'What do you do for a living?'

'I work for a film distributor.'

'Where is your office?'

'Dharamtala.'

'What's the name of this company?'

'Koh-i-noor Pictures.'

'How long have you worked there?'

'Seven years.'

'What did you do before that?'

'I . . . nothing, just little chores in the house that needed to be done.'

Samaresh Mallik had folded his hands and stuffed them between his knees, a clear sign that Feluda's questions had done nothing to put him at his ease.

'Can you throw any light on this mysterious business of Mr Sen's disappearance?'

Samaresh Babu remained silent.

'Did you know he had received a threat?' Feluda went on.

'Yes.'

'Is your room on the ground floor?'

'Yes.'

'Did anyone from outside ever visit Mr Sen?'

'Oh yes, every now and then.'

'Did you happen to notice anyone recently? I mean, anyone you hadn't seen before?'

'No. But . . .'

'What?'

'I noticed a few young men lurking in this area. I had never seen them before.'

'Where exactly did you see them?'

'At the crossing near our house.'

'What were they doing?'

'They appeared to be keeping an eye on this house.'

'How old were they?'

'Between twenty and twenty-five, I'd say.'

'How many were there?'

'Four.'

Feluda stopped and thought for a while. Then he said, 'Thank you, Mr Mallik, you may go now.'

Was any of this going to be of any use? I could not tell. However a chat with Ambuj Sen's wife proved to be extremely useful. We met her in a smaller sitting room on the first floor. Mrs Sen was a good-looking woman and, as we soon realized, just as bright. She must have been over forty, but looked a lot younger.

Feluda began by apologizing to her for any inconvenience.

'Not at all,' she replied. 'Having read a number of detective stories—including your own—I am aware of the kind of job you have to do. How will you learn anything unless you meet everyone and ask questions?'

'I'm so glad you appreciate that. OK, so let me begin by telling you what my biggest problem is. You do know about the threat your brother-in-law received, don't you?'

'Yes.'

'Did you see that note?'

'Yes.'

'I asked Ambar Babu if he could recall any instance where he might have harmed someone. He told me he could not. What I didn't specify at the time was that I wasn't just speaking of the recent past. Something might have happened a long time ago. There are times when people wait for ages to take revenge. What I want to ask you now is whether you are aware of any such event, going ten, even twenty years back?'

Mrs Sen remained silent for a few moments, looking faintly

worried. Then she said slowly, 'Well, I suppose I ought to tell you . . . you see, I recalled this incident only last night. In fact, I haven't yet told my husband about it.'

'Go on.'

'It . . . was an accident.'

'Accident?'

'Yes. If happened a year before Runa was born. My brother-in-law used to drive his father's car in those days. It was an Austin. Anyway, one day he happened to run a man over in Shyambazar. The man died.'

'I see. Can you remember anything else, either of you?' Feluda asked.

'The family was not very well off,' Ambuj Sen said. 'The man used to work as a clerk somewhere.'

'Can you remember his name?'

'No. I'm afraid not.'

'He had a wife and three children—a son and two daughters. The boy was about fourteen, the girls were younger,' Mrs Sen added. 'My brother-in-law gave his widow five thousand rupees.'

'Yes, and he gave up driving from that day. It's all coming back to me now,' said Ambuj Babu.

'Hm. That means that young boy is now about twenty-five. No doubt the death of his father led to many hardships and deprivations. Five thousand rupees could not have lasted long, could it?'

'I suppose not. Unfortunately, I cannot remember any other detail,' Mrs Sen said, shaking her head.

'Neither can I,' her husband put in.

'Did your brother ever keep a diary?'

'No, not that we are aware of.'

Feluda rose to take his leave.

'Thank you very much, Mrs Sen,' he said, 'you've been most helpful. I think I am beginning to see my way through.'

'You are very welcome, Mr Mitter. I do hope you will be able to solve this case,' she said, with genuine concern in her voice.

THREE

There was no point in disturbing Mr Sen's old and ailing mother, so we said goodbye to the Sens and got into their Ambassador. Their driver, Bilash Babu, took us to the riverside and parked the car in front of the Happy Restaurant.

'This is where Mr Sen used to get out of the car,' he said, 'and then he used to start walking in that direction,' he pointed to the southern side. 'He always came back in exactly an hour.'

'Did you usually wait in the car?'

'Yes, sir.'

'How long have you been working for Mr Sen?'

'Nine years.'

'Then you wouldn't know about the accident, I suppose?'

'What accident?'

'About twelve years ago, Ambar Sen had run a man over and killed him.'

'Ambar Babu?'

'Why is that so surprising?'

'I didn't know he could drive at all.'

'He stopped driving after that incident.'

'I see. It might not have been his fault. Sometimes pedestrians don't obey traffic rules either. It is not fair to blame the driver each time an accident takes place. In fact, I am surprised more people don't get run over every day!'

'Could you describe what happened when Mr Sen did not return from his walk this morning? What did you do?'

'When he didn't show up after an hour, I drove up to Hastings to look for him. I stopped from time to time to ask people if anyone had seen him. At one or two places, I even got out of the car to look for him. His heart wasn't particularly strong, you see, so I was afraid he might have had a stroke or something.'

'Were there a lot of people about?'

'Well yes, quite a few people normally come here for morning walks. But Mr Sen used to go towards the new Howrah Bridge, where it's always quiet. If a couple of strong men were to jump out of a car and kidnap him, I don't think he'd get even the chance to shout for help. I mean, if that's what happened, it's not surprising that no one saw or heard anything.'

We then drove slowly up to Hastings, but could see nothing

suspicious on the way.

The next two days passed without any news from Palm Avenue. Jatayu turned up in the evening on Thursday, and said, 'What news of Ambar Sen, Felu Babu?'

On being told that he had disappeared, his eyes nearly popped out. 'What! Disappeared? And you thought it was all a big joke? It's amazing, isn't it, how all your cases—even the seemingly insignificant ones—always turn out to be thrilling in the end?'

'We haven't yet reached the end of this one, Lalmohan Babu. Anyway, tell me about your new neighbour, that great scholar called Mrityunjay Som. How is he?'

'Great scholar? Ha! He's nothing of the sort.'

'No? Only a couple of days ago you were prepared to swear he was the best. What made you change your mind?'

'I don't want to talk about it.'

'Why not?'

'I am too embarrassed, Felu Babu. I couldn't possibly tell you what happened.'

'Come on, of course you could. You've known me for years, so why should you feel embarrassed to tell me anything?'

After a little more persuasion, Lalmohan Babu came clean. 'Just imagine, Felu Babu,' he said, 'this man hadn't heard of you! When I told him I knew you, he looked totally blank and said, "Who is Pradosh Mitter?"'

'Is that all? Never mind, Lalmohan Babu, it does not matter. After all, I had not heard of this great scholar either, had I? I mean a double MA from Herbert . . . there can't be too many of those, I'm sure.'

This seemed to reassure Lalmohan Babu. 'Yes, you are right. How is it possible to know every single soul in this big, wide world? Besides, this man has spent most of his life abroad. So I guess one ought to forgive him.'

The phone rang before Feluda could say anything. It was Ambuj Sen from Palm Avenue. They had received another anonymous note, he said. On Feluda's request, he read it out on the phone:

> If you wish Ambar Sen to be restored to you in one piece, get twenty thousand rupees in hundred-rupee notes, put it all in a

bag and leave the bag by a pillar on the south-eastern side of Princep Ghat, at 6.30 p.m. tomorrow (Friday). If you try informing the police or a detective, the consequences would be disastrous. This is your only chance to get Ambar Sen back.

'Very well, there is no need to take any decision right now,' said Feluda. 'We've got nearly twenty-four hours to work things out. I have a few things to do tomorrow, but I'll come to your house in the afternoon around two o'clock and tell you what to do next. But you must get the money somehow. That is very important.' He put the phone down.

'Er . . . didn't the note say something about not informing a detective?' Lalmohan Babu asked immediately.

'Yes, so it did,' Feluda replied briefly.

Things had suddenly started to move like a speeding rocket. Twenty thousand rupees was a lot of money, but what could the Sens do but pay up?

After five minutes of complete silence, Feluda spoke again.

'Lalmohan Babu, could I use your car tomorrow?'

'Of course, any time. When do you want it?'

'Say around half past nine in the morning? I need to go out. I don't think I'll take more than a couple of hours to finish my work. Then I'll send your car back, but could you please return at five o'clock?'

'Very well.'

Feluda lapsed into silence after this.

True to his word, Lalmohan Babu sent his car at half past nine the following morning. Feluda went out alone, so I couldn't tell where he went or what he did. But I did notice that when he returned at twelve o'clock, the expression on his face had changed totally.

'What are you planning to do, Feluda?' I asked hesitantly.

'Well, I think the ransom must be paid. But we've got to ignore the threat about going to a detective.'

'What does that mean? Are you going to be present when they come to collect the money?'

'Felu Mitter does not panic so easily.'

'And what about us?'

'You two will also have to be there, in case I need your help.'

I stared. What on earth had he decided to do?

We left for Palm Avenue straight after lunch. Ambuj Sen was

waiting for us.

'I couldn't sleep a wink last night, Mr Mitter,' he said anxiously as we stepped in. 'Who knew this would happen?'

'I am afraid you are going to have to pay the entire amount,' Feluda replied solemnly, 'there is no other way to get your brother back.'

'Haven't you worked things out yet?' Runa asked suddenly, emerging out of a door.

'Yes, Runa. I have solved most of it, and I hope to clear up this evening what little remains of the mystery. At least, I am going to try very hard.'

'Oh, that's all right, then.' Runa sounded profoundly relieved. If her hero failed in any way, her little heart would have been broken, it seemed.

'So what do you suggest we do?' asked Ambuj Sen.

'Have you got the money?'

'Yes. Naturally we did not have all that cash at home, so I sent Samaresh to the bank this morning.'

'May I please see the money and the bag you are going to put it in?'

Ambuj Babu sent for both. I had never seen such a lot of money in cash. Ten small packets were made, each containing twenty hundred-rupee notes, held together by a rubber band. All ten packets were then transferred into a bag, which began to look like a well-fed tortoise.

'Very good,' Feluda said, 'that's all settled, then. We should leave at quarter to six.'

Ambuj Babu started. 'What! You mean you will go yourself?'

'I cannot allow a criminal to come and coolly walk away with your money. I know the most important thing here is to get Ambar Babu back, but if nothing is done to catch his kidnappers, they may well attack someone else. Please do not worry about anything, Mr Sen. I will take adequate precautions, as I always do.'

'In that case . . .'

'Listen to me carefully. You must go in your car with the money. Drive towards the new Howrah Bridge, where it's relatively quiet. Park your car at least two hundred yards away from Princep Ghat. Then ask your driver to take this bag and leave it by the pillar as suggested. I will remain in the vicinity, to make sure nothing goes wrong. Then we'll meet in front of the Happy Restaurant. Drive straight on and wait there for me. If I manage to catch the culprit, needless to say he, too, will be with me.'

Ambuj Sen began to look rather uncertain. I could not blame him. The amount involved was not insignificant, and who could tell what a pack of hooligans might decide to do?

Lalmohan Babu turned up at half past four.

'I have never handled such a case before,' Feluda declared as soon as he walked in. 'It is totally unique.'

I still could not see what was so special about it, but did not say anything.

'What is the plan for this evening?' Lalmohan Babu asked.

'Listen carefully. You, Topshe, take the car and go to the Happy Restaurant at half past five. Have something to eat there and get out at six-fifteen. Leave the car in front of the restaurant and walk over to the ghat with the pillars. You'll see a small pavilion with a domed roof just before you reach the ghat. Go there and sit on a bench. You must look as though your only aim is to have a casual walk by the river. Try keeping an eye on the ghat without making it obvious. Wait until six-forty and then go back to your car. I shall come and meet you there.'

FOUR

It was almost the end of February, but it still felt quite cool. The days, however, were now longer than in winter, and until six o'clock, it stayed reasonably bright. By the time we left the restaurant after a cup of coffee and a plate of chicken cutlets, it was a quarter past six.

On our way to Princep Ghat, Lalmohan Babu began taking deep breaths every now and then, saying, 'Aaaaah!' in order to impress upon passersby that we wanted no more than to enjoy the fresh evening air. It was not a convincing act at all, but luckily, there were so few people about, and even the bhelpuriwallas had been left so far behind, that it did not really matter.

It took us ten minutes to reach the pavilion Feluda had mentioned. We found ourselves a bench. After a few moments, Lalmohan Babu glanced around and said, 'Can you see your cousin anywhere?'

I could not see anyone at all, except boatmen in little boats on the river. The tall pillars around the ghat, each of them a hundred and fifty years old, towered over the water. It was quickly getting dark. If anyone crept up to any of those pillars to either leave a bag or take it, the chances of being seen were almost nil.

'Look, over there!' Lalmohan Babu hissed, clutching at my sleeve. I had seen him too. A man wearing white trousers and a dark jacket with a bag in his hand was quietly approaching one of the pillars. Bilash, Ambar Sen's driver. He disappeared behind the pillar and emerged again a few seconds later. Now his hand was empty. He walked on until he reached the main road, then he turned right and disappeared behind a tree.

It was now past six-thirty and almost totally dark. I could see nothing except the first row of pillars. Just for a second I thought I saw something move in the dark, but that could well have been my imagination.

Then we saw Mr Sen's car go past and turn in the direction of the Happy Restaurant. Three young boys in jeans came walking along after this, followed by an elderly European gentlemen with a walking stick. All of them went in the same direction as the car.

We rose to our feet, and made our way back to our own car in ten minutes. But where was Feluda?

'Salaam, babu!' said a voice from inside the car. I peered quickly and saw an old man sitting next to the driver. He was wearing a lungi. Around his shoulders was a snuff-coloured wrapper, and on his face a heavy stubble.

Feluda! Disguised as a Muslim boatman. Before either of us could say anything, Ambuj Sen arrived from across the road. Feluda greeted him, hurriedly explaining why he was in disguise. 'I had to hide in one of those boats, since the ghat is clearly visible only from the river.'

'But what happened, Mr Mitter? What did you see?'

Feluda shook his head slowly. 'Very sorry, Mr Sen,' he said.

'What do you mean?'

'The man escaped with the money before I could get to the ghat.'

'What! You mean all that money, and the man . . . are both gone?'

'Yes, I am afraid so. I told you I was sorry.'

Ambuj Babu stared blankly at Feluda. To tell the truth, my own head was reeling. I had never seen Feluda defeated like this.

'You'll have to tell the police,' Feluda said. 'I suggest you go back home. Your brother ought to return now, I'll join you there, only give me a little time to get changed. I can hardly walk into your drawing room looking like this.'

We came back home simply so that Feluda could get into some decent clothes. He also needed to wash his hands which were stained black. 'Coal tar,' he told me when I asked him what it was. But he did not say whether it was a part of his disguise, or whether he had stained his hands accidentally.

It was nearly half past seven by the time we set off for Palm Avenue. Nobody spoke on the way except Lalmohan Babu, who said, 'It was a brilliant disguise, Felu Babu. Pity it did nothing to help you.' Feluda made no reply.

Runa greeted us at the door. 'Uncle has come back!' she shouted in glee.

Ambar Babu, we were told, had returned only ten minutes before our arrival. He rose from a sofa as we went in and came forward to clasp Feluda's hands in his own and shake them warmly. Ambuj Babu, his wife, and Samaresh Mallik were all present in the room.

'Where had they hidden you? What exactly happened?' Lalmohan Babu asked with a big smile.

'Oh my God, I hardly know where to begin . . .'

'Don't,' said Feluda, raising a hand. 'Don't say anything at all, because if you open your mouth, Mr Sen, you will simply have to use your imagination again. Please note that I used the term "imagination", not "lies".'

'Hurrah! Hurrah!' Runa jumped up and down with joy. 'Feluda has guessed it. He has caught you out!'

Feluda lit a Charminar. 'Yes,' he said slowly, 'you had all got together in a conspiracy, hadn't you? I have worked that out, though the reason for it is still a mystery.'

'Please allow me to explain everything,' Ambar Sen laughed. 'The reason for all this is my little niece. Yes, sir. You see, she worships you. She is convinced you can never be fooled, and that you are incapable of making a mistake. So I said to her one day that I could get you involved in a totally bogus case. And that was it. That was how this whole business started. We've all had a role to play.'

'You mean it was something like a family drama?'

'Exactly. I taught everyone what to say. I knew more or less what kind of questions you might ask, so I got everyone in my family—including the servants—to rehearse and memorize their lines. The chief female role was, of course, played by my sister-in-law, who told you that fictitious story about my accident. I didn't think you'd ever manage to get to the bottom of it. In fact, my brother and I even had a bet on it. Now I suppose I'll have to pay him a hundred rupees. Needless to say, the one who is the happiest and most relieved at your success is little Runa. If her hero had failed, she'd have been quite inconsolable. But anyway. Mr Mitter, do tell us what made you suspicious in the first place. How on earth did you guess?'

'There were two clues, both of which I found in your study. The first was a cash memo from Himalaya Opticals. They told me that you had had new glasses made a week ago. You had even ordered golden frames. But no one in your family knew about it; nor had anyone seen you wear them. The question was, why did you have them made at this particular time? What did you need them for?

'The second thing that struck me as odd was the calendar on your desk. Its date had not been changed for three days. No one ever changed the date except yourself. What made you neglect your duty?

'Then an idea occurred to me. What if this business of being kidnapped was not true? What if you were only pretending to have been captured by a gang of unknown hooligans? If this was the case, you would naturally need to go into hiding somewhere, and that might require leaving your home a couple of days before the supposed kidnapping, just to get used to a new place. To be on the safe side, I thought, you might even have got yourself some sort of a disguise, which would explain the new glasses.'

'Right! You are absolutely right!' Runa shouted again.

I suddenly noticed Lalmohan Babu. He was pacing up and down like a caged tiger. What was the matter with him? I opened my mouth to ask, but he stopped abruptly and raised his arms.

'Eureka!' he exclaimed.

'Ah, so you've finally got it, have you? Can you recognize him?' Feluda asked.

'Of course. Mrityunjay Som.'

Ambar Sen burst our laughing.

'Our first meeting in the park took place purely by accident, I assure you. What happened was that my place of hiding was actually a friend's house not far from where you live. I had no idea you lived in that area. When you introduced yourself, I could scarcely believe it. Who could have imagined I'd run into a member of Mr Mitter's team? Then I thought I might pull your leg, just a little. You saw me again in Mr Mitter's house, but failed to recognize me without my disguise.'

'All right, Mr Sen. I think that explains most things, but not all. We cannot say the whole mystery has been solved, can we?' Feluda asked.

Ambar Sen stopped laughing instantly, for Feluda had spoken these words in a serious tone.

'Where did the money go?' Feluda continued, sounding decidedly grim. The air suddenly became charged with tension.

Ambar Sen gave Feluda a piercing look and said, 'Mr Mitter, I am something of an amateur detective myself. What if I were to tell you it was you who took the money just to keep us guessing for a while? When there's no real criminal, no one's actually been kidnapped, where could the money have gone?'

Feluda shook his head. 'No, Mr Sen, I'm afraid your deductions are quite wrong. At Princep Ghat this evening, there was someone else, apart from myself, also in disguise.'

'Really? Did you see him?'

'Yes, but I didn't recognize him.'

'I see, but why did you let that bother you? If you knew the man was in disguise, you should have caught him then and there!'

'No, that would not have been dramatic enough. You like drama, don't you? I think exposing the man in front of you would be much more dramatic. It is my belief that he is present in this room. But I have to be absolutely sure.'

There was a pindrop silence in the room. I cast a sidelong glance at Runa. Even she had turned pale.

'Bilash Babu, could you please check your shoes?' Feluda asked.

Bilash Babu was standing near the door. 'My shoes?' he said ruefully. 'What is there to check? They're smeared with coal tar. My feet kept getting stuck to the ground when I came back from the ghat after leaving that bag there.'

'I had spread coal tar around that particular pillar,' Feluda told us, 'because I had reason to suspect someone. All of you had made up tales for me. But the pack of lies this person told me was different from . . . why, where are you going?'

The only route of escape was blocked by the solid frame of Bilash

Babu. He reached out and caught the person who was trying to slip out quickly. It was Samaresh Mallik. 'Take off your sandals, Mr Mallik, and let everyone have a look. Bilash Babu might be able to help.' Mr Mallik remained still, like a statue. Bilash Babu bent down and took off one of his sandals. Like his own shoes, it was covered with tar. There could be no doubt that Mr Mallik had been to Princep Ghat.

'Your Koh-i-noor Pictures went out of business two years ago, didn't it?' Feluda went on. 'How could you go round telling people you were still working there? How did you manage all this while? Where did you get the money from?'

Mr Mallik did not answer. Bilash Babu was still holding him tight, looking as though he had no intention of letting him go until the police arrived.

'I must say you have only me to thank for exposing this man. You had no idea, Mr Sen, did you? And you certainly would not have left a bag full of cash by that pillar unless I had insisted, and said I myself was going to be present there. Anyway, Mr Mallik has now got twenty thousand rupees. If he doesn't return it to you himself, you are of course free to call the police. They have various methods of dealing with such people. My job here is over. I think it's time for us to go.'

At these words, Lalmohan Babu and I rose to our feet, but were obliged to sit down again.

'Go? Most certainly not!' exclaimed Mrs Sen. 'You think I will let you go without making amends for having told you so many lies? No, you cannot go without having dinner with us tonight.'

'Besides,' Ambar Sen put in, 'some of that twenty thousand should definitely go to you. How can you leave without taking what is your due?'

'And today all three of you have come together. Won't you stay to sign my autograph book?' Runa piped up.

Lalmohan Babu clinched matters.

'End well that all's well!' he declared.

The Gold Coins of Jehangir

ONE

'Hello can I speak to Mr Mitter, please?'

'Speaking.'

'Namaskar. My name is Shankarprasad Chowdhury. I live in Panihati. You don't know me, but I am calling you to make a special request.'

'Yes?'

'I'd like you to visit my house here in Panihati. It is by the Ganges. It's about a hundred years old and is called Amaravati. Locally it's quite well-known. I'm aware of the kind of work you do, and that you're normally accompanied by your cousin and your friend, so I'm inviting all three of you. Do you think you could come next Saturday, say around ten in the morning? You could stay the night and go back the following morning.'

'Are you in trouble of some kind? I mean, you said you knew about my profession, so I wonder . . . ?'

'Yes, why else would I need to seek your help? But I'm not going to talk about it on the phone. I think you'll enjoy staying in my house. You'll be well looked after—I can guarantee that—and you'll get a chance to exercise your brain.'

'Well, I must confess I am free this weekend.'

'In that case, please say yes. But I must mention something else.'

'What is it?'

'There will be a few other people here. I don't want them to know who you are—at least, not right away. There's a special reason for this.'

'You mean we should come in disguise?'

'No, no, that will not be necessary. After all, you're not a film star, so I don't think the others are familiar with your appearance. All you need to do is choose yourselves three different roles. I can even suggest what roles you might play.'

'Yes?'

'My great-grandfather Banwarilal Chowdhury was a strange man. I'll tell you about him when we meet, but you could pretend you have come to collect information about him to write his biography. In fact, I really think it's time his biography was written.'

'Very well. What about my friend, Mr Ganguli?'

'Do you have a pair of binoculars?'

'Yes.'

'Then why don't you turn him into a bird-watcher? I get plenty of birds in my garden. That'll give him something to do.'

'All right; and my cousin could be the bird-watcher's nephew.'

'Good idea. So I'll see you on Saturday, at around ten?'

'Yes, I'll look forward to that. Thank you and goodbye!'

Feluda put the phone down and repeated the whole conversation to me. He ended by saying, 'Some people speak with such genuine warmth and sincerity that it becomes impossible to turn down their request. This Mr Chowdhury is such a man.'

'But why should you even think of turning him down? From what he told you, there's a case waiting in Panihati for you. Surely you have to think of earning some money, at least occasionally?'

Over the last couple of months, Feluda had refused to accept a single case. He did this often after a spate of great activity, during which he might have had to work on more than one case. Then he would take some time off and spend his days studying different subjects. His current passion was the primitive man. He found an article by an American scientist called Richard Leaky in which it was suggested that the actual process of evolution took far longer than is generally believed. This got Feluda terribly excited. He paid five visits to the museum, went three times to the National Library and once to the zoo.

'Do you know what the latest theory says?' he told me once. 'It says man came from a particular species of apes called the "killer ape". That's why there is an inherent tendency towards violence in man.'

The chances of encountering violence in Panihati seemed remote, but I knew Feluda would welcome the opportunity to get out of Calcutta for a couple of days. In fact, we all enjoyed short trips to neighbouring towns.

We left for Panihati on Saturday morning in Lalmohan Babu's Ambassador. His driver being away, Feluda took his place. 'What a responsibility you've thrust upon me, Felu Babu,' Lalmohan Babu remarked as we set off. 'A bird-watcher? Me? I've never seen anything except crows and sparrows where I live. What use are these binoculars to me, and these two books you have told me to read?' The two books in question were Salim Ali's *Indian Birds* and Ajoy Hom's *The Birds of Bengal*.

'Don't worry,' Feluda reassured him. 'Just remember a crow is *Corvus splendens*, and a sparrow is *Passer domesticus*. But you needn't try to learn the Latin names of all the birds you might see—that'll only make you stutter. All you need do is throw in ordinary English names like drongo, tailor-bird or jungle babbler. If even that is difficult, just keep peering through your binoculars. That'll do.'

'I see. And what about a new name for me?'

'You are Bhabatosh Sinha. Topshe is your nephew. His name is Prabeer. And I am Someshwar Roy.'

We reached Mr Chowdhury's house in Panihati at five minutes to ten. The Gurkha at the gate opened it as he saw our car approach. Feluda drove gently up a cobbled driveway. The house was huge, and it had a massive compound. Whoever designed it must have been impressed by English castles, for the general pattern of the house reminded me instantly of pictures of castles I had seen. There was a garden on one side in which grew a number of flowers. It had a greenhouse in one corner, behind which an orchard began.

Mr Chowdhury was waiting for us at the door. 'Welcome to Amaravati!' he said, smiling, as we got out. He appeared to be about fifty, was of medium height and had a clear complexion. He was dressed in a pyjama-kurta and carried a cheroot in one hand.

'My cousin Jayanta arrived yesterday. I've told him everything, but he's not going to tell the others who you really are. I trust him entirely,' said Mr Chowdhury.

'Very well. But are the others already here?'

'No, I'm expecting them in the evening. Please come in; you can have a little rest, and we can talk more comfortably inside.'

We went in and sat on a wide veranda that overlooked the river. It was beautiful. I noticed a few steps going down to the edge of the water. It appeared to be a private bathing ghat.

'Is that ghat still in use?' Feluda asked.

'Oh yes. My aunt lives here, you see. She bathes in the Ganges every day.'

'Does she live alone?'

'No, no. I've been living here for the last couple of years. I work in Titagarh. That's closer from here than from my house in Calcutta.'

'How old is your aunt?'

'Seventy-eight. Our old servant Ananta looks after her. She's more or less in good health, except that she's lost most of her teeth and has had to have cataracts removed from both her eyes. Besides, she's turned a little senile—she can no longer remember names, she complains of not having eaten even after she's been fed, sometimes she gets up in the middle of the night to crush paan leaves for herself, for she can't chew on paan any more . . . you know, that kind of thing. She suffers from insomnia, too. If she gets two hours' sleep every day, she's lucky. She could have stayed in Calcutta, but after my uncle died, she decided to come and live here.'

A bearer brought tea and sweets on a tray. 'Please help yourselves,' Mr Chowdhury invited. 'Lunch is going to be delayed. I think you'll like the sweets. You don't get this kind in Calcutta.'

'Thank you,' Feluda replied, picking up a steaming cup from the tray. 'Well, Mr Chowdhury, you know who I am. It'll help if you told me who you are and what you do. I hope you don't mind?'

'No, no, of course not. I asked you to come here simply to tell you a few things, didn't I? Very simply, I am a businessman. A successful businessman, as you can see.'

'Has your family always had a business?'

'No. This house was built by Banwarilal Chowdhury, my great-grandfather.'

'The same man whose biography I am supposed to be writing?'

'That's right. He was a barrister. He used to practise in Rampur. In time, he became quite wealthy and came to Calcutta. Then he decided to move here and had this house built. In fact, he died in this house. My grandfather, too, was a barrister, but his passion for gambling and drinking ate heavily into his savings. It was my father who started a business and eventually strengthened our financial position again. I simply carried on what my father had started. Things at present are not too bad. I only feel sorry to think about the possessions of Banwarilal that my grandfather sold to settle his gambling debts.'

'What about your cousin?'

'Jayanta did not join me in my business. He works for an engineering firm. I believe he earns quite well, but of late he's started to play poker in his club. Clearly our grandfather's blood runs in his veins. Jayanta is five years younger than me.'

I noticed that Feluda had switched on the microcassette recorder that we had brought back from Hong Kong. It was now so much easier to record what a client told us.

'Well, that covers my relatives. Let me tell you something about a few other people,' Mr Chowdhury added.

'Before you do that,' Feluda interrupted, 'please allow me to ask a question. Although it's almost gone, I can see traces of a white *tika* on your forehead. Does that mean—?'

'Yes, it's my birthday today. My aunt put that *tika*.'

'Oh, I see. Is that why you've invited your friends this evening?'

'There will be only three people. I had invited them last year to celebrate my fiftieth birthday. I had no wish to invite people again on my birthday this year. But there's a special reason why I had to.'

'And what is that?'

Mr Chowdhury thought for a minute. Then he said, 'If you will be so kind as to come with me to my aunt's room upstairs, I can explain things better.'

We finished our tea and rose. The staircase going up was through the drawing room. I was greatly impressed by the beautiful old furniture, the chandeliers, the carpets and the marble statues that filled the large drawing room.

'Who else lives on the first floor apart from your aunt?' asked Feluda, quickly climbing the stairs.

'My aunt's room is at one end. I have a room at the other. When Jayanta visits us, he, too, sleeps in a room on my side of the building.'

We crossed the landing and entered Mr Chowdhury's aunt's room. It was a big room, but only sparsely furnished. Through one of its open doors came a fresh cool breeze. The river must lie on that particular side. An old lady was sitting on a mat by the side of the open door, prayer beads in her hand. Next to her on the mat was a hand-grinder, a few paan leaves in a container and a big fat book. It must be either the *Ramayana* or the *Mahabharata*, I thought. The old lady glanced up and peered at us through thick lenses.

'I have a few visitors from Calcutta,' Mr Chowdhury informed her.

'So you decided to show them this ancient relic?' asked his aunt.

We went forward to touch her feet. 'It's very good of you to have come,' she said. 'There's no point in telling me your names. I couldn't remember even a single one. Why, I often forget my own! It doesn't matter, I suppose, my days are numbered, anyway. I only have to wait for the end . . .'

'Come this way, please.'

We turned as Mr Chowdhury spoke. The old lady went back to her prayer beads, mumbling under her breath.

Mr Chowdhury led us to the opposite end of the room where there was a huge chest. He took out a key from his pocket and began unlocking it. 'What I am going to show you now,' he said, 'belonged once to my great-grandfather. Many of his clients in Rampur were Nawabs, who often gave him expensive gifts. In spite of his son having sold most of them, what remains today is not insignificant. Take a look at these!'

He picked up a small velvet bag and turned it over on his palm. A number of gold coins slipped out. 'These are said to have been used by Jehangir,' said Mr Chowdhury. 'A sign of the zodiac is engraved on each.'

'But you've only got eleven pieces here. Surely there are twelve zodiac signs?'

'Yes. One of the coins is missing.'

We exchanged puzzled glances. Missing? Why was it missing?

'But there are other interesting objects as well,' Mr Chowdhury continued. 'Look, there's this golden snuff box from Italy. It's studded with rubies. There's a goblet made of jade, also studded with rubies and emeralds, and a large collection of rings and pendants made of precious stones. I will show you those in the evening when the others are here.'

'You keep the key to this chest, don't you?' Feluda asked.

'Yes. There is a duplicate which is kept in my aunt's wardrobe.'

'But why haven't you kept this chest in your own room?'

'My great-grandfather used to live in this room. It was he who had placed the chest in this corner. I saw no reason to remove it. Besides, we have very reliable guards at the gate and my aunt spends most of her time in this room. So it's quite safe to leave it here.'

We returned to the veranda downstairs. Feluda switched on his recorder again and asked, 'How does a single coin happen to be missing?'

'That's what I want to talk to you about. You see, last year on my birthday, I had invited three people. One of them was my business partner, Naresh Kanjilal. The second guest was Dr Ardhendu Sarkar. He lives here in Panihati. The third was Kalinath Roy, an old friend from school. I had lost touch with him completely. He contacted me after thirty-five years. Each one of these guests had heard of my great-grandfather's possessions, but none had seen any of them. That evening, I told Jayanta to take out the little bag of gold coins and bring it down to the drawing room. He did so, and I spread all twelve out on a table. We were bending over these to get a better look when suddenly, there was a power cut. Mind you, this was nothing unusual. One of the bearers brought candles in less than two minutes, and I put the coins back in the chest. Rather foolishly, I did not count them then for it never occurred to me that one might go missing. The next day, when it did dawn on me that counting the pieces might be a good idea, it was too late. My guests had left, and the coin showing the sign of cancer had vanished.'

'Are you sure you yourself had put the coins away?'

'Oh yes. But just think of my predicament, Mr Mitter. The three outsiders were all my guests. I have known my business partner for twenty-five years. Dr Sarkar is a well-known doctor here; and Kalinath is an old friend.'

'But are they totally honest? Do you happen to know that for a fact?'

'No, and that's why I'm so utterly confused. Take Kanjilal, for instance. Many businessmen are often dishonest in their dealings, but I've seen Kanjilal lie and cheat without the slightest qualm. It disturbs me very much. He knows this and often laughs at me. He says I should give up my business and become a preacher.'

'And the other?'

'I don't know too much about the doctor. He treats my aunt occasionally for rheumatism, that's all. But Kalinath . . . he makes me wonder. He rang me one day purely out of the blue, and said the older he was getting, the more inclined was he becoming to look back. He missed his childhood friends, so he wanted to come and see me.'

'Did you recognize him easily after all these years?'

'Yes. Besides, he talked of our years in school at great length. There's no doubt that he is my old classmate. What worries me is that he never tells me what he does for a living. I have asked him many times, but all he has ever said is that he, too, is a businessman. I don't know any other detail. He's a talented enough person—very jolly and cheerful, and clever with his hands. He knew magic in school and, in fact, is even now quite good at performing sleight of hand.'

'But your cousin was also in the room, surely?'

'Yes. He wasn't standing anywhere near the table, though. He had seen the coins before, so he wasn't interested. If anyone stole it, it must have been one of the other three.'

'What did you do when you realized one of the coins had gone?'

'What could I do? Anyone else would have reported the matter to the police and had these people's houses searched. But I couldn't do this. I've played bridge with them so often. For heaven's sake, I have always treated them as my friends! How could I suddenly turn around and call one of them a thief?'

'Does that mean you did nothing at all, and so none of them realizes he might be under suspicion?'

'That's right. In the last twelve months, I've met them on many occasions, but they've all behaved absolutely normally. Not one of them ever appeared uncomfortable in my presence. Yet, I know that one of them must be the culprit.'

We all fell silent. What a strange situation it was! But what was one supposed to do now?

Feluda asked the same question a few seconds later. 'I have a plan, Mr Mitter,' Mr Chowdhury replied. 'Since none of these people think I suspect them, I have invited them again to look at some of the other valuable possessions of Banwarilal. For the last few weeks, we've been having a power cut on the dot of seven every evening. Today, I shall place these objects on the same table a few minutes before seven. When the lights go off, I expect the thief would not be able to resist the temptation to remove something else. The total value of these pieces would be in the region of five million rupees, Mr Mitter. If something does get stolen this time, you can stop pretending to be a writer and start an investigation immediately.'

'I see. What does your cousin have to say about all this?'

'He didn't know anything about my plan until last night. He got quite cross at first. He said I should have gone to the police a year ago, and that it was too late now for you to do anything.'

'May I say something, Mr Chowdhury?'

'Yes, certainly.'

'The thief simply took advantage of your mild and easygoing nature. Not too many people would have hesitated to accuse one of their guests of stealing, if they were as sure of their facts as you seem to be.'

'I know. That's really why I sought your help. I know you will be able to do what I couldn't.'

TWO

We had lunch a little later. Mr Chowdhury's cook produced an excellent meal, including hilsa from the Ganges cooked in mustard sauce. We met Mr Chowdhury's cousin, Jayanta, at the dining table. He seemed a most amiable man, not very tall but well-built.

'I'm going to rest for a while,' said Mr Chowdhury after lunch. 'Please feel free to do what you like. I'll meet you at teatime.'

We decided to explore the grounds with Jayanta Babu.

On the western side of the house was a wall with pillars that went right up to the river. A slope began where the wall ended, leading to the river-bank. Jayanta Babu took us to see the garden. He was passionately fond of flowers, roses in particular. He spoke at some length on the subject. I learnt for the first time that there were three hundred types of roses.

On the northern side was another gate. Most people in the house used this gate to go out if they wanted to go to the main town, Jayanta Babu told us. There was another flight of steps on this side, also going down to the river. 'My mother—the old lady you met this morning—uses these stairs when she goes to bathe in the river,' said Jayanta Babu.

We came back to our room after a few minutes. Jayanta Babu went to the greenhouse to look at his orchids. We had been given two adjoining rooms on the ground floor. There were three other rooms across the passage. Presumably, those were meant for the other three guests.

Lalmohan Babu took one look at the large, comfortable bed and said, 'Hey, I feel like having a nap, too. But no, I must read those books you gave me.'

'Feluda,' I said when he had gone, 'have you thought about the plan this evening? Even if there is a power cut at seven, what happens if the thief does not steal anything this time? How will you catch him?'

'I can't. At least, not without studying all three people carefully. Anyone with a tendency to stealing would have a subtle difference in his behaviour. It shouldn't be impossible to spot it if I watch him closely. Don't forget that a thief is a criminal, no matter how polished and sophisticated his appearance might be.'

Soon, the sound of two cars stopping outside the front door told us that the guests had arrived. Mr Chowdhury came to fetch us himself when tea had been laid out on the veranda, and introduced us to the others.

Dr Sarkar lived within a mile, so he had come walking. About fifty years old, he had a receding hairline and specks of grey in his hair. But his moustache was jet black.

Naresh Kanjilal was tall and hefty. He was dressed formally in a suit. 'I am very glad you've decided to write Banwarilal's biography,' he said to Feluda. 'I've often told Shankar to have this done. Banwarilal was a remarkable man.'

Kalinath Roy turned out to be a fun-loving man. He was carrying a shoulder bag, possibly containing equipment for magic. He smiled as he met Lalmohan Babu and said, 'Who knew a bird-watcher would go carrying an egg in his pocket?' Then he quickly slipped a hand into Lalmohan Babu's pocket and brought out a smooth white stone egg. 'What a pity!' he said, shaking his head regretfully. 'I was planning to have it fried!'

It was decided that after dinner, Mr Roy would hold a small magic show for us.

It had started to get dark. The last few rays of the sun shone on the water. A cool breeze rose from the river. Mr Kanjilal and Mr Roy went for a walk. Lalmohan Babu had been fidgeting for some time. Now he rose to his feet with the binoculars in his hand and said, 'I thought I heard the cry of a paradise flycatcher. Let me see if the bird is anywhere around.' I looked at Feluda as Lalmohan Babu went out busily; but, seeing that Feluda had kept a perfectly straight face, I managed to stop myself from bursting into laughter.

Dr Sarkar took a sip from his cup and turned to Mr Chowdhury. 'Where is your cousin? Is he still roaming in his garden?'

'You know how he feels about his flowers.'

'True. But I told him to wear a cap if he were to spend long hours out in the sun. Has he taken my advice?'

'Do you think Jayanta would ever take a doctor's advice? You know him better than that, don't you?'

Feluda was watching the doctor covertly, a Charminar in his hand.

'How is your aunt?' Dr Sarkar asked.

'Not too bad. But she was complaining of having lost her appetite. Why don't you pay her a visit?'

'Yes, I think I'll do that. Excuse me.'

Dr Sarkar got up and went upstairs. Jayanta Babu returned from the garden as soon as he left, grinning broadly.

'Why, what's so amusing?' Mr Chowdhury asked.

Jayanta Babu poured himself a cup of tea and turned to Feluda, still grinning. 'Your friend is trying desperately to pass himself off as a bird-watcher. I found him in the garden peering through his binoculars, looking dead serious.'

Feluda laughed. 'Well, virtually everyone present here will have to do a certain amount of acting today, won't he? Your cousin's plan has a heavy element of drama in it, don't you think?'

Jayanta Babu stopped smiling.

'Do you approve of my cousin's plan?' he asked.

'Why, don't you?'

'No, not in the least. The thief, I am sure, is far too clever to fall for something so obvious. You think he doesn't know we've discovered that a gold coin is missing?'

'Yes, Jayanta, you're quite right,' replied Mr Chowdhury, 'but I still want to give it a try. Call it simply a whim, if you like, or the result of reading too many detective novels.'

'Do you want to take out every single object from the chest?'

'No, no, just the snuff box and the goblet. They're both in an ivory box. Dr Sarkar is with your mother right now. You must go to her room the minute he returns and get me those two things. Here's the key.'

Jayanta Babu took the key with marked reluctance.

Dr Sarkar returned in five minutes. 'Your aunt is just fine,' he said happily. 'I left her on the veranda, eating rice and milk. She's going to be around for quite some time, Mr Chowdhury. She is in pretty good health.'

Jayanta Babu left without a word. 'Why are you still sitting around?' Dr Sarkar asked Feluda. 'Let's go out and get some fresh air. You'll never get such clean air in Calcutta.'

All of us got up and went down the steps. I spotted Lalmohan Babu behind a marble statue in the garden, still peering through the binoculars.

'Did you find the paradise flycatcher?' Feluda asked him.

'No. But I think I saw a jungle babbler.'

'Lalmohan Babu, it is now time for the birds to return to their nests. In a few minutes, you won't be able to find anything except perhaps an owl.'

There was no sign of either Naresh Kanjilal or Kalinath Roy.

Where had they gone? Could they be in the orchard behind the greenhouse?

'Hey, Naresh, where are you hiding?' called Mr Chowdhury. 'And Kalinath, where have you got to?'

'I saw one of them go into the house.' said Lalmohan Babu.

'Which one?'

'I think it was the magician.'

But Lalmohan Babu was wrong. It was Naresh Kanjilal who emerged from the house, not Kalinath Roy. 'The temperature drops very quickly the moment the sun goes down,' he said upon seeing us, 'so I had gone inside to get my shawl.'

'Where's Kalinath?'

'Why, he left me as soon as we reached the garden. He said he had learnt a new trick to turn old, wilted flowers into fresh new ones, so . . .'

Mr Kanjilal could not finish speaking. He was interrupted by Mr Chowdhury's old servant, Ananta, who came rushing out of the house, shouting and waving madly. 'Why, Ananta, whatever's the matter?' Mr Chowdhury asked anxiously.

'Come quickly, sir. It's Jayanta Babu. He fell . . . upstairs . . . he's lying on the stairs, unconscious.'

THREE

Each one of us sped upstairs without a word. We found Jayanta Babu lying just outside his mother's room on the landing, about three feet away from the threshold. He had hurt the back of his head. Blood had oozed out on the floor, to form a small red pool.

Dr Sarkar was the first to reach him. He sat down by Jayanta Babu and quickly took his pulse. Feluda joined him a second later. He was looking grave, and frowning deeply.

'What do you think?' asked Mr Chowdhury in a low voice.

'His pulse is faster than it should be.'

'And that wound on his head?'

'He must have got it as he fell. I got tired of telling him to wear a cap when working in the sun.'

'Concussion—?'

'It's impossible to tell without making a proper examination. The trouble is, I didn't bring my medical kit today. I think he should be removed to a hospital right away.'

'That's not a problem. I have a car.'

Feluda helped the others in carrying Jayanta Babu to the car. He remained unconscious. Kalinath Roy met us on the staircase.

'I had stepped into my room just for a second to take some medicine—and this happened!' he exclaimed.

'Shall I come with you?' asked Mr Chowdhury as Dr Sarkar got into the car.

'No, there's no need to do that. I'll give you a ring from the hospital.'

The car left. I felt very sorry for Mr Chowdhury. What an awful thing to happen on one's birthday. Besides, now his plan wouldn't work, either.

We went into the drawing room and sat down. But Feluda sprang to his feet almost immediately and went out of the room with a brief 'I'll be back in a minute'. He returned soon enough, but I couldn't tell where he had gone. Mr Chowdhury continued to speak normally, even going so far as to tell his guests a few stories about his great-grandfather. But clearly it wasn't easy for him to remain calm and cheerful, when he must have been feeling anxious about his cousin.

Dr Sarkar rang an hour later. Jayanta Babu had regained consciousness and was feeling better. He would probably come back home the next day.

This piece of news helped everyone relax, but the chief purpose of our visit seemed to have been defeated. Mr Chowdhury made no attempt to bring out any objects from the chest and, in fact, after declining his offer to show us films on video, we returned to our room soon after dinner. The magic show also got cancelled.

As soon as we were back in our room, Lalmohan Babu asked the question I had been dying to ask for a long time.

'Where did you disappear to when we were all in the drawing room?'

'I went to Mr Chowdhury's aunt's room.'

'Why? Just to see how she was doing?' Lalmohan Babu sounded sceptical.

'Yes, but I also pulled at the handle of that chest.'

'Oh? And was it open?'

'No. I don't think Jayanta Babu got the chance to open it. He seemed to have fallen on the floor before he got to the room.'

'But where's the key?' I asked.

'I don't think Mr Chowdhury thought of looking for it. Everything happened so quickly.'

I opened my mouth to speak, but at this moment, Mr Chowdhury himself came into the room. 'I am so sorry about everything,' he said, 'but thank goodness Jayanta is feeling better. This happened once before. Sometimes his blood pressure drops alarmingly.'

'What else did Dr Sarkar say?'

'That's what I came to tell you. I didn't want to say anything in front of the others. You see, I had forgotten all about the key. Now, the doctor tells me Jayanta hasn't got it. Perhaps it slipped out of his pocket as he fell.'

'Did you look for it?'

'Oh yes, I looked everywhere on the landing, the stairs and even outside the front door. That key has vanished.'

'Never mind. You have a duplicate, don't you?'

'Yes, but that's not the point. The mystery hasn't been solved, has it? That's what's worrying me. I couldn't even give you the chance to exercise your brain!'

'So what? I wouldn't consider this visit entirely fruitless. I've seen this beautiful house and enjoyed your wonderful hospitality. That's good enough for me, Mr Chowdhury.'

Mr Chowdhury smiled. 'It's very kind of you to say so, Mr Mitter. Anyway, I shall now bid you good-night. Your bed tea will arrive at six-thirty, and breakfast will be served at eight.'

Lalmohan Babu spoke in a whisper when Mr Chowdhury had gone. 'Could this be a case of attempted murder?' he asked. 'After all, both Mr Kanjilal and Mr Roy had gone into the house.'

'Surely murder was unnecessary to get what they wanted? All they had to do was make sure Jayanta Babu was unconscious.'

'What do you mean?'

'Just that. How long would it take, do you think, to remove a key from the pocket of an unconscious man, unlock the chest, take what was needed and then slip the key back where it had been found?'

I hadn't thought of this at all.

'If that is the case,' I said, 'then we have two suspects instead of three—Kanjilal and Roy.'

'No,' Feluda shook his head, 'it's not as simple as that. If someone else had struck him unconscious, Jayanta Babu would have said so the minute he opened his eyes in the hospital. He didn't. Besides, his mother was in the room throughout. Surely she'd have said something if anyone other than a family member started to open the chest? I could pull at the handle only because her back was turned for a second.'

I didn't know what to say. So I went to bed, though I couldn't go to sleep. Feluda was still pacing in the room. What was keeping him awake, I wondered. After a few minutes, Lalmohan Babu returned from his own room.

'Have you looked out of the window?' he asked. 'I have never seen things bathed in moonlight like this. It's a crime to stay indoors on such a night!'

'Yes, you are right,' Feluda began moving towards the door. 'Let's go out. If you must turn into a poet in the middle of the night, you should have witnesses.'

Outside, Amaravati and its surroundings were looking more beautiful than they had done during the day. A thin mist covered everything on the other side of the river. The reflection of the moon shimmered in the dark, rippling water. The sound of crickets in the distance, the smell of hasnuhana, and a fresh breeze combined together to give the atmosphere a magical quality. Feluda looked at the nearly full moon and remarked, 'Man may have landed there, but who can ever take away the joy of sitting in moonlight?'

'There's a terrific poem about the moon,' declared Lalmohan Babu.

'Written, no doubt, by that man who was a teacher in your Athenium Institution?'

'Yes. Baikuntha Mallik. No one in our foolish, miserable country ever gave him his due, but he's a great poet. Listen to this one. Tapesh, listen carefully.'

We had been talking in soft tones. But now, Lalmohan Babu's voice rose automatically as he began to recite the poem.

'O moon, how I admire you!
A silver disc one day,
or half-a-disc as days go by,
or a quarter, or even
just a slice, oh my,
like a piece of nail, freshly cut,
lying in the sky.
After that comes the moonless night,

there's no trace of you.
As you, my love, are hidden from sight,
untouched by moonlight, too!'

Lalmohan Babu stopped and, unaware that I was trying desperately hard not to laugh, said seriously, 'As you can see, Tapesh, the poem is actually addressed to a lady.'

'Well, certainly your recitation has caused a lady to come out of her room,' Feluda observed, staring at the balcony on the first floor. This balcony was attached to Mr Chowdhury's aunt's room. The old lady, clad in her white sari, had stepped out of her room and was standing on the balcony, looking around. She remained there for about a minute. Then she went back inside.

We turned towards the river and sat on the steps of the ghat for more than half an hour. Finally, Feluda glanced at his watch and said, 'It's nearly one o'clock. Let's go.' We rose, and stopped still as a strange noise reached our ears.

Thud, thud, clang! Thud, thud, clang!

Slowly, we climbed the steps of the ghat and made our way back to the house.

'Is someone digging a s-secret p-passage?' Lalmohan Babu whispered.

My eyes turned towards the old lady's room. That was where the noise appeared to be coming from. A faint light flickered in it.

Thud, thud, thud, thud, clang, clang!

But another light was on in one of the rooms in the far end. I could actually see someone through the open window. It was a man, talking agitatedly. A few seconds later he went out of the room.

'Mr Kanjilal,' Feluda muttered, 'in Mr Chowdhury's room.'

'What could they have been talking about so late at night?'

'I don't know. Perhaps it was something to do with their business.'

'Why, couldn't you sleep, either?'

All of us started as a new voice spoke unexpectedly. Then I noticed the magician, Kalinath Roy, coming out of the shadows.

That strange noise hadn't stopped. Mr Roy raised his head and looked at the open window of the old lady's room. 'Have you figured out what's causing that noise?' he asked.

'A hand grinder?' said Feluda.

'Exactly. Mr Chowdhury's aunt often wakes in the middle of the night and decides to crush paan leaves in her grinder. I've heard that noise before.'

Mr Roy took out a cigarette from his pocket and lit it. Then he shook the match slowly until it went out, and gave Feluda a sharp, knowing look.

'Why do you suppose a private investigator had to be invited to act as Banwarilal's biographer?' he asked casually. I gasped in astonishment. So did Lalmohan Babu.

Feluda laughed lightly. 'Oh, I'm glad someone recognized me!' he said.

'There's a lot that I know, Mr Mitter. I've been through so much that my eyes and ears have got accustomed to staying open at all times.'

Feluda looked steadily at him. 'Will you come to the point, Mr Roy? Or will you continue to speak in riddles?'

'How many people have you met who can speak their minds openly? Most people do not want to open their mouths. Unfortunately, I am one of them. You are the investigator, it is your job to speak openly and reveal all. But let me tell you one thing. You can forget about using your professional skills here in Shankar's house. Do spend a few days here, if you like, have fun and enjoy yourself. But if you meddle in things that don't concern you, you'll get into trouble.'

'I see. Thanks for your advice.'

Kalinath Roy went back into the house.

'It seems he knows something vital,' Lalmohan Babu observed.

'Yes, but that's not surprising, is it? After all, he was here last year. He may have seen something.'

'Or maybe Mr Roy himself is the thief?' I said. 'Don't you remember what Mr Chowdhury said about his sleight of hand?'

'Precisely,' Feluda nodded.

FOUR

I woke at six-thirty the following morning as my bed-tea arrived. But Feluda appeared to have risen long before me.

'I've been for a walk. Went to see the town,' he told me.

'What did you see?'

'Oh, a lot of things. The main thing is that now I'm convinced our visit isn't going to be a waste of time.'

Lalmohan Babu entered the room at this moment and declared that he hadn't slept so soundly for a long time.

'I think the old lady upstairs also slept well last night. She got up much later than usual this morning,' Feluda remarked.

'How on earth do you know that?'

'Ananta told me. He said she was late for her visit to the river. Normally she goes to the ghat at six every morning.'

The three of us were sitting on the veranda. Mr Chowdhury joined us in ten minutes. He had had his bath, and looked quite fresh.

'I'm afraid I've been recognized,' Feluda told him. 'Your old classmate knows who I am.'

'What!'

'Yes. You were right about him. He knows much more than he lets on.'

'So should I tell everyone else the truth, do you think?'

'Yes, but if you do that, you'll also have to tell them why I am here. I mean, your secret can no longer remain a secret, can it?'

Mr Chowdhury began to look worried and unhappy. But before he could say anything, Mr Kanjilal and Mr Roy appeared together. Almost in the same instant, a car tooted outside the front door. Feluda, Lalmohan Babu and I went with Mr Chowdhury to see who had arrived. The other two remained on the veranda.

A black Ambassador with a red cross painted on one side was standing outside. Dr Sarkar and Jayanta Babu got out and came walking towards us. The wound on Jayanta Babu's head was now dressed. Some of his hair had had to be shaved for this purpose. 'I am so very sorry,' he said to his cousin. 'I ruined your birthday, didn't I? Actually, my blood pressure—'

'Yes, Mr Chowdhury is aware of the details,' Dr Sarkar cut in. 'You're fine now, and there is no cause for concern. But no more roaming in the sun for you.'

'You'll stay for a cup of tea, won't you?' invited Mr Chowdhury.

'Yes, a cup of tea would be very nice, thank you.'

'Where are the others?' asked Jayanta Babu.

'They're on the veranda.'

Dr Sarkar and Jayanta Babu went off to join the others. Mr Chowdhury was about to follow them, but Feluda's words stopped him. 'Wait, Mr Chowdhury, there's something we need to do before we go back to the veranda,' Feluda said. There was something in his tone that made Mr Chowdhury look up in surprise.

'What is it?'

'You said your aunt had the duplicate key to the chest in her room. Would she give it to us now?'

'Yes, certainly if I asked her for it. But—'

'I need to open it and see what's inside. Yes, now.'

Without another word, Mr Chowdhury led us upstairs. We found his aunt getting ready to go for her bath.

'What!' Mr Chowdhury exclaimed. 'How did you manage to get so late today?'

'God knows. I just overslept. This doesn't happen very often, of course, but sometimes . . . I don't know . . .'

'I need the duplicate key to the chest.'

'Why? What have you done with yours?'

'I can't find it,' said Mr Chowdhury, a little helplessly. His aunt opened her wardrobe, and found a large bunch of keys which she handed to him silently. Then she left the room.

Mr Chowdhury went to open the chest. For some odd reason, Feluda stopped for a second to pick up the hand grinder from the floor and inspect it briefly.

'Oh my God, I don't believe this!'

Startled by Mr Chowdhury's scream, Lalmohan Babu dropped the book by Salim Ali he had been carrying under his arm.

'That little bag of gold coins and the ivory box have both disappeared, I take it?' Feluda asked calmly. Mr Chowdhury swallowed, unable to speak.

'Lock up your chest again, Mr Chowdhury, and then let's go downstairs. The time has come to reveal the truth. Please tell the others who I really am, and also tell them that I would be asking them a few questions.'

Mr Chowdhury pulled himself together with a supreme effort, and we trooped down to join the other guests on the veranda.

'I'd like to tell you something,' began Mr Chowdhury, and spoke briefly about what had happened on his previous birthday and what he had discovered only a few minutes ago.

'I could never have imagined that one of my close associates would do such a thing in my own house,' he finished, 'but there is no doubt at all that a gold coin was stolen last year, and now other things are missing. I am therefore asking Mr Mitter, who is a well-known investigator, to make a proper investigation. He would now like to ask you a few questions. I hope you will be good enough to answer them honestly.'

No one spoke. It was impossible to tell what each one of them was thinking. Feluda addressed his first question to Dr Sarkar. It came as a complete surprise to me.

'Dr Sarkar, how many hospitals are there in Panihati?'

'Only one.'

'Does that mean that was where you took Jayanta Babu last night and that was where you rang from?'

'Why do you ask?'

'I'm asking this question because I went to that hospital this morning. Jayanta Babu hadn't been taken there.'

Dr Sarkar laughed. 'But I never said I was calling from the hospital, did I, Mr Chowdhury?'

'Well then, where were you calling from?'

'From my house. Jayanta Babu regained consciousness in the car, which meant that his injury was not as serious as I had thought and there was no concussion. So I decided to take him to my house to keep him under observation overnight.'

'All night. Now let me ask Jayanta Babu something. You took a key from your cousin yesterday. Was it still in your hand when you fell?'

'Yes, but I wouldn't know what happened to it afterwards.'

'It should have fallen somewhere on the landing, or in the vicinity of where you were found lying. But no one could find it.'

'So? How am I responsible for that? Why don't you stop beating about the bush, Mr Mitter, and tell us what you really mean?'

'One more question, and then I'll speak my mind, I promise you. Dr Sarkar, are you aware of a substance called *alta*?'

'Yes, isn't it a red liquid women use on their feet? I know my wife does, occasionally.'

'And you're also aware, aren't you, that at one glance it would be difficult to tell the difference between *alta* and blood, especially if the light was poor?'

Dr Sarkar cleared his throat and nodded.

'Very well. I shall now tell you all what I really think.'

Feluda paused. All eyes were fixed upon him.

'It is my belief,' he continued, 'that Jayanta Babu didn't lose consciousness at all. He only pretended to do so. He was in league with Dr Sarkar, because it was necessary for both of them to leave the house.'

'Nonsense!' shouted Jayanta Babu. 'Why should we do that?'

'So that you could return in the dead of night.'

'Return?'

'Yes. You came in through the smaller gate on the northern side, and crept up to your mother's room.'

'That's too much! If I did that, wouldn't my mother have got to know? Are you aware that she doesn't get more than two hours' sleep every night?'

'Yes, I do know she's an insomniac. But what if she had been given something to make her sleep? What if Dr Sarkar had dropped something into her bowl of milk and rice? A strong sleeping pill, perhaps?'

Neither Dr Sarkar nor Jayanta Babu said anything. Both were beginning to lose their colour and look uncomfortable.

'You had to come back,' Feluda went on, 'because this time you couldn't afford to get things wrong. You had to ruin Mr Chowdhury's plan for the evening and get back into the house much later to steal. The theft might not have been discovered for a long time. But you had lost the key you had been carrying, so you had to use the duplicate kept in your mother's wardrobe. While you were doing this, you suddenly heard my friend reciting poetry, and got a bit nervous. You obviously hadn't realized that others in the house were awake, and strolling outside. So you decided to wrap yourself in one of your mother's white saris and come out on the balcony, simply so that we could see a figure and assume it was your mother. Then you went back inside and started to use the hand grinder in the hope that that would make your act more convincing. My suspicions were aroused even then, for you were banging an empty grinder. If it had had paan leaves in it, it would have made a different noise.'

'So what are you accusing me of?' Jayanta Babu asked, making a brave attempt to sound casual. 'That I pretended to be unconscious? Or that I tampered with my mother's food? Or that I stole back into her room and opened the chest?'

'Ah, you admit doing all these things, do you?'

'That doesn't mean a thing, does it? None of these is a punishable offence. Why don't you speak of the real event?'

'Because there isn't only one event to speak of, Jayanta Babu, there are two. Let me deal with them one by one. The first is the theft that occurred a year ago.'

'And what do you know about it? For heaven's sake, you weren't even there!'

'No. But there were others. Someone happened to be standing right next to the thief. He'd have seen everything.'

Mr Chowdhury spoke this time. He sounded greatly distressed. 'What are you saying, Mr Mitter? If someone saw it happen . . . why, surely he'd have told me?'

Instead of giving him a reply, Feluda suddenly turned to face Kalinath Roy. 'What trouble were you talking about, Mr Roy, when you told me to keep away from this case?'

Kalinath Roy smiled. 'Revealing an unpleasant truth can always lead to trouble, can't it, Mr Mitter? Just think of poor Shankar. I only wanted to spare his feelings.'

'You needn't have bothered,' Mr Chowdhury said crossly. 'If you know anything abut this case, Kalinath, come clean. Never mind about my feelings. We've wasted enough time.'

'He couldn't tell you what he had seen, Mr Chowdhury,' Feluda said before Mr Roy could utter another word, 'for that would have meant a great deal of financial loss for him. And that was why he didn't want me to catch the thief, either. You see, he's been milking the thief dry these past twelve months.'

'What! Blackmail?'

'Yes, Mr Chowdhury, blackmail. But what Mr Roy didn't know was that the thief had an accomplice. He had noticed only one person remove that gold piece. But I think it was his constant demands for money that forced the thief to think of stealing a second time. And so—'

'No!' cried Jayanta Babu, a note of despair in his voice. 'You're wrong. There was nothing left to be stolen. Banwarilal's other valuable possessions had already gone! That chest is empty.'

'Does that mean none of my allegations are false or baseless? You admit—?'

'Yes! But who . . . who stole the other stuff last night? Why don't you tell us?'

'I will. But before that I want a full confession from you. Go on, tell us, Jayanta Babu, did you and Dr Sarkar get together last year and steal one of the twelve gold coins of Jehangir?'

'Yes. I admit everything. Mr Mitter's absolutely right.'

Feluda quietly took out his microcassette recorder and passed it to me.

'I . . . I can only beg for forgiveness,' Jayanta Babu continued, casting an appealing glance at his cousin. Dr Sarkar sat with his head in his hands.

'Dr Sarkar has still got that gold coin,' Jayanta Babu added. 'We'll return it to you. We . . . we were both badly in need of money. But when we tried to sell the first coin, we realized the whole set would fetch a price a hundred times more, so . . .'

'So you decided to remove the remaining eleven pieces?'

'Yes. But we were not the only ones capable of stealing. Anyone who can blackmail . . .'

'. . . Can well be a thief? True. But Mr Roy did not steal anything from that chest.'

'How do you mean?'

'The remaining coins and other objects were removed by Pradosh Mitter.'

As everyone gaped in silence, Feluda left the veranda and went to his room. When he returned, he had the little bag of coins and the ivory box in his hands. 'Here you are, Mr Chowdhury,' he said, 'your great-grandfather's possessions are all safe and intact. You'll find the rings and pendants, too, in that box.'

'But how . . . ?'

'I began to smell a rat, you see, when I found *alta* on the floor instead of blood, and there was no sign of the key. So I was obliged to pick your pocket, Jayanta Babu, when I helped the doctor to carry you to the car. Thank goodness you had kept the key in your right pocket. I couldn't have taken it if it had been in the other one. The others came and sat down in the drawing room after you had gone. I took this opportunity to rush upstairs, open the chest and take everything away. I could tell they were no longer safe in your mother's room. Luckily, she was already asleep, so she didn't see me open the chest . . . Well, here's your key, Mr Chowdhury. Now you must decide what you want to do with the culprits. I have finished my job.'

On our way back to Calcutta, Lalmohan Babu made us listen to another poem by Baikuntha Mallik. We heard him in silence, without offering any comments on its poetic merits. It was called 'Genius', and it went thus:

The world has seen some amazing men,
Who knows of what stuff is made
their brain?

Shakespeare, Da Vinci,
Angelo, Einstein,
I salute you all,
each hero of mine!

Crime in Kedarnath

ONE

'What are you thinking, Felu Babu?' Lalmohan Babu asked. It was a Sunday morning. The three of us were sitting in our living room, chatting as usual, Lalmohan Babu having driven all the way from his house in Gorpar to join us. There had been a shower earlier, but now the sun was scorching. Our ceiling fan was moving with great gusto, since on Sundays power cuts were rare.

'I was thinking of your latest novel,' Feluda replied.

On the first of Baisakh, Jatayu's new novel, *The Astounding Atlantic*, had been released. By the fifth, four thousand and five hundred copies had been sold. 'What about my latest novel? How can that possibly give you food for thought?'

'What I was thinking, simply, was this: no matter how exaggerated or unreal your plots are, you manage to get away with it simply by being able to tell a good story. Despite all their weaknesses, your books are immensely enjoyable.'

Lalmohan Babu began to look deeply gratified, and was about to say something suitable, but Feluda continued, 'That made me wonder if any of your ancestors had also been writers.'

The truth was that we knew very little about Lalmohan Ganguli's family. All he had told us was that his parents were no more, and he was a bachelor.

'My ancestors? I have no idea who they were, or what they did, more than four generations ago. Nobody in the last three generations was a writer, I can tell you that.'

'Didn't your father have brothers?'

'Yes, he had two brothers, one older and the other younger than him. The older one was called Mohinimohan Ganguli. He practised homoeopathy. When I was a child, being ill automatically meant going to my uncle and being given arnica, or rhus tox, or belladonna. My great-grandfather was Lalit Mohan Ganguli. He was a paper merchant. He had a shop called L.M. Ganguli & Sons. Both my grandfather and father looked after our family business, but after my father's death, things became rather difficult. The shop changed hands, although the name L.M. Ganguli & Sons was retained for some time.'

'What about your father's younger brother? Your uncle? Wasn't he interested in running the business?'

'No, sir. I saw my uncle, Durgamohan Ganguli, only once in my life. I was born in 1936. Seven years before that, in 1929, he had become a freedom fighter, and joined the terrorists. The Assistant Commissioner in Khulna—which is now in Bangladesh—used to be a Mr Turnbull. Durgamohan tried to shoot him. He didn't succeed in killing him, but the bullet hit Turnbull's chin, causing a great deal of damage.'

'And then?'

'Then nothing. Durgamohan disappeared. The police never found him. Perhaps the passion for adventure is something I got from my uncle.'

'When did you see him?'

'He returned home once, after Independence, in 1949. That was my first and last meeting with him. The man I saw was utterly different from the daredevil I had heard so much about. Terrorism and pistols were a thing of the past. Durgamohan had become quiet and withdrawn—in fact, much more of a spiritual character than anything else. He stayed at home for a month, then vanished again.'

'Do you know where he went?'

'As far as I can remember, he left to work in a forest—something to do with supplying timber.'

'He didn't get married?'

'No, he didn't.'

'But surely you have other siblings, and cousins?'

'I have an older sister. Her husband works in the railway, and they're posted in Dhanbad. My uncle has three daughters, no sons. All three are married and scattered in various corners of the country. We exchange postcards after Durga Puja, but other than that I have no contact with them. Frankly, I don't think family ties are so important. I mean, I value friendship much more. I am so close to you and Tapesh, you can see that for yourself. Now, has that anything to do with a blood relation? I don't really . . .'

He had to stop, for there was a knock at the door. This wasn't unexpected, for a man called Umashankar Puri had made an appointment to see Feluda at half past nine. It was now 9.33.

I opened the door to let Mr Puri in. He turned out to be a man of medium height, clean-shaven, with salt-and-pepper hair parted on the right. For some strange reason, the parting in his hair made me feel uneasy. Perhaps it was simply that so few men parted their hair on the right—probably one in a hundred—that it seemed positively odd.

'You appear to have left in a hurry,' Feluda remarked as soon as greetings had been exchanged and Mr Puri had been offered a seat.

'Yes, but how did you guess?' he asked in amazement.

'All your nails on your left hand are neatly clipped. I can see one nail is still stuck to your jacket. But except for two nails, your right hand . . .'

'Oh yes, yes. I was clipping those just before coming here. I got a trunk call before I could finish, and then it was time to leave, so . . .' he laughed.

'Anyway, tell me now how I may be able to help you.'

Mr Puri stopped laughing. He was quiet for a few seconds, trying to collect his thoughts. Then he said, 'Your name was recommended to me by the Maharaja of Bhagwangarh. He spoke very highly of you. That is why I am here to seek your assistance.'

'I am honoured.'

'The problem is—' he stopped, then took a deep breath and started again. 'What I am afraid of is that there may be an unfortunate incident. Can you help me to try and avoid it?'

'I couldn't make promises, Mr Puri, without a few more details. What exactly do you think might happen?'

Mr Puri couldn't make an immediate reply, for Srinath came in at this moment with tea and biscuits. Mr Puri picked up a biscuit and said, 'Have you heard of Rupnarayangarh? It used to be a princely state.'

'It does seem to ring a bell. Is it somewhere in Uttar Pradesh?'

'Yes, that's right. It's 90 km to the west of Aligarh. Thirty years ago, its chief was Raja Chandradeo Singh. I was the manager of the estate. Although the country had become independent, small states like ours could still be run privately without too much interference from the government. Chandradeo Singh was then fifty-four, but was strong and very active. He went on shikar, played tennis and polo, and exercised regularly to keep fit. The only thing that bothered him sometimes was an occasional attack of asthma. Who knew one day it would suddenly grow so much worse that the Raja would become totally incapacitated? But that's what happened. I cannot even begin to describe how horrible his attacks were. In six months, the man who couldn't sit still became completely confined to bed. No doctor could help him, no medicine worked. He couldn't breathe, he couldn't eat, he couldn't sleep, or talk, or move.

'When we were about to give up hope altogether, we heard about a Bhavani Upadhyaya. He lived in Haridwar, and apparently knew of some ayurvedic medicine that could cure asthma. Dozens of people had already gone to him and were fully recovered.

'Having heard this, I went to Haridwar myself and tracked him down. He was quite well-known in that area. He turned out to be a very simple man, who lived quietly in a small cottage. When I explained why I had gone to find him, he agreed readily to go to Rupnarayangarh with me, and treat the Raja. His medicine would take ten days to take effect, he said. He would spend those ten days in the estate. If there was no improvement in that time, he would return to Haridwar without taking a single paisa.

'You may find it difficult to believe, but the Raja's health was restored in not ten, but three days. By the fourth day, it seemed as though he had never been ill. It was really a miracle. Upadhyaya said he would go back to Haridwar, and could he please be paid fifty rupees for the medicine? The Raja laughed at the idea. "How can you save my life, bring me back from death's door, and say all I need to pay you is fifty rupees?" he asked Upadhyaya. But Upadhyaya was a man devoid of greed. He refused to take anything more.

'Raja Chandradeo Singh, however, paid no attention. He was rather different from most men. All his emotions—joy, grief, generosity—were stronger than others. Despite Upadhyaya's objections, he decided to give him a most valuable pendant. It was made of solid gold, studded with pearls, rubies, emeralds and diamonds. Thirty years ago, its value would have been in the region of seven hundred thousand.'

'What did Upadhyaya do? Did he take this pendant willingly?'

'Oh no, no. He seemed greatly distressed by the offer. He said, "I am a simple man. What would I do with a locket like that? Besides, who is ever going to believe I was given it? Won't everyone assume I had stolen it from somewhere?"

'The Raja said to him, "No, why should they? We are not going to tell everyone, are we? This is simply between you and me. But if it will make you happier, I will give you a written document, stamped with my royal seal, saying that I have given you this piece of jewellery out of my own free will, as your reward for treating me."

'It was only after this that Upadhyaya agreed to accept the Raja's offer, with happiness and gratitude.'

'How many people knew about this? I mean, apart from the Raja, Upadhyaya and yourself?'

'The Maharani knew about it, as well as her two sons—Suraj and Pavan. Suraj was then in his early twenties, a very good and kind young man, which is something of a rarity in royal families. Pavan was only fifteen. In my own family, my wife and my son, Devishankar, learnt about the Raja's generosity. Devi was five or six years old at the time. The Raja may have mentioned it to someone else in his later years, I don't know. I certainly did not tell anyone. In the last thirty years, the press did not pick up this story even once. You know very well what reporters and journalists are like. If word had leaked out, do you think they'd have let it remain a secret?'

'That is true. People who knew certainly seemed to have kept their lips sealed.'

Mr Puri continued, 'Chandradeo Singh lived for another twelve years. He was succeeded by Surajdeo, although, of course, by then, no one would call him a Raja. However, he was the principal owner of the estate and all other property of his father.'

'Did you continue to be the manager?' Feluda asked.

'Yes. I tried very hard to keep the estate going by developing new projects, going into business, and making sure its future was secure; but unfortunately, Suraj was not really interested in these things. His only passion in life was books. He used to spend nearly sixteen hours in his library every day, refusing to discuss business matters with me. How much could I achieve all on my own? Soon, the financial status of the estate started to deteriorate.'

'Your own son must have grown up by now.'

'Oh yes. I sent him to a school in Aligarh. From there he went to college in Delhi, and then started his own business there. He did not return to Rupnarayangarh.'

'Is he your only son?'

'Yes. Anyway, I was struggling to keep the affairs of the estate in order. Sometimes I thought of giving it all up and going away to Moradabad, which is where I come from. But I had grown very attached to Rupnarayangarh, I couldn't leave it just like that.'

Mr Puri stopped briefly to light a cigar. Then he said, 'I am now coming to the most important part of my story, which will explain why I am here. Please bear with me. What happened was this: about a week ago, Chandradeo's younger son, Pavan, came to me rather unexpectedly. The first thing he said was, "Give me the name and address of the man who cured my father." Naturally, I asked him why he wanted it, was anyone ill? To that he said no, no one was ill.

He needed to contact Upadhyaya simply in connection with a television film he was making.

'I knew Pavan was interested in photography, but had no idea he was now into making films. I said to him, "You mean you're going to show this man in your film?" He said, "Of course. I am also going to tell everyone about the pendant he was given. I doubt if anyone has ever been given such a big reward for curing an ailment." At this, I was obliged to tell him that Upadhyaya himself had certainly not wanted any publicity. But he gave me a lecture on how it was the duty of those working for our television to inform the public about all important events, no matter when they had occurred. Besides, Upadhyaya might well change his mind about not wanting any publicity once Pavan had spoken to him. So would I just give him his address?

'After this, there was nothing I could do, but tell Pavan where Upadhyaya lived. He thanked me and left.'

'How old would Upadhaya be now?'

'He'd be in his seventies. When he came to Rupnarayangarh, he was not a young man.'

Feluda said nothing for a few moments, but looked steadily at Mr Puri. Then he asked, 'Did you come here simply to ensure that nobody found out about Upadhyaya's secret?'

Mr Puri shook his head. 'No, Mr Mitter. It is not just that. I am deeply concerned about Chandradeo's pendant. If Pavan is making a film, he needs a great deal of money. Perhaps he has made arrangements, I don't know. What I do know is that a locket like that would be enough to remove all his financial worries.'

'But that would mean adopting unfair means, wouldn't it?'

'Yes, certainly.'

'What kind of a man is Pavandeo?'

'He has inherited both the strengths and weaknesses of his father. He's a good sportsman, and a very good photographer. But he gambles a lot. He's lost quite a lot of money in poker. He can be totally reckless at times, but I have known him to be surprisingly thoughtful and generous. Like his father, he has a complex character, and it is not easy to get to know him well.'

'So what would you like me to do?'

'I would simply like you to make sure no one gets the chance to adopt unfair means.'

'Is Pavandeo going to Haridwar?'

'Yes, but not immediately. He'll take at least a week to set out, for he's busy taking shots of the palace right now.'

'If I agreed to take this case, I couldn't leave immediately either. It would take me a while to reserve seats on a train. But assuming that I did agree, how would I recognize Pavandeo?'

'I thought about that. Here's his photo. This was published in a magazine last month, after he won a billiard championship. You may keep it. And . . . er . . . would you like me to pay you an advance?'

'Not now. If I decide to take a case, I expect an advance payment of a thousand rupees. This is non-refundable. If the case turns out to be successful, I take another thousand.'

'Very well. Please think it over, Mr Mitter. I am staying at the Park Hotel. Let me know what you decide by four o'clock this afternoon. If your answer is yes, I will come back with your advance payment.'

TWO

I knew Feluda would agree to take the case. He had recently started to record conversations with his clients on a microcassette recorder, which he had bought in Hong Kong. With Mr Puri's permission, his conversation with Feluda had been recorded as well. In the afternoon, Feluda played the whole thing back and listened to every word carefully. Then he switched the machine off and said, 'This case is quite different from what I usually get. That is reason number one why I think I ought to take it. Reason number two is the chance to visit Haridwar and Hrishikesh again. After all, isn't that where I spent some of my early days as a detective?'

Yes, indeed. How could I ever forget it was in Haridwar that the case of the stolen Emperor's ring took a new turn?

He rang Mr Puri and told him of his decision. Mr Puri returned in just half an hour and paid him his advance. When he had gone, Feluda spoke to our travel agent and told him to book three seats on the Doon Express, as soon as possible.

Two days later, something totally unexpected happened. Mr Puri sent us a telegram from Rupnarayangarh. It said: REQUEST DROP CASE. LETTER FOLLOWS.

Drop case? Why? No client had ever done this to us before. A couple of days later, Mr Puri's letter arrived. What it said briefly was that Pavandeo Singh had changed his mind. He would still find and interview Bhavani Upadhyaya, but would only show how he spent his time treating the sick. He would mention that Upadhyaya had once treated and cured the Raja of Rupnarayangarh, but would say nothing about the pendant. There was therefore no need for Feluda to travel all the way to Haridwar.

Feluda replied to Mr Puri by sending another telegram: DROPPING CASE, BUT GOING AS PILGRIMS. His curiosity had been aroused. He would go simply as a tourist all right, but would certainly keep his eyes and ears open. To be honest, I was very pleased by this, for I wanted to meet both Bhavani Upadhyaya and Pavandeo.

All this had happened a few days ago. We were, at this moment, sitting in a four-berth compartment of the Doon Express. The train had stopped at Faizabad, and we were sipping hot tea from clay pots.

'You said you had once visited Haridwar,' Feluda said to Lalmohan Babu. 'When was that?'

'Oh, when I was only a child, just about two years old. I have no memory of the place at all.'

'Are you going only to Haridwar, or do you intend to see other places as well?'

This question came from our fellow passenger, an elderly gentleman who was sitting next to Lalmohan Babu. His thin hair was mostly white, but his skin wasn't wrinkled, and his strong white teeth appeared to be his own. There were a few laughter lines around his eyes, and from the way his eyes twinkled, it seemed he was ready for laughter any time.

'We have some work in Haridwar,' Feluda answered. 'When that gets done, we might try and see other places. We haven't really thought about it yet.'

The gentleman raised his eyebrows. 'What! You don't mean to say you haven't thought about going to Kedar and Badrinath? You must never miss those places, if you are travelling all that distance, anyway. You can go to Badrinath by bus. Buses don't go right up to Kedar, and you have to walk the last few miles, but at your age that shouldn't be a problem. And for your friend, there would be dandis and ponies. Have you ever ridden a pony?' he asked, looking at Lalmohan Babu.

Lalmohan Babu finished his tea, threw the pot out of the window and said gravely, 'No, but I have ridden a camel in the Thar desert. Have you had that experience?'

'No, I'm afraid not,' the gentleman shook his head, smiling, 'I have never been anywhere near a desert. My field for roaming is restricted to the mountains. I have been to Kedar and Badri twenty-three times. It's got nothing to do with religious devotion. I go back just to look at their natural beauty. That itself is a spiritual experience, I can tell you. If I didn't have a family, I'd quite happily live there. I have also been to Jamunotri, Gangotri, Gomukh, Panchakedar and Vasukital. Allow me to introduce myself. I am Makhanlal Majumdar.'

Feluda said 'namaskar' and introduced us.

'Very pleased to meet you,' said Mr Majumdar. 'A lot of people are going to all these place now, thanks to road transport. They are not pilgrims, they are picnickers. But, of course, buses and taxis can do nothing to spoil the glory of the Himalayas. The scenic beauty is absolutely incredible.'

We reached Haridwar at 6 a.m.

This time, there didn't seem to be as many pandas as last time. We stopped at the railway restaurant for a cup of tea and snacks. Feluda asked its manager about Upadhyaya. What he told us came as a shock.

Bhavani Upadhyaya had left Haridwar more than three months ago, and gone to Rudraprayag.

'Who can talk to us about him? Is there anyone here who knew him well?'

'You can try talking to Kantibhai Pandit. He used to be Upadhyaya's landlord.'

'Does he live in Laxman Mohalla?'

'Yes, yes. He and Upadhyaya were next-door neighbours. Go there, and ask anyone. They'll take you to Kantibhai's house.'

Feluda thanked him and paid the bill. We decided to go to Laxman Mohalla immediately.

Kantibhai Pandit turned out to be a man in his mid-sixties, with a clear complexion and sharp features. He had heavy stubble on his face, and he peered at us through bifocal lenses. He seemed quite surprised on being told we wanted to ask him about Upadhyaya.

'What is going on?' he asked. 'Why this sudden interest in Upadhyaya, I wonder? Someone else came to ask about him only about three days ago.'

'Do you remember what he looked like?'

'Yes, certainly.'

'See if it was this man.' Feluda took out Pavandeo Singh's photograph and showed it to Mr Pandit.

'Yes, yes, this is the man who came to see me. I gave him Upadhyaya's address in Rudraprayag.'

'I'd be very grateful if you could give it to me, too.' Feluda offered him one of his cards. One look at it brought about a marked change in Mr Pandit's behaviour.

'Oh, do please sit down,' he said busily. 'I'm sorry I made you stand all this while.' When we were all seated, he added, 'Is anything wrong, Mr Mitter? What's happened?'

'Nothing has happened yet,' Feluda smiled, 'but there is a chance that something might. I am going to ask you a straight question, Mr Pandit. I'd appreciate a straight answer.'

'Yes?'

'Did Mr Upadhyaya have something of great value among his personal possessions?' Mr Pandit smiled back at Feluda. 'I have already had to answer this question. I will tell you the same thing that I told Mr Singh. Mr Upadhyaya had given me a small bag and asked me to keep it in my safe. I locket it away, but I have no idea what it contained. He didn't tell me, and I didn't ask.'

'Did he take it with him to Rudraprayag?'

'Yes, sir. But there is something else that I think you should know. About six months ago, before Upadhyaya left, two men came to see him one day. One of them was probably a Marwari, he looked like a rich man. They spent nearly an hour with him, talking and arguing. I don't know what exactly was said, but after they had gone, Upadhyaya came to me. He said, "Panditji, today I have conquered one of the deadly sins. Mr Singhania tried to tempt me—oh, he tried very hard—but I didn't give in." Those were his words.'

'Did you ever tell anyone else about Upadhyaya's possession?'

'Look, Mr Mitter, a lot of people knew that he had something to hide. Some even used to make fun of him behind his back, about this great secret. I . . . I sometimes sit with my friends and have a drink in the evening, so something may have slipped out when I wasn't completely sober—I really don't know. But most people here respected Upadhyaya so much that no one would have tried to find out what he had hidden in a safe.'

'Was there any particular reason why he left for Rudraprayag?'

'He told me he had met a sadhu at a ghat. Talking to him had brought about a serious change in Upadhyaya. He became more withdrawn. I often found him sitting quietly in his room, lost in thought.'

'Did he take all his medicines with him?'

'There wasn't much to take. All he had were a few jars of herbs and roots, some pills and ointments, that was all. Yes, he took them with him. But I think eventually he'll give up ayurveda altogether and become a full-fledged sanyasi.'

'He was not married, was he?'

'No. He had no attachments at all. He told me the day he left, "Two, paths were open to me. One meant indulgence and running after comforts and luxuries. The other meant sacrifice and austerity. I decided to choose the latter."'

'Did he give you his new address before he left?'

'Oh no. I got it from the postcard he sent me from Rudraprayag.'

'Do you have it with you now?'

'Yes.' Mr Pandit went inside and came back with a postcard, which he handed to Feluda. I couldn't read what was written on it, but could see that it had been written in Hindi. Feluda read it quickly, said, 'Most interesting,' and returned it to Mr Pandit. God knew what was so interesting in the card.

Finally, Mr Pandit himself arranged a taxi for us. It would take us first to Rudraprayag, and then we could go wherever we liked. The Garhwali driver was called Joginder Ram. He seemed very friendly and cheerful. All of us took an instant liking to him. Feluda told him we'd have an early lunch in Hrishikesh and leave for Rudraprayag at twelve o'clock. Hrishikesh was fifteen miles from Haridwar. There was nothing to see in Haridwar itself. The river looked dirtier than it had when I saw it last. Every quiet corner in the town seemed to have been filled by new buildings; all the walls were covered with handwritten advertisements. It was necessary for us to go to Hrishikesh, since we'd need to arrange our accommodation in Rudraprayag. We could stay in a dharamshala. Every town in the vicinity had the old and famous Kalikamli dharamshalas, but we were sure Pavandeo would not be staying in one of them.

Luckily, before we left Hrishikesh, we could book a double room in the rest house run by the Garhwal Mandal Vikas Nigam in Rudraprayag. They agreed to put an extra bed in the same room for Lalmohan Babu. We had a quick lunch, and left for Rudraprayag as planned. A few miles later, I saw Laxmanjhoola on our right. Like Haridwar, it had been spoilt by hideous new structures, but even so, memories of our adventure regarding the Emperor's ring gave me goose pimples.

Rudraprayag was famous for two reasons. The first was Jim Corbett. Anyone who has read *The Man-eating Leopard of Rudraprayag* will always remember the patience, perseverance and courage with which Corbett had hunted down the man-eater fifty-five years ago. Our driver Joginder said he had heard his grandfather talk of Corbett. He cared very deeply for the local Garhwalis, and they loved him just as much.

The second thing that made Rudraprayag important was that it was possible to go to both Kedarnath and Badrinath from here. Two rivers—Mandakini and Alakananda—met in Rudraprayag. If one followed Alakananda, one could get to Badrinath; Mandakini would take one to Kedar. Buses went to Badrinath. But to get to Kedarnath, one had to walk, or ride in either a dandi or on horseback the bus route finished in Gaurikund, 14 km before Kedar.

Rudraprayag was 140 km from Hrishikesh. Even if we could go at 30 km an hour, we couldn't reach there before dark. We would pass through three towns on the way, Devprayag, Keertinagar and Srinagar. The last was the capital of the Garhwal district, it had nothing to do with the capital of Kashmir.

The road, built through forests and hills, was going up and down. Occasionally, the trees parted to reveal green plateaus in the distance, on which stood sweet little villages, like picture postcards.

However, I could not concentrate on the scenery. My mind kept going back to Bhavani Upadhyaya and the valuable pendant in his possession. If a sanyasi, who had no other earthly possessions, decided to hang on to just one thing, there was bound to be trouble. Someone somewhere would want to take it from him. Besides, I was still puzzled about why Mr Puri told Feluda to forget the whole thing. He did provide an explanation in his letter, but was that really the truth? Or was I reading too much into it, just because such a thing had never happened before?

Lalmohan Babu broke the silence. 'I was never good in either geography or history,' he confessed. 'You have often pointed this out, haven't you, Felu Babu? So will you now kindly explain where we are? I mean, which part of the country is it, exactly?'

Feluda took out his large map, produced by the Bartholomew Company.

'Look, here is Haridwar, and we are on our way to Rudraprayag. Here it is, can you see it? That means, on the east is Nepal and on the west is Kashmir. We are in the middle. Now do you understand?'

'Ye-es. It's all quite clear to me now, absolutely crystal clear.'

THREE

By the time we reached Rudraprayag, after a brief stop in Srinagar to have a cup of tea, it was nearly five o'clock. Rudraprayag was a fairly large town, with its own school, college, hospital and post office. A signboard used to hang over the spot where Corbett had killed that famous leopard. 'But it broke a few years ago, and nobody replaced it,' Joginder informed us.

We went straight to the rest house. It was just outside the main town, in a quiet and peaceful spot. The first thing we heard on our arrival was that the road to Kedar had reopened and buses were running again. Apparently, it had been blocked for many days due to a landslide. As things turned out, this was a stroke of luck, but we did not realize it until much later.

The manager of the rest house, Mr Giridhari, had not heard of Feluda, but that did not stop him from being most kind and hospitable. He said he had read many Bengali authors in translation, Bimal Mitra and Shankar among them. 'They are my favourite authors,' he beamed.

A few minutes later, we met another guest, who had got stuck in Rudraprayag because of the landslide. Unlike Mr Giridhari, he recognized Feluda instantly. 'I am a journalist, I have heard of many of your cases,' he said. 'Your photograph was published in the newspapers in northern India after the Sukhtankar murder case in Allahabad. That's how I could recognize you. My name is Krishnakant Bhargav. I am very proud to meet you, sir.'

The man was about forty years old, of medium height and had a thick beard. Mr Giridhari naturally became curious on learning that Feluda was an investigator.

'There is no trouble here, I hope?' he asked anxiously.

'There can be trouble anywhere, Mr Giridhari, but we haven't come here to look for trouble. Actually, all we're looking for is a man called Bhavani Upadhyaya.'

'Upadhyaya? But he's no longer here!' exclaimed Mr Bhargav. 'I came here simply to write a story on him. When I reached Haridwar, I heard he had come here. So I came here, and discovered he had gone to Kedarnath. That's why I decided to follow him there. Now that the road is open again, I intend leaving tomorrow morning. He's a very interesting character.'

'Is he? I'm looking for him because I believe he treats the sick, and can work wonders. You see,' Feluda lowered his voice, glancing rather pointedly at Lalmohan Babu, 'this friend of mine is mentally disturbed. He behaves quite normally most of the time, but just occasionally, his problem flares up. He starts talking absolute gibberish, and can even get violent at times. A lot of doctors have seen him in Calcutta, but nothing has worked. So when I heard of Upadhyaya, I thought he might be able to help. At least it's worth a try, don't you think?'

After the first few seconds of stunned disbelief, Lalmohan Babu caught on quickly. In order to prove Feluda right, he tried to bring an expression of wild insanity to his face, but succeeded only in looking like the Nepali mask that hangs in our drawing room.

Mr Bhargav nodded sympathetically. 'Then you, too, must look for him in Kedarnath. He didn't go to Badri, for I didn't find him there. But I hear he has become a sanyasi, so he may have changed his name.'

At this moment, an American car drew up outside the gate. Three men got out of it and came walking towards us. The leader of this team was easy to recognize, for we had all seen the photo Mr Puri had given Feluda. It was Pavandeo Singh of Rupnarayangarh. The other two were obviously his chamchas. Pavandeo took a cane chair and sat down on the veranda. We were sitting only a few feet away, drinking tea. 'No luck,' Pavandeo said, shaking his head, 'we've just been to Badri. Upadhyaya isn't there.'

'What amazes me,' Mr Giridhari remarked, 'is that everyone in this rest house is looking for Upadhyaya for a different reason. You want to include him in your film, Mr Bhargav wants to write a story on him, and Mr Mitter wants to get his friend treated.'

Pavando's men were carrying television equipment. He was holding a camera with a huge lens.

'A tele lens?' Feluda asked.

'Yes. I took it with me to film the melting snow on the peaks of Badrinath. Actually, the main equipment I am using is compact enough for one person to handle. That includes sound. My friends will go with me as far as Gaurikund. I will film the rest of it myself.'

'Does that mean you are going to leave for Kedarnath tomorrow?'

'Yes, first thing in the morning.'

'Will you be interviewing Upadhyaya if you can find him?'

'Yes, certainly. This film is being made for an Australian television company. I will naturally show the mountains and the snow and all the rest of it, but the interview with Upadhyaya will get a lot of footage. He's such an amazing character. What he did to my father was nothing short of a miracle.'

I watched Pavandeo Singh closely. This man bore little resemblance to what Umashankar Puri had told us. Feluda, I noticed, did not mention Mr Puri at all.

We left the rest house shortly afterwards, to go and have our dinner in town. When the waiter came to take our order, Lalmohan Babu suddenly banged a fist on the table and demanded an omelette. 'An armadillo's egg! That's what I want!' he said loudly. Feluda was obliged to explain to him that his insanity was something he didn't have to prove all the time, particularly when nobody from the rest house was in sight. If he kept behaving strangely without any reason, the chances of getting thrashed were very high.

'Well, you're right,' Lalmohan Babu conceded, 'but if I get a suitable opportunity, don't think I'm going to miss it.'

We returned straight to the rest house as we wanted an early night. Pavandeo's room was not far from ours. The sound of clinking glass and loud laughter told us he was with his two friends and Mr Giridhari, having a good time.

'I must admit one thing, Felu Babu,' Lalmohan Babu said, stretching out on his bed. 'In spite of what Mr Puri told us about Raja Chandradeo's younger son, he struck me as a most amiable man.'

'Surely you're aware that looks can be deceptive? Besides, nature often bestows cruelty and beauty in the same creature. Can you think of an animal more beautiful than the Royal Bengal tiger? Then consider the peacock. A creature of incredible beauty, right? Just think of the damage one peck of its beak can cause. You have seen it for yourself, haven't you?'

'Yes. Yes, I suppose that's true.' Lalmohan Babu rose, grabbed his alarm clock and began twisting its switch viciously, a wild look slowly creeping into his eyes.

Clearly, he felt he had to do full justice to his role.

FOUR

We came out of the rest house and found our taxi at five-thirty the following morning. Joginder was ready and waiting for us. Pavandeo's American car was standing near ours, being loaded with film equipment. He could not possibly leave for another half an hour. But the chances were he would catch up with us without any problem, and then overtake us.

As we were about to get into our car, the man himself came striding towards us, as though he had something important to say.

'Last night,' he said to Feluda, 'Mr Giridhari had a glass too many, and revealed your identity. I'd like to ask you a straight question.'

'Yes?'

'Did Umashankar send you here to keep an eye on me?'

'Even if he did, Mr Singh, I would certainly not tell you about it, for that would be a breach of confidentiality. It would also be rather foolish. However, I have to admit Mr Puri has nothing to do with my presence here. We are going to Kedarnath purely as tourists. If something untoward does happen, I will naturally not stand by and be a passive spectator. I would like to meet Bhavani Upadhyaya myself, for something special has made me immensely curious about him, although I am not at liberty to tell you what it is.'

'I see.'

'May I now ask you a question?'

'Sure.'

'Are you going to show that famous pendant in your film?'

'Of course, assuming that Upadhyaya has still got it with him.'

'But don't you realize that will put his life at risk? At the moment, nobody knows he has got something so valuable; but your film will be seen by thousands. Do you think it's fair to expose his secret like that?'

'Mr Mitter, if he has truly become a sanyasi, that locket should have no meaning for him. I will ask him to give it to a museum. It originally belonged to the Maharaja of Travancore. Its workmanship is absolutely exquisite. If he donates it to a museum, Upadhyaya's name will always be remembered. You bet I am going to show it in my film, and I hope you will not try to stop me.'

Pavandeo stormed off, having spoken the last few words with a great deal of emphasis. Mr Bhargav joined us as soon as he left. 'I wish I had known you were also going to Kedar,' he said. 'I could have gone with you, and shared the information I've got regarding Upadhyaya.'

'Really? Who—or what—is the source of your information?'

'Well, I spoke to Mr Singh's brother, Surajdeo, in Rupnarayangarh. But the interesting details came from their eighty-year-old bearer. He said Upadhyaya had treated the former Raja Chandradeo Singh, and cured him of asthma.'

'I see.'

'In order to show his appreciation, the Raja gave him one of his most precious pieces of jewellery. Nobody outside the family knew of this until now. Can you imagine what this will mean to the press? Oh, what a story! What a scoop!"

'Good for you, Mr Bhargav. You'll be able to make a lot of money out of this, won't you?'

'Maybe. But I can tell you one thing, Mr Mitter. That locket is not going to remain with Upadhyaya for long. Do you really think Pavandeo is here just to make a telefilm? Don't be surprised if your professional skills are soon called for.'

'It wouldn't surprise me, Mr Bhargav. I always keep myself ready for any eventuality.'

Mr Bhargav said goodbye and left.

'A clever man!' Lalmohan Babu observed.

'All good reporters and journalists are clever. They have to be, for in their job they often have to do a bit of detective work. He has shown a lot of initiative by interviewing an old retainer. Sometimes servants come to know of things that their masters are blissfully unaware of. But even so . . .' Feluda broke off.

'Even so, what?' I prompted. I could see something was bothering him.

'I don't know. Something in that man makes me uneasy. I just can't put my finger on it.'

We finally got into our car and started our journey. The road ran by the side of Alakananda. Only a few minutes later, we entered a tunnel. When we emerged from it, the river had changed. It was now Mandakini that flowed by our side, and it would stay with us right up to Kedarnath, which was where its source was supposed to be.

Feluda was still frowning. His next words explained why he was so annoyed.

'I am very cross with that man Giridhari. I had no idea he was so utterly irresponsible. What Pavandeo just told me was, I suppose, natural enough, coming from him. But it shows he and Umashankar Puri did not talk about Upadhyaya's pendant after Mr Puri returned from Calcutta. Now, if that is the case, why did he send me that telegram and the letter? The whole thing seems even more mystifying now. God knows who is telling the truth, and who can be trusted. I am only glad we didn't drop our decision to come here, even if we did agree to drop Mr Puri's case.'

Gaurikund was only 80 km from Rudraprayag; but the road went up and down the hills so frequently that it took much longer to get there than one might expect. Thirty kilometres from Rudraprayag stood Agastyamuni, at 900 metres. Guptakashi was 9 km from there, standing at 1800 metres. From there one had to go to Son Prayag, where Son Ganga joined Mandakini. Gaurikund was 8 km from Son Prayag. Its elevation was 2250 metres.

Our woollen clothes were packed into a small bag which we had taken with us. Our heavy luggage was in the rest house, waiting to be collected on the way back. Lalmohan Babu had not forgotten to bring his Rajasthani cap to protect his bald dome. We stopped briefly in Agastyamuni to slip our warm clothes on. As we were doing so, an American tourer went past us. Pavandeo put a hand out to wave, so we were obliged to wave back at him. We were on our way once more, ready to fight the cold. Mandakini could be seen occasionally on our left; but, in the next instant, it would go way down below a gorge. The sound of its waves was drowned at times by Lalmohan Babu's voice. He kept reciting a line from a poem; 'Do you know why/The waves do rise so high?' From the way he said it, over and over, it was obvious that was the only line he knew. Finally, a stern look from Feluda made him stop.

It was ten o'clock by the time we reached Guptakashi. We were all rather hungry by this time, so we decided to stop at a tea stall. Its owner provided hot jalebis, kachauris and steaming tea, to which we did full justice. Joginder said one of his brothers lived close by, so he'd take just five minutes to go and meet him.

'Ah, that gives me the chance to see those temples,' said Lalmohan Babu, trotting off in the direction of the temples of Chandrasekhar Mahadev and Ardhanarishwar.

From Guptakashi, it was possible to see Ukhimath high in the hills. It was in Ukhimath that the daily puja of Kedareshwar was held between November and April every year, when heavy snow blocked the road to Kedar.

Lalmohan Babu returned in a few minutes, but there was no sign of Joginder. Feluda and I began looking for him, when suddenly Pavandeo's car reappeared. What was he doing here? He should have been miles ahead of us, surely?

He stopped and came out when he saw us. 'We stopped here to take photos of the peaks of both Badri and Kedar,' he informed us. 'Guptakashi is the only place from where one can do that. But now we must press on, for we must get there before daylight starts to fade.' He waved again and went away.

Where on earth was Joginder? We were still looking around, when Mr Bhargav appeared. I had already spotted his car and had been wondering what was taking him so long. He said he had been interviewing a priest from the temple in Kedarnath, who happened to be visiting Guptakashi. Now he must be off on his way to Son Prayag and Gaurikund.

Mr Bhargav left, and was almost immediately replaced by a young boy of about fifteen.

'Taxi number 434?' he shouted. 'Are you a passenger in 434?'

'Yes, yes. Why, what's the matter?' Feluda asked him anxiously.

Joginder was hurt, the boy told us. He had come to inform us because he knew Joginder, and had just found him. We told Lalmohan Babu to wait in the car, and followed the boy.

Joginder was lying on the ground. Blood oozed from the back of his head. It seemed a very quiet area; there were no more than six houses in the vicinity. Joginder was still breathing, but Feluda ran and took his pulse. There was no time to worry about who had attacked him. The most important thing was to get him seen by a doctor.

'There is a hospital and a dispensary here,' the boy told us. 'I can drive.' Eventually, it seemed the only sensible thing we could do was to place Joginder in the car and let the boy drive us to the hospital.

The doctor who examined him said his injury might have been a lot worse. He dressed the wound, and said there was really nothing else he could do. Joginder would remain in pain for some time, but was sure to get better. All this took an hour and a half. We told Joginder we'd take another taxi to get to Kedar, but he insisted on driving us himself.

'Do you have any idea who hit you?' Feluda asked him.

'No, babu. He struck me from behind.'

'Do you have any enemies here?'

'No, no, I have no enemies at all.'

I knew what Feluda was thinking. If anyone had an enemy, it was us. Someone unknown did not want us to go to Kedarnath. The best way to stop us from going, or at least delay our arrival there, was to hurt our driver, obviously.

'Look, Feluda,' I said, once we were on our way again, 'I have been thinking. Could it be that Pavandeo came to know that Mr Puri had been to see you? And then maybe he made him send that telegram and write that letter, simply to make sure you didn't pose a threat to him?'

'Good thinking, Topshe. I've thought of it, too. If that is the case, it shows Pavandeo has full control over Umashankar Puri.'

'Why wouldn't he?' Lalmohan Babu pointed out. 'Pavandeo is, after all, one of the owners of the estate. A prince! What is Umashankar? Only one of his employees, right?'

'Right. If the young "prince" decided to throw his weight around, I don't think he'd consider the difference in age between Umashankar and himself. But I bet he didn't imagine I'd turn up anyway, in spite of the telegram and the letter!'

'Does that mean Pavandeo is responsible for the attack on poor Joginder?'

'Who else could it be, especially since Joginder claims there's no one who might wish to cause him harm?'

'Excuse me, sir,' Lalmohan Babu said, 'but I don't like that journalist chap.'

'Why not? I must admit I have my own reservations about him, but why don't you like him?'

'If he is a journalist, why doesn't he keep a pen? I noticed he didn't have a pen in the front pocket of his jacket. Yesterday, I saw him put it on. There wasn't a pen even in the inside pocket, or in the pocket of his shirt.'

'What if he has a cassette recorder, like me?'

This was a possibility that had clearly not occurred to Lalmohan Babu. He was silent for a few seconds. Then he said, 'Well then, that's a different matter. The truth is that I don't like men with heavy beards.'

'I see. May we now discuss a few practical arrangements?'

'Such as?'

'Which would you prefer—a horse, or a dandi?'

'Whatever you decide, Felu Babu, is fine by me.'

'I hope you have some idea of the road to Kedar?'

'Ha ha ha ha ha!'

'Why, what's so funny?'

'My idea, Felu Babu, is far more vivid than yours. You see, my favourite poet, Baikuntha Mallik, visited Kedar years ago and wrote a poem about his journey. I have read it many times, and am fully aware of what to expect.'

'Good. Well then, I think you would find a dandi easier to manage than a horse. Horses usually have a tendency to walk near the edge of the cliff. You'll find it very difficult to cope with all that tension. Tapesh and I will walk.'

Lalmohan Babu gave Feluda a steely glance. Then he said, 'Why do you keep underestimating me? You really think I'll take a dandi, while you two go walking? I am telling you, Felu Babu, either I walk together with you, or I don't go at all.'

'Very well, that's settled, then. We're all walking.'

'Now may I ask you something?'

'Certainly.'

'If we have been recognized by everyone, what is the purpose of our visit?'

'That would depend on who finds Upadhyaya first.'

'Suppose we do?'

'Then we must tell him everything. If he has indeed become a sanyasi, he may well wish to give the locket away. We should find out who he'd like to give it to. Pavandeo may get there before us. Because of his regard for his father, Upadhyaya may agree to be interviewed, and allow the young prince to take photos of the pendant. But no one—not even Pavandeo—must take it from him without his approval. But then, we have no evidence to prove Pavandeo does want to grab it for himself. We are merely assuming that it was he who had forced Mr Puri to put me off the case. Maybe his sole intention is to make a film, and nothing else. We don't know. In fact, we don't know anything for sure, do we?'

I said, 'But what about Mr Bhargav? He's looking for Upadhyaya as well, isn't he?'

'Well, I think Bhargav would be happy if he got a couple of photographs, one of Upadhyaya himself, and the other of the pendant. If he can get those, at least for a few days he'll find himself quite comfortably off.'

As we were talking, our car had climbed up to 3,000 metres. At least, that was what Joginder said. Judging by the sudden drop in the temperature, he was probably right. A number of tall peaks were visible from here, but I didn't know what they were called. We should reach Gaurikund in fifteen minutes. It was a quarter past five by my watch. Although the mountain peaks were still shining bright, the shadows were getting longer among the pines and rhododendrons.

Soon, our car climbed down again and turned a corner. A number of houses and traffic on the road told me we had reached Gaurikund. It was clear that we would have to spend the night here, and start for Kedar the next morning. Even if we left fairly early, it would take us all day to get there. A meeting with Upadhyaya could take place only after tomorrow.

Gaurikund was a small, but busy town, chiefly because there was a bus terminus here. A large number of passengers were arguing over prices of horses, dandis and kandis. A kandi was like a basket, in which one could be carried. Presumably, some people found it convenient; but its appearance did nothing to inspire confidence.

We had not made arrangements for an overnight stay. But it turned out accommodation was not a problem at all. Local pandas let out rooms. They even provided bedding, quilts and blankets. The rooms were small, with such low ceilings that if Feluda stood up straight, his head nearly touched it. The charges were low, and all of us thought the arrangements were fine, especially since we were not going to spend more than one night.

The first things we saw on arrival was the yellow American car that belonged to Pavandeo Singh. He and his team must have reached Gaurikund at least four hours before us. They had probably already hired horses and left for Kedarnath. If so, he would get more than a day in Kedar.

Mr Bhargav would probably also get there tonight.

So many people, with one common aim—tracking down Bhavani Upadhyaya.

FIVE

All of us slept soundly that night. Our alarm clock woke us at five o'clock. We were ready to leave in a few minutes.

The number of people who were already out and about was quite amazing. People from virtually every corner of the country were present, including a large number of Bengalis. Most of them were travelling in groups. Many families had several generations travelling together, ranging from grandfathers in their seventies, to grandchildren barely five years old.

It took me only a few seconds to spot Pavandeo Singh. He was in the process of hiring two horses. What was he still doing here? I had assumed he had already gone to Kedarnath.

'Good morning!' he greeted us. 'I got delayed in Son Prayag yesterday. The scenery there was so beautiful, I had to stop to take photos. I am now going to go up to Kedarnath alone. I'll carry my camera and sound equipment with me, on one horse. The other will take all the new and unused film.'

Feluda returned his greeting and moved away. 'There is no end to the mysteries,' he remarked. 'Could it be that he's appointed someone in Kedar to find Upadhyaya?' There was no time to ponder over this, for it was time to get going.

'Are you still determined to walk with us?' Feluda asked Lalmohan Babu.

'Yes, sir. I may not be able to keep pace with you at all times, but—'

'Oh, don't worry about that. You walk at whatever pace you find comfortable. Since there is only one road, and one destination, we'll all get there sometime, never fear. Here, take this.'

Feluda handed Lalmohan Babu one of the walking sticks he had bought for us. Nearly every traveller to Kedarnath was crying a similar stick. It was wooden, but the pointed end was covered by iron.

We left on the dot of six. Lalmohan Babu took a deep breath and shouted, 'Jai Kedar!' with such vigour that I began to feel afraid he might have spent half his energy at one go.

The road to Kedarnath was narrow and rocky. At times, there wasn't even enough room for two people to stand side by side. There were steep hills on one side, and on the other were deep ravines. The Mandakini flowed with great force below these. There was little vegetation on the way, except for certain patches where large leafy trees created a green canopy over our heads; but these were few and far between. Those who were walking frequently had to stand aside to make way for horses and dandis. One had to stay as close to the hill as possible, for going near the edge of the road was extremely dangerous. One single careless step could lead to a fatal accident.

Feluda and I did not find it too difficult to walk uphill, possibly because we both did yoga regularly. Lalmohan Babu tried very hard not to show what a struggle it was for him. He walked in complete silence, catching up with us when we reached flatter surface. 'I can now see what made Tenzing so famous!' he declared, panting slightly.

Twenty minutes later, something happened to delay our arrival in Kedarnath by another half an hour.

A large boulder suddenly came rolling down a slope at great speed. This was so totally unexpected that it took us a few seconds to realize what was happening. Although no one was seriously hurt, a certain amount of damage could not be avoided. The boulder brushed against Feluda's arm and smashed his HMT watch. Then it knocked the walking stick from the hand of an elderly man, making it fly towards the edge of the cliff and disappear into the gorge below, perhaps to land directly in the gushing Mandakini.

By this time, Feluda had collected himself and decided to act. He began climbing up the slope with the agility of a mountain goat, as I stood gaping after him, marvelling at his strength and stamina. How could he do it, so soon after having climbed uphill for many miles? But there was not a second to be lost. I followed him as quickly as I could. By the time I reached him, Feluda had already caught the culprit. He was clutching at the collar of a young man, pushing him against a tree. The man could not have been more than twenty-five. He had turned visibly pale, and was freely admitting to having pushed that boulder deliberately. He had apparently been paid by someone to do this. The man took out a new, crisp ten-rupee note to show us he was telling the truth.

'Who paid you?' Feluda demanded.

'I don't know him. He is a man from my village, but I don't know him personally. I did it only for the money.'

There was no reason to doubt his word. We'd never learn from him who was really responsible. This man was no more than a hired hand.

Feluda grabbed the woollen wrapper the man was wearing, and tied him to the tree with it. 'I'm bound to find a police constable somewhere. When I do, I'll send him to you,' he told him.

Lalmohan Babu sighed with relief when we joined him. 'How

worrying, Felu Babu! Anything could have happened if that boulder hit you. Who is it that wants to prevent your reaching Kedarnath so desperately?'

We didn't know the answer, so we simply resumed walking. A little later, we reached a place called Ramwara. Nearly everyone stopped here to rest for a while. There were dharamshalas here, as well as tea stalls. Lalmohan Babu deserved a short period of rest, so we decided to stop for half an hour. Ramwara was at a height of 2500 metres. The scenery around us was absolutely fantastic. Lalmohan Babu went into raptures, recalling scenes from the *Mahabharata*. He declared eventually that he would have no regret if he fell and died on the way, for no one could possibly have a more glorious death.

'Really?' Feluda teased him. 'You must remember, sir, that considering the amount of rubbish you have always fed your readers, you are liable to spend a good many years in hell. So what good will a glorious death do?'

'Heh! Who's afraid of a few years in hell? Why, even Yudhishthir wasn't spared, was he?' Lalmohan Babu waved a hand dismissively.

In the remaining three and a half miles, only one thing happened that's worth mentioning. The tall spire of the temple of Kedarnath came suddenly into view after leaving Ramwara. Most of the travellers stopped, shouting, 'Jai Kedar!' Some folded their hands and bowed, others lay prostrate on the ground. But only a few moments after we resumed walking, it vanished behind a mountain. We could see it again only after reaching Kedarnath. I learnt afterwards that the brief glimpse we had caught earlier was considered a special darshan. It was called *deo-dekhni*.

SIX

It was half past five in the evening by the time we reached Kedarnath. It had not yet started to get dark, and the mountain tops were all shining bright.

It is impossible to describe what one feels on reaching a flat plateau after climbing uphill for several hours on a steep and narrow road. The feeling uppermost in my mind was a mixture of disbelief, reassurance and joy. With this came a sense of calm, peace and humility. Perhaps it was those peaks which towered over everything else that made one feel so humble. Perhaps it was this feeling that evoked religious ardour, a reverence for the Creator.

A large number of people were sitting, standing, or lying on the rocky ground, overcome with emotion, unable to say or do anything except shout, 'Jai Kedar!' The famous temple stood surrounded on three sides by heavy snow. We walked through the crowd to find ourselves somewhere to stay. There was a hotel here called Hotel Himlok, but it was already full, as was the Birla guest house. Finally, we went to a Kali Kamliwali dharamshala. They gave us mattresses, blankets and razais, at a very nominal charge.

By the time we finished booking a room, it was past six o'clock and the temple had closed. It would open only at eight the next morning, we were told. So we went off to find what we needed the most: a hot cup of tea. There was a stall not far from our dharamshala. The streets of Kedar reminded me of the streets of Benaras. Most of the roadside shops were selling incense, flowers and Vermillion. They would shut down in November, and until April, the town would remain totally deserted.

I had expected Lalmohan Babu to want to rest after our difficult journey. But he said he had never felt more invigorated in his life. 'There is new life in every vein in my body,' he said. 'Tapesh, such is the magic of Kedar.'

Three steaming cups of tea were placed before us. The tea had been brewed with cinnamon. I could smell it as I raised a cup to my lips.

'Did you find Upadhyaya?' asked a voice. It was Pavandeo Singh, standing a few feet away. In his hand he still held his camera. The equipment for recording sound was strapped to his belt.

'No, we came only about half an hour ago,' Feluda told him.

'I got here at two-thirty and made some enquiries. As far as I can make out, he has become a full-fledged sanyasi. I think he even dresses like one. So you can imagine how difficult it's going to be to single out one sanyasi amongst so many. Besides, he is very likely to have changed his name. At least, no one I asked seemed to know anyone called Upadhyaya.'

'Well, we must keep trying, mustn't we?' Feluda said.

Pavandeo nodded and left. He was still a mystery to me.

We finished our tea and got up to leave. Another familiar voice spoke unexpectedly.

'Ah, so you've arrived finally. Wasn't it worth the effort?'

It turned out to be Makhanlal Majumdar, the man we had met on the train.

'Oh yes, most certainly,' Feluda smiled. 'I think we're still in a daze. This is so incredible.'

'I am so glad you came. Did you finish your work in Haridwar?'

'No, which is why we're here. You see, we're looking for someone who used to live in Haridwar. When we went there, we were told he'd gone to Rudraprayag. So we followed him there, but by then he had left for Kedarnath.'

'Who are you trying to find?'

'A man called Bhavani Upadhyaya.'

Mr Majumdar's eyes nearly popped out. 'Bhavani? You came looking for Bhavani, and you didn't tell me!'

'Why, do you happen to know him?'

'Know him? My dear young man, I have known him for seven years, ever since he cured my ulcer with just one pill. I met him shortly before he left Haridwar. I noticed a change in him. He seemed very detached. He said he wanted to go to Rudraprayag. I told him Rudraprayag was not the same any more, what with buses and tourists and everything. If he wanted peace and quiet, he should go to Kedarnath. Still, he went to Rudraprayag first, perhaps to give it a try. But now he is here.'

'Where can we find him?'

'Not in the main town. He now lives in a cave. Have you heard of Chorabalital? It's now called Gandhi Sarovar, I believe.'

'Yes, yes.'

'The river Mandakini begins her journey from Chorabalital. You have to go behind this place, and make your way through rocks and snow for about three miles. There is no proper road. Then you will see a lake. That is the Sarovar. Bhavani lives in a cave near that lake. His surname has disappeared completely. People now know him as Bhavani Baba. He lives in complete seclusion. No one lives anywhere near him. If you are really keen, you may try finding his cave tomorrow morning.'

'Have you met him?'

'No, not this time. But some of the local people told me about him. Just occasionally, he comes here for food. Actually, fruit and vegetables are all he needs to keep going for days.'

'Thank you very much indeed, Mr Majumdar. You've done us an enormous favour. But do you think anyone here might know of his past?'

'Yes, there's every possibility of that. After all, he hasn't given up practising altogether. I heard he has cured a local child of polio. But, very soon, I think he'll stop seeing patients, and become a total recluse.'

'One last question. Can you tell me which part of the country he comes from?'

'To be honest, I never asked him. He always spoke to me in very good Hindi, without traces of a regional accent. Anyway, good luck!' Mr Majumdar left.

Lalmohan Babu had left us a while ago, and was talking to someone. He now joined us once more, and said, 'We're wanted in the Birla guest house.'

'Who wants us?' Feluda asked.

The man who had been talking with Lalmohan Babu stepped forward and said, 'Mr Singhania.'

Feluda frowned. Then he turned to me and whispered, 'This may well be the same Singhania who had gone to see Upadhyaya in Haridwar, It can't do us any harm to go and meet him.' To Singhania's messenger, he said, '*Chaliye*.'

The guest house was very close to the temple. It took us barely three minutes to get there. I noticed on the way that it was beginning to get dark, although the sun still shone on some of the peaks, making them turn red and pink and golden.

I was surprised to see how clean the guest house was. Perhaps this was the best place in town, at least in terms of cleanliness. God knows what their food was like. In any case, I had heard all one could get in Kedar was potatoes.

Our guide took us to the first floor of the building, and ushered us into a fairly large room. Four mattresses lay on the floor. Three bulbs shone rather dimly from the ceiling. Kedarnath did have electricity, but the voltage was clearly very low.

A minute later, the man who had summoned us came into the room.

SEVEN

I felt a sudden stab of disappointment on seeing Mr Singhania. Perhaps it was his name that had made me think of lions and, subconsciously, I was expecting a man with a personality to match the majesty and ferocity of that animal. The man who walked in was of medium height, and everything else about him was so ordinary that it took me a while to accept that this indeed was the wealthy and powerful man who had gone to tempt Mr Upadhyaya. Only his thick moustache seemed to give him an air of importance.

'My name is Singhania,' he said. 'Please sit down.'

We sat on two mattresses. He took the third, and sat facing us.

'I am aware how well-known you are, Mr Mitter, but so far I haven't had the chance to meet you,' he began.

'Nobody wants to meet me unless they are in trouble,' Feluda replied lightly.

'Possibly, but I am not in trouble.'

'I know that. In fact, I had heard of you. But I wasn't sure that you were the same Singhania.'

'I'd be very interested to know how you learnt my name.'

'Did you ever go to Haridwar?'

'Oh yes.'

'Did you meet a man called Bhavani Upadhyaya there?'

'I did, but how do you know about it?'

'Mr Upadhyaya's landlord told me someone called Singhania had come to meet his tenant, together with another man.'

'What else did he tell you?'

'You had apparently made a proposition that Upadhyaya found immensely tempting, but he managed to overcome that temptation.'

'What a strange man, this Upadhyaya! I have never seen anyone like him. Can you imagine this, Mr Mitter? His monthly income never exceeded five hundred rupees, as he treated the poor without charging a penny. I offered him five hundred thousand. You know about the pendant he was given, don't you? Originally, I believe it used to belong to the Maharaja of Travancore.'

'Yes, I've heard that, but what I'd like to know is who told you. I was given to understand that only a handful of people who were close to Chandradeo Singh knew about it.'

'You're right, Mr Mitter. It was one of this handful of people who told me. I have a business in Delhi. I buy and sell precious stones and jewellery. Umashankar Puri's son, Devishankar, came to me and told me about this pendant. He wanted me to buy it, and naturally, expected a commission. So I went to Haridwar, but Upadhyaya refused to part with it, even at the price I offered. Puri lost all interest, but I did not. I simply cannot give up the idea of buying it. I have come here to make one last attempt. If Upadhyaya has renounced the world and become a sanyasi, why should he want to hang on to an earthly object like that? Doesn't it seem strange? Maybe if I made another offer, he'd agree to sell it this time?'

'So why don't you approach him?'

'That is impossible.'

'Why?'

'He now lives in such a remote corner that I couldn't possibly visit him there. May I ask you something?'

'Yes?'

'What are you doing here?'

'I have come, Mr Singhania, chiefly as a traveller. But I have got a lot of regard for Upadhyaya. If I see anyone trying to harm him, I shall certainly do my best to stop that person.'

'Does that mean you are acting as a free agent? I mean, no one has employed you to be here on their behalf?'

'No. Why?'

'Would you agree to work for me?'

'What would you like me to do?'

'Go and see Upadhyaya, and persuade him to sell me that pendant. I will give you ten per cent of five hundred thousand. If Upadhyaya does not want to take any money for himself, I am prepared to give it to a member of his family, or whoever he thinks deserves to be paid.'

'But are you aware that someone else is interested in this pendant?'

'Yes. You mean Pavandeo Singh, don't you? To be honest, I didn't know until this evening. A reporter called Bhargav came and met me here. Who knew reporters would chase me even in Kedarnath? Anyway, it was he who told me. But I believe Singh is here simply to make a film.'

'Sure. But Upadhyaya and his pendant will play a major role in his film.'

Mr Singhania began to look utterly helpless.

'Please, Mr Mitter,' he begged, 'please help me.'

'Did you mention anything to Bhargav?'

'No, of course not. I told him I was only a pilgrim here.'

'Bhargav himself is interested in Upadhyaya, but only as material for a scoop.'

'You haven't answered my question.'

'Look, all I can promise to do is this: if I find Upadhyaya, I will pass on what you've just told me. I personally feel if he doesn't want to keep the pendant with him any more, he'd like to give it to someone. I don't think he'll agree to sell it. So let's not make any firm arrangements right now. I will let you know what happens if I can get to meet him at all.'

'Very well. Thank you, Mr Mitter, thank you very much.'

It was dark outside. The town of Kedarnath was slowly going to sleep. The lights in the houses, the shops as well as the streets were all so dim that they didn't really make much difference. In the middle of it all, one light shone very brightly. Curious, we made our way to it, and found Pavandeo Singh filming the streets of Kedar with the help of a battery-operated light. He stopped as he saw us, and asked, 'Any luck with Upadhyaya?'

Instead of giving him an answer, Feluda asked him a question. 'Where are you staying here?'

'I have got a room in a private house. The house belongs to a panda. It's not far from here. See that lane on the left? I'm in the third house one the right.'

'OK. I'll get back to you,' Feluda said. We began walking back to our dharamshala.

A few seconds later, Lalmohan Babu suddenly remarked, 'I don't know what kind of a person Pavandeo Singh really is, but that man Singhania is a crook.'

'What makes you say that?'

'Maybe you couldn't see it from where you were sitting, but I did. He had a small tape recorder in his pocket. I saw him switch it on as soon as you started speaking. He's got the whole conversation on tape.'

'Well then, Mr Ganguli, I make a much better crook, wouldn't you say?' Feluda took out his mircrocassette recorder. 'Do you think that I—' he couldn't finish. A man had emerged from the shadows and hit him on his shoulder as he was speaking. I saw Feluda sway and then fall to the ground, without being able to do anything to defend himself. The lane we were passing through was totally deserted. No doubt the attacker had taken the fullest possible advantage of this.

He tried to run away after that one blow. I stood stupefied, but only for a moment. Some odd instinct made me leave Feluda, and chase the other man instantly. Ten seconds later, I had caught him by his shoulders and pinned him against the wall. He kicked at me, and began to push me away; but Lalmohan Babu's weapon shot out at him, and he fell down, crying in pain. I looked with some surprise at the weapon, which was nothing but his walking stick with a sharp pointed end. Deliberately, or otherwise, Lalmohan Babu had managed to hit this man on the head. I could see, even in the semi-darkness, blood gush forth from an open wound. But the man was obviously quite strong. He struggled to his feet in spite of his injury, and ran again, this time quickly melting into the darkness.

We turned to Feluda, and helped him to his feet. He did not say anything, but it was clear that he was hurt and in pain. Luckily, our dharamshala was not far. He said only one thing on the way: 'So the goondas have made it to Kedarnath!'

By an enormous stroke of luck, it turned out that there was a doctor staying in the dharamshala. He was a Bengali, who happened to recognize Feluda. So he received extra special care. His shoulder had a nasty cut. The doctor washed it with antiseptic lotion, then put a band-aid on it. 'It's impossible to tell without taking an x-ray whether you've fractured your shoulder or not,' he said.

'Never mind about that. Fracture or no fracture, you couldn't make me stay in bed, I promise you,' Feluda grinned.

When we asked him about his fee, the doctor shook his head vigorously.

'No, no, I cannot charge a fee for doing so little,' he said. 'You know, Mr Mitter, this is my third visit to Kedar. Each time I come back, I find the natural beauty of the place quite unspoilt, but the number of antisocial elements appears to be on the increase. I suppose the improvement in road transport is responsible for this. While it has made Kedar accessible to thousands of pilgrims and tourists, it has also made it easier for these elements to spread crime and vice where it simply did not exist before.'

The manager of the dharamshala had informed the local police without being told. When an inspector turned up, Feluda spent a long time speaking to him. I couldn't hear what exactly he told him, but could see that the inspector was listening carefully and nodding in agreement.

Mr Bhargav arrived as soon as the inspector left. 'What is this I hear about you being attacked?' he asked, sounding both surprised and concerned.

'It was nothing, Mr Bhargav. A detective learns to take these things in his stride. It was probably only a local goonda, interested more in my wallet than my person. But he didn't succeed in taking anything.'

'You mean this is not connected in any way with your investigation?'

'What investigation? I am here merely to meet Upadhyaya.'

'I see. Have you discovered where he lives?'

'Have you?'

'No one here knows anyone called Upadhyaya.'

'Then perhaps he has changed his name.'

'Yes, maybe.'

Feluda did not reveal anything of what we knew. Bhargav left, looking faintly disappointed.

Since we had another early start the following morning, we had dinner at half past eight and prepared to go to bed. Feluda, however, had other plans. To my amazement and considerable annoyance, he said, 'You two can go to bed. I'm going out now, but will soon be back.'

'Going out? Where? Feluda, you can't! I know your shoulder's still hurting, and you need to rest.'

'I need to see Pavandeo. It's urgent.'

'What! You can't go straight into the enemy camp.'

'Look, Topshe, this has happened to me before. The shock of a physical attack makes my mind function much better. I now realize Pavandeo is not our enemy.'

'No? Then who is?'

'You'll see for yourself, very soon.'

'What will you do if you go out, and find him waiting for you?'

'I have got my weapon with me. Stop worrying, and go to sleep. It doesn't matter what time I come back. Tomorrow's programme remains the same. We are leaving for Gandhi Sarovar at half past four.'

Feluda went out, his revolver in his pocket and a big torch in his hand.

'What admirable courage!' Lalmohan Babu exclaimed.

EIGHT

I could not tell when Feluda had returned at night. When I woke, shortly before half past four in the morning, he was already dressed and ready to go. Lalmohan Babu and I took ten minutes, and then we set off. Dawn had only just started to break. The streetlights were still on, looking more apologetic than ever.

We passed the temple and reached the open area behind it. Feluda suddenly turned to me and said, 'You used to be able to whistle pretty loudly. Can you still do it?'

Somewhat taken aback, I said, 'Yes, of course. Why?'

'You must whistle when I tell you to.'

I looked at him curiously, but knew better than to press for an explanation. We kept walking, using our walking sticks. Without those, it would have been extremely difficult to walk on the slippery, rocky surface, most of which was still covered with snow. A little while ago, we had had to cross the river, stepping rather gingerly across a makeshift bridge of wooden planks. Mandakini was little more than a stream here. Everywhere I looked, I could see high mountain peaks, but I had no idea what they were called. The tallest of these had started to acquire a pinkish glow in the early light of dawn.

My hands and face felt absolutely frozen. Lalmohan Babu spoke, through chattering teeth, 'T-t-t-opshe will wh-whistle, but wh-what am I going t-to do?'

'You? You need do nothing but hold that stick of yours over your head, and whirl it in the air. This will prove both your bravery and your insanity.'

'V-very w-well.'

Half and hour later, a flat, grey area came into view. It was surrounded by endless rocks and stones. That had to be the Sarovar. Even so, I looked at Feluda and asked, 'Is that the—?' Feluda nodded in silence. To the west of the lake was a large rocky mound. It could well contain a small cave. The whole thing was at least two hundred and fifty yards away.

For sometime now, Feluda had been glancing around, as though he was looking for something specific. Now his eyes seemed to rest on an object. I followed his gaze quickly and saw one leg of a tripod, peeping out from behind a large boulder. Silently, Feluda made his way to it, closely followed by us.

A few seconds later, we found Pavandeo Singh peering through his camera. He was using his telephoto lens like a telescope.

'I can see the cave quite clearly,' he said as we reached him, 'but he hasn't yet come out of it.' Then he passed the camera to Feluda, who passed it to me after a brief look.

The surface of the lake was still, reflecting the faint pink in the sky. I had to turn the camera a little to the left to locate the cave. A saffron flag was stuck between two stones right next to it.

As I looked, the sanyasi slowly stepped out of the cave. In those strangely beautiful surroundings, it seemed as though he had stepped onto a stage, to take part in some heavenly play. He was facing the east, waiting to welcome the rising sun.

'Topshe, we have to get going,' Feluda whispered. Rather reluctantly, I turned to go.

'Don't worry,' Pavandeo said reassuringly. 'I'll stay here with my camera.'

We walked on, as quickly as we could, trying to hide whenever possible behind boulders and smaller hills. It was a shade brighter now, but there was no noise anywhere. It seemed almost as if nature was waiting with bated breath for something extraordinary to happen.

Soon, we got much closer to the sanyasi. I could see him clearly, as well as the flag near his cave. He was wearing a brown wrapper over his saffron clothes. We were moving toward the north; the sanyasi was still facing the east.

Then I noticed something strange. On the mound that had initially hidden the cave from sight, a small light was moving around. There was no doubt that it was being reflected from a piece of metal. Before any of us could say anything, a man suddenly slipped out from behind the mound. He was wearing an overcoat, with its collar turned up. It was impossible to see his face, but it was easy enough to recognize, even from a distance, the small object he was carrying in his hand. It was a revolver.

The sanyasi, totally unaware of what was going on, continued to stare at the sun. Feluda spoke under his breath, 'I am going to deal with this. I want you to wait behind the boulder and keep an eye on things. Whistle as loudly as you can when you hear a gunshot.'

Feluda began to walk towards the cave without making the slightest noise. He stopped a few seconds later and hid behind another boulder. Now he could see the man with the gun, but that man could not see Feluda. We were about twenty yards away, but even so, Lalmohan Babu and I could both see each character in this play.

Now Feluda took out his own revolver. As he did so, the sanyasi turned his face in the direction of the man in the overcoat. A split second later, a shot rang out to destroy the uncanny silence that had enveloped us so far. I saw the gun being knocked out of the other man's hand, and falling on the snow a few away. He swayed and sat down quickly, clutching his right hand with his left.

Then I remembered Feluda's instruction, and whistled with all my might. Several figures in police uniform emerged at once from behind various rocks and boulders.

'Topshe! Lalmohan Babu! You can come out now,' Feluda called.

We ran as fast as we could and joined him in front of the sanyasi's cave.

The sanyasi had probably not yet grasped the full implications of what had just happened, but his calm dignity remained unruffled. He only looked at us in surprise.

And the man with the revolver? He hadn't moved an inch, but we could now see his face.

Why, this way none other than the journalist, Krishnakant Bhargav!

He was surrounded by policemen, but they appeared to be waiting for instructions from Feluda. 'Take his beard off!' Feluda said. One of the constables peeled it off immediately. The face that emerged seemed vaguely familiar, but everything fell into place when, a second later, Feluda himself removed the woollen cap that covered his hair.

'Heredity is a funny business,' Feluda observed. 'Not only are the lobes of his ears exactly like his father's, but this man also learnt to part his hair on the right. No wonder he made me feel so uneasy each time I looked at him.'

But what would it mean? Was this man really—? I didn't even have to ask.

'Yes,' Feluda answered my unspoken question, 'you are looking at Umashankar's only son, Devishankar Puri.'

NINE

We now looked at the sanyasi. He was still looking perplexed.

'The sound of that gunshot upset me,' he said. 'I'm sorry I took so long to pull myself together. Please forgive me.'

'What happened was not your fault. But you must now bring out that bag you have been guarding for over thirty years. Surely you have realized by now that we are your friends? Is it in your cave?'

'Yes, where else could it be? That's my only earthly possession!'

Once of the constables disappeared into the cave and came back with a small red bag in his hand. The sanyasi opened it. What slipped out first was a rolled sheet of paper. It was a statement from Raja Chandradeo Singh, confirming that the pendant was given to Bhavani Upadhyaya as a reward. It was stamped with his royal seal.

A smaller bag came out after this, from which emerged the famous pendant. Each little stone in it shone and glittered in the sun. It was not difficult to see that it had been created by an extraordinarily gifted craftsman. Its beauty left us speechless for several seconds.

Feluda was the first to recover. 'Now,' he said gently, 'it would help us greatly if you could tell us who you really are.'

'Who I really am? What are you talking about?'

'Couldn't you tell us your real name? The name you were given by your Bengali parents?'

The sanyasi did not even try to hide his amazement. 'You know so much about my past? Who told you I was a Bengali?'

'No one. But I saw a letter you had written in Hindi. Some of the letters written in the devnagari script looked suspiciously like Bengali letters. Besides, on a shelf in your house in Haridwar, I found a torn page from a Bengali book.'

'Really? You have an exceptionally brilliant mind.'

'May I please ask another question?'

'Yes?'

'Is Upadhyaya really your surname, and are you really called Bhavani?'

'What do you mean? Are you implying I am . . .'

'Isn't Upadhyaya only a portion of Gangopadhyaya, and isn't Bhavani a name for Durga? If I were to say your real name was Durgamohan Gangopadhyaya, would that be wrong?'

'Oh my God! K-k-k-ka-ka-ka-ka . . .'

'Why are you cawing so loudly, Lalmohan Babu? Have you

suddenly turned into a crow?'

'N-no. It's Kaka! My uncle, Durgamohan, isn't it? Oh God, can it really be true?' Durgamohan looked at Lalmohan Babu in profound surprise.

'Kaka, I am Lalu!' Lalmohan Babu went forward to touch his feet. The sanyasi put his arms around him and said, 'The Almighty does move in mysterious ways, doesn't He? Who knew I would be reunited with my only nephew like this? But now that I have, I have nothing left to worry about. That pendant is rightfully yours. I have no use for it any more.'

'Yes, I can see that. If you give it to me, Kaka, I can keep it in a bank locker. You may not know about it, but of late I have been making a lot of money by writing crime stories for children. But who knows, public demand changes so quickly, they may not want to read my stuff one day. If I knew I had the pendant tucked away somewhere, I'd feel a lot. . . you know . . . reassured!'

The Acharya Murder Case

ONE

It was at Lalmohan Babu's insistence that we finally went to see a 'jatra'. It was called *Surya Toran* and was staged by the well-known group, Bharat Opera. At the end of it, we had to admit it was a good show. The story and the acting bordered on melodrama, but in spite of that, the performers managed to hold the attention of the audience throughout. Obviously, they were all experienced actors, and the writer knew what would interest the public.

'It was a bit like the stories I write, wasn't it?' Lalmohan Babu remarked as we came out. If you were to look at the whole thing critically, you could probably find a thousand flaws in it. Yet, it kept you entertained for hours. Wouldn't you agree, Felu Babu?'

We both did. What Lalmohan Babu wrote inevitably lacked depth and serious thought. But he was amazingly popular among his readers. Every new book he wrote remained on the best-seller list for at least three months. He published only two books every year, one in April and the other in October. Of late, the factual errors in his books had grown minimal, since in addition to having his manuscripts corrected by Feluda, he had started to consult various encyclopaedias.

The reason why I mentioned *Surya Toran* is that the case I am going to write about was related to a man who used to work for Bharat Opera. His name was Indranarayan Acharya. It was he who had written the play, as well as the songs. He had also joined the orchestra and played the violin, we were told. A gifted man, no doubt. The problems that arose involving him eventually turned out to be so very complex that Feluda had to use each of his grey cells to unravel the tangled web.

Ten days after we had been to see *Surya Toran*, Mr Acharya himself rang us and made an appointment with Feluda. Feluda asked him to come the following Sunday at ten o'clock in the morning. By the time he arrived, we had been joined by Jatayu. Mr Acharya turned out to be slightly taller than most men and was clean-shaven. A man in his early forties, his hair had only just started to turn grey.

Feluda told him how much we had enjoyed seeing his play, and said, 'You are obviously what's known as a man of many parts. How did you manage to learn so many different things?'

Mr Acharya laughed lightly, 'The story of my life is somewhat strange, Mr Mitter. You'll realize how odd my connection with the world of jatras is when I tell you about my family. Have you ever heard of the Acharyas of Bosepukur?'

'Yes, yes. It's a well known family. Wasn't Kandarpanarayan Acharya one of your ancestors? The one who went to England and adopted a lifestyle as lavish as that of Prince Dwarkanath Tagore?'

'Yes, that's right. Kandarpanarayan was my great-grandfather. He went to England in 1875. He had many interests, music being one of them. The violin I play was bought by him. I have two brothers, Devnarayan and Harinarayan. Both are older.

'Harinarayan is interested in music like me, but he doesn't play any instrument. He's more interested in western classical music. All he ever plays are records and cassettes. He's a chartered accountant by profession. Devnarayan is a businessman. Our father, Keertinarayan, is still alive. He is seventy-nine. He was a barrister, though now of course he's retired. So, you see, coming from such a background, normally a man like myself wouldn't get involved with jatras. But I've had a flair for writing and a passion for music ever since I was a child. I did go to college, but didn't wait to finish my graduation. A special tutor taught me to play the violin. And I had already begun writing songs. So I went straight to my father and told him I wanted to join a group of artistes who worked together to stage jatras. Father has a certain weakness for me, possibly because I am his youngest. He agreed. That's how I began. Now I earn as much as my other brothers. I'm sure you know how well-paid jatra workers are.'

'Oh yes!' Lalmohan Babu exclaimed. 'The leading actors are paid something like twenty thousand rupees every month.'

'I do not wish to sound presumptuous,' Mr Acharya went on, 'but if Bharat Opera is well-known today, it is chiefly because of contributions I have made. My plays, my songs and my violin are the biggest attractions . . . and this is where the problem lies.' He stopped as Srinath came in with the tea.

'Are you talking of pressure from rival groups?' Feluda asked, lifting his cup.

'Yes, you're right. Many other groups have been making rather tempting offers for quite a long time. I have been in two minds—after all, one can't always ignore a good offer, can one? But, on the other hand, I've been with Bharat Opera for seventeen years. They've looked after me all this while and treated me with utmost respect. I cannot let them down. So I've had to play one group against another, simply to give myself more time to think things over. But . . . matters have now come to a head, which is why I've come to you today. An attempt was made three days ago to cripple Bharat Opera—for good—by removing me.'

'What do you mean?'

'In simple English, by murdering me.'

'What makes you say that?'

'I was attacked physically. My shoulder still hurts.'

'Where were you when you were attacked?'

'Our office is in Muhammad Shafi Lane, which is just off Beadon Street. That is where rehearsals are held. The lane is almost always dark, and quiet. When I stepped into the lane that evening, there was a power cut, making matters worse. As I made my way to the office, someone sprang up and hit me with a heavy rod. I think his intention was to strike my head, but he missed and hit my shoulder instead. Luckily, two of our actors arrived within minutes and found me lying on the ground, crying in pain. They were also on their way to the office. It was they who carried me there and took care of everything. I was carrying my violin, which had also fallen to the ground.

'My biggest worry was that it might have been damaged, but later I discovered it wasn't. Now, Mr Mitter, you must tell me what to do.'

Feluda lit a Charminar. 'At this moment, there is really nothing that I can suggest, except that you should go to the police. There is no reason to assume that the man who attacked you had been sent by a rival group. He may well have been an ordinary petty thief; perhaps all he wanted was your wallet. So do tell the police and get back to me if something else happens. That's all I can tell you. But what you told me about your family was most interesting. I could never have imagined anyone from such a family would join a jatra.'

'I was known as the black sheep of the Acharya family,' said Mr Acharya. 'At least, that's what my brothers used to call me.'

He left soon after this. When he had gone, Feluda sat quietly for a few minutes, smoking in silence. Then he blew out a couple of smoke rings and said, 'Just imagine, only a hundred years ago, Kandarpanarayan Acharya had gone to England and lived like a prince. Today, his great-grandson is trying to seek help after being attacked in a small lane in Calcutta. What a difference in their situations, although they're only three generations apart!'

'But,' Lalmohan Babu remarked, 'the change has occurred only in Indranarayan's case. From what we just heard, his two brothers are still living pretty lavishly, in keeping with their family tradition.'

'Whatever it may be,' Feluda said, 'I'd love to learn more about these people. Perhaps one day we should visit Bosepukur.'

Who knew Feluda's wish would come true and we'd find ourselves in Bosepukur in just a few days?

TWO
(INDRANARAYAN'S STORY)

Samrat Ashok would be ready in two days. On that score, at least, Indranarayan had nothing to worry about. If the truth were known, he had written four other plays and all were ready. But he hadn't said anything to the owner of Bharat Opera. He knew very well that not every play could be a guaranteed success. The mood of the audience changed frequently, and a sensible playwright had to judge very carefully what kind of stories or what themes would prove popular. In that context, *Samrat Ashok* was going to be well suited to current tastes.

No, Indranarayan wasn't worried about his play. What was causing him anxiety was something quite different. It was now ten in the night. The manager of Binapani Opera, a man called Ashwini Bhaur, was expected to call in a few minutes. This would be his fifth visit. Another group called Nobo Natya had also sent its manager to speak to him, but they were not as big and powerful as Binapani. Both wanted him to leave Bharat Opera and join their own group. After seventeen years with Bharat Opera, Indranarayan naturally found it difficult to make a decision. God had given him a special gift that had made him famous. But he also had a strong sense of loyalty.

His mind went back to the night when he had been attacked. Perhaps what Pradosh Mitter had said was right. Perhaps it had no connection with other rival groups. Indranarayan had so far been quite unaware of how strongly the feeling of rivalry ran between various theatre groups. Now he knew. However, on that particular night, it must have been an ordinary thief who had hit him with the simple intention of knocking him unconscious to steal his wallet. If he had seriously wanted to crack his skull open, surely he could've done so? Thank goodness those two boys turned up when they did. It was because of their timely arrival that even his wallet was safe. There had been around a hundred and fifty rupees in it that day.

Santosh, the bearer, came in with a slip. 'Ashwini Bhaur', it said.

'Ask him to come in,' Indranarayan told him. Ashwini Bhaur came in and took a chair.

'What's going on?' he asked.

'You tell me,' Indranarayan replied.

'I've nothing new to tell you, Mr Acharya. This is my fifth visit. You must make a decision now, one way or another.'

'Yes, I know that. But surely you realize I need to think things through? I can't just leave Bharat Opera after so many years without giving them sufficient notice.'

'Yes, but you won't be the first one to switch from one group to another. You know about Sanjay Kumar, don't you? Didn't he leave New Opera after ten years and go over to Bharat? It happens all the time. Besides, how can you ignore the amount we're offering you? We know how much you're getting from Bharat. Fifteen thousand, right? We're going to give you twenty. Your annual income will be in the region of two hundred and fifty thousand. You'll be very well looked after and treated with as much affection and respect as you are in Bharat. Your name will be highlighted in the credits. We'll accept all your terms, as far as we possibly can.'

'Look, Ashwini Babu, I'll take another day or two to finish this play I am writing. Please wait until it's been written, and it's out of my mind. Right now, I can't think of anything else. Could you come back after three days?'

'All right. But does that mean—?'

'I wouldn't ask you to come back if my intention was to disappoint you. But you must consider my position too. Money isn't everything, is it? If Bharat Opera come to know about your offer, they may decide to increase my salary to match it. What would you expect me to do if that happened? And that isn't all. A long-standing relationship like this cannot be wiped out in a day.'

'Very well, I will leave you in peace now, Indra Babu, and come back a week later. You ought to be able to make a final decision in that time. Keeping people hanging in suspense isn't very nice, is it? Well, goodbye, Indra Babu. Good night.'

'Good night.'

Indranarayan rose from his chair and went with Mr Bhaur to see him off at the front door. Then he returned and went back to writing. He was very happy with the way the last scene was coming along. If he could keep it up till the very last line, *Samrat Ashok* might well turn out to be the most successful play he had ever written.

Indranarayan went on writing. A few green flies flew in through an open window and began buzzing around. This happened every night. It was most annoying, as were regular power cuts. Of late, however, the power supply had improved. Indranarayan waved the flies away and turned his attention to his play. He had to get on with his job.

But he couldn't go on for long. Totally unbeknown to him, a shadowy figure slipped into his room and walked stealthily up to his chair to stand directly behind him.

Then it raised an arm and struck a blow with an iron rod. Instantly, a curtain of darkness fell before Indranarayan. His eyes closed, forever.

THREE

I gave a violent start as I opened the newspaper.

Indranarayan Acharya had been killed in his own house, the day before yesterday. How strange! He had come to visit us only ten days ago.

Feluda had already read the news. He shook his head with deep regret.

'I couldn't save him even after he came to me for help. But at that stage there was nothing for me to work on. How could I have given him any help?'

A small thing was bothering me. 'First he was attacked in an alley,' I said, 'and then someone broke into his house to kill him. I must say the killer has enormous daring.'

'You can't say that without looking at the victim's house and seeing for yourself which room he stayed in. Besides, if someone was desperate to kill him, he wouldn't hesitate to steal into his house, would he?'

'I guess not. But they didn't ask you to make an investigation, did they?'

'No, they obviously decided to go to the police. But I happen to know the local inspector, Monilal Poddar. He might be able to give us some information.'

I had met Monilal Poddar before. Plump and heavily moustached, he was a cheerful man who often teased Feluda, but at the same time, respected him a great deal.

As it happened, we didn't have to wait for the police to tell us anything. Indranarayan's father, Keertinarayan, himself sent word to Feluda. Three days after the murder took place, our door bell rang at nine in the morning. The visitor turned out to be a man in his early forties, his appearance smart and polished. I found him wiping his face when I opened the door. Although it was October, it was still pretty warm. 'I hope you'll forgive me for barging in like this,' he said, 'but I simply couldn't get through on the telephone. I have been sent here by the old Mr Acharya—Keertinarayan. You may have heard of the murder in his house. He'd like your assistance in the matter.'

'I see. And you are—?'

'Oh, sorry. I should have introduced myself first. My name is Pradyumna Mallik. I am currently writing the biography of Kandarpanarayan Acharya, the one who had gone to England. I used to work for a newspaper, but I gave that up and became a full-fledged writer. At this moment, I am working as Keertinarayan's secretary and collecting material for my book. Keertinarayan, as you may know, used to be a barrister. He retired four years ago. His health isn't very good.'

'Why does he want my help? Haven't they told the police?'

'Yes, his sons informed the police. But the old man himself has different views. He's very fond of crime fiction. He feels this is a job for a private investigator. He'll pay your fee, naturally.'

'Have you learnt anything further about the murder?'

'No, not really. Someone stood behind Indranarayan and struck him on the head with a blunt instrument. He was seated at his desk at the time. According to the police surgeon, he was killed between twelve and half past twelve at night. His room was on the ground floor. He had a bedroom and a study. He used to work until quite late every night. You're aware of his connection with the jatra, aren't you?'

'Yes. In fact, Indranarayan had met me before he died, and told me quite a few things about himself and his family.'

'Well then, that makes things easier. Indranarayan had had one visitor that night. It was the manager of Binapani Opera. I think his name is Ashwini Bhaur. He came at ten o'clock, and the bearer, Santosh, said he heard him having an argument with Indranarayan. But he left at eleven. The police have already spoken to him. No one knows if he came back later. There is a door at the back that is often left unlocked until about one o'clock. The servants go out of the house after dinner to meet their friends, and normally don't return until well after midnight. So if Mr Bhaur returned an hour later and slipped in through the back door, no one could have seen him. But anyway, you will obviously make your own enquiries, provided you agree to take on the job. If you do, you can visit Keertinarayan at eleven today. He'll be free at that time.'

I knew Feluda would agree, for he had developed a curiosity about the Acharyas and had enjoyed his meeting with Indranarayan. It was agreed that we would reach Bosepukur by eleven. Mr Mallik wiped his face once more and left.

'What's that piece of paper doing here?' Feluda asked a few moments after he had gone. I noticed a folded piece of paper lying in one corner of the settee which had been occupied by Mr Mallik. I picked it up and passed it to Feluda, who unfolded it and spread it out. It said:

HAPPY BIRTHDAY
HUKUM CHAND

The words had been written with a ballpoint pen.

Feluda frowned for a few seconds, staring at these words. Then he said, 'Hukum Chand . . . the name sounds familiar. Perhaps the message is going to be written on a birthday cake. Hukum Chand may be a friend of Keertinarayan. Or perhaps Mr Mallik had been told to send a telegram with that message.' Feluda folded the paper again and put it in his pocket. 'What we must do now is inform the third Musketeer. We have to use his car and, in any case, he's going to be most displeased if we leave him out.'

Lalmohan Babu turned up in his green Ambassador within an hour of being told, having waited only to have a quick shower and dress smartly. 'It seems we'll spend these Puja holidays solely trying to solve this mystery,' he said when Feluda finished filling him in. 'It's good in a way. I always find it hard to fill my time after finishing a novel. This will give me something to do. Oh, by the way, my neighbour, Rohini Babu, happens to know the Acharyas. He said he had never seen such a strange family. Apparently, the sons don't get on with their father; neither is there any love lost between the brothers. It's hardly surprising someone in that family's been killed.'

We left for Bosepukur. When our car drew up at the portico of the Acharya residence, it was five minutes past eleven. A servant opened the door as we rang the bell. Mr Mallik was standing behind him. 'I heard your car arrive,' he said. 'My room is also on the ground floor. Please come with me, I'll take you to Mr Acharya.'

The house was huge, large enough to be called a mansion. Kandarpanarayan himself might have had it built, or perhaps it had been built even earlier, possibly a hundred and fifty years ago. We went up a wide wooden staircase, our feet making quite a racket. Large oil paintings of ancient Acharyas hung by the stairs. A marble statue stood where the stairs ended. A number of vases stood here and there, most of which appeared to be Chinese. A grandfather clock stood on one side. There was a veranda, from which one could see a hall down below. It was, I learnt later, a music hall. A row of rooms stood on the other side of the veranda. Mr Mallik took us to one of these. It was a living room, well-furnished with sofas and a carpet and two small chandeliers. Lalmohan Babu and I sat on a sofa. Mr Mallik left to call Mr Acharya. Feluda paced restlessly for a while, then took a smaller sofa.

Keertinarayan Acharya arrived in two minutes. He was clean-shaven, and his complexion was remarkably fair. Most of his hair was white, but I was surprised to note that even at his age, some of it had still remained black. He wasn't particularly tall, but there was something in his personality that would make him stand out in a room full of people. As a barrister, he must have been successful. He was dressed in a silk kurta-pyjama, over which he wore a mauve dressing gown. The glasses he wore were of the kind that's known as 'half-glass'.

'Which one of you is the investigator?' he asked.

Feluda introduced himself and the two of us. Jatayu's name made Mr Acharya raise his eyebrows.

'A writer of crime stories? Why, I've never read any of your stuff!'

'What I write,' Lalmohan Babu said as modestly as he could, 'simply isn't good enough for a discerning reader like yourself.'

'Even so, if you can write crime stories, there must be an investigator in you. See if between yourselves you can find a solution to this mystery. Indra was my youngest child. He had been rather neglected in his childhood. But he never complained, or did anything to cause me concern. He was always fond of music. When it became clear that he wasn't really interested in studies, I decided to let him develop his other interests in whatever way he fancied. Even as a child, he used to write songs and plays. He even played the violin. My grandfather had brought a violin from Europe—the Strings of Amity.'

'What? Strings of what?'

'Amity. My grandfather had a rather strange sense of humour. The violin, for some obscure reason, was called the Strings of Amity. He called his first Lagonda car his Pushpak Rath; a gramophone record was a Sudarshan Chakra . . . and so on. I could spend hours telling you about my grandfather. The truth is, Mr Mitter, Indra's death has shaken me profoundly. That is the simple reason why I have asked you to investigate. I do realize being associated with jatras could not have been something an Acharya might feel proud of, but lately Indra was being paid fifteen thousand rupees a month. Now, how many people can achieve that? And how could Indra have got to this stage unless he had real talent? I myself was fond of the theatre and music. So I saw no reason to try and stop him. He could have fallen into bad company, but he didn't. All he ever seemed to care about was his work. In no way did he bring shame or dishonour to his family. On the contrary, I should think he did just the opposite.'

'Did you know he had been attacked recently? If the blow had landed on his head instead of his shoulder, he'd probably have been killed.'

'Yes, I did come to know about it. In fact, it was I who told him to consult you.'

'What do you think is the motive behind his murder? Rivalry between one jatra company and another?'

'I couldn't say. That's for you to find out, isn't it? All I can say is that if Indra had any enemies at all, they were sure to have been from one jatra company or the other. He didn't know many people outside that world. As I told you before, his only passion was his work.'

'The police must have met everyone and asked questions already.'

'So they did. But there's no reason why you cannot do the same, although you won't find either of my other sons at home. They'll be back in the evening. If you wish to ask Pradyumna anything, you may do so. Besides, there are all the servants and my daughter-in-law. She is my second son Hari's wife. My eldest, Devnarayan, is a widower. Hari has a daughter called Leena. She was very attached to Indra. Oh, by the way, how much is your fee?'

'I take a thousand in advance. Then, if everything works out well, I take another thousand when a case is finished.'

'I see. Very well. I will give you a cheque for a thousand rupees right away. You see, Mr Mitter, I am nearly eighty, a diabetic and I've suffered a stroke. Anything can happen to me any time. I'd like to see my son's killer caught and punished before I die.'

'I will do my best, I assure you. May I ask you something?'

'Yes?'

'Do you happen to know anyone called Hukum Chand?'

'No, I don't think so. I used to know a Hukum Singh, but that was many years ago.'

'Thank you.'

Feluda decided to start his enquiries with Pradyumna Mallik. He came in as soon as Mr Acharya left. 'The inspector wants to see you,' he said.

'Who, Mr Poddar?'

'Yes, he's waiting downstairs.'

The three of us made our way back to the ground floor. Lalmohan Babu hadn't said a word, but I knew he had listened carefully to the entire exchange. He had told me once that it was the duty of a writer to observe and take, in how people talked and what they said. 'Besides,' he had added, 'I don't think, Tapesh, that we help your cousin in his work as much as we should. We need to keep our eyes and ears open. Being just a passive spectator is of no use to anyone, is it?'

Monilal Poddar grinned from ear to ear on seeing us.

'As a piece of metal to a magnet, eh?' he asked Feluda.

'You could say that. But I was expecting you to have solved the mystery by the time I got here.'

'Well, it's a relatively simple case, I think. Just a matter of rivalry and jealousy between groups. The victim was a big asset to Bharat Opera. So other groups were trying to buy him off. When that proved difficult, they got someone to kill him just to damage Bharat Opera anyhow. Theft might have been a motive, too. Someone had been through his papers on his desk. Perhaps he was looking for a new play.'

'Have you spoken to the manager of Bharat Opera?'

'Yes, but have you heard what Binapani Opera did? Their manager, Ashwini Bhaur, came to see Indranarayan the same night. He tried hard to tempt him, even offered to pay him twenty thousand a month. But Indranarayan made no commitment. His loyalties were still with Bharat Opera. Mr Bhaur left at a quarter to eleven. The murder took place between twelve and half past twelve. The rear entrance was open. According to the bearer, Indranarayan was still working in his room, playing the violin occasionally. Perhaps he was writing or composing a new song. That was when he was killed. Struck on the head by a heavy, blunt instrument as he was leaning over his desk, writing. The killer couldn't have found a better opportunity.'

'Have you found the weapon?'

'No. Indranarayan's room on the ground floor was tucked away in a corner. All the servants had gone out after dinner. The chief bearer, Santosh, apparently goes out every evening for a drink or two with his mates. By the time he returns and locks the back door, it's usually one o'clock. The front door was locked, naturally, and there was a chowkidar. But anyone could have slipped in through the back door, there was no one to see or hear anything. There is a little lane behind the house called Jodu Naskar Lane. It must have made things very easy for the killer.'

'May I please see the victim's bedroom and study?'

'Of course, you're most welcome. But I'd be grateful if you could pass on any new information you might get, just as I've told you everything I knew. It will help us both, don't you see . . . heh heh heh!'

FOUR

We left Inspector Poddar and went to see Indranarayan's bedroom. It was at the end of a long veranda. His study was only a few feet away. The back door was just across the veranda, so if anyone did come through that door, it must have taken him only a few seconds to get to the study.

The bedroom was sparsely furnished. We could see nothing except a bed, a cupboard and a couple of suitcases. Then we went to his study. There were two large shelves on one side, stacked with endless papers and files and folders. Perhaps every line Indranarayan had ever written over the last seventeen years was stored on those shelves. A door led to the veranda outside. On its right was a desk and a chair. Obviously, that was where the murder had taken place. A fountain pen, two ballpoints, pencils, ink, a paperweight and a table lamp were strewn about the desk. Besides these was a violin case.

'Let's have a look at the Strings of Amity,' Feluda said, opening the case. The violin inside looked almost new. Clearly, Indranarayan had taken very good care of this instrument. It must be a hundred years old, I thought. Feluda shut the case again.

Apart from the desk, there was a sofa in the room, a chair and a small marble side-table. On the wall hung two framed certificates of merit given to Indranarayan, an English landscape and a photograph of Ramakrishna Paramahansa.

We sat down on the sofa. Mr Mallik took the chair. A servant brought four glasses of lassi and placed them on the side-table. Feluda took a sip from a glass, and began his questions.

'Where is your own room, Mr Mallik?'

'Diagonally opposite this one. That room in the far end of the veranda is the library. Mine is next to it.'

'When do you usually go to sleep?'

'Quite late at night, occasionally later than one o'clock. I do my main work—that is, collecting information on Kandarpanarayan—only at night. I began by interviewing Keertinarayan. He was twenty-two when his grandfather died, so he had had the chance to get to know him a little. When I finished talking to him, I started studying old letters and diaries and other documents.'

'Does that mean you were awake that night when Indranarayan was killed?'

'Yes, I must have been. But you see, that music hall stands between my room and this one. It is impossible to see or hear anything from that distance.'

'How did it get to be known that Ashwini Bhaur from Binapani Opera had come to visit that night?'

'Santosh knew about it. The police found the piece of paper he had sent in through Santosh with his name on it. It was Santosh who noted what time Mr Bhaur left.'

'Couldn't you hear Indranarayan play his violin?'

'I might have. But he played almost every night, so there was no reason for me to pay any special attention. I couldn't tell you definitely whether I heard him play that particular night or not.'

'Did Kandarpanarayan keep a diary regularly?'

'Yes, but only for fifteen years. He started when he was twenty-five and stopped at the age of forty.'

'That means there's a record of his visit to England?'

'Oh yes. It's an amazing account. He made a lot of friends there, and moved freely among the aristocracy. Then he went to France from London. After spending some time in Paris, he went to the French Riviera. As you know, there are famous casinos in this area, and it's a sort of Mecca for gamblers. Kandarpanarayan won a few lakhs in roulette. A rare achievement for a Bengali, especially at that time.'

'Where did the Acharyas have the zamindari?'

'In Kantipur, East Bengal. They owned a lot of land.'

Feluda lit a Charminar and inhaled deeply. 'Who discovered the body?' he asked after a short pause.

'Santosh. He returned at quarter to one, and saw that the light in this room was still on. So he came to check if Indranarayan was still working here, and discovered what had happened. Then he ran across to tell me, and I went upstairs to wake the others.'

'Who decided to go to the police?'

'Devnarayan. Old Mr Acharya was against the idea, but his son did not listen to him.'

'How did you get on with Indranarayan?'

'Very well, I think. I had interviewed him, too, particularly about his violin. He told me its quality was exceptionally good, and its sound more melodious than any he had ever heard. No one had touched it for nearly seventy years. But when Indranarayan began playing it, he realized what a superb instrument it was.'

'What did you think of him as a person?'

'He was a man in love with his work. He used to come to the library occasionally to consult books on history, especially when be began writing a historical play. Kandarpanarayan's son—Keertinarayan's father, that is—Darpanarayan had done his MA in history. So the library has a good collection of history books.'

'I see. Could you now please tell me a little about the other brothers? The eldest is Devnarayan, I gather. The second brother's called Harinarayan, and Indranarayan was the youngest. Is that right?'

'Yes.'

'Indranarayan was a bachelor. And I believe Devnarayan is a widower?'

'Yes, that's right. His wife died seven years ago.'

'Doesn't he have children?'

'Yes, but they are grown up. His son's in America, studying. His daughter's married. She lives in Pune.'

'What kind of a man is Devnarayan?'

'Very reserved and serious.'

'What does he do?'

'He works for the Stockwell Tea Company. I believe he is a very senior officer there.'

'When does he normally get back from work?'

'Not before half past nine. He goes to his club after work. That's where he spends most evenings.'

'Did he seem greatly disturbed by his brother's death?'

'To tell you the truth, Mr Mitter, the three brothers weren't particularly fond of one another. The two older brothers looked down upon Indranarayan for his association with jatras.'

'But Keertinarayan was very fond of his youngest son, wasn't he?'

'Absolutely. He loved Indranarayan most of all. I have no doubt about this since I have heard Keertinarayan say many things that implied he was partial to Indranarayan in many ways.'

'Has Keertinarayan made a will?'

'Yes, I think so.'

'In that case, even his will may show his fondness for Indranarayan.'

'Yes, of course.'

Feluda paused once more to light another cigarette. Lalmohan Babu had brought out his little red notebook and started to scribble in it. Perhaps a possible plot for a new story had suddenly occurred to him.

'Now I need to know about the second brother,' Feluda resumed. 'What does he do?'

'He's a chartered accountant. He works for Skinner & Hardwick.'

'What's he like?'

'Well, he's married with a family, so there's an obvious difference with Devnarayan. On the whole, he's a cheerful man, very fond of western music.'

'Records and cassettes?'

'Yes, but only on Sundays. On other days, he goes to his club and returns around ten in the night.'

'Which club does he go to?'

'Saturday Club.'

'Does his brother go to the same club?'

'No, he goes to the Bengal Club.'

'Harinarayan has a daughter, I believe.'

'Yes, Leena. She's about fourteen, a very intelligent girl. She goes to the Calcutta Girls' School, and is learning to play the piano. She was devoted to her uncle. His death has upset her very much.'

'And her father? Is he not upset?'

'If he is, he doesn't show it. He always seemed to consider himself superior to his younger brother.'

'Perhaps neither brother liked the fact that Indranarayan was earning a lot of money from jatras?'

'Perhaps.'

'I must talk to both brothers myself. When do you think I should call?'

'If you come on Saturday in the morning, you'll find both at home.'

'OK. Tell me, when did you start working on this biography and what made you do it?'

'I started six months ago. What happened was that I decided to write a novel, set in the nineteenth century. So I went to the National Library to do a bit of reading, and found references to Kandarpanarayan Acharya. This made me curious and I made some enquiries. Then I came to know that his family lived here. So I met Keertinarayan one day, and told him what I wanted to do. He agreed to let me stay here to do my research, on one condition: that I worked as his secretary, for which he'd pay me separately. This was fine by me, so I left my old job and moved in. I work exclusively for Keertinarayan, but I don't think anyone else in the family has ever had any objection to my research. I seem to get on quite well with everyone.'

'I see. Oh, by the way—' Feluda took out his wallet and brought out a piece of paper. It was the same paper that had 'HAPPY BIRTHDAY, HUKUM CHAND' written on it.

'This must have slipped out of your pocket when you came to visit us. What is it? A message on a birthday cake, or a telegram?'

Mr Mallik appeared totally taken aback. 'Why,' he said, looking at the piece of paper Feluda held out, 'I've never seen this before! I couldn't have had it in my pocket. Who is this Hukum Chand? I have no idea!'

'How did you get to our house?'

'I took a bus.'

'Was it crowded? Could someone have dropped it in your pocket?'

'Yes, that's possible. But why should anyone do such a thing? It just doesn't make any sense!'

'Never mind. If this doesn't belong to you, I think I'll keep it with me,' said Feluda, putting the message back in his wallet.

There was no doubt that this piece of paper was part of a bigger mystery.

FIVE

We had gone to Bosepukur on a Thursday, and were supposed to go back there on Saturday. We were therefore free on Friday. Lalmohan Babu turned up in the morning, although he normally came only on Sunday. The beginning of a new case was clearly causing him great excitement.

He flopped down on a chair and said, 'There's lots to do, isn't there? Surely we must visit some of these jatra companies?'

'Certainly. Since you're here already, let's take your car and go to Bharat Opera.'

'And then I suppose we need to find the manager of Binapani, Ishan—'

'No, not Ishan. Ashwini. Ashwini Bhaur. Yes, we have to speak to him as well. Topshe, go and find their address.'

I looked it up in the telephone directory and discovered it was in Suresh Mallik Street.

'I know where it is,' Lalmohan Babu informed us. 'I used to go there regularly at one time. There used to be a gym.'

'You used to go to a gym?' Even Feluda couldn't hide his surprise.

'Yes, believe me. I did push-ups and used barbells, and a chest expander. When I eventually stopped going there, my chest measured forty-two inches. Not bad for a man of my height, eh?'

'So what happened to that chest and those muscles?'

'They . . . disappeared. What would a writer do with muscles, anyway? Whatever muscles I have left are in my brain. But I still walk a lot, miles daily. That's why I can still keep up with you.'

We left after a cup of tea. Lalmohan Babu's driver got very excited on being told where we were going. He had seen many shows staged by Bharat Opera and knew about the murder. 'It was Indra Acharya alone who made Bharat Opera what it is today. If you can catch his killer, sir, you will do us all a great service,' he said to Feluda.

The traffic being heavy today, it took us forty-five minutes to reach Bharat Opera in Muhammad Shafi Lane. A dark, middle-aged man greeted us as we entered.

'Who would you like to see?' he asked lazily.

Feluda produced his card. The man's demeanour underwent a swift change. His expressionless eyes began glinting with interest.

'Are you looking for Sarat Babu, our proprietor?'

'Yes, that's right.'

'Just a minute, please.'

The man disappeared behind a door. We found ourselves a bench and a chair and sat down. Lalmohan Babu glanced around and said, 'You wouldn't say this company was doing so well just by looking at this room, would you?'

The same man came back in a couple of minutes and said, 'Please come with me. Sarat Babu's office is upstairs.'

We went up a narrow staircase. I caught strains of a harmonium. Were people rehearsing somewhere in the building? Even if they had lost a valuable member of their team, the show had to go on.

The office of the proprietor, Sarat Bhattacharya, was very different from the room downstairs. It was a large and spacious room, with a big table in one corner surrounded by several sturdy chairs, photographs of artists gracing the walls and a huge Godrej almirah placed opposite the table. A fan whirred noisily overhead.

The man seated behind the table was obviously the proprietor. He was bald, except for a few grey strands around his ears, his eyebrows thick and bushy, his age possibly between fifty and sixty-five.

'You are Pradosh Mitter?' he asked, looking at Feluda.

'Yes, and this is my friend, Lalmohan Ganguli, who writes crime thrillers,' Feluda replied.

'Oh, you are the famous Jatayu? Very pleased to meet you, sir.

Everyone in my family is a devoted fan.'

Lalmohan Babu coughed politely, then we sat down. Feluda began speaking.

'Indranarayan's father asked me to investigate his son's murder. That's why I'm here.'

Sarat Babu shook his head. 'What can I tell you, except that his death has almost destroyed my company? I could perhaps get someone to write good plays, but no one could ever write the kind of songs Indra Babu wrote. They were superb, utterly beautiful. People used to flock to our shows just to hear his songs.'

'We've heard he was being tempted to leave your group and join another.'

'That may well be. But it had no effect on Indra Babu. He was very close to me, he'd never have left my group. He was only twenty-five when he first came to me. I gave him his first break. He often used to tell me how grateful he was because of that. But now . . . I've been crippled, my company paralysed.' Sarat Babu stopped to wipe his eyes. Then he went on, 'Someone attacked him a few days before the murder. You knew that, didn't you? Well, I couldn't say for sure whether that is related to the actual murder. After all, there's no dearth of petty thieves in this area. But anything could have happened if those boys hadn't turned up. There really isn't anything more I could tell you. If you must make enquiries, go to Binapani. Whoever did this, killed not just Indra Babu but Bharat Opera as well.'

We rose and said goodbye. It was time now to make our way to Binapani. It didn't prove too difficult to find their office. Rehearsals were in full swing. We could hear many voices, raised high and trembling with emotion—a prerequisite of all jatras. It didn't take us long to find the manager. One look at Feluda's card made him lose his temper.

'Is this to do with the murder in Bosepukur?' he bellowed.

'Yes,' Feluda replied, 'I've been asked to investigate. I'd like to ask you a few questions since you had met the victim just before he was killed.'

'The police have already been here and asked a thousand questions. Why must you do the same? Anyway, I know nothing about the murder. I had gone simply to make him an offer, which he more or less accepted. I told him Binapani was strong and big enough to pay him much more than Bharat. I wanted him to join our company, Mr Mitter. As such, I wanted him to stay alive. Neither I nor our company stood to gain anything by his death.'

'No? Not even if it meant harming your chief rival, nearly destroying them?'

'No, sir. We wouldn't stoop so low, ever. Yes, we do try to get artists from other groups to leave them and join our own. But we wouldn't dream of actually taking someone's life just to damage a rival company. No way!'

'All right. You just said Indranarayan had more or less accepted your offer. Can you prove it?'

'I had originally made my offer in writing. I can show you the reply he sent me.'

A postcard was dug out of a file and handed to Feluda. 'I am considering the proposal you have made,' Indranarayan had written, 'Please contact me in a month.' This meant he hadn't rejected Binapani's offer outright. He had been tempted.

'Did you have an argument that night?' Feluda asked.

'Look, I spent some time trying to convince him, make him see how much better off he'd be if he accepted our offer. Now, I may have raised my voice while speaking, I don't know. I wouldn't call it arguing. In any case, Indra Babu was a very level-headed person. That's why his work was always so good. He told me it was hard for him to end his relationship with Bharat Opera. He was writing a new play for them, and couldn't make a final decision until it was finished. Then he would get in touch with me again. That was all. Those were his last words. I came away after that, at a quarter to eleven.'

We thanked Mr Bhaur and left.

'It's more complicated than I thought,' Feluda remarked a little later, as we sat having coffee in a restaurant in Chowringhee.

'You mean you no longer think Binapani hired a professional killer?' Lalmohan Babu asked.

'No, I don't think Binapani had anything to do with it. But the question is, who did? Who could have wanted him out of the way, and why? He seems to have known very few people, and those who did know him, all say they liked him very much. Of course, what Mr Bhaur just told us need not be true. Who knows, Indranarayan may well have refused his offer. We have only Mr Bhaur's word that he didn't. After all, there were no witnesses.'

'What about the people in the house?'

'Yes, that possibility cannot be ruled out. Keertinarayan was very fond of his youngest son. In fact, he liked him the most. If it came to be known that Keertinarayan had made a will in which he had left Indranarayan more than his other two sons, either of them might have wanted to remove Indranarayan from the scene.'

'Hey, that's brilliant!' Lalmohan Babu said admiringly.

'No, there is a problem with that. You see, murder isn't all that easy. No one can kill another human being unless there is the most pressing need to do so. In this case, certainly at this moment, we are unaware of any such need either of those brothers might have felt. So let's not jump to any conclusions before both brothers have been interviewed.' Feluda stopped speaking, but continued to frown.

'Now what's bothering you?' I asked.

'The second brother, Harinarayan.'

'What about him?'

'He's fond of music, western classical. I know very little about it, so I'd be at a disadvantage, wouldn't I? How could I possibly ask him anything about a subject I myself know almost nothing of?'

'Is that all? Felu Babu, I can help you out. I have an encyclopaedia of western music; just one volume, seven hundred and fifty pages. You'll get from it whatever information you need.'

'Really? What are you doing with an encyclopaedia like that?'

'It's a part of a set. There are many other sections including science and medicine and history and art.'

'Good. Do you think you could let me have that volume sometime today?'

'Of course, no problem. For you, sir, any time.'

'Thank you.'

We left the restaurant and went straight to Lalmohan Babu's house. Feluda got his book, and we returned in a taxi.

After this, it became impossible to speak to Feluda for the rest of the day. He disappeared into his room clutching the encyclopaedia, and shut the door firmly behind him.

SIX

We returned to Bosepukur at ten on Saturday morning. The first person we met was Harinarayan's daughter, Leena. She had heard a private investigator had been hired and was eager to talk to us. It turned out that she was also an admirer of Feluda's, so talking to her became easier.

'Your uncle was very fond of you, wasn't he?' Feluda began.

'Yes, but it wasn't just that. We were more like friends. He used to read out to me everything he wrote and ask for my views. If I wanted anything changed, if something didn't sound right, I'd say so; and Uncle would then change it.'

'What about songs?'

'Those, too. I was always the first to hear a new song.'

'Are you fond of music?'

'I'm learning to play the piano.'

'Western music?'

'Yes, but I like Indian music, too. I loved my uncle's music. I can sing a little.'

'Did your uncle ever tell you he was thinking of leaving Bharat Opera?'

'I knew that Binapani had offered him a lot of money. But I don't think he'd have left Bharat. He often used to tell me his roots were with Bharat. If he plucked those out, he couldn't live anywhere else.'

'He was writing a new play. Did you know about this?'

'Yes, There were many other plays he had written. I don't think anyone knows about them. *Samrat Ashok* wasn't finished. These others are all complete, but none of them has been staged. Besides, there must be at least twenty new songs that haven't been used. And rough drafts for more plays . . . you know, just ideas jotted down, outlines written. There may be ten or twelve of those.'

We were talking to Leena in Mr Mallik's room, which was next to the library. He had told us as we had arrived that his research was now complete, and he was going to return to his house in Serampore to write his book.

'But you are aware, aren't you, that you cannot leave this house until this whole business has been settled?' Feluda asked him.

'Oh yes, the police made that very clear.'

'If you leave, who will work as Keertinarayan's secretary?'

'I'll get someone else to replace me, that shouldn't be a problem. Once I get busy writing that biography, I won't have time for anything else.'

Feluda got up and began pacing, inspecting the room and occasionally staring out to check what else could be seen from it. I followed his gaze and realized that one could see the door to

Indranarayan's study. From the library, however, neither his study nor his bedroom was visible. Through another window in Mr Mallik's room one could get a view of the lane that ran behind the house. It was called Jodu Naskar Lane, I remembered.

Feluda finished his questions. Leena had already told her father about us. Now she took us to meet him in a sitting room on the first floor. It was a fairly large room, tastefully furnished and full of antiques and curios. On a shelf was hi-fi equipment for playing records and cassettes, flanked by two stereo speakers.

There were striking resemblances between father and daughter. Harinarayan was a good-looking man, with a very fair complexion like all the other men in his family. But he seemed larger and fatter than the others.

'I have heard of you both,' he said, looking at Feluda and Lalmohan Babu. 'What can I do for you?'

Feluda did not come straight to the point. 'You've got quite a collection,' he said, looking at the records and cassettes stacked on one side.

'Yes, I love western classical music. Indian music does not appeal to me.'

'Who's your favourite composer?'

'I like Tchaikovsky very much; and Schumann, Brahms and Chopin.'

'That means you're more fond of the Romantic era than any other.'

'Yes, you could say so.'

'Your younger brother used to play the violin. But he wasn't interested in western music, was he?'

'No. He was very different. I hear he had a lot of talent, but I never felt like going to a jatra. My wife and my daughter went a few times.'

'Do you happen to have a theory of your own regarding your brother's murder?'

'Theory? Well, I think he died because of the company he kept. People who work in jatra companies are often . . . well, they're not always educated and from good backgrounds, are they? Who knows who Indra had got involved with? He may have had a disagreement with one of his cronies. It's impossible to say what might have happened. Since nothing valuable was stolen from his room, one can only assume the motive was revenge. If you must make enquiries, go and speak to the people he used to hobnob with. I don't think you'll get much from any of us.'

'Was it your elder brother who informed the police?'

'Yes, but I was in full agreement with him. Isn't that the obvious thing to do when there's been a murder? How many people would call in a private investigator without first going to the police? I know my father wanted to do that, but then he's always been somewhat eccentric. God knows how he managed to work as a barrister.'

'He was very fond of Indranarayan, wasn't he?'

'That's another instance of his eccentric behaviour. He doesn't like anything traditional, or anyone who conforms to accepted norms. In this respect he is very much like our ancestor, Kandarpanarayan.'

Feluda did not ask him anything more. He thanked him and we rose. It was clear Harinarayan Acharya was not going to tell us anything useful.

The oldest of the Acharya brothers, Devnarayan, was sitting in a cane chair on the veranda that faced the west. In front of him was a table with cold beer standing on it. He offered it to us after greetings had been exchanged, but we refused.

'Was it my father's idea to employ a private detective?' he asked.

'Yes,' Feluda laughed, 'no one else seems to have any faith in my abilities.'

'A private investigator is all right in a novel or a film. This is real life.'

The words were spoken in a dry tone. I had seldom seen a man look so serious.

'You have come to ask me about Indra, haven't you?' he went on. 'Well, what can I say? In my view, he was the black sheep of our family. He brought us great dishonour. We became the laughing stock among our friends. People in my club used to come up to me and ask me how Indra was doing in his jatra company, how many songs he had written, were they popular, was he still playing the violin . . . and I hardly knew where to look. It was so embarrassing. And then this awful thing happened. Who could have dreamt something like this would happen to my own brother? But I'd say he brought it on himself. Frankly, I have no sympathy for him. And let me tell you, Mr Mitter, I am not greatly impressed by you, either. It's obvious a jatra company hired a killer and got him to steal into our house to kill my brother. Try and catch him. Why are you wasting your time here? Mind you, anyone associated with jatra might be a potential criminal. You may well find yourself looking for a needle in a haystack.'

There was no point in asking anything further. We said goodbye to Devnarayan and came down. Feluda turned to Mr Mallik.

'There's something I am sorely tempted to take a look at,' he said. 'I mean the diaries Kandarpanarayan had kept while he was in England. How many are there?'

'Two. He spent a year there.'

'May I borrow both for a few days?'

'Certainly.'

Mr Mallik got the diaries and gave them to Feluda. 'Thank you very much,' said Feluda, placing them in his shoulder bag. Then we came back home.

SEVEN

'How do you find things, Felu Babu? What conclusions have you drawn?' Lalmohan Babu asked, helping himself to a large handful of daalmut. We had returned from Bosepukur about fifteen minutes ago, and Srinath had just brought in tea and daalmut for all of us.

Feluda lit a Charminar. 'What has become clear is that it's not just a case of one jatra company trying to harm another. There's much more to it than that. We cannot eliminate the two brothers, although we've learnt nothing about them except that neither cared for Indranarayan. If one of them was in need of money, he might well have had a motive to kill. If their father has made a will, he will now have to change it. Naturally, the two remaining brothers will get much more now than they'd have got otherwise.'

'I didn't like Devnarayan. Have you ever seen anyone so cold and unfriendly?'

'We shouldn't judge anyone simply after one meeting in their house. I'd like to see both brothers in their clubs. At least, I want to find out what they do there.'

'How will you manage that?'

'Easy. Two of my old classmates are members. They'll be able to tell me. The one who goes to the Saturday Club is called Bhaskar Deb. The other's a member of the Bengal Club. He's called Animesh Som.'

'I've only heard of these clubs. Never been inside any of them.'

'You wouldn't find anything in there that might amuse or interest you, Lalmohan Babu. You don't drink or play cards or billiards, do you? What would you do in a club?'

'Yes, that's very true.'

Feluda stood up and got to work, although it took seven attempts to get through to Animesh Som. After a few minutes of conversation, he put the phone down and told us what his friend had said. Apparently, Devnarayan went to his club regularly and spent most of his time drinking. He didn't seem interested in either playing a game or in meeting people. But he read all the newspapers that came from London. And rumour had it that there was labour unrest in his office. The workers might go on strike any day.

Feluda picked up the phone again and rang Bhaskar Deb. This time, he got through at once. This is how his conversation went:

'It that Bhaskar? This is Felu, Pradosh Mitter.'

'You are a member of the Saturday Club, aren't you?'

'I wonder if you can tell me something about one of your members, Harinarayan Acharya?'

'Yes, yes, he's the one whose brother was killed. What kind of man is Harinarayan? You must know him.'

'What? A gambler? Plays poker, does he, on high stakes? Have you ever played with him? He must have got that trait from his great grandfather.'

'In debt? And that debt is increasing every day? Why doesn't he stop? Good heavens, it must be a serious problem if . . . anyway, thanks a lot, you've been most helpful. I've been asked to investigate, you see, so I thought I'd get a few details. Thanks again and goodbye.' Feluda replaced the receiver. 'Just imagine!' he said to us, 'Harinarayan Acharya is up to his neck in debt, but doesn't let on. A real cool customer, I must say. But would he kill his own brother for that? Wouldn't he be more likely to steal or embezzle funds from somewhere?'

'Felu Babu,' Lalmohan Babu said excitedly, looking as though a new idea had suddenly dawned on him, 'this is getting more and more complex. If he killed to get a bigger share in his father's will, he'd obviously have to wait until his father died. So . . . that means Keertinarayan's life is now at risk!'

'You're getting very good at this, Lalmohan Babu. Yes, what you just said could well be true.'

'In that case, shouldn't we warn Keertinarayan?'

'Look, Lalmohan Babu,' Feluda said, pulling his chair closer, 'I have said this before, and I will say it again. Murder isn't easy. A police constable is guarding that house every day. Everyone knows the victim was Keertinarayan's favourite child. Now if Keertinarayan himself is killed, suspicion will fall immediately on the two brothers. Neither will be able to escape. The police will naturally do their job, but so will I. Both brothers will be in big trouble, and they know it. Besides, Keertinarayan is old and ailing. He's not going to live very long, in any case. So I don't think he's in any immediate danger of being killed. What we have to remember is what Bhaskar just told me about Harinarayan. His behaviour at home was so normal that I don't think anyone could ever guess what he was really up to. I used to think people fond of music were always gentle and straightforward. But this man . . . well, obviously I was mistaken. It's weird!'

'That whole family is weird, if you ask me,' said Lalmohan Babu somewhat irritably, and picked up the *Statesman* from the centre table. Feluda watched him, then suddenly seemed to notice something on the back page of the newspaper. He snatched it from Lalmohan Babu, and read the whole page carefully. Then he put it down and said, 'I see.' A minute later, he said, 'Now I understand.' Another thirty seconds later, he added, 'Now it's clear.'

Lalmohan Babu lost his patience. 'What is clear?' he demanded.

'It's quite clear to me, my friend, that my knowledge is sadly limited. There's a lot I still have to learn.'

I could tell Feluda was trying purposely to create a mystery, to lead us on. A few moments later when he suddenly remarked, 'We're going to have a new experience today,' I knew it was a part of a deliberate plan.

'What do you mean?' Lalmohan Babu asked innocently.

'We're going to the races.'

'What! The races? Why?'

'I've wanted to, for many years. We're free this evening, so let's go. Just think, this extraordinary event takes place every Saturday in our own city, and yet we've never seen what it's like. It's time we witnessed it. One should experience everything in life, at least once.'

'Well said, Felu Babu!' Lalmohan Babu's voice held suppressed excitement. 'I've often thought of going to the races myself. The reason why I didn't was my fear of being spotted by an acquaintance, and then getting the reputation of being a gambler.'

'That won't happen.'

'How can you be so sure?'

'All of us will be in disguise.'

Lalmohan Babu jumped to his feet. 'Oh, what a good idea! Can you give me a French beard?'

'Yes, it would suit you.'

'Great.'

Feluda had always been very good at putting on disguises, but so far we had seen him use make-up only on himself. Today, by the time he finished working on us, we were startled to see our own reflection in the mirror. Lalmohan Babu had a beard and long wavy hair; I had a moustache and an untidy beard. My hair looked overgrown and unruly. Feluda himself had a thick, military-style moustache and was wearing a wig that made his hair look as though it had been cut very short. Even a close friend would have found it difficult to recognize any of us.

Soon, we arrived at the race course. I had never expected to find myself there. If there was any place where millionaires would stand rubbing shoulders with beggars from the street, it was here. Nowhere else in Calcutta could anyone hope to see a scene like this.

The race hadn't yet started. We took this opportunity to roam around in the crowd. A large area had been fenced off and all the horses were being walked in it. Feluda told me this area was called a 'paddock'. There was a building in the distance with rows and rows of windows. All bets were being placed through these windows. Like everyone else, we had bought little booklets. Lalmohan Babu was turning its pages with grave concentration, in order to make his acting more authentic.

We spent about half an hour at the race course. The first race started quite soon. We watched the horses run, and heard the crowd call desperately to the horses they had placed their money on; and then, suddenly Feluda said, 'Our purpose has been served, so why bother any more? Let's go back.'

I had no idea what purpose had been served, but knew that Feluda wouldn't tell me even if I asked. So without another word, we came out, found Lalmohan Babu's car and climbed back into it.

EIGHT

Inspector Monilal Poddar rang us on Sunday. 'Have you made any progress?' he asked Feluda.

'No. I'm trying to get to know the people in that house, without which I'm not going to get very far. It's a rather complicated case.'

From what Inspector Poddar then told us, it appeared that there was even now a great risk of the Acharya household being burgled. Since it was known that there were loads of new and original plays and songs still in existence, it was highly likely that whoever had had Indranarayan killed would also try to steal his works. There was an area in Bosepukur where notorious miscreants lived. It was the inspector's belief that the bearer, Santosh, was in league with these people and might actually help them break into the house.

'Is that little lane behind the house being watched?' asked Feluda.

'You mean Jodu Naskar Lane? Oh yes.'

'Do you think you could ask your men to withdraw just for one night?'

'So that a potential burglar might feel tempted?'

'Exactly.'

'Very well. Just tell me when you'd like me to remove my men, and I'll do it.'

Mr Poddar rang off. It was half past seven in the morning. Only a few minutes later, the phone rang again. This time, it was Pradyumna Mallik. 'I have been trying your number for half an hour!' he said breathlessly. 'Something terrible has happened. Last night, at around midnight, a thief got into Indranarayan's study. One of the servants must have helped him get in for the constable guarding the rear entrance didn't see him at all. I heard a noise, and came out of my room to look. At this, the man tried running away. I ran after him and even managed to catch him, you see, but he gave me such a hard push that I fell down and hurt my knee. He escaped, and now I'm walking with a limp!'

Feluda put the phone down.

'It does seem that the main motive behind the murder was to steal Indranarayan's works,' he said to me. 'If a writer's songs are so very popular and if it gets to be known that he left behind as many as five new plays and nearly twenty unused songs, obviously all jatra companies would wish to lay their hands on these. Strictly speaking everything should go to Bharat Opera. But, of course, their rivals would like to make sure they get nothing.'

'But,' I ventured to say, 'how could anyone have learnt about all these songs and plays unless Indranarayan himself had told them? Maybe he wasn't as loyal to Bharat Opera as people seem to think. Maybe he had made up his mind about joining some other group.'

'In that case, who killed him? And why?'

'Perhaps he had given his word to Binapani, and so a third group decided to step in and remove him altogether.'

Feluda nodded silently. Clearly, he had already thought of this possibility, but was nowhere near finding a solution. He took out his famous blue notebook and began scribbling in it. What was he thinking of now? Why was he looking so serious? I simply couldn't tell.

Lalmohan Babu arrived as usual at nine o'clock.

'May I keep your encyclopaedia for another couple of days?' Feluda asked him.

'Of course. You may keep it for two months, I don't mind at all.'

'Thank you. I've learnt a lot from it about melody, harmony, polyphony, counterpoint. Even in the history of music there have been mysteries and unsolved crime. Mozart had apparently been fatally poisoned by another composer called Salieri. But no one ever really got to the bottom of it.'

'I see. What are you plans for today?'

'You haven't heard the latest. Someone got into Indranarayan's study last night, but thanks to Mr Mallik, he couldn't steal anything. I think that house should be kept under observation tonight.'

'Tonight?'

'Yes, say around half past eleven.'

'How?'

'Remember that back lane? The rear door of the house opens on to it. We could sit on the pavement and keep an eye on that door.'

'Sit on the pavement? What will people think if they see three gentlemen sitting on a pavement in the middle of the night? It'll look decidedly fishy.'

'No, it won't, for the three men won't look like gentlemen at all.' My heart leapt suddenly. Was Feluda talking of disguises again? What kind of disguise? Feluda provided the answer even before I could ask.

'Have you ever played cards?' he asked Lalmohan Babu.

'Cards? Why, yes. I've played as a child, simple games. . .'

'OK, that's all you need to know. You won't confuse between clubs and spades, diamonds and hearts, will you?'

'No, no, of course not.'

'Fine. We'll dress as Oriya cooks, and play "twenty-nine". We'll have to include your driver, Haripada. I'll organize our costumes and make-up. Don't open your month unless you have to. And if you do, remember to speak with an Oriya accent.'

'OK.'

Lalmohan Babu's eyes took on a new glint. Even I began to feel very excited. The plot had certainly started to thicken. Lalmohan Babu left at twelve o'clock, agreeing to return at seven and have dinner with us. Then we'd get dressed and go over to Jodu Naskar Lane at eleven. It had struck us all as a quiet and peaceful place. We'd sit under a lamp-post and start playing. Haripada offered to bring a pack of cards in the evening, and an old cotton sheet. Lalmohan Babu would have to be taught the basic rules of 'twenty-nine' before we left.

The only person who didn't appear even remotely excited was Feluda. He spent the whole day reading the music encyclopaedia, while I forced myself to sit quietly and turn the pages of a magazine.

Lalmohan Babu arrived with his driver on the dot of seven. Since this time we had to dress a lot more simply, it took us much less time to put on our disguises, and we were ready by ten-thirty. Feluda had dropped a packet of tea leaves in a bucket of water, and then soaked four white dhotis in it. When they were dry, they looked crumpled and dirty. We wore these, and wrapped cotton shawls around our shoulders. Haripada hadn't forgotten the cards and the sheet. Lalmohan Babu was shown how to play the game, and allowed to practise a couple of times. When we set off, I heard him mutter under his breath, 'Jack-ace-ten-king-queen-eight-seven.'

We parked our car in a dark corner on the main road and walked over to Jodu Naskar Lane. Not a soul was about. On Feluda's request, Mr Poddar had removed the constable on duty. The house of the Acharyas stood sprawling. Among the room from which this lane could be seen was the library and Mr Mallik's room. The back door was at the far end, where the rooms ended. It was closed. Lights were on both in the library and Mr Mallik's room, but it was impossible to tell which of the two he might be in.

We spread the sheet under a lamp-post and began playing. Feluda brought out a packet of paan from under his shawl and passed it around.

'Keep your paan tucked inside your mouth, and don't spit,' he whispered, looking at Lalmohan Babu.

A clock—possibly the grandfather clock in the big house—struck eleven.

'Nineteen,' called Lalmohan Babu. He was Feluda's partner. Feluda now produced a packet of beedis, gave one to Haripada and lit one himself. Still there was no one to be seen except a rickshaw-walla where the lane ended, but he was fast asleep. It was probably a moonless night for the sky seemed darker than usual, although there were no clouds.

'*Turupo maruchi kain*?' asked Lalmohan Babu. I looked at him in surprise. I had no idea he could actually speak in Oriya. Feluda probably thought this was going too far, so he said, 'Sh-sh!' giving Lalmohan Babu a warning glance. Although we were supposed to be playing only to kill time, 'twenty-nine' was such an interesting game that I soon lost all track of time, until the clock struck the half-hour. Good heavens, was it half past eleven already? The others seemed just as deeply engrossed in the game. Lalmohan Babu picked up a beedi absentmindedly, tried to light it, failed and threw, it away. A few minutes later, a dog barked somewhere. Another barked back at the first one and, at this precise moment, Feluda laid a hand on my knee. I looked up quickly.

A man had turned into the lane and was walking towards us. He was wearing a dhoti and a kurta and, like us, a grey cotton shawl. It was quite nippy out in the open. He passed us by and crossed over to the other side. Now he was walking alongside the Acharyas' house, past all the windows that overlooked this lane. Then he stopped in front of the door.

Tap, tap, tap!

He knocked three times. I could hear him knock only because I was straining my ears. The door opened, making a crack just about wide enough for the man to pass through. By now we had all recognized him.

It was the manager of Binapani Opera, Ashwini Bhaur.

A little later, the clock struck twelve. Fifteen minutes had passed since Mr Bhaur's arrival. He came out only a couple of minutes later. Was he carrying anything in his hands? I couldn't see, for both his hands were hidden under his shawl. He began walking rapidly, and soon disappeared from sight.

Our vigil was over and very successful, too. I glanced at Feluda. 'Let's finish this game. Then we can go,' he said under his breath.

NINE

Feluda rang Mr Mallik from his room the following morning. I picked up the extension in our living room and heard the whole conversation.

'Hello, Mr Mallik?'

'Yes, how are you?'

'Fine, thanks. Is everything all right?'

'Why, yes! I think so.'

'Could you please do something for me? Go and see if everything's OK in Indranarayan's study. Yes, I'll hold.'

Mr Mallik disappeared, but was back in thirty seconds.

'Oh my God, Mr Mitter, there's been a disaster!'

'Disaster? What's happened?'

'Every new play and all the new songs have gone.'

'I had guessed as much. That's why I rang.'

'What can it mean?'

'Another mystery has been added to all the others, that's all.'

'Will you come here now?'

'I'll go, if need be. But before that I must speak to the police.'

Feluda replaced the receiver, then picked it up again to dial Inspector Poddar's number.

'Hello, Mr Poddar? Thank you every much for removing your man from duty last night. It really worked. I hope you're keeping an eye on Ashwini Bhaur. He stole some valuable papers from Indranarayan Acharya's room last night.'

'This man is a crook,' Mr Poddar said. 'He cannot even give us a proper alibi. He left the deceased alive and well, he says, but apparently Bhaur did not return home immediately. His story is that he took a taxi and it broke down on the way. I don't think that's true. What progress have you made?'

'I have made good progress, I should say, but you may not agree with some of my views or accept my conclusion since we've approached this case from different angles.'

'Never mind the angle or your views. All I want is that the culprit should be caught.'

I knew Feluda was not going to tell me what he had meant by different angles, so I didn't even bother to ask. Feluda said goodbye to Inspector Poddar and told me he was going out. 'I have to put in an advertisement in the personal column of the *Statesman*. I'm in need of a good violin.'

A small advertisement appeared the next day. If anyone wanted to sell a violin, preferably made abroad and in good condition, they were asked to write to a box number.

Two days later, Feluda received a response to this advertisement. He read the letter and said, 'Lowdon Street. That's where I have to go.' An hour later, he was back.

'They were asking for far too much,' he announced, looking glum.

'Is this sudden interest in a violin simply the result of reading that encyclopaedia? You mean you seriously want to learn to play it, at your age?'

'It is,' declared Feluda solemnly, 'never too late to learn.'

This mystified me even more, but Feluda refused to say another word. Lalmohan Babu turned up later in the day and took me aside to make a complaint. 'I like everything about your cousin, Tapesh, except his habit of sinking into silence every now and then. Why can't he tell us what he's thinking?'

The next day, which was a Saturday, Feluda suddenly seemed to have cheered up. I even heard him humming under his breath. 'We must visit Keertinarayan Acharya today. I'll ring him now,' he said.

'Have you finished your investigation?' Mr Acharya asked when Feluda called him.

'Yes, I think so. But I need to have a meeting in your house to explain everything. Your two sons and Mr Mallik would have to be present.'

'That's no problem. They're all at home. What time should we expect you?'

'Ten o'clock.'

Feluda rang Inspector Poddar after this and told him to reach Bosepukur by ten. 'We need you to be there, for today this story is going to reach its climax,' he said.

Lalmohan Babu arrived at nine. We had a cup of tea, and left at nine-thirty.

We were taken to the same sitting room on the first floor where we had first met Keertinarayan. He was waiting for us. 'Go and call the others, Pradyumna,' he said. Mr Mallik left to call his two sons.

Devnarayan was the first to arrive.

'I hear the police have made a lot of progress,' he said irritably. 'Why then do we have to listen to a lecture from this man?'

'I have made a lot of progress, too, Mr Acharya, but in a different way. Besides, murder is not the only crime committed in this case. I think you ought to know that. I will try to explain everything very clearly.'

Devnarayan grunted and sat down. The pipe that always seemed to dangle from his lips had had to be abandoned for the moment, possibly out of respect for his father. Maybe that was the real reason why he was so cross.

Harinarayan arrived in a few minutes. He didn't say anything, but his brows were knitted in a deep frown. So obviously, he wasn't feeling very pleased, either.

Feluda began speaking when everyone was seated.

'Indranarayan Acharya was killed on the night of 7 October between twelve and half past twelve. When I began to think of a possible motive for the murder, I learnt that he had been his father's favourite child. If Keertinarayan had made a will, it was very likely that he had left most of his assets to Indranarayan. In the event of Indranarayan's death, this would naturally have to be changed. However, even if a new will meant a greater share for the two remaining brothers, neither could actually get anything until their father died. There was therefore no immediate gain for them after Indranarayan's death.

'Another fact was brought to my attention. I learnt that Binapani Opera had been trying to get Indranarayan to leave Bharat and join their own company. But Indranarayan had refused to do so. As such, Binapani might well have hired a killer to do the job, with the sole purpose of causing Bharat Opera irreparable loss. Binapani's manager, Ashwini Bhaur, had met Indranarayan that same night. He was killed about an hour after Mr Bhaur left.

'Leena then told us something very useful. We learnt from her that Indranarayan had written five plays and nearly twenty songs which had never been used. I don't have to spell out how valuable these must be to any jatra company. Whoever killed Indranarayan did go through the papers on his desk, but did not take anything, possibly because he didn't have enough time. Last Sunday, Ashwini Bhaur came and took everything away.

'It then became clear that the most likely motive for the murder was stealing Indranarayan's works. However, an outsider could not have done it. He wouldn't have known what these plays and songs looked like, or where they were kept. Someone from within the family would have had that information. It was also much easier for someone in the house to steal these papers after the murder, when there would have been ample time and opportunity. Now, I had to find out if anyone in this family was facing a financial crisis. I made some enquiries and was told that Harinarayan had lost heavily in cards and owed people a lot of money. Yet, I couldn't see him going to the extent of killing his brother, stealing his papers and then selling them to a jatra company. Who, then, needed money so desperately? As I was trying to work this out, I discovered something accidentally.

'When Mr Mallik called on us on Keertinarayan's request, a piece of paper had dropped out of his pocket. The words written on it were "Happy Birthday" and "Hukum Chand". When I showed this piece of paper to Mr Mallik, he said it did not belong to him; nor did he have any idea how it might have got into his pocket. I thought no more about it until last Saturday, when my eyes happened to fall on the last page of the *Statesman*. There was information about race horses. I realized instantly that "Happy Birthday" and "Hukum Chand" were names of horses. This made me suspect that Mr Mallik went to the races, but wanted to keep it a secret. I went to the race course the same evening, and saw Mr Mallik placing bets. There could be no doubt after this that he was a gambler. People who frequently go to the races are often in need of money. If he had suffered heavy losses, Mr Mallik certainly had a motive for killing Indranarayan and a suitable opportunity. Mr Mallik was in his room that night, supposedly working. It would've taken him only a few minutes to walk across, past the music hall, and get into Indranarayan's study.

'Mr Mallik, it turned out subsequently, was not only a killer, but also a liar. He didn't lie to me only about going to the races. He rang me one day to tell me a thief had stolen into Indranarayan's room and, in trying to chase him away, Mr Mallik had fallen and hurt his knee. As a result of this, he said, he was walking with a limp. This morning, however, I noticed that on at least two occasions he forgot to limp.

'Ashwini Bhaur came here at a quarter to twelve last Sunday night, and took the plays and the songs from Indranarayan's room. I know this for a fact because when he came, I was sitting outside with my friends, playing cards. We all saw him. The light was on in Mr Mallik's room. It is my belief that it was he who stole all the vital papers and then made a deal with Binapani. It was he who let Mr Bhaur in that night, and it was he whom Mr Bhaur paid. If any of this is wrong or untrue, perhaps Mr Mallik will be good enough to correct me.'

Mr Mallik didn't say a word. His face had turned pale, his body was trembling. He sat staring at the floor. Behind him stood Inspector Poddar. There were two other constables in the room.

'That explains the mystery behind Indranarayan's murder,' Feluda resumed, 'but that isn't all. Let me tell you about the second crime. On my first visit to this house, one little thing had struck me as odd. It was Indranarayan's violin. I couldn't see how an instrument that was a hundred years old could look so new. But I knew nothing of violins then, so I paid no attention. What I did learn the same day was that Kandarpanarayan used to call his violin "The Strings of Amity". Recently, I have had the chance to read two things: one was a music encyclopaedia, and the other was Kandarpanarayan's diary. I learnt from the encyclopaedia that in the sixteenth and seventeenth century in Italy, there had been various violin makers who had reformed and made great improvements on the instrument, both in its appearance and sound. Three names among these violin makers are revered even today: Antonio Stradivari, Andrea Guarneri and Nicolo Amati. All of them had lived in the seventeenth century. Amati was the first among these men to bring about a revolution in the making of violins in Cremona.

'I did not see the connection between "Amati" and "amity" until I read Kandarpanarayan's diary.' Feluda took out a piece of paper from his pocket and read from it. 'This is what he wrote: "I bought an Amati today from a musician who was sunk in debt and who sold it to me for two thousand pounds. It has a glorious tone."

'Two thousand pounds in those days would have equalled twenty thousand rupees. Today, a violin like that would fetch at least a hundred thousand rupees.

'Such an old and extraordinary violin was lying around in this house, being played occasionally by Indranarayan. How many people were aware of its real value? I don't think either Keertinarayan or Devnarayan had any idea. But two people knew about it. One of them was Pradyumna Mallik, who had read Kandarpanarayan's diary; and the other was Harinarayan, who knew about western classical music. He must have known about violins and their makers. At any rate, I am sure he knew that the name of the maker is always inscribed inside a violin. You can see it if you peer through the gaps by the side of a violin. These gaps are shaped like the letter "S".

'My suspicions fell on Harinarayan the minute I realized "amity" stood for "Amati". It was obvious that the real Amati had been removed after Indranarayan's death and replaced by a newer and cheaper version. The original had been sold. I put in an advertisement in a newspaper, offering to buy a good quality violin, made abroad. A Mr Rebello wrote in response to my advertisement. He turned out to be an antiques dealer. He told me he had an old violin which he could sell me for one hundred and fifty thousand rupees. I asked him if he had bought it from Harinarayan Acharya. He told me that he had and said it was the only Amati in India.

'That, I think, explains everything about the second crime. And that, Mr Acharya, is the end of my lecture.'

No one spoke. Not a single voice uttered one word in protest. There was not a single denial from either criminal. Inspector Poddar arrested Mr Mallik and took him away. Harinarayan continued to sit still like a statue, holding his head in his hands. Devnarayan left the room in silent disgust.

After a long time, Keertinarayan sighed. 'If only Hari had had the sense to tell me about his debts, I would've helped him out, and we'd never have lost such a valuable possession. But I still can't believe what Pradyumna Mallik did. How could he be so totally dishonest, how could he stoop so low? Now, of course, there's no question of allowing him to write my ancestor's biography. All I can hope for is that he gets his just desserts.'

Mr Acharya said all that, but it was still important to him that the biography of Kandarpanarayan be written. After a while, he turned to Lalmohan Babu.

'You are a writer of thrillers, aren't you?' he asked. 'Why don't you try writing about Kandarapanarayan's life? You'll find his life more full of mystery and thrill than anyone else you've ever heard of.'

Lalmohan Babu bowed, with as much modesty as he could assume. 'Please don't, sir . . . I am immensely honoured, but I am only a very small and ordinary writer. I'm not even worthy of your consideration.'

Much later, on our way back, he made a confession to Feluda.

'Me? Write someone's biography in a house where there's been a murder? Are you mad? Long live my pot-boilers, long live my hero Prakhar Rudra, and—above all—long live The Three Musketeers!'

Murder in the Mountains

ONE

'Good news?' Feluda asked Lalmohan Babu the minute he came into the room. I didn't notice anything special, but Feluda went on, 'I knew from the way you rang the bell twice that you were eager to share some important news with us, though I couldn't tell whether the news was good or bad. Now it's obvious it's good news.'

'How did you guess?' Lalmohan Babu asked. 'I didn't even smile.'

'No, but there were a few things that gave you away. Number one, your appearance. You have taken extra care today. That yellow kurta you're wearing is new, you used a new blade to shave and the whole room is already reeking with your aftershave. Besides, you don't usually come here before nine. It is now seventeen minutes to nine o'clock.'

Lalmohan Babu laughed. 'Yes, you're absolutely right. I couldn't rest in peace until I came and told you what had happened. Do you remember Pulak Ghoshal?'

'The film director? The one who made a Hindi film based on your story, *The Buccaneer of Bombay*?'

'It wasn't just a film, Felu Babu, but a super-hit film. He had told me he wanted to make another film from one of my stories. We" he's going to do it now.'

'Which story is this?'

'The one with all the action in Karakoram. But Karakoram has been dropped. The action's now in Darjeeling.'

'Darjeeling? How could Darjeeling ever compare with Karakoram?'

'I know, I know. But something's better than nothing, isn't it? Apart from that, they're going to pay me a lot more than last time. Forty thousand, no less.'

'What! It takes me two years to earn that much!'

'Well, their total budget is 5.6 million rupees. Forty thousand for the writer is nothing. Do you know how much their top stars get paid?'

'Yes, I have some idea.'

'Then why are you surprised? Rajen Raina will play the hero in this film. He will get more than a million. And the villain's role has gone to Mahadev Verma. His rates are even higher. He's done only five films so far, but all five have had silver jubilees.'

'Really? Well then, if Pulak Ghoshal is a pal of yours, how come he hasn't invited you up to Darjeeling?'

'But he has! That's what I came to tell you. He's asked not just me, but all three of us. I did say to him there was no need for a formal invitation, we'd go on our own. What do you say, Felu Babu?'

I couldn't remember when we were last in Darjeeling. All I could remember was that it was there that Feluda began his career as an investigator. I was only a young boy then, and he had to tick me off pretty frequently for my naivete and ignorance. Now he had started to introduce me as his assistant. If he had done that before, people would simply have laughed at him. Over the last few years, I had thought many times of going back to Darjeeling for a holiday, but Feluda had become so busy that there never seemed to be any time. He was also earning much more. Of the five cases he had handled in the last six months, he had solved all except the case of a double murder in Chandannagore. His work had been highly appreciated everywhere, and he had been paid well. Only three months ago, he had bought a colour television, and a large number of old books, in which he seemed greatly interested. I had realized by now that Feluda was not really bothered about saving money. He liked spending what he earned, but not necessarily always on himself. He often bought little gifts for Lalmohan Babu, simply to show him how much he appreciated all the help he gave us, whenever we needed it. The aftershave he was wearing now had been given by Feluda. Lalmohan Babu had declared he would use it only on special occasions. Today was obviously such an occasion for him.

Our Puja holidays were about to start. Feluda had already decided not to accept any more cases for a few months. So I didn't think he would object to a visit to Darjeeling. He loved the place, anyway. I had often heard him commenting on the variety Bengal could offer. 'It may only be an accident of geography,' he told me once, 'but can you think of any other state that has lush green farmland, dry and arid areas, a forest like the Sunderbans, huge rivers like the Ganga, Padma and Meghna, an ocean at its bottom and the Himalayas at its top?'

'Well?' Lalmohan Babu asked a little impatiently, sipping the tea Srinath had just brought in. 'Do you want to go or not?'

'Wait, I'd like one more detail before I make up my mind.'

'Yes?'

'When would you like us to go?'

'A part of the film unit has already reached Darjeeling. But they're not going to start shooting before next Friday. Today is Sunday.'

'I am not really interested in watching the actual shooting. Are they going to work outdoors, or have they—?'

'Have you heard of Birupaksha Majumdar?'

'The managing director of the Bengal Bank?'

'He was the MD, but is now retired. A mild cerebral stroke made him retire at the age of fifty-two.'

'I see. But isn't he a rather talented man? He used to be a sportsman, I think?'

'Yes. He was once the national billiards champion. And I think he was a shikari, too.'

'Yes, I have read one of his articles on shikar and hunting.'

'He comes from a very well-known family. His ancestors used to be the zamindars in a place called Nayanpur in East Bengal. They have a huge house in Darjeeling. It's built like a bungalow, and has sixteen rooms. That is where Mr Majumdar stays. Pulak has got his permission to use a couple of rooms to take a few shots in. The rest of the shooting will take place all over Darjeeling. The film unit will stay at Mount Everest Hotel. We could book ourselves somewhere else.'

'Yes, that will be better. I don't like the idea of seeing too much of the film unit. We could stay in one of the new hotels Darjeeling's now got.'

'I saw an advertisement for Hotel Kanchenjunga,' I put in.

'Yes, so did I.'

'Very well, Felu Babu. I'll make the arrangements.'

It took us three days to complete all the arrangements.

We reached the airport on Thursday, 30 September to find that Pulak Ghoshal was on the same flight. With him were the hero, heroine and villain of the film. Lalmohan Babu's story didn't have a heroine at all, but clearly the director had found it necessary to introduce her in the film version. Pulak Babu grinned on seeing Feluda. 'I'm so glad I chose one of Laluda's stories. I wouldn't have met you again otherwise, would I? But I do hope you won't have to get involved in an investigation this time!'

Then he introduced us to his hero, Rajen Raina, heroine, Suchandra, and villain, Mahadev Verma. Suchandra was pretty, but was wearing rather a lot of make-up. Rajen Raina—who I could recognize easily enough—looked cheerful and smart. He had a short, carefully trimmed beard. He was as tall as Feluda and looked quite fit. Although he was newcomer, he looked at least forty to me. But perhaps his age was something skilful make-up could hide. I didn't think there was any man in the whole country who might fit the description of Lalmohan Babu's hero in his book. Prakhar Rudra's height was six-and-a-half feet, his chest measured fifty inches, his nose was sharp as a sword and his eyes glowed like burning coal at all times.

Mahadev Verma struck me as the most interesting. His eyes drooped, a slight smile lurked around his lips, under his nose was a thin moustache that curled upwards, and he looked as though he wouldn't think twice before killing another human being. Both he and Raina were wearing cologne. Feluda told me afterwards that the one Verma was wearing was called Denim, and Raina's was called Yardley Lavendar.

We were told at the airport that our flight to Bagdogra had got delayed by an hour. So we all went to the airport restaurant for a cup of coffee. It was actually Pulak Babu's idea, the three of us went as his guests.

Mahadev Verma and Feluda got talking in the restaurant. Since I was sitting next to Feluda, I heard the whole conversation.

'You've been working in films for a few years, haven't you?' Feluda began.

'Yes, three years. Before I joined films I used to travel a lot. I've seen most parts of the country, including Leh and Ladakh. When I was in Kashmir, I happened to meet the director of a film that was being shot in Srinagar. It was he who gave me my first break. Now, of course, I couldn't even think of leaving films.'

Lalmohan Babu had been fidgeting in his seat. Now he promptly asked the question that was clearly trembling on his lips.

'How do you like the character you're going to play in this film?'

'It's a very powerful character. Oh, I like it. That scene, especially, where I hold the heroine in front of me and call the hero loads of cruel names, and the hero is helpless to do anything although he has a revolver in his hand—ah, that scene is truly dramatic!'

Nowhere in Lalmohan Babu's book did a scene like this appear. The eager smile with which he had asked his question faded quickly at Mr Verma's reply. But Mr Verma hadn't finished. He turned to Feluda again.

'Mr Ghoshal said you were a detective. I believe detectives can tell a lot of things about a person within minutes of having met him. Can you tell us anything about me?'

Feluda laughed. 'A detective isn't a magician. What he can see is usually based on his powers of observation, and his knowledge of human psychology. To me, you appear somewhat disappointed.'

'What makes you say that?'

'You keep looking around as you speak, and I think you've realized that no one in this restaurant has recognized you. I saw you glance around, and heave a deep sigh. But Rajen Raina has been recognized, and a lot of people have already come up for his autograph. You even took off your dark glasses in the hope that that might help people recognize you. But when it didn't work, you put them back on again.'

Mahadev Verma sighed again. 'You are absolutely right, one hundred per cent. If I am seen in Bombay in a public place, I am instantly surrounded by a crowd. But here . . . Perhaps Bengalis don't often watch Hindi movies?'

'Oh yes, they do,' Lalmohan Babu assured him. 'The only thing is that three of your films haven't yet been released here. I don't normally keep a track of what's happening to Hindi film actors, but I did make a few enquiries about the man who was going to play the villain in my film.'

'I see,' Mr Verma sounded relieved. 'Anyway, Mr Mitter's powers of observation are terrific, there's no doubt about that.'

Our flight was announced soon after this, so we all left hurriedly for the security check. Feluda had transferred his Colt revolver to his suitcase, which had already been taken to the plane. In the past, we had got involved in criminal cases so many times even when we were on holiday, that these days Feluda refused to take any risks. He never stirred without his revolver.

We went through security and reached the departure lounge. Within ten minutes it was announced that our flight was ready for departure. The three of us and all members of the film unit got into the plane. My heart danced with excitement at the thought of seeing Darjeeling again, and being at a height of 6,000 feet. It was going to be quite cold there since it was nearly October. Even that gave me an odd thrill. Somehow, I felt another adventure awaited us. But when I mentioned this to Feluda, he snapped, 'Where on earth did you get that idea? Has a single thing happened yet to indicate an adventure? If you get your hopes up without any reason whatsoever, they're only going to be dashed. Just remember that.'

After this, I didn't dare make any comment about the future.

TWO

Hotel Kanchenjunga turned out to be quite neat and clean. Each room had a telephone and a heater, the bathroom had running hot water, the linen was crisp and spotless—in short, it was a place that cheered one up instantly. We were going to be in Darjeeling for ten days. If the place we were going to stay in wasn't reasonably satisfactory, it could become a serious irritant.

Our journey had been eventless. Lalmohan Babu had taken out his Rajasthani leather-and-wool cap on reaching Sonada and put it on. 'To protect my head and ears,' he explained. Then he began to concentrate on the scenery, and said 'Beautiful!' at least a million times. Finally, over a cup of tea in the Kerseong railway restaurant, he made an honest confession. This was his first visit to Darjeeling, he told us.

'What!' Feluda raised his eyebrows. 'You mean you have never seen Kanchenjunga?'

'No, sir,' Lalmohan Babu admitted, sticking his tongue out in embarrassment.

'Oh God, how I envy you!'

'Why?'

'Because you've no idea what a treat is in store for you. Only you among the three of us will get to experience the tremendous impact of seeing Kanchenjunga for the first time. You are very lucky, Mr Ganguli.'

It was possible to see Kanchenjunga even from Kerseong, if the sky was clear. But it had been quite cloudy today. By the time we reached Ghoom, daylight had started to fade and the clouds hadn't gone. Lalmohan Babu had, therefore, not yet had his treat. This was, of course, a special feature of visiting Darjeeling. Even at the end of one's holiday, Kanchenjunga could well remain unseen. If that happened, I would certainly be extremely disappointed. I had seen it before, but was very anxious to see it again. This was an experience that one could never get tired of.

We left our luggage in the hotel and went out for a walk. We had to walk uphill for about five minutes before we reached the Mall. It was dark by this time, and the streetlights had been switched on. The shops in the Mall were also lit up. 'Felu Babu, why aren't there any cars anywhere?' Lalmohan Babu asked, puzzled.

'Cars and other vehicles aren't allowed to run in many parts of Darjeeling. The Mall is one such place. You can walk here, or ride a horse. Have you ever ridden before?'

'N-no. But then, I have taken a ride on a camel, haven't I? A horse would be child's play in comparison, surely?'

A little later, we ran into Mr Birupaksha Majumdar. The film crew were out for a walk, like ourselves. Pulak Ghoshal strode forward to meet us. He was accompanied by a gentleman wearing a suit and a felt hat. This is Mr Majumdar,' he said, 'we're going to shoot a part of the film in his house. He's very kindly given us his permission. And these are—' Pulak Babu finished making the introductions.

'What have you to do with the shooting?' Mr Majumdar asked, looking at Feluda.

'To be honest, nothing at all. But this friend of mine writes crime thrillers. The story the film is based on was written by him.'

'Very good. He writes crime stories, and you are an investigator. That's a wonderful combination. I seem to have heard your name before. Has it come out in the papers a few times?'

'Er . . . yes. I helped solve a case in Bosepukur last year. This was reported in the press.'

'That's right. That's why your name sounded so familiar. You see, I collect press cuttings; not routine ordinary stuff, but if the news has a touch of drama about it, it goes into my collection.

'This has been my hobby since I was seventeen. I have thirty-one scrapbooks. Now that I'm retired, I spend some of my time turning the pages of these scrapbooks, just as some people read old books. But now I've got a helper. Rajat—my secretary— cuts out the pieces I want and pastes them for me. That's how I've got the cuttings that I mentioned to you.'

By this time, we had passed the fountain that stood in one end of the Mail, and had started to walk towards the main road. 'I have run out of my medicine,' Mr Majumdar said. 'Why don't you come with me to the chemist?' We accompanied him to the shop just across the road. What he bought turned out to be pills called Trofnil. The chemist handed him thirty-one of these, sealed in aluminium foil. 'It is an anti-depressant,' Mr Majumdar told us. 'I cannot sleep unless I take one of these. What I've got here will last me a month.'

We came out of the shop. 'I'd like to visit you one day and look at some of your scrapbooks,' Feluda said.

'Oh, sure. You are most welcome. I can even show you reports on cases that haven't yet been solved. These go back twenty years.'

'How interesting!'

'But then, my life is no less interesting. Sometimes I toy with the idea of writing an autobiography, but then I tell myself it wouldn't be of any use, since I couldn't obviously tell all my stories exactly the way they happened. An autobiography should be totally honest, devoid of secrets and lies. At least, that's my belief. Anyway you must come and visit me one day.'

'We'd love to. When is the best time for you?'

'In the morning. I normally go for a walk in the evening. If you go beyond Mount Everest Hotel, you'll find a road that goes up the hill. You have to take this road. I think you'll find my house easily enough—it's a bungalow called Nayanpur Villa. There's a large garden around it.'

Mr Majumdar raised his hand In farewell and left. We saw him get on a horse. There was a man to help him.

'Perhaps his doctors don't allow him to walk up a hill, which would explain the horse,' Feluda observed. 'A very nice gentleman, I must say.'

Members of the film unit were all busy looking at the shops. Pulak Babu came forward and asked, 'How did you like Mr Majumdar?'

'It was a pleasure to meet him. He may be getting on, but he's still young at heart.'

'True, and he takes a lively interest in everything. He was asking me a lot of things about the shooting.'

'Who else is there in his house?'

'He has a secretary called Rajat Bose. Apart from him there are three servants, a mali and a man to look after his horse. Mr Majumdar is a widower. He has a son and two daughters. His son lives in Calcutta. He's supposed to be coming here soon. The daughters are both married. I don't know where they live.'

'Mr Majumdar seems to have a fascinating hobby.'

'You mean collecting press cuttings?'

'Yes. He reminded me of an uncle of ours. Uncle Sidhu.'

I had been thinking of Uncle Sidhu, too. But he cut out anything that struck him as interesting, not just reports about murder and crime.

Pulak Babu took his leave. There was a lot to do, he said. They would take a few outdoor shots tomorrow, but the real work with the artists would start from the day after, in Mr Majumdar's house.

We went to the Keventer's open-air restaurant after Pulak Babu and his team left, and ordered three hot chocolates. Lalmohan Babu took a long sip with great relish, and said, 'Felu Babu, my heart tells me this visit won't go to waste.'

'Well, why should it? We've come to Darjeeling for a holiday, the weather's beautiful, and the air free of pollution. You'll feel your health getting better in no time. Of course our visit isn't going to go to waste!'

'No, no, that's not what I meant,' Lalmohan Babu replied, with a knowing smile.

'What did you mean, Mr Ganguli?'

'I am thinking of your profession.'

'My profession? What about it?'

'Something tells me your services are going to be required.'

Feluda lit a Charminar. 'The problem is not related to my profession, Lalmohan Babu, but yours. You can't give up looking for mysteries in every corner. I have no idea why you should get such a feeling, but what I can tell you is that if something untoward did happen, Felu Mitter wouldn't just stand by and do nothing.'

'Ah, that's what I like to hear from ABCD! That's just the right attitude, sir.'

ABCD was a title Lalmohan Babu had conferred on Feluda. It stood for Asia's Best Crime Detector.

I said nothing, but somehow Birupaksha Majumdar had struck me as a mysterious character. Why did he spend all his time in Darjeeling, year in and year out, collecting information on crime? Of course, that did not necessarily mean that he himself was likely to get involved in anything suspicious. I suppose it was only our past experience that made me feel like this. I had lost count of the number of times we had gone on holiday, only to find ourselves mixed up in some mystery or the other. Perhaps that was the only reason why I, too, wondered whether Feluda would once again have to put his skills to the test.

Let's just see what happens, I told myself.

THREE

'Sublime!' said Lalmohan Babu. I had never heard him use this word earlier. But before I could say anything, he added, 'Heavenly, unique, glorious, magnificent, indescribable—oh, just out of this world!'

The reason for this burst of excitement was simple. He had risen in the morning, and had seen Kanchenjunga from his window. It had just started to glow pink in the early morning sun. Unable to contain himself, Lalmohan Babu made me join him in his room. 'One can't really enjoy such a thing unless the joy is shared, you see,' he explained. This remark was then followed by a stream of superlatives.

Feluda had seen it, too, but not from our room. He had finished doing yoga and left the hotel long before I woke up. He returned after a walk from the Mall to the Observatory Hill, just in time for our first cup of tea. 'Each time I see Kanchenjunga,' he declared, 'I seem to grow younger. Thank goodness the new buildings that have cropped up in most places have made no difference to the road to and from the Observatory Hill.'

'I feel just the same, Felu Babu. Life seems worth living, now that I've seen Kanchenjunga.'

'Good. I'm very glad to hear that, for it shows you have still retained a few finer feelings, in spite of all the nonsense you write.'

Lalmohan Babu let that pass. 'What are we going to do today?' he asked.

We were in the dining hall, having breakfast. Feluda tore off a piece of omelette and put it in his mouth. 'I'd like to visit Mr Majumdar today. His house is going to be very crowded from tomorrow. Today is probably the only day we can have a quiet and peaceful meeting in his house. I consider it my duty to cultivate a man like him.'

'Very well, just as you say.'

We left at half past eight. We had to go down the Mall, past Das Studio and Keventer's, and walk for three-quarters of a mile to get to Mount Everest Hotel. The road to Mr Majumdar's house began after that. As it happened, we had no difficulty in finding it. It was a sprawling old bungalow, made of wood, with a red tiled roof. A well-kept garden surrounded it. Behind it stood a pine forest and, beyond that, a steep hill. The mali working in the garden came forward on seeing us.

'Is Mr Majumdar at home?' Feluda asked.

'Yes. Who shall I say—?'

'Just tell him the people he met yesterday are here to see him.'

The mali disappeared inside the house. While we waited outside, I kept looking at the house and admiring its surroundings. Kanchenjunga was clearly visible in the north, now a shimmering silver. Whoever had chosen this spot to build a house clearly had good sense as well as good taste.

Mr Majumdar and the mali came out together.

'Good morning! Do come in,' Mr Majumdar invited. We went through a white wooden gate with 'Nayanpur Villa' written on it, and joined our host. He must have been very good-looking once, I thought. Even now, he certainly didn't look as though he might be ailing. Another gentleman had come out with him. He was introduced as Rajat Bose, his secretary. A man of medium height and a clear complexion, Mr Bose was wearing a dark blue polo neck sweater over brown trousers.

We were taken to the drawing room. There was glass case in one corner, crammed with silver trophies of various shapes and sizes. These had obviously been won by Mr Majumdar in sports competitions. A leopard skin was spread on the floor, and on the wall hung the heads of two deer and a bison. We sat on two sofas.

'My son, Samiran, is coming this evening,' Mr Majumdar told us. 'I don't think you'll find any similarities between him and me. He is a businessman, very involved with the share market.'

'Is he coming on holiday, or is it strictly business?'

'He said he had taken a week off. But he's very restless, just not the type to sit at home and relax, even for a few days. He's almost thirty, but is showing no signs of getting married. God knows when he'll settle down. But never mind about my son. Tell me about yourselves.'

'We came here to hear about you,' Feluda said.

'Then I hope you've got all day,' Mr Majumdar laughed. 'I have led a very colourful life. Until I was about forty, there was very little that I didn't do—sports, both indoor and outdoor, shikar, just name it. But afterwards, I was put in charge of a bank, which meant handling enormous responsibilities. So I had to cut down on most other activities, and concentrate on my job.'

'But you still had your favourite hobby?'

'You mean collecting press cuttings? Oh yes. I never gave that up. Rajat can show you a sample.' He nodded at Mr Bose, who got up and went into the next room. He returned with a fat scrapbook, and handed it to Feluda. Lalmohan Babu and I moved from where we were sitting to get a closer look.

It was a remarkable object, undoubtedly.

'I can see that you've got cuttings from a London newspaper as well,' Feluda remarked.

'Yes. A friend of mine is a doctor in London. He has my instructions to send me copies of any sensational news he gets to read.'

'Murder, robbery, accidents, fires, suicide . . . you've got them all, haven't you?'

'Yes that's right.'

'But what were you telling me about a criminal case that hasn't yet been solved?'

'Yes, there is such a case. I can show you the relevant report. There is one more case like that, though you won't see a cutting, for the press didn't get to hear about it.'

'What happened?'

'No, please don't ask me to explain. I'm afraid I couldn't tell you anything more. Go, Rajat, please get the 1969 volume.'

Mr Bose came back with another scrapbook.

'This particular report appeared sometime in June, in the *Statesman*. The headline, as far as I can remember, said, "Embezzler Untraced".'

'Here, I've got it,' said Feluda, quickly turning the pages. He read the first few lines, then looked up and exclaimed, 'Why this is about your own bank!'

'That is why I cannot forget it. A young man called V. Balaporia used to work in our accounts department. One day, he disappeared with 150,000 rupees. The police did their best, but couldn't catch him. I was then the Deputy General Manager of the bank.'

'I seem to remember the case vaguely,' Feluda said slowly. 'You see, before I became a full-time investigator, I used to read a lot about real life crime. This one happened such a long time ago that I can't now recall all the details.'

By this time, Lalmohan Babu and I had read the report.

'Even at that time, I had wished we could get hold of someone like Sherlock Holmes or Hercule Poirot,' Mr Majumdar shook his head sadly. 'A private detective might have been able to do something. Frankly, I haven't got a lot of faith in the police.'

Feluda turned a few more pages, glanced briefly through some of the other cuttings, then returned it to Mr Bose with a polite 'Thank you'.

A bearer came in with coffee on a tray. I was faintly surprised to see him. He had such a bright and polished air about him that it would've been quite difficult to guess he was a servant. We picked up our cups from the tray.

'We saw your horse outside,' Feluda said, 'is that what you normally use to go around?'

'I stay at home all day, going out only once in the evening. My habits are quite different from others. In fact, my daily routine has become decidedly strange since my retirement. I told you I suffer from insomnia, didn't I? Do you know what I do? I sleep in the afternoon—but that, too, after taking a pill with a glass of milk. I set the alarm for 5 p.m., after which I have a cup of tea, and then I go out. I spend my nights reading.'

'Don't you sleep at night at all?' Feluda asked, surprised.

'No, not even a wink. I believe my grandfather had a similar habit. He was a powerful zamindar. At night, he used to go through his papers, check his accounts and do whatever else was required to look after his land and property. During the day, he used to take opium and sleep the whole afternoon. By the way, if you wish to smoke, please do so. I wouldn't mind.'

'Thank you,' Feluda said, lighting a Charminar. I looked at Mr Majumdar again. He was nearly sixty, but he neither looked nor behaved like it.

'The shooting starts here tomorrow, doesn't it? It may mean a lot of stress and strain for you.'

'Oh no, I don't mind in the least. I'll be in one end of the house, on the northern side. The shooting will take place at the opposite end. That director struck me as a very nice chap, so I couldn't refuse.'

Before anyone else could say anything, a jeep came and stopped outside. Some members of the film unit got out of it. Pulak Ghoshal crossed the garden and knocked on the door.

'Come in, sir!' Mr Majumdar called out. Pulak Babu came in, followed by Raina and Mahadev Verma.

'We are on our way for some outdoor shooting,' Pulak Babu said. 'We thought we'd just drop by and say hello. You haven't met these actors, have you? This is Rajen Raina and that's Mahadev Verma. One is the hero and the other's the villain.'

'Very pleased to meet you. Why don't you stay for coffee?'

'No, thank you, Mr Majumdar. We haven't got the time today. Besides, from tomorrow we'll be spending almost the whole day in your house. Oh, incidentally, your secretary said you normally sleep in the afternoon. We'll have to have a generator working near this house. I hope that won't disturb you?'

'No, I don't think so. I always shut my door and all the windows, and draw the curtains. No noise from outside can reach me.'

I noticed Mr Majumdar casting piercing looks in the direction of Raina and Verma. After a brief pause, he added, 'I can now tell people I've met two film stars. I hadn't had the good fortune before.'

Pulak Babu turned to Lalmohan Babu. 'Laluda,' he said, 'I have a request.'

'Yes?'

'I have a fairly sharp memory, Laluda. I distinctly remember you playing a role in a play we had organized in the Gorpar Friends' Club, way back in 1970.'

'Heavens, Pulak, I haven't forgotten it, either. It wasn't a very easy role, was it? My first and last performance as an actor!'

'No, no, not your last performance.'

'What do you mean?'

'Yes, I'm coming to that. You see, the local Bengali Club had promised to provide a couple of men for small roles. But now they're saying most of their people have gone on holiday to Calcutta. I feel very let down. There is one particular role, you know, of the villain's right-hand man—'

'Who? Aghorchand Batlivala?'

'Yes.'

'But he appears only in two scenes.'

'I know. That's why I need your help. I'll get someone to go and give you your lines this evening. Please don't say no. I know you can do it. You'll have to work with me for just three days.'

'But. . . but . . . I don't look like a villain's right-hand man, do I? Besides, we came to Darjeeling just for ten days!'

'That's plenty of time, I don't need more than a few days, I told you. With full make-up, a short beard and a wig, you'll most definitely look the part. Tell me Mahadev, haven't I made the right choice?'

'Sure. Absolutely!' Mahadev Verma grinned.

'Have you ever smoked a cigar, Laluda?'

'I used to smoke, but I gave up cigarettes ten years ago,' Lalmohan Babu replied.

'Never mind. You must have a cigar in your hand. And wear dark glasses.'

Lalmohan Babu's eyes began glinting. I could tell he wasn't going to need much persuasion.

'OK, Pulak, since you're in a spot, I must try and help you out, mustn't I? Besides, a guest appearance in my own story might be quite a good idea, come to think of it. But I must insist on one thing.'

'What is it?'

'There must be an "am" after my name in the credits. I refuse to be known as a professional actor. People must know I am only an amateur. All right?'

'OK, sir.'

I seized this opportunity to put in my own request.

'May I please come and watch the shooting?' I asked.

'Of course, dear boy, of course!' said Pulak Ghoshal.

FOUR

Pulak Ghoshal and his team left. We had finished our coffee, so Feluda rose to his feet. 'We ought to leave now, I think,' he said. 'I hope we shall soon meet again.'

'Pardon?' said Mr Majumdar, sounding as though he was miles away. But then he pulled himself together, and said quite naturally, 'Oh, all right. Yes, I hope so, too.' We came out of Nayanpur Villa and began walking back to our hotel.

Feluda didn't say a word on the way back. For some reason, he also seemed rather preoccupied. But, over lunch, he turned to Lalmohan Babu and said, 'Why, Mr Ganguli, you are a dark horse! We've known you for years, and yet you didn't tell us about your acting career! You played a difficult role in a play, did you?'

Lalmohan Babu transferred a piece of a fish-fry into his mouth, and said, 'Well, to be honest, Felu Babu, there are loads of things about myself that I have never mentioned. I was the North Calcutta Carrom Champion in 1959, did you know this? I have many records in endurance cycling. Then I won a medal in a recitation competition—not once, mind you, but three times. This is not the first time I've had an offer to act in a film. Even twenty years ago, I had received such an offer. This bald dome that you now see was then covered by thick, curly hair. Can you imagine that? but I didn't accept that offer. No, sir. My mind was already made up. I wanted to become a professional writer, just to see if it was possible to earn enough simply by writing. An astrologer had told me it would work. "There's magic in your pen, you must write," he had said. He was right. But I never thought so much success would come my way.'

'I see. There is one little thing I must point out, Lalmohan Babu.'

'What?'

'You said you gave up smoking ten years ago. Now if you are made to smoke a cigar, the result may well be disastrous.'

'Hey, you're quite right. What do you think I should do?'

'I suggest you buy some cigars and start practising. Don't inhale the smoke. If you do, you're bound to start coughing and that will mean the end of every shot.'

'Yes, thank you for the advice, sir.'

We had a little rest in the afternoon, then we left for a walk at four o'clock. We wanted to walk to the Observatory Hill. There was a wonderful view of Kanchenjunga one could get from the northern side of the hill.

Lalmohan Babu bought a packet of "cigars from the first tobacconist he could find. The first drag very nearly resulted in disaster, but he managed to avoid it somehow. I noticed a cigar in his hand had brought about a change in his whole personality. He seemed a lot more sure of himself, striding ahead with great confidence, looking around with a slight smile on his lips. He had clearly started to play the role of Aghorchand Batlivala.

The next left turn brought Kanchenjunga into view. The last rays of the sun were shining directly on it, making it glow like a column of gold. Lalmohan Babu opened his mouth, but refrained from bursting into adjectives. By the time we returned to the Mall after going round the hill, it was past five and the sun had disappeared behind the hill. A small crowd had gathered near the horse-stand. A closer look revealed the film crew, who were returning after a day's shooting, followed by a large number of onlookers. But the people seemed pretty civilized, so I didn't think they would create any disturbances. Raina and Verma both had to stop a few times to sign autographs. Then the whole group turned left into Nehru Road and went in the direction of their hotel.

'Good evening!' called a voice.

It was Birupaksha Majumdar, riding his horse. He climbed down as we got closer.

'I forgot to tell you something this morning,' he continued, lowering his voice. 'I heard this from my mali, so I couldn't tell you how reliable his information is.'

'What did he tell you?'

'Apparently, over the last few days, a man has been seen lurking outside our gate, keeping an eye on the house.'

'You don't say!'

'My mali has been with me for years; I don't really have any reason not to believe him.'

'Has he been able to describe this man?'

'Yes, but not very well. All he's told me is that the man is of medium height and is unshaven. He disappears behind a tree each time the mali tries to get a closer look. But he smokes, for the mali has seen some smoke rising from behind the tree.'

'Can you think of a reason why anyone should want to keep an eye on your house?'

'Yes. There is a valuable object in my house. It is a statue of Krishna, made of *ashtadhatu*. It used to be in a temple in Nayanpur. Many people here have seen it, and many others might know that I have it with me.'

'Where do you keep it?'

'On a shelf in my bedroom.'

'Don't you keep it under lock and key?'

'I stay awake all night, and I always have my revolver close at hand. So I don't think a burglar would get very far, even if he broke into my house.'

'Might there be some other reason why anyone would wish to attack your house?'

'All I can tell you is that there is every possibility someone may wish to harm me. Please don't ask me to explain—I'm afraid I couldn't tell you more. If something untoward does happen, Mr Mitter, can I count on your support?'

'Of course. That goes without saying.'

'Thank you. I feel a lot better now.'

At this moment, a man of about thirty was seen walking towards us.

'Come here, Samiran, let me introduce you to my friends,' said Mr Majumdar. 'This is my son, Samiran, And this is Mr Pradosh Mitter, and Mr Lalchand—no, sorry, Lalmohan . . . Ganguli, isn't it?'

'Yes, sir.'

'And this is Tapesh, Pradosh Mitter's cousin.'

We exchanged greetings. Samiran Majumdar was a smart looking man, and was dressed just as smartly in a red jerkin. 'You are a famous detective, aren't you?' he said to Feluda.

'I don't know about being famous, but detection is certainly my profession.'

'I love reading fiction. I'd like to have a long chat with you one day.'

'Certainly. I'll look forward to it.'

But you'll have to excuse me today. I'm out shopping, you see.'

Samiran Majumdar left. His father got back on his horse. 'I should make a move, too. See you soon.'

'Yes. Don't hesitate to call me, if need be. We're staying at Hotel Kanchenjunga.'

While we were talking, a man had appeared and thrust a piece of paper into Lalmohan Babu's hand. It turned out that he had been sent by Pulak Ghoshal, and the paper contained his lines for tomorrow. 'They wrote out my Hindi dialogue in the Bengali script,' he said. 'Very thoughtful of them, I must say. I cannot read Hindi very well.'

'How many lines have you got?'

'Er . . . three and a half.'

'Very well, bring them to my room later. We must have a rehearsal and make sure you speak Hindi better than you can read it.'

We went back to Keventer's for a cup of hot chocolate. It was quite nippy outside, especially as the sky was clear this evening. Quite a few stars were out already, and even the Milky Way was faintly visible.

'May I join you?'

All of us were startled to find an elderly gentleman standing behind an empty chair at our table, smiling slightly. He must have been in his early sixties, wore glasses and had salt-and-pepper hair.

'Yes, certainly,' Feluda invited.

'I know who you are,' the gentleman looked at Feluda. 'I read an interview with you in a magazine about a year ago. It included your photograph.'

'Yes, I remember that.'

'You must forgive me for barging in like this. You see, I live next to Mr Majumdar's house. I saw you go in there this morning. My house is called The Retreat, and I am Harinarayan Mukherjee.'

'Namaskar. This is my friend, Lalmohan Ganguli; and here's my cousin, Tapesh.'

'Namaskar. Have you come here to work on a case?'

'No, I'm here purely on holiday.'

'I see. I just wondered . . . I mean, if you see a detective going into Mr Majumdar's house . . .'

'Why, is he in trouble?'

'Well, one hears lots of rumours about him.'

'Ah. No, I don't think he's in trouble of any kind; neither do I think one should pay any attention to rumours.'

'Yes, yes, you're quite right.'

It seemed to me that Feluda deliberately avoided mentioning our last conversation with Mr Majumdar. After all, we didn't know this man. Besides, he had barged in, uninvited.

It was quite dark by this time, and the restaurant wasn't particularly well lit. But, even in that dim light, I could see Lalmohan Babu studying his lines, speaking the words softly.

'I'll take my leave now, Mr Mitter. Very pleased to have met you,' Mr Mukherjee said, rising. He was gone a second later.

'I think he's lived here for a long time,' Feluda remarked.

'What makes you say that?'

'He's used to the cold. Didn't you see he was wearing only a woollen shawl over a cotton shirt? He wasn't even wearing socks. I'd like to get to know him a little better.'

'Why?'

'Because of what he implied today. He may have some information. Who knows?'

I sipped my chocolate, thinking of the people we had met since our arrival, and all that they'd told us. If this went on, there could well be an explosion.

I had no idea it would come so soon.

FIVE

A member of the film unit, Mr Nitish Som, turned up soon after breakfast the following morning to collect Lalmohan Babu. Feluda and Lalmohan Babu had worked very hard the previous evening to make sure he got his lines right.

'Mr Ghoshal said he'd like you to wear your own clothes, but we don't yet know what colour would be suitable. So could you pack everything you've got here?' Mr Som asked.

'May I go with you?' I said. Mr Som thought for a minute and replied, 'Why don't you come around eleven? We're not going to start shooting before twelve this afternoon. I am taking Mr Ganguli away only because we need to have enough time to do his make-up. But if you come at eleven, you'll be able to see our little ceremony to mark the mahurat—you know, the starting of our shooting. After that, if you like you can stay on and have lunch with us.'

Lalmohan Babu left with his suitcase at eight-thirty. Feluda and I went out half an hour later, to walk down Jalapahar Road. 'It makes no sense to spend the whole morning in the hotel!' Feluda declared.

The morning, as it happened, was as beautiful as the day before. The sun shone brightly, and Kanchenjunga stood out in all its glory. The Mall was quite crowded today. Loads of people had arrived to spend their Puja holidays. We passed the horse-stand, and continued walking. Feluda lit a cigarette. He was trying very hard to give up smoking, but he couldn't do without one after breakfast.

'What do you make of it, Topshe?' he asked, looking at the scenery.

'The only person who struck me as interesting was Birupaksha Majumdar.'

'Yes, but that is only because you have learnt a lot of interesting things about him. A man who doesn't sleep at night, spends his time collecting pieces of sensational news, tells you there's a mystery in his life but refuses to divulge the details, and keeps a valuable statue on an open shelf in his bedroom, most certainly cannot be classified as ordinary.'

'His son hardly opened his mouth.'

'True. In fact, that stuck me as odd. He appeared as though he was afraid to say very much, in case he said something he shouldn't.'

'And Rajat Bose?'

'What did you think of him?'

'I think his eyesight isn't very good, but he's decided not to wear glasses. Didn't you see him bump against a chair?'

'Excellent. Perhaps he does have glasses, but they're either broken or lost. I think it's things in the far distance he cannot see. I'm sure his close-range vision is fine, or he couldn't have brought out those scrapbooks.'

'What about the hero from Bombay and the villain?'

'You tell me. Let's see how much you've observed.'

'I noticed something strange yesterday.'

'What?'

'Mr Majumdar seemed upset—no, not exactly upset—but didn't he suddenly grow kind of preoccupied when he met Raina and Verma?'

'Yes. But his mind keeps wandering, doesn't it? As if there's something on his mind, all the time. We may learn what it is if we can ever get to hear what the local rumours say about him.'

We returned to the hotel an hour and a half later. I left again at eleven-thirty. 'Don't worry about me,' Feluda said, 'I'll try to get to the gumpha on top of the Observatory Hill. You just go and enjoy yourself.' I reached Nayanpur Villa in about twenty minutes. The first thing that greeted me was the noise from a generator, but I couldn't see it. One of the unit members saw me, and came forward to take me inside. The shooting was going to take place in the southern side of the house. We hadn't seen this part of the house yesterday. One of the rooms was very brightly lit. All doors and windows had been sealed to keep out natural light. Perhaps the scene to be shot would show something happening at night.

But where was our Jatayu?

Oh, there he was! It took me a few seconds to recognize him. A beard and a wig had transformed his appearance totally. He really was looking like a villain. On catching my eye, he walked over to me and said gravely, 'What do you think? Will I do?'

'Oh, sure. I hope you remember your lines?'

'Of course.'

At this moment, Pulak Babu called from the set. 'Laluda!'

Lalmohan Babu ran to grab a chair opposite Mahadev Verma, who was sitting on a small sofa, stroking his moustache.

'Look, Laluda,' said Pulak Babu, 'let me explain what I want you to do . When I say "Action!", you must take out a cigar from your pocket and put it in your mouth.

'Mahadev will take out a cigarette. Then you must bring out a matchbox, light Mahadev's cigarette, and then your own cigar, leaning back in your chair. I will then say "yes". You must then inhale, and speak your first line. That will end the shot. Remember, this is chiefly your shot, for the camera will show your face, and Mahadev's back. All right? Here's a cigar and a matchbox.'

'All right.'

The camera started rolling a minute later. 'Sound!' said Pulak Babu, 'Action!' Lalmohan Babu put the cigar in his mouth, but failed to light the match. I saw him clutching a matchstick the wrong way round, and striking the plain end against the box helplessly. 'Cut, cut! Laluda, please—!'

'Sorry, sorry. I'll be more careful the next time.'

In the second shot, he lit his cigar successfully, but inhaled quite a lot of smoke and began coughing and spluttering. Pulak Babu had to shout, 'Cut!' once more. But the third shot went without a single hitch, and ended in a round of applause for the villain's assistant.

It took Pulak Babu another five hours to call it a day. I noted with surprise that Lalmohan Babu did not make a single mistake after the first two shots. He did have to go to the bathroom twice, but that may have been because it was cold, rather than the fact that he was nervous. Pulak Ghoshal declared himself totally satisfied.

'My man will call for you at the same time tomorrow morning,' he said.

'There is no need to send anyone. I can come here on my own.'

'No, no, I can't let you do that. All our artists are always escorted by someone from the unit. It is our normal practice.'

Ten minutes later, Lalmohan Babu's make-up had been removed and we were on our way back to the hotel in one of the jeeps of the production team.

On reaching the hotel, Lalmohan Babu came straight to our double room instead of going back to his own. He threw himself down on my bed without a word. Before Feluda could say anything, I told him how well he had performed and how that had been appreciated by everyone in the unit.

'Oh, good. This opens up a whole new dimension to your career, doesn't it? A famous writer, and a brilliant film actor!'

Lalmohan Babu had been lying with his eyes closed. Now he suddenly opened them and looked straight at Feluda. 'Oh God, I nearly forgot. Felu Babu, I have to tell you something very important.'

'What is it?'

'Listen carefully. We had our lunch break today at half past one. I went to the bathroom as soon as work stopped. There is a bathroom in the southern wing where the shooting is taking place, but I found it crammed with stuff Pulak is using to get his sets ready. So I had to go to another bathroom in the other wing, where Mr Majumdar lives. In fact, one of the production assistants showed me where it was. It was quite separate, not attached to a bedroom. I washed my hands and was coming out, when I heard Mr Majumdar's voice. I couldn't tell you which room he was in, but it wasn't far from the bathroom. I heard him say, "You are a liar. I don't believe a single word you say." He wasn't speaking loudly, but he sounded distinctly annoyed.'

'Oh? That obviously means he was still awake.'

'Yes. I heard he takes his pill at half past one. When I came out of the bathroom, it must have been at least one thirty-five, perhaps a couple of minutes more.'

'What did the other person say?'

'I couldn't hear him. Lunch was ready by that time, and the others were waiting for me, so I had to come away quickly. But there is no doubt that the words I heard were spoken by Mr Birupaksha Majumdar.'

'That means he was speaking either to Rajat Bose or his son, Samiran.'

'Yes, maybe.' Lalmohan Babu yawned and suddenly changed the subject.

'I noticed something else, Felu Babu. These famous film stars from Bombay aren't really as good as they are supposed to be.'

'Why do you say that?'

'I had a shot with Raina after lunch. It was a simple shot, and he had very few lines. Still, he kept getting them wrong, and we ended up having as many as five takes.'

'These things happen, Lalmohan Babu. Sometimes even an old and established actor can have an attack of nerves.'

'As for myself,' Lalmohan Babu announced, 'I have lost all my nervousness. I have nothing to worry about now.'

SIX

The explosion came the next day. But, before I explain how it happened, I must describe what the day was like.

It was cloudy, so Kanchenjunga couldn't be seen. Feluda and I went out in the morning for a bit of shopping. Then we took a walk down Birch Hill Road before returning to our hotel. I left for Nayanpur Villa at eleven. Lalmohan Babu was already there, having practised his new lines to perfection. He had five lines today, and wasn't required to light a cigar in a single shot. This gave an added bounce to his step.

Pulak Ghoshal took seven shots with Lalmohan Babu. He was free by half past four. 'There's a jeep waiting, Laluda,' Pulak Babu said, 'you can go back any time.'

'Since I've managed to finish early today, Pulak, I think I'll walk back.'

'Very well, just as you wish.'

'I like their tea,' Lalmohan Babu confided when Pulak Ghoshal had gone, 'so why don't we wait until tea is served?'

By the time we had had tea, it was five o'clock. It took us another half an hour to reach the hotel. We found Feluda putting on his jacket rather hurriedly.

'Going out?' I asked. Feluda gave me a startled look.

'But you were there! Didn't you hear anything?'

'We left more than half an hour ago. No, we didn't hear anything. What's happened?'

'The old Mr Majumdar has been murdered.'

'Wha-a-a-t!' Lalmohan Babu and I yelled together.

'He rang me at about half past twelve,' Feluda told us. 'He said he had something important to tell me, so he'd see me here in the evening. And then this happened.'

'Who told you?'

'His son. Samiran Majumdar rang me five minutes ago. He said he had informed the police, but would like me to be there as well. It was he who found the body, when he went to see why his father hadn't got up even after five. The door was shut, but not locked or bolted. Apparently, Mr Majumdar always left his door unlocked. Someone stabbed him in the chest. Their family doctor has already confirmed that stabbing was the cause of death. Whatever shooting remained has naturally been cancelled, and until the police finish their enquiries, it will have to stay cancelled. Anyway, I am going there. Would you like to come with me, or would you rather stay here?'

'Stay here? Felu Babu, how could we stay here after such news? Let's go!'

We reached Nayanpur Villa at quarter past six. It was dark by this time, and had started to rain. Everyone from the film unit was still present. Pulak Ghoshal came forward to meet us. 'What a terrible affair!' he exclaimed. 'None of us can quite believe it. What a nice man he was, so very accommodating.' I had already seen a police jeep standing outside. An inspector was waiting on the front veranda. He stretched out an arm towards Feluda. 'I have heard a lot about you, Mr Mitter. I am Jatish Saha.'

'Pleased to meet you, Mr Saha,' Feluda shook hands, 'what exactly happened?'

'He was killed in his sleep, as far as one can make out.'

'The weapon?'

'A dagger. It's still there, stuck in his chest. I believe it belonged to the victim. He had it in his room.'

'Has your own surgeon examined the body?'

'No, he hasn't yet arrived, but we're expecting him any minute. Why don't you come in?'

Mr Majumdar's bedroom was quite large. Lalmohan Babu and I remained standing near the door. Feluda went in with the inspector. The body was covered with a white sheet.

'I'd like to tell you something,' Inspector Saha said to Feluda, taking him aside. 'We'll carry out our own enquiries in the usual way. But if you want to make an independent investigation, please fee! free. The only thing I'd ask you to do is share your findings with us. If we learn anything useful, I'll make sure you get to hear of it.'

'Thank you. You needn't worry, Mr Saha. You'll certainly get my full cooperation; and I don't think I'll get very far without yours.'

Samiran Majumdar entered the room, looking pale and dishevelled.

'My sympathies, Mr Majumdar. You were the first to discover the body, weren't you?' Feluda asked.

'Yes. My father set his alarm always at five. Then he used to go and sit on the veranda, where Lokenath used to bring him his tea. Today, when he still hadn't appeared at quarter past five, I wondered what the matter was. So I came in here to check, and . . . found this!'

'This must be difficult for you, but do you have any idea who might have done this, and why?' Feluda continued with his questions pacing in the room, his eagle eyes taking in every detail.

'No. But I've noticed there's something missing in this room.'

'What?'

'A small statue of Krishna, made of *ashtadhatu*. It was a very old family heirloom and most valuable.'

'Where was it kept?'

'On that shelf over there, next to the dagger that was used.'

'Why did you keep such a valuable object out in the open? Why wasn't it locked away in a chest?' Inspector Saha wanted to know.

'Baba never slept at night. Besides, he always had his revolver with him. So none of us ever thought there was any danger of theft.'

'Well, now it looks as though robbery was the motive. How much was it worth, do you think?'

'At least sixty-five thousand. Although there were eight metals, it was chiefly made of gold.'

Feluda picked up a pencil from a bedside table and said, 'The point is broken, and the broken portion is lying right here.' There was a small writing pad on the table. Feluda bent over it, and murmured, 'The top page was torn off, I think.' Then he began inspecting the floor around the table, kneeling to get a closer look. Only a few seconds later, he said, 'Got it!' He rose to his feet again, a small piece of paper in his hand. He quickly read what was written on it, and passed it to the inspector. Mr Saha cast a quick glance at it, and gave an involuntary exclamation. '*Vish*? You mean he was poisoned?' he asked in profound amazement.

'That's what it looks like, doesn't it? The last two letters are so crooked that it seems he died just as he finished writing them, which explains the broken pencil and this piece of paper that came loose and fell under the table.'

'But why should he write "poisoned"? It's so obvious he was stabbed to death.'

'Hm, I can't understand it either.' Feluda frowned, then turned to Samiran Babu. 'Do you know where your father's sleeping pills were kept?'

'In a bottle, in the dining room. Lokenath used to take them out of the aluminium foil and pour them into the bottle as soon as Baba bought a fresh supply.'

'Could you bring that bottle here, please?'

Samiran Babu left, and took a long time to return. When he finally came back to the room, he was looking even paler and more distressed.

'That bottle's gone!' he whispered through white lips.

Feluda, however, didn't seem to find this surprising. 'The day before yesterday,' he said calmly, 'your father bought thirty-one of those pills. We saw him. Tell me, Mr Saha, if thirty were mixed in somebody's drink, wouldn't that be enough to kill him?'

'What pills are you talking about?'

'Trofnil. Anti-depressant pills.'

'Oh. Yes, that may well be possible.'

'And if that was the case, it would be quite right to call the pills "poison", wouldn't it?'

'Certainly.'

'Well, that would at least explain why he wrote that word. But . . .' Feluda was still frowning, 'If a dying man wanted to write something before his death, surely he'd want to write the name of his murderer, rather than how he had been murdered?'

'Yes, you're right. But obviously Mr Majumdar didn't do that. Why don't we speak to the bearer, Lokenath?'

Feluda nodded and looked at Samiran Babu, who left to find Lokenath. I noticed that Feluda hadn't stopped frowning.

'Mr Majumdar came to watch the shooting today,' Lalmohan Babu said, 'Lokenath came to look for him at around half past one. But Mr Majumdar didn't go back immediately.'

'That means his routine today was slightly upset.'

'Looks like it. I think he was finding it quite interesting to watch us shoot. I saw him talking to both Raina and Verma. He seemed to be asking a lot of questions.'

Samiran Babu returned once more. The expression on his face suggested he hadn't come back with good news. But none of us were prepared for what he blurted out. 'Lokenath's missing!' he said.

'Missing?' Even Feluda couldn't hide his surprise.

'Yes. He's apparently been missing since one-thirty. All our servants have their lunch together at two o'clock every day. Lokenath didn't even eat with them. No one knows where he's gone, or what time he left.'

'Have you spoken to Mr Bose? Maybe he sent him out somewhere?'

'No. He knew nothing about this. He says he spent half an hour resting in his room straight after lunch, and then went for a walk in the pine wood. He does this almost every day. He doesn't believe in afternoon siestas.'

I knew this was true, for I had gone for a little walk in the wood myself during the lunch break. I had seen Rajat Bose coming back from there.

'How long have you had Lokenath?' Inspector Saha asked.

'About four years. Our old bearer died after an attack of hepatitis. That's when Lokenath arrived, with excellent references. Besides, he seemed to be educated and quite intelligent. In fact, he used to help Baba and Mr Bose in keeping the scrapbooks up to date.'

'Well then, maybe if we can trace this fellow, we can solve this case! May I use your telephone, please?' Inspector Saha said.

'Yes, certainly,' replied Samiran Babu and went out with the inspector.

'I don't understand this at all, Felu Babu. Why should anyone stab him if he was dead already?'

'Difficult to say. It could simply be that the killer wished to make sure. He may have returned to the room after giving him that poisoned drink to steal the statue, and may have seen him move in his sleep. After all, pills do take a few minutes to start working, don't they? So the killer decided not to take any chances, and finished him with the dagger. Then he slipped away with the statue.'

'So when do you think he wrote the word *vish*?'

'Before he was stabbed. He may have realized his drink had been tampered with, and started to write a message. But he lost consciousness after writing that single word. I cannot think of any other explanation at this moment.' Feluda sounded distinctly unhappy.

Inspector Saha returned. 'It makes perfect sense to me,' he said, having heard Feluda's explanation. 'But anyway, I've put my men on the job to track down Lokenath. In the meantime, I have to interview the whole film unit as well as every member of this household.'

'I think I ought to tell you something,' Lalmohan Babu said. 'Not everyone had permission to use the bathroom in the northern wing. The only people allowed were Pulak Ghoshal, the cameraman Sudev Ghosh, Raina, Verma and me.'

'That means not everyone had reason to go there. Very well, I shall interview only the people you just mentioned.'

'Why-what, even m-me?' Lalmohan Babu began to look just a little bit unsure.

'Of course,' said Feluda seriously, 'you are certainly among the people who had the opportunity.'

'Who are the people actually living in the house?' Inspector Saha asked, looking at Samiran Babu.

'Apart from myself, there's Rajat Bose, our servant Bahadur and the cook, Jagadish.'

'Very well. Where should we start?'

SEVEN

Pulak Ghoshal came to our hotel at half past nine the next morning.

'Have the police finished asking questions?' Feluda asked him.

'Yes. None of us could go home before half past nine last night. Who could ever have imagined something like this would happen? We can't start shooting until the police give the all-clear. Samiran Babu has said we may go ahead once the police finish their investigation, but who knows how long that might take? I'm trying not even to think about the financial loss we'll have to suffer because of this.'

Lalmohan Babu clicked his tongue in sympathy.

'However,' Pulak Babu added a shade more cheerfully, 'there's something I have seen in the past. If the production of a film gets temporarily stopped for some reason, it goes on to become a smash hit. Besides, Laluda, your story is totally unbeatable.'

Inspector Saha turned up half an hour after Pulak Babu left. 'No sign of Lokenath,' he said, 'but we're still looking for him. My men are working even in Siliguri. I think it's just a matter of time before we find him. He may be hiding in a tribal colony at the moment, but he's bound to be caught sooner or later. I am positive he'll try to go to Calcutta and sell the statue there. It's strange, isn't it, what greed can do to an otherwise simple man?'

'I believe you've finished interviewing people in the house.'

'Yes. It proved one thing: everyone, without a single exception, was avidly curious to see how a film is shot. All of them admitted to having spent considerable time watching the shooting. Even Mr Majumdar changed his routine. That is most remarkable, for his life ran with clockwork precision.'

'How many people would have had the opportunity, do you think? Let's not worry about the motive as yet.'

'Well, there are two things to be considered here. One, pouring poison into the victim's glass of milk; and then stabbing him to steal the statue. Lokenath got the glass of milk ready at around half past one and went to call Mr Majumdar. He could have dropped the remaining thirty pills into the glass; or, in his absence, someone else might have slipped in and done that. Rajat Bose says he was reading in his room at that time. Samiran Majumdar also says he was in his own room. Neither can prove it. Bahadur and Jagadish were watching the shooting. This happens to be true.'

'What did your surgeon say about the time of murder?'

'According to him, the victim was stabbed between 2.30 and 4 p.m. There is no doubt that the cause of death was stabbing, or there wouldn't have been so much bleeding.'

'Could anyone say anything about Lokenath?'

'No. Everyone was engrossed with the shooting.'

Lalmohan Babu cleared his throat. 'If I must be questioned, why don't you ask your questions now? Let's get it over with.'

'Very well. Technically, I should have interviewed you last night, along with the others, but I didn't insist as you're a friend of Mr Mitter's. Anyway, let's hear from you what happened yesterday.'

'I got there at nine o'clock,' Lalmohan Babu began. 'It took me an hour to finish my make-up. There is a veranda right next to the room where the shooting is taking place. All the actors normally wait on that veranda to be called to the set. While we were waiting there, something happened, at about half past ten. Mr Majumdar arrived and asked Raina and Verma to go with him. They were back in five minutes. Raina told me Mr Majumdar had shown them an old family heirloom. Now I know it was that statue of Krishna.'

'I see. What happened next?'

'At eleven o'clock, Verma and I were called. Pulak started taking the shot in just ten minutes. Four shots were taken before lunch. I had to go to the bathroom after the second one. It must have been around half past twelve.'

'Did you see anyone on the way?'

'No. I was called back to the set within minutes of my return. The third shot was taken half-an-hour later, after a rehearsal. After that, I had a few minutes' rest. I spent that time sitting on the veranda.'

'Alone?'

'No. Raina and Verma were both with me. Mr Majumdar came back for a while. It was during this time that I saw Lokenath come and tell him his milk was ready. Mr Majumdar left after another five minutes. At quarter to two, Pulak took the fourth shot, with just me in it. We broke for lunch at half past two, and I went back to the bathroom to wash my hands. Raina and Verma followed me.'

'Who went to the bathroom first?'

'I did. Then I returned straight to the southern side. It took us twenty minutes or so to finish eating. After that I just sat on the veranda. Tapesh was with me.' I nodded in agreement.

Lalmohan Babu continued, 'I couldn't tell you where Raina and Verma were at this time. We resumed working at around three o'clock. My fifth shot was over at half past three, after which there was a break for thirty-five minutes to get the lights ready.'

'What did you do during that time?'

'I chatted with Raina and Verma on the veranda. Tapesh sat with us.' I nodded again.

'Verma has travelled a lot, all over the country. He was telling us about his experiences.'

'You mean the three of you were together throughout, until the lights were ready?'

Lalmohan Babu frowned. Then he said, 'I'm not sure. I think Verma got up and left for about five minutes. Raina was regaling us with gossip from the film world, and then—'

'That'll do, thank you,' Inspector Saha interrupted him. 'I think I've got everything I needed to know. But do you remember having seen Lokenath at all after half past one?'

Lalmohan Babu shook his head. 'No, I don't think I did.'

'Very well. Thank you very much.' Then he looked at me. 'Tapesh, you were there as well, weren't you? Do you have anything to say?'

'I agree with everything Lalmohan Babu has just told you. At half past two, I went for a walk in the pine wood behind the house. I saw Rajat Bose returning from there. He appeared to be slightly out of breath.'

'He told me the same thing. Apparently, he often goes for a walk in the pine wood soon after lunch. By the way, when you had your lunch, did anyone from the Majumdar household ever join you?'

'No. Pulak asked Samiran Majumdar and Rajat Bose to have lunch with us, but both declined.'

'I see. That reminds me, we didn't find any fingerprints on the handle of that dagger.'

'No, I didn't think you would,' said Feluda. 'I need to ask you something, Mr Saha. It's about the time of the murder. Isn't it far more likely to be half past two rather than half past four?'

'Why do you say that?'

'If Lokenath is the culprit, surely he'd have mixed all the pills—there would have been twenty-nine, not thirty—in Mr Majumdar's glass of milk as soon as he could? I mean, if he did that at half past one, why should he wait for another three hours before trying to steal the statue, and then stabbing his victim? He'd have wanted to clear out right away, don't you think?'

'Yes, that's a good point. But if he did kill at half past two that still fits in with the surgeon's report.'

Inspector Saha rose. 'Thank you very much for your help,' he said, 'I must go now. I have more work in Nayanpur Villa. Goodbye.' But he stopped at the door and turned around. 'Mr Mitter, why are you still frowning?' he asked.

'Oh, that's nothing!' Feluda tried to dismiss it with a wave of his hand. 'You see, I am so used to handling complex cases that this one is striking me as far too simple. This is a totally new experience for me. I am finding it difficult to accept.'

'You must be mad. We in the police are always immensely relieved if a case turns out to be easy and simple. Perhaps that's the difference between a police officer and an amateur private detective!'

Inspector Saha left. Feluda continued to look worried, but finally shook his head and said, 'The inspector's right. I shouldn't worry so much. They'll find Lokenath, and that will be that. Let's go for a walk down the Mall.'

There weren't many people about in the Mall. It was cold and misty. We found an empty bench. The mist got thicker in a few minutes. It became difficult to see anything beyond a few yards. If anyone came out of the mist, it seemed as though he had appeared out of nowhere. So we were considerably startled when the figure of an elderly gentleman emerged suddenly from the haze, and stopped before us.

'Namaskar,' he said, looking at Feluda.

EIGHT

'Namaskar,' Feluda replied, returning his greeting.

'Yesterday, we met briefly at Keventer's, if you remember.'

'Yes, of course. You are Harinarayan Mukherjee, aren't you?'

'That's right. I must say you have a sharp memory. May I sit here with you for a few minutes?'

'Certainly.'

Feluda moved aside to make room for him on the bench. He sat down between Feluda and Lalmohan Babu.

'You live near Nayanpur Villa, don't you?'

'Yes. I've lived here for eleven years.'

'I see. You must have heard of the tragedy, so close to your house.'

'I have indeed. It's all very sad, but not totally unexpected, is it?'

'Is that what you think?'

'I say this because I had known Birupaksha Majumdar a long time. I cannot say we were intimate friends, for he was somewhat reserved by nature; but I had heard a lot about him.'

'How?'

'I spent nearly ten years in a place called Neelkanthapur in Madhya Pradesh. I was a geologist, working on the local rocks. Mr Majumdar once came to Neelkanthapur, at the invitation of Raja Prithvi Singh, to go tiger hunting on his estate. They had known each other for some time. Mr Majumdar was then in his mid-thirties, I think. Both men had one thing in common. Neither liked to shoot from a high machaan, or even from an elephant. They wanted to go on foot, without taking the help of beaters, and shoot a tiger at close range from the ground. That's what led to that terrible accident.'

'Why, what happened?'

'Mr Majumdar hit a man instead of a tiger.'

'What!'

'Yes. It's the truth.'

'You mean a local villager, or someone like that?'

'No. That might have made matters simpler. The man who died was a professor of history in a college, and a Bengali. He was called Sudheer Brahma. Although he taught history, his main interest in life was ayurveda. While the Raja and Mr Majumdar were looking for a tiger, he was roaming around in the forest looking for herbs. Unfortunately, he was draped in a yellow wrapper. Mr Majumdar saw a flash of yellow through some thick foliage, and mistaking it for a tiger, fired a shot. The bullet went straight into Brahma's stomach. He died instantly.

'Prithvi Singh had to spend a lot of money and pull a lot of strings to keep this quiet. I should know, for I was a friend of Sudheer Brahma. Mr Majumdar got away with it that time, but in his heart he obviously knew he was a criminal. He had killed a man, never mind if it was only by mistake. He hadn't paid for it, had he? So how long do you suppose he could go on living, weighed down by this awful load of guilt?'

'Do you happen to think there is a link between the present tragedy and what happened so many years ago?'

'You are a detective, Mr Mitter, you know about murder and motives. Perhaps I ought to tell you something. Sudheer Brahma had a son called Ramesh. He was sixteen when his father died. Naturally, he hated the idea of the whole thing being hushed up and the killer of his father going scot free. He told me he'd somehow settle scores with the killer when he grew up. He ought to be thirty-eight now.'

'Have you been in touch with him all these years?'

'No. I left Neelkanthapur twenty years ago. Then I spent a few years in Chhota Nagpur. Finally, I retired and came to Darjeeling. I don't know if you've seen my house. It's only a small cottage. I live there with my wife. My son works in Calcutta, and my daughter's married.'

'I see. Do you have reason to believe Ramesh Brahma is in Darjeeling at this moment?'

'No. But to be honest, if he came and stood before me today, I doubt that I could recognize him after twenty-two years. All I can tell you is that he had seemed absolutely determined to avenge his father's death.'

Mr Mukherjee finished his tale. It was undoubtedly a strange tale, and one that I knew would give Feluda fresh food for thought.

'Thank you very much indeed, for telling us all this,' he said to Mr Mukherjee. 'Even if Sudheer Brahma's son isn't here, the very fact that such an event had occurred in Mr Majumdar's life is surprising. Mind you, he had hinted that there was something in his life he couldn't talk about, and you yourself had vaguely mentioned something similar, but I could never have imagined it to be this! If you say you were actually present in Neelkanthapur when it happened, I see no reason to doubt your word.'

There seemed no point in continuing to sit in one place. All of us rose to our feet, and Mr Mukherjee said goodbye. We began walking towards Observatory Hill. The familiar frown was back on Feluda's face. He had clearly decided it was no longer an easy and simple case. 'God knows if Mr Mukherjee's story is going to help or hinder my thinking,' he remarked, walking through the mist. 'My thoughts, at this moment, are a bit like this place—covered by a haze, muddled and unclear. If only I could see a ray of sunshine!'

A Nepali with a horse emerged from the mist. 'Would you like a horse, babu?' he asked. But we ignored him and walked on. The road curved to the left; on the right was a gorge. We turned left, trying to steer clear of the edge on our right. The railing by the side of the road was practically invisible. On a clear day, it was so easy to see Kanchenjunga from here, but today it seemed as though we were surrounded by an impenetrable white wall.

Soon, the railing ended. We had to be doubly careful now, for if we went just a little too close to the edge on our right, there was every chance of slipping straight into the gorge. I was concerned to note that Feluda seemed so preoccupied that he was moving to the right, every now and then. Then he'd check himself and come back to the left side, closer to the hill. Lalmohan Babu kept muttering, 'Mysterious, mysterious!' Once I heard him say, 'Hey, do you think the word "mysterious" has anything to do with "mist"?'

Neither of us could reply, for we had all heard a noise and stopped. It was the sound of hurrying footsteps, coming from behind us. Whoever it was, was clearly in a hurry and we'd have to let him pass. But although the sound got louder, we couldn't see anyone, until—suddenly—a shadowy figure materialized from nowhere and pushed Feluda hard in the direction of the gorge. Unable to maintain his balance, or do anything to tackle his attacker, Feluda went right over the edge. The figure disappeared with the same suddenness with which it had appeared, before any of us could see its face. Lalmohan Babu screamed. I remained still like a statue, aware of what had happened, but unable to move.

At this moment, two Nepalis appeared, walking from the opposite direction. They stopped immediately, and asked, '*Kya hua,* babu?'

I finally came to life, and told them. '*Ek minute thahariye, hum dekhte hain*,' said one of them. A second later, both men vanished from sight, climbing down the hill with remarkable ease. We still stood foolishly, wondering what the men might find. But in less than thirty seconds, the mist began to lift, rapidly and miraculously. Vague outlines of trees and other objects became visible, almost as if an unseen hand had lifted a veil. I glanced around anxiously.

What was that down below?

A tree. A rhododendron. A man seemed to be wrapped around its trunk. Feluda! Oh yes, there couldn't be a mistake. I could see his brown jacket and red-and-black scarf. The two Nepalis had seen him, too. They reached him a couple of minutes later, and helped him to his feet. Feluda stood up somewhat unsteadily.

'Feluda!' I cried.

'Felu Babu!' shouted Jatayu. Feluda looked up, then slowly raised a hand to indicate he wasn't seriously hurt. Our two Nepali friends—an absolute Godsend in our moment of crisis—held his hands and guided him up the hill again. It wasn't easy, but in about five minutes, Feluda was back with us. He was panting, his forehead was bleeding, and he had scratched his palms which showed streaks of blood.

'*Bahut, bahut shukriya*!' he said to his rescuers. They grinned, dusted him down and said he should go straight to the clinic in the Mall for first aid.

We thanked them once more, and began walking back to the Mall. 'Tapesh, do you have any idea who the man might have been?' Lalmohan Babu asked me. I shook my head. I had seen nothing of his face except his beard. Even that had somehow seemed to be false. 'How are you feeling now?' Lalmohan Babu turned to Feluda.

'Sort of wrecked,' Feluda replied. 'If it wasn't for that tree, I would have broken every bone in my body. But this is exactly what I needed. Such a severe jolt has opened up my brain again. I have already found a very helpful clue. I think I am finally getting somewhere, Lalmohan Babu, though it is now obvious that the case is neither simple nor easy.'

NINE

The doctor on duty at the clinic was called Dr Bardhan. He examined Feluda thoroughly, and confirmed his injuries were not serious. But he was naturally curious to know what had happened, and we were obliged to tell him.

'But who should want to attack you like this?' he asked, puzzled. In order to explain that, Feluda had to tell him who he was. Dr Bardhan grew round-eyed.

'You are the most famous investigator, *the* Pradosh Mitter? I have read so much about your cases, but never thought I'd get to meet you in person. Are you here to look into the death of Mr Majumdar?'

'I am involved in it now, yes.'

'He was one of my patients.'

'Really?'

'Yes. A man with the most extraordinary will power. No one could tell how much he had suffered and, in fact, was still suffering. He kept himself busy with his hobby, and went about riding everywhere.'

'What do you mean by suffering? Do you mind telling me?'

'Well, to start with, his health wasn't very good. Then he lost his wife seven years ago. She died of cancer. Apart from all that, there were problems with his son.'

'You mean Samiran Babu?'

'Yes. He was quite a gifted young man, but speculation in the stock exchange ruined him totally. He's now up to his neck in debt. I felt very sorry for Mr Majumdar. Samiran was, after all, his only son. Since I was his doctor, he used to tell me many things, share his worries with me that he wouldn't with anyone else. I am sure Samiran decided to visit this time only to ask his father for more money. But Mr Majumdar, I know, was so angry and disappointed with his son that he wouldn't have helped him out. He may even have given him an ultimatum. The whole thing is so unpleasant, so shameful, I really fee! sad to think about it. Particularly ever since the murder. I feel afraid it isn't over, something else might happen. I couldn't tell you what, but I cannot shake off this feeling.'

'Do you know if he made a will?'

'No. But if he did, I'm sure he left everything to his son, unless he changed it recently.'

'Thank you, Doctor,' said Feluda, 'you have no idea how much you've helped me. I came here to get first aid. But you've given me aid of a very different kind. It's an added bonus. I cannot thank you enough.'

Dr Bardhan waved his thanks aside and refused to accept a fee.

When we came out of the clinic, Feluda said, 'If you two wish to have a little rest, you can go back to the hotel. I must go to Nayanpur Villa. I have to begin my investigation all over again, keeping in mind every new thing I've learnt today. In my eyes, the whole case seems entirely different now.'

Lalmohan Babu and I both said we had no intention of returning to the hotel. If Feluda could carry on working in spite of his brush with death, there was no reason for us to retire quietly. I couldn't stop marvelling at his stamina. He had rolled at least a hundred feet down the hill.

By the time we reached Nayanpur Villa, the mist had almost totally gone. The house had a rather sombre air about it, but the beauty that surrounded it was as breathtaking as ever. Rajat Bose came out as we got closer to the front veranda. Perhaps he had heard our footsteps on the cobbled driveway.

'Namaskar,' Feluda greeted him, 'I can see that you're feeling at a loose end. I need your help, Mr Bose.'

'Yes?'

'Do you think I might see Mr Majumdar's study? I'd like to see your room as well, if I may, and ask some questions.'

'Very well. Please come in.'

'Where is Samiran Babu?'

'He is probably having a bath.'

'OK, let's sit in the study.'

We followed Mr Bose to the rear portion of the northern wing. Mr Majumdar's study was large, tidy and comfortable. The pine wood behind the house was partially visible through a window. A heavy mahogany table stood before the window, together with two chairs. At the far end were other chairs and sofas for visitors. We walked over to this side. Feluda did not come with us. He took his time inspecting the room, occasionally picking up objects from the table. I saw him pick up a paper-knife and look at it closely.

'It's got quite a sharp blade,' he remarked, 'one could even kill with a small knife like this!'

'I think it's one of a pair, Felu Babu,' Lalmohan Babu piped up. 'Pulak has used the other one on his set. In one of the scenes, the villain uses it to scratch his back.'

Even from a distance the knife looked sharp and sort of lethal. Feluda put it back on the table.

Rows of shelves stood on one side, packed with long, thick ledgers—Mr Majumdar's scrapbooks. We had seen two of these already. Feluda took out a couple more and glanced idly through them. 'Who used to cut out and paste these before you came?' he asked Mr Bose.

'Mr Majumdar used to do it himself.'

'Did he leave this job entirely to you after your arrival?'

'More or less. Lokenath helped me sometimes.'

'You mean the bearer?'

'Yes. He had finished school. He could read and write very well indeed.'

'That's unusual in someone working as a bearer. Could you tell us why he had chosen such a job?'

'Mr Majumdar paid him well.'

'I see. He chose a fine way to show his gratitude, didn't he?'

Mr Bose said nothing. Feluda continued to walk around the room, looking at and touching objects as he asked his questions.

'What did you do before coming here?'

'Work in a private firm.'

'Where?'

'In Calcutta.'

'How long did you stay in that job?'

'Seven years.'

'Did Mr Majumdar put in an advertisement for a secretary?'

'Yes.'

'What are your qualifications?'

'I have a degree in commerce. I graduated in 1957.'

'What about your family? Where are they?'

'I'm not married. My parents are both dead.'

'Brothers and sisters?'

'I have none.'

'You mean you are totally alone in this world?'

'Yes.'

'What is this photograph?'

Feluda had picked up a framed photograph from a shelf. It was a group photo, possibly of staff in an office. There were about thirty-five people, most of them standing in rows. Only a handful of people sat in chairs in the front row.

'It was taken many years ago, when Mr Majumdar used to work for Bengal Bank. One of their managing directors was leaving. This photo was taken on the day of his farewell. Mr Majumdar was the Deputy Director then.'

Feluda peered at the photo closely. 'It doesn't appear to contain the names of all these people. I can recognize Mr Majumdar, though.'

'Perhaps there was a list at the bottom of the photograph. It may be hidden under the frame.'

'May I keep it with me for a couple of days?'

'Of course.'

Feluda passed the photo to me. Lalmohan Babu and I looked at it. It wasn't any different from the usual group photos taken in offices.

Mr Majumdar was sitting in a chair. The man sitting next to him was probably the departing managing director.

'Now I need to know how you spent your time on the day of the murder,' Feluda said, taking out his notebook from the pocket of his jacket. He opened it and ran his eyes through the notes on a particular page. 'Mr Majumdar used to come to his study at half past eleven every morning. You had to be here at that time, and you worked with him until half past twelve. Is that correct?'

'Yes.'

'What did you work on that morning?'

'Chiefly his correspondence. Mr Majumdar knew a lot of people, both in India and abroad. They wrote to him regularly. Replying to those letters took up a lot of time.'

'What were you doing before Mr Majumdar joined you at half past eleven?'

'The film unit arrived soon after breakfast. I was standing on the veranda on the other side, and watching them getting ready for the first shot.'

'Which one was it?'

'It had Verma and Mr Ganguli in it.'

Lalmohan Babu gave a slight nod to confirm the accuracy of this statement.

'What time would that have been?'

'Probably eleven o'clock. I'm not sure, I didn't look at my watch. I left in a few minutes and came here.'

'OK. What did you do when you finished your morning's work? Did you have lunch with Mr Majumdar and his son?'

'Yes.'

'What did you do after that?'

'It was almost one o'clock by the time we finished eating. I went to my own room straight after that and spent half an hour reading.'

'What were you reading?'

'A magazine—*Readers' Digest*.'

'And then?'

'Around two, I went for a walk in the pine wood. It's a beautiful place. I go there whenever I can.'

'So I've gathered. What did you do after that?'

'I returned around half past two and went back to my room to rest. I came out of my room at four o'clock and started to watch the shooting again. Mr Ganguli was in the shot being taken.'

Lalmohan Babu nodded once more.

'When Mr Majumdar did not make an appearance after five o'clock, didn't you find it odd?' Feluda went on.

'Frankly, I had lost track of time. There was this noisy generator running all the time, and dozens of people coming and going and shouting; it was so distracting I forgot to look at my watch.'

'How was Mr Majumdar as a boss?'

'Very good.'

'He didn't get angry or impatient with you?'

'No. He was most amiable.'

'Were you happy with your salary?'

'Yes.'

'Lalmohan Babu told us about something he had heard the day before the murder, when he went to use the bathroom. He heard Mr Majumdar's voice saying, "You are a liar. I don't believe a single word you say." Who do you think he might have been talking to?'

'I can't think of anyone except his son.'

'Didn't father and son get on?'

'He was disappointed with his son, in some ways.'

'How do you know that?'

'He said things in my presence that seemed to imply it. You know, things like "Samiran has become rather reckless", or words to that effect. He loved his son most undoubtedly, but that didn't stop him from ticking him off every now and then.'

'Do you know if he left a will?'

'I'm not sure, but as far as I know, he did not.'

'What makes you say that?'

'He had once said to me, "I feel just fine at the moment. I'll make a will only if my health gets any worse."'

'That would mean all his assets would go to his son.'

'Yes, naturally.'

'May I now see your room?'

'Sure. Please come with me.'

Rajat Bose's room was rather sparsely furnished. There was a bed, a small wardrobe, a table and a chair. On the wall was a bracket, from which hung a shirt, a brown pullover and a towel. A suitcase stood in one corner, with 'R.B.' written on it. On the table were strewn a few paperbacks and magazines.

'A Hindi magazine!' Feluda exclaimed.

'Yes. I spent my childhood in Kanpur, you see, That's where I learnt Hindi. My father was a doctor there. I moved with my mother to Calcutta when he died.'

We came out of his room. 'Did you know Mr Majumdar used to take sleeping pills?'

'Oh yes. I used to buy them for him sometimes. He liked to get a whole month's supply.'

'Hm. All right, thank you very much. I'd like to speak to Samiran Babu now.'

Samiran Babu had had his bath, and was in his room, reading a newspaper. He hadn't shaved since he was in mourning. Feluda tried talking to him, but he didn't say very much. However, he admitted to having frequent arguments with his father. 'Baba wasn't like this before. He changed a lot after his illness,' he said.

'Would it be wrong to say you changed, too, which might have caused him distress?'

'Some of my speculations went wrong, but that can happen to anyone, in any business.'

'Did you have an argument the day before your father was murdered, say around half past one in the afternoon?'

'Why, no!'

'Did you ever ask your father for financial support?'

'Yes, why shouldn't I? He had made a lot of money.'

'Did you know your father hadn't made a will?'

'Yes. He had told me once he wouldn't leave me a penny if he did decide to make a will.'

'But now you're going to inherit everything.'

'Yes, so it would seem.'

'Most of your problems are going to be solved now, right?'

'Right. But I don't understand what you're trying to imply. Surely you don't think I killed my own father?'

'Suppose I do? You certainly had the motive, as well as the opportunity, didn't you?'

'How could I have poisoned his drink? Lokenath got his milk ready, didn't he?'

'Yes, but don't forget he left it in the room and went away to call your father. You could have tampered with it then. Besides, you had every opportunity to stab your father. You must have known there was an excellent weapon in the same room.'

Samiran Babu gave a twisted smile. 'Have you gone totally mad, Mr Mitter? Why aren't you thinking of the missing statue? Would I bother with a small statue if I knew I was going to get every penny my father owned?'

'Who knows, Mr Majumdar, you might have been in a hurry to get hold of ready cash? After all, even if you inherited everything, you wouldn't have got it all in a day, would you? The whole legal process would have taken a while, and you knew it.'

'Well then, where has Lokenath gone? Why did he run away? Why don't you try to catch the real culprit instead of wasting your time here?'

'I have a reason for coming back here, Mr Majumdar. A very good reason.'

'All right. I don't even wish to hear what it is. All I can tell you is that it is simply by chance that I've got involved in this awful business. I am certainly not your man. You'll have to look elsewhere to find the killer.'

TEN

We returned to the hotel. Feluda said after lunch that he wanted to take the framed photograph to a studio on the Mall. 'Then I must go and see Inspector Saha at the police station,' he added. 'I need some information urgently, which I think the police could get far more easily. If you two want to go anywhere, do so. I am not going to go out when I return. All I want to do then is think. This case hasn't yet formed a definite shape. A few things are still unclear . . . still hazy.'

Feluda left. Lalmohan Babu and I decided to go for another walk. A cool breeze was blowing outside, which made walking very pleasant.

'There's something you haven't yet seen,' I said to Jatayu. 'It's the pine wood behind Mr Majumdar's house. I went there for only a couple of minutes, but I thought it was a beautiful place. Would you like to go there?'

'Do we have to go through his house to get there?'

'Oh no. The main road forks to the left, which goes straight to the wood. Haven't you noticed it?'

'No, can't say I have. But if that is the case, let's go.'

We left. Feluda's words kept ringing in my mind. He had definitely found a powerful clue, but of course he wasn't going to talk about it unless he had thought it all out. We would have to put up with long periods of silence when he got back.

'Tapesh,' Lalmohan Babu said on the way to the wood, 'tell me something. Where is the mystery in this case? Lokenath killed his employer and vanished with the statue. Surely that's all there is to it? Why doesn't your cousin simply leave it to the police? They'll find Lokenath and deal with him. End of story.'

'How can you say that? You've known Feluda for years. Have you ever seen him get worked up about anything unless there was a good reason? You saw for yourself how he was attacked. Surely Lokenath wasn't responsible for that? Besides, Mr Majumdar himself had killed someone, even if it was an accident. Then there was that case of someone in his bank stealing a lot of money. He was never caught. Above all, you yourself told us you heard Mr Majumdar shouting at somebody. We don't know who he was shouting at. So many questions need to be answered. How can you say it's a simple case?'

By this time we had reached the wood. It wasn't just beautiful, but also remarkable in other ways. I realized there were many other trees and plants in addition to pine. I could recognize juniper, fir and rhododendron, all of which were in abundance; I did not know the names of the other plants. Some of the bushes had red, blue and yellow flowers. Since the sky was overcast, the whole place seemed darker today. We walked on, feeling as though we were passing through a huge church with endless tall pillars. Nayanpur Villa occasionally came into view through gaps in the trees, but the deeper we went into the wood, the farther the house seemed to recede. It felt just a little creepy to make our way through the dark shadows in the wood. There was no noise, not even the chirping of birds, and certainly there was no question of running into other people. Perhaps that was why Lalmohan Babu was prompted to remark, 'If anyone was murdered here, it would probably take a month to find his body.'

We walked on. The house had disappeared altogether. Suddenly, a bird called; but I couldn't tell what bird it was. My eyes fell on another gap between the trees, and I realized the clouds had dispersed for the moment, so I could see a portion of Kanchenjunga. I turned towards Lalmohan Babu to tell him to have a quick look before it vanished again. To my surprise, I found him standing still, gaping at something with his mouth hanging open.

What had he seen?

I followed his gaze and realized with a shock what it was. Close to the fallen trunk of a tree was a large bush. Protruding from behind it were two feet. No, two shoes. That was really all we could see.

'Should we take a closer look?' Lalmohan Babu whispered.

Without making a reply, I went forward to peer behind the bush. I had seen those shoes before. Where had I seen them?

It all became clear a second later.

A dead body was lying on the ground.

We recognized him instantly. It was Mr Majumdar's missing bearer, Lokenath.

He, too, had been stabbed, but the weapon was nowhere in sight.

Not far from the body, scattered on a rock were the broken remains of a glass bottle, and a lot of small white pills. At least, they must have been white once. Lying on the damp ground had made them turn brown.

We didn't waste another moment. We ran back to the hotel, to find that Feluda had just returned. 'Felu Babu, what sensational—' began Lalmohan Babu, but I stopped him before he could begin to get melodramatic. I told Feluda in a few words what we had seen.

Feluda rang the police station immediately. Within five minutes, two police jeeps arrived at our hotel. Inspector Saha got out of one. The other had four constables in it. We returned to the pine wood.

'Stabbed!' the Inspector exclaimed. 'We were looking for him in local villages. Of course we had assumed he was still alive. Your friend and your cousin get full credit for this discovery, Mr Mitter. We are very grateful to you both.'

The police took the body away. We came back to the hotel once more.

'Now the whole thing's taken a completely unexpected turn, hasn't it?' Lalmohan Babu asked, flopping down on a chair.

'Yes, you're right. But it's turned not towards darkness, Lalmohan Babu, but towards light. All I need is a few pieces of information. Then everything's going to fall into place.'

Inspector Saha rang Feluda later in the evening. From the way Feluda gave his lopsided smile and said, 'I see' and 'Very good', I could tell he had got the information he was waiting for.

'If that's the case, I think you should ask everyone to gather in Mr Majumdar's drawing room tomorrow morning at ten,' Feluda said to Mr Saha. 'We must have everyone from Nayanpur Villa, and a few people from the film unit—Pulak Ghoshal, Rajen Raina, Mahadev Verma and Sudev Ghosh. Your own presence, need I tell you, is absolutely essential.'

ELEVEN

The telephone in our room began ringing at seven the following day. We were already up, sipping our bed tea. Feluda stretched out an arm and picked it up. I heard him say only two things before he put it down. 'What!' he said, and 'I'll be ready in five minutes.' Then he turned to me and added, 'Go and tell Lalmohan Babu to get ready. We have to go out at once.'

I did as I was told without asking questions. Where were we going? No one told me, until a couple of police jeeps arrived again, and we were told to get into the first one with Inspector Saha. It turned out that the constable who had gone to Nayanpur Villa early this morning to tell them about the meeting had learnt that Samiran Majumdar had received a phone call only fifteen minutes before the constable's arrival. He had left for Siliguri, apparently on some urgent work. Since Feluda felt there would be no point in having the meeting without him, we were on our way to see if our jeep might catch up with his vehicle.

I had never been driven at such speed on a winding, hilly road. Luckily, the driver seemed to be extremely skilful, and there was no mist today. We passed Ghoom, Sonada and Tung in half an hour. Normally, it would have taken us at least forty-five minutes. Inspector Saha had sent word to Kerseong and Siliguri, but it had not been possible to give the number of the taxi in which Samiran Babu was travelling. Trying to find its number would have taken up a lot of time, Inspector Saha said.

We reached Kerseong fairly soon, but there was no sign of Samiran Majumdar's taxi. 'Take the short cut through Pankhabari,' Inspector Saha said to the driver. Our jeep left the main road. The other one went ahead, following the regular route.

It is impossible to describe just how winding the road to Pankhabari was. Lalmohan Babu shut his eyes, and said, 'Let me know if you see the taxi. I'm not going to open my eyes if I can help it. I'd feel sick if I did.'

Fifteen minutes later, after going up a road that coiled itself like a snake round the hill, we came round a hairpin bend. Our driver pressed his foot hard on the brake, for there was a taxi standing almost in the middle of the road. Its driver was trying to change a punctured tyre, and Samiran Majumdar was standing some distance away, smoking impatiently. He seemed both startled and apprehensive at the sudden appearance of our jeep.

All of us got out. Feluda and Inspector Saha strode ahead.

'What . . . what is it?' Samiran Babu asked, turning visibly pale.

'Nothing,' Feluda replied, 'it's just that there's going to be a meeting in your own house at ten this morning. We feel you must be present there, and really it's far more important than the one you set off to attend. So could you please pay your taxi driver, and join us? Don't forget your suitcase.'

In three minutes, we were on our way back to Darjeeling. No one spoke on the way.

By the time we reached Nayanpur Villa, it was a quarter to ten.

'Since Lokenath is still missing, could you please ask your other servant, Bahadur, to make coffee, for at least a dozen people?' Feluda asked.

We went to the drawing room. More chairs had been brought from the next room.

The team from the Mount Everest Hotel arrived almost as soon as Bahadur came in with the coffee. Pulak Ghoshal looked openly surprised. 'What on earth's the matter, Laluda?' he asked.

'Haven't got a clue. Your guess is as good as mine. But the purpose of this meeting is to throw light on everything that's been baffling us since the murder. Mr Pradosh Mitter is in charge of the lighting.'

'Good. Can we start shooting again?'

'I couldn't tell you. Just be patient, all will be revealed soon.'

'I'll keep my fingers crossed. I've been directing films for twelve years, and finished making seventeen films in that time; but never before have I got involved in something so messy.'

I felt sorry for Pulak Babu. The total budget for his film had originally been 5.6 million rupees. God knows how much they'd finally end up spending if the shooting kept getting delayed.

Everyone found chairs and sat down, looking distinctly uneasy. I glanced briefly at the whole group. Feluda was sitting on my left, and Lalmohan Babu on my right. The others, including Mr Saha and Samiran Majumdar, were scattered all over the room. Bahadur and the cook, Jagadish, were also present. Four constables stood near the door.

We finished our coffee. A rather attractive clock on a shelf chimed ten times. Feluda stood up as soon as the last note faded away. He was the only one in the room who appeared perfectly calm. Even Inspector Saha was cracking his knuckles occasionally.

Feluda cleared his throat and began speaking.

'In the last few days, a few mishaps have occurred in this house. Perhaps they would not have happened if the usual routine of the house hadn't been upset totally by the arrival of the film unit. Most people had their attention taken up by the shooting, so it became easier for the culprit to do what he wanted.

'The first among the tragedies was the death of Mr Birupaksha Majumdar, the owner of this house. His death struck me as very mysterious. It seemed obvious to everyone that his bearer, Lokenath, had killed him to steal a valuable statue, and disappeared the same afternoon. But I could not accept this. I am going to explain the reason in a few minutes. Before I do so, I'd like to tell you two things involving the deceased.

'The first is related to embezzlement of funds. While Mr Majumdar was working as the managing director of the Bengal Bank in Calcutta, a young employee called V. Balaporia vanished with 150,000 rupees. He has not yet been traced.

'The second incident took place in Neelkanthapur, Madhya Pradesh. The local Raja, Prithvi Singh, invited Mr Majumdar to go on shikar. They wanted to kill a tiger. Mr Majumdar went to the forest with the Raja, and saw something moving behind a bush.

'Mistaking it for a tiger, he fired his gun and realized that he had actually hit a man, not a tiger. The man was called Sudheer Brahma. He was a professor of history, but his interest in ayurveda had brought him to the forest to look for herbs. He died on the spot. Raja Prithvi Singh went to a lot of trouble to keep this quiet, to save his friend's reputation.

'Sudheer Brahma had a sixteen-year-old son called Ramesh. Deeply distressed by his father's death and the way in which his killer was allowed to get away with it, Ramesh vowed to take revenge. Somehow, when he grew up, he would find the killer and pay him back. I heard this from Mr Majumdar's neighbour, Harinarayan Mukherjee, who was present in Neelkanthapur at the time and knew the Brahmas. There is no way to prove this story; but Mr Majumdar himself had hinted to me that there was a scandal in his past that had somehow been kept from the press. It was for this reason that I believed what Mr Mukherjee told me.

'Allow me now to return to the death of Birupaksha Majumdar. The person who had the best motive and opportunity to kill him was his own son, Samiran. He had lost heavily in the stock market and was in debt. Do you deny this, Mr Majumdar?'

Samiran Majumdar shook his head mutely, staring at the floor.

'Do you also deny that you stood to gain all your father's assets if he died?'

Again, Samiran Babu shook his head without looking up.

'Very well. Let me now examine the way in which he was murdered. Mr Majumdar used to take a sleeping pill with a glass of milk every day after lunch. His bearer Lokenath used to prepare the drink. Two days before his death, he had bought a whole month's supply. When he died, there should have been twenty-eight pills left. But the bottle containing the pills could not be found. So naturally we all assumed he had been poisoned. Besides, we found a piece of paper with the word "vish" written on it, which removed any lingering doubt. But that wasn't all. He had also been stabbed. It seemed therefore that his killer had returned a few minutes after Mr Majumdar had drunk his milk, and finished his job with a knife, in case the pills didn't work.

'The question that now arose was, what might have been the motive for this gruesome murder? The answer was simple: the statue of Krishna made of *ashtadhatu* was missing. The killer had clearly run off with it.

'I had my doubts about this theory, as I've said before. Nevertheless, the police were convinced Lokenath was the murderer as well as the thief. Yesterday, we realized how utterly wrong it was to blame Lokenath. My friend and my cousin discovered, purely by accident, Lokenath's dead body in the pine wood behind this house. He, too, had been stabbed to death. Beside his body lay a broken bottle, and scattered around were the remaining pills. This could only mean that not only was Lokenath innocent, but he had actually tried to save his employer from being poisoned by running away with the whole bottle of pills. Someone killed him on the way. This could only mean one thing: Mr Majumdar's death was caused by his stab wounds, not by poison.

'Let me now tell you of certain things I experienced myself.

'I was curious about one of the inhabitants of Nayanpur Villa, although initially I had no reason to suspect him. It was Mr Rajat

Bose. He told me in answer to my questions that he had a degree in commerce, and had finished his graduation in 1957.

'My enquiries revealed that no one by the name of Rajat Bose had obtained a degree in commerce that particular year.'

I quickly glanced at Mr Bose. He was looking both upset and tense.

'Can you explain this, Mr Bose? Did you tell me a lie, or is my information wrong?' Feluda was looking straight at him.

Rajat Bose cleared his throat a couple of times. Then he took a deep breath, and spoke very rapidly. 'I did not murder Birupaksha Majumdar, but God knows I wanted to. Oh yes, I did, a thousand times. He killed my father, and then he paid and bribed people to hush it all up. He was a criminal!'

'Believe me, Mr Bose, I have every sympathy with you on that score. But now I'd like you to answer a few more questions, and I want the truth.'

'What do you want to know?' Mr Bose was still breathing hard.

'On the day of the murder, Lokenath had mixed a single pill in a glass of milk—as he did every day—and went to call Mr Majumdar, who was watching the shooting. The glass of milk as well as the bottle of pills were both lying in the empty dining room. You tried to seize this opportunity to pour the remaining pills into the milk, didn't you?'

'Look, I already told you I wanted to avenge my father's death.'

'Yes, but Lokenath came back before you could actually put your plan to action. Isn't that right? He saw what you were about to do, and you decided he should never get the chance to open his mouth.'

'He was a fool! I wanted him to help me. I told him everything—but he refused.'

'So you attacked him, didn't you? He managed to struggle free, and ran towards the pine wood with the bottle of pills. You followed him with a weapon in your hand—that sharp paper-knife in Mr Majumdar's study. You did manage to catch him, but before you actually struck him with your weapon, he threw the bottle on a rock, and it broke to pieces. Tell me, isn't that exactly how it happened?'

Mr Bose didn't reply. His sudden burst of courage had petered out completely. Now he broke down, and covered his face with his hands. Two constables walked over to him and stood behind his chair.

'I have another little query. The initials "R.B." on your suitcase stand for Ramesh Brahma, don't they? You started calling yourself Rajat Bose simply to keep the same initials?'

Mr Bose nodded silently.

After a brief pause, Feluda resumed speaking.

'Yesterday, something else happened. There was an attempt on my own life. Someone took advantage of the thick fog, and tried to push me into a gorge.'

This piece of information was greeted with complete silence from his audience.

Everyone was staring at Feluda, simply hanging on to his words.

'I couldn't see his face, but could make out that he was wearing a false beard. When he actually pushed me towards the edge of the cliff, I caught a faint whiff of a scent. It was Yardley Lavender. It wasn't altogether an unfamiliar scent. I had smelt it before, sitting in the restaurant in Dum Dum airport.'

Rajen Raina spoke unexpectedly, 'I use that scent myself, Mr Mitter. But if you think no one uses it except me, you couldn't be making a bigger mistake.'

Feluda smiled. 'I knew you would say that. I haven't yet finished speaking, Mr Raina.'

'Very well. What else do you have to say?'

Instead of giving him a reply. Feluda looked at Inspector Saha, who quietly passed him a briefcase. Feluda took out an envelope from it, and the framed group photo of all the employees of Bengal Bank.

'Do you recognize this photograph, Mr Raina?' Feluda asked.

'I have never seen it before.'

'No? But you yourself are present in the group!'

'What do you mean?'

Feluda opened the envelope and took out another photo. It was the enlargement of a single face.

'I have to admit I had to work in this one,' Feluda said. 'I drew the beard, for when the photo was taken, you didn't have it. Now can you recognize the fellow? It's a photo of Mr V. Balaporia, who used to work in the accounts department of Bengal Bank.'

Mr Raina didn't bother to ask for the photo to get a closer look. He began wiping his face nervously. I peered at it and saw that the face staring at the camera was of Raina himself.

'How were you to know the person in whose house you were going to shoot would turn out to be an ex-boss? Much less did you anticipate that he would recognize you instantly. But it took you no time to judge just how badly your film career was going to be affected if any scandal from your past got to be known. Mr Majumdar had told you you had been recognized, hadn't he? You denied it, to which he said, "You are a liar. I do not believe a single word you say."

'Well, that takes care of the motive. If we now look for an opportunity to kill, remember there was a forty-five-minute break during lunch. You could easily have slipped into Mr Majumdar's room during that time. When he had taken you and Mr Verma to look at that statue of Krishna, you must have noticed the dagger lying next to it on the shelf.'

Inspector Saha rose and made his way to where Raina was sitting. Pulak Ghoshal was sitting next to him, clutching his head. I could well imagine his profound distress. Lalmohan Babu leant towards me, and whispered, 'I don't understand one thing. Why should Mr Majumdar write the word "vish"?'

Feluda heard him. 'I am coming to that,' he said. 'When Mr Raina walked into Mr Majumdar's room, he woke unexpectedly and saw him. Even after being stabbed, he remained alive for a few seconds, and tried to write the killer's name during that time. Unfortunately, he couldn't finish. Mr Raina, can you tell us the full name Mr Majumdar had tried to write?'

Rajen Raina remained silent.

'Shall I tell everyone, then?'

Raina didn't speak.

'Very well. I learnt through my enquiries that the "V" in Balaporia's name stood for "Vishnudas". It was this name that Mr Majumdar was trying to write moments before his death. He didn't get beyond "Vish".'

'Sorry! Oh God, I am so sorry!' wailed Vishnudas Balaporia, alias Rajen Raina. Feluda now turned his eyes on Samiran Majumdar.

'I am a mere child, compared to him!' Samiran Babu exclaimed, meeting Feluda's gaze.

'True. Please be good enough to open your suitcase now, and take out the statue of Krishna,' Feluda said dryly.

Pulak Ghoshal joined us at Keventer's in the evening.

'Darjeeling proved to be quite unlucky,' he observed morosely. 'I think I'll reshoot in Simla. Rajen Raina can be replaced by Arjun Mehrotra. What do you think of that?'

'Brilliant!' said Lalmohan Babu, 'I think he'll really suit the part. But. . . you'll still retain the bits I appear in, won't you?'

'Of course. I'll go back and start shooting in November, which means I can finish by February. I have another four films to work on. Each one of them must be done by the end of next year.'

'What! All four of them, one after the other?'

'Yes. I'm not doing too badly, I must admit, by the grace of God!'

Feluda turned to Lalmohan Babu.

'I think we can give him the same title you bestowed on me,' he said.

'How?' Lalmohan Babu asked, raising his eyebrows. 'How would you get ABCD?'

'Asia's Busiest Cinema Director.'

The Magical Mystery

ONE

Magic was among the many things that Feluda knew a lot about. Even now, occasionally, I caught him standing before a mirror, with a pack of cards, practising sleight of hand. It was for this reason that when we heard that a magician called Surya Kumar had arrived in Calcutta, the three of us decided to go to his show one day. The third person, naturally, was our friend, Lalmohan Ganguli (alias Jatayu), the writer of popular crime thrillers. The organizers of the show were well known to Feluda, so we only had to ask before we were given three tickets for seats in the front row.

When we arrived, about thirty percent of the auditorium was empty. The show started. The items presented were not bad, but there was something lacking in the personality of the magician. He had a goatee, and was wearing a silk turban studded with sequins. But his voice was thin, and that was where the problem lay because a magician's job is to talk incessantly. He has to have a good voice.

One of the things that happened as a result of our sitting in the front row was that the magician called Jatayu to the stage to hypnotize him. Hypnotism, it turned out, was something the man knew well. He handed a pencil to Jatayu and said, 'This is a bar of chocolate. Take a bite. How do you like it?' Lalmohan Babu bit the pencil in his hypnotized state and answered, 'Lovely. Delicious chocolate!'

He remained on the stage for five minutes. In that time, the magician made a complete fool of him, which the audience enjoyed hugely. Even after he came to his senses, it seemed as if the sound of applause would never die down.

The next day was a Sunday. Lalmohan Babu arrived from his house in Gorpar, as usual, in his green Ambassador, on the dot of nine o'clock. We continued to talk about the magic show. 'That man,' said Feluda, 'hasn't quite made it yet, has he? So many seats were empty yesterday. Did you notice?'

'Yes, but he certainly knows hypnotism,' Lalmohan Babu observed. 'You must give him full credit for making me do all those weird things. My God, I chewed a pencil and thought it was a chocolate. Then he had me bite a stone and declare it was a sandesh. Just imagine!'

Srinath came in with the tea, and with his arrival, came the sound of a car stopping outside our house. This was followed quickly by a knock on the front door. We were not expecting anyone. I opened the door to find a man of about thirty.

'Is this Pradosh Mitter's house?'

'That's right,' Feluda said. 'Please come in.'

The gentleman stepped in. He was slim, fair and wore glasses. He looked quite smart.

'I tried quite hard to get you on the phone,' he said, sitting in one corner of our sofa, 'but I just couldn't get through. So I decided to come in person.'

'That's all right. What can I do for you?'

'My name is Nikhil Burman. You may have heard of my father, Someshwar Burman.'

'The man who used to perform Indian magic?'

'Yes.'

'One doesn't hear his name any more. Has he retired?'

'Yes, about seven years ago. He hasn't performed in that time.'

'But he never did perform on a stage, did he?'

'No. He used to perform sitting on the ground on a mattress, surrounded by people. He was quite well known in some princely states. Many rajas watched his shows. He also travelled quite a lot to gather information on Indian magic. His findings are all described in a large notebook. He calls it his manuscript. What has happened, you see, is that someone wants to buy it from him. He's been offered twenty thousand rupees. My father cannot make up his mind about whether or not he should sell it. So he'd like you to read his manuscript and give him your views.'

'May I ask who has made the offer?'

'Another magician. Surya Kumar Nandi.'

How amazing! Only yesterday, we were at Surya Kumar's show. This was telepathy! At least, that's what Feluda would call it.

'Very well,' Feluda replied, 'I'll have a look at your father's notebook. This will give me the chance to meet him, which is something I should like very much.'

'Baba, too, is an admirer of yours. He says it's only rarely that one can find a man as intelligent as you. Could you visit us in a day or two? Baba is at home every evening.'

'All right. We can come this evening, if you like.'

'Splendid. Say, around half past six?'

'Fine.'

TWO

Someshwar Burman's house—a massive affair—was in Rammohan Roy Sarani. He came from a family of zamindars in East Bengal, but had been residing in Calcutta for a long time. Most of the rooms in his house were now lying empty. Apart from servants, there were only five people in the house: Someshwar Burman, his son Nikhil, Mr Burman's secretary, Pranavesh Roy, his friend Animesh Sen, and an artist called Ranen Tarafdar. He was said to be drawing a portrait of Someshwar Burman. We learnt all these facts from Mr Burman himself. It was difficult to guess his age, because his hair was almost wholly untouched by grey. His eyes were bright, as the eyes of a magician ought to be. We were all seated in the living room on the ground floor. Nikhil Babu ordered some tea for us.

'My father was a homoeopath,' Someshwar Burman told us. 'He had a thriving practice. I studied law, but never worked as a lawyer. My grandfather had been a tantrik. Perhaps it was he who influenced me. I was interested in magic even as a young boy. I remember watching an old magician in a park in Allahabad. The sleight of hand he could perform was just amazing. That's what made me get more interested in traditional Indian magic. What is shown on a stage is always done with the help of equipment and gadgets. That does not mean anything to me. Indian magic depends purely on the dexterity of the magician. That's what I call real magic. So once I'd finished college, I left home to learn this kind of magic. and gather as much information as I could. I was lucky to have a father who was both understanding and generous. He was happy to see me take an interest in something new. In our family, you see, people have always worked in different fields. There have been doctors, lawyers, singers, actors, the lot. And many of them were very successful in their chosen profession, just as I was as a magician. Rajas used to invite me to their states. I used to sit on the floor in their palaces, and pull off trick after trick, before a gaping audience. I earned a lot of money, too, though I did not have a set fee. What I received was always far in excess of my expectations.'

The tea had arrived by this time. Feluda picked up a cup and said, 'Tell us something about your manuscript. I hear you have written about Indian magic?'

'Yes,' Someshwar Burman replied. 'I'm not aware of anyone else having worked in this area. I've often written articles about my research and findings, which is how some people have come to know about the existence of my manuscript. That's the reason why Surya Kumar came to me, or else he could never have known that such a manuscript existed. Mind you, he had heard my name as a magician long ago.'

'Does he want to buy your manuscript?'

'That's what he says. He came straight to my house. I liked the young man; in fact, I could feel a certain amount of affection for him. But I cannot accept his offer. It is my belief that the work I have put into writing that manuscript is very important, and certainly worth more than twenty thousand. That's why I want you to read it. You know a lot about a variety of subjects, don't you? I have read about your cases. That's the impression I got.'

'Very well. I'll be glad to read your manuscript.'

Someshwar Burman turned to his secretary. 'Pranavesh, go and get that notebook.' His secretary left.

'We went to Surya Kumar's performance yesterday,' Feluda told him.

'How did you like it?'

'Well, it was so-so. The only thing he's really good at is hypnotism. Everything else was done with the help of gadgets.'

Someshwar Burman suddenly picked up a biscuit from a plate, and closed his hand over it. He opened his hand in the next instant, but the biscuit had gone. It came out of Lalmohan Babu's pocket a second later.

'That's terrific!' Feluda exclaimed. 'Why did you stop performing? You're obviously so gifted.'

Mr Burman shook his head. 'No, I do not wish to have shows any more. Now I must spend all my time over my manuscript. If the book is ever published, I do think people will find it useful. No other book has been written on this subject.'

'In that case, I will certainly read what you have written, and return your notebook the day after tomorrow, in the evening. Is that all right?'

'Yes, certainly. Thank you very much.'

Feluda told me the next day that he had finished reading the entire manuscript. It appeared that he had spent the whole night on it. 'The man's handwriting is beautiful, and it's a gold mine. When it's published, I'm sure the book will be an enormous success. Mr Burman must not part with his manuscript even for fifty thousand rupees, let alone twenty!'

In the evening, we returned to Mr Burman's house and Feluda told him what he thought. Mr Burman seemed quite reassured by Feluda's words. 'That certainly takes a load off my mind!' he said. 'I was in a dilemma, you see, but if you liked the book so much, I think I know what to do. Pranavesh is typing it out. He has told me how impressed he's felt by some of the facts I have described. My friend Animesh has also said the same thing. Now I can refuse Surya Kumar's offer without any hesitation. Oh, by the way, someone stole into my room last night.'

'What!'

'Yes. I woke before he could take anything. In fact, he ran away as soon as I said, who is it?'

'Has anything ever been stolen from your house before?'

'No, never.'

'Is there anything valuable in your room?'

'Yes, but I keep it in a safe. They key to the safe is always kept under my pillow'.

'Do you mind telling me what it is? I am deeply curious.'

'No, I don't mind at all.'

Mr Burman rose and went upstairs. He returned in about three minutes, and placed something on the table. It was a six-inch high statue of Krishna, with a flute in his hand.

'It's studded with five different gems,' Mr Burman informed us, 'Diamonds, rubies, sapphires, coral and pearls. I have no idea about its value.'

'I think it's priceless, and exquisite. How long have you had it?'

'Raja Dayal Singh of Raghunathpur gave it to me, in 1956. He was very impressed by my performance.'

'Don't you have a chowkidar?'

'Oh yes, and four servants. Perhaps the thief was known to one of the servants'.

'Or he might be one of the residents of this house.'

'What! What a terrible notion!'

'Detectives often say such things. There's no need to take me seriously'.

'Thank God.'

'You are a widower aren't you?'

'Yes.'

'Is Nikhil your only son?'

'No. Nikhil is my younger son. The elder—Akhil—finished college at the age of nineteen and went overseas.'

'Where?'

'He did not tell me. There have been a few oddly restless characters in my family. Akhil was me of them. He said he wanted to work in Germany, and left in 1970. He never contacted me after that. Perhaps he's still in Europe, but there's no way I can find out.'

'Does your secretary Pranavesh know about this statue?'

'Yes. He's like a son to me. Besides, he has to go through all my personal papers, anyway.'

'I see. Perhaps you should put it back in the safe. I have seldom seen anything so beautiful.'

'Shall I tell Surya Kumar my answer is no?'

'Of course.'

Feluda rose. 'I'd like to look at your compound, if I may,' he said. 'I want to see how the intruder might have got into the house.'

'The easiest way would be through the veranda,' Someshwar Burman replied. 'I think my chowkidar has been a little slack in his duties.'

The veranda overlooked a garden. It did not seem as if anyone bothered to look after it. The house was surrounded by a fairly high compound wall. Scaling it would not be easy. There were no trees near the wall, either.

Feluda spent about fifteen minutes, inspecting the grounds. Finally, he said, 'No, it's no use. I cannot be sure whether the burglar came from outside, or whether it was someone from the house.'

THREE

Someshwar Burman rang us the next day to say that he had spoken to Surya Kumar and told him he would not sell his manuscript.

'I've just thought of something,' said Lalmohan Babu, when Mr Burman had rung off.

'You see, my next novel is going to be about a magician. So I was wondering if I could meet Surya Kumar and talk to him. How should I go about it, do you think?'

'Try his hotel,' Feluda said, 'The organizers of his show should be able to tell you where he's staying. Just give them a ring.'

'All right.'

It took Lalmohan Babu fifteen minutes to contact Surya Kumar and make an appointment with him. Surya Kumar agreed to come to our house at half past nine the following morning.

'You'll have no difficulty in recognizing me,' Lalmohan Babu told him. 'I was hypnotized by you the other day.'

The next day, Surya Kumar arrived in a Maruti, very punctually at nine-thirty. Lalmohan Babu had turned up about twenty minutes before that. Surya Kumar seemed a little taken aback on meeting Feluda. 'You seem rather familiar. I didn't quite catch your name,' he said.

'I am Pradosh Mitter. You may have seen my photo in a newspaper.'

'Pradosh Mitter? You mean Pradosh Mitter, the investigator?'

'Yes,' Feluda admitted with a laugh.

'It's a privilege to meet you, sir!'

'I am no less privileged to have met you. We've never had a famous magician in our house before.'

Lalmohan Babu began his questions when we had all had our tea.

'How long have you been holding shows?'

'For nearly twelve years.'

'Did you learn magic from someone?'

'I worked as a magician's assistant for five years. He was called Nakshatra Sen. He was quite old. He had a stroke on the stage, in the middle of a show, and died soon afterwards. There was no one to claim his equipment and all the other paraphernalia, so I took it and began my own career.'

'Do you have to travel all over the country?'

'Yes. I've been to Japan and Hong Kong as well.'

'Really?'

'Yes. I have an invitation from Singapore next year.'

'Don't you have a family?'

'No. I am a bachelor.'

'Do you still have to practise and rehearse everything, or is that no longer necessary?'

'Not all of it. But every day, I spend a couple of hours practising sleight of hand. Being in regular practice is absolutely essential.'

Feluda intervened at this point.

'You have met Someshwar Burman, haven't you?'

'Yes, I believe you wanted to buy his manuscript?'

'Yes.'

'I thought it might be a good idea to add a few items of Indian magic to the ones I usually show. My own items follow the western style of magic. But Mr Burman refused to sell. I had offered him twenty thousand. But I don't really mind. I've come to know him well, and we've got a good relationship. I really respect the man. He has invited me to go and stay with him for a few days, once my shows are over.'

'When is the last one?'

'This Sunday.'

'Where will you go next?'

'I'd like to take a week off. I need a break. Then I'll go to Patna.'

Lalmohan Babu had a few more questions for him. Surya Kumar left in a few minutes. He struck me as quite a pleasant man.

'All his clothes and his shoes were foreign, bought possibly in Hong Kong, or Japan,' Feluda remarked. 'He's clearly fond of the good things in life, like most magicians.'

'Well, he certainly seems to have grown quite close to the Burmans,' Lalmohan Babu observed. 'Or why should he be invited to go and stay with them?'

FOUR

The rest of the week passed eventlessly. What happened after that came as a bolt from the blue. The following Tuesday, Someshwar Burman rang us to say that one of his oldest servants, Avinash, had been murdered, and the little statue of Krishna had vanished! It was a double tragedy.

Feluda called Lalmohan Babu immediately, and told him to go straight to Mr Burman's house. We left in a taxi.

By the time we got there, the police had arrived. Inspector Ghosh knew Feluda. 'A case of burglary, nothing else,' he said. 'The murder was not premeditated. Avinash happened to see the burglar, I think, and the burglar realized it. So Avinash had to go. The main aim of the culprit was to steal that statue from the safe. There's been another case of burglary recently.'

'But no one except the people in this house knew about the statue.'

'In that case, someone in this house is involved, I should think. There's Mr Burman's son, his secretary, his friend, the artist—Ranen Tarafdar, isn't it?—and the magician, Surya Kumar. He arrived only yesterday. Any one of them could be guilty of the crime. If that is the case, our job becomes so much simpler.'

'When did the murder take place?'

'Between one and three o'clock in the morning.'

'Did the bearer try to stop the intruder?'

'That's what it looks like, doesn't it?'

We went into the house. Someshwar Burman was sitting in the living room on the ground floor, clutching his head. Also present in the room was everyone else in the house. Some were sitting, others standing.

'Will you please tell me what exactly happened?' Feluda asked Mr Burman. 'How long had this bearer worked for you?'

'Thirty years. He was totally devoted to me. I cannot believe he is no more.'

'Where was he killed?'

'On the ground floor. Perhaps Avinash woke up just as the thief was making his escape with the statue of Krishna. Then he tried to catch the thief, so the thief stabbed him with a knife.'

'Can you tell me what the sleeping arrangements are in this house?'

'You've seen my bedroom. Animesh and I have our rooms upstairs. All the other bedrooms are on the ground floor. Yesterday, when Surya Kumar arrived, I gave him a guest room, also on the ground floor.'

'I see. No one outside this house knew about that statue, is that right?'

'Yes. Yet, I cannot imagine anyone from this household getting involved in such a thing.'

'Whoever did it would have had to take the key from under your pillow. How come that did not wake you?'

'I take a sleeping pill every night, and sleep very soundly.'

'What happened to the key to the safe?'

'It is still there. It was left hanging from the lock.'

'Has the murder weapon been found?'

'No.'

Inspector Ghosh walked into the room at this moment. 'I have questions for all of you,' he said.

'Would you mind if I asked some more questions after you've finished?' Feluda wanted to know.

'No, not at all. I know a lot about your work and your methods,

Mr Mitter. Or I wouldn't have let you come in. We don't usually encourage private detectives.'

Inspector Ghosh took more than an hour to finish his task. We waited, and drank a lot of tea. Although Mr Burman was still in a state of shock, there were no lapses in his duty as a host.

We had stepped out and were in the garden when Inspector Ghosh joined us. 'I am through. You can take over now,' he said to Feluda.

Feluda decided to start with Mr Burman's son, Nikhil. We were shown into his room. 'What do you do for a living?' Feluda began.

'I have an auction house in Mirza Ghalib Street.'

'What is it called?'

'The Modern Sales Bureau.'

'I have seen your shop.'

'I see. That's where I usually am, from ten o'clock in the morning to six in the evening.'

'How is your business doing?'

'Quite well, I think.'

'Are you interested in art?'

'My work is such that I often come across objects of art. I have learnt a lot through my work.'

'How long have you been doing this work?'

'Seven years.'

'How old are you?'

'Thirty-three.'

'How old is your elder brother?'

'He must be thirty-six. He's older by three years.'

'Were you two close?'

'My brother was not close to anyone. He did not talk much, nor did he have many friends. He did not seem to care for anyone, to tell you the truth, not even me.'

There was something funny about Nikhil Burman's voice, and the way he spoke. But I could not put my finger to what it was.

'Didn't your brother write to you from abroad?' Feluda continued.

'No. He did not write to anyone.'

'Have you never taken an interest in your father's magic shows?'

'Of course I have. But Baba held most of his shows out of town. I did not get to see those.'

'Did you ever think of learning magic yourself?'

'No. I was happy just watching.'

'Do you have any idea as to who might be responsible for yesterday's tragedy?'

'No, none at all. I did tell Baba to keep that statue in a bank. But he paid no attention to what I said.'

There were no more questions for Nikhil Burman. We thanked him and went to find Someshwar Babu's friend, Animesh. He was in his room.

'What do you do for a living?' Feluda asked him.

'Nothing. My father was a lawyer. He built a multi-storey building, which was rented out. I manage with the rent I get each month.'

'How long have you known Someshwar Burman?'

'Nearly twenty years.'

'How did you happen to meet him?'

'I used to dabble in astrology at one time. Someshwar came to consult me. He had just started his career as a magician. I told him about his bright future. Five years later, he came back to thank me. That was the start of our friendship. When his wife died, Someshwar asked me to come and stay with him, probably to get over his loneliness. I agreed, and have been living in his house since. It's almost fifteen years since the day I arrived.'

'When did you first see the statue of Krishna?'

'I knew about it even before Someshwar did. You see, I had already predicted that he would acquire such an object one day. He showed it to me as soon as it was given to him.'

'Do you have any theories as to who could have burgled the house and committed the murder?'

'I think the burglar knew one of the servants. It is my belief that he opened the safe only to steal money. Then he saw that glittering statue, so he took it. I cannot believe that any other occupant of this house could be linked with it in any way,'

FIVE

Pranavesh Babu, Someshwar Burman's secretary, told us that he had been working for Mr Burman for the last five years. He had his own house in Bhowanipore, but seeing that many of the rooms here were lying empty, Mr Burman had suggested that he stay in the same house.' Pranavesh Babu had seen no reason to object.

'How is Mr Burman as an employer?'

'Wonderful. I have no complaints at all.'

'How do you like your work?'

'I feel amazed by some of the facts Mr Burman has collected. I can't tell you how many new things I have learnt just by typing his notes for him.'

'How long do you work every day?'

'Until eight or nine o'clock in the evening.'

'You sleep on the ground floor, don't you?'

'Yes.'

'Do you usually manage to sleep well?'

'Yes, most of the time.'

'Wasn't your sleep disturbed last night by a noise, or something else?'

'No. I heard what happened only this morning.'

'Do you suspect anyone in this house? If no one but the residents of this house knew about that statue, then the culprit might still be here!'

'That could well be the case. Am I not one of the suspects myself?'

'Yes, you are.'

'The police officers will search the whole house, I believe. But it should not be difficult to find a place to hide a tiny object like that. All one has to do is retrieve it once the coast is clear.'

The artist who was drawing Mr Burman's portrait was also staying in the house. He would have to remain here until his job was done. I found this man somewhat peculiar, possibly because of his appearance—he had a thick beard, and his hair came down to his shoulders. He also spoke very little. But from what I had seen of the unfinished portrait, he was a good artist.

His room was also on the ground floor. Feluda knocked on his door. He opened it and looked enquiringly at us.

'I have a few questions to ask,' Feluda said.

'Very well. Please come in.'

His room was quite untidy, as I had expected. Feluda took a chair, I a stool, and Lalmohan Babu sat on the bed.

'You are Ranen Tarafdar?'

'Yes.'

'How long have you spent in this house?'

'I've been here since the day I began the portrait, six weeks ago.'

'How long do you usually take to finish a portrait?'

'If it's a full figure, and if I can get a couple of hours' sitting every day, it usually takes me six weeks.'

'Then why is it taking you longer this time?'

'Because Mr Burman doesn't like sitting for me for more than an hour every day. Besides, he's grown quite fond of me, so he'd like me to stay here permanently. He likes having a lot of people around him. One of his sons is living abroad. His daughter is married, and his wife is dead. Mr Burman began feeling extremely lonely after his wife passed away. So he decided to fill his empty house with people. At least, that's what I think.'

'Where did you train as an artist?'

'I spent three years in Paris. Before that, I was in the Government College of Art in Calcutta.'

'Do you manage to make a decent living out of making portraits?'

'No, not any more. Photography has wiped out the popularity artists once enjoyed as makers of portraits. I have gone into abstract painting myself. If Mr Burman had not come forward to sponsor me, I would have been in dire straits.'

'Did you know about the stolen statue?'

'Yes. Mr Burman had shown it to me. "You are an artist, you will be able to appreciate its real value," he had said.'

'What do you think about the theft and the murder?'

'I do not think anyone in this house was involved. Perhaps the thief opened the safe to take some money from it, then saw the statue purely by chance. He gave in to temptation, took it, and then came face to face with Avinash before he could get away. So he had to get rid of Avinash. Self defence must be the only motive behind the murder. I cannot think of anything else.'

'Thank you.'

Feluda rose. There were two men left to be interviewed: Surya Kumar and Someshwar Burman. We went to Surya Kumar first. He seemed quiet and somewhat depressed, possibly because the disaster had occurred the same day as his arrival here.

'You are an unfortunate man!' Feluda remarked.

'You can say that again! Mr Burman invited me so warmly, and I was so glad to accept. . . and look what happens on my first night. I can hardly believe it.'

'Didn't you hear any noise?'

'Nothing at all. I tend to sleep rather soundly, without waking even once during the night. So I heard nothing.'

'Have you got to know everyone in this house?'

'No. I've met them, but that's about all. Someshwar Babu is the only person I know.'

'Didn't you see the statue that was stolen?'

'No, how could I? I don't even know what it looked like. A statue of Krishna, that's all I've heard.'

'Yes, but it was made with five different gems. As beautiful as it was valuable. It must be worth more than a hundred thousand rupees. Will you continue to stay here?'

'Someshwar Babu wants me to. He said to me, "There cannot be any question of asking you to leave. I'm just sorry that your stay couldn't be more pleasant."'

'If you're going to be around, could I come back and ask you further questions, if need be?'

'Of course. Any time.'

We thanked him and made our way to Someshwar Burman. He was still looking stunned.

'I can understand how devastated you must be feeling,' Feluda said, 'but since I am here, I must ask you a few questions, if only to satisfy my curiosity.'

'Go ahead. This is your job, after all.'

'You just didn't realize what had happened, did you? I mean, you saw and heard nothing at all?'

'No. All I can say is that I am very badly shaken by this whole thing. Avinash was a very good man, a good worker. And now I have lost not just him, but also my precious statue. Raja Dayal Singh had given it to me himself. He had picked it up with his own hands, and passed it to me. "You are the artist of all artists, you deserve nothing less," he had said. Besides . . .' Mr Burman broke off suddenly, and seemed lost in thought.

A few moments later, he spoke absently: 'Did I make a mistake? I hope so, because if it turns out to be true, it will be doubly painful for me.'

'What are you talking about?'

'Don't ask me, please. I couldn't tell you.'

'Didn't you realize . . . or sense . . . anything?'

'Yes, I did. But even so, I could do nothing.'

'That sounds quite mysterious, Mr Burman. Do you mind clarifying what you mean? That would make things a lot simpler, you see.'

'No, Mr Mitter. Please don't ask me to say anything more. Please . . . may I be left alone now? I'd be very grateful.'

'Of course, Mr Burman.'

We got to our feet. 'There's just one thing I'd like to say,' Feluda commented. 'If I were to carry on my own investigation regarding the tragedy here, would you have any objection?'

'No, no, certainly not. The culprit must be caught, no matter who it is.'

SIX

When we returned home, Lalmohan Babu said, 'Someshwar Burman's words were most mystifying, weren't they?'

'Yes, you're right,' Feluda replied.

'I think he suppressed quite a few facts.'

'Yes, I got that impression, too.'

'What do you think of the whole thing?'

'I am not totally in the dark, that much I can tell you. But I need to find out more about the world of magic. There's the auction house to consider as well. Let me go there and have a look. You two sit and chat here.'

There was something I had to say to Feluda before he disappeared. 'Feluda,' I said, 'did Nikhil Burman's words . . . or, rather, his voice . . . well, did that strike you as odd?'

'If it did, that's hardly surprising. But you have to work out why that is so.'

Feluda left, without adding anything further. Lalmohan Babu was following his own train of thought. 'I don't like that artist chap,' he said. 'Mind you, I am prejudiced against all men with thick beards.'

'Did you like Surya Kumar?'

'He, too, is a little strange. But I don't think he'd have gone around breaking safes open on his first night. After all, he wasn't familiar with the house or its occupants, was he? How was he to know who slept where, which room had the safe, and where its key was kept? But what I am sure of is that the thief was ready for murder. I mean, when he came face to face with the bearer, he could simply have knocked him unconscious, couldn't he? Surely, that's all he need have done to get away with his loot? No, I think he came clutching a knife, fully prepared to kill.'

'Yes, you may be right.'

'I wish we knew what was on Mr Burman's mind. What did he start to say, and then why did he change his mind? Why did he clam up like that? I think there's an important clue hidden in what he was saying.'

Before I could say anything, the phone rang. I picked it up and said, 'Hello.'

'Is Mr Mitter there?' asked a voice. Inspector Ghosh.

'No, he's had to go out for a while.'

'Please tell him when he gets back that the culprit has been caught. A thief called Gopchand, recently released from prison. He hasn't confessed, but we know for sure that he wasn't home last night. Please tell your cousin. I'll call him again once we get this man's confession. Your cousin can relax.'

I replaced the receiver, feeling a little let down. This was too easy. This was not what I wanted.

Feluda returned in an hour and a half. I told him at once about the inspector's call. He appeared quite unperturbed. 'I learnt a few things,' he said, hardly paying any attention to what I had just told him. 'Surya Kumar's shows aren't doing all that well. The same goes for Nikhil Burman's business and his auction house. And Ranen Tarafdar never went to the Government College of Art. Whether he went to Paris or not, I don't know.'

'So what do we do now?' Lalmohan Babu asked.

'I've nearly finished my investigation. All that remains to be done is revealing the truth. Let me call Inspector Ghosh.'

When he got through, the first thing Feluda said to the inspector was, 'I can't accept the solution you're offering me, Mr Ghosh.' After a pause, I heard him say, 'I think the killer is one of the residents of that house. Let's do one thing. I know who the real culprit is. I'd like to announce it to everyone in Someshwar Burman's house. Why don't you come there, too? Hear me out, then say what you have to say. Please do this for me. And come prepared to arrest the murderer. Thank you.'

He put the phone down. 'The inspector agreed. Gopchand—ha! How could he even think—? Honestly, when the police do something like this, I begin to lose my faith in them.'

Feluda picked up the phone again and rang Someshwar Burman, to tell him that we would be calling on him in the evening, and that we would like everyone in the house to be present.

We reached Mr Burman's house at five o'clock, to find that Inspector Ghosh had already arrived with two constables.

When everyone was seated, Feluda began speaking.

'The first question that arose in this case was whether the burglar had come from outside or not. Someone had stolen into Mr Burman's bedroom a few days before the final tragedy. I happened to visit this house the next day. I went round the house and inspected the grounds. It seemed to me that breaking into the house was really quite difficult. One might climb up a pillar on the veranda to gain access to the first floor, but climbing down that way, particularly if one was carrying anything, would be extremely tricky. So my suspicions fell on those who lived in the house, and I had no doubts about the object the thief had his eye on.

'After what happened yesterday, I met everyone and asked a lot of questions. From what Someshwar Babu told me, I could gather that he had seen the thief, but had done nothing to stop him from stealing. Perhaps the sight of the thief had left him totally stunned. But he could not have known that the theft would be followed by murder. There could be only one motive behind the theft—whoever took the statue was suddenly in need of a great deal of money.

'Now, let's look at the people who live in this house. Ranen Tarafdar had a commission, and was working on it. His financial position, at least temporarily, was sound. There was no reason for him to steal. Animesh Babu had been here for years, well looked after by his friend. He, too, could be ruled out.

'Let's now consider Nikhil Burman. He runs an auction house, but I have learnt that his business is not doing very well. If he could lay his hands on that statue of Krishna and sell it, he could easily get enough money to settle his debts. It is my belief that the first attempt at removing the statue had been made by Nikhil Burman. But he failed.'

'You are making an allegation without any evidence!' Nikhil Babu cried.

'I haven't finished,' said Feluda. 'You did not succeed, even if you tried. So why are you getting all worked up? I am not claiming that my reasoning is totally faultless. All I am doing at the moment is guessing. You are free to raise objections, but please remember that what happened the first time is not important. We must concentrate on the real theft and murder.

'A new person arrived in this house between the first failed attempt at theft, and the second successful one. It was the magician, Surya Kumar. I know for a fact that his shows are not drawing as much attention as he'd like. Many seats were lying empty even on the day we had been to it. Could Surya Kumar be the thief? He was clearly in need of money.'

Surya Kumar broke in: 'You are forgetting, Mr Mitter, that I knew absolutely nothing about Mr Burman's safe, or the statue of Krishna in it!'

'Surya Kumar, allow me to ask you a question,' Feluda went on, 'Someshwar Burman appeared to like you a lot, didn't he?'

'Yes, certainly. He would hardly have invited me to stay here, if he did not like me.'

'Do you have any idea why he seemed to have grown so fond of you?'

'No.'

'What if I said you reminded him of his first son? In fact, I think he believed that you were his elder son. Am I wrong, Mr Burman?'

'But . . . but . . . how could my own son do this to me?' Someshwar Burman cried in dismay.

Feluda continued to speak relentlessly. 'Surya Kumar's voice is quite thin, which affects his overall personality. Nikhil Burman's voice is also similarly thin. One might change one's appearance by wearing a wig and a beard, but it's more difficult to alter one's voice. Your voice gave you away.'

'You're right, Mr Mitter. I recognized Akhil from his voice,' Someshwar Babu admitted.

'Right. Does that mean Surya Kumar knew about the statue?'

'I might have known about it,' said Surya Kumar, alias Akhil Burman, 'but the statue was not there in the safe. I stole nothing.'

At these words, a babble broke out in the room. Everyone began talking at once. I felt totally taken aback myself. If the statue was not there in the safe when Surya Kumar opened it, where had it gone?

'The statue was missing all right,' Feluda declared. 'You could not steal it. So you are not a thief, Mr Akhil Burman. But you are a murderer.'

'I don't understand. Where's my Krishna gone?' Someshwar Burman demanded.

'Here it is.'

Feluda took the statue out of his pocket and placed it on a table.

'A thief broke into your house, not twice but thrice. I decided to take precautions as soon as I heard that Surya Kumar was going to stay in this house. When I noticed the similarity between his voice and Nikhil Burman's, I could tell that Surya Kumar was none other than his brother, Akhil. But he made no attempt to tell the truth about himself. That could only mean that he had some evil designs. Then I discovered that his income was far from satisfactory. He was steeped in debt, and his shows were running at a loss. So I felt that the statue of Krishna should not be allowed to remain in the safe. I had to bribe your chowkidar pretty heavily to get into your house. Then I climbed a pillar to get to the first floor, before I could find Someshwar Babu's bedroom. Getting the key from under his pillow might have been difficult, but I have practised card tricks, too. So I know something about removing objects quietly, without disturbing anything else. Mr Burman did not wake up. So I could do my job and leave in the same manner. Sadly, I could not prevent the murder.'

Inspector Ghosh, by this time, had reached Surya Kumar and was standing by his side. 'In this particular case, Akhil Burman, your magic or your hypnotism is not going to work,' Feluda told him.

Someshwar Burman rose and gripped Feluda's hand. 'If my Krishna is safe today, it is only because of you. I don't know how to thank you, Mr Mitter!'

Lalmohan Babu had the last word, when we returned home. 'Felu Babu,' he said, 'until today, I used to admire you. Now, I have to say my admiration is mixed with fear. Who knew you were such an ace burglar?'

take precautions as soon as I heard the [illegible], a [illegible] was going to [illegible] in this job [illegible] hand [illegible] the [illegible] his voice [illegible] I [illegible] right. But [illegible] and the truth [illegible] that I said [illegible] Then I [illegible] the [illegible] and [illegible] that the [illegible] that [illegible] pretty [illegible] I could find [illegible] the [illegible] might have been [illegible] and card tricks too [illegible] everything else [illegible] I [illegible] the [illegible] you [illegible] know [illegible]

[illegible]

The Case of the Apsara Theatre

ONE

We had been watching Sherlock Holmes on television. Feluda seemed greatly impressed. 'Don't Holmes and Watson both seem as though they have stepped straight out of the pages of a book? If Holmes hadn't shown us the way, taught us about method and observation, what would modern detectives have done? We owe so much to his creator, Conan Doyle.'

Jatayu was in full agreement. 'What amazes me is the number of stories the man wrote. How could he have thought up so many different plots? I have had to pull at my hair so frequently to get together even a rough outline for a story that I have actually gone bald!'

Lalmohan Babu, I thought, was being unusually modest. He had written forty-one novels so far. Even if his plots did not show a great deal of originality or variety, it was no mean achievement to be one of the most popular writers in Bengal. Yet one had to admit that his stories had improved considerably since he had come to know Feluda.

It was raining outside and we had just finished having tea and daalmut. 'Dear Tapesh,' said Lalmohan Babu, 'do you think Srinath could be asked to make us another cup of tea?'

I rose and went inside to tell Srinath. When I returned, there was the sound of a car stopping outside our house, followed by the ring of the doorbell. I opened the door to find a man of medium height, clean shaven, possibly in his mid-forties standing there.

'Is this where Pradosh Mitter lives?' he asked me.

'Do come in,' Feluda invited, 'and you can put that by the door,' he added, indicating the umbrella our visitor was carrying.

The man did as he was told, then sat down on a sofa.

'I am Pradosh Mitter, and this is my friend, Lalmohan Ganguli,' Feluda said.

'Namaskar. Thank goodness I found you at home. I did try to ring you, you know, but couldn't get through.'

'I see. What can I do for you?'

'I'm coming to that. First let me introduce myself. My name is Mahitosh Roy. I don't expect you to recognize my name, but I am an actor—in the theatre, not films—and a few people know about me.'

'You are in Apsara Theatre, aren't you?'

'Yes, that's right. I am currently acting in a play called *Prafulla*.'

'Yes, I had heard that.'

'I have come to you, Mr Mitter, because I think I may be in danger.'

'Oh? Why do you say that?'

'I have been receiving threats. I have no idea who might be sending these, but they are all in writing. I brought them with me.'

Mahitosh Roy took out four pieces of paper from his pocket and placed them on a table. One of them said 'WATCH OUT!' The second one said 'YOUR DAYS ARE NUMBERED'. The third and the fourth said 'PAY FOR YOUR SINS' and 'THIS IS THE END. SAY YOUR LAST PRAYERS'. The messages had all been written in capital letters. It was impossible to tell if the same hand had written each one.

'Did these arrive by post?' asked Feluda.

'Yes, in the last seven days.'

'Can't you even take a guess as to who might have sent them?'

'No, I honestly can't imagine who'd bother to do such a thing.'

'Can't you think of anyone who might have a grudge against you?'

'Look, I work in the theatre. There are always petty jealousies among actors. I've been with Apsara for two years. Before that I was with Rupmanch. When I joined Apsara, I was asked to replace another actor. He didn't like it, naturally, and is probably still angry.'

'What is this man called?'

'Jaganmoy Bhattacharya. He had started to drink very heavily. That's why he had to go. I couldn't tell you where he is now.'

'Can you think of anyone else?'

'I have a younger brother, who I don't get on with. He fell into bad company and was led astray . . . Our father got fed up with him after a while, and eventually left whatever assets he had, solely to me. My brother was naturally upset by this. He lives separately, we hardly see each other. But I can't think of anyone else who might hold anything against me.'

'All right. But do you know what the problem is? In a situation like this, I can't really do anything except ask you to be careful about where you go and who you see. Where do you live?'

'Ballygunj. My address is Five Panditia Place.'

'Do you live alone?'

'Yes. I have a cook and a bearer. I am not married.'

'I see. I'm sorry, Mr Roy, but I really can't do anything at this stage. All these notes were posted in different places, so I can't even start an enquiry in any particular place. Usually, people who send threatening notes do not actually carry them out. All they want to do is cause fear and anxiety, and that is what this person—or persons—is doing to you. I think it would be better for you to go to the police.'

'The police?' Mr Roy sounded a little dismayed.

'Why, do you have anything against them?'

'No, no, of course not.'

'Well then, I suggest you go straight to your local station and lodge a complaint. Tell them exactly what you have told me.'

Mr Roy rose. Feluda went to the front door to see him out. Then he returned to his seat and said, 'There was a white mark on one of his fingers. He used to wear a ring until recently. I wonder what happened to it?'

'You mean he might have sold it?' Lalmohan Babu asked.

'Yes, that's highly likely. His shoes were in pretty poor shape too. He has only a small role in *Prafulla*. The lead is played by the star of Apsara Theatre, Nepal Lahiri.'

'But who could be harassing him like this?'

'Impossible to tell. It could be one of the two people he mentioned, who knows? I didn't really think I could take this case. Anonymous threats—written or spoken—seldom come to anything. Why, I have received any number of threats ever since I started working. If I were to take them seriously, I'd never be able to step out of the house!'

But the threats received by Mahitosh Roy were not empty ones. We learnt this three days later.

TWO

It was a small report, published in one of the dailies. The actor from Apsara Theatre, Mahitosh Roy, had disappeared. Apparently, he used to go for a walk by the lake in the evening, unless there was a show. The day before yesterday—on Monday, that is—he was free, so he went for his walk, but did not return. His bearer informed the police, but he had not been found as yet.

Feluda seemed annoyed when he read the report. 'I told him to be careful,' he said, frowning. 'I said he shouldn't take any undue risks. Who asked him to leave his house and go out purely unnecessarily?

Still, I suppose I ought to visit his house since he did come to me for help. Do you remember his address?'

'Five Panditia Place, Ballygunj.'

'Good. I was just testing your memory.'

Five Panditia Place turned out to be a small house with two storeys. Mr Roy lived on the ground floor. His bearer opened the door. We told him who we were. He stepped aside and asked us to come in.

'Your master had come to me to ask for help. He was receiving threatening notes. Did you know about that?' Feluda asked.

'Yes, sir. I had been with him for twenty-two years. He used to tell me everything. I had told him not to go out of the house unless it was necessary, but he didn't listen to me. That evening, when he didn't return even after nine o'clock, I went to look for him myself. I knew the exact spot where he liked to walk and the bench where he often sat. But I couldn't find him anywhere. Then a whole day passed, he still did not come back. I even went to the police, but they couldn't find him, either.'

'Do you think you could come with us now and show us the spot where you think Mr Roy might have been seen last?'

'Very well, sir.'

'What is your name?'

'Dinabandhu.'

We took a taxi and reached the lake. Dinabandhu pointed out a bench under a tree by the lake, where Mr Roy used to sit after he finished walking. Apparently, it was his doctor who had insisted on this daily exercise. At this moment, there was no one in sight. Feluda took this opportunity to inspect the bench and its immediate surroundings closely. Five minutes later, he found a small brass container in the tall and thick grass behind the bench.

'Why, this used to belong to my master!' exclaimed Dinabandhu.

Feluda opened the container. There were a few pieces of supari in it. Feluda put it in his pocket.

'Did you go to the Bhawanipore police station?' Feluda asked.

'Yes, sir.'

'Very well. We'll now drop you at your house, and then have a chat with the police.'

Most OCs in Calcutta knew Feluda. The one in Bhawanipore was Subodh Adhikari. A stern, yet cheerful man, he greeted us with surprise. 'What brings you here so early in the morning?' he asked.

We took two chairs. 'It's about the disappearance of a Mahitosh Roy,' Feluda explained.

'I see. Inspector Ghose was handling that one. Let me call him. Would you like a cup of tea?'

'Yes, please. Thank you.'

Our tea and the inspector arrived together. He and Feluda shook hands.

'I am here to enquire about Mahitosh Roy. I believe he is missing?' Feluda said.

'Yes. I think he's been killed. We found a few threatening letters in his house. All anonymous, of course. If he was killed, and his body thrown into the lake, it would be impossible to find it, especially if something heavy was tied to it. But how come *you* are interested in this case?'

'Well, Mr Roy had come to see me before he vanished, about those notes, you see. Have you worked out how you are going to proceed?'

'We are still making enquiries. He used to work for Apsara Theatre. We have spoken to a few people there, but didn't get very far. There were rivalries between actors, but nothing strong enough to warrant a murder.'

'How was Mr Roy doing financially?'

'He was earning twelve hundred rupees a month. He had no family, so he managed to get by. Mind you, we don't know for sure that he's been murdered. It may be that he's simply gone into hiding.'

'I went to the spot where he used to sit after a walk, by the lake. I found one of his belongings there, hidden in the grass. It is a small brass container. He kept supari in it.'

'Really? Then perhaps it *is* murder. Perhaps this container fell out of his pocket during a struggle with his assassin.'

'Yes, that is a possibility.'

'Very well, we'll continue with our investigation and keep you informed, Mr Mitter.'

'Thank you, I'll be in touch.'

We finished our tea and left the police station.

'I think we ought to visit Apsara Theatre,' said Feluda as we came out. 'Go and ring Lalmohan Babu from that chemist's shop and tell him to join us.'

I made the phone call and then we took a taxi. Apsara Theatre was in Shyambazar.

THREE

We found Lalmohan Babu waiting for us outside Apsara Theatre.

'What's up?' he asked.

'Haven't you seen the papers today?'

'Yes, of course. Mahitosh Roy has vanished, hasn't he?'

'Not just vanished from his house, Lalmohan Babu. He may well have vanished from this earth.'

'What!'

Feluda quickly filled him in.

'So what are we going to do now?' Lalmohan Babu demanded.

'Let's start by speaking to the manager here.'

We had been standing outside on the pavement. Now we entered the building. The chowkidar at the gate told us that the manager, Kailash Banerjee, was in his office.

There was an antechamber before one could get to Mr Banerjee's room. We were asked to wait there while one of the staff took Feluda's card in to inform the manager. He returned a minute later and said, 'You may go in now.'

We stepped into the manager's room. Kailash Banerjee was short, dark and stout. A thin moustache graced his upper lip. He appeared to be about fifty.

'I have heard of you, Mr Mitter, but I cannot quite understand why you wish to see me,' he said when we were all seated.

'I need some information about one of your actors. The one who is missing,' Feluda told him.

'Who, Mahitosh? But the police have been here already. They asked a lot of questions.'

'Yes, I know. I am interested because Mahitosh Roy had come to me shortly before he disappeared. He was worried about the threats he had received.'

'Written threats? My God, does that mean he's been killed? I thought he was simply hiding from his creditors.'

'No, it is not as simple as that.'

'I see. Mind you, his absence has not caused us too many problems. I've found a temporary replacement already. The police came yesterday, but we couldn't really help. Mahitosh did not have a single close friend here. He was rather aloof and reserved. A reasonably good actor, I'd say, but not good enough to play the lead. It was his ambition to play the hero in the same play we are staging now.'

'Are you telling me he had no enemies?'

'I just told you, sir, that he had neither friends nor enemies.'

'Didn't you once have an actor called Jaganmoy Bhattacharya?'

'Yes, but he was asked to leave a long time ago.'

'Mahitosh Roy replaced Bhattacharya, didn't he?'

'Yes, yes, that's right. I had totally forgotten about it.'

'Do you have Bhattacharya's address?'

'I do, but it's his old address. He may well have moved from there.'

'Never mind. That's a chance we'll have to take.'

'Very well.'

Mr Banerjee rang a bell. A young man of about twenty-five appeared.

'Get Jaganmoy Bhattacharya's address and give it to Mr Mitter,' Mr Banerjee said to him.

The young man returned in a couple of minutes with the address: 27 Nirmal Bose Street. Lalmohan Babu said he knew where it was. Apparently, it wasn't far from Apsara. We thanked Mr Banerjee and left.

Luckily, it turned out that Jaganmoy Bhattacharya had not moved from his old address. His servant took Feluda's card in, and then returned to take us to his master.

We found Jaganmoy Bhattacharya sitting on a divan. He looked ill. He made no attempt to rise even when he saw us trooping in.

'What does a detective want from me?' was his first question.

'Information. Did you once know an actor called Mahitosh Roy?'

'Know him? Not really. All I know is that he arrived, and my own career was destroyed. But I hear he's disappeared.'

'Not just disappeared. He's probably been killed.'

'Killed? Oh. Well, frankly, I can't say I am greatly distressed to hear this. He put an end to my livelihood. That's the only thing I remember about him.'

'Mr Roy had received anonymous notes threatening him. Do you think you might be able to tell us who—?'

'You mean you want to know if *I* had sent them to him?

'Well, you still appear to bear him a grudge.'

'No, sir. You mentioned Mahitosh Roy, and so I was reminded of what his arrival had done to me. All that is now in the past, Mr Mitter. I don't spend my days planning revenge, I assure you. I am now working somewhere else, and I've given up drinking. What I earn isn't much, but I manage. My only problem now is asthma. Apart from that, I am fine. If you hadn't reminded me of Mahitosh, I would not have thought of him at all. Honestly.'

'Did you ever see him after you left Apsara?'

'No, not even on the stage. I never went back to Apsara after they got rid of me.'

FOUR

Three months had passed since then. There was no trace of Mahitosh Roy, so there didn't seem to be any doubt that he had been killed. We went back to Apsara Theatre one day to see if they had heard anything, but drew a blank. All we learnt was that a new actor had been employed to replace Mahitosh Roy. His name was Sudhendu Chakravarty. He was said to be a good actor.

Feluda had managed to contact Mahitosh's brother, Shivtosh. It turned out that the two brothers had not been on speaking terms for many years.

'Why is that?' Feluda had asked. 'Was your family property the only reason?'

'What other reason do you need to look for? My brother used to try very hard to please our father. I am not like that at all. I went my own way, did my own thing. My father didn't like it. Both he and my brother thought I didn't count, just because I was the younger one. So my father cut me out of his will. Naturally I resented this, and Mahitosh and I drifted apart. That's not surprising, is it?'

Shivtosh Roy spoke with considerable bitterness. It seemed to me that he still held a big grudge against his brother.

'Would you like to say anything about his disappearance? If he really has been killed, surely you realize that you could be a prime suspect?'

'Look, I didn't see my brother at all in the last five years. I had absolutely nothing to do with him. I didn't even go to the theatre.'

'Can you remember what you were doing the day Mahitosh Roy disappeared, say between 6 and 8 p.m.?'

'I was doing what I do every evening—playing cards with my friends.'

'Where?'

'Sardar Shankar Road. Number eleven. It is the house of one Anup Sengupta. You can go and speak to him, if you like.'

Feluda did, and Mr Sengupta confirmed that Shivtosh Roy had most certainly been at his house at that particular time. He was a regular visitor there. Feluda was therefore obliged to drop him as a suspect.

Lalmohan Babu turned up the next day and said, 'Look, Felu Babu, this case isn't a case at all. I can't see why you're losing sleep over this one. Why don't you take a short break? I can feel a new plot taking shape in my mind, and you need a change of air to clear your head, so let's go out.'

'Where to?'

'Digha. We've never been to Digha, have we?'

'Very well. In all honesty, I can't see this case being successfully concluded. Mahitosh Roy's killer is never going to be captured.'

We left for Digha the next day, having booked ourselves at the tourist lodge. It was a very comfortable place to be in, and the sea wasn't far. I noticed Lalmohan Babu had brought a pair of new red swimming trunks.

The first two days passed quietly. On the third day, Feluda picked up the newspaper in the evening, as they took all day to reach Digha from Calcutta. He glanced at it and gave a sharp exclamation.

'I don't believe this!'

'What's the matter?' Lalmohan Babu and I cried in unison.

'Someone else from Apsara Theatre has been killed. Nepal Lahiri… he was their hero, he always played the lead. What is going on?'

I took the paper from Feluda and read the report quickly. Nepal Lahiri, it said, was returning home in a taxi on the evening of the murder. He stopped it on the way to see a friend. This friend's house happened to be in a small alley. Someone stabbed Mr Lahiri as he stepped into the alley. The police had started their investigation. Mr Lahiri's wife and twelve-year- old son had been unable to shed any light on the matter.

'What do we do now?' asked Lalmohan Babu.

'We return to Calcutta, and you go back to Apsara to ask some questions.'

'Me? Why me?'

'Because I sprained my ankle while bathing in the sea this morning. I can tell that by tomorrow I'll be in considerable pain.'

'Well then, I suggest we go back to Calcutta tonight. You can rest your ankle far better if you're at home.'

'Do you think you can manage to take my place?'

'Heh, Felu Babu, I ought to have learnt something of your style after spending so many years with you!'

We returned to Calcutta the same evening. Lalmohan Babu agreed to come to our house the following morning, so that Feluda could brief him properly. Then he and I would go to Apsara Theatre.

Lalmohan Babu arrived punctually, and we were able to leave by ten. Feluda had given us clear instructions on what to do. Lalmohan Babu seemed very pleased with this development. 'I often felt sorry that I couldn't help your cousin more actively,' he told me, 'but now I think I've got the chance to make amends. Look!' He took out a card from his pocket. 'I had this printed last night. What do you think of it?'

I looked at the card. It said: LALMOHAN GANGULI, WRITER.

'This is good. Very smart!' I told him. He nodded happily.

By this time we had reached Apsara Theatre. We gave the chowkidar one of these new cards and asked him to take it in to the manager. Three minutes later, we were told to go in.

Kailash Banerjee failed to recognize us. 'Look,' he said a little impatiently, 'we've got a lot of problems today. If you've come here about a new play, I'm afraid I cannot discuss it right now. Can you come back in a few days, please?'

Lalmohan Babu raised a hand in protest. 'No, no. I haven't brought you a new play. I am here representing Pradosh Mitter, the investigator. He's not well, so he couldn't come himself. We were with him when he came here to investigate the disappearance of Mahitosh Roy.'

'Yes, yes, now I remember. What do you want to know? It's all been reported in the press. I have nothing further to add.'

'I have only one question, sir—was Nepal Lahiri also getting anonymous letters, like Mahitosh Roy?'

'Yes, but he ignored the first few and didn't tell anyone. Then, about three days ago, he showed me one of them. Said he had got the first one ten days ago.'

'What did it say?'

'Just the usual, making unspecified threats. Written in capital letters. I told Nepal to take care, but he fancied himself as a real-life hero, just because he played the hero on stage. So he said, "Pooh, this kind of stupid stuff doesn't bother me!" And now look what happened to him.'

'Where did he live?'

'Twenty-seven, Nakuleshwar Bhattacharya Lane.'

'He was married, wasn't he?

'Yes.'

'Who is this friend he had stopped to see? Do you have any idea?'

'Well, if he stopped to go into an alley, it may have been Sasadhar Chatterjee. He lives in a small alley. He's an actor, too. Works for Rupam Theatre.'

'Did Nepal Lahiri have any enemies here in Apsara?'

'How should I know? Every successful actor is bound to have enemies, and people who'd envy him. Nepal was envied by people in our rival companies as well. They knew how badly Apsara was going to be affected if Nepal left us.'

'Does that mean your productions have come to a standstill?'

'We've had to cancel the last show of *Prafulla,* which was scheduled for tonight. Then we were going to work on a new play called *Alamgeer.* Nepal was to play the main role. Now we're trying out another actor. He's new, but he's already got a heavy beard and seems very well suited to the part. He won't need any make-up at all. His acting isn't bad, either. We'll have to manage somehow, won't we?'

Now I suddenly remembered something Feluda had asked us to get.

'Do you think we could have the names and addresses of all your main actors? Mr Mitter might wish to speak to some of them,' I said.

Mr Banerjee called his secretary, who gave us a list of the necessary names and addresses.

'Where does this friend live? I mean, the one he was going to see? Sasadhar Chatterjee, did you say?' Lalmohan Babu asked.

'It was mentioned in the press report. Moti Mistri Lane. That's where he was killed.'

'Thank you.'

There didn't seem to be any point in staying any longer. We said 'namaskar' and took our leave.

FIVE

Moti Mistri Lane turned out to be so narrow that we had to park our car outside on the main road. The owner of a paan shop told us where Sasadhar Chatterjee lived. We found the house and knocked on the door. It was opened by a middle-aged man.

'Yes?' he looked at us enquiringly.

'We'd like to meet Sasadhar Chatterjee. Is he home?'

'I am Chatterjee. How can I help you?'

Lalmohan Babu took out another card and passed it to Mr Chatterjee.

'You are the famous writer, Lalmohan Ganguli?' Mr Chatterjee asked, his eyes glinting.

'I don't know about being famous, but I am the writer, yes,' Lalmohan Babu replied with unusual modesty.

'Why, I have read every book you've ever written! But what brings you here?'

'I have been sent here by my friend, Pradosh Mitter.'

'I know of him, too. Please come in.'

At last, we stepped into his room. A large bed occupied most of it, but there were two chairs as well. Lalmohan Babu took one of these and said, 'We are making enquiries regarding the murder of Nepal Lahiri. Can you tell us anything about it?'

'What can I say? He was killed even before he could get to my house. One of our local boys came and told me what had happened. Nepal and I had been friends for twenty-two years, although we worked for different companies.'

'Did he have any enemies?'

'Of course he did. He was important and well established, the star of Apsara. Many other actors envied him.'

'Can you think of anyone in particular?'

'No, I am afraid not. He never mentioned anyone's name. Nepal was a bit reckless, it never bothered him what others said or felt. He knew how good he was, and how much in demand. Various rival companies had made him tempting offers, but his loyalties were with Apsara. That's where he had started his career, you see.'

'Did he tell you about the threatening notes he had been sent?'

'Yes, but he didn't seem perturbed at all. The fact is, an astrologer had once told him he'd live until the age of eighty-two. Nepal believed him. He also believed that he'd continue to work until that age, and would actually die on the stage.'

Mr Chatterjee sighed. 'I really don't have anything more to say,' he added. 'I feel rather depressed, to tell you the truth.'

We took the hint and rose. Then we thanked him and left.

We returned home straight after this to make our report. Feluda seemed very pleased with Lalmohan Babu. 'Well done, Mr Ganguli!' he said. 'You worked just as efficiently as a professional investigator. The only thing that remains to be done now is interviewing the other top actors of Apsara—the ones that knew Nepal Lahiri well. Some might have been jealous, but others might have been close to him.'

'How is your ankle?' I asked him.

'Much the same. I don't think I can go out for another couple of days. By the way, when you speak to the other actors, don't forget the new one.'

'No, no, of course not.'

Lalmohan Babu was duly gratified by Feluda's praise. 'It was a new experience for me,' he said happily. 'Now I don't think your job is as difficult as it seems.'

'No. The only difficult part is arriving at the truth.'

'Yes, that's true; and I certainly cannot claim that I can find out the truth just by asking a few questions. But, Felu Babu, I can tell you this: if you saw me today, even you would not have recognized me.'

'Really?'

'Really. I was a different man.'

Feluda laughed and changed the subject. 'Were they having rehearsals this morning?' he asked.

'Yes, I think so. They're planning to stage *Alamgeer* quite soon,' I replied.

'In that case, ring the manager before going and ask him what time might be convenient to speak to everyone.'

'Very well.'

'Did you see the police there?'

'No. There were no policemen.'

'Perhaps they were in plain clothes. I am going to ring Inspector Bhowmik and ask him how far they have got. He must be in charge of this case.'

SIX

A conversation with Inspector Bhowmik revealed that the police suspected a gang of criminals. Apparently, Nepal Lahiri had been wearing an expensive watch which was missing when the police found his body. Plain robbery might well have been the motive behind his murder.

'You mean there's no connection between the theatre and this murder?' Feluda asked.

'No, I don't think so. A particular gang—most of them ex-convicts—has been active in that area for some time. We found the knife Lahiri had been stabbed with, but there were no fingerprints. However, we are pretty sure we can catch the culprits soon, perhaps in two or three days. We may not need your services this time, Mr Mitter.'

Feluda put the phone down and said, 'Ring the manager now. We need to talk to those actors.'

I got through to Kailash Banerjee on my third attempt.

'The police have already been here and spoken to everyone. But if you must go through the whole process again, come here at half past ten on Thursday. Rehearsals start at eleven. You'll have to finish your business in half an hour,' Mr Banerjee said.

'You need to speak to only four people,' Feluda told me after I had replaced the receiver. 'The top three in Apsara and the new recruit.'

Lalmohan Babu and I reached Apsara a little before ten-thirty. Today, Lalmohan Babu appeared even smarter and more confident. His whole demeanour had changed.

When we told the manager we wanted to speak to only the top three actors and the latest arrival, he said, 'In that case, you had better start with Dharani. Dharani Sanyal. He is our seniormost artiste. He's been with us for twenty-six years.'

We were sitting in the antechamber attached to the manager's room. Dharani Sanyal entered a few minutes later. About fifty years old, he had thick long hair like a lion's mane, and rather droopy eyes.

'I am Dharani Sanyal,' he said. 'You two are detectives, I believe?'

'Yes,' Lalmohan Babu said quickly, without bothering to explain. 'We are investigating the death of Nepal Lahiri.'

'Nepal was getting strange anonymous notes,' said Dharani Sanyal. 'I told him to take care, but he paid no attention. God knows why he had to go to Moti Mistri Lane. It's not a safe area at all. If he didn't see his friend for a few days, what difference would it have made? I even told him to inform the police, but he just laughed. A similar thing had happened to one of our other actors, Mahitosh Roy. But Mahitosh was not a star. His disappearance was no major loss to the company.'

'Did Nepal Lahiri have any enemies?'

'Certainly. Envy is pretty common, particularly among actors. But if you want me to mention names, or tell you who might be a suspect, I am afraid I couldn't help you.'

'Did he ever visit your house?'

'No. We met here three times a week. I didn't know him well enough to want to meet him on other days as well.'

'What were you doing at the time when Nepal Lahiri was killed?'

'I was at the house of a friend, Kalikinkar Ghoshal, attending a session of keertan. You can have this verified, if you like.'

'All right. Thank you, no more questions.'

Dharani Sanyal left, and was replaced by Dipen Bose: slightly younger than Sanyal, clean shaven, short curly hair, a cigarette dangling from his lips.

'Nepal and I joined this theatre together. I was ambitious like him, but not as gifted. Nepal had real talent,' he said.

'Did you envy him?'

'Yes, frequently. I often thought how nice it would be if Nepal could be removed from my path. He was the one stumbling block in my way to stardom.'

'You are very honest, Mr Bose. Didn't you ever think of acting upon your thoughts?'

'Oh no. I am a very ordinary man, and I have a family to think of. Planning and carrying out a murder is something I'd never do, except perhaps on the stage. I might get dramatic ideas because I act in plays, but carry them out in real life? No, sir, not me!'

'Where were you that evening when Mr Lahiri was killed?'

'At a cinema. But I cannot prove it. I never keep old stubs.'

'What film did you see?'

'*Heartthrob*.'

'How was it?'

'Awful.'

'All right, you may go now.'

The third actor was called Bhujanga Ray. He seemed to be a little more than fifty, his eyes were sunken, his cheeks hollow, his nose hooked, and his hair thin.

'How did you get on with Nepal Lahiri?' Lalmohan Babu asked him.

'Nepal was my best and closest friend in Apsara.'

'Do you have anything to say about his death?'

'It is the biggest tragedy in many years that's hit not just Apsara, but the whole world of theatre. Nepal was a remarkable actor. We never clashed, for he always played the lead, and I did smaller characters.'

'Did you know about the threats he was receiving?'

'Yes, he told me when he got the first one. I warned him immediately not to take it lightly, and to stop going to Moti Mistri Lane. That area crawls with criminals. But Nepal decided to ignore the whole thing. He was convinced he'd live to be eighty-two.'

'Does that mean you think he was killed by an ordinary armed robber?'

'What else is one supposed to think? His watch was missing, wasn't it? It was an Omega, worth at least seven thousand.'

We had no further questions for him. Bhujanga Ray thanked us and left.

The new actor, Sudhendu Chakravarty, came in next. I was slightly startled to see him, for with a thick beard and moustache, he looked as if he was made up for a part and about to go on stage. He told us he had started to grow a beard the minute he heard Apsara were going to produce *Alamgeer.* Before that he only had a moustache.

'Where were you before you joined Apsara?' Lalmohan Babu asked him.

'Nowhere. I mean, I was not a professional actor. I occasionally did small roles in plays for private clubs, that was all. But although I run a small business selling plywood, acting has always been something of a passion. For years, I stood in front of a mirror and played various roles from different plays, learning the lines until I was word perfect. Now I don't need to do that, but the passion has remained.'

'Have you got a role in *Alamgeer*?'

'I have been promised one, yes. It may well be the lead. Nothing's finalized yet.'

'Where do you live?'

'Amherst Row.'

'What will happen to your business?'

'I will give it up. I was doing it only because I hadn't got a proper break. Now I can be a full-time actor.'

There was only one question left to be asked.

'Did you get to know Nepal Lahiri?'

'Only a little. But I had seen his acting many times before. I used to admire him a lot.'

SEVEN

Feluda listened to our report attentively. Then he said, 'I can see that you've managed pretty well without me.'

'Well, asking questions is simple enough,' said Lalmohan Babu. 'But I cannot figure out what the answers add up to. Frankly, I am very much in the dark. If Lahiri was killed by an armed robber, the police will certainly catch him. Where is the mystery in all that?'

'No ordinary robber would send anonymous notes before killing a man in an alley.'

'Ye-es, I guess that's true. Do you think the same person killed both Mahitosh Roy and Lahiri?'

'Yes, either the same person, or two different people from the same gang.'

'Yes, but the motive—?'

'It could be that one of the other theatre companies had these two men killed. It will take Apsara a long time to replace two of their main actors, and re-establish themselves. A rival company could easily gain from their loss.'

Feluda's foot was still painful. Perhaps he'd have to have an x-ray. He placed his injured foot on a coffee table, leant back on the sofa and said, 'You've done a lot today. Let me now do my share of the work.'

'What are you going to do?'

'Think. There is a faint glimmer, but that needs to get brighter . . . and so I need to think.'

'Very well, Felu Babu. You think as much as you need to. I am going to sit here very quietly and have a cup of tea. Tapesh, could you please go and tell Srinath?'

When I returned after telling Srinath to make us a fresh pot of tea, I saw Feluda frowning, his eyes closed. Was he going to solve the mystery without stepping out of the house?

A little later, he suddenly asked, 'Did any of these actors appear to have an addiction of any kind? For instance, did any of them smoke?'

'Yes, Dipen Bose did. Bhujanga Ray, I think, takes snuff; and

Sudhendu Chakravarty was chewing supari.'

'I see.'

Silence fell again. Lalmohan Babu poured himself a cup of tea when Srinath brought it, and began drinking it with great relish. I picked up a magazine and leafed through it. Feluda received a great number of magazines every month, some of which went straight into the wastepaper basket.

The silence continued for five minutes. Then Feluda opened his eyes. They were shining with excitement.

'Lalmohan Babu!' he called, his voice low.

'Yes, sir?'

'This Sudhendu Chakravarty, the newcomer . . . was he of medium height?'

'Yes.'

'And he had a clear complexion?'

'Yes.'

'Age between forty and forty-five?'

'Why, yes! What is this, Felu Babu? Do you know the man?'

'Not just I. You know him, too.'

'What do you mean?'

'I think I've got it. . . but first let me ring Inspector Bhowmik.'

I dialled the number, and passed him the receiver.

'Inspector Bhowmik?' I heard him say. 'This is Pradosh Mitter. Look, it's about those actors from Apsara Theatre. I have just worked out who killed Nepal Lahiri. No, it wasn't one of your ex-convicts. I will tell you everything, but I'm afraid you are going to have to come to me. I am still quite immobile. Yes, you can come in an hour, that'll be fine. See you then.'

He put the receiver down and found Lalmohan Babu and me gaping at him.

'All right, I won't keep you in suspense any longer,' he said with a smile. 'You are dying to know who it was, aren't you? This whole business was laughably simple on one hand, extremely complex on the other. Hats off to the murderer . . . he had even Felu Mitter completely stumped for a while. His motive was envy, pure envy . . . and nothing else. Nepal Lahiri had to be removed, so that someone else could take his place.'

'What about Mahitosh Roy? He wasn't a great star or anything.'

'That is why *he* was not killed.'

'What!'

'Yes, Mahitosh Roy did not die. He just disappeared, simply so that he could orchestrate the whole thing from behind the scene. What he told me here—about receiving threats and then his own sudden disappearance—was all part of a plan. It was done just to create the impression that he had been murdered. He is actually still alive, living at a new address, and he's given himself a new name. That brass container was dropped in the grass to make sure it was found, and we assumed that he had been attacked, killed and his body thrown into the lake.'

'What a brain that fellow has!'

'It took him three months to grow a beard. Then he returned to Apsara, taking care to change his voice whenever he spoke. Actually, a beard can alter one's appearance completely. He knew he wouldn't have any difficulty in filling the gap left by Mahitosh Roy. Apsara was looking for a new face.'

'Sudhendu Chakravarty!'

'Exactly. The only thing he couldn't give up was his habit of chewing supari, but he should have known better than to have it in your presence. But there's no doubt that his evil plans would have succeeded, if you two hadn't helped me out. That man's ambition has turned him into a ruthless killer. He took Nepal Lahiri's watch just to pull the wool over our eyes. But then, he didn't know he'd be up against Felu Mitter and his team, did he? Now he's going to regret ever having come to me!'

Feluda was absolutely right. Inspector Bhowmik rang us the next morning to confirm everything that Feluda had told us.

Lalmohan Babu took me aside and whispered into my ear: 'Now I know where the difference lies between your cousin and myself.'

'Where?'

He tapped his head with a finger, and said sadly, 'In here!'

Peril in Paradise

ONE

'Where are we going this year?' asked Lalmohan Babu, helping himself to a handful of savoury chana and washing it down with hot tea. 'It's now so infernally hot here in Calcutta that I think we've got to escape!'

'Where would you like to escape to?' Feluda queried. 'You're the one who's so interested in travelling. I could quite happily remain in Calcutta all year.'

'You're not working on a case right now, are you?'

'No.'

'Well then, let's get out of here.'

'Yes, but where to?'

'To the hills, naturally. I mean mountains . . . and that means the Himalayas. I don't consider Vindhyachal or the Western Ghats as mountains. Where I want to go, Felu Babu, is where *everyone* wants to go. Some say your entire life is a waste of time if you haven't seen this place.'

'Where is it?'

'Haven't you guessed, even after so many hints?'

'Paradise on earth?'

'Exactly. Kashmir. Why don't we go there, Felu Babu? We've both earned quite a lot of money, don't you think? You haven't got a family, nor have I. So why don't we travel when we can, and enjoy ourselves? Do say yes. We could go from here to Delhi, then take a plane to Srinagar.'

'Srinagar isn't the only place worth seeing. There's Pahalgam, Gulmarg, Khilanmarg—'

'OK, OK, we'll see everything worth seeing. Let's spend a couple of weeks in Kashmir, shall we? I can't think of a plot unless I travel. I have to write a new novel before Durga Puja, don't forget.'

'That shouldn't worry you. Do what everyone else is doing—pinch ideas and events from foreign thrillers.'

'Never. *You* would be the first one to make fun of me if I did. Don't deny it, Felu Babu, you know you would. Your jibes are sharper than a knife.'

'Very well then, shall we stay in a houseboat?'

'In Srinagar?'

'You can't stay in houseboats anywhere else. We could take one on Dal Lake. But it will be expensive, let me warn you.'

'Who cares? Let's just have some fun.'

'All right, we'll stay in a houseboat in Srinagar, a tent in Pahalgam and a log cabin in Gulmarg.'

'Splendid!'

The idea of going to Kashmir had clearly appealed to Feluda. He went to the tourist office after Lalmohan Babu left and brought back a number of leaflets.

'Since we've made the decision to go there, let's not waste any time,' he said. 'Today's Monday, isn't it? We could leave on Saturday.'

'It'll be cold in Kashmir, won't it?'

'Yes, so we must be adequately prepared for it. Lalmohan Babu ought to be warned—he'd feel the cold much more than either of us!'

Our warm clothes were duly fetched from the dry cleaners. We decided to spend the first week in Srinagar. The tourism department booked a houseboat for us. It was large enough for a whole family, so it would suit us perfectly. I tried to imagine what it might feel like to stay in a luxury boat. Perhaps it would be the same as the 'baujras' or pleasure boats zamindars had used in Bengal many years ago. I saw in the leaflets that they looked like little cottages. There were also pictures of smaller boats that carried people from one end of the lake to the other. The houseboats remained stationery.

'There's such a lot to see in Srinagar!' I said to Feluda, having read all the literature. 'Look, there are the Mughal gardens, and the river Jhelum, and lakes, and poplars, eucalyptuses and rows of chinar . . . have you seen these pictures, Feluda? It's truly beautiful, and so are Pahalgam and Gulmarg. If we can climb up to Khilanmarg at eleven thousand feet, I believe it's possible to get a wonderful view of Nanga Parvat. Can we see everything in two weeks?'

'Oh yes!' Feluda laughed.

We left by air the following Saturday, as planned. This time, we were given seats in different rows. I saw Lalmohan Babu talking animatedly with the gentleman sitting next to him.

'Who was that man?' I asked him curiously when we reached the airport in Delhi.

'He's called Sushant Som. He works as a secretary. His boss is a retired judge. They're both going to Srinagar, with some other people, and will also stay in a houseboat. He recognized your cousin, and asked me if we were working on a case. I was tempted to say we were, but then I changed my mind and told him the truth.'

Our flight to Srinagar was not going to leave for another three hours. So we went to the restaurant for a cup of tea. Here we ran into Mr Som. He smiled as he saw us and walked over to our table. 'My name is Sushant Som,' he said, shaking hands with Feluda. 'I am very pleased to meet you. I am one of your many admirers, you see. I'm sure my boss would like to meet you, too.'

Four other men had just walked into the restaurant. Mr Som approached this group, whispering something to the oldest of them. The old gentleman glanced at us, then walked across. Feluda stood up.

'Please, please, there's no need to get up,' said the gentleman. 'I am Siddheshwar Mallik. I have spent virtually all my life dealing with crime, but this is the first time I have come face to face with a real-life private detective!'

'Dealing with crime? You mean—?'

'I used to be a judge. I have sent a lot of men to the gallows. Now I've retired. My health isn't what it used to be and I have to travel with a doctor in tow. But this time I am also accompanied by my son, a bearer and my secretary. Sushant is a most efficient man. I really don't know what I'd do without him.'

'Will you be staying in Srinagar?'

'Yes, but we'd like to visit a few other places.'

'We have a similar plan. Are you going to take a houseboat?'

'Yes. I stayed in one in nineteen sixty-four; it's a unique affair. Er . . . I didn't quite catch your name? . . .' Mr Mallik looked enquiringly at Lalmohan Babu.

'Lalmohan Ganguli,' he replied. 'In a way, I am also involved with crime. I write thrillers.'

'Really? Well then, all that's missing here is a criminal! Very well, we shall see you again in Srinagar.'

TWO

The aerial view of Srinagar was quite different from the one that greeted my eyes as we climbed out of the plane. Both were beautiful, but in different ways. It also became instantly clear that Srinagar was not like Darjeeling, Simla, or even Kathmandu, which I had seen before. When I saw the lake and the river Jhelum on our way to the city, I realized just how unique Srinagar was, both in its location and appearance.

Our destination was the Boulevard, the road which ran by the southern side of Dal Lake. Small steps went down to the water, where little boats called shikaras were waiting to take passengers. Just as Venice has its gondolas, Srinagar is famous for its shikaras. Our houseboat was called *The Water Lily.* A special shikara was waiting to take us to it. We climbed into it, taking our luggage with us. Several houseboats stood in a row, at a distance of fifty yards. Then the lake became much wider and I couldn't see any more houseboats. They were all parked on the western side of the lake.

It was not difficult at all to climb up to the boat from the shikara. There was an open area in front of the rooms. One could sit there, or take the stairs that went up to the upper deck for a better view of the surroundings. The first room as we entered the boat was the living room. It was well furnished with flowers in a vase, paintings on the wall and a small library. Behind this was the dining room, two bedrooms and a bathroom. The kitchen was in a smaller boat, attached to the rear. In short, it provided every comfort on the lake that one might find in a private bungalow in town.

'You have to thank me for this!' Lalmohan Babu declared, grinning broadly. 'It was really my idea to come here, wasn't it?'

'Sure. You are a writer, Lalmohan Babu. All good ideas ought to come from you. Anyway, let's have a cup of tea and then go for a ride in our shikara.'

There were two bearers in the houseboat to look after us. They were called Mahmudia and Abdullah.

By the time we finished our tea and got into the shikara, the sun was about to set. Although it was May, it was quite cool. We had to wear our warm clothes when we went out. Feluda said, 'I don't think we'll have time for anything but a tour of the lake. We'll start our sightseeing from tomorrow. See that hill behind the Boulevard? Its height is 1000 feet. There's a temple at its top—the temple of Shankaracharya. It is said to have been built by Emperor Ashok's son. To the east of the lake are the Mughal gardens. We must see Nishad Bagh, Shalimar and Chashma Shahi. I believe there's a spring in Chashma Shahi. Its water is supposed to be like nectar, both in taste and in its power to improve one's appetite.'

'What is that little island in the middle of the lake?' I asked.

'It's called Char Chinar. There are four chinar trees on it, one in each corner.'

Mahmudia and Abdullah began rowing. We passed about ten houseboats on our left and were soon at the spot where the lake widened. The retired judge, Mr Mallik, and his team had taken two houseboats. Mr Sushant Som waved from the lower deck of one of these and shouted: 'Do drop in on your way back for a cup of tea!'

When I saw the lake properly, it took my breath away. I haven't got words to describe its beauty. Its water was as clear as crystal. There was no wind, so like a mirror, its surface reflected the mountains. Lotuses bloomed everywhere. Our shikara made its way through these. Lalmohan Babu, deeply moved, first began reciting poetry, then stopped abruptly and started humming under his breath. When I asked him what he was singing, he replied, 'An Urdu ghazal.' I had to turn my face away to hide a smile.

The sun had set, but at this time of the year, it stayed light for quite some time. When we began our return journey, it was nearly half past seven; but it wasn't yet totally dark.

Sushant Som was still standing on the deck of their houseboat which was called *Rosemary.* He waved again. We stopped our shikara and went up.

'Welcome!' said Mr Som. 'Let's have some tea.'

Mr Som was sharing this boat with Mr Mallik's son, Vijay. The old Mr Mallik, his doctor Harinath Majumdar, and their bearer, Prayag, were in the next boat, called *Miranda.*

We climbed to the top deck after tea had been ordered.

'Are you any good at cards? Poker or rummy?' Mr Som asked Feluda.

'I haven't played for a long time. But yes, I can play most games. Why do you ask?'

'People are hard at it downstairs, in the living room.'

'People?'

'Vijay met two other men in the plane from Delhi. One of them is called Sarkar. I don't know the name of the other man. All three are gamblers.'

We were offered comfortable chairs. I still found it difficult to take everything in. Calcutta seemed to have faded away in the far distance. I might have been on a different planet. Some foreign tourists had moved into the boat on our right. Through an open window, I could see men and women dancing to western music.

Feluda turned to Mr Som. 'How long ago did Mr Mallik retire?' he asked.

'Five years ago, when he turned sixty.'

'But judges don't have to retire at sixty, do they?'

'No, but his health wasn't very good. He has angina, you see. He didn't really wish to retire, but his doctor was most insistent. Actually, his ailment may be a result of a psychological dilemma.'

'How do you mean?'

'He has sentenced many people to death. Sometimes he tells me, "I am going to pay for this in my old age." I suppose if one knows one has taken a life—even if it's in the interests of law and justice—that is bound to affect one's mind. He used to keep diaries. I have got all his diaries now, for I am writing the story of his life, although it will be published as an autobiography. Every time he passed a death sentence, he put a red cross against that date in his diary. Sometimes these crosses are accompanied by a question mark. That shows he wasn't always convinced that he had done the right thing. Do you know what he's been doing lately? His doctor—Dr Majumdar—is a good medium. Mr Mallik uses him to speak to the spirits of the people who he condemned, and asks them if they had really committed a murder. If they say yes, Mr Mallik feels reassured. So far, no one has found fault with his judgement.'

'Really? Are you going to hold seances here in Srinagar?'

'No, not straightaway, perhaps. But they'll start in a day or two. Why, are you interested?'

'I certainly am,' Feluda replied, 'but whether my presence would be welcome or not is a different matter.'

'I can ask him. I don't think he'll refuse, for he was very pleased to meet you. Besides, his seances are no secret. Everything that's disclosed will go into the book. I am keeping a record of every minute detail.'

'In that case, I'd be grateful if you'd ask him about me.'

'Certainly.'

We finished our tea, chatted for a few more minutes, then returned to *The Water Lily*. Lalmohan Babu flopped down on a sofa and said, 'Highly interesting man, this judge sahib.'

'True,' Feluda agreed, 'but he isn't the first judge to have reacted like this. I have read of other cases, both here and abroad, where ex-judges have questioned their own verdicts.'

'I see. But I hope you'll remember to include me, Felu Babu, when you seek his permission. I've never witnessed a seance. I can't miss this opportunity!'

THREE

The next four days passed quickly. We saw the various sights of Srinagar. Lalmohan Babu, who had brought a Hotshot camera, started taking photos of almost everything he saw. Then he took his finished roll to the local branch of Mahatta & Co. and had it developed. The photos had come out pretty well, I had to admit, but when Lalmohan Babu called his effort 'highly professional', I could not agree with him.

Mr Mallik and his party accompanied us one day to see Nishad Bagh, Shalimar and Chashma Shahi. This gave us the chance to get to know him better. 'Sushant tells me you are interested in seances,' he said to Feluda. 'Is that true? Do you believe in such things?'

'I have an open mind on the subject,' Feluda replied. 'I have read a lot on spiritualism. Plenty of well-known and learned people have said it is possible to contact the dead. So I see no reason to scoff at the whole idea without examining it thoroughly. However, I am fully aware of the fraud and deception that often takes place in this particular area. It all depends on the genuineness of the medium, doesn't it?'

'Dr Majumdar is a first rate medium. Why don't you come and watch us one day?'

'I'd like to, thanks. May I bring my cousin and my friend?'

'Sure. I have no objection to anyone, provided they have enough faith. Why don't you come to our boat this evening? Do you know what kind of people I am trying to contact?'

'People you sentenced to death?'

'Yes. I want to find out if my judgement was wrong at any time. So far there's been no such indication.'

'Do you speak to just one dead person at a session?'

'Yes. The doctor finds it quite strenuous to handle more than one.'

'What time should we call on you?'

'Ten o'clock at night. We could all sit down together after dinner. There shouldn't be any noise at that time.'

We went over to Mr Mallik's boat straight after dinner. Five chairs had been arranged around a table in the living room. We took our seats and got to work without wasting another minute. 'Tonight,' Mr Mallik told us, 'we shall try to speak to a Bihari boy called Ramswarup Raaut. He was hanged for murder ten years ago. Despite certain misgivings and doubts, I passed the sentence because the jury found him guilty, and the murder had been a brutal one. But in these ten years, I have often wondered if I had made a mistake. Did I send an innocent man to his death? The case against him had been very cleverly prepared and it seemed he was indeed the culprit, yet . . . anyway, are you ready, doctor?'

'Yes.'

All the curtains had been drawn. The room was totally dark. To my right sat Feluda, and on my left was Lalmohan Babu. To Feluda's right Mr Mallik was seated and beside him was Dr Majumdar, who completed the circle.

'Ramswarup Raaut was only nineteen,' Mr Mallik went on. 'His features were sharp, his complexion fair. He had a thin moustache. The deceased had been stabbed to death in a small alley in Calcutta. Raaut did not look like a vicious killer. You must try to picture him and concentrate on the image. I will ask the questions; the answers will come in Raaut's voice, through Dr Majumdar.'

We sat in silence for fifteen minutes. Then, suddenly, I felt the table move. The movement increased, until it began to rock violently. We waited with bated breath.

A minute later, Mr Mallik asked his first question: 'Who are you?'

'My name is Ramswarup Raaut.'

Dr Majumdar spoke. But his voice sounded totally different. I gave an involuntary shiver. Mr Mallik went on, 'Were you hanged in 1977?'

'Yes.'

'Are you aware that I was responsible for the sentence passed on you?'

'Yes.'

'Did you kill that man?'

'No.'

'Who did?'

'Chhedilal. He was a most cunning man. He framed me. The police arrested me, not him.'

'I could tell when I saw you in court that you could not have planned a murder like that. Yet, I had to pass the death sentence on you.'

'There's no point in worrying about it now.'

'Can you forgive me?'

'Oh yes. I can forgive you easily. But many of my relatives and friends are still alive. They may continue to hold you responsible for my death.'

'I am not concerned with them. It's your forgiveness that matters.'

'Then you have it. Death wipes out anger, jealousy, desire for revenge—everything.'

'Thank you. Thank you very much.'

Mr Mallik rose and switched on the lights. Dr Majumdar appeared to be unconscious. It took us a few minutes to rouse him. What a strange experience! I looked at Feluda, but his face told me nothing.

'I feel a lot better now,' Mr Mallik said. 'I knew my verdict had been wrong in Raaut's case. Now that I know I have been forgiven, my heart feels lighter.'

'Do you hold seances only to reassure yourself?' Feluda asked.

'Partly. Do you know what I really think? Sometimes I seriously wonder whether one man has any right at all to send another to his death.'

'What about murderers? I mean real criminals, not people like Raaut. Shouldn't they be punished?'

'Of course. They may be given long and hard prison sentences, but death? No, I no longer think that's fair. Everyone—even criminals—should be given the chance to mend their ways.'

It was nearly eleven o'clock. We rose to go back to our own boat.

'We are going to Gulmarg the day after tomorrow,' Mr Mallik said before we left. 'Why don't all of you come with us?'

'We should like that very much, thank you. Are you going to stay there?'

'Just for a night. We could go to Khilanmarg from Gulmarg. It's only three miles away—you can walk, or go by horse. Then you can come back with us and spend the night in Gulmarg. Our travel agent will make all the arrangements for you. Shall I ask Sushant to speak to him?'

'Yes, please.'

We said good night and returned to our boat. Feluda said only one thing before going to bed: 'I cannot really agree with Mr Mallik's views. If a murder is committed, then the killer—the real killer, of course—should not be spared. If he has taken a life, he has no right to live. I think age and illness have both affected Mr Mallik's mind. But this has been known to happen to other judges. I suppose it's natural enough.'

'Just think, Felu Babu,' Lalmohan Babu observed, 'how much power a judge is given. One stroke of his pen can take or save a life. Surely anyone with a conscience and a sense of responsibility will wish to use this power only with extreme caution?'

'Yes, you are absolutely right.'

FOUR

Gulmarg was totally different from Srinagar. There were no lakes, or rivers or gardens. What it had was soft, smooth, velvety grass on meadows and slopes, spread over a range of mountains, like rippling green waves. Then there were pine forests and a handful of wooden houses dotted over the valley. It looked as pretty as a picture. In the summer, golfers arrived to play golf in Gulmarg. In the winter, the same slopes, covered with snow, offered skiing.

We had taken a taxi up to Tangmarg, which was twenty-eight miles from Srinagar. The last four miles to Gulmarg had to be covered on horseback. Lalmohan Babu had been duly warned before leaving Calcutta about the possibility of riding a horse. 'Don't worry, it's easier than riding a camel,' Feluda had told him. None of us could ever forget his plight in Rajasthan when he had been forced to ride a camel, many years ago. Thus reassured, Lalmohan Babu had gone to the extent of bringing proper riding breeches. Now, as he dismounted, he declared there was nothing to riding a horse, it was a piece of cake.

As planned, Mr Mallik and the others had travelled with us. We were all going to spend the night here, then go to Khilanmarg in the morning. Khilanmarg was another three miles away and two thousand feet above Gulmarg. Then we would return to Srinagar.

We had been given two adjoining cabins to stay the night. Ours was smaller than Mr Mallik's. Three members of his team turned up to see us in the evening, as we were sitting out on our balcony, sipping tea. We recognized two of them—they were Sushant Som and Mr Mallik's son, Vijay. But the third man was a total stranger. A good-looking man, he must have been in his early thirties. All three appeared to be in the same age group.

'Allow me to introduce him,' Mr Som said. 'This is Arun Sarkar. He is a businessman from Calcutta, but we got to know him in Srinagar. He is one of the gamblers. That should make it easier to place him!'

Everyone laughed. 'Perhaps you can guess why we are here,' Mr Som went on. 'Both these men were eager to meet a real-life private investigator. Mr Ganguli here is a famous writer, too, isn't he?'

Lalmohan Babu tried to smile modestly.

'Tell us about some of your cases,' Vijay Mallik said to Feluda. 'We're really interested.'

Feluda had to oblige. When he had finished describing a couple of his best-known cases, Arun Sarkar asked, 'Is this your first visit to Kashmir?'

'Yes. When I saw you, Mr Sarkar, I thought you were a Kashmiri yourself. Have you visited Kashmir many times?'

'Yes. As a matter of fact, I spent a few years of my childhood in Srinagar. My father was the manager of a hotel. Then we left Srinagar and went to Calcutta more than twenty years ago.'

'Can you speak the local language?'

'A little.'

Feluda now turned to Vijay Mallik. 'Aren't you interested in your father's work? I mean, the seances—?'

Vijay shook his head emphatically. 'My father has become senile,' he said. 'He keeps talking about withdrawing the death penalty. Can you imagine allowing a murderer to get away with his crime? What could be more unfair?'

'Is your father aware of your views?'

'I don't know. You see, I am not very close to my father. We usually leave each other alone.'

'I see.'

'But if what he's doing is bringing him peace of mind, I see no reason to object.'

'What about your mother?'

'My mother's no more. She died four years ago.'

'Do you have siblings?'

'I had a brother. He was much older than me. He went to America and was working there as an engineer, but he died last year. His American wife never came to India. I have a sister, too. She's married and lives in Bhopal.'

'You are not very interested in Kashmir and its scenic beauty, are you?'

'No, I am not. But how did you guess?'

'It's pretty obvious from the way you spend most of your time indoors, playing cards.'

'You're right. I am a rather prosaic sort of a person. Mountains and rivers mean very little to me. A few friends and a pack of cards are enough to keep me happy.'

Arun Sarkar smiled at this. 'I am different,' he said. 'I like cards *and* I enjoy the scenery. Perhaps that's because of my early years in Kashmir.'

'Anyway,' Vijay Mallik rose to his feet. 'It's time we went. I managed to rope in Sushant today. Are either of you interested in cards?'

'We were planning to go for a walk right now,' Feluda replied. 'You'll play all evening, won't you?'

'Yes, certainly until eleven.'

'Very well, I'll drop by when we get back.'

'OK, see you then.'

All three left with a friendly wave. 'Why don't we save the walk until after dinner?' Lalmohan Babu suggested.

'So be it!' said Feluda.

We had told the cook to make rice and chicken curry for dinner. The meal he produced at half past eight was really delicious. We finished it quickly, then set out for our walk, eager to see the town of Gulmarg at night.

It was a quiet place, although its streets were not totally deserted. The people we saw were chiefly tourists, foreigners outnumbering Indian visitors. Lalmohan Babu was still trying to sing a ghazal, his voice trembling occasionally because of the cold.

'You're feeling cold and uncomfortable, aren't you?' Feluda asked him after a while.

'Ye-es, but I am not complaining, Felu Babu. Cold it might be, but the air's so clean and pure. Most refreshing, isn't it?'

'So it is. However, I don't think we should stay out late. Come on Topshe, let's get back.'

We made an about turn, passed the main street and made our way through a stretch that had no houses or any other sign of habitation. Our cabins were on the other side of this open space. It was here that something completely unexpected happened.

An unknown object came flying through the air and shot past

Feluda's ear with a whoosh, missing it by less than an inch. Then it struck against a tree and fell to the ground. Feluda was carrying a torch. He shone it quickly on the object. It was a large stone. Had it not missed its target, Feluda might well have been badly injured.

The big question was: who could have done such a thing? We had only just arrived here. Nothing untoward had happened yet to warrant an investigation. Sometimes, we were threatened or attacked as an investigation got under way. At this moment, that was out of the question. What, then, could be the reason behind this?

When we were back in our cabin, Feluda said, looking grave, 'I don't like this at all. It is obvious that my presence here is unwelcome, someone would like to have me out of his way. That can only mean a criminal activity is being planned. There is absolutely no way of guessing what it might be.'

'I hope you brought your revolver, Felu Babu?' Lalmohan Babu asked anxiously.

'Yes, I always take it with me wherever I go. But how can I use it, when nothing has actually happened?'

'We'd better take every possible care, Felu Babu. Let's make sure all doors and windows are locked and bolted at night. We mustn't take any chances. But isn't it absolutely amazing? I mean, why do troubles start the minute we set off on a holiday?'

Feluda did not reply. After a brief pause, he simply said, 'You two can go to bed. I'll just go and have a game of poker with the boys next door. I should be back in an hour.'

FIVE

The next morning, we left for Khilanmarg at nine o'clock, after a quick breakfast. We had to walk uphill for three miles, to climb the additional two thousand feet. Only old Mr Mallik chose to take a horse. The rest of us decided to go on foot. There were nine of us in the group, including Arun Sarkar and Prayag (Mr Mallik's bearer). The way to Khilanmarg was most picturesque. There were colourful flowers on both sides of the path.

I have found new energy in these seven day,' Lalmohan Babu declared. 'Covering two thousand feet doesn't strike me as a problem at all.'

We began our journey. The others dispersed in smaller groups, but the three of us stayed together. It took us two hours to reach Khilanmarg. The sight that met our eyes as we got to the top rendered us completely speechless. There was snow on the ground as well as on all the peaks immediately visible. Stretched below us, right up to the horizon, was a green valley, complete with shimmering lakes and rippling rivers. Behind it rose Nanga Parvat, sculpted against the sky, tall and majestic.

'I don't think there is any view in Kashmir more beautiful than this!' Feluda exclaimed softly.

Lalmohan Babu took out his camera. 'Come on everyone, let's have a group photo!' he called. 'Stand on the snow here, please. It'll make a fantastic picture.'

A sudden commotion from the other group made me tear my gaze away from the mountains. Then I heard Mr Mallik's voice: 'Vijay? Where is Vijay?'

A quick glance told me Vijay Mallik was the only person missing. Could he simply have fallen behind? It did not seem likely. They had not been walking together, it was true; but a single member could not have got totally separated from everyone else without a good reason. Sushant Som spoke next: 'Why don't you wait here, Mr Mallik? Let me go and have a look.'

'We'll go with you,' said Mr Sarkar and the doctor.

We, too, joined the search party, retracing our steps slowly over the path we had just climbed up. My heart beat faster. Where had the man gone?

'Vijay!' Mr Som called loudly. There was no reply.

We continued to climb down. About fifteen minutes later, Lalmohan Babu stopped suddenly, staring at a bush. Feluda followed his gaze and ran over to the bush immediately. Through its leaves, a man's foot was sticking out. Or—strictly speaking—it was a mountain boot.

'Mr Som! Over here!' Feluda yelled. Mr Som ran across, followed by the others.

Vijay Mallik was lying on his stomach, unconscious. Feluda felt his pulse and said, 'He's alive. I think he received a blow on his head, which made him faint.'

Luckily, there was a stream nearby. One of the men ran to bring water from it. Vijay Mallik opened his eyes when his face had been splashed with water a few times.

'Where? . . .' he asked, looking around in a puzzled fashion.

'How did this happen?' Feluda asked sharply.

'Someone . . . pushed . . .'

'It seems as if you fell from quite a height, rolling down the hill.'

'Yes . . . I remember bending over a flower . . .'

'You struck your head against this tree trunk. That's what broke your fall, I think, but you lost consciousness with the impact.'

'Yes . . . perhaps . . . '

'Do you think you could get up?'

Feluda put his arms round Vijay's shoulders and helped him to his feet. Vijay swayed unsteadily for a few moments, then managed to stand upright. Feluda looked at his head and said, 'There's a swelling, but no bleeding. You may well be in pain for a few days. I suggest we go back immediately. We'll try to get you a horse; in the meantime, walk slowly. When we're back in Gulmarg and you're feeling better, I'd like to talk to you.'

Vijay seemed to have recovered a little. He raised his hand gingerly and felt the swelling on his head, then started walking. I wondered confusedly who had done this to him. Why had he been attacked?

It was evening by the time we reached Gulmarg. We went straight to our cabin.

'We must have a cup of tea before we do anything else,' Feluda announced, calling the bearer a second later. Then he lapsed into silence. I noticed his brows were knotted in a heavy frown.

Much to our surprise, just as we had finished having our tea, Vijay himself arrived at our cabin, accompanied by Mr Sarkar and Mr Som. 'I had to come and see you, Mr Mitter,' he said. 'I have never felt so perplexed in my life.'

'Can you think of anyone here who might have a grudge against you?'

'No. Who could it be, unless it was either of these men here, or Dr Majumdar? That's a preposterous idea!'

'You did not run into any old acquaintance in Srinagar?'

'No.'

'Is there anyone back in Calcutta who might bear you a grudge?'

'Not that I am aware of.'

'Did you go to college in Calcutta?'

'Yes, Scottish Church.'

'And was your student life more or less troublefree?'

'Er. . . no, not exactly.'

'Oh? Why not?'

'When I was in my second year in college, I fell into bad company. I began taking drugs.'

'Hard drugs?'

'Yes. I tried cocaine . . . and morphine.'

'What happened next?'

'My father came to know. He was still working as a judge. He tried very hard to make me give up drugs, but couldn't.'

'Even so you finished college?'

'Yes. I was a brilliant student, as it happened.'

'Were you at home throughout?'

'Initially, yes. But once I had left the university, I felt I had to get out. So I left home and travelled to Uttar Pradesh. I met an extraordinary man in Kanpur. His name was Anandaswamy. He was a sadhu, and he made me see the error of my ways. It was really nothing short of a miracle. I finally came to my senses, and went back home. I haven't touched drugs since. My father was very pleased to have me back. He forgave me completely.'

'How old were you at the time?'

'Twenty-seven or twenty-eight.'

'What did you do next?'

'My father found me a job in a private firm. I am still working there.'

'You have a special weakness for cards and gambling, haven't you?'

'Yes, that is true.'

'Has that ever created a problem?'

'No.'

'If I were to ask you whether you had any enemies, what would you say?'

'As far as I know, there is no one who might want to kill me. There may be people who envy me for small things; but then, nearly everyone has enemies like that. Even you must know people who dislike you, or envy your success.'

'That's true. Let me now ask you something about other people. How long have you known Dr Majumdar?'

'He's been our family physician for the last fifteen years.'

'I see. I've now got a question for Mr Som.'

'Yes?'

'How long have you been working as Mr Mallik's secretary?'

'Five years, ever since he retired.'

'How long has the bearer Prayag worked in his house?'

'About the same length of time, I should think. Mr Mallik's old bearer, Maqbool, died rather suddenly. Prayag was appointed in his place.'

'Very well. I think we'll give it a rest now. But may I ask you further questions later, if that becomes necessary?'

'Of course,' replied Vijay Mallik.

SIX

'Back to square one, Felu Babu?' Lalmohan Babu asked. We were back in our houseboat in Srinagar, and were sitting on the upper deck, having tea.

'Yes, so it would seem,' Feluda replied solemnly. 'Crime and mysteries seem to chase me every time I go on holiday and plan to relax for a while. But I must admit I have never felt so puzzled in my life. There's nothing I can work on, no leads at all.'

He finished his tea and lit a Charminar. Then, after a brief pause, he added, 'I ought to ask Mr Som to lend me Mr Mallik's diaries.'

'Why? What good would that do?'

'That's difficult to tell. But of course I'll have to get Mr Mallik's permission. That's why I must ask Mr Som.'

'You can do that right away. Look, there he is!'

Mr Som was in a shikara, returning from the Boulevard. Judging by the parcels in the boat, he had been out shopping. Feluda leant over the railing and called, 'Hello Mr Som! Could you stop here for a moment?'

Mr Som's shikara slowly made its way to our boat.

'Did you bring Mr Mallik's diaries with you?' Feluda asked.

'Yes, all twenty-four of them.'

'Do you think I might borrow them? I mean, two or three at a time? I couldn't really work on this case unless I learnt something more about Mr Mallik and his family. The diaries might help.'

'All right, let me ask him.'

'Thank you.'

'I don't think he'll object. He has already told you so much about his life.'

Mr Som left, but returned half an hour later with four old diaries.

'Mr Mallik agreed at once,' he told us. 'He said once his book is. published, everyone will come to know everything, anyway. In any case, the criminal cases he talks about were all reported in the press, so they're no secrets.'

'Thank you. I will let you know when I finish these, and get a few more . . . Topshe, why don't you and Lalmohan Babu go and see Manasbal Lake? I need to stay indoors to work.'

'Oh by the way,' said Mr Som. 'Aren't you planning to go to Pahalgam?'

'Yes, we certainly are.'

'When do you want to go? It might be better if you came with us. We're going there the day after tomorrow.'

'Very well.'

I stared at Manasbal Lake in wonder. Its water was so clear that I could see all the underwater vegetation. I had never seen a lake with such amazingly clear water.

Lalmohan Babu was similarly impressed, but I could see that he was thinking about Feluda and his investigation. 'I can't see why your cousin is reading all those diaries,' he remarked after a while. 'Surely those who have been hanged already will not come back to commit a fresh crime?'

'No, but Feluda must have his own reasons.'

Manasbal was eighteen miles from Srinagar. By the time we got back, it was half past six. Feluda was still in the living room, reading a diary. 'I have finished reading eleven of them,' he told us. 'Each one was interesting.'

'Really? But did it do you any good? I mean, can you now see your way forward?'

'It isn't always' possible to tell in advance what good a certain activity might do. All I am interested in, right now, is gathering information; and I've learnt some new things today, not only from the diaries. For instance, Vijay Mallik came and told me that when he was pushed, he felt something cold and metallic touch his neck. I think it was a ring, but that doesn't really help because three people were wearing rings yesterday—Mr Som, Mr Sarkar and Prayag. If the culprit was someone outside this group, there's no way we can catch him. Dozens of people must wear rings.'

'Yes, but how many went to Khilanmarg yesterday?'

'I can remember a group of Punjabis. There were five of them. Three were on horseback.'

'I don't think anything unpleasant is going to happen now, Felu Babu.'

'I hope you are right. Who wants problems in paradise, especially when I can't exercise my brain?'

Feluda finished reading the remaining diaries the next day.

'What did they tell you?' Lalmohan Babu asked.

'There were six cases, in which Mr Mallik seemed sure that the accused should have been sent to prison, not hung. He was very unhappy about the sentences he had himself passed. One case in particular involved a Kashmiri called Sapru. Mr Mallik felt such remorse after sentencing him to death that he developed angina soon afterwards, and had to retire.'

Pahalgam was sixty miles from Srinagar. It was a small town in the Lidar valley. The river Lidar flowed by its side. It was not a large river, but moved with considerable force. Many foreigners came to catch trout in it. Snow-covered mountains were visible from Pahalgam. A few hotels had been built recently, but it was still possible to stay in tents by the river. That was what we decided to do.

We left in four taxis, and reached Pahalgam by twelve o'clock. To the west of the river stood hills, without any sign of habitation. To the east lay the town, complete with hotels, restaurants and shops. Like everything else we had seen so far in Kashmir, it looked absolutely enchanting.

When we arrived, our tents were being put up. They were special tents, almost like apartments, including bedrooms, dining rooms and even attached bathrooms. We had one tent; Mr Mallik had been given two. The river was only about twenty yards away. The sound of its gushing waters did not stop even for a second.

'I had seen people live like this only in Hollywood westerns,' Lalmohan Babu enthused. 'Who knew one day I would be staying outdoors?'

After lunch, we saw Mr Som making his way to our tent.

'Have you had lunch?' he asked.

'Yes, we've just finished.'

'There's a place called Chandanwadi, eight miles from here. Did you know that?'

'Isn't there a bridge there that stays covered by snow throughout the year?'

'Yes.'

'Do you plan to see it?'

'Yes. Would you like to come with us?'

'Certainly, but we've only just arrived. Why don't we look at Pahalgam today, and go to Chandanwadi tomorrow?'

'That's what I was going to suggest myself. I only came to invite you today.'

'Thank you. Perhaps we really ought to travel together. I could keep an eye on things. What's happened already is bad enough. I wouldn't hesitate to call it attempted murder. Vijay Mallik is a lucky man to be alive today.'

'We could leave tomorrow after lunch, say around two. We'll have to take horses and ride the eight miles.'

Mr Mallik came out of his tent, calling his bearer: 'Prayag! Prayag!'

Prayag was washing his hands in the river. He did not reply.

'Perhaps he can't hear you because of the noise from the river,' Feluda remarked.

'No, he's a little deaf. I usually have to call him at least three times before he can answer me.' Mr Mallik shouted again. This time, Prayag heard him and came running.

'Bring me my walking stick,' Mr Mallik ordered.

'Ji, huzoor,' said Prayag and went inside. I saw Feluda give Prayag a sharp glance, but could not figure out why.

In the meantime, Vijay and Mr Sarkar had emerged from their tent. Mr Sarkar was probably planning to stay with the Malliks throughout their tour.

'We're going to Chandanwadi tomorrow,' said Mr Som. The others nodded approvingly. Feluda turned to us. 'Why don't you get a couple of chairs from the tent and sit here by the river?' he said. 'I want to go for a walk. That ought to clear my head.'

'When will you be back?'

'In an hour, I should think.'

'I hope you've got your reliable weapon with you?'

'Oh yes.'

Feluda left. Lalmohan Babu and I sat outside, enjoying the scenic beauty of Kashmir. The others returned to their tents. Lalmohan

Babu said he had thought of a plot for his next novel and described it to me. I listened to him carefully, then suggested a few changes. All this took about an hour and a half. Sitting by the river was so pleasant that we nearly lost track of time, but Lalmohan Babu suddenly looked at his watch and exclaimed, 'It's two hours since your cousin left! Surely he should have been back by now?'

I gave a start. I had completely forgotten about Feluda.

'What should we do?' Lalmohan Babu went on. My years with Feluda had taught me to take quick decisions. I stood up. 'Let's go and look for him,' I said.

'All right.'

We had seen Feluda go up a narrow path. We went the same way, slowly climbing up a hill. The path ran through a pine wood, but we were no longer in a mood to appreciate its beauty. Something awful must have happened, or Feluda would have been back by now.

In half an hour, my worst suspicions were confirmed. We found Feluda sprawled on the ground behind a bush. My throat went dry immediately. I could barely move. It was Lalmohan Babu who leapt forward and felt his pulse.

'It's all right, he's alive!' he cried. A few seconds later, Feluda groaned and sat up slowly. Then he felt the back of his head and made a face. 'This time he did not miss,' he said to me. 'Whoever it was, Topshe, hit his target most accurately.'

'Can you get up?'

'Yes, yes, my head's aching; there's nothing wrong with my legs.'

He rose to his feet, leaning on us for support. Then he took a couple of cautious steps and said, 'OK, I think I can walk now.' Lalmohan Babu released his arm and said, 'Did you see who did it?'

'No. That would have solved the entire mystery, Lalmohan Babu. Our culprit isn't a fool. I have to think very hard, look at everything from a different angle. I need more time . . .'

We returned to our tent. Later that night, Mr Mallik called us over for another seance. We had seen one before we left Srinagar, during which the spirit of someone called Shasmal had appeared and admitted that he was indeed a murderer, so the sentence passed on him was fully justified.

This was to be our third seance. Tonight, Mr Mallik wanted to speak to Sapru, the same Kashmiri man Feluda had told us about. Dr Majumdar was a very good medium indeed. Sapru arrived within minutes.

'Why have you called me here?' he asked.

'I was the judge at your murder trial. I was responsible for your death.'

'You passed the sentence . . . yes, I am aware of that.'

'I don't think you committed the murder.'

'You're right, I didn't. It was committed by a man called Haridas Bhagat. The police went off on the wrong track and arrested me. But none of that matters any more.'

'I have been worried since 1978. I have had no peace.'

'Would you like me to say I forgive you?'

'Yes!'

'Very well then, I do. But I cannot speak for my family. They may never be able to forgive you.'

'That does not matter. I am only interested in your forgiveness.'

'You may set your mind at rest. I have nothing against you. Goodbye!'

The seance was over. Mr Mallik looked visibly relieved.

We returned to our tent. I was so tired that I fell asleep almost as soon as my head touched the pillow.

SEVEN

The next morning, Feluda shook me awake. One look at his face told me something disastrous had happened.

'Mr Mallik has been murdered!' he said briefly.

'*Wha-at!*'

My scream woke Lalmohan Babu.

'Last night,' Feluda went on, 'someone stabbed him in the chest after midnight. Then he smashed his head in as well, just to make sure, I suppose. It's a horrible sight.'

Lalmohan Babu and I sprang to our feet, threw some warm clothes on and came out of our tent. I could hardly believe what I had just heard.

Everyone else was gathered outside Mr Mallik's tent, looking baffled and distressed. Vijay Mallik had left to inform the police. The main town wasn't far, so it shouldn't be long before the police came.

Dr Majumdar had been the first to discover the body. The weapon had not been found.

'It will probably never be found,' I thought to myself. 'No doubt it's been thrown into the river. God knows how far it's already travelled with the gushing waters!'

But it wasn't just a case of murder. A valuable diamond ring Mr Mallik used to wear on the third finger of his right hand (given to him by a Gujarati client) was missing.

Feluda was talking to Dr Majumdar. 'When did Mr Mallik go to bed last night?' he asked.

'Much before any of us did. Normally, he used to retire by nine o'clock, unless he wanted to sit up late for a seance.'

'You are a doctor. Can't you tell us when he might have been killed?'

'At a guess, I'd say he was killed between two and two-thirty in the morning. But a police surgeon will be able to fix the time of death far more precisely.'

'You didn't hear any noises last night? Nothing that might have disturbed your sleep?'

'No. I sleep very soundly, Mr Mitter. I hardly ever wake up at night. But I am an early riser. I got up as usual at six-thirty this morning, and discovered what had happened. Prayag had risen before me, but had gone out of the tent without looking in on his master. So he didn't see anything.'

'Do you have any idea who might have done this?'

'No, none whatsoever.'

At this moment, a police jeep arrived and stopped a few feet away. Vijay climbed out of it, followed by a police officer in uniform. 'I am Inspector Singh,' he said to us. 'I am taking charge of this case. Where's the dead body?'

Vijay took him inside. We remained where we were. A couple of constables and a photographer followed them in and began their work. I had seen this many times before, so this time I felt no curiosity. Besides, I had no wish to see Mr Mallik's dead body. All I could think of was how he had been worried about sentencing innocent people to death, and now he was dead himself. Would his killer ever be caught and brought to justice?

Feluda had moved to one side and was standing alone. Lalmohan Babu went over to talk to him. 'What's the matter, Felu Babu?'

'I was trying to unravel a tangle—now I am more confused than ever. That's the matter, Lalmohan Babu. Now let's see if the police can do anything.'

'Don't tell me you have given up?'

'No, no, of course I haven't. I know a lot of things the police don't. But what I can't make out is whether everything is linked together, or whether they are all separate incidents. Someone threw a stone at me, and someone pushed Vijay Mallik. Was it the same person? And did he also commit the murder? But then, if the main motive was theft, then anyone could have walked in to steal the diamond ring and been forced to kill its owner. But—' Feluda stopped. After a few seconds, he added, 'I cannot rule out murder by a burglar, but what I really think is that someone known to Mr Mallik is responsible for his death.'

'Known to him? Who?'

'Everyone he's been travelling with, including Mr Sarkar. Don't forget the golden ring he wears. It has the letter "S" engraved on it.'

I failed to see how this was significant, but couldn't ask because at this moment, Inspector Singh and Vijay Mallik emerged from the tent.

'Do all three tents belong to one single party?' the inspector asked.

'No. The first two are ours. The third is Mr Mitter's.'

'Mr Mitter?'

'Pradosh Mitter. He is a well-known private investigator from Calcutta.'

Inspector Singh frowned a little, then walked across to us. 'Mr Mitter? Are you the one who helped solve the murder case in Rajgarh?' he asked.

'Yes, that's right.'

The inspector offered his hand and shook Feluda's. 'Pleased to meet you, sir,' he said. 'The officer who worked with you on that case—Inspector Vajpayee—is a good friend of mine. I have heard a lot about you. In fact, he had nothing but praise for you.'

'That is very kind of him. But I am here at this moment purely by chance. I wasn't called in to solve any crime. You mustn't think I am going to interfere in your work.'

'No, I wasn't thinking that at all. But since you know the family already, why don't you proceed with your own investigation? I think it was the job of an outsider, you know. The man who stabbed Mr Mallik was left-handed. Everyone present here, I can see, is right-handed. Anyway, please feel free to make your own enquiries, if you so wish.'

'Thank you. I can't just stand by and do nothing, Inspector Singh.

You see, I was attacked too. Not once, but twice.'

'Good heavens, I didn't know that! Oh, by the way,' the inspector turned to Vijay, 'What do you want to do with the body? Would you like to take it back to Calcutta?'

'No, there is no need to do that. There is no one left in my family. My mother and brother are both dead.'

'Very well, I will make arrangements for a funeral here. But you must understand one thing. Until certain things become a little clearer, no one from your own party can leave Pahalgam. You are all under suspicion, and I'd like to ask you questions in due course . . . yes, each one of you.'

EIGHT

Inspector Singh stayed on for the next three hours to question everyone. He had a word with Feluda first of all.

'Did you hear anything suspicious last night?'

'No. The noise from the river tends to drown every other sound.'

'Yes, that's true. That's an advantage for a criminal, isn't it? By the way, I haven't met your companions.'

'Sorry, let me introduce them. This is Lalmohan Ganguli, he's a writer; and that's my cousin, Tapesh.'

Inspector Singh asked us the same questions, then allowed us to go into town. The three of us found a restaurant and ordered tea and omelettes. No one had had the chance to have breakfast.

'What surprises me,' said Lalmohan Babu, munching thoughtfully, 'is that when the culprit couldn't kill the son, he decided to kill the father.'

'It may not necessarily be the same man. Someone might have had something against Vijay Mallik, but a totally different person might have attacked his father.'

'My suspicions have fallen on someone.'

'Who?'

'Dr Majumdar. He's supposed to be a doctor, a man of science; and, at the same time, he's speaking to the dead. It's peculiar, don't you think?'

'Perhaps. It's true that he had the best opportunity, since he slept only a few feet away from the deceased. But what motive could he possibly have had? Stealing that diamond ring? If so, he must be in desperate need of money. But there's nothing to indicate that he is.'

'What about Vijay Mallik?'

'He stands to gain a lot, there's no doubt about that. Mr Mallik was pretty wealthy, and Vijay will get all his assets—unless, of course, Mr Mallik made a will and left his money to someone else.'

'But why should Vijay want to kill his father? He's got a good job, he earns reasonably well. Why should he be in need of a vast amount of money? I mean, killing another human being isn't child's play, is it?'

'No, it most certainly isn't, and like you, I cannot see what pressing motive Vijay could have had.'

'Sushant Som? What about him?'

'Qualified and efficient, a man Mr Mallik used to depend on quite heavily. No discernible motive there, either.'

'Well then . . . suppose it was a case of revenge? Surely Mr Mallik had loads of enemies?'

'True. That's what I've been thinking. Just consider the number of people he had sent to the gallows.'

'But . . . well, revenge can be ruled out at least in his son's case, I think.'

'Absolutely, which brings us back to square one.'

After lunch that afternoon, Feluda said he wanted to go for another walk, this time in the main town. Only a long walk would clear his head.

'Keep your weapon with you, Felu Babu, even if you're only going into town,' Lalmohan Babu advised him.

We went and sat by the river again. Mr Som came and joined us.

'A bolt from the blue, wasn't it?' he said, sounding upset.

'Yes, please sit down,' I offered him a chair. What he had said was quite true. We were all still feeling dazed.

'What does the inspector say?' Lalmohan Babu asked.

'He seems to think it's likely that a burglar did it. That ring was very expensive, you see. There was a big diamond, surrounded by emeralds. Although Pahalgam is a small town, burglaries do occur. It's been on the increase ever since tourists began coming here in large numbers. Even thirty years ago, it was a perfectly peaceful and safe area.'

'Are you confined to your tents?'

'No, we are allowed to go into town, but we cannot leave Pahalgam.'

'When is the funeral?'

'This evening.'

Feluda returned at five o'clock. I couldn't help feeling worried while he was gone, but he said now that the police were involved in the case, it was much safer for him to be out and about. Whoever had attacked him wouldn't dare risk being caught by the police.

'I am very glad to hear that, Felu Babu, but did your long walk help you?' Lalmohan Babu asked.

'Yes, it certainly did. But I need to go back to Srinagar, or I couldn't really bring this case to a close.'

'When do you want to go?'

'Tomorrow.'

'What about us?'

'You two should stay on here. I hope to be back in a couple of days. Don't worry about anything. You couldn't possibly be in a more beautiful place, could you?'

'No, but why do you have to rush off to Srinagar? Have you seen the light?'

'Yes. I really had gone blind, I ought to have seen it before.'

'But still there is partial darkness, you reckon?'

'Right, and that's why I have to go back to Srinagar. But before I go, I have to ask a few questions. Let's start with Prayag.'

Mr Som returned to his tent and came back with Prayag. We then went to our own tent.

'Have a seat, Prayag,' Feluda said. Prayag sat down.

'I am going to ask you some questions. I want honest and correct answers. All right?'

'Yes, sir.'

'How long have you worked for the Malliks?'

'Five years.'

'Where were you before?'

'With Mr Jacob. I was his bearer. He lived in Park Street.'

'How did Mr Mallik get you?'

'Mr Jacob was leaving for England. He did not need me any more. So he wrote a letter to Mr Mallik and I took it to him.'

'How did Jacob and Mallik know each other?'

'They went to the same club.'

'What's your full name?'

'Prayag Mishir.'

'Who else is there in your family?'

'No one. My wife is dead. I have two daughters, but they're married. I live alone.'

'I see. Didn't you hear any noise last night?'

'No, sir.'

'Who could have killed your master?'

'I have no idea, sir. I could never have imagined this might happen.'

'Very well, you may go now.'

Prayag left. Feluda got Mr Som to call Dr Majumdar.

'Do you mind if I ask you a few questions?'

'No, go ahead.'

'You are a doctor. Did you really approve of the way Mr Mallik tried to contact the dead?' Dr Majumdar shook his head. 'No, I certainly did not. I told him many times not to meddle in these matters. I also pointed out that a judge was only a human being. If he made an error in passing a verdict, there was really no need to torture himself with it. What was done was done.'

'That's true. But when did *you* realize you had this special power to act as a medium?'

'Many years ago, at least twenty-five years back.'

'Do you have any idea who might have killed him?'

'No, none at all.'

'What do you think of his son?'

'Vijay? He got into a lot of trouble when he was younger—drugs and all that, you see. But later—whether under the influence of a sadhu or something else, I do not know—he recovered and is now leading a perfectly normal life.'

'Isn't gambling one of his weaknesses?'

'I couldn't really comment on that, Mr Mitter. I have never gambled in my life. I know nothing about it.'

'Very well. Where does Vijay work?'

'Chatterjee & Co., import and export.'

'I see. Thank you, Dr Majumdar. That's all for now.'

Dr Majumdar returned to his tent. Mr Som looked enquiringly at Feluda.

'I'd like to speak to Mr Sarkar now,' Feluda said. Mr Som looked profoundly startled.

'Mr Sarkar?'

'Why do you find that surprising?'

'Well, he's an outsider, isn't he? I mean, he just happened to be with us. He didn't know Mr Mallik or any of us earlier.'

'That may be so. But how do you know he isn't in need of money? Anyone can kill anywhere if they need money urgently and desperately.'

'All right, I will go and get him.'

Mr Sarkar arrived in a few minutes.

'Please take a seat,' Feluda said to him.

'I had come here on holiday,' Mr Sarkar remarked, taking the chair he was offered, 'simply to have a good time. Who knew such a terrible tragedy was in store?'

'True. But there's nothing to be done, is there, except to try to accept what's happened?'

'You're right. What would you like me to tell you?'

'How old were you when you left Kashmir?'

'Twelve.'

'You went straight to Calcutta?'

'Yes.'

'Did your father work as a hotel manager in Calcutta also?'

'Yes.'

'Which hotel?'

'The Calcutta Hotel.'

'Are you a graduate?'

'B Com.'

'What do you do for a living?'

'I work in an insurance company—Universal Insurance. The office is at 5 Pollock Street in Calcutta.'

'Did you know Mr Mallik before?'

'Oh no. I came to know him only after reaching Kashmir. I met Vijay on the plane from Delhi, and discovered we had many things in common. So we quickly became friends.'

'Are you fond of gambling?'

'Yes, you could say that, but it isn't a passion with me. Not like Vijay.'

'Why did you decide to come to Kashmir?'

'To see how much it had changed. To compare it with my childhood memories.'

'How long did you intend spending here?'

'Ten days originally. But now God knows how long we'll have to stay here.'

'May I see the ring you're wearing?'

'Certainly.'

Mr Sarkar took his ring off and passed it to Feluda. It was made of gold. A blue hexagonal shape was engraved on it and, in the middle of it, was the letter 'S', inscribed in white. Feluda thanked him and returned the ring.

'I have no more questions for you, Mr Sarkar.'

'Thank you.'

NINE

Feluda took a taxi to Srinagar the next day, soon after breakfast. 'I think I'll be back the day after tomorrow, but I may be delayed by a couple of days. So don't worry,' he said.

Inspector Singh arrived at nine o'clock in his jeep and went to have a word with the others. Then he walked into our tent.

'Where is Mr Holmes?' he asked with a smile.

'He just left for Srinagar,' I told him.

'To work on this case?'

'Yes.'

'But why? This case is easy, clear as crystal.'

'How?'

'It's that bearer who did it. He had the opportunity. He was sleeping in the same tent, wasn't he? That diamond ring must have tempted him. After all, how much does a bearer earn?'

'Are you going to arrest him?' Lalmohan Babu asked.

'Right now, I am simply taking him to the police station for further questions. I know now that he's left-handed. I asked him to write his name. He used his left hand. Even so, he's still denying having killed his master. So I am taking him away.'

'That ring has to be recovered as well,' Lalmohan Babu commented.

'Yes, I am sure he'll tell us where he's hidden it once we've had the chance to speak to him properly.'

Was Feluda's visit to Srinagar purely unnecessary? A complete waste of time? I couldn't bring myself to believe the case was as simple as Inspector Singh had made it out to be. If it was, Feluda would not have gone to so much trouble. I knew he had gone to

Srinagar simply to call Calcutta from there. He knew lots of people in Calcutta who'd get him any information he wanted.

At the same time, didn't the inspector say Prayag was left-handed? But could he really have been stupid enough to think he could get away with it? Didn't he know he'd fall under suspicion immediately?

Inspector Singh left in a few minutes, taking Prayag with him. I felt quite sorry for the man for he was looking frightened and had tears in his eyes. I knew only too well what the police could do to get a confession from a suspect. I had heard Feluda express regret on this matter more than once. 'The police are often very good in their work, very committed,' he had said to me, 'but they are devoid of mercy.' But then, sometimes they have no choice. If stern action was necessary to get a vital piece of information, how could anyone blame them for being ruthless? Certainly, under specific circumstances, the police could act far more effectively than a private detective.

Mr Som paid us another visit. 'Mr Mitter has gone to Srinagar, I believe,' he said.

'Yes,' I replied.

'I must say I am surprised to see how much he's prepared to do for us, even without being asked.'

'He wouldn't wait to be asked. He's taken the whole thing as a challenge, you see. He cannot stand being confronted by an unsolved mystery and will do anything to get to the bottom of it.'

Mr Som nodded. After a while, Lalmohan Babu asked, 'Had you started writing Mr Mallik's biography?'

'Yes. Mr Mallik was checking and correcting what I was writing, and we were making very good progress. It would have been a most interesting book.'

'Now the whole project is going to be shelved?'

'Yes, I can't see what else can be done.'

'Tell me, do you think Prayag did it?'

'No, I would never have thought he'd have the nerve. But the police . . .'

'Did you know about the attack on Mr Mitter?'

'What! No, I had no idea. What happened?'

'Someone hit him with a heavy object, perhaps a stone. Luckily, he wasn't badly hurt. But it's clear that someone has objections to his presence here, and would like him out of the way.'

'Why doesn't he ask for police protection?'

'No, he'd rather die than do that, although he'd always be prepared to help the police.'

'Are you still playing poker?' Lalmohan Babu asked.

'Oh no. None of us can think of anything but Mr Mallik's death. Cards have been forgotten.'

Feluda did not return the next day. Lalmohan Babu and I took ourselves off to see Shikargah Lake and an old Shiv temple. Both of us felt it was better to stay away from our tent. Mr Mallik's death was still casting a shadow over everyone's thoughts. We felt suffocated in such a sombre atmosphere.

On the third day, just as I was wondering what we should do to keep ourselves occupied, Feluda arrived in a taxi at about ten o'clock. Lalmohan Babu and I went out eagerly to greet him, both of us asking questions. He raised a hand and said, 'Patience, patience. You will be duly rewarded, I assure you.'

'Just tell me if your head feels clear,' Lalmohan Babu implored.

'It does, but it wasn't easy to unravel the tangled mess. It's a very complex case.'

'When will you tell us everything?'

'I have to speak to the inspector first.'

'He has already caught the murderer.'

'What! Who's been arrested?'

'Prayag.'

'Oh God! I mustn't waste another second. I'm off to the police station now.'

Feluda left at once. By the time he got back, it was almost time for lunch.

'We're having a meeting at three o'clock, in the other tent,' he announced. My heart skipped a beat. Feluda's revelations at the end of a case were always incredibly dramatic. Only those who had seen him do it before would understand why I reacted like that.

A police jeep arrived soon after three. Inspector Singh got out of it and found Feluda.

'Can you believe that a police inspector might be interested in crime stories?'

'You mean *you* read them?' Feluda laughed.

'Yes, I am passionately fond of detective novels. I am now reminded of quite a few famous stories, Mr Mitter, though I have no idea what you're going to reveal in a few minutes.'

'You shall learn soon enough.'

We went into the other bigger tent. Everyone else was already gathered there. Vijay Mallik, Mr Som, Mr Sarkar and Dr Majumdar were seated on chairs. Prayag was standing in a corner. He looked exhausted. The police had obviously been thorough in their questioning.

TEN

Feluda rose from his chair and glanced at the assembled group. Then he poured himself a glass of water from a jug, drank some of it, and began speaking.

'Mr Mallik is no longer with us. I am going to start by talking about him. Siddheshwar Mallik worked as a judge for thirty years before ill health forced him to retire. But it could also be that he had lost some of his faith in the entire system of law and justice. He had started to question the validity of the death penalty. I am not going to discuss whether or not he was right in thinking what he did. I am merely going to describe events as they occurred.

'Mr Mallik used to keep diaries. There was something special about these. He used to mark the days on which he passed a death sentence by writing the name of the condemned man and putting a red cross against it. If he wasn't entirely satisfied that his verdict was justified, he used to put a question mark against that cross. I have seen Mr Mallik's diaries. There were six question marks, which meant he had doubts about six men. They might have been innocent, but Mr Mallik had to send them to their deaths.

'Now I would like to draw your attention to something else. Mr Mallik expressed his doubt about the accused, but nowhere in his diaries did I find any mention of the family or friends of these men. I don't think he ever thought about the feelings of parents or wives or children, or anyone who might have known these men closely. But it is not difficult to imagine the pain these people must have suffered.

'As soon as I realized this, I began to wonder if Mr Mallik himself might have been murdered by one of these people, who might have felt he was responsible for the death of an innocent man. The desire for revenge can be kept alive for many years. The more I thought about it, the more likely did it seem.

'Now, the question was: could any one among those present here be a relative or friend of a man hanged for murder, though he might not have been the real culprit?

'Dr Majumdar could be ruled out immediately, as he had been Mr Mallik's physician for fifteen years. This left me with four people: Mr Som, Vijay Mallik, Mr Sarkar and Prayag. Vijay could be dropped from the list since none of his friends had been sentenced to die. The same rule applied to Mr Som. So, in the end, I was left with only Mr Sarkar and Prayag. Now I'd like to ask Prayag a question.'

Prayag stood in silence. Feluda looked straight at him. 'Prayag,' he said, 'when you were washing your hands in the river the other day, I saw that two letters from the English alphabet had been tattooed on your right arm: "HR". What do these letters stand for?'

Prayag swallowed. 'They don't mean anything, sir,' he said slowly. 'I wanted to have a tattoo done on my arm. The fellow who did it put those letters there, that is all.'

'Are you telling me that they are not your initials? Nothing to do with your name?'

'No, sir. My name is Prayag Mishir.'

'Really? Suppose I tell you it's not? You fail to respond often enough if anyone calls you Prayag. But you're not really deaf, are you? You can hear perfectly well at other times. Why is that?'

'I am called Prayag Mishir, sir. That is my name.'

'No!' Feluda shouted, 'Tell me what the "R" stands for. What is your surname?'

'What . . . what can I say?'

'The truth. This is a matter of life and death, can't you see? Stop telling lies.'

'Well then, sir, you tell everyone what you know.'

'Very well. The "R" stands for Raaut. Now tell us your full name.'

Suddenly, Prayag broke down. 'He . . . he was my only son, sir,' he sobbed, 'and he didn't kill anyone. But the case against him was so strong, he was so cleverly framed that he had to die. My only son . . . hanged!'

'You still haven't told us your name.'

'Hanuman Raaut. That is my real name. But. . . but I did not kill my master, nor did I steal that ring. I swear I didn't!'

'Did I say you were being accused of murder and theft? All I wanted to know was your name.'

'Then . . . then please, sir, please forgive me.'

'No, Hanuman Raaut, you cannot be forgiven completely. Tell us the whole truth.' Hanuman Raaut stared blankly at Feluda.

'You did not kill your master, it is true,' Feluda went on, 'but you tried to kill someone else, didn't you?'

'No, no.'

'Yes!' Feluda said coldly. 'You wanted to teach your master a lesson, didn't you? You held him responsible for your son's death. So you wanted him to feel the same sorrow and the same pain. Wasn't it you who tried to kill Vijay Mallik? Didn't you push him down the hill in Khilanmarg? You used your left hand, didn't you, on which you wear a ring?'

'But . . . but he didn't die. He is still alive!'

'Attempted murder, Hanuman Raaut, is a serious offence. You will not hang for murder, but what you did was utterly wrong. You cannot escape the consequences.'

Hanuman Raaut did not try to speak after this. Two constables took him away. Feluda drank some more water, then resumed speaking.

'Let me now move on to something else. Something far more serious than what poor Hanuman Raaut did. Yes, I am talking of murder, the wilful destruction of a human life. Whoever took Mr Mallik's life must pay for it by giving up his own. The death penalty in this case would be fully justified.'

Feluda stopped. Every eye was fixed on him. The noise from the river was the only sound that could be heard.

'There is someone in this room I've already spoken to. But I'd like to ask him some more questions,' Feluda went on. 'Mr Sarkar!'

Mr Sarkar moved in his chair.

'Yes?' he said.

'When did you arrive in Srinagar?'

'I arrived with you, by the same flight.'

'There is an "S" engraved on your ring. What does it stand for?'

'My surname, of course—Sarkar.'

'But Mr Sarkar, I have checked with Indian Airlines. On that flight from Delhi, there was no Sarkar on the list of passengers. There was a Sen, two Senguptas, one Singh and one Sapru.'

'But . . . but . . .'

'But what, Mr Sarkar? Why did you feel you had to change your name? Do tell us.' Mr Sarkar remained silent.

'Shall I tell you what I think?' Feluda asked. 'I think you are

Manohar Sapru's son. The same Sapru who had been sentenced to death by Mr Mallik. You look very much like a Kashmiri. Meeting Mr Mallik was an accident, but the minute you recognized him, you decided to change your name and befriended Mr Mallik's son. This gave you the chance to move together with his group, and look for a suitable opportunity to strike. That opportunity came in Pahalgam.'

'But how can you say that? This crime was committed by a left-handed man!'

'Mr Sapru, don't forget I have seen you deal cards. It may have escaped everyone's attention, but I saw you use your left hand.'

Mr Sarkar—I mean Sapru—suddenly lost his temper.

'All right, I stabbed him!' he cried. 'I don't regret that for a minute. He was responsible for my father's death. My father wasn't guilty, but he was hanged because Mallik said so. I was only fifteen at the time. But. . . wait a minute!' Sapru seemed to remember something. 'I did not steal his ring. I only killed him!' he added.

'That's right,' Feluda replied. 'You did not remove the ring. Someone else did that.'

There was complete silence in the room once more. Feluda's eyes moved away from Sapru. 'Vijay Mallik! You have been losing heavily at cards, haven't you? I have made enquiries in Calcutta. I've got various sources of information, I even have friends in the police. You are up to your neck in debt, aren't you?'

Vijay did not answer.

'You were probably uncertain as to whether your father had left you anything in his will. So you hit him in order to snatch the ring from his finger.'

'Hit him? What do you mean?'

'I mean that your father was attacked by two different people. One was Sapru, the other was you. He died from his stab wounds—there is medical evidence to prove that. So Sapru is his real killer. But you were taking no chances, so you crushed his head with a heavy object. It is for the court to decide whether you should be tried for theft or murder, but certainly you are both going to be arrested.'

There was nothing more to be said. Inspector Singh and his men took the culprits away, and we returned to our tent.

'One thing still bothers me, Felu Babu,' said Lalmohan Babu on our return, 'and you didn't shed any light on this matter. Who attacked you, not once but twice?'

'I didn't shed any light, Mr Ganguli, because I was not sure about the answer. It was undoubtedly one of the three culprits—most probably it was Prayag. He had the opportunity each time. He could slip out unseen. It doesn't seem likely that either Vijay Mallik or Sapru would have left their group to follow me. Anyway, that is now irrelevant. It did not affect the main investigation. Take it as a failure on my part.'

'Oh? But that's good news, Felu Babu. It is very reassuring to know that even a super sleuth like you can fail or make mistakes sometimes.'

'Are you trying to be modest, Lalmohan Babu? There's no need. A super sleuth I might be, but I could never write like you, not in a million years.'

'Thanks for the jibe!'

[illegible] about [illegible] could [illegible] that [illegible]

[illegible]

[illegible]

[illegible]

Shakuntala's Necklace

ONE

'Look,' said Lalmohan Babu, 'I have been with you since your visit to Jaisalmer and the golden fortress there, but before that you had been to Lucknow and Gangtok, hadn't you? I didn't know you then, so I have not had the chance to see these two places. I am particularly interested in Lucknow. It's got so much history. Why don't we go back there in the Puja holidays this year?'

The idea appealed to both of us. Feluda loved Lucknow. I was quite young the last time we had been there, when Feluda had solved the mystery of the stolen diamond ring that had once belonged to Aurangzeb. If we went back to Lucknow, I knew I'd enjoy seeing it more than I had done the last time.

It didn't take Feluda long to make up his mind. 'Yes,' he agreed. 'I must admit any mention of Lucknow makes me feel quite excited. It's a beautiful place. How many cities in the country have a river flowing through it, tell me? Besides, it still hasn't lost the old Mughal atmosphere. You can find signs of life from the time of the nawabs, and of course the mutiny of 1857. You're right, Lalmohan Babu. I had been wondering where we might go this year. Let's go back to Lucknow.'

Feluda was earning pretty well these days. He was easily the best known among all the private investigators in Calcutta. He usually got seven or eight cases every month, and he charged two thousand for each. Even so, it wasn't possible to get anywhere near Lalmohan Babu. He had once told us that his annual income was in excess of three hundred thousand. He published two new books every year, and each ran into several editions.

We completed all the arrangements without further ado. Feluda bought three first-class tickets on the Doon Express. It would leave Howrah at 9 p.m., reaching Lucknow at half past six in the morning. He also made our hotel bookings at the Clarks Avadh.

'We couldn't really enjoy ourselves if we didn't stay somewhere comfortable,' he said.

'What's Avadh?' Lalmohan Babu wanted to know.

'Avadh is the Urdu name for Ayodhya.'

'You mean Lucknow is in Ayodhya?'

'Yes, sir. Didn't you know that? The name "Lucknow" has come from "Laxman".'

'Laxman? You mean, as in the *Ramayana*?'

'Right. Clarks Avadh is the best hotel in Lucknow. The river Gomti flows by it.'

'Lovely. Avadh-on-the-Gomti, one might call it. Is it going to be cold?'

'Take a woollen pullover. The evenings may well be cool. Or a warm waistcoat will do, depending on whether you wish to wear western clothes, or dress as a traditional Indian.'

'I think I'll take both.'

'Good.'

'A lot of Bengalis live in Lucknow, don't they?'

'Oh yes. Some families have been there for several generations. There's a Bengali Club where they have Durga Puja every year. Who knows, you may even find people who have read your books!'

'You think so? Should I take a few copies of my latest, *Shaken in Shanghai*?'

'Take a dozen. Why stop at only a few?'

We left on the fifth of October, which was a Saturday. The station was absolutely packed. We were shown into our compartment by a railway official who happened to recognize Feluda. We had been given a lower and two upper berths in a four-berth section. We thanked the official and took our places. The fourth berth was already occupied by a middle-aged man, sporting a thin moustache. He moved aside to make room for us. We didn't have much luggage. Feluda and I had packed our clothes in one suitcase, and Lalmohan Babu had brought his famous red leather case. A friend of his had brought it specially for him, all the way from Japan.

'How far are you going?' asked our fellow traveller when we were all seated.

'Lucknow,' Lalmohan Babu replied. 'What about you?'

'I am also going to Lucknow. That's where I live. My family has been settled in Lucknow for years—we go back three generations. Are you on holiday?'

'Yes.'

Feluda spoke this time: 'I can see three letters on your suitcase: H J B. These are rather unusual initials. Would you mind if I asked your name?'

'Not at all. My name is Jayant Biswas. The "H" stands for Hector. I am a Christian. Everyone in my family has a Christian name.'

'Thank you. Please allow us to introduce ourselves. I am Pradosh Mitter, this is my cousin Tapesh and that's my friend, Lalmohan

Ganguli.'

'Pleased to meet you. You may have heard of my mother-in-law. She used to be an actress in silent films, and was quite well known.'

'What was her name?'

'Shakuntala Devi.'

'Good heavens!' Lalmohan Babu exclaimed. 'She was a major star in her time. One of my neighbours has old issues of the *Bioscope* magazine. He used to be a regular film buff in his youth. I've seen Shakuntala Devi's pictures in those old magazines, and read articles on her. She wasn't a Bengali, was she?'

'No, she was an Anglo-Indian. Her real name was Virginia Reynolds. Her father, Thomas Reynolds, was in the army. He could speak fluent Urdu. He married a Muslim singer. Virginia was their daughter.'

'Highly interesting,' Lalmohan Babu remarked, 'but she didn't work in a single talkie, did she?'

'No. She married a Bengali Christian before talkies began to be made in India. Then, when she was expecting her first child, she retired from films. Her first two children were girls, the third was a boy. I married her second daughter in 1960. My wife's sister married a Goan. Their brother has remained a bachelor.'

Feluda spoke again: 'Didn't a maharaja give Shakuntala Devi a valuable necklace at one time?'

'Yes, that's right. It was the Maharaja of Mysore. He was so moved by Shakuntala's acting that he gave her that necklace. Even in those days, it was worth a hundred thousand rupees. But how did you learn about it? Shakuntala stopped acting before you were born.'

'True. But I read a report about it fifteen years ago. This necklace was stolen and then recovered by the police, wasn't it?'

'Right. Shakuntala was alive at the time. She died only three years ago, at the age of seventy-eight. There were stories about the necklace even after her death. But how did you manage to remember something you had read fifteen years ago? You must have a very sharp memory.'

'I have always been interested in news on crime. And yes, I can usually recall things I've read. Perhaps I should tell you the whole truth. You see, my profession is related to crime and criminals.'

Feluda took out one of his cards and offered it to Jayant Biswas. He took it, raising his eyebrows. 'A private investigator! Oh, I see.

That's why your name sounded familiar. You have a pet name, don't you?'

'Yes. I am called Felu.'

'That's right. Feluda. My daughter's an ardent admirer of yours. She has read all your stories. I am very glad to have met you.'

Feluda now turned to Lalmohan Babu. 'I don't know if his name has reached Lucknow,' he said, 'but he is a very well-known writer in Bengal. He writes under the pseudonym of Jatayu.'

'Really? Who knew I'd get to meet two famous personalities tonight in the same compartment? Where will you be staying in Lucknow?'

'The Clarks Avadh.'

'I see. I live on the other side of the river, in Badshah Bagh. I will contact you in Lucknow. All of you must come and have a meal with us. My wife is a great cook, and Mughlai food is her speciality. And of course my daughter's going to be thrilled to meet her hero.'

'Thank you,' said Feluda. 'We'd be very glad to come. Perhaps we can see that famous necklace?'

'Oh sure. That's not a problem at all, since it's with me. I mean, my wife has got it.'

'That's a bit odd, isn't it? Surely it should have been given to Shakuntala's elder daughter? Didn't you say you had married the younger one?'

'Yes. The reason is quite simple. Virginia—I mean Shakuntala—was deeply fond of my wife, Suneela. Suneela is extremely talented. A gifted actress, she might have gone into films and become a famous star like her mother. But she chose to be a simple housewife instead.'

'Suneela? Doesn't she have a Christian name?'

'Yes. Her full name is Pamela Suneela.'

TWO

I went to sleep at ten o'clock and woke at half past six. Breakfast was served when we reached Buxar. We were supposed to reach Mughalsarai at a quarter to nine. Lunch would be served at twelve-thirty, our bearer told us. By that time we should have reached Pratapgarh.

Mr Biswas turned out to be an early riser. After breakfast, he said,

'Someone I know is travelling in the next compartment. Let me go and say hello to him.'

Lalmohan Babu, I noticed, had had a shave and was looking quite fresh. He was currently using imported razors. A friend had brought him twenty from Kathmandu. Each lasted three or four shaves, then had to be discarded.

'What will you do when you run out of these?' Feluda asked him. 'Go back to ordinary Indian blades?'

'No, sir,' Lalmohan Babu grinned. 'I rather like to indulge myself when if comes to shaving. I buy Wilkinson blades from New Market.'

'But that's really expensive.'

'Yes, but I don't have any other expenses to handle, do I? I live alone, so I like to spend my money on myself.'

'We contribute quite a lot to your expenses, Lalmohan Babu. Just think how often we use your car?'

'Heh, that's hardly a problem. We are the Three Musketeers, remember? How can one of them travel in his own car, leaving the others to look for taxis? I never heard anything so ridiculous.'

Feluda lit a Charminar and went into the corridor for a walk. He returned in five minutes and said, 'I found Mr Biswas and another man deep in conversation in coupe number one. He appeared to be an Anglo-Indian, although his complexion wasn't all that fair.'

'Did you hear what they were saying?' Lalmohan Babu asked curiously.

'I only heard what this other man was saying. He said, "I can give you just three days." That was all.'

'Did it sound like a threat?'

'Difficult to say. One has to raise one's voice so often in a moving train. Perfectly harmless words may sound like a threat.'

A little later, Mr Biswas came back with the man he had been speaking to. 'I thought you might like to meet Mr Sukius,' he said to Feluda. 'He's a well-known businessman of Lucknow; and a connoisseur of art.'

'I hope we will meet again in Lucknow. Mr Biswas and I are old friends,' Mr Sukius said, shaking hands with Feluda. He left soon after we had been introduced to him.

Feluda turned to Mr Biswas as he returned to his seat. 'You told us your mother-in-law's real name was Virginia Reynolds,' he said. 'Do you know anything about the history of their family? How long have they been in India?'

'Virginia's grandfather, John Reynolds, came to India in 1827. He was nineteen at the time. He joined the Bengal regiment. During the mutiny of 1857, he was posted in Lucknow. He fought bravely for a long time, but was eventually killed. His son Thomas was also in the Bengal regiment and, like his father, was posted to Lucknow after a while. He decided to settle there. He learnt to speak Urdu, began to smoke a hookah, take paan and use attar. Since he was fond of music and dancing, he got professional singers and dancers to perform regularly in his house. Sometimes he even dressed in Indian clothes. In other words, his lifestyle was no different from that of a nawab in Lucknow. People called him "Thomas Bahadur". In the end, he fell in love with a kathak dancer called Farida Begum and married her. They had two sons, Edward and Charles. Neither went into the army. Edward became a lawyer and Charles went to manage a tea estate in Assam. He never returned to Lucknow. Thomas and Farida's third child was Virginia. She was born with her father's pale skin, but her mother's dark hair and eyes. When she began acting in films, she looked beautiful, and not unsuitable in the role of an Indian woman. She spoke both Urdu and English.

'As I told you before, she married a Bengali Christian. He was called Percival Motilal Banerjee. He was, in fact, the producer of Shakuntala's films. It was he who got Virginia to join films and change her name to Shakuntala. He made a lot of money from films. Virginia's father, Thomas Reynolds, had virtually no savings. He might have died a pauper, but Virginia stepped in and took care of her old father.

'Percival and Virginia had two daughters and a son. The eldest is called Margaret Susheela. She is married, as I told you, to a Goan called Saldanha. He owns a shop selling musical instruments.

'I married their second daughter, Pamela Suneela, in 1960. I am in the business of imports and exports. I've told you about my daughter. I have also got a son. Victor Prasenjit. My daughter's called Mary Sheela. I tried to get my son to join me, but he wasn't interested in running a business. He usually does what he likes. Sheela finished college two years ago. She is quite a gifted actress, but her main interest is in journalism. She's started writing for various publications. I've read her articles. They're really good.'

Mr Biswas stopped and lit a cigarette, having offered one to Feluda.

'Interesting,' Feluda said briefly.

'Highly romantic!' Lalmohan Babu declared. 'Tell me, has your wife ever worn that necklace?'

'Yes, she's worn it to a few parties. But usually it stays locked in a chest. You'll see how valuable it is when I show it to you.'

'I can't wait!' Lalmohan Babu cried.

'You'll have to be patient, Mr Ganguli, for just another four days,' Mr Biswas told him.

THREE

We had been in Lucknow for the last three days. My mind kept going back to our first visit—Emperor Aurangzeb's diamond ring, Dr Srivastava, Bonobihari Babu's amazing zoo, Haridwar and, finally, our spine-chilling adventure on the way to Laxmanjhoola.

On that occasion we had stayed with a friend, not in a hotel. Clarks Avadh had probably not even been built at that time. It was a really good hotel. We had been given a double and a single room. Both overlooked the river. When the sun set every evening on the other side of the Gomti, it was a sight worth seeing. The food, too, was excellent. We had stayed in many hotels in various parts of the country, but I couldn't recall a single place where the food had been quite so delicious.

Lalmohan Babu had seen most of the important sights in these three days. We had begun with the Bara Imambara. Its huge hall—unsupported by pillars—made my head reel once more. Lalmohan Babu was speechless. All he said, as we left, was: 'Bravo, nawabs of Lucknow!'

The Bhulbhulaiya nearly made him faint. When Feluda told him the nawabs used to play hide-and-seek with their begums in this maze, he grew totally round-eyed.

The Residency was another surprise. 'This . . . this is like going back in time, Felu Babu! I can almost hear the cannons and smell the gunpowder. My word, did the sepoys really cause such a lot of damage to this strong and sturdy building?' Lalmohan Babu exclaimed.

On the fourth day, we went out to the local market to buy bhoona peda, a sweetmeat Lucknow is famous for. On our return to the hotel, we found an invitation to dinner. It had been sent by Hector

Jayant Biswas, inviting us to attend his silver wedding anniversary in two days time. There was a map enclosed with the invitation, which showed clearly where his house was located. We already knew it was on the other side of the river. With a map like that, we should have no difficulty in finding it.

Mr Biswas rang us in the evening. 'All of you must come,' he said. 'You'll get to meet some other people, and of course I'll show you Shakuntala's necklace.'

We spent the next two days looking at the Chhota Imambara, Chattar Manzil and the zoo. Lalmohan Babu was most impressed to find animals in the open and not locked in cages. 'The Calcutta zoo should also be like this!' he proclaimed.

In the evening, we took a taxi to Mr Biswas's house. The map we had been sent was a very good one. Our driver found his house quite easily. It was a bungalow, large and sprawling. Flowers bloomed in the big front garden. A cobbled driveway led to the front door. When we rang the bell, a bearer in uniform opened the door. We could hear voices from the living room. Mr Biswas came out quickly. 'I am so glad you could come!' he said warmly. 'Do come in and meet the others.'

We followed him into the room where a few other people had assembled. Perhaps many more were expected. The first person we were introduced to was Mr Biswas's wife, Pamela Suneela. She had clearly been good-looking at one time. Her daughter—Mary Sheela—was attractive and smart. Her son, however, was just the opposite: he sported long, thick, unruly hair untouched by a comb, an unkempt beard and a moustache. His name was Victor Prasenjit.

Mrs Biswas's sister and brother-in-law—Mr and Mrs Saldanha were also present. Mrs Saldanha may have been pretty once, but had now put on a lot of weight. Her husband, on the contrary, was very thin. He seemed to be about sixty. I remembered being told he sold musical instruments. There was no one else in the room apart from these family members.

The room was fairly large. I was surprised to find that a screen had been put up in one corner. Opposite it stood a projector. I looked enquiringly at our host. 'We have got a print of the last film in which Shakuntala Devi appeared. We'd like to show one reel from it before dinner,' he explained. 'You'll see her wearing that famous necklace.'

That should be quite interesting, I thought. Mary Sheela came up to speak to Feluda.

'I am a fan of yours. I would love to have your autograph but, right now I haven't got an autograph book. I'll buy one and call on you at your hotel before you leave,' she said.

A bearer came in with a tray of drinks. We picked up three glasses of orange juice. Samuel Saldanha approached us. 'My shop is in Hazratganj,' he said. 'Why don't you come and see it one day? I should be very pleased if you did.'

'Thank you. Do you sell Indian instruments?'

'Yes, we sell sitars, as well as western instruments.'

At this moment, we were joined by another gentleman. Judging by the resemblances between him and Mrs Biswas, he was her brother. But his skin and his eyes were lighter, which made him look more European than Indian. He picked up a glass of whisky and turned to us.

'I am Albert Ratanlal Banerjee, Jayant's brother-in-law,' he said. 'You are—?'

Mr Biswas stepped forward and quickly introduced us. 'Private detective?' Ratanlal raised his eyebrows. 'Are you here working on a case?'

'No, no,' Feluda smiled. 'I am here purely on holiday.'

Another man emerged from the house. He seemed to be about the same age as Mr Saldanha. Perhaps he lived here. I looked at him in surprise. His clothes were dirty, he hadn't shaved for a couple of days and his hair hung down to his shoulders. He was a total misfit among the other people.

Mr Biswas laid a hand on his shoulder and brought him over to us. 'Meet Mr Sudarshan Som,' he said. 'He is an artist, a well-known painter of portraits. He did many portraits of Shakuntala. He's been living with us since his retirement.'

I had never heard of an artist retiring so early. Now I noticed the portrait of a woman in one corner of the room. Was that Shakuntala Devi? She must have been about forty when that portrait was painted, which meant she had already given up films. Sudarshan Som picked up a whisky from a tray. For some odd reason, I felt a little sorry for the man. Samuel Saldanha and Ratanlal had started a loud argument on current politics. Mr Som went and joined them.

I kept wondering when we'd get to see the necklace. Mrs Biswas and her sister were moving among the guests, making sure they were being looked after. Mrs Biswas stopped as she saw Feluda and exclaimed, 'What is this? Just orange juice? Don't tell me you don't drink!'

'No, I don't, Mrs Biswas,' Feluda replied with a smile. 'In my profession, it is best to keep a clear head at all times.'

'But I always thought private detectives drank a lot.'

'Perhaps you got that idea from American crime thrillers.'

'Yes, perhaps. I am very fond of reading thrillers.'

'Oh, by the way,' Feluda couldn't help saying, 'your husband offered to show us your mother's necklace.'

'Yes, of course! I am so sorry, Mr Mitter, ! completely forgot. Sheela!'

Sheela came over to her mother.

'Yes, Ma?'

'Be a sweetheart, and bring me your grandmother's necklace. Mr Mitter would like to see it. You know where the key is kept.'

'Yes,' she said and left immediately.

'Don't you keep the key with you?' Feluda asked.

'No, it is kept in the drawer of my dressing table. We hardly open the chest. It is perfectly safe, really. The few servants we've got are all old and trustworthy. Suleman, who opened the door for you, has been with us for thirty years.'

Sheela returned in three minutes, carrying a dark blue velvet box. Her mother took it from her and opened it. 'Here it is,' she said, turning the open box towards us.

Each of us gave an involuntary gasp. Never before had I seen a piece of jewellery with such exquisite craftsmanship. It was a golden necklace with a delicate design, studded with diamonds and pearls and many other precious stones.

'A remarkable object,' Feluda said. 'Truly a unique piece. Do you have any idea how much it's worth today?'

'I don't know . . . in excess of two hundred and fifty thousand, I should imagine.'

'I see. Go and put it back, Sheela. It's best not to keep something valuable like this out for long.'

Sheela left with the necklace.

I had noticed that Sheela's brother was making no attempt to talk to us. In fact, he looked distinctly uncomfortable and was obviously not enjoying himself. Perhaps he was one of those young men who cannot feel at ease unless they are with their own set of friends.

The round of drinks was coming to an end. I saw a man come in and start fiddling with the projector. After a while, he called out to Mr Biswas, 'I am ready.'

'All right. Ladies and gentlemen, we are now going to watch a part of the last film Shakuntala Devi featured in. Suleman, please switch the lights off.'

The room was plunged in darkness. The projector began running noisily. A second later, the first scene appeared on the screen. 'This film was made in 1930,' Jayant Biswas told us. 'Just before talkies began to be made in India.'

I watched Shakuntala Devi with some interest. She was undoubtedly a beauty—even today, one didn't often get to see such a beautiful woman in films. It was clear why she was so successful. She had touched the hearts of people—from maharajas to. paanwalas—not merely because of her looks, but also because of her acting. Despite the drawbacks of a silent film and the overtly theatrical style of acting, Shakuntala Devi emerged as a gifted performer.

The film ran for ten minutes. All the lights were switched on again, and people began talking. Suddenly I realized someone had slipped in while the room was dark. It was Mr Sukius. He had presumably not been invited, for I heard him apologize for barging in. Mr Biswas waved aside his apologies and asked him to stay for dinner. Only a few minutes later, a bearer appeared at the door to announce that dinner had been served.

When we returned to our hotel after a sumptuous meal, it was a quarter past eleven. The party must have continued for quite a while after our departure.

FOUR

Feluda shook me awake the next morning. I sat up quickly.

'What is it, Feluda?'

He looked grim. 'Mr Biswas rang me just now. Shakuntala's necklace has been stolen.'

'Oh my God!'

'Get ready as quickly as you can. I'll go and tell Lalmohan Babu. We must go back there after breakfast. I believe everyone except Mr Sukius has already arrived after they heard the news.'

'Haven't the police been informed?'

'Yes, but they want me as well.'

We reached Mr Biswas's house by half past eight. The cheerful atmosphere of the night before was replaced today by a sombre silence.

'I can't help feeling I am responsible,' Feluda said. 'That necklace was taken out yesterday only because I asked to see it. It may well have nothing to do with the theft, but I thought I ought to tell you how awful I feel.'

The police had already appeared. The inspector in charge greeted Feluda with an outstretched arm. 'Mr Pradosh Mitter?' he said, shaking hands, 'I have heard of you. I am Inspector Pandey.'

'Pleased to meet you, sir.'

'I assume you'd like to make your own enquiries?'

'Yes, but only after you've finished.'

'Thank you.'

Inspector Pandey began asking questions. It was gradually revealed that when the last guest had left after midnight, Mrs Biswas retired to her bedroom and suddenly felt like looking at the necklace once more. As she confessed herself, 'It is probably only my vanity that made me want to open the chest and look at the necklace. I had just watched my mother wear it on the screen and it looked lovely on her. So I thought I'd put it round my own neck and see how I looked. But . . . but when I took out the key from my dressing table drawer and opened the chest, I couldn't find it anywhere. I called my daughter immediately and asked her if she had put it back. She was absolutely sure that she had. It had always been kept in that chest. Where else could she have put it, anyway?'

'You had a dinner party last night, didn't you?' the inspector asked.

'Yes,' Mrs Biswas replied.

'When did it start and how long did it continue?'

'It went from a quarter to eight to midnight.'

'Mrs Biswas, did you go straight to your room after the party was over?'

'Yes.'

'And how long was it before you discovered the necklace was missing?'

'About fifteen minutes.'

'You didn't leave your room during that period?'

'No.'

'That means it was stolen during the party.'

'So it seems,' Mr Biswas remarked. 'When my daughter brought the necklace out to show it to Mr Mitter, the party was in full swing.'

'After that, Miss Biswas, did you put the necklace back where you had found it? Did you go back to your mother's room straightaway?'

'Of course!' Mary Sheela said firmly. 'I didn't waste even a second.'

'Perhaps I ought to mention, Inspector, that soon after the necklace was taken away, all the lights in the living room were switched off to screen a film. The room remained dark for ten minutes.'

'How many servants do you have?'

'Three. A cook and two bearers.'

'How long have you had them?'

'Fifteen years or more. Suleman, the old bearer, has been with us since the time of my father-in-law,' Mrs Biswas said.

'Then there is only one conclusion to be drawn,' Inspector Pandey declared. 'If you think your servants are all above suspicion, the necklace was taken by one of those present at the party. I am sorry, Mr Biswas, but every reason points that way.'

I—and possibly Feluda and Lalmohan Babu—could only agree with him. Inspector Pandey now turned to Feluda.

'Mr Mitter, who are your companions?'

'Sorry, I should have introduced them before. This is my cousin, Tapesh; and that's my friend, Lalmohan Ganguli. He is a well-known writer.'

'How long have you known him?'

'More than five years.'

I looked at Lalmohan Babu. He had turned pale. For a moment, I tried to picture him as a thief. Even at this critical moment, I nearly laughed out loud.

Fortunately, the inspector changed the subject. 'How many people live in this house?' he asked.

'Apart from my wife and myself, my two children and Mr Som, the artist.'

Mr Som was present in the room with all the others. His stubble was heavier today which made him look even more haggard.

'What about the others?' Inspector Pandey went on.

'Mr Saldanha and his wife live in Clive Road. Mrs Saldanha and my wife are sisters.'

'I can see one more gentleman.'

'Yes, he is my wife's brother, Ratanlal Banerjee.'

'Was there anyone else at the party?'

'Only one other person. In fact, he had not been invited, but he happened to drop by. It was Mr Sukius. He arrived while the film was being shown. I saw him only when the lights came on.'

'What does Mr Sukius do?'

'He is a collector of antiques and art objects. He is also a professional moneylender.'

'Did he ever show an interest in that necklace?'

'Yes. He wanted to buy it, but I refused to sell.'

'I see.'

Inspector Pandey was silent for a few moments. Then he said, 'I think we are agreed that one of the guests at dinner removed the necklace. The question is: where has it gone?'

Mr Biswas cleared his throat. 'If you wish to search us and the house, please feel free to do so.'

'Yes, I'm afraid I am going to have to do that. I've arranged a couple of women police officers to search the women. The house will have to be thoroughly searched.'

No one raised any objection. Only Mr Saldanha said, 'I have to go and open my shop at ten o'clock. I'd be grateful if you could search me first and allow me to leave before ten.'

Feluda was silent all this while. Now he said, 'I am going to go back to the hotel. If you find the necklace, Mr Biswas, please let me know. If you don't, I will come back this evening.'

We returned to our hotel. Lalmohan Babu joined us in our room.

'Can you remember how many times this has happened before? I mean, this business of going on a holiday and getting mixed up in a mystery? Telepathy, that's what it must be!' he observed.

'All right then, Lalmohan Babu, let me test your memory,' Feluda laughed. 'I have tested Topshe often enough, but not you.'

'Very well sir, I am ready.'

'Let me ask you something about Shakuntala Devi's family.'

'All right.'

'What are the names of her three children?'

'The elder daughter is called Susheela.'

'Yes, but there's a Christian name before that.'

'Oh yes. The Christian name . . . ah . . .'

'Topshe, do you remember?'

Luckily, I did. 'Margaret,' I said.

'Good. What is Mrs Biswas called, Lalmohan Babu?'

'Pamela Suneela.'

'Right. Her brother?'

'Ratanlal. Albert Ratanlal Banerjee.'

'Fine. Now tell me the names of the Biswas children.'

'Mary Sheela and Prasenjit. I can't remember his Christian name.'

'Victor. Margaret Susheela came with her husband. What's he called?'

'Samuel Saldanha.'

'Very good. Who else was there?'

'That artist fellow. What's his name, now? . . .

Topshe?'

'Som. Sudarshan Som.'

'Well done.'

'Don't mind my saying this, Felu Babu, but I didn't like that man.'

'Why not?'

'He looked weird, as if he was really quite mad. Hadn't shaved for days, his clothes hadn't been washed probably for weeks! . . .'

'Artists don't always keep themselves spruced up. They don't often live by social norms.'

'Perhaps, but in my view he and one other person are the prime suspects.'

'Who is this other person?'

'Victor Prasenjit Biswas. Looks like a hippie, a good-for-nothing. But I noticed he wasn't drinking.'

'Perhaps that was because his father was present.'

'Could be. Anyway, there was someone else present at the party.'

'You mean Mr Sukius?'

'Correct. He wanted to buy the necklace, didn't he?'

'He is an art collector. Any art collector would want to buy something so beautiful. That is to say, he'd want to buy if he had sufficient resources. If he didn't, he might try to get it through unfair means. We know nothing about Sukius or his financial status. Let's not waste any more time in idle speculation. We're free until Mr Biswas rings us in the evening. What about a trip to Kaizer Bagh?'

'Excellent idea, Felu Babu. If getting involved in a case meant going back without seeing all the important sights of Lucknow, I'd be very disappointed.'

FIVE

Jayant Biswas rang us later, as promised. The police had been meticulous in their search, but the necklace had not been found. They had even questioned the servants, to no avail.

'I'll come over, Mr Biswas,' Feluda told him. 'Now I'll start my own investigation. It won't clash with what the police are doing, I assure you.'

We took a taxi from the hotel, crossed the Gomti bridge and reached Mr Biswas's house. It still wore a rather forlorn air.

Suleman opened the door once more and showed us into the living room. Mr Biswas was seated on a sofa. He rose as we entered the room.

'They couldn't find it,' he said, shaking his head sadly.

'That's hardly surprising. A clever thief like that would never leave it lying about, would he?'

'Would you like to search the house yourself?'

'No, no. I only want to speak to everyone in your family. Who is at home right now?'

'My wife, my daughter and Mr Som. I don't think my son is back yet.'

'I see. I also need to talk to Mr Saldanha and Mr Sukius.'

'That shouldn't be a problem. I'll give you their addresses.'

'Very well. Let me start with you.'

'Go ahead. You wouldn't mind a cup of tea, would you?'

'No, that would be very nice, thank you.' Suleman was told to get four cups of tea. Feluda lit a Charminar and began his questions.

'You told the police Mr Sukius had wanted to buy that necklace. How long ago was that?'

'About a year ago.'

'How did he learn about the necklace?'

'Lots of people know about it. It's been written about more than once. When my mother-in-law died, the *Pioneer* published a short biography which mentioned the necklace. Sukius is really a moneylender. I mean, that's how he's made his money. Normally, one doesn't associate a moneylender with anything as refined as art and aesthetics. But Sukius is different. I have been to his house. He has exquisite taste.'

'How did he react when you refused to sell the necklace?'

'He was naturally very disappointed. He had offered two hundred thousand. I might have agreed, but my wife wouldn't dream of parting with it. And now, the very same . . .' he left his sentence unfinished and sighed.

'Do you suspect anyone?'

'No. I still feel perfectly amazed. I cannot believe one of my old and trusted servants did it. Yet, who else would have stolen it? Why would they do such a thing?'

'You are a businessman, aren't you?'

'Well yes, I have a small firm. We handle exports and imports.'

'How well are you doing?'

'Not bad, Mr Mitter. I have a partner. We run the firm together.'

'What's he called?'

'Tribhuvan Nagar. We began our careers as clerks in a merchant firm. Thirty years ago, we gave that up and formed our own company.'

'What's the name of your company?

'Modern Imports & Exports.'

'Where is your office?'

'Hazratganj.'

Suleman came back with the tea. We helped ourselves.

'I have one more question,' said Feluda.

'Yes?'

'While the film was being shown yesterday, did you see anyone move or go out of the room?'

'No.'

'Does your son work anywhere?'

'No. I tried to get him to join me, but he refused.'

'How old is he?'

'Twenty-five.'

'What's he interested in?'

'God knows.'

'Thank you, Mr Biswas. May I now speak to your wife?'

'Certainly. But she's very distressed, you understand.'

'I promise I won't take long.'

Mr Biswas went inside to fetch his wife. We had finished our tea by this time. When Suneela Biswas arrived, she looked as if she had spent a long time crying. Despite that, the resemblances she bore to her mother seemed more pronounced today. She said in a low voice:

'You wished to ask some questions, I believe?'

'Yes, only a few. I won't keep you long.'

'Very well.'

'When your mother gave you her famous necklace instead of your elder sister, how did your sister react?'

'She had guessed what my mother was going to do.'

'How?'

'She was my father's pet, I was mother's. She gave me that necklace three years before she died. My sister and I never spoke about it, so really I couldn't tell you how she reacted.'

'Are you and your sister close to each other?'

'Yes. We're getting closer as we're growing older. When we were young, there was a feeling of rivalry between us.'

'You were fond of acting, weren't you?

'Yes. That's why my mother was so proud of me. Susheela—my sister—was never interested in acting.'

'What about your daughter?'

'She's taken part in plays in school and her college. Then she received a few offers from film producers, but did not accept.'

'What does she want to do?'

'Go into journalism. She's already started writing. She wants to be independent and have a career of her own.'

'Do you suspect anyone of having stolen your necklace?'

'No. I cannot help you at all, I am afraid.'

'Did you see anyone leave their seat during the film show last night?'

'No. I thought everyone was totally engrossed in the film.'

'Thank you Mrs Biswas, no more questions for you.'

Suneela Biswas said goodbye and went inside.

Feluda turned to Mr Biswas once more.

'I'd like to see Mr Som, if I may.'

'Sure.'

Mr Biswas disappeared inside and sent Mr Som. Mr Som had shaved this morning, which made him look slightly less unsavoury. He sat on the small sofa opposite Feluda and lit a cheroot. I had seen him smoking a cheroot last night too. A pungent smell filled the room.

'How long have you lived in this house?' Feluda began.

'About fifteen years. Shakuntala Devi herself had brought me here.'

'Didn't you mind having to depend on someone's charity?'

'I had very little choice in the matter, Mr Mitter. I had already crossed fifty. Arthritis affected my right thumb so badly that I could no longer paint. I had no money. If Shakuntala Devi hadn't given me a home, I'd have starved out there in the streets. Of course I didn't like having to depend on anyone. But Shakuntala and her family were very kind, and then young Prasenjit and Sheela also seem to be very fond of me. So now I don't mind so much. I have got used to the idea.'

'Don't you have an income at all?'

'Not really. Some of my old paintings sell occasionally, at very low prices. That brings me virtually nothing. I manage on the allowance Mr Biswas pays me every month. I have a room, and I eat with the family. Cheroots are the only luxury I allow myself, although I have cut down on them.'

'Do you suspect anyone regarding the missing necklace?'

Mr Som remained silent for a few seconds. Then he said, 'I don't suspect any of the servants.'

'Is there anyone else?'

Mr Som fell silent again. 'Look,' Feluda urged, 'if you don't tell me exactly what you think, it makes my job that much more difficult. You do want the necklace to be recovered, don't you?'

'Of course.'

'Well then?'

'There is someone I am not sure of.'

'Who?'

'Prasenjit.'

'Why do you say that?'

'He has changed such a lot. He doesn't speak properly with anyone in the family, not even me. Perhaps he's fallen into bad company. Perhaps he's into drugs, or gambling . . . or something else for which he needs money. I know he hasn't got a job, and the money he gets from his father is never enough. Sometimes he comes to *me* to borrow money, he's that desperate. I've tried talking to him, to make him see reason, but I have failed.'

'I see. Did you see anyone move or walk away when the film was being shown yesterday?'

'No. My eyes never left the screen.'

'All right, Mr Som. That's all for now. Thank you very much, and could you please send Mary Sheela?'

Mr Som left in search of Sheela. She arrived in a few minutes. Dressed in a salwar-kameez, and devoid of jewellery, she looked the perfect modern young woman.

'What were you doing, Sheela?' Feluda asked her when she was seated.

'I was writing an article.'

'For a magazine?'

'Yes, on how to decorate a room.'

'Oh? Are you interested in interior decoration?'

'Yes. I would like to become a decorator one day.'

'Have you had any training?'

'No, no formal training; but I have read quite a lot on the subject.'

'Can you draw?'

'A little. I learnt a few things from Uncle Sudarshan. He used to encourage me a lot when I was a child.'

'How do you get on with your brother?'

'I don't. Not any more. He hardly ever speaks to me. Yet, once we were very close.'

'Do you mind? Does this change in him upset you?'

'It used to. Now I've grown accustomed to it.'

'You did put the necklace back in its usual place, didn't you?'

'Yes, of course! And I replaced the keys.'

'Do you have any idea how it disappeared?'

Sheela smiled, 'No, how should I? You're the detective!'

'Yes, but a detective has to ask question to get at the truth. You know that, don't you?'

'Yes.'

The bell rang before Feluda could speak again. Suleman opened the door and let Prasenjit in. He seemed slightly taken aback to see us, but recovered quickly.

'Detection in progress?' he sneered.

'I was simply asking your sister a few questions. I'm glad you're back because I'd like to do the same with you. Do you mind?'

'Yes, I do. The police tried to question me, too. I didn't answer any of their stupid questions.'

'But I am not the police.'

'That makes no difference. I am not going to open my mouth.'

'Then you will automatically become a suspect.'

'I don't care. Suspicion alone isn't enough to send anyone to prison, is it? Where's the evidence? You have to find the necklace before you can say it's in my possession!'

'Very well, Prasenjit. If you're not prepared to cooperate, there's nothing we can do. We cannot force you to talk to us.'

Feluda rose. Lalmohan Babu and I followed suit.

'Before I go,' he said to Sheela, 'May I please see the layout of your house?'

'Certainly.'

Sheela took us inside. There was a dining room behind the living room. This was followed by Mr and Mrs Biswas's bedroom, which had an attached bathroom. Connecting doors in their bedroom led to a room on either side, which belonged to Sheela and Prasenjit. These also had attached bathrooms. Mr Som's room was next to Prasenjit's.

We returned to the living room.

'I am going to visit you soon with my autograph book,' Sheela said.

'You'd be most welcome,' Feluda replied. 'But please give me a call before you come. If you simply turned up at the hotel, I might not be in. By the way, could I please see your father again?'

Sheela went and called her father.

'Have you finished?' Mr Biswas asked.

'Yes, more or less. Your son didn't allow any questions, unfortunately.'

Mr Biswas shook his head regretfully. 'I am sorry about that, Mr Mitter. Prasenjit is like that . . . I have almost given up on him.'

'Never mind. I wanted to see you about something else. Do you think Mr Saldanha will be at his shop?'

'Yes, I should think so. It's only half past five.'

'Could you give me his telephone number please, and tell me where his shop is?'

Mr Biswas tore a page off a small pad lying next to the telephone and quickly wrote down the shop's address and phone number.

'May I ring him from here?' Feluda asked.

'Yes, of course.'

Mr Saldanha himself answered the phone and told Feluda to go there straightaway.

'There are two other people I have to see,' Feluda said to Mr Biswas. 'Your brother-in-law, Ratanlal and Mr Sukius. I think I'll save the latter until tomorrow.'

'Ratanlal lives in Frazer Road. Let me give you his address as well. The best time to get him is after seven o'clock.'

SIX

I had no idea Saldanha & Co. in Hazratganj was such an old shop. Its threadbare look startled me.

Mr Saldanha was sitting behind a desk. The shop was going to close in fifteen minutes. There was no one except an assistant. Mr Saldanha smiled as he saw us arrive.

'Welcome, Mr Mitter. Do sit down.'

We were offered three chairs.

'I hope we haven't caused you any inconvenience by coming here?' Feluda asked.

'Oh no, not at all. We're about to close, anyway. You may ask me what you like; then when we're finished here. I'll take you to my house. You could have a cup of coffee and meet my wife.'

'That would be very nice, thank you. I would like to ask your wife a few questions as well. You see, I have to speak to everyone who was present at the party.'

'That's all right. I don't think she'll mind.'

'Very well. Let me begin with you. How old is this shop?'

'Nearly seventy years. My grandfather started it. It was Lucknow's first music shop.'

'There must be other music shops now?'

'Yes, there are two more, both owned by Goans. One belongs to de Mello, the other to Noronha. One of them is not far from here. Sadly, we have not been able to keep up with the times. You can tell that, can't you, from the appearance of this shop?'

'Are you saying that your business isn't doing all that well?'

'What can I say, Mr Mitter? It's the age of competition, isn't it? If I could get my son to join me, perhaps his young ideas would help. But he studied medicine, then went off to America. He's earning a lot of money there, but his old Dad has to look after this old shop. I have a few faithful customers, so I do get by, but things have changed. No one respects simplicity and honesty any more. Everyone wants glamour.'

Feluda made sympathetic noises, then moved to his next question.

'Do you have anything to say about the tragedy that occurred last night?'

'I hardly know what to say. When that necklace went to my sister-in-law, Margaret—my wife—broke down completely. She loved that necklace and was bitterly disappointed it wasn't given to her. And who could blame her? It was so extraordinarily beautiful . . absolutely priceless.'

'You mean you agree that it was unfair of Shakuntala Devi to have given it to her younger daughter, even in the eyes of God?'

'Yes. Why else would Pamela suffer such a tragedy?'

'But who could have taken it? Do you have any idea?'

'No, Mr Mitter, I cannot help you at all in this matter.'

'Are you aware that your sister-in-law's son has fallen into bad company?'

'I had guessed as much, yes.'

'He is probably into drugs. He needs a great deal of money regularly.'

Mr Saldanha clicked his tongue regretfully. Then he said, 'That may be so, Mr Mitter, but I cannot believe he'd steal and sell such a prized possession. No, that seems quite far-fetched.'

'Did you see anyone go out of the room during the film show?'

'No, but I saw Sukius come in.'

'Thank you.'

It was time to close the shop. We got to our feet. When we reached Mr Saldanha's house in his car, it was a quarter past six and quite dark. Like Mr Biswas's house, it was a bungalow, but smaller in size. The drawing room appeared rather bare. Mr Saldanha obviously wasn't as wealthy as his brother-in- law, and his wife not that keen on interior decoration.

'Margaret, you have visitors!' called Mr Saldanha. Margaret Susheela arrived a moment later. 'Oh, it's you!' she said, smiling a little. But the smile did nothing to hide the look of exhaustion on her face.

'Please sit down, Mrs Saldanha,' Feluda said. 'Perhaps you don't know that Mr Biswas asked me to investigate this business of the stolen necklace.'

'I had guessed.'

'May I ask you a few questions in this regard?'

'Yes, certainly.'

Mr Saldanha got up, 'Let me go and get changed, Mr Mitter; and I'll get us some coffee.'

He went inside. Margaret Susheela took a chair and looked at Feluda.

'How long have you been married?' Feluda began after a short pause.

'Thirty-five years.'

'Your son is in America, I believe. Do you have any other children?'

'A daughter. She's married. Her husband owns an apple orchard in Kulu. That's where they live.'

'What's the difference in age between you and your sister?'

'Just two years.'

'Have you always been close?'

'We were very close when we were little. We played together, wore similar clothes, went to the same nursery school.'

'What happened when you grew older?'

'When I was about fifteen, I realized our mother was much more fond of Pam than she was of me. There was a reason for this. Pamela was better looking and far more talented. She was good at acting, elocution and music. She even fared better in studies. I could feel my mother's affection moving away from me. She gave Pam all her attention. Our father loved me a lot, but that didn't seem to make up for the loss of mother's affection. I felt quite jealous of Pam. And then . . . then that necklace was given to her. I have never felt so let down in my life. I was the elder daughter. It should have come to me. It took me a long time to get over my disappointment.'

'What about now? Are you still jealous of her?'

'No. All that's history now. We are very fond of each other. You saw us yesterday. Did we appear distant?'

'Not at all.'

'It's not just love that I feel for my sister. Sometimes I even feel pity.'

'Pity? Why is that?'

'My brother-in-law's business is not doing well. They are in trouble. Money has become a serious problem.'

'Really?'

'Yes. I am saying this to you in absolute confidence. Pam's husband has piled up a lot of debts, and is drinking heavily.'

'But only yesterday they threw a party!'

'I know. I can't imagine how they did it. My husband and I were very surprised to receive an invitation.'

'Perhaps things are better now.'

'Perhaps. But even two months ago, my sister often used to come to me and tell me of her problems. Sometimes she cried. Besides, their son isn't . . . you know about their son, I assume?'

'Yes.'

'I just hope you're right and things have improved in their house.'

'Do you have any idea who might have stolen the necklace?'

'None whatsoever. It's a big mystery to me.'

'Don't you suspect Prasenjit?'

'Prasenjit? Pam's son?'

Mrs Saldanha pondered for a while. Then she said slowly, 'Perhaps I ought to mention this. When that film was being screened, Prasenjit was sitting next to me. He left his seat during the show. I do not know where he went.'

'Did you see anyone else move?'

'No. I was engrossed in the film. I saw it after twenty years.'

'Thank you, Mrs Saldanha. No more questions.'

We had coffee after this, and left. As we emerged outside, Feluda said, 'Albert Ratanlal. Then we can call it a day.'

We went to Ratanlal's flat from the Saldanhas' house. I was surprised by the opulence that greeted my eyes, in direct contrast to the house we had just left. The flat was large—in fact, very large for one person. The sitting room was filled with expensive furniture and various *objets d'art*. Ratanlal was lounging in a sofa, listening to ghazals on a hi-fi stereo. He was dressed in a silk dressing gown, and a pipe hung from his mouth. The whole room reeked with the smell of attar.

He switched off the stereo as he saw us enter and said, 'Why, whatever's the matter?'

'I have a few questions to ask you, Mr Banerjee,' Feluda explained, 'regarding the theft last night. I have to speak to everyone who was present.'

'Everyone?'

'Yes. Sukius is the only person left. I'll go to him tomorrow.'

'Do you think I might be the thief?'

'No. But I do think you might help me catch whoever it was.'

'Mr Mitter, I am not in the least bit interested in the theft.'

'How can you say that? What was stolen was not just valuable, but such an exquisitely beautiful object. How can you be totally disinterested in it?'

'It was a gift from the Maharaja of Mysore, so obviously it was expensive. There's nothing surprising about that.'

'But it was so precious to your mother!'

'So what? Look, neither my mother's jewellery nor her career in films is of any interest to me. I think all films are rotten, certainly silent ones.'

'What, may I ask, do you do for a living?'

'Yes, you may. I am the assistant manager in a mercantile firm.'

'And you cannot help us in any way?'

'No. I am very sorry, but I have nothing to say to you.'

'One last question—did you see anyone move during the film show?'

'No. I wasn't watching the film, however. It was boring. I saw Sukius come in.'

'Thank you. Goodbye, Mr Banerjee . . . I see that you're fond of Indian music, like your grandfather.'

Ratanlal made no comment. He simply switched on the stereo again. We came away.

SEVEN

The next day, Feluda said, 'Why don't you two go to Dilkhusha? I have a few things to do. I must make an appointment with Sukius, and also speak to Inspector Pandey.'

Lalmohan Babu and I left after breakfast. Instead of taking a taxi, we took a tonga this time. It was his idea, since he had heard Feluda and I had ridden in tongas during our last visit.

'Can you tell me the history of this place, dear Tapesh?' he asked on the way. I told him what I knew: 'Early in the nineteenth century, Nawab Sadat Ali had this building built, though he did not live here permanently. He brought his friends over sometimes, to have a good time for a few days. It had a most scenic view. Deer roamed in his gardens. Sadly, now the whole place is in ruins, but there is a beautiful park next to it. To the north of Dilkhusha is the famous La Martiniere School. Claude Martin, who was a Major General, built this school in the eighteenth century. You can see it from Dilkhusha.'

It did not take us long to inspect the ruins. 'It's like watching history unfold itself!' Lalmohan Babu enthused. Then we went for a walk in the park, little knowing what an unpleasant experience awaited us.

At first, the park appeared to be empty. Perhaps it was in the evening that most people came here. We made our way through beds of flowers. Soon, a portion of a bench behind a tree came into view. This was followed by voices. What we saw as we passed the tree made my heart jump.

Prasenjit and a couple of other boys of the same age were sitting on the bench, smoking. Their hair was dishevelled, their eyes looked glazed. Now there could be no doubt that Prasenjit was a drug addict. Unless something was done soon, it would be too late for him to make a comeback. Hard drugs made an addict lose all sense of right and wrong. Sometimes people didn't even hesitate to kill.

It took Prasenjit a few seconds to notice us. When he did, his lips spread in a slow, cruel smile.

'I can see the detective's chamchas. Where's the super sleuth himself?' he asked. His voice sounded hoarse, his speech was slurred.

'He didn't come with us,' Lalmohan Babu replied shortly.

'No? Well, it's his loss. He missed witnessing this tremendous scene!'

We remained silent.

'Has the thief been caught?' Prasenjit's voice held open contempt.

'No, not yet.'

'I am the prime suspect, aren't I? Because I need money. Everyone knows that. I have to borrow money all the time . . . just for a glimpse of heaven . . . for an hour or two. Listen—I can tell you this—I wouldn't be foolish enough to steal that necklace. Do you know why? Because I don't need to. My luck has changed. I've been making a lot of money lately. Yes, yes . . . gambling, what else? If I have to borrow money sometimes, it's only because once you've had a taste of heaven, you cannot stop. Why don't you try it, Mr Thriller Writer? Your writing's bound to improve . . . you'll get thousands of new ideas, I promise. Come on, are you game?'

Still we said nothing. What could we say, anyway?

'Remember just one thing, both of you!' Prasenjit suddenly leapt to his feet. His voice was still hoarse, but had a sharp edge to it. Before either of us could ask him what he meant, he took out a flick knife from his pocket and pointed it at us. We were both considerably startled by the speed with which the blade sprang out.

'If I hear that anyone has come to know about my hanging around in this park, I will know who has blabbed. And then you will learn how sharp this knife is. Now clear out from here!'

There was no reason to stay on. We had already seen and heard too much. Lalmohan Babu and I retraced our steps, found another tonga and returned to our hotel. Neither of us spoke on the way back.

We found Sheela in our room, an autograph book in her hand. She stood up on seeing us.

'I'd better be going now,' she said, turning to Feluda. 'I've already taken up quite a lot of your time. Thank you for the autograph. Good luck with your detection!'

When Sheela had gone, Lalmohan Babu described our recent experience. Feluda shook his head sadly. 'There was something odd about the look in his eyes,' he said. 'It was pretty obvious he took drugs. I feel sorry for his parents. A bleak future is all that's in store for him.'

'But does that mean it was he who stole the necklace?' Lalmohan Babu asked.

Feluda made no reply. After a brief pause, he suddenly said, 'Oh by the way, you'll have to go out again, I am afraid.'

'Why?'

'Mr Sukius's telephone seems to be out of order. We'll have to go to his house to make an appointment to see him. I would have gone myself, but Sheela turned up. And now I don't want to go out. I need to think. There's something shaping up in my mind . . . I have to sit quietly and think it through. If you left now, you might get him at home. Go on, Topshe, call a taxi.'

Lalmohan Babu appeared quite pleased by this. 'I was getting tired of all those questions,' he confessed as we climbed into a taxi. 'Now we've got something different to do.'

We found the house easily enough. We told our driver to wait for five minutes and rang the bell. It was a large house. It looked at least fifty years old, but was well maintained. A marble nameplate on the gate bore Sukius's name.

A bearer opened the door.

'Is Mr Sukius in?' Lalmohan Babu asked.

'Yes, sir. May I please have your name?'

'Tell him Mr Mitter has sent his cousin and his friend to see him. We won't take long.'

'Please wait here.'

The bearer disappeared. When he returned less than a minute

later, his whole demeanour had changed. He looked as though he had seen a ghost. His eyes were bulging, his body was trembling and he could barely speak.

'What's the matter? What happened?' we asked in unison.

'P-p-please c-come with me!' he managed, motioning us to follow him.

We went through the drawing room to what appeared to be a study. It was packed with glass cases, some filled with books, others with objects of art. In the middle of the room was a big table. Behind it was a revolving chair. Seated on this chair, leaning forward on the table, was Mr Sukius. His head was resting on the table. The back of his white shirt was soaked with blood. Although his eyes were open, I knew he was dead. Rarely had I seen a sight so horrible.

I heard Lalmohan Babu give a gasp. I myself felt quite stupefied. Lalmohan Babu was the first to recover.

'When did you last see him alive?' he asked the bearer.

What the poor man mumbled amounted to this: Mr Sukius was in the habit of retiring to this room every morning after breakfast. He had no secretary, so he had to deal with his own correspondence and other paperwork. His bearer had instructions not to disturb him at this time of the day unless it was necessary to do so. This morning, Mr Sukius had had breakfast as usual and then disappeared into his study. The bearer found him like this when he came to inform him of our arrival.

'Did anyone else come to see him?' Lalmohan Babu asked.

The bearer shook his head vigorously.

There was an open window behind Sukius's chair. It had no grills. The murderer had undoubtedly gained entry through the window. There was no need for him to have come through the front door.

'Your telephone isn't working, is it?'

'No, sir. It hasn't been working for two days.'

'But—'

I interrupted Lalmohan Babu. 'Never mind about calling the police. Let's go back and tell Feluda. Let him decide what's to be done.'

'OK. Let's do that.'

EIGHT

We reached the hotel in ten minutes. When Feluda heard our story, he put aside the blue notebook he had been studying and put on his jacket. Then, without a single word, he went out of the room with the two of us in tow. His brow was deeply furrowed.

On reaching Sukius's house, he asked the bearer: 'You have a driver, don't you?'

'Yes, sir.'

'Send him to me.'

When the driver arrived, Feluda told him to take the car to the nearest police station to report the murder. The driver left.

We then went into the study.

'Stabbed,' Feluda said briefly, glancing at the body. 'But the weapon has been removed.' Then he bent over the desk and said, 'He was writing a letter when he was killed.'

I had noticed it, too. Nearly a whole page had been filled. Then I heard Feluda exclaim, 'Why, it was a letter to me! Well, in that case . . . I suppose I have a claim on it, even if it isn't right to touch anything before the police arrive.' So saying, he tore off the top sheet from the writing pad, folded it and put it in his pocket. Then he moved to the window and leant out. There was a passage outside—about four feet wide—beyond which was the compound wall of the house. Any able-bodied man could have scaled that wall.

'It is obvious that the murderer was not an educated gentleman,' Feluda observed. 'As far as I can see, this is the work of a hired goonda. Ordinary burglary can be ruled out since nothing has been disturbed. The stuff in this room would be worth at least a hundred thousand rupees. A burglar would have helped himself to at least some of it. The question is: who hired a man to kill Sukius?'

'Well, we need to learn something about Sukius's history, don't we?' Lalmohan Babu suggested. 'I mean, how much do we know about him?'

'It's not as if we know nothing. At least we know what a strange character he was. How many moneylenders are interested in building up a huge collection of antiques and art objects? That's pretty uncommon, isn't it? I believe his letter to me will also reveal a few things about the man.'

'Aren't you going to read it?'

'Yes, at the right time, in the right place. It had "confidential" written on it, which you clearly didn't see. I don't think Sukius saw his killer. So the letter cannot possibly contain his killer's name.'

The police arrived in ten minutes. We met Inspector Pandey again. He shook hands with Feluda. 'You seem to have taken a lead in this case, Mr Mitter!' he smiled.

'That's how it might seem, but it's all yours. Inspector. I am not going to meddle in it at all because I know that won't do any good. Just let me know if you catch the murderer.'

'What! Are you leaving?'

'Yes. But I may see you again in a day or two. I've nearly solved that case of the missing necklace.'

'Really? My suspicious have fallen on the young Biswas boy. Do you think that's right?'

'I couldn't say. Please forgive me.'

'We've got definite proof that he's taking drugs. We're having him followed.'

'Well, best of luck. You've now got a murder on your hands. Tell me something: I know it's possible in most places in the world to hire a killer. Lucknow, I take it, is no exception?'

'Not at all. It is perfectly possible to do that here.'

'Thank you. That's all I needed to know. Goodbye.'

NINE

Feluda did nothing over the next couple of days except accompany us to the remaining sights worth seeing in Lucknow. I had never seen him behave like this when he was in the middle of a case. On the third day, I couldn't help asking him. 'What's the matter with you, Feluda? Have you given up?'

'Oh no. Half the mystery's solved, dear boy. I need help from the police to solve the other half. Pandey has called me twice already. I think I'll get the final news in two days.'

'Why do you need the police to help you? Is it to do with the death of Mr Sukius?'

'Yes.'

'What about the missing necklace?'

'There's nothing to worry about on that score. The necklace is fine.'

'Really? So all you have to do is find the killer? Surely you've got some ideas about who might have done it?'

'Oh, I've got ideas all right, but no proof. I'll get enough evidence, I am sure, the minute that hired killer is caught by the police. I have definite ideas about who had hired him.'

Another day passed. In the meanwhile, we took Lalmohan Babu to see the museum. He had practically finished his sightseeing of Lucknow. We were supposed to return to Calcutta in two days.

That afternoon, Feluda finally got the phone call he was waiting for. He spoke to Inspector Pandey, then replaced the receiver quietly.

'What did he say, Feluda?' I asked eagerly.

'The case is over, Topshe. They caught the man, a fellow called Shambhu Singh. He's made a full confession and agreed to expose the real culprit. The knife that had been used to stab Sukius with, has also been found.'

'So what happens now?'

'We now raise the curtain. At seven o'clock this evening, in Jayant Biswas's house, all will be revealed.'

Feluda had to make a lot of phone calls after this. The first one was naturally to Mr Biswas. 'Very well, Mr Mitter,' he said, 'but would you mind telling all the others to come here? You've got their phone numbers, haven't you?'

We reached Mr Biswas's house at a quarter to seven. I felt both deeply anxious and curious. Feluda had said nothing after making the last phone call. Inspector Pandey arrived at five minutes to seven, together with two constables and a man in handcuffs. That was obviously the hired murderer.

The others arrived within ten minutes. There were five people from the Biswas household, the Saldanhas, and Ratanlal Banerjee. The big drawing room could accommodate everyone quite easily.

'What is this farce?' asked Ratanlal, taking a seat.

'You may call it a farce, Mr Banerjee, but I think to the others it's a serious matter,' Feluda replied.

'Have you found the necklace?' asked Mrs Biswas in an urgent whisper.

'You'll get the answer to your question in due course,' Feluda said to her. 'Please bear with me.' Then he ran his eyes over the assembled group and announced, 'The mystery has been solved. Needless to say, nothing could have been achieved without the assistance of the police. All I want to do now is explain what happened. I hope all your questions will be answered as I proceed.'

'I hope you won't take long. I have a dinner to go to,' Ratanlal muttered.

'I will take not a second longer than is necessary. May I begin?'

There was a moment's silence. Then Mr Biswas said, 'Please do.'

Feluda started to speak again, 'The chief thing to remember is that we had two cases on our hands: the stolen necklace and the murder of Mr Sukius. I questioned each one of you. Some of you lied to me, or tried to hide things, or just refused to answer me. Suspicion could fall on many of you regarding the necklace. Young Prasenjit here has got into the unfortunate habit of taking drugs. He needs money all the time. Sometimes he can borrow it, at other times he is lucky at cards. The second suspect might have been Mr Sudarshan Som. He has spent a large part of his life depending on charity. He might have stolen the necklace in a desparate attempt to start life afresh. Then there was Mr Saldanha. His shop isn't doing well at all. He is certainly in need of money. Only one person seemed above suspicion. It was Mr Biswas, because he said his business was flourishing, he had enough money. However, someone else told me that that was not the case. Mr Biswas was apparently going through a rough patch financially, which had led to his drinking heavily. Of course, whether this information was correct or not is another matter.

'Let me now turn to the murder of Mr Sukius. He was writing a letter when he was killed. It was addressed to me, and he had nearly finished it. The reason why he was writing was that he was leaving for Kanpur the same day. He knew he couldn't meet me, so he tried to tell me in a letter all that he knew.

'I learnt two things from his letter. One, Jayant Biswas had finally agreed to sell Shakuntala's necklace to him, for two hundred thousand rupees. He was going to pass it on to Mr Sukius three days after their agreement. But Sukius was killed before this three-day period was over.

'Two, there is someone present in this room who had borrowed fifty thousand rupees from Mr Sukius six weeks ago. He had promised to return the amount with interest in a month, but despite several reminders, failed to keep his promise. Mr Sukius then threatened to take legal action. He was killed because whoever had borrowed the money didn't want him to tell me any of this. Sadly for him, things didn't work out quite the way he had planned. His accomplice—a hired hooligan—did his job and killed his quarry, but did not remove the letter the deceased had been writing. Obviously, he had no idea what had been said in that letter. The police have now arrested this man and he has offered to show us who had employed him.'

Feluda turned to Inspector Pandey. 'Ask your man to come over here, please.'

The man in handcuffs and the constable were waiting at the far end. At a nod from the inspector, they brought the man forward.

'Tell me, Shambhu Singh, do you see the man who hired you to kill Mr Sukius?' Feluda asked slowly.

The man ran his gaze swiftly through the group.

'Yes, sir,' he replied.

'Can you point him out?'

'Easily. There he is!' Shambhu Singh raised his handcuffed hands and pointed. The pipe from Ratanlal's mouth fell to the ground with a loud clatter.

'What nonsense is this?' he barked.

'Nonsense or farce, your game is up, Mr Banerjee,' Feluda said calmly. A second later, he continued to speak as everyone sat tense and taut in their seats.

'Will you tell us why you borrowed that large sum of money, Mr Banerjee?' Feluda asked.

'I will not!'

'Very well. Allow me to speak for you. What you spent was always in excess of your income, wasn't it? Sukius wrote to me about your visits to singers and dancers and the kind of money you spent on them. When we went to your flat, we could smell attar. Perhaps you had been entertaining a singer, who was hurriedly sent inside when we rang the bell? You do not use attar yourself, do you? If you were in the habit of using attar yourself, you would have used it on the day of the party. This may well be a trait you inherited from your grandfather. He, too, was fond of all the good things in life, I believe. And like you, money had become a serious problem for him in his old age. His daughter had helped him out. You turned to Sukius.'

'Oh my God!' Ratanlal whispered, his head bent low. 'I am finished.'

Inspector Pandey and a constable went over to him.

'I haven't finished,' Feluda went on. 'We still have the first mystery to explain. Mr Biswas wanted to take the necklace and sell it to Sukius, but someone else got hold of it before him.'

'Who?' Mrs Biswas gasped.

'Let me clarify something. At first, most people assumed someone had crept out of the room during the film show and removed the necklace. But that was not the case. I had been standing behind the projector. The room wasn't totally dark and I did remove my eyes from the screen from time to time to look at the others. If anyone left the room, I would certainly have seen him, or her. No one did. Prasenjit was restless. He left his seat and moved to a different chair, but he remained in the room. Then Mr Sukius came in. That was all.'

'So when . . . how? . . .' Mrs Biswas could barely speak.

'The necklace was taken *before* the film began.'

'Yes, I know that,' Mrs Biswas now sounded a little impatient. 'Sheela went and took it out. Then she brought it here, so you could look at it.'

'Ah yes. But did she put it back?'

'Of course she did.'

'No. Sheela did not put it back, but kept it with herself. I had realized this, but couldn't see why she should have done so. At first it was in her room. Then, much later, she dug up a flower pot and hid it in there. This is something I learnt from Sheela herself. Look, here's your necklace.'

Feluda took out the necklace from his pocket and placed it on a coffee table. Everyone gasped in unison.

'But . . . but. . . why did she do such a thing?' Mrs Biswas asked, casting a perplexed glance at her daughter.

'Because the night before, she had overheard you and your husband talking. Her room is next to yours, and there's a communicating door. This door happened to be open. She heard you tell your husband that you had finally overcome your reservations and were willing to sell the necklace to Sukius. Sheela did not want such a precious heirloom to be lost. So she did the only thing she could have done, and removed it from sight. It is because she did so that you can still say it's yours. I do hope it will never leave this house. You must not let go of something like this. It would be nothing short of a crime, Mrs Biswas!'

'Felu Babu,' Lalmohan Babu asked when we were back in our hotel, 'Lucknow means good-fortune-right-at-this-moment, doesn't it?'

'Luck-now? Yes, if you want to put it like that.'

'Well, who is the lucky one here?'

'Why, you are! Didn't you get to witness the brilliance of my intelligence, all for free?'

'And think of the Biswas family,' I put in. 'Aren't they lucky to have a clever girl like Sheela *and* to have their necklace back?'

'True,' Lalmohan Babu agreed. 'A girl like Sheela is one in a million. What do you say, Felu Babu?'

'If there is anyone who appreciates the real value of Shakuntala's necklace,' Feluda declared, 'it is Mary Sheela Biswas.'

Feluda in London

ONE

'I bought a new television, but it didn't do me any good,' Lalmohan Babu complained. 'There's really nothing worth seeing. I tried watching the *Mahabharata*, but had to switch it off after just five minutes.'

'It's a pity you're not interested in sports,' Feluda said. 'If you were, you could have watched some good programmes. Tennis, cricket, football . . . everything's covered, games played both here and abroad.'

'Doordarshan had written to me recently, saying they'd like to make a TV serial from one of my stories.'

'That's good news, isn't it?'

'Yes, I suppose so, though I cannot imagine who might play Prakhar Rudra, my hero. Can you think of an actor in Bengal who might suit the part? I mean, it's not like America, is it? They even found someone to play Superman! He looks as though he's climbed out of the pages of the comic!'

Durga Puja had started. A song from a Hindi film was being played on a loudspeaker. We could hear it clearly from our living room. When he had finished complaining against Doordarshan, Lalmohan Babu tried singing the same song, but had to give up soon. His grandfather was supposed to have been a classical singer, but he himself could not sing even a single note without going out of tune.

We had already had tea, but were wondering whether to have a second round, when a car stopped outside our house. The door bell rang a moment later.

I opened the door to find a tall and handsome gentleman. His complexion was as fair as a European's.

'Is this where Pradosh Mitter lives?' he asked.

'Yes, please come in.'

I showed him into our living room. Dressed traditionally in a dhoti and kurta, he had a sophisticated air about him.

'Please sit down,' Feluda offered. 'I am Pradosh Mitter.'

Our visitor took a sofa and looked enquiringly at Lalmohan Babu. 'He is my friend, Lalmohan Ganguli,' Feluda explained. Lalmohan Babu said 'namaskar', but our visitor did not respond. He appeared somewhat preoccupied. There was a few seconds' silence.

'I heard about you from one of your clients,' he said finally. 'Sadhan Chakravarty.'

'Yes, I worked for him last year. How can I help you? Is there a particular problem?'

'I don't even know whether it merits being described as a problem. You must decide that. But yes, there is something bothering me.'

He took out an envelope from his pocket. In it was a photograph. He brought it out carefully and handed it to Feluda. I peered over Feluda's shoulder and saw two young boys—seventeen or eighteen years old—standing together, smiling at the camera. Both were dressed in shirts and trousers. It was an old photo and its colour had faded considerably.

'Can you recognize any of these boys?' our visitor wanted to know.

'The one on the left is you,' Feluda replied.

'Yes, that's the one I can recognize too.'

'The other one must be your friend.'

'Presumably, but I have no idea who he is. I found this photo only recently, while going through some old papers in a drawer. There's only one thing I'd like you to do: find out who this boy is. I mean, I need to know where he is now, what he does for a living, how did he and I happen to meet, the lot. I will, of course, pay your fee and any other expenses.'

'Haven't you made enquiries on your own?'

'Yes, I've shown the photo to a few old classmates who now go to the same club as me, but none of them could remember that other boy. If you look at the photo carefully, you'll see it's impossible to tell whether the boy is Indian or not.'

'Well, his hair is dark, but his eyes seem light. Why, did you know many foreigners when you were young?'

'I spent five years in England as a young boy. Four of those years were spent in school, then I did one year of college. My father was a doctor there. Then we returned to India. The problem is, I had a serious accident before we left. I fell off my bicycle and fractured my skull. As a result, I suffered partial loss of memory. Even today, I cannot recall anything of the years I spent in England.'

'Surely you know which school and college you went to?'

'My father told me, many years ago. I went to a college in Cambridge. I don't remember its name, nor could I tell you the name of the school.'

'Have you received any treatment to bring back this lost memory?'

'Yes. Conventional medicine hasn't helped. Now I am trying ayurvedic stuff.'

'What happened when you returned from England?'

'I was admitted to St Xavier's College here in Calcutta. My father made all the arrangements. I wasn't fully recovered.'

'Which year was that?'

'1952. I joined the intermediate year.'

'I see.'

Feluda stared at the photo for a few moments. Then he said, 'Do you think this other boy is related to some special incident? Some particularly significant event in your life?'

'Yes, the thought has indeed crossed my mind. Sometimes, I feel as if I can recall a few things vaguely. This boy's face keeps coming back to me, but for the life of me I cannot remember his name, or where I met him. It's an extremely awkward situation. We must have been close friends. I'd be very interested to learn if he's still around somewhere and whether he remembers me, I realize it won't be a simple task to trace him, but perhaps you won't mind the challenge?'

'Very well, I'll take the job. But obviously, I cannot tell you how long it might take to finish it. Suppose I have to go to England to make enquiries?'

'If you do, I will pay for you and your assistant to go and stay there. I will also get you the foreign exchange you'll be allowed to take from here. That must tell you how keen I am to get to the bottom of this mystery.'

'Is your father still alive?'

'He's no more. He died five years after we returned from England. My mother died ten years ago. I have a wife and a daughter. My daughter's married. She lives in Delhi. Here's my card.'

I looked curiously at the card. Ranjan K. Majumdar, it said. The address given was 13 Roland Road, followed by a telephone number.

'Thank you, I'll be in touch. I may well need to ask you more questions.'

'I will do my best to answer them, Mr Mitter, but I've already explained the basic problem. Shall I leave the photo with you?'

'Yes, I'll get a copy made and return the original to you. Oh, by the way, I need to know where you work. I mean, what do you do for a living?'

'Sorry, I ought to have told you myself. I am a chartered

accountant. I did B. Com from St Xavier's. My firm is called Lee & Watkins.'

'Thank you.'

'Thank *you*, Mr Mitter. Goodbye.'

With a general nod in our direction, Mr Majumdar left.

'A unique case,' Lalmohan Babu commented when he had gone.

'No doubt about that. I don't think I've ever handled a case like this.'

'May I see the photo?'

Feluda handed him the photo of the two boys. Lalmohan Babu looked hard at it, frowning. Then he shook his head.

'Mr Majumdar was right. It's impossible to tell whether that boy is English or Indian. How on earth will you proceed, Mr Mitter?'

'I'll think of a way. Leave it to me, Mr Ganguli.'

TWO

Feluda knew a chartered accountant called Dharani Mukherjee. He rang him the same day. Mr Mukherjee said he knew Ranjan Majumdar very well since both were members of the Saturday Club. On being asked what kind of a man Mr Majumdar was, Mr Mukherjee said he was quiet and reserved, and did not speak to many people. Usually, he was seen sitting alone. He drank occasionally, but never in excess. Mr Mukherjee knew that he had spent a few years in England in his childhood, but could tell us nothing more.

The next day, Feluda got hold of a list of students who had attended the intermediate year at St Xavier's in 1952. 'I think I've heard of one of them. He's a homeopath,' said Feluda, quickly scanning the list. 'Topshe, see if you can get me the telephone number of Dr Hiren Basak.'

I found his number in two minutes. Feluda rang up and made an appointment to see him the next morning at half past eleven.

Lalmohan Babu turned up the next day to find out if we had made any progress. We went to Dr Basak's chamber in his car. The crowded waiting room bore evidence of the doctor's popularity. His assistant greeted us and took us straight into the consulting room.

Dr Basak rose as he saw us, a smile on his face.

'What brings you here, Mr Mitter? You don't fall ill often.'

'No, no, it isn't illness that's brought me here today, Dr Basak. I've come only to ask you some questions as a part of my investigations.'

'Yes?'

'Were you a student at St Xavier's?'

'Yes, I was.'

'Will you please look at this photo and tell me if you can recognize these boys?'

Feluda took out the photo from its cellophane wrapper and gave it to Dr Basak. He had already returned the original to Mr Majumdar. This was a copy he had had made. The doctor frowned as he looked at it. 'I seem to recognize one of them,' he said after a while. 'He used to be in my batch. I think his name was Ranjan. Yes, that's right. Ranjan Majumdar.'

'And the other one? I am more interested in him.'

'No, sorry, Mr Mitter. I never saw the other boy in my life.'

'Didn't he go to St Xavier's? I mean, wasn't he in your batch as well?'

'No, I am certain of that.'

Feluda put the photo away.

'Would there be any point in speaking to any of your other batchmates?'

'No, I don't think so. It'll only be a waste of time.'

'Even so, I'd be very grateful if you could do something for me.'

'I am willing to do what I can.'

Feluda took out the list of students. 'Please go through this and tell me if you know how any of these men might be contacted.'

Clearly, he was not going to give up easily. Dr Basak ran his eyes over the list and said, 'I know one of them. He's a doctor, too; but he practises orthodox medicine. Dr Jyotirmoy Sen. He lives in Hastings. You'll get his address from the telephone directory.'

'Thank you. Thank you very much, sir.'

We came out and got into the car. 'Look, Felu Babu, why are you assuming that the other boy was a classmate?' Lalmohan Babu asked as we drove off. 'One can make friends anywhere, surely? Not one of my present set of friends had ever studied with me.'

'You're right. I think in the end we'll have to put in an advertisement in the press with the photo, but in the meantime let's see what this other doctor has to say.'

Dr Jyotirmoy Sen was not available for the next three days. But he agreed to see us in his house on the fourth day, at half past nine. He normally left for his clinic at ten, he said. He had heard of Feluda, and appeared duly impressed.

Lalmohan Babu collected us in his car, and we reached Dr Sen's house on the dot of nine-thirty. His house was large and well kept, so presumably here was another doctor with a thriving practice. A bearer showed us into his drawing room. 'The doctor will be with you shortly,' he said and disappeared.

'Who will you ask him about? Ranjan Majumdar, or the other boy?' Lalmohan Babu asked, lowering his voice.

'Let's see if we can get anything more on Ranjan Majumdar. We don't know a great deal about our client, do we? As for the other boy, I don't think Dr Sen can help.'

The doctor arrived as soon as Feluda finished speaking.

'You must be Pradosh Mitter,' he said, taking a chair, 'although you're better known as Feluda, aren't you? And you two must be Tapesh and Jatayu. Everyone in my family devours the stories Tapesh writes, so all of you are quite familiar to me. How may I help you?'

'Take a look at this photograph. Can you recognize either of these boys?'

'Yes, one of them is Ranjan Majumdar. I remember him pretty well. I don't know the other one.'

'He wasn't in your class?'

'No. I'd have remembered him if he was.'

'I'd like to ask you a few questions about Ranjan Majumdar.'

'Go ahead. We were close friends in college. We attended lectures together, went to movies together. If he missed a class, I stood in for him at roll-call, and he often did the same for me. But now we've lost touch.'

'What was he like as a person?'

Dr Sen frowned slightly. 'A little eccentric. But we didn't really mind that.'

'Eccentric? Why do you say that?'

'Well, he had very strong nationalistic feelings. I mean, no young man of that age ever spoke or felt like that about the country. Perhaps this was something he had inherited from his grandfather, Raghunath Majumdar, who was a terrorist once. He fought very hard against the British. Ranjan's father went to England, but came back because of some disagreement he had had with an Englishman.

The whole family had this funny trait.'

'Mr Majumdar went to school in England, didn't he?'

'Yes, but he never spoke about it. He had a terrible accident in England. I assume you know about it?'

'Yes, he told us.'

'As a result, he lost his memory. He couldn't remember anything of his life in England. Five years—or more—were totally wiped from his mind.'

'Supposing he had made a friend there, or met someone special, is there any way one could find out?'

'I can't see how, unless his lost memory came back. That has been known to happen in many cases. But let me tell you this, Ranjan was not an ordinary young man. I don't know how he lived in England, or what he did as a student there, but when I met him in college, I could tell he was different from all the others. He had a distinct personality of his own, even at that young age.'

We went to Mr Majumdar's house the next day.

'Any progress?' he asked.

'Well, we've established that your friend in the photo did not go to college with you here in Calcutta. Now I wish to take a step that requires your approval.'

'Yes?'

'I'd like to publish the photo of this other boy and see if anyone can recognize him. If it came out in papers in Calcutta and Delhi, I think that should be enough.'

Mr Majumdar thought for a minute.

'Will my name be mentioned anywhere?'

'No, not at all. All I'm going to say in the notice is that if anyone can recognize the boy, they should contact me, at my address.'

'Very well. You must do what you have to for your investigation. I have no objection, Mr Mitter.'

THREE

Five days later, Feluda's little advertisement came out in the Statesman in Delhi and Calcutta. Nothing happened on the first day. 'It can't be anyone from Calcutta, I guess. If it was, we'd have heard by now,' Feluda said to me.

On Wednesday, Feluda got a call from a tourist staying in the

Grand Hotel. His name was John Dexter. He was travelling with a group of Australians, and had seen the photo—purely by chance—in Delhi. This made him come to Calcutta to talk to Feluda. Since he was leaving for Kathmandu in the evening, he would have to see us in the afternoon, he said. 'Would it be all right if I called at your house at one o'clock?' he asked.

'Yes, of course. Thank you for taking so much trouble.'

Feluda sounded excited. He had not really expected the little notice to work.

A taxi drew up at our front door a little before one. Feluda opened the door and admitted a middle-aged white gentleman.

'Mr Mitter?' he said, offering his hand, 'I am John Dexter.'

'Pleased to meet you,' Feluda shook his hand. 'Please sit down.'

Mr Dexter sat on our settee. His face and arms had a deep tan. He had clearly been travelling in India for some time.

'You saw that photo in the *Statesman*?'

'Yes, that's why I am here. I told you on the phone. I was amazed to see a photo of my cousin, Peter Dexter, after such a long time and in a foreign country.'

'Are you sure it was your cousin?'

'Absolutely. Peter and I are first cousins. But I left England and went to Australia when I was quite young. Then I lost touch with Peter and his family. In fact, I am no longer in touch with my own family in England. So I couldn't tell you where Peter is at present, or what he does. All I can tell you is that Peter's father, Michael Dexter, used to be in the Indian Army. I think he went back to England after 1947.'

'Was Peter his only son?'

'Oh no. Michael Dexter had seven children. Peter was his sixth. His eldest son, George, was also in the army.'

'Where did Michael Dexter live in England?'

'In Norfolk. I couldn't give you the whole address, not even the name of the town. Sorry.'

'Never mind. You have been most helpful.'

Mr Dexter rose. His companions were waiting for him in the hotel. Feluda thanked him again and saw him off to his taxi.

We went to see Ranjan Majumdar the next day.

'Did your plan work?'

'Yes, that's what I have come to tell you. That boy was English, called Peter Dexter.'

'How did you find out?'

Feluda told him about John Dexter's visit. Mr Majumdar grew a little thoughtful. 'Dexter?' he muttered, 'Dexter . . . Dexter . . .'

'Can you remember anything?'

'Only vaguely. Something unpleasant happened, I think . . . but no, it's no more than a feeling. There are no definite memories.'

'Does your memory return occasionally?'

'Yes, sometimes I feel as if I can recall certain incidents. But there's no one I might ask to see if any of it is true. My parents were the only people who knew what had happened in England. Both are now dead.'

'Well, one thing has become quite clear. No one in Calcutta can tell us anything more about Peter Dexter.'

'Yes, I realize that, but . . .' Mr Majumdar grew preoccupied again.

'Would you like me to drop the case?'

Mr Majumdar suddenly pulled himself together. 'No, no, of course not. I want to know where he is, where he works, whether he remembers me, everything. When can you leave?'

'Leave? Where to?' Feluda was taken aback.

'London, where else? You've got to go to London!'

'Yes, that would be the next logical step.'

'Do you both have valid passports?'

'Oh yes. We've had to travel abroad before. I have no other case at the moment, so I could go any time.'

'Good. I'll arrange tickets for you.'

'A friend of ours will go with us—at his own expense, of course.'

'Very well. Let my secretary have his name. He'll make the necessary arrangements for all of you. We use a good travel agent, who can book you into a hotel in London.'

'How long would you like me to stay there?'

Mr Majumdar thought for a minute. Then he said, 'Give it a week. If you fee! you're just not getting anywhere, you can come back after that. I'll tell my secretary to make your return bookings accordingly.'

'Thank you. If I return without having traced the whereabouts of your friend, I will not accept a fee from you.'

'Have you ever failed in a case, Mr Mitter?'

'Not as yet.'

'Then you won't fail in this one either.'

FOUR

'UK!' Lalmohan Babu stared, his eyes round with surprise. Feluda had just finished telling him of the latest developments. He was clearly not prepared for a visit to the UK.

'You will have to bear your own expenses, Lalmohan Babu. Mr Majumdar is paying for Topshe and myself.'

'I know that. I can afford the trip, I assure you. You may be a busy and famous detective, but don't forget I earn much more than you. Just tell me what I have to do.'

'Take enough warm clothes to last you a week. I hope you haven't lost your passport?'

'No, sir. It's kept carefully in my almirah.'

'In that case, you have to do nothing else except pay Mr Majumdar whatever is required in Indian rupees. He will make your bookings and arrange foreign exchange. His travel agent is handling all the arrangements.'

'Where are we going to stay in London?'

'Probably in a three-star hotel.'

'Why only three star?'

'Because if he tried to climb any higher, Mr Majumdar might well go bankrupt. Do you have any idea how expensive London hotels are?'

'No. Tell you what, I've just thought of something. One of my neighbours is a businessman. He goes abroad every year. He might be able to give me a few extra dollars. What do you say?'

'It would be going against the law.'

'Please, Felu Babu, you don't always have to act like a saint. Everyone tries to take extra foreign exchange. That doesn't make them all criminals, does it?'

'Very well, Mr Jatayu. I agree, much against my better judgement, mind you.'

We were booked to travel by Air-India on a Tuesday. The plane would leave Calcutta soon after midnight and go to Bombay, where we would catch a connecting flight to London. The hotel we were booked at was called the Regent Palace, in Piccadilly Circus. Feluda said it was a very good place to be in, right in the heart of the city. He had been reading a lot of guide books on London, and studying various maps.

He rang Mr Majumdar the day before we left. I heard him speak for a couple of minutes, then he said goodbye and rang off. 'I asked him if his father had been attached to a hospital, but he said he did not know; nor could he remember where they used to live. Never mind, one of my friends is a doctor in London. Let's see if he can help.'

Feluda's work had taken us to so many different places, but I never thought we'd go to London. When Lalmohan Babu arrived to pick us up on his way to the airport, he said, 'I was trying to tell myself to stay calm for, after all, every Tom, Dick and Harry goes to London these days. But I just couldn't help getting excited. Do you know what my pulse rate was this morning.' One hundred and ten. Normally it never goes beyond eighty.'

It wasn't just the thought of going to London that made him feel pleased. I knew he had managed to get quite a few extra dollars from his neighbour.

Feluda said nothing in reply. He was doing everything that needed to be done, but was speaking very little. Perhaps he had not yet worked out how he'd proceed. I certainly didn't have a clue. There was virtually nothing to go on. Lalmohan Babu noticed his silence and remarked, 'Frankly, Felu Babu, I can't imagine why you took this case. Have you ever handled anything like this before, with so little information?'

'No, but if I hadn't taken the case, how could you have gone to London.

'Yes, there is that, of course.'

Our plane took off on time and we soon reached Bombay. When it was announced that our connecting flight was ready for departure, I looked at my watch. Normally, at this time I would be in bed, fast asleep. But today, I wasn't feeling sleepy at all.

'I feel wide awake too,' Lalmohan Babu told me, fastening his seat belt. 'I slept for a couple of hours this afternoon, you see. I say, doesn't this remind you of the story of Pinocchio? He got swallowed by a whale, didn't he? This jumbo jet seems like a whale to me. I could be sitting right inside its tummy! How will it climb into the air with so many people inside it? Amazing stuff!'

The amazing stuff happened soon enough. When the plane began to rush down the runway, making an ear-splitting noise, Lalmohan Babu kept his eyes closed. As the bright lights of Bombay grew smaller, I saw Lalmohan Babu's lips move, possibly in a prayer for a safe journey. Then the noise grew less and the hostess announced that we could unfasten our seat belts. We were sitting in the non-smoking section of the plane. Feluda usually smoked frequently, but could go without doing so for several hours, if he had to.

'Aren't they going to show a film?' Lalmohan Babu asked.

They did, but it was such a' boring film that I put my headphones away and went to sleep.

When I woke, bright sunlight was streaming in through the windows. Feluda said he too had slept for two hours. Only Lalmohan Babu had been awake throughout.

'I will make up for it when we get to our hotel,' he said.

I looked out of the window, but there was nothing to see except the snow-covered Alps. On learning the name of the range, Lalmohan Babu asked, 'Shall we get to see Mont Blanc?' He pronounced the 't' and the 'c'.

'Yes,' Feluda replied, 'but if you are going to visit Europe, you had better learn the correct pronunciations of European names. It's "Maw Bleau".'

'You mean several letters are silent?'

'Yes, that's natural enough in French.'

Lalmohan Babu muttered 'Maw Bleau, Maw Bleau' a few times. Finally, we landed at Heathrow half an hour later than our scheduled time of arrival. After we had been through immigration control and collected our baggage, Feluda said, 'There are three ways to get to central London: by bus, taxi or by tube. A taxi would be too expensive, and a bus would take too long. Let's try the tube. According to my map, it would go through Piccadilly.'

'What is the tube?'

'It is like our metro rail, except that there are many more lines. The map looks like a maze, but once you get to understand how it works, travelling by tube is the easiest thing to do in London. I'll get you a map tomorrow.'

FIVE

Our hotel was large and comfortable, but not all that expensive. 'Mr Majumdar's travel agent is a sensible fellow, I must say,' Lalmohan Babu commented. He seemed very pleased with everything he saw, from the underground stations to the red double-decker buses.

'See how handsome these buses are?' he said admiringly, looking out of the window. 'We have double-decker buses too. Why do you think ours look as though they've been chewed and then spat out?'

After lunch, Feluda said, 'If you're not feeling tired, go and have a walk down Oxford Street. You'll see London at its busiest.'

'What about you? What are you going to do?'

'I am going to call my friend, Bikash Datta. Didn't I tell you I had a friend here? Let's see if he can give us any information.'

We were not particularly tired, so we decided to go out. Feluda managed to get through to his friend almost immediately. When he rang off, he was smiling. 'Bikash was amazed to hear my enquiries had brought me to London. But he told me something useful.'

'What?'

'There's an old doctor here—an Indian, who came to London as a medical student soon after the Second World War, then stayed on to work as a GP. A man called Nishanath Sen. He is apparently, a very kind and helpful man. He might have known Mr Majumdar's father. Bikash gave me the address of his clinic. I think I'll try meeting him.'

Feluda got to his feet. 'If we must take shots in the dark, we may as well start with Dr Sen.'

We left the hotel together. Feluda went in the direction of the tube station, having told us how to find Oxford Street. Lalmohan Babu and I pulled out woollen scarves and wound them round our necks as we began walking. October in London was decidedly cool.

There were plenty of Indians on the street, which was probably why Lalmohan Babu said, 'I feel quite at home, dear Tapesh. Mind you, the roads are so good here that that is enough to remind me I am not at home!'

A little later, staring wide-eyed at the milling crowds on Oxford Street, he exclaimed, 'A sea of humanity, Tapesh! A veritable ocean!'

What was amazing was the speed with which everyone was walking. Why was every single person in such a hurry? We had to increase our own pace, or we'd have been trampled in the rush. The street was lined with huge departmental stores, with the most tempting objects in their show windows. I could now see the famous names I had only heard of: Marks & Spencer, Boots, Debenhams, D. H. Evans, John Lewis. Selfridges, I knew, was at one end of Oxford Street. But I had no idea it was so big.

'Let's go in,' I said and pushed Lalmohan Babu through a revolving door. Neither of us had ever seen anything like it. It was crammed with people. We could hardly take a step forward without being pushed and jostled. I held Lalmohan Babu's hand tightly, in case he got lost. Every conceivable consumer product appeared to be available in this shop.

'I never knew,' Lalmohan Babu remarked as we finally emerged in the stationery department, which was relatively less crowded, 'that it was possible to have a human traffic jam. But, dear boy, how can we go back without buying anything here?'

'What would you like to buy?'

'See the number of pens and writing material they've got? If I could buy a pen, that would be enough. I mean, I could write my next novel with a pen I bought in London, couldn't I?'

'Of course. Why don't you choose one?'

It took him five minutes to find one he liked. 'Three pounds thirty pence. What's that in rupees?' he asked.

'Nearly seventy-five,' I replied.

'Good. A pen like this in Calcutta would cost not less than two hundred.'

'Really? Well then, take it. The payment counter's over there.'

'What . . . what do I have to tell them?'

'Nothing. Just give this pen to that lady over there, and she'll tell you what you have to pay. Then you give her a five pound note because I know you haven't got any coins, and she'll give you the change, and put your pen in a Selfridges paper bag. That's all.'

'How do you know all this? This is only your first day!'

'I have been looking at other people. So have you, but you haven' really observed anything.'

Two minutes later, he returned smiling, clutching his pen wrapped in a bag.

'Would you like a cup of tea?' I asked.

'Good idea, but where could we go?'

'There's a cafe here, upstairs.'

'Very well, let's go.'

We took the escalator to the top floor and found the cafe and, luckily, an empty table. It didn't take us long to finish our tea. By the time we crossed the 'ocean of humanity' in Oxford Street again and reached our hotel, it was half past four. Feluda was back already.

'Did you get an idea of what England is like?' he asked with a smile.

'Oh Felu Babu, I haven't got words to describe my feelings.'

'Why? The books you write seem to suggest you have an endless stock of adjectives. Why are words failing you now?'

'There's only one word I can think of: super-sensational. I am caught in a dilemma, Felu Babu.'

'A dilemma? How come?'

'Should I simply see the sights of London, or should I see how you're conducting your enquiries?'

'My enquiries have only just begun. There's nothing to see. I suggest you see as much of London as you can. If I come across anything interesting, I shall certainly let you know.'

'Did you get to meet that doctor?'

'Yes, but he was so busy with his patients there was no time to talk. He told me to go to his house tomorrow morning. He lives in Richmond.'

'Where's that?'

'We can take the tube from Piccadilly and change to District Line at South Kensington. That will take us straight to Richmond. Dr Sen will meet us at the station. Bikash was right. He is very friendly and kind. But all he could tell me today was that he knew Ranjan Majumdar's father, nothing more.'

We spent the evening watching television in our room, then had an early dinner. I fell asleep the instant my head hit the pillow.

SIX

I woke the next morning to an overcast sky and a faint drizzle. Feluda and Lalmohan Babu put on their macintoshes and I wore my waterproof jacket when we left the hotel soon after breakfast.

'Mr Jatayu,' said Feluda, 'this is the normal weather in England. The bright sunshine you saw yesterday was really the exception, not the rule.'

'But I bet roads here don't get waterlogged!' Lalmohan Babu commented.

'No; but then, a really heavy downpour—so common in Calcutta—is something of a rarity here. A steady, soft drizzle is what the English are used to.'

Passengers on the underground seemed in as much of a hurry as the people in Oxford Street.

'This speed is infectious, isn't it?' Lalmohan Babu said, walking as fast as he could. 'Look, even we are walking far more quickly than we'd do back home.'

We reached Richmond at eleven o'clock. Dr Sen had told Feluda how long it would take us to get there from Piccadilly. We found him waiting outside the station. He was a good-looking man in his early sixties.

'Welcome to Richmond!' he said, smiling at Feluda. It had stopped raining, but the sky was still grey.

Feluda returned his greeting and introduced us. 'You are a writer?' Dr Sen asked Lalmohan Babu. 'I can't remember when I last read something written by an Indian writer.'

'Why, don't you go back home from time to time?'

'The last time I went was in 1973. There's no reason for me to go back, really. My whole family is here in Britain. I have two sons and two daughters who have all grown up and left home. They are married with children and live in different parts of the country. My wife and I live here in Richmond.'

His car was parked little way away. 'It's not so bad here,' he said, unlocking the doors, 'but in London the parking problem is quite a serious one. If you went to see a film somewhere in central London, you might well have to park half a mile away from the cinema.'

We got into the car. Feluda sat in the front and fastened his seat belt. Lalmohan Babu looked at me enquiringly. 'It's the law in this country,' I explained quickly. 'Front seat passengers, and of course the driver, are required to have their seat belts on.'

Dr Sen's house was a little more than a mile from the underground station. On our way there, I saw a few branches of some of the shops in Oxford Street. Richmond was clearly not a small area.

His house was in a quiet spot, surrounded by trees. Their large, green leaves had patches of yellow and brown. There was a small, immaculate front garden, behind which stood a beautiful two-storey house, like something out of a picture postcard.

We were shown into the living room. A fire burnt in the fireplace, for which I was glad since it was cold and damp outside. A middle-aged English lady entered the room as soon as we were seated.

'This is my wife, Emily,' Dr Sen said. We introduced ourselves.

'Would you like a cup of coffee?' she asked with a smile.

'That would be very kind, thank you,' Feluda replied.

Dr Sen sat down on a couch and turned to Feluda. Mrs Sen left the room.

'All right. What is it that you want to know, Mr Mitter?' Dr Sen asked.

'You told me yesterday you knew Ranjan Majumdar's father. I am collecting information on Ranjan.'

'I see. Ranjan's father, Rajani Majumdar and I came to England together in 1948. He was older than me by about sixteen years. By the time I got to know him, I had finished studying medicine in Edinburgh and was working in London. Rajani Majumdar was attached to St Mary's Hospital. We happened to sit next to each other at a play. I even remember which play it was: *Major Barbara.* We got talking during the intermission and I realized he was a doctor too. His wife was with him. They used to live in Golders Green, and I in Hampstead. I wasn't married at the time.'

'What about his son?'

'His son was in school.'

'Do you remember which school he went to?'

'Yes. It was Warrendel, in Epping. Then he went to Cambridge.'

'Which college?'

'As far as I can recall, it was Trinity.'

'What kind of a man was Dr Rajani, Majumdar?'

Dr Sen was quiet for a minute. Then he said, 'Peculiar.'

'Peculiar? Why do you say that?'

'Well, I think there was a certain rather strange trait in his family. His father, Raghunath Majumdar, had been a terrorist in his youth. I mean, he was supposed to have made bombs and attacked British officers when he was only a teenager. But, later, he became a heart specialist. By the time he began to practise as a consultant, he had lost all his earlier hatred against the British. It was he who sent Rajani to England. He wanted to see his son work in England and his grandson receive his education there. Seldom does one find such a complete change of heart. But when Rajani began working here, he kept thinking the British still looked down upon Indians. I tried explaining to him that a few isolated cases of racism did not mean every English person was a racist, but he wasn't convinced. In the end, he left England because of something a patient of his said to him—something trivial and insignificant, which he ought to have ignored.'

'By then I assume his son had had that accident?'

'Yes. What is his son doing now? He must be around fifty.'

'Yes. He is a chartered accountant.'

'That means the year he spent in college here was a total waste. He must have had to start afresh when he went back.'

'Yes. By the way, did you know any of Ranjan's friends?'

'No. I never met any of them, nor was anyone's name in particular ever mentioned to me.'

'I see.'

Mrs Sen came in with the coffee. Feluda asked nothing more about Ranjan Majumdar. We left soon afterwards. Dr Sen insisted on driving us back to the station.

SEVEN

We took the tube to Epping the next day and reached Warrendel School at half past three in the afternoon. The main building was behind a huge sports ground. It was probably two hundred years old. Feluda wanted to find out if Ranjan Majumdar had really been a student there and whether there had been a Peter Dexter in his class.

A hall porter met us at the front door.

'I would like some information about one of your ex-students. He studied here many years ago, in the late forties,' Feluda told him. The porter took us to what looked like a library. 'Mr Manning here may be able to help you,' he said.

Mr Manning was seated behind a desk, writing busily in a notebook. Feluda cleared his throat softly. He looked up.

'Yes?'

Feluda explained what he wanted.

'Right. Which year did you say?'

'1948.'

Mr Manning rose and fetched a fat ledger from a shelf. Then he put it on his desk and sat down again.

'What name did you say?' he asked, quickly leafing through the pages.

'I didn't. The name's Majumdar. Ranjan Majumdar.'

'I see. Majumdar . . . Majumdar . . .' he began running his finger through a list and stopped abruptly. 'Yes, here it is. R. Majumdar.'

'Thank you. Could you check another name for us, please? Dexter. Peter Dexter. Was he in the same batch?'

'Dexter . . . no, I see no Dexter here.'

'Oh. Would you be so kind as to look up the 1949 list as well? Maybe Dexter came a year later?'

Mr Manning was most obliging. Sadly, though, there was no mention of Peter Dexter in the 1949 list, either. There was no point in wasting more time.

'Thank you very much indeed,' Feluda said to Mr Manning. 'You have been most helpful.'

On our way back to Piccadilly, Feluda said, 'If we went to Cambridge and made enquiries, I am pretty sure we could learn something about Dexter. Still, I think it might not be a bad idea to put a small notice in the personal column of the Times.'

'What will you say in your notice?'

'If anyone knows anything about a Peter Dexter of Norfolk, he should contact me at my hotel.'

'What do you think you are going to achieve by this?'

'I don't know. Look, if we simply went to Cambridge, we might find his name in an old list of students. But that wouldn't tell us anything about the man, would it? An ad in a paper might bring better results, who knows?'

'But that will take three or four days, surely?' Lalmohan Babu asked.

'No, the ad should come out in two days. If we get a free day, we'll explore London. There's so much to see. Have you heard of Madame Tussaud's?'

'Where there are the waxworks of famous people?'

'Yes, then there are the art galleries, the Houses of Parliament, Big Ben, St Paul's Cathedral . . . you might get blisters on your feet walking, but you couldn't finish seeing everything in a day.'

'When will you go to the office of the *Times*?'

'Today. Hopefully, the notice will come out the day after tomorrow.'

'OK then, we can spend all day tomorrow just sightseeing, can't we?'

'Certainly.'

Madam Tussaud's was a remarkable place. Even the porters who stood in front of certain rooms were made of wax and amazingly lifelike. The chamber of horrors gave me the creeps.

When we came out of Madam Tussaud's, Feluda began walking without telling us where we were going. Puzzled, Lalmohan Babu and I followed him silently. Suddenly, my eyes fell on a sign fixed high up on the wall of a building, that told me which street we were in. 'Baker Street', it said. Sherlock Holmes used to live in 221-B Baker Street. Now I knew what Feluda was looking for. As it turned out, there was no house with that number, but we found number 220. That was good enough. Feluda stood before that building and murmured softly, 'Guru, you showed us the way. If I am an investigator today, it is only because of you. Now I can say coming to London was truly worthwhile.'

I knew how deeply Feluda admired Holmes and his methods. He had told me how the creator of Holmes, Conan Doyle, had once killed the famous detective. But his readers had made such an enormous fuss that he was obliged to bring him back.

I realized that seeing the sights of London would have remained incomplete if we hadn't seen Baker Street.

EIGHT

Two days later, Feluda's ad came out in the *Times*. Surprisingly enough, someone rang Feluda the very next day at 8 a.m.

'A man called Archibald Cripps,' Feluda told me, replacing the receiver. 'He sounded rather aggressive. But he said he could tell me something about Peter Dexter. He'll be here in half an hour. Go and tell Lalmohan Babu. This may prove to be quite interesting.'

Lalmohan Babu was dressed and ready. He came over to our room and said he had never dreamt a little notice like that would fetch such a quick result.

At a quarter past nine, someone knocked at our door. The man who entered looked as rough as were his manners. He glared at Lalmohan Babu and said, 'Well? Who're you? Mitter?'

'No, no. He is,' Lalmohan Babu pointed quickly at Feluda.

'I am Cripps,' our visitor scowled. 'What do you want to know about Dexter?'

'To start with, where is he now?'

'He is in heaven.'

'Oh, I am sorry to hear that. When did he die?'

'Many years ago, when he was in Cambridge.'

'Was he a student there?'

'Yeah. Like an idiot, he tried to row on the river Cam.'

'Why should that make him an idiot?'

'Because he couldn't swim, that's why. The boat capsized. He drowned.'

'He had many siblings, didn't he?'

'Yeah. Five brothers and two sisters. I only know what happened to two of them—George, who was the eldest and Reginald, the youngest. George was in the Indian Army. He came back after your independence. He used to say only the Sikhs and Gurkhas were any good in India. The rest were either crooks or just bloody idle. None of the Dexters liked Indian niggers.'

'Niggers? There are no niggers in India, Mr Cripps. In fact, even in America, blacks are no longer called niggers.'

Feluda's face was set. 'You appear to be in agreement with the Dexters, Mr Cripps,' he added.

'You bet I am! They were right, absolutely right.'

'In that case, I don't want this conversation to go any further. Thank you for your time.' The coldness in Feluda's voice seemed to soften Mr Cripps.

'Look here,' he said a shade more politely. 'I didn't mean to offend you.'

'No?'

'No. I said all that because Reginald's name came up. He was the youngest of the lot. He's still in India, in a tea estate. But he won't be there for long.'

There was a pause. Feluda simply stared at Mr Cripps, saying nothing.

'—Because he has cancer,' Cripps went on. 'He went to India just to make money. He has no affection for the country.'

Feluda stood up. 'Thank you, Mr Cripps. I don't need to learn anything more.'

Cripps got to his feet, looking rather uncertain. Then he said, 'Good day!' and strode out of the room.

'What an awful man! But you set him straight, Felu Babu. I am very glad about that. I mean, putting an Englishman in his place here in London is no joke, is it?'

'Never mind, he's gone now. At least we learnt something useful. Peter Dexter *was* in Cambridge and died in a boating accident.'

'So what do we do now?'

'We haven't much time. Don't forget we must return the day after tomorrow. Let's go to Cambridge today, straight after lunch.'

We left at one-thirty, catching a train from Liverpool Street station. It took us an hour to reach Cambridge. The trains in Britain ran faster and, like the buses, were clean and well maintained.

Cambridge was a beautiful place. The university, with all its ancient glory, stood in its centre. There were several colleges, but Dr Sen had told us Ranjan Majumdar had gone to Trinity. So we made our way there. We were directed to a Mr Tailor, who had access to old records.

'Yes,' he said, checking through some papers. 'In 1951 a boy called Ranjan Majumdar was admitted to this college, and there was a Peter Dexter in his class.'

'I believe Dexter drowned in the river. Is that right?'

'Sorry, I am afraid I wouldn't know. I've been working here only for the last seven years. What you can do is speak to old Hookins. He's our gardener, been working here for forty years. You'll probably find him in the garden.'

'Thank you.'

We had to ask a couple of people before Hookins was pointed out to us. He didn't look very old, though all his hair had turned white. We found him trimming a hedge.

'You've been here a long time, haven't you?' Feluda began.

'Yes,' Hookins replied, 'but I'm soon going to retire. I am sixty-three, you know, although I can work as hard as any other man. My house in Chatworth Street is two miles from here. I come walking every day.'

'How do you get on with the students? Do you come across many of them?'

'Oh, all the time. They love me. Many of them stop by for a chat, some even offer me a smoke, or a beer. I get on very well with them.'

'Can you remember things that happened in the past? How good is your memory?'

'Pretty good, though sometimes I forget things that happened recently. Why do you ask?'

'Can you cast your mind back forty years ago?'

'What for?'

'Boys here take boats out on the river, don't they?'

'So do girls.'

'Yes, but can you remember an instance where a boat capsized and a boy died?'

Hookins was silent for a few moments. He had stopped smiling. 'Yes,' he said slowly. 'I remember. It was very sad. An English boy—can't remember his name. He couldn't swim, so he drowned.'

'Didn't he have an Indian friend?'

'Yes, I think he did.'

'Was this Indian boy in the boat with him?'

'Maybe he was . . . maybe . . .'

'Where were you when it happened?'

'I wasn't far, just sitting behind a bush, taking a break. I was smoking, I think.'

'Did you actually see anything?'

'No. I ran to the river only when I heard cries for help. But I could not save the boy.'

'Then you must remember if there was anyone else in the boat.'

Hookins frowned, lost in thought. Then he sighed and shook his head.

'No, sir. I can't remember anything else. It was my wedding day too. Yes, sir, that's why I remember the day so well. Later in the afternoon, I got married to Maggie—the best wife one could have.'

NINE

We returned to London. Much to our surprise, another Indian rang Feluda the next morning. It was a South Indian gentleman called Satyanathan.

'I saw your ad in the *Times*, Mr Mitter,' he said on the phone, 'but I couldn't ring you earlier as I was a little busy. I could tell you a few things about Peter Dexter. Would it be all right if I came to your hotel at eleven?'

'Sure.'

Mr Satyanathan arrived on time. He was quite dark, but his hair was totally white.

'I'm sorry I couldn't contact you before,' he said, taking a seat.

'Do you live in London?'

'Yes, in north London—in Kilburn. I teach in a school. Peter Dexter and I went to college together.'

'Really? Do you remember a Ranjan Majumdar?'

'Oh yes. He and Peter were friends, though they fought a lot.'

'Why?'

'It was chiefly because of Peter's attitude towards Indians. He hated them. The only reason why he treated Ranjan differently was the colour of Ranjan's skin. He was fair enough to pass off as a European. Peter used to say to him: you are half English, I think, you cannot be a genuine Indian.'

'How did Peter treat you?'

'Need I spell it out? You can see for yourself how dark I am. He used to call me a dirty nigger. I didn't have the courage to protest.'

'Do you remember Peter's death?'

'Of course. I even remember the day. It was the day before Whit Sunday. Peter should never have got into a boat when he couldn't swim.'

'Who else was with him?'

'Ranjan.'

'Are you sure?'

'Absolutely. The sight of Ranjan standing with his clothes dripping wet still keeps coming back to me. I was in my room when it happened. I rushed out only when I heard our gardener Hookins shouting outside. Ranjan had jumped into the river to save his friend, but it was too late. Reginald went in next, but even he couldn't save his brother.'

'Reginald was Peter's younger brother, wasn't he?'

'Yes, younger by only a year. He was exactly the same. He used to get into trouble frequently with Indian boys, saying nasty, provoking things. The authorities had given him several warnings, to no avail. It was Reginald's belief that Ranjan could easily have saved Peter, but didn't. That's what he went around telling everyone: he deliberately let him drown.'

'Ranjan Majumdar did not spend more than a year in Cambridge, did he?'

'No. He, too, had a serious accident. His family took him back to India after that.'

Mr Satyanathan had no further information to give. He rose, said goodbye and left. When Feluda came back to the room after seeing him off, he was frowning. Later, over lunch, Lalmohan Babu commented, 'Why, Felu Babu, you seem dissatisfied. What might be the reason?'

'I feel doubtful about something.'

'What is it?'

'Well, I can't help feeling Hookins did not tell us all he knew. For some reason, he kept certain facts to himself.'

'What are you going to do about it?'

'There's only one thing we can do. Let's go back to Cambridge and find his house. He told us the name of his street. Do you remember what it was, Topshe?'

'Chatworth Street.'

'Good. I think all we need to do is ask the police in Cambridge. They'll tell us how to find it. I' believe the English police are most helpful.'

After lunch, Feluda said he had to go out briefly for some work. We'd go to Cambridge when he got back. There were frequent trains to Cambridge, so getting there would not be a problem.

We finally left at half past four. It was dark by the time we reached Cambridge. The streetlights had been switched on. We came out of the station and began walking down the main road. Feluda spotted a constable in a few moments.

'We're looking for Chatworth Street,' he said to him. 'Could you please point us in the right direction?'

The man gave us such excellent directions that we had no difficulty in finding it. It took us about half an hour to get there. Chatworth Street was a narrow lane, very obviously not a posh area. There was no one about, except a man who came out of his house to pick up a fat cat sleeping near his gate. Feluda hastened his speed to speak to him before he disappeared.

'Excuse me, do you happen to know where Mr Hookins lives?'

'Fred Hookins? Number sixteen.'

We thanked the man, and found the house easily enough. Each house had its number clearly written. When we knocked on the front door of number sixteen, Hookins himself opened it.

'You! What are you doing here?'

'May we come in,' please?'

'Yes, certainly.' Hookins moved aside to let us go through. We stepped into a small lounge.

A settee and a chair seemed to fill the whole room. We sat down.

'Well?' Hookins looked enquiringly at Feluda.

'I'd like to ask you a few more questions.'

'About the drowning?'

'Yes.'

'I've already told you all I know.'

'I'd like to ask some different questions, if I may.'

'All right.'

'Mr Hookins, do you seriously believe that someone sitting in a boat that's only cruising along a river very slowly can fall into the water and drown?'

'Any boat can capsize in a storm. There was a high wind that day.'

'I went to a library today and found the report published the day after the accident. It mentions Peter Dexter's death, but there's no mention of a storm. I looked at the weather report for that day. The wind speed had been 20-25 mph. Would you call that a very high wind?'

Hookins did not reply. In the silence that followed, all I could hear was a table clock ticking away.

'You are hiding something, Mr Hookins. What is it?'

'It happened so long ago . . .'

'Yes, but it's important. You were very close to one of those two boys, weren't you?'

Hookins cast a startled look at Feluda. His eyes held both surprise and suspicion.

'What do you mean?' he asked.

'I have spotted two objects on that shelf over there: a Ganesh and an ivory Buddha. Where did you get those?'

'Ron gave those to me.'

'Ron? You mean Ranjan?'

'Yes. I called him Ron, and sometimes I called him John.'

'I see. Now tell me this: didn't you hear anything *before* you heard Peter cry for help? Remember, you must not tell lies before Indian gods, or you'll rot in hell forever.'

'I couldn't hear what they were actually saying. I only heard their voices.'

'That means they were talking loudly?'

'Perhaps . . . perhaps . . .'

'Do you know what I think? I think they were fighting, having a violent argument. Peter stood up in his anger, and then lost his balance. The boat did not capsize, but he fell into the water.'

'Yes, yes, yes!' Hookins blurted out, 'Peter tried to attack Ron . . . he would have hit him . . . but the boat gave a sudden lurch and he . . . he just fell over.'

'Does that mean Peter was responsible for his own death?'

'Of course.'

'But consider something else. Your Cam isn't a big river. In our country we would call it a canal. Now, it can't be easy to drown in a small river like that when there's someone trying to get you out.'

'I saw him drown, with my own eyes!'

'You're still hiding something from us, aren't you? Mr Hookins, I have travelled thousands of miles in search of the truth. I will not leave until I have it. You must tell me what really happened. Why did Peter Dexter drown so easily?'

Hookins looked around helplessly, like a cornered animal. Then he broke down.

'All right, all right!' he cried. 'You want the truth? I'll give it to you. When Peter fell into the water, he was unconscious.'

'Unconscious?' Feluda gave Hookins a sharp glance. Then he said under his breath, 'I see. Ranjan was rowing, wasn't he?'

'Yes.'

'That means he had an oar in his hand?'

'Yes.'

'So he used it as a weapon? He struck Peter with his oar, Peter lost consciousness and fell out of the boat. Ranjan jumped in after him, but actually did nothing to save Peter. He only pretended to be trying to help him. In other words, it was Ranjan who was responsible for Peter's death.'

Hookins struck his forehead with his palm. 'I didn't want to cause you any pain. That's why I was trying to hide the truth. Had I been in Ranjan's shoes, I'd have done exactly the same. Peter was abusing him loudly. He was saying: "It's only your skin that's white. If I scratch it, I'll find it's black under the surface. You are nothing but a dirty black native." If Ranjan lost his head after this, can anyone blame him?'

'Was there any other witness?'

'Yes, only one.'

'Who?'

'Reginald.'

'Reginald Dexter?'

'Yes. We were both sitting by the river, smoking. We both saw what happened, we heard every word. But later, I said Peter tried to attack Ron and fell into the water. I said this to protect Ron. But Reginald went around telling the truth. Luckily for Ron, everyone knew how he felt about Indians. So no one believed him. Thank God for that. Ron was such a nice boy, so kind and generous.'

'But surely there was an inquest?'

'Of course.'

'You were asked to give evidence, presumably?'

'Yes.'

'And you told the same lies?'

'Yes. I was determined to save Ron. We told the same story, and we stuck to it.'

'What about Reginald?'

'He was called by the coroner, too; and naturally he described what had really happened. But he was so obviously a racist that no one took him seriously. The coroner thought he was making things up just to get Ranjan into trouble. The official verdict was death by accident.'

Feluda rose. 'Thank you, Mr Hookins. I have no more questions.'

It was time for dinner by the time we got back to our hotel. As we were collecting our keys, one of the receptionists looked at Feluda and said, 'Mr Mitter?'

'Yes?'

'There's a telegram for you.'

Feluda opened it quickly. It had been sent by Ranjan Majumdar. It said: CAN RECALL EVERY THING. RETURN IMMEDIATELY.

'Perfect timing,' Feluda remarked. 'We've finished our job, we're going back tomorrow and now Mr Majumdar's memory comes flooding back!'

On the flight back home, Feluda said we should go straight to Mr Majumdar's house from the airport. Our flight was supposed to land in Calcutta at 1 p.m. I felt deeply concerned. What was Mr Majumdar going to do, now that he knew he had once killed someone?

Lalmohan Babu's car met us at the airport. The driver was told to take us to Roland Road.

My heart gave a sudden jump as Mr Majumdar's house came into view. Why was a police van standing in front of it?

We clambered out and went in quickly. The familiar figure of Inspector Mandal met us at the front door. He looked grim. 'It happened at around eight o'clock this morning,' he said without any preamble.

'What happened?'

'You haven't heard? Mr Majumdar has been killed. Apparently, an Englishman come to see him early this morning. No one knows who he was. Would you like to make your enquiries, Mr Mitter?'

'No.'

Lalmohan Babu arrived at our house at seven-thirty the next morning. He seemed greatly disturbed. 'Have you seen today's paper?' he asked breathlessly. 'Page five in the *Statesman*?'

Feluda picked up the paper. Neither of us had had the chance to look at it. The front page had news of Mr Majumdar's death.

'Page five, page five!' Lalmohan Babu cried impatiently. 'Look at the third column!'

Feluda read it out slowly:

Suicide in hotel room

The staff and guests in a hotel in Sadar Street were disturbed last night by the sound of a gunshot. Enquiries revealed that the guest in room number seven had shot himself. He was found lying on the floor, a revolver in his hand. According to the hotel register, his name was Reginald Dexter. He had come from a tea estate called Khoirabari, near Darjeeling.

The Mystery of the Pink Pearl

ONE

'What is there to see in Sonahati?' asked Lalmohan Babu.

'Well, according to this book I've been reading, called *Travelling in Bengal,*' Feluda replied, 'there ought to be an old Shiv temple and a large lake. I think it's called Mangal Deeghi. It was built by one of their zamindars. Even twenty years ago, Sonahati was little more than a village. Now it has a school, a hospital and even a hotel.'

Lalmohan Babu looked at his watch and said, 'Another ten minutes, I should think.' It was a new quartz he had bought recently. 'The way it keeps time is really most terrific, he had told us.

We were on our way to Sonahati at the invitation of their Recreation Club. We were accompanied by one Navjeevan Haldar, who was a famous professor of history, and had written several books. The club had organized a joint reception for Prof Haldar and Feluda. We would spend two days in Sonahati, staying at the house of the wealthiest man there, called Panchanan Mallik. He was also the president of the club. Rumour had it that he was a collector of antiques.

'I didn't really think you'd accept this invitation,' Lalmohan Babu remarked, looking at Feluda.

'I just wanted to get out of Calcutta for a couple of days,' Feluda replied. 'At least the air in Sonahati will be cleaner. Besides, a friend of mine—Someshwar Saha—lives there. He's a lawyer. We used to be classmates. I am looking forward to seeing him again.'

Our train reached Sonahati more or less on time. A small group came towards us as soon as we got out. Two of them were carrying garlands, which they promptly placed around Feluda and Prof Haldar's necks. The man who had garlanded Feluda said, 'Namaskar. I am the secretary of our club. My name is Naresh Sen. It was I who wrote to you. And this is Panchanan Mallik.'

A middle-aged man stepped forward, a welcoming smile on his lips. I noticed he had gold buttons on his kurta.

'We are deeply honoured to have you here,' he said. 'I hope you won't find it too inconvenient to stay in my house. I mean, we couldn't offer you *all* the facilities of a big city.'

'Please don't worry about that. I'm sure we'll all enjoy ourselves,' Feluda said.

'You are a well-known personality as well, I hear,' Mr Mallik turned to Lalmohan Babu.

'Well, I . . . I do a bit of writing,' Jatayu tried looking modest.

Mr Mallik's blue Ambassador was parked outside the station. We climbed into it.

'I have heard about your collection,' Feluda remarked as we drove off. 'In fact, I think I read a report on it somewhere.'

'Yes, it's an old passion of mine. I have collected quite a few things. Prof Haldar here may be particularly interested for many of the items have a historical significance. My latest acquisition is the Maharshi's shoe.'

'The Maharshi's shoe? What does that mean?' Lalmohan Babu asked, puzzled.

'Don't you know about it? Prof Haldar, I am sure, has heard the story.'

'Let's hear it.'

'Maharshi Debendranath, Rabindranath Tagore's father, was an extremely wealthy man, as you all know. Once he received an invitation from a maharaja. He knew many other rich people had been invited. So he went and saw that the others had turned up in their most expensive clothes. Everywhere he looked, he saw silk kurtas, jamavar shawls, gold chains and priceless jewels. But what was he dressed in? Tight white pyjamas, a long white achkan and a plain white shawl. People were amazed. Why was he dressed so simply? Then they saw his feet. The Maharshi was wearing a pair of white naagras, on which shone two huge diamonds.'

'My word! And you've got those shoes?' Lalmohan Babu exclaimed.

'One, I've got only one of them. The diamond is still fixed on it. I'll show it to you.'

Mr Mallik's house was large, surrounded by a big garden. There could be no doubt about his own affluence. The car stopped under the portico. Two bearers and a chowkidar were waiting near the front door.

'Show these people to their rooms,' Mr Mallik said to one of the bearers as we got out. 'And see that lunch is served at one o'clock.'

We were taken up a marble staircase. 'Your reception is in the evening. It's likely to be quite cold at that time,' Mr Mallik told us. 'I hope you have brought enough warm clothes?'

'We have, thank you.'

Three rooms at the end of a passage had been made ready for us.

Prof Haldar disappeared into his, and the three of us went into the one meant for Feluda and myself. It was a spacious room, and its floor was embedded with pieces of china. A little hole in the wall near the ceiling told us there had once been a hand-pulled fan in this room.

'This pattern is called crazy china,' Feluda informed us, looking at the floor. Then he added, 'Mr Mallik's money came from copper mines. One of my clients knows him very well.'

'I see. Hey, have you noticed the difference in the air?' Lalmohan Babu asked. 'It is clean and pure, isn't it?'

It certainly was. There was no noise pollution either. Traffic was nonexistent. I had not heard one single horn from a car or a rickshaw since the moment of our arrival. My ears would get a rest here, I thought.

A bearer arrived, carrying three glasses of sherbet on a tray. As soon as we had finished drinking it, he returned to say lunch had been served.

TWO

Mr Mallik was undoubtedly a most hospitable man. The number of dishes on the table bore evidence of that. I had no idea there could be so many different types of fish curry. Feluda seldom ate a lot during meals, but Lalmohan Babu—a gourmet—enjoyed his meal with obvious relish. But then, he had an additional reason to feel pleased. Mr Mallik kept asking him about his writing, which gave him the chance to brag about himself.

'Allow me now to show you a part of my collection,' said Mr Mallik after lunch. We went back to the first floor, turning left instead of right this time. Mr Mallik's bedroom, study and museum were all on this side of the building.

We were shown a wide range of curios. Each of them, we were told, had once belonged to a famous character in history. The diamond-studded naagra was the first object we saw, followed by Tipu Sultan's snuff box, Robert Clive's pocket watch, Siraj-ud-daula's handkerchief and Rani Rashmoni's paan box. All of us made the right admiring noises, but I couldn't help feeling somewhat sceptical. How could anyone be sure that each item had really belonged to all those well-known people? After all, it wasn't as if their names were written on anything. As we were returning to our rooms after thanking our host, Prof Haldar muttered under his breath: 'What did you make of it, Mr Mitter?'

'Not very convincing, was it?'

'Convincing? Not a single thing was genuine. That naagra had a distinct smell of new leather!'

We had about three hours left before the reception. A bearer came to call us at a quarter to six. We were all dressed by this time. Feluda had donned a traditional dhoti and kurta (in which he looked quite handsome, I had to admit); and Lalmohan Babu was wearing a beautifully embroidered Kashmiri shawl, which he said had once belonged to his grandfather.

It was dark by the time we reached the place where the function was going to be held, but we found an abundance of lights, ranging from powerful spotlights to tiny coloured bulbs. The actual presentation of the citations came at the very end. It was preceded by songs and dances and reading of poetry. Every performer was clearly doing his utmost to impress Feluda. Feluda responded by clapping with great enthusiasm as they left the stage.

The citations were read out eventually before being handed to the two recipients. Whoever had written them out had a beautiful handwriting. A few reporters surrounded Feluda afterwards. In answer to their questions, Feluda said he was not working on a case at the moment, and was enjoying a break.

Prof Haldar went back home with Mr Mallik after the function ended, but we stayed on as Feluda's friend, Someshwar Saha, had invited us to dinner. He arrived as the crowd began to disperse.

'Can you recognize me?' he asked with a smile.

'Easily,' Feluda replied. 'You've got a moustache now, but otherwise you haven't changed.'

'And I might say the same about you, except that your eyes seem sharper and you look a lot smarter. How many cases have you handled so far?'

'No idea,' Feluda laughed. 'I've lost track.'

'Look, here's someone very keen to meet you,' Mr Saha gently pushed forward a gentleman who was standing behind him. 'Meet Jaichand Boral. He lives here, and it was he who designed that citation.'

'Really? Very pleased to meet you, sir. We were all admiring your handwriting.'

Mr Boral smiled shyly. 'Thank you, Mr Mitter, thank you very much. I never thought I'd hear praise from you. I am one of your ardent fans.'

'Mr Boral is going to join us for dinner,' said Mr Saha. 'Come on, let's go. My house is only ten minutes from here.'

Mr Saha's house turned out to be small and compact. His wife and ten-year-old son greeted us. 'Dinner will soon be ready,' Mrs Saha said, offering us drinks.

When we were all seated, Mr Saha pointed at Mr Boral. 'He has something to tell you. I think you're going to find it interesting.'

'Oh? What is it, Mr Boral?'

Mr Boral smiled again. 'Nothing much, Mr Mitter. It's just something related to my family.'

'Oh, do tell us!' Lalmohan Babu leant forward in his chair. Even the hint of a story always made him excited.

Mr Boral put his glass down on a table.

'I work here now as a simple schoolteacher,' he began, 'but we were originally a family of jewellers. In fact, even now we own a small shop in Calcutta. An uncle of mine looks after it. My great great grandfather had started this business. He used to sail round the coast to buy and sell precious gems. He found something near Madras, which has survived till this day. I would like to show it to you.'

'Have you got it with you now?'

'Yes.'

Mr Boral took out a brown handkerchief from his pocket. It was knotted around a small object. As he untied it, a tiny red velvet box slipped out. He opened it and held it forward. In it lay a pearl.

'Good heavens, it's a pink pearl!' Feluda exclaimed.

'Yes, sir. It is pink, but I don't know if that makes it special in any way.'

'What! You come from a family of jewellers and you don't know?' Feluda sounded unusually agitated. 'Out of all the pearls that are available in India, a pink pearl is the most rare and, therefore, the most expensive.'

'Hey, I didn't even know a pearl could be anything but white!' Lalmohan Babu remarked.

'Pearls come in many hues—white, red, black, yellow, blue, pink. Look, Mr Boral, you must not go about carrying such a precious object in your pocket. If you have a safe in your house, keep it there.'

'Yes, Mr Mitter, it always stays in a chest. I hardly ever take it out. But tonight, I wanted you to see it, so . . .'

'Have you shown it to anyone else?'

'Just one other man. He's a writer. He came to my house last week, saying he was writing a book on the merchants of Bengal in the nineteenth century. I showed it to him, but no one else.'

'Very well. But is it generally known that you have got it?'

'Er . . . yes. You see, this writer went and told a reporter. A report came out the next day.'

'In the local papers?'

'Yes, three different papers picked up the story. It was published only yesterday.'

'Did it actually say the pearl was pink?'

'Yes, unfortunately.'

'That is bad news, Mr Boral,' Feluda sounded serious. 'Let me emphasize one thing. Please do not show it to anyone else. You have no idea how valuable it is. If you sold it, it would fetch enough money not just for yourself, but also for the next two generations in your family to live in comfort.'

'Really? Thank you very much for telling me this, Mr Mitter. I am much obliged.'

Before he put it away, each of us held the pearl in our hand and had a good look at it. Feluda said it wasn't just its colour that was remarkable, but also its shape, which must add to its value.

'The only unfortunate thing is this business of the press report,' Feluda clicked his tongue in annoyance. 'I hope it won't cause you any problems.'

'If it does, should I contact you?'

'Yes, you must. Someshwar here has my address and telephone number. Don't hesitate to give me a call. If necessary, you can bring that pearl to Calcutta.'

THREE

We left for Calcutta the next morning. Prof Haldar accompanied us, but Feluda did not mention the pink pearl even once in his presence. All he said on reaching home was, 'I wish the press hadn't got hold of the story!'

Two days passed eventlessly. On the third day, we were both in our living room, I reading and Feluda clipping his nails, when the telephone rang. Feluda answered it, spoke briefly, then put it down.

'That was Boral,' he informed me.

'Is he here in Calcutta?'

'Yes. He said he had to see me urgently. He is coming at half past five. He sounded both excited and disturbed. Topshe, go and call Lalmohan Babu.'

It was necessary to tell Lalmohan Babu, for he'd have been quite disappointed if we had left him out. 'If I'm not involved right from the start, Felu Babu, I cannot understand how things develop, and then I cannot think well enough to be able to help you!' he had once complained.

Lalmohan Babu arrived at five and, exactly half an hour later, Jaichand Boral turned up, just as Srinath came in with the tea.

Mr Boral looked tired and haggard. In the last couple of days, two national dailies had published the story of the pink pearl, which had clearly added to his worries. He quickly finished the glass of water Srinath offered him, then shook his head ruefully.

'Who knew a small report in the press would create such havoc? I have to tell you three things. First, a cousin of mine—Motilal Boral—has written to me, saying that if the pearl is sold, he wants a share of the proceeds since it is a family heirloom, not just my personal property. Motilal lives in Benaras. He runs a cinema. His letter openly implies that I have tried to deceive him by never telling him about the pearl.'

'I see. What's the second thing?'

'I received one more letter, from a man called Suraj Singh in Dharampur, which is in Uttar Pradesh. It was once a princely state. Suraj Singh appears to be a most powerful man in Dharampur for he wrote from Dharampur Palace. He says he has a huge collection of pearls, but he doesn't have a single pink one. So he'd like to buy the one I've got, and wants me to name a price.'

'OK, what about the third thing?'

'That's really the reason why I am here. It's really worrying me, Mr Mitter. Someone actually turned up at my house the day before yesterday. I think he was a Marwari. Judging by his clothes and the number of rings he was wearing—he even had a diamond stud in one ear—he was a very wealthy man. He said he collected antiques and art objects. I guess he sells them abroad at hefty prices.'

'And he wanted your pearl?'

'Oh yes. He offered me fifty thousand for it. I said I needed three days to think it over. He's visiting Calcutta at present. He has a house in Chittaranjan Avenue. So he gave me his address and said he must have my answer by ten o'clock tomorrow morning. He seemed totally determined to get the pearl. If I refuse, he might offer a bit more . . . after that, if I still don't agree, Mr Mitter, who knows what he might do?'

'What is this man called?'

'Maganlal Meghraj.'

Even Feluda was stunned for a few seconds by this revelation. Maganlal! Why did this man keep coming back into our lives? None of our adversaries in the past had been as dangerous as Maganlal. We had already dealt twice with him. Why did he want Mr Boral's pearl?

'Look, Mr Boral,' Feluda said eventually, 'you'll have to refuse his offer. That pearl is worth at least five times the amount he's offered you. He will sell it to a foreign buyer. That's what he does for a living . . . most of the time, anyway. We know him well.'

'But what if he doesn't listen to me? He did say nothing could stop him from getting it.'

'Yes, he would say that. Tell you what, why don't you leave your pearl with me? If you take it with you, Maganlal will definitely grab it. He would not hesitate to kill you, if he had to.'

'My God! What am I going to tell him, Mr Mitter?'

'Simply say that you didn't bring it with you since you decided not to sell it. After all, you cannot be expected to roam the streets of Calcutta with something so valuable in your pocket.'

'Very well, I will leave it with you. Here it is.'

Mr Boral took out the same handkerchief and handed over the red velvet box to Feluda, who locked it away in the Godrej safe that stood in his bedroom. Then he returned to the living room and said, 'What will you say to Suraj Singh? He is not going to give up easily, either.'

'Even so, my answer must be no. We've had that pearl for a hundred and fifty years. I have no wish to lose it. It's not as though I'm in desperate need of money. I manage pretty well with my own income—I own some farmland and then I have my salary.'

'All right. Let's see what happens tomorrow. You must tell me everything before you go.'

Mr Boral finished his tea and left.

'I can hardly believe Maganlal's got involved in this!' Lalmohan Babu exclaimed when he had gone. 'God knows what he'll do this time.'

'He may have put us in some tricky situations, Lalmohan Babu, but we outwitted him each time, didn't we? What happens this time depends entirely on Mr Boral and what he tells Maganlal. I only hope Maganlal doesn't get to know that Boral came to see me.'

'You took a great risk, Felu Babu. Did you really have to keep the pearl here?'

'Yes, there was no other way. If I had allowed Mr Boral to keep it with him, it would most certainly have gone to Maganlal tomorrow morning.'

FOUR
(JAICHAND BORAL'S STORY)

It did not take Mr Boral long to find Maganlal's house. The exterior of the house was most uninviting; but once he had stepped in, Mr Boral was surprised to see how neat and tidy the place was.

A bearer came down and took him to Maganlal. 'Jaichand Boral is here, huzoor,' he said, stopping outside a room at the far end of a passage.

'Come in!' called the gruff voice of Maganlal Meghraj.

Mr Boral walked into the room and took a sofa. Maganlal was seated on a mattress spread on the floor.

'What have you decided?' he asked.

'I am not going to sell the pearl.'

Maganlal was silent for a minute. Then he said slowly, 'You are making a mistake, Mr Boral. No one refuses my offer and gets away with it. Are you hoping to get a bigger amount?'

'No. I simply wish to keep it in the family. It's been with us for five generations.'

'You are not doing very well in life, are you? I saw your house in Sonahati. How much do you earn? Two thousand a month? Just think for a moment. If you sold that pearl to me, you'd get a lot of cash, just like that. Why are you being so foolish?'

'It's a matter of family pride. I couldn't explain it to you.'

'Where is that pearl?'

'I haven't got it.'

'You mean you didn't bring it here with you?'

'No, I didn't. There was no reason to, since I wasn't going to sell it to you.'

Maganlal rang a bell. The man who appeared almost instantly was tall and hefty. He looked enquiringly at his master.

'Ganga, search this man,' Maganlal ordered.

Ganga pulled Mr Boral to his feet. A thorough search yielded a wallet, a handkerchief and a small box of paan-masala.

'All right, give the stuff back to him.'

Ganga returned every object.

'Sit down.'

Mr Boral sat down again.

'I learnt in Sonahati that your club had given a reception for Pradosh Mitter.'

'Yes, that's right.'

'Did you meet him?'

'Why should I tell you? I don't have to answer all your questions.'

'No. There is no need to answer my question because I already know what happened. My men watched your movements from the minute you got off your train at Howrah. You checked into a hotel called Jogamaya, right?'

'Right.'

'You left your hotel at five o'clock and took a taxi. Then you went to Felu Mitter's house, correct?'

'If you know everything, why are you still asking questions?'

'That pearl is now with Felu Mitter.'

Mr Boral said nothing. Maganlal looked at him steadily. 'You have done something very stupid, Mr Boral. If you gave me your pearl, I'd have paid you fifty thousand rupees for it. Now, I will still get the pearl—sooner or later—but you won't get a single paisa.'

Mr Boral rose. 'May I go now?'

'Yes. I have nothing more to say. But I feel sorry for you.'

FIVE

Mr Boral came to our house at around twelve o'clock and told us what Maganlal had said.

'What do you want to do with the pearl now?' he asked. 'Should I take it back with me?'

'Maganlal knows I have got it here. He's an extremely cunning man. I shouldn't be surprised if he actually came here himself. I realize you are anxious to take the pearl back to your house, but believe me, it will be safer here. If you keep it, Maganlal will take it from you, by hook or by crook. We can't let that happen.'

'Very well. Let's wait until Maganlal leaves Calcutta. Once he's out of the way, I can come back and collect it from you.'

'Yes, that would be far better. Are you going back to Sonahati today?'

'Yes, by the evening train.'

'All right. Don't forget to let me know if anything untoward happens.'

The next morning, Someshwar Saha rang us from Sonahati. Mr Boral, he said, was attacked on his way back from Calcutta. He was struck on the head and he lost consciousness. When he came to, he found his belongings strewn all over. Someone had clearly gone through everything looking for a specific object.

'Maganlal did this!' I exclaimed when Feluda told me what Mr Saha had said.

'Of course. He obviously decided not to take chances. Thank God the pearl was not with Mr Boral.'

Lalmohan Babu dropped by in the evening, and was told of the latest development.

'This can mean only one thing, Felu Babu,' he declared. 'Maganlal will now try speaking to you. He must know for sure that you have got Boral's pearl.'

Barely five minutes later, a car stopped outside our house and then the doorbell rang. I opened it to find the object of our discussion standing there, beaming at me.

'May I come in, Tapesh Babu?' asked Maganlal.

'Certainly.'

Maganlal stepped in. Still dressed in a black sherwani and a white dhoti, he didn't seem to have changed at all.

'I have often wanted to visit your house, Mr Mitter. After all, we're such old friends, aren't we?' he remarked jovially. 'Hello Uncle, how are you?'

Lalmohan Babu stiffened. Maganlal had treated him so awfully on two previous occasions that he was clearly finding it difficult to relax in his presence.

'Fine, thank you,' he croaked after a while.

'Would you like a cup of tea?' Feluda asked politely.

'No, sir. I am not going to take much time, Mr Mitter. Perhaps you can guess why I am here?'

'Yes, perhaps I can.'

'Then let's not beat about the bush. Where is that pearl?'

'Mr Boral doesn't have it. At least that much you ought to know, since the men you sent to attack him did not find it.'

'My men?'

'Yes, who else would do such a thing?'

'Please don't talk like that, Mr Mitter. There is no evidence that those men were mine.'

'I don't even have to look for evidence, Maganlalji. A crook of your stature has his own style. I would recognize your style anywhere.'

'Is that so? Well, let me ask you again: where is that pearl?'

'With me.'

'I need it.'

'Too bad. You cannot always have what you need, or what you want.'

'Maganlal always gets what he wants. Why are you wasting your time talking? I want that pink pearl. If you don't give it to me, you know very well I have the means to take it from you.'

'Then you will have to resort to those means, won't you? You won't get it from me, Maganlalji.'

'No?'

'No.'

'Very well,' Maganlal rose. 'I will take my leave now. Goodbye, Mr Mitter. Goodbye, Uncle.'

'Goodbye,' Lalmohan Babu answered in a faint voice.

Maganlal stopped at the door and turned back. 'I am prepared to give you another three days,' he said, looking straight at Feluda. 'Today is Monday. Tuesday, Wednesday, Thursday. Think it over. Do you understand me?'

'Perfectly.'

Maganlal went out. Lalmohan Babu stared after him, shaking his head. 'I don't like this, Felu Babu,' he said. 'Why don't you give him the pearl and be done with it? How long can you keep it here, anyway? Boral will take it back sooner or later, won't he?'

'Yes, but not when there is even a remote chance of its failing into the wrong hands. I will return the pearl to its rightful owner only when I can be sure that Maganlal is out of the way.'

'What about that maharaja who is also interested in the same pearl? We know nothing about him, do we?'

'No, but there is someone who can tell us something about the man: Uncle Sidhu. I haven't been to see him for a long time. Let's visit him today.'

'What is that man called? Can you remember his name?'

'Suraj Singh.'

'And the place?'

'Dharampur, in Uttar Pradesh.'

We got into Lalmohan Babu's car and reached Uncle Sidhu's house in five minutes. We found him in his room inspecting an ancient scroll with a magnifying glass. He looked at us coldly.

'Who are you? I don't think I know any of you.'

Feluda laughed. 'You must forgive me, Uncle. I know it's a long time since I last visited you, but I've had so many cases that it simply didn't leave me any time for socializing. At least it means I am doing well in my work. You should be pleased.'

This time, Uncle Sidhu smiled. 'Felu Mitter,' he said, 'I have known you since you were a child of eight. You had killed a mynah with your airgun and brought the dead bird to show me. I had said to you, "It is a sin to kill a poor defenceless creature. Promise me you won't do it ever again." You understood, and stopped using your airgun. Of course I am glad you're doing well. But don't try boasting about it. I might have been a detective, too. I had—and still have—exactly what it takes. But that would have meant being tied down to a job, so I didn't bother. I am a bit like Sherlock Holmes's brother, Mycroft. His brain was even sharper than Sherlock's, but he was too lazy to do any serious work. Sherlock used to consult him sometimes. Anyway, what made *you* come here today?'

'I need some information about a man.'

'Who?'

'Have you heard of a place called Dharampur?'

'Certainly. It is in UP, seventy-seven miles to the south of Aligarh. It was once a princely state. Even today, there is no rail connection, one has to get there by road.'

'Then you must know about Suraj Singh.'

'Good heavens, is he still alive?'

'Yes.'

'He is quite a character. A multi-millionaire, he owns a chain of hotels; and has a stupendous collection of jewels. The best in India.'

'What's he like as a person?'

'I've no idea. Never met the fellow. But I do know this: men like Suraj Singh don't fall into a category. If you went to visit him, you might well find him a kind and hospitable man. But the same man would go to any length—even murder—to get what he wanted. Naturally, he wouldn't do it himself. He must have a lot of people working for him. He himself will never break the law, but his job will get done.'

Feluda thanked Uncle Sidhu, and we left. I couldn't quite see why and how we might have to deal with Suraj Singh, but when I mentioned this to Feluda, he replied, 'Since he's taken the trouble to write to Boral, it's obvious he's pretty keen to buy that pearl. I'd be very interested to see how far he'd go to get it. I'm glad we went to see Uncle Sidhu today.'

SIX

Maganlal had given us three days to give an answer. Feluda made no attempt to contact him in these three days. What happened on the fourth day left us reeling with shock.

It was a Friday. I got up as usual and finished doing yoga, which I had started to do recently, inspired by Feluda. By the time I finished. it was half past six. Normally, Feluda joined me at this time, bathed and fully dressed. There was no sign of him today.

I went to his room and found the door ajar. A slight push made it open widely. What I saw was totally amazing. Feluda was still lying on his bed, fast asleep. He should have been up more than an hour ago.

I went over to him quickly and tried to wake him. When he didn't respond even to some vigorous shaking, it dawned upon me that he was unconscious. Automatically, my eyes went to the Godrej safe. It was open, its contents lying on the floor.

Quickly, I felt his pulse. That—thank God!—appeared normal. I ran back to the living room and rang Dr Bhowmik, our family physician. He arrived in ten minutes. Feluda began stirring as the doctor started to examine him.

'Someone used chloroform, I think,' said the doctor. 'But how did he get in?'

It took me a minute to work that out. The side door to the bathroom, through which our cleaner came in every day, was open.

Feluda opened his eyes in about fifteen minutes. 'You'll be fine,' Dr Bhowmik said reassuringly. 'In just a few minutes, you're going to feel like your old normal self. What you need to check is whether anything has been stolen. Your safe is still hanging open.'

'Topshe, open the bottom drawer.'

I did, but couldn't find the red velvet box Mr Boral had left with us. His pink pearl had gone.

Feluda shook his head and sighed. 'Who can I blame but myself? I did bolt that door last night, I remember that. But the bolt had become rather loose. I noticed it a few days ago, but didn't get round to getting it fixed. Oh, I could kick myself!'

Dr Bhowmik left. I rang Lalmohan Babu and fold him what had happened. He came as soon as he could.

'Look, Felu Babu, I knew something like this would happen. I did try to warn you, didn't I? If they could come straight into your room and actually chloroform you, just think how dangerous these people are! What are we going to do now?' he asked.

Feluda, having recovered, was drinking a cup of tea. 'I am not going to tell Boral about this. At least, not immediately. Let's see if I can get that pearl back.'

The telephone rang. It was Someshwar Saha from Sonahati. Feluda spoke for about three minutes before replacing the receiver.

'Boral's got some fresh news. He's heard again from Dharampur. Singh still wants the pearl for his collection. He's offered one hundred and fifty thousand. Boral is now thinking of selling the pearl—after all, it's not a small amount. Besides, he's had to face so many problems lately that he's told Someshwar he'd be quite happy to get rid of it. Suraj Singh is going to Delhi for a week. He'll travel to Sonahati after that and meet Boral personally.'

'Then we've got to retrieve that pearl from Maganlal!'

'Of course. Topshe, see if Maganlal is listed in the telephone directory.'

I grabbed the directory and quickly found the right page. 'Yes, he is. Sixty-seven, Chittaranjan Avenue.'

'OK. Let me finish my tea, then we'll leave.'

'But are you feeling all right?'

'Oh yes. I am one hundred per cent fit.'

'Why don't you tell the police?'

'The police couldn't possibly tell me anything I don't know already. I don't wish to waste their time.'

It was ten minutes past nine when we reached Maganlal's house. 'God knows what he'll do this time,' muttered Lalmohan Babu as we walked in. But, as it turned out, Maganlal was not at home. He had left for Delhi that very morning.

'Did he go by air?' Feluda asked his bearer.

'No, sir. He went by train.'

We left. 'Isn't it odd,' Lalmohan Babu remarked, 'that the two people interested in the pearl have both gone to Delhi?'

'Yes, but we ought to get that verified.'

Feluda had friends everywhere, including the railway reservations office. We went there straight from Maganlal's house and Feluda found a man he knew, called Aparesh.

'How many trains left for Delhi this morning?'

'Only one. It left Howrah at 9.15 and will reach Delhi tomorrow at 10.40 a.m.'

'Now can you check your list and tell me if a Mr Meghraj went to Delhi by that train?'

Aparesh went through a reservation list and replied, 'Yes, here you are. Mr M. Meghraj, first class AC. But he wasn't booked to go to Delhi.'

'No? Then where's he gone?'

'Benaras. He'll get there tonight at half past ten.'

'Benaras?'

I felt surprised, too. But then, didn't Maganlal have his headquarters in Benaras?

'How many trains are there that will reach Benaras tomorrow morning?'

'There are two that leave at a reasonable time. One is the Amritsar Mail. It leaves at 7.20 in the evening and reaches Benaras at 10.05 a.m. The other's the Doon Express which will leave tonight at 8.05 and get to Benaras at 11.15 tomorrow morning.'

Feluda booked us on the Amritsar Mail. Had it not been for Aparesh's help, we'd never have got three reserved seats at such short notice. The only trouble was that we didn't have enough money. So we had to go back home and return to the railway booking office by twelve o'clock.

Lalmohan Babu left immediately to pack a suitcase.

'Take enough clothes to last you a week. I've no idea how long we might have to stay. And don't forget it's very cold over there,' Feluda warned him.

Our train left on time. The journey was eventless, except that Feluda bought a newspaper the following morning in which we read an important report. A group of American traders was visiting India. Suraj Singh was one of the Indians they were dealing with. That explained why Singh had gone to Delhi.

We reached Benaras only fifteen minutes later than the scheduled time.

SEVEN

Although this was my second visit, I still felt startled and strangely moved by the sight of the ghats and the streets of Benaras. We checked in at the Calcutta Lodge, where we had stayed before. Niranjan Chakravarty was still the manager there.

When Feluda asked him if he had a vacant room, he said, 'For you, sir, I will always be able to find a room. How long do you want it for?'

'I don't really know. Let's say a week.'

We were given a mini dormitory, like the last time. It had four beds in it, but the fourth was unoccupied. Since we had already had breakfast on the train, Feluda wanted to get cracking immediately.

'What exactly are you suggesting we do, Felu Babu? Walk straight into the lion's den?' Lalmohan Babu wanted to know.

'Yes, but you don't have to come with us, if you'd rather stay here.'

'No, no, of course not. We are the Three Musketeers, remember?'

We had to pass the temple of Vishwanath to get to Maganlal's house. The sights and the smells were very familiar. Nothing had changed in the past few years. Perhaps nothing would, even in the future.

We left the temple behind us and reached a relatively quiet spot. It all came back to me quite clearly. A left turn from here would take us to Maganlal's house.

'Have you decided what you're going to say?' Lalmohan Babu asked.

'No. I don't always prepare and rehearse my lines. Sometimes it's best to play things by the ear.'

'Is that what you want to do this time?'

'Yes.'

Here was Maganlal's house, with paintings of two armed guards by the front door. They were standing as before, with their swords raised high, but their colour seemed to have faded a little. We slipped in through the open door and stood in the courtyard.

'Koi hai?' Feluda shouted. When no one answered, he said, 'All right, let's go upstairs. We must meet the man, so there's no point in waiting here.'

Maganlal's room was on the second floor. I remembered we had had to climb forty-six steps to get there. No one stopped us on our way. As we reached the second floor and emerged at one end of a long passage, we found a man sitting near the stairs, rubbing tobacco leaves in his hand. He gave us a startled look.

'Who are you looking for?' he asked.

'Seth Maganlal. Is he here?'

'Yes, but he's having his lunch. Why don't you wait in his drawing room? I'll show you where it is.'

We followed the man into a room that I recognized instantly. This was where Maganlal had made a knife-thrower throw large, vicious looking knives around Lalmohan Babu, who had fainted at the end of the 'show'. Then, when we met him later in Kathmandu, he had dropped LSD into Lalmohan Babu's tea. Fortunately, our Jatayu came to no harm, but the whole episode had caused us a great deal of anxiety.

'Felu Babu,' said Jatayu as soon as we were seated. 'Please decide what you're going to say. I can't think of anything at all.'

'Don't let that worry you. You are not required to speak. I am.'

'Did you bring that thing with you?'

'That thing' clearly meant Feluda's revolver.

'Yes, I did. Do try to calm yourself. It's very difficult to tackle a tricky situation like this if one of my companions starts showing his nervousness.'

Lalmohan Babu did not say anything after this. We continued to wait for what seemed like ages. A wall clock ticked away, from somewhere came the sound of a drum, and I could smell food being cooked. Where was Maganlal?

'How long does he take to finish a meal?' Lalmohan Babu sighed impatiently. Almost immediately, a man entered the room. Judging by his size and bulging muscles, he was a wrestler. He went straight to Feluda and said, 'Stand up.'

'Why should I?'

'I have to search you.'

'Who's told you to do that?'

'The master.'

'Maganlal?'

'Yes.'

Feluda made no attempt to rise. The man caught him by his shoulders and pulled him to his feet. There did not seem to be any point in putting up a resistance, for the man was far stronger than Feluda.

The first thing that he found was the revolver. This was followed by Feluda's wallet and handkerchief. Then he turned to Lalmohan Babu and myself. Our pockets yielded no weapons. Finally, the man returned everything to us, except the revolver which he took away at once. His departure was followed by the sound of someone clearing his throat outside the room. A second later, Maganlal came in.

'Why are you hounding me like this, Mr Mitter?' he demanded, sitting down on a mattress. 'Haven't you learnt your lesson? What good is it going to do, anyway? You'll never get that pearl back.'

'You consider yourself very clever, don't you Maganlalji?'

'Sure, and so do you. I couldn't have run my business so successfully if I didn't have the brains, could I? If I wasn't clever, Mr Mitter, I could not have brought that pearl straight out of your bedroom.'

'Oh? And what pearl would that be?'

'The pink pearl!' Maganlal shouted, sounding intensely annoyed. 'Do I have to describe it to you? You know very well what I'm talking about.'

'No, Maganlalji,' Feluda said slowly, with unruffled calm. 'There is something *you* don't know. That pearl is a white pearl—a cheap, cultured white pearl, painted pink to fool you and your men who broke into my house. The real pink pearl has gone back to its rightful owner. Actually, you are not half as clever as you think.'

I listened to Feluda's words, absolutely amazed. How could he tell so many lies with a straight face? Where did he find such courage? I cast a quick glance at Lalmohan Babu. He was staring at the floor, his head bowed.

'Is that the truth, Mr Mitter?'

'Why don't you check it out?'

Frowning darkly, Maganlal rang a silver bell. The same large and hefty man answered it.

'Call Sunderlal from his shop. Tell him Maganlal wants to see him. Now.'

The man left. A few seconds passed in silence. Maganlal opened a paan box and stuffed a paan into his mouth. Then, shutting it again, he asked a strange question:

'Do you know any Tagore songs?'

I glanced quickly at him. He was looking at Lalmohan Babu.

'Why don't you answer me, Uncle? You can't be a Bengali and not know a Tagore song!'

Lalmohan Babu shook his head silently.

'No? You really don't? You expect me to believe that?'

Feluda spoke this time: 'He does not sing, Maganlalji.'

'So what? He'll sing now, for me. Sunderlal will take at least ten minutes to come here. Uncle will entertain us in the meantime. Come on, Uncle, get up and come and sit by me on the mattress. You'll find it easier to sing from here. Get up, get up. If you don't there's going to be trouble.'

'Why do you always make fun of him?' Feluda asked angrily. 'What's he done to you?'

'Nothing. That's why I like him so much. Go on then Uncle, get going.'

Lalmohan Babu was forced to rise this time and do as he was told. He went and sat down on the mattress and began singing, 'Let all be awash in this fountain of life'. The poor man could not sing at all, but he carried on nevertheless, for nearly five minutes. After that, he stopped abruptly and said, 'I don't know the rest.'

Maganlal had been tapping the top of his cash box in rhythm with the song. He nodded and said, 'That is enough. You were very good Uncle. Now go back to your sofa.'

Lalmohan Babu returned to where he had been sitting before. Just as he flopped down on the sofa, Maganlal's henchman came back, accompanied by an old man wearing thick glasses.

'Come in, Sunderlalji,' Maganlal opened his cash box and took out the little red velvet box Mr Boral had left with us. From it he extracted the pearl and asked, 'Did you know a pearl could be pink?'

'*Pink?*'

'Yes.'

'Well . . . yes, I have heard of pink pearls, but never seen one in my life.'

'You've been running a jeweller's shop for fifty years, and you've never seen one? Very well, just take a look at this. Tell me if you think it's genuine.'

Sunderlal took the pearl from Maganlal and held it gingerly between his thumb and forefinger, peering at it closely. I noticed that his hands were trembling slightly. He examined it for nearly a minute before saying, 'Yes, sir. It's a genuine pearl, and certainly it's pink. I never imagined I'd get to see something like this.'

'Are you sure it's not a fake?'

'I do not see any reason to think so, sir.'

Maganlal took the pearl back. 'All right, you may go now,' he said. Sunderlal left.

'You heard him, Mr Mitter,' Maganlal glared at Feluda. 'This pearl is genuine. You lied to me.'

'Will you try to sell it to Suraj Singh?'

'Why should I tell you? It's none of your business.'

'You'll now go to Delhi, I suppose?'

'What if I do?'

'Suraj Singh is in Delhi right now.'

'I am aware of that.'

'Do you mean to say you have nothing to do with Suraj Singh?'

'I am saying nothing, Mr Mitter, not a word. This whole business regarding the pink pearl is over now, the chapter's closed.'

'All right. Kindly allow us to leave since you won't talk, and return my property which your man confiscated.'

Maganlal rang the bell again. 'Give him back his revolver, and let them go,' he said irritably.

The revolver was duly returned to Feluda. We left immediately.

'How do you feel now?' I asked Lalmohan Babu as we emerged on the veranda.

'Better, thank you. God knows how he can guess a man's weak point. I have never sung a Tagore song for five minutes in my entire life!'

We reached the front door.

'I hope you realize, Lalmohan Babu,' Feluda said, stepping out, 'That we managed to find out something rather important today.'

'Something important?'

'Yes, sir. Now we know where that pearl is kept.'

'Yes, but. . . hey, are you planning to take it back from him?'

'Of course.'

EIGHT

We returned to our hotel. The manager, Niranjan Chakravarty, called from his room on seeing us: 'Mr Mitter, you have a visitor here. He's been waiting for you for quite some time.'

We went into the manager's room and found a man of about forty-five sitting opposite him. He rose as we entered.

'Namaskar. My name is Motilal Boral.'

'Namaskar. Are you Jaichand's cousin?'

'Yes, his first cousin. I own a cinema here.'

'Yes, he told us. Come to our room, we can talk more comfortably there.'

The four of us trooped upstairs to our room.

'Where is that pearl now? Is it still with Jaichand?' asked Motilal, sitting down on the fourth empty bed.

'No.'

'No?'

'Have you heard of Maganlal Meghraj?'

'Oh yes. I couldn't have spent twenty-three years in Benaras without having heard of Maganlal.'

'He has got the pearl.'

'But why? He's not a collector. He exports things, doesn't he? Buys stuff at a low price and then sells it abroad. Or so I've heard.'

'Yes, that's right. Only this time, he is going to sell it to Suraj Singh of Dharampur.'

'Really? Is Suraj Singh going to come here?'

'No. He's in Delhi, and Maganlal is going to go there very soon.'

'What are you going to do?'

'We shall travel to Delhi, too, if we can get hold of that pearl.'

'If Maganlal cannot sell it, will my cousin get paid?'

'Of course, provided Suraj Singh keeps his word.'

'The strange thing is that I did not even know our family possessed such a valuable object. You see, I left Sonahati when I was only fifteen, and never went back. Jai found the pearl and he kept it all these years without telling anyone. I wrote to him only when I read the newspaper report. His first letter said he was not going to sell it, but I heard from him only yesterday. He now seems to have changed his mind. Here's his letter.'

He took out a folded piece of paper and passed it to Feluda. Feluda read it quickly and handed it back.

'He has offered you thirty thousand rupees. Are you happy with that?'

'Not really, but I am not going to argue. Something is better than nothing, isn't it? But are you sure Maganlal has got the pearl?'

'Absolutely. We saw it with our own eyes.'

Motilal thought for a while. Then he said, 'Let me get this straight. If you get the pearl, you yourself will go and sell it to Suraj Singh. Is that right?'

'Right. You will get your share, and the money that remains will go to Jaichand.'

'So somehow we must get that pearl back.'

'Yes. Can you help me in this matter?'

'What would you like me to do?'

'Find me a few people who wouldn't mind doing something rather reckless.'

Motilal frowned, lost in thought. Then he looked straight at Feluda. 'Look, Mr Mitter,' he said, 'running a cinema isn't good enough these days. I mean, I don't make enough money that way. Most people like to watch videos at home. So I've had to think of doing other things to add to my income.'

'You mean things not entirely straightforward?'

'Yes, something like that; but without actually breaking the law.'

'Does that mean you do know of people who might agree to work for me?'

'Yes. In fact, Manohar—who used to be Maganlal's right-hand man—has joined me. I can arrange a couple of other men besides him.'

'That's brilliant.'

'Just let me know what needs to be done.'

'Come to the Gyan Bapi Masjid with your men at midnight. We'll meet you there.'

'All right.'

'Felu Babu,' Lalmohan Babu said anxiously, 'have you really thought this through?'

Feluda ignored him. 'Maganlal's current right-hand man is extremely strong. He'll have to be dealt with,' he told Motilal.

Motilal smiled. 'Don't worry about that. Manohar is a wrestler, too; plus he is an intelligent man.'

'Very well then. See you later tonight, at Gyan Bapi.'

Motilal stood up. 'By the way,' he stopped at the door, 'do you know where Maganlal has kept this pearl?'

'Yes, we saw it.'

'Good.'

Motilal Boral left. Feluda, too, got to his feet and said, 'I need to speak to Mr Chakravarty. It'll only take a minute. After that, we'll go and have something to eat. I am absolutely famished.'

NINE

There was something particularly eerie about the silence during the night in Benaras. This was possibly because, during the day, every street was filled with people, sounds, smells and colours. When we reached Gyan Bapi at midnight, everything was wrapped in darkness and all I could hear was a dog barking in the distance.

We had to wait for about five minutes. Just as Feluda finished his cigarette and crushed its stub with his shoe, a voice called softly: 'Mr Mitter!'

Four dark figures emerged from an alley. 'I brought three men,' said Motilal's voice. 'Are you ready?'

'Sure,' Feluda whispered back. 'We know our way. Let's go.'

We began walking. Both Motilal and Feluda seemed to be very familiar with the way to Maganlal's house. They were walking fast even in the dark. Only one streetlight shone in a corner. In its dim light I could see that one of Motilal's companions was as tall and muscular as Maganlal's man. That was obviously Manohar.

We stopped at the mouth of the alley that led to Maganlal's house. 'Please wait here,' Feluda said to Lalmohan Babu. 'We'll take about twenty minutes, I should think.'

The others left before either Lalmohan Babu or I could speak. They soon vanished from sight. We stood a little foolishly, unsure of what to do. Lalmohan Babu broke the silence after a couple of minutes.

'I can't imagine why your cousin had to go and get mixed up with those hooligans.'

'He'll explain everything, I am sure.'

'I don't like this at all.'

'Sh-h. I don't think we should talk.'

Lalmohan Babu fell silent again. If I strained my ears, I could hear the sound of a harmonium and ghungrus, coming from the far distance. I looked at the sky. Millions of stars winked back at me. I had never seen quite so many of them. Now I realized there was a very faint light, perhaps being cast by all those stars. There was no moon.

How long was it since we were left here waiting? Ten minutes? Fifteen? It seemed like hours. It felt strange to think that Maganlal's house was being burgled less than fifty yards away, but there was no noise, absolutely no way of telling what was going on inside.

Five minutes later, I heard footsteps coming back. Yes, it was Feluda and the others.

'Right, let's get back,' he said as they got closer.

'Mission—?' Lalmohan Babu began breathlessly.

'—Accomplished!' Feluda finished his sentence. Then he turned to Motilal Boral.

'Thank you very much for your help, Mr Boral. I'll make sure you get your share when that pearl is sold.'

We started walking back to the hotel. The other men waved, and disappeared into the darkness. None of us spoke on the way. As soon as we were back in our room, Lalmohan Babu burst into speech, unable to contain himself a moment longer: 'Come on, tell us what happened!'

'First look at this.'

Feluda took out the red velvet box from his pocket and placed it on his bed.

'Shabaash!' exclaimed Lalmohan Babu. 'How did you get it? There was no violence, I hope?'

'Yes, there was, I am afraid. There had to be. But the only person who received a blow on his head was Maganlal's henchman. Manohar did that. No one else was injured.'

'How did you open that cash box?'

'How is a locked object normally opened, Lalmohan Babu? I used a key.'

'What! Where did you get it?'

'From Maganlal.'

'How? Good heavens, what did you use? Magic?'

'No, sir. Not magic, but you might call it medicine. Supplied by a doctor our manager happens to know.'

'What nonsense are you talking, Felu Babu? What was supplied?'

'Chloroform,' Feluda replied with a grin. 'Tit for tat. Now do you understand?'

We took the Delhi Express the next evening, reaching Delhi at 6 a.m. the following day. Having stayed at Janpath Hotel during our last visit to Delhi, we went there straight from the station. Feluda began ringing various other hotels as soon as we were taken to our room. It took him ten minutes to find out where Suraj Singh was staying.

'Yes sir, Mr Singh is staying with us,' said a voice from Taj Hotel. 'Room number 347.'

'Could I speak to him, please?'

Luckily, Suraj Singh was in his room. Feluda told him he wanted to see him regarding the pink pearl. Mr Singh agreed immediately to see us in his room at six o'clock the same evening. We spent the afternoon eating at a Chinese restaurant and looking at the shops in Janpath. Then we went back to the hotel for a rest before leaving again at a quarter to six.

Feluda rang from the lobby at Taj Hotel to inform Mr Singh of our arrival. We were told to go up to his room.

The man who opened the door when we rang the bell turned out to be his secretary. 'Please sit down,' he said. 'Mr Singh will be with you in a minute.'

The three of us sat on a large sofa. It wasn't really just a room, but a whole suite. We were in the sitting room. Suraj Singh appeared shortly. One look at him was enough to tell us he was immensely wealthy. He was wearing an expensive suit, a golden tie-pin and a gold pen peeped from his front pocket. On his fingers he wore more than one gold ring, studded with precious stones. He was perhaps in his mid-fifties, although only a few strands of hair at his temple had turned grey: The rest of his hair was jet black, as was the rather impressive moustache he sported.

'Which one of you is Mr Mitter?' he asked.

Feluda rose and introduced himself. Mr Singh nodded, but continued to stand.

'What's your connection with the pink pearl?'

'I am a private investigator. Jaichand Boral left the pearl with me for safe keeping.'

'Really? How do I know you didn't steal it from him? Why should I believe you?'

'I couldn't prove anything, Mr Singh, if that's what you mean. You'll just have to take my word for it. I did not steal the pearl from Mr Boral. He gave it to me.'

'No, I am not prepared to accept that without sufficient evidence.'

'Very well. In that case, Mr Singh, you cannot buy the pearl. It will go back to Boral'

'No, you have got to give it to me.'

'I am not obliged to do anything of the sort. No one can force me.'

In a flash, Suraj Singh produced a revolver. This was followed by an ear-splitting noise. It took me a second to realize the noise had come from Feluda's Colt, not Singh's revolver. Feluda had realized what Mr Singh was going to do the instant he had moved his hand, and so had taken out his own weapon and fired it.

Mr Singh's revolver was knocked out of his hand. It fell on the carpet with a thud. I saw him glance again at Feluda. But, this time, his eyes held respect, not contempt.

'I once killed a tiger from a distance of forty yards, but your aim is far better than mine,' he admitted frankly. 'All right then, give me that pearl. I will write you a cheque.'

Feluda handed him the velvet box. Mr Singh took out the pearl from it, holding it gently. He turned it around, looking at it from different angles. His eyes gleamed with hope and excitement. Finally, he said, 'I'd like to have it examined by an expert. You wouldn't mind, would you? After all, I am going to pay an awful lot of money for it.'

'Fine, go ahead.'

'Shankarprasad!' Suraj Singh called. A neat little man of about forty emerged from the adjoining room. He wore glasses with a golden frame.

'Sir?'

'Take a good look at this pearl. Is it genuine?'

Like Sunderlal, Shankarprasad peered closely at it, frowning in concentration. A minute later, he gave it back to Mr Singh.

'No, sir,' he said.

'What! What do you mean?'

'This is not a genuine pink pearl, sir. It's only an ordinary cultured white pearl. Someone painted it pink, that's all.'

'Are you sure?'

'Absolutely.'

Suraj Singh turned to Feluda. His face had turned scarlet, he was shaking all over.

'You . . .' he muttered, clearly finding it difficult to speak, 'you . . . were trying to sell me a fake? You scoundrel!'

Feluda appeared totally astounded. 'I don't understand!' he exclaimed. 'Perhaps Jaichand Boral made a mistake. Maybe it was a fake pearl all along, but he didn't know it.'

'Shut up! Put that gun away.'

Feluda lowered his hand.

'Here's your stupid pearl!' Suraj Singh thrust the pearl and the little box into Feluda's hand.

'Now get out!' he barked.

The three of us walked out like three obedient children. I stole a glance at Feluda as we got into the lift. His brows were creased in a deep frown.

It was quite late at night by the time we reached our house in Calcutta two days later. Feluda had barely spoken during the journey.

The next morning, however, I heard him humming under his breath. It was the same song Lalmohan Babu had been forced to sing for Maganlal. He said nothing when I entered his room, but continued to move about restlessly, still humming. I felt quite pleased by this for I hate to see him depressed.

Lalmohan Babu arrived in five minutes. We heard his car toot outside. I opened the door; but before I could say anything, Feluda strode forward to greet him.

'Good morning!' he said, folding his hands and bowing low, 'Please do come in, O Clever One!'

Considerably taken aback, Lalmohan Babu stopped at the threshold and stuttered, 'D-does this m-mean you have . . .?'

'Yes, sir. I don't like being in the dark, Mr Ganguli, so it's impossible to keep me there for long. I have worked out the truth: you and my dear cousin were in it together, weren't you? Your own jeweller created the false pearl, right? But how, and when—?'

'I'll tell you, I'll tell you. Oh God, I'll be glad to make a confession!' Lalmohan Babu came in and sat down. 'Please forgive me for doing this, Mr Mitter, and don't be cross with your cousin, either. He helped me all right, but it wasn't his idea. You see, when you paid no heed to Maganlal's threat, I began to feel most concerned. He gave you three days to make up your mind—Tuesday, Wednesday, Thursday. I came back here on Tuesday, remember? You went off to get a haircut. Tapesh found your keys in your absence and opened your safe. Then he passed me Boral's pearl. I took it to my jeweller immediately, and he made a duplicate the same day. I returned on Wednesday and got Tapesh to slip it back into your safe. What I did was purely out of concern for your welfare, believe me.'

'I do. It was an admirable plan. Where is the real pearl?'

'With me, safe and sound. When you told Maganlal it was fake, for a minute I thought you had seen through everything.'

'No. I would never have thought you capable of such deviousness. I was bluffing before Maganlal and hoping his jeweller would simply say he couldn't tell if the pearl was genuine. How was I to know the old man would make a mistake and declare that it was?'

'Jaichand Boral will get a better offer, I am sure.'

'He already has, from an American millionaire. I found a letter from Someshwar waiting for me. He's been offered three hundred thousand rupees.'

'Oh good. I *am* pleased for him.'

Feluda now turned to me. I braced myself for a sharp tap on my head, or at least a long lecture, but all Feluda did was place his hand very gently on my shoulder.

'Let me give you a word of advice,' he said. 'When you write about this case, do not reveal what the two of you did until you get to the end of the story. It will hold the suspense, and your readers will enjoy your story all the more!'

[illegible]

[illegible] Wednesday, Thursday [illegible]

[illegible] Wednesday [illegible]

[illegible] the next [illegible]

[illegible]

[illegible] him [illegible]

[illegible]

[illegible] hand [illegible]

[illegible]

[illegible]

Dr Munshi's Diary

ONE

Today we were having samosas with our tea instead of daalmut. Lalmohan Babu had brought these from a shop that had recently opened in his neighbourhood.

'It's a shop called Let's Eat, and the samosas they make are absolutely out of this world!' he had told us a few days ago.

Having just demolished the ones he had brought, Feluda and I found ourselves in full agreement.

'Have you worked out the plot of your next book?' Feluda asked Jatayu.

'Yes, sir, including the title: *Flummoxed in Florence*. My hero, Prakhar Rudra, behaves like Pradosh Mitter in this book.'

'Really? He's a lot sharper, is he? And brighter?' Feluda laughed.

'You bet!'

'What about his creator? Is he any smarter?'

'Well, Felu Babu, all these years of hovering around you was bound to have had some effect.'

'Yes, but I shall be convinced only if you can pass a test.'

'A test? What kind of a test?'

'An observation test. Tell me, do you notice any change in me—or my appearance—since yesterday?'

Lalmohan Babu got up, stepped back and looked carefully at Feluda. After a few seconds of scrutiny, he shook his head. 'No, I can't spot any difference at all.'

'Then you've failed, and so has Prakhar Rudra. I cut my nails, after about a month, only minutes before you arrived. If you look at the floor, you'll find some bits there, shaped like the crescent moon.'

'Oh. Oh, I see what you mean.'

Lalmohan Babu looked a little crestfallen. Then he perked up and said, 'Very well. Now you tell me if you can spot any changes in me.'

'Shall I?'

'Yes, do.'

Feluda put his empty cup down on a table and picked up his packet of Charminar. Then he said, 'Number one, you had used Lux until yesterday. Today I can smell Cinthol. A result of ads on TV?'

'Yes, quite right. Anything else?'

'You are wearing a new kurta. The top button is open, presumably because you found it difficult to insert it in the buttonhole. Normally all your buttons are in place.'

'Correct!'

'There's more.'

'What else?'

'You take garlic every morning, don't you? I can smell it as soon as you come and sit here. Today I can't.'

'Yes, I know. My servant gets it ready for me, but today he forgot. He's getting quite careless. I had to have a stern word with him. Garlic is a wonderful substance, Felu Babu. I've been taking it regularly since '86. My whole system—'

Before he could continue this eulogy on garlic, the doorbell rang. I opened it to find a young man of about the same age as Feluda. Feluda stood up.

'Please come in,' he said.

'Are you—?'

'Yes, I am Pradosh Mitter.'

The man sat down on a sofa and said, 'My name is Shankar Munshi. You may have heard of my father, Dr Rajen Munshi.'

'The psychiatrist?'

'Yes.'

'I seem to have read something on him recently. Wasn't there a press report with his photograph?'

'Yes, you're quite right. You see, my father has kept a diary for over forty years. It is now going to be published by Penguin as a book. Father is well known as a psychiatrist, but there is a different area in which he has had quite a lot of experience: shikar. He gave up hunting twenty-five years ago, but he recorded his experiences in his diary. Penguin haven't yet seen any of it, but have offered to publish it since the diary of a psychiatrist who is also a shikari is bound to be something unique. However, they do know that my father has been writing interesting articles in medical journals, so in his own way he is already an established writer.'

'Was it your idea to have that report published in the press?'

'No, that was done by the publishers.'

'I see.'

'Anyway, let me now tell you why I am here. My father has always been very proud of the fact that he has only recorded the unvarnished truth in his diary. In talking about some of his cases, he has mentioned three men, although he has used just the first letter of their names. These are A, G and R. All three are now successful and well known in society. Many years ago, they had all done something terribly wrong, but they managed to evade the law. None of them was caught. Since my father has not used their full names, he is safe and knows he cannot be sued. Still, he rang them as soon as Penguin made their offer, and told them he was going to write about all three cases. A and G were initially not very happy about this; but when Father explained that their true identity was not going to be revealed, they gave their consent, albeit a little reluctantly. R raised no objection at all.

'Yesterday, as we were sitting down to have lunch, our bearer brought him a letter which had just been delivered. He grew so grave upon reading it that I had to ask him what was wrong. That was when he told me about these three people. Until then, I had had no idea.'

'Why not?'

'Because my father never spoke about his patients or his diary. He . . . he's a bit peculiar. All he has ever seemed to care about is his work. My mother, myself, our family . . . none of this appears to have any meaning for him. My own mother died when I was three. Then my father remarried, but he and my stepmother are not very close, either. In fact, my stepmother, too, has always held herself a little aloof from me. I used to be looked after by an old servant when I was a child. So I grew up rather distant from both parents. The good thing was that if I didn't get my father's love, I didn't get any interference from him, either. I was free to do what I liked, without any parental supervision or control.'

'And you didn't read his diary?'

'No. No one has read it.'

'I see. Going back to this letter, was it from one of these three people your father spoke to?'

'Yes, yes. Look, here it is.'

Shankar Munshi took out an envelope and passed it to Feluda. Lalmohan Babu and I stood behind him and read the letter when Feluda took it out. It was signed A. It said, 'I take back my word. If you get your diary published, you'll have to delete the portions in which you've mentioned me. This is not a request, but a command. If you do not obey it, you will pay for it, very heavily.'

'I have a question for you. How did your father get to know what these people did?'

'That's a rather interesting story. All three got away with what they had done, but their own conscience began to trouble them. A deep regret for their action, combined with a fear of making a slip somewhere and being caught out turned them into psychiatric cases. My father had made quite a name for himself, so all three came to him for treatment. Naturally, they had to tell him exactly what had happened and the reason for their fear. Without knowing these details, my father could not have treated them. In time, they recovered and went back to leading normal lives.'

'Is A the only person to have threatened your father?'

'Yes, so far. But my father's not too sure about G. He may well do the same.'

'Do you know what terrible crimes these men are supposed to have committed?'

'No; nor do I know their real names, or what they are now doing. But I am sure my father will tell you what he has never told me, or anyone else.'

'Did he ask to see me?'

'Yes, certainly, that's why I am here. One of his patients mentioned your name. He asked me if I had heard of you, so I said you were very well-known in your profession. At this, Father said, "A good detective has to be a good student of psychology. I'd like to speak to Mr Mitter. A threat like this is going to cause a great deal of disturbance—that's the last thing I want right now." So here I am. Do you think you can come to our house at ten o'clock on Sunday?'

'Yes, of course. I'd be glad to help, if I can.'

'Good. We'll see you on Sunday. Our address is 7 Swinhoe Street, and the house is called Munshi Palace.'

TWO

Seven Swinhoe Street did not seem to be the house of a doctor at all. Close to the front door stood a Royal Bengal tiger, over which the head of a bison was fixed on the wall.

Shankar Munshi met us downstairs, then took us to their living room on the first floor. The walls of this room also bore evidence of Dr Munshi's years as a shikari. How did he get the time to kill so many animals if he was a busy doctor?

He arrived in less than a minute. All his hair had turned white, I noted, but he was still quite strong and agile. He shook Feluda's hand and said, 'You appear very fit. You do physical exercises every day, don't you? Good, good. I am so glad you decided not to neglect your body even if you have to use your brain so much more in your job.'

Then he glanced at us. Feluda made the introductions.

'Are these people trustworthy?' Dr Munshi asked.

'Absolutely,' Feluda replied. 'Tapesh is my cousin and Mr Ganguli is a very close friend.'

'I see. I have to make sure, you see, because today I am going to tell you who the three men are, about whom I have written in my diary. I know you cannot help me unless you know the truth, but I don't want another soul to hear of it.'

'Please don't worry about it, sir,' Lalmohan Babu reassured him. 'No one will learn anything from us.'

'Very well.'

'We have already heard about the written threat,' Feluda said.

'Something else has happened, Mr Mitter. I received a verbal threat as well, on the telephone last night at around half past eleven. He was totally drunk, I think. It was Higgins. George Higgins.'

'The G in your diary?'

'Yes. He said, "I was a fool to accept what you told me. I am still running the same business that I used to when I went to you for treatment. In my field, I am virtually the only man who runs such a business. So loads of people are likely to recognize me simply from my initial. Leave me out of your book." I could hardly reason with a drunkard. So I put the phone down. I can see that talking to these people on the phone won't do. I really ought to visit them and have a face-to-face chat. But I am so busy with my patients every day that I don't think I shall ever find the time. That's why I'd like you to see them on my behalf. You'll have to visit only A and G. I've spoken to R. He doesn't think anyone will recognize him just from his initial.'

'I see. Who *are* these three people?'

'Have you got a pen and piece of paper?'

Feluda took out his notebook and his pen.

'A stands for Arun Sengupta,' Dr Munshi went on. 'He is the general manager of McNeil Company, and the vice president of Rotary Club. He lives at 11 Roland Road. You'll get his telephone number from the directory.'

Feluda noted everything down quickly.

'G is George Higgins,' said Dr Munshi. 'His business is to catch wild animals and export them abroad for foreign television. His address is 90 Ripon Street. He is an Anglo-Indian. I am not going to tell you who R is, unless it becomes absolutely necessary to do so.'

'What crime did A and G commit?'

'Look, I'll let you take my manuscript and read it. Read the whole thing, and then tell me if you think I have written anything so damaging about anyone that they can sue me.'

'Very well. In that case—' Feluda had to stop, for three men had entered the room. Dr Munshi introduced them.

'These people live with me, apart from my wife and my son. All of them wanted to meet you when they heard you were coming. This is my secretary, Sukhamoy Chakravarty; and this is my brother-in-law, Chandranath.'

Sukhamoy Chakravarty was probably no more than forty. He wore glasses. Chandranath was much older, possibly in his mid-fifties. For some reason, he looked as if he didn't have a job or an income of his own and that he merely lived with the Munshis.

'And this is one of my patients, Radhakanta Mallik. He's still under treatment. He'll remain here until he recovers fully.'

Radhakanta Mallik—a man in his late thirties—seemed oddly restless, blinking every now and then and cracking his knuckles. Why was he so nervous? If that was his ailment, he seemed a long way from recovery.

After greetings had been exchanged, Mr Mallik and Chandranath left, but Sukhamoy Chakravarty remained in the room. 'Please get my manuscript and give it to Mr Mitter,' Dr Munshi told his secretary. Mr Chakravarty went out and returned in a couple of minutes, carrying a thick, heavy envelope.

'That is the only copy,' Dr Munshi told us. 'Sukhamoy will type it out before we pass it on to the publishers.'

'Don't worry, I'll handle it very carefully. I am fully aware of its value,' Feluda replied.

We rose to take our leave. Shankar Munshi saw us off at the front door. We got into Lalmohan Babu's green Ambassador and left. On our way back, Lalmohan Babu spoke suddenly: 'I have a request, Felu Babu!' he said.

'What is it?'

'I want to read that manuscript after you. You'll have to lend it to me for a couple of days, please don't say no.'

'Why are you so keen?'

'I love reading tales of shikar. I find them quite irresistible . . .

please, Felu Babu, do not refuse.'

'All right. You may take it, but only for a day. Dr Munshi stopped going on shikar after 1965. A day should be enough to read the chapters where he speaks of animals and hunting. Remember, Lalmohan Babu, you must return the manuscript the day after you take it home.'

'OK, OK, I won't forget. I promise!'

THREE

Although Dr Munshi's writing was quite clear and legible, it took Feluda three days to finish reading his manuscript, which ran to 375 pages. But the delay was partly due to the fact that Feluda had to stop every now and then to make notes in his own notebook.

On the fourth day, Lalmohan Babu turned up.

'Have you finished?' he asked as soon as he stepped in.

'Yes.'

'So what is your view? Is it safe to publish that book as it stands?'

'Absolutely. But what I think is not going to make any difference to those men who are convinced they are going to be recognized. I don't think they'll stop at anything to prevent its publication.'

'What, even murder?'

'That's right. Take A, for example. Arun Sengupta. His ancestors were wealthy zamindars. When he was a young man, Sengupta was a middle-ranking bank officer. But he had inherited his forefathers' passion for spending money. So he ran up heavy debts, even borrowing from kabuliwallas.'

Kabuliwallas, Feluda had told me once, were men from Kabul, who made a living out of lending money at a very high rate of interest. They had left the country now, but once the sight of kabuliwallas standing at streetcorners, carrying heavy sticks, was pretty common.

'A time came when the amount he owed became so enormous that Sengupta got absolutely desperate. He stole forty thousand rupees from his bank. However, he did it with great cunning, so that no suspicion could fall on him. A junior officer was blamed, who had to spend a few years in jail.'

'I see!' Jatayu cried. 'This was followed by great pangs of conscience, then that became a psychological problem, and so he had to see Dr Munshi. But now . . . now this Sengupta is an important man. That can only mean Dr Munshi's treatment worked beautifully, and Sengupta recovered.'

'Correct. Dr Munshi has mentioned the success of his treatment, but nothing else. Nevertheless, it is not difficult to imagine how Sengupta must have changed his lifestyle, and gone from strength to strength to reach the position he is at today. So he is naturally anxious to remove any possibility—however remote—of being exposed and ridiculed.'

'I see. What about the other two?'

'I cannot tell you who R is because Dr Munshi has said nothing about his real identity. Apparently, he knocked a man down while driving. The man died, but R got away with it simply by bribing a few people. His own conscience did not spare him, however, and so he ended up at Dr Munshi's clinic. Anyway, his case isn't so important since he has raised no objections. What is interesting is the case of George Higgins.'

'What did Higgins do?'

'You know he exports wild animals, don't you? Well, in 1960 a Swedish film director came to Calcutta to make a film in India. He needed a leopard for his film. Someone told him about Higgins, so he met him at his house. It turned out that he did have a leopard, but it was not for export. It was his own, Higgins treated it as his pet. The Swedish director paid a lot of money to hire the animal for a month. He promised to return it, safe and in one piece, within a month. But that did not happen. The leopard was killed by some villagers, as was described in the film script. When the director eventually visited Higgins and told him what had happened, Higgins was so outraged that he lost his head. In a fit of insane rage, he caught the Swedish man by the throat and throttled him to death. When he realized what he had done, fear replaced fury—but even so, he did not fail to think of a plot to save himself. First, he took a knife and made deep wounds all over the body of his victim. Then he found a wild cat among the animals he kept in his collection in his house. He released the cat from its cage, and shot it. It then looked as if the cat had somehow escaped and attacked the film director. Higgins shot the cat, but the director was already dead. This ruse worked, and the police believed his story. However, Higgins began having nightmares. Night after night, he saw himself being dragged to the gallows and hung by the neck. These terrible dreams soon drove him to seek help from Dr Munshi. Munshi helped him recover, and you know the rest.'

'Hmm, very interesting. What should we do now?'

'I have to do two things. Number one, I must hand over the manuscript to you; and number two, I must ring Arun Sengupta.'

Lalmohan Babu took the proffered packet with a big smile. 'Are you going to meet Sengupta?' he asked.

'Yes, there's no point in waiting any more. Topshe, go and find his number. Arun Sengupta, 11 Roland Road.'

The phone rang as soon as I picked up the directory. It was Dr Munshi. Arun Sengupta had sent him another letter. Feluda spoke quickly, noting down the details of the letter. Then he put the phone down and read it out to us:

> I give you seven days. In that time, I wish to see it reported in every newspaper in Calcutta that your diary is not going to be published due to some unavoidable reason. Remember, only seven days. If you do not do as you are told, these warnings will stop and I will get down to direct action. Needless to say, the results will not be happy—at least, not for you.

I found Sengupta's number and dialled it quickly. Luckily, I got through at once. Then I passed the receiver to Feluda, and heard his side of the conversation:

'Hello, could I speak to Mr Arun Sengupta, please? . . . My name is Pradosh Mitter . . . Yes, that's right. Can I come and see you? . . . Really? How strange! What's the matter? . . . Certainly. When would you like me to be there? . . . All right. See you then.'

'Just imagine!' he exclaimed as he replaced the receiver. 'He said he was about to call me himself.'

'Why?'

'He didn't want to talk about that on the phone. He'll tell us everything in person, he said.'

'When does he want to see you?'

'In half an hour.'

FOUR

Eleven Roland Road was a house with two storeys, built during

British times. A bearer in uniform answered the door, and took us upstairs. The wooden stairs were covered by a carpet.

Mr Sengupta arrived in a couple of minutes, wearing a, dressing gown and bedroom slippers. In his hand he held a cheroot.

'Can I offer you a drink?' he asked after we had introduced ourselves.

'No, thank you. We don't drink,' Feluda replied.

'I hope you won't mind if I have a beer?'

'No, of course not.'

Mr Sengupta called his bearer and told him to bring us tea, and a glass of beer for himself. Then he turned to Feluda.

'If you don't mind, Mr Sengupta,' Feluda said before he could speak, 'Could you first tell me why you were keen to meet me? I will then tell you the reason why I wanted to come here.'

'Very well. Have you heard of G.P. Chawla?'

'Guru Prasad Chawla? The businessman?'

'Yes.'

'One of his grandsons—?'

'Yes, he's missing. Possibly kidnapped.'

'I read about it in the papers.'

'I have known Chawla for many years. The police are doing their best, but I suggested your name to Chawla.'

'I am sorry, Mr Sengupta, but I am already working on a case. I couldn't take on another one.'

'I see.'

'In fact, I am here regarding this case I am handling right now.'

'Really? What's it about?'

'It involves Dr Munshi.'

'What!'

Mr Sengupta jumped to his feet. 'Munshi told you about me? Then in just a few weeks the whole world will come to know who A is, when they read his book.'

'Look, Mr Sengupta, I know how to keep a secret. You may trust me. But no good can possibly come out of sending repeated threats to Dr Munshi.'

'Why shouldn't I threaten him? Have you read his book?'

'Yes.'

'What did you think?'

'He has mentioned something that happened thirty years ago. In these thirty years, there has been embezzlement of funds in at least five hundred banks. It is very likely that many of the other culprits have names that also start with A. You have nothing to fear.'

'Has Munshi mentioned the name of my bank?'

'No.'

'There were two officers there who had suspected me at the time. I had gone to them to borrow some money, but neither had agreed.'

'Mr Sengupta, let me assure you again—you have no cause for concern. Besides, what do you think you are going to gain by sending these notes? Dr Munshi has done nothing to break the law. You couldn't possibly take any legal action against him. Surely you aren't thinking of doing anything illegal?'

'If I find myself in trouble, Mr Mitter, I am not going to worry about the law. Since you know my history, you must also know that I would not hesitate to take drastic measures.'

'You seem to have gone quite mad, Mr Sengupta. You are not the same man you were thirty years ago. You are well-known now, and highly respected. Why should you want to risk losing your position in society by doing something stupid?'

Mr Sengupta did not reply immediately. He sat in silence, sipping his beer. Then his face softened a little. He finished his remaining drink in one gulp, put the glass down on a table and said, 'All right, damn it! Let him go ahead.'

'Does that mean there will be no more threats from you?'

'Yes, yes, yes. I will stop—but, let me remind you, if I see even a hint of any trouble whatsoever . . .'

'I know, I know. You have made yourself quite clear, Mr Sengupta. I will pass on your message to Dr Munshi.'

FIVE

True to his word, Lalmohan Babu returned the manuscript the following day. Feluda thanked him and said, 'I am afraid we haven't got time for a cup of tea. I spoke to G; he wants to see us in half an hour.'

The man who opened the door at 90 Ripon Street was bald, but had white hair round his ears. The rather impressive moustache he sported was also totally white.

'Mr Mitter? I am George Higgins,' he said. He shook hands with all of us, then took us to his living room. It was a big house with a large compound. I noticed two big cages, one of which contained a tiger, and the other a hyena. I might as well be in a zoo, I thought.

'You are a detective?' Mr Higgins asked Feluda when we were all seated.

'Yes, a private one,' Feluda replied.

'I see. So . . . you've spoken to Munshi, have you? I must admit he helped me a lot when I was in trouble.'

'If that is so, why did you threaten him?'

Higgins was silent for a few moments. Then he said, 'Well, one reason for that was I had had a bit too much to drink that night. But tell me, is it not natural that I should feel anxious? Do you know what my father was? Just a station master. And look at me! I have done so well in life, simply through my own efforts and hard work. I have a monopoly in this business. I am well-known as the only man who deals with exporting animals. If Munshi's book is published, and if his readers can recognize me simply from the initial G, can you imagine how badly my business is going to be affected?'

In reply, Feluda had to repeat what he had told Arun Sengupta. There was nothing George Higgins could do legally; and if he decided to break the law in the hope of saving his reputation, things could only get worse.

'Is that what you really want?' Feluda asked him, raising his voice a little. 'Do you think doing something unlawful will enhance your prestige?'

Higgins fell silent once more. Then I heard him mutter: 'I don't regret having killed that Swedish swine. If I could get the chance, I'd kill him again. Bahadur . . . my leopard . . . how I loved him! . . . He was only four years old. And that stupid oaf had him killed, for nothing!'

No one said anything in reply. Higgins seemed lost in thought. Finally, he looked up and suddenly slapped the arm of his chair. 'Very well,' he said clearly. 'Go and tell Munshi I don't give a damn what he does with his diary. I don't care if I am recognized. Nothing can harm my business. I know it.'

'Thank you, Mr Higgins. Thank you very much.'

Feluda had already rung Dr Munshi and told him about Arun Sengupta. Now we went to his house to report on George Higgins. Besides, the manuscript had to be returned.

Dr Munshi thanked us profusely and said to Feluda, 'You have done a splendid job, Mr Mitter. You may go home and relax now.'

'Are you sure?' What about R?'

'He's all right, he'll never raise any objections. Don't worry about R, Mr Mitter. Send me your bill and I will pay it immediately.'

'Thank you.'

We came back. 'Felu Babu,' said Jatayu on reaching home, 'can you really call this a case?'

'You can call it a mini case; or a case-let.'

'Yes, I guess that's quite apt.'

'What amazes me is that all these people committed serious crimes, and yet continued to live normal lives. No one was caught and punished by the law.'

'Exactly. That's what I was thinking, too. I was trying to remember how many people I knew closely thirty years ago, and what eventually happened to them. After hours of thinking, I could remember just one man. A fellow called Chatterjee. I used to go to the cinema with him, see football matches, spend hours in the coffee house.'

'Where is he now?'

'God knows. I cannot even recall how I lost touch with him. He just vanished from my life.'

Lalmohan Babu dropped by for a chat the next day.

'Why do you appear a bit depressed?' he asked Feluda. 'Is it because you are out of a job?'

'No, sir. I am not depressed. It's just that I am still very curious about R. I wish I knew who he was. I can't rest easy until I find that out. It would have been simpler if R had also made threats.'

'Rotten, rubbish, ridiculous!' said Lalmohan Babu emphatically. 'Let R go to hell. You're being paid in full, aren't you?'

'Yes.'

'Well then, you should forget the whole thing, Felu Babu.'

The phone rang. I answered it. It was Shankar Munshi. I passed the receiver to Feluda.

'Hello?' said Feluda and listened intently for the next few seconds. A deep frown appeared between his brows as Shankar Munshi began speaking. Then he simply said 'hmm' and 'yes' a couple of times before putting the phone down.

'I can hardly believe what I just heard,' he said, turning to us. 'Dr Munshi has been murdered, and his manuscript is missing.'

'My God!'

'We thought the case was over, didn't we? This is just the beginning.'

We left immediately in Lalmohan Babu's car without wasting another second.

The police had already arrived at Munshi Palace. The inspector in charge—Inspector Shome—happened to know Feluda. 'He was killed in the middle of the night,' he said. 'Struck on the back of his head by a heavy instrument.'

'Who was the first to find the body?'

'His bearer. He took him a cup of tea at six o'clock, as he did every day. That's when he saw what had happened. Dr Munshi's son was not at home. We were informed by his secretary.'

'Have you finished speaking to everyone?'

'Yes, but you can start your own investigation, Mr Mitter. I know your work will not hinder ours. There are only four people to question, anyway. But there is also Mrs Munshi. We haven't yet asked her anything.'

Feluda thanked the inspector, and we made our way to the living room upstairs. Shankar Munshi came with us. 'I had feared many things,' he said with a sigh as we entered the living room, 'but not this!'

'I know it cannot be easy for you, but I will have to ask questions and it may be simple if I start with you.'

'Very well. What would you like me to tell you?'

We sat down. I couldn't help glancing at the heads of all the animals that graced the walls. Who could have guessed that such an expert shikari would one day be killed himself?

Feluda began: 'Is your room on the first floor?'

'Yes. My room is in the northern side. Father's was in the south.'

'Did you go out this morning?'

'Yes.'

'Where did you go?'

'To get hold of our doctor. His phone is out of order. I knew that he goes for a long morning walk every day near the lake. So I went out to catch him on the way. I have been getting a headache for the last few days. Perhaps my blood pressure has gone up.'

'Couldn't your father have checked your blood pressure at home?'

'No. That's another example of my father's peculiar behaviour. He refused to treat people of his own family even for minor ailments. We had been told to consult Dr Pranav Kar.'

'I see. Let me tell you something, Mr Munshi. You said your father was indifferent towards you. That is not true. He mentions you frequently in his diary.'

'Very surprising.'

'Didn't you ever want to read it?'

'No. I haven't got the patience to read such a long handwritten manuscript.'

'I assume what he has written about you is true and correct?'

'It would be so only from my father's point of view. I mean, he wrote what he felt to be true and correct. My point is, when did he get the chance to find out what I was really like? He was so totally preoccupied with his patients all the time, he did not know me at all.'

'Do you have any idea what his monthly income was?'

'No. But judging by the amount he spent, his income might well have been in the region of thirty thousand.'

'Did you know he had made a will?'

'No.'

'He made it last year, on the first of December. A portion of his savings will go to psychological research.'

'I see.'

'His will includes you too.'

'I see.'

'Can you throw any light on this murder?'

'No, none at all. It's come like a bolt from the blue.'

'And the missing manuscript?'

'That may have been stolen by one of the three people he's mentioned in it. I mean, one of them might have hired a man to break into the house and steal it. They had all visited this house before. They knew which was his consulting room. They also knew that the next room was his office. That was where the manuscript used to be kept.'

'Your front door is always kept locked at night, I presume?'

'Yes, but there is a spiral staircase at the back of the house that's used by the cleaners. A thief could have sneaked in using those stairs.'

'I see. All right, that's all for now. Could you please send in Mr Chakravarty?'

Dr Munshi's secretary, Sukhamoy Chakravarty, entered the room a minute later, and took a chair at a little distance. Feluda began his questions.

'Tell me, this manuscript that got stolen . . . was it always kept lying around?'

'No. It was kept in a drawer, but the drawer was never locked. This was so because neither Dr Munshi, nor I, could ever have imagined it might be stolen.'

'When did you realize it was missing?'

'This morning. I had planned to start typing it today. But when I opened the drawer to take it out, it wasn't there!'

'I see. How long have you been working as Dr Munshi's secretary?'

'Ten years.'

'How did you get this job?'

'Dr Munshi had put in an advertisement.'

'What kind of work did you have to do?'

'Handle his appointments, and his correspondence.'

'Did he get a lot of letters?'

'Yes, quite a few. Various societies and associations from foreign countries used to write to him regularly. He used to travel abroad every couple of years to attend conferences.'

'Are you married?'

'No. I have no family, except my widowed mother and an aunt.'

'Do you live with them?'

'No. I live here. Dr Munshi gave me a room on the ground floor. I have lived here ever since I started. My mother and aunt live in Beltola Road, number thirty-seven. I visit them occasionally.'

'Can you throw any light on this murder?'

'I am afraid not. I can understand about the stolen manuscript. After all, there had been a number of threats, and there were people who did not want to see it published. But the murder strikes me as completely meaningless.'

'How was Dr Munshi as an employer?'

'Very good. He was always very kind and affectionate towards me, appreciated my work and paid me well.'

'Did you know that if his book got published, the copyright would have passed to you after his death?'

'Yes, he had told me.'

'Would the book have sold well, do you think?'

'Yes, the publishers certainly seemed to think so.'

'That would have meant a fat income from the royalties, wouldn't it?'

'Are you implying I killed Dr Munshi just to get the royalty from the sale of his books?'

'It is a strong motive, surely you cannot deny that?'

'But I have got plenty of money. Enough for my own needs. Why should I kill my employer when I am not in any dire need of it?'

'I cannot answer that question yet, Mr Chakravarty. I need a little time to arrive at the truth. Anyway, I have no more questions for you.'

'Would you like to talk to anyone else?'

'Yes, please. Could you send Dr Munshi's brother-in-law? Thank you.'

Lalmohan Babu turned to Feluda when Mr Chakravarty had gone.

'What do you think, Felu Babu? Is the disappearance of the manuscript a separate issue, or is it linked with the murder?'

'Let's find the gun first, only then can we jump it.'

'What is that supposed to mean?'

Feluda made no reply.

SIX

Dr Munshi's brother-in-law arrived almost instantly. From the way he kept mopping his face, it seemed as if he was feeling nervous for some reason.

'Please sit down,' Feluda invited. He took a chair.

'Your name is Chandranath, I gather. What is your surname?'

'Basu.'

'You've been living here for about fifteen years, is that correct?'

'Yes, but how did you . . . ?'

'I have read Dr Munshi's diary. I know a few things about you, but would like you to confirm everything, if you don't mind.'

Mr Basu wiped his face again.

'Did Dr Munshi actually ask you to come and live here?'

'No. It was my sister's idea.'

'Did Dr Munshi agree readily?'

'No.'

'So how . . .?'

'He agreed . . . only when my sister . . . requested him repeatedly.'

'You haven't got a job, have you?'

'No.'

'Are you given an allowance every month?'

'Yes.'

'How much?'

'Five hundred.'

'Is that sufficient?'

Mr Basu averted his gaze and looked down at the carpet without making a reply. It was obvious that five hundred rupees a month was inadequate for him.

'You went to college, didn't you? You studied up to the intermediate year, I think?'

'Yes.'

'How were you as a student? Average? Or worse than that?'

Mr Basu remained silent.

'You failed in your first year at college, didn't you? Was that the reason why you never got a job?'

Mr Basu nodded, still looking at the floor.

'Do you do any work in this house?'

'Work? Well yes, I help with the shopping . . . I go to the chemist, if need be . . . things like that.'

'I see. Is your bedroom on the first floor?'

'Yes.'

'Where exactly is it? How far from Dr Munshi's room?'

'Quite close.'

'Close? You mean your room is right next to his?'

'Ye-es.'

'What time do you usually go to bed?'

'Around ten-thirty.'

'And when do you get up?'

'Six o'clock.'

'Do you have anything to say about this murder?'

'No, no. Nothing at all.'

'Very well. You may go now, but please send Radhakanta Mallik. I have some questions for him as well.'

Radhakanta Mallik arrived in a few moments, threw himself

down on a sofa and began shaking his head and waving his hands rather violently. 'I know nothing about this murder . . . absolutely nothing . . . not a thing! . . .'

'Please calm down. Have I said that you're suspected of knowing anything?' Feluda asked.

'No, but you *will* say it eventually. I am not a fool. I know you detectives. I hate this whole idea of having to answer endless questions. I am going to tell you all I know. Just hear me out. When I first arrived here with an ailment, I did not know what it was called. Dr Munshi told me it was persecution mania. I had started to suspect everyone around me of being my enemy, and I mean everyone—all family members, neighbours, colleagues, the lot. It seemed as if they were all lying in wait. Each of them would attack me, if only they got the chance. This was something I had never experienced before. I cannot even recall when it started. But what I do know is that it reached a point when I could not sleep at night. I didn't dare close my eyes, in case I was attacked in my sleep.'

'Did Dr Munshi's treatment work?'

'Yes, but progress was rather slow. He wanted me to stay here for another couple of weeks. Then he said I could go home. But now . . . it's all over.'

'Will you go home right away?'

'Yes, as soon as the police let me leave.'

'You have a job, presumably?'

'Yes, I work for Popular Insurance.'

'All right, you may go now.'

After Radhakanta Mallik left, Feluda went alone to inspect the body and the place of the murder. The murder weapon had not yet been found. The police surgeon had arrived in the meantime and said that Dr Munshi had been killed between four and five in the morning. The manuscript had not been found, but the police were still looking for it. Inspector Shome had offered to let Feluda know immediately if they found it.

'Is it possible to talk to Mrs Munshi?' Feluda asked the inspector.

'Yes, I think so. She's taken it quite well, I must say. A brave lady!'

The three of us went to Mrs Munshi's room. She was sitting on her bed with her back to the door, facing a window. She turned her head to look at us when Feluda knocked on the open door. I gave a start. Mrs Munshi looked exactly like her brother. Were they twins?

'Namaskar,' Feluda said. 'My name is Pradosh Mitter. I am a

private investigator. I am here to investigate your husband's death. I am sorry to disturb you, but—'

'—You'd like to ask me some questions. Is that it?'

'Yes, if you don't mind.'

Mrs Munshi looked away. 'Go ahead,' she said in a flat voice. Her face did not bear any traces of tears. Her eyes were expressionless.

'Do you have anything to say about this whole tragic business?'

'What can I say? It's his diary that's responsible, I am sure of it. I told him so many times not to have it published. People in our society have not learnt to face facts, and live with the truth. Many of them would have been hurt, angry and upset. But he . . .'

'Mrs Munshi, I have read the book that was going to be published. I don't think there was anything incriminating in it.'

'I am pleased to hear that.'

'Are you and Mr Basu twins?'

'Yes.'

'When you suggested he come and live here permanently, what did your husband say?'

'He agreed, somewhat reluctantly.'

'Why was that?'

'He could not accept the idea that my brother didn't have a job. He himself was so totally devoted to his own job that he couldn't imagine how anyone could live without one.'

'Thank you, Mrs Munshi. That's all I needed to know.'

SEVEN

It was past twelve o'clock by the time we got back home. We invited Lalmohan Babu to have lunch with us, and he agreed.

'A remarkable woman!' he said, turning the regulator of our fan to its maximum speed, and stretching out on his favourite couch. 'So calm and collected even at a time like this—and look at her brother! Just the opposite, isn't he?'

'Perhaps that is why she is so fond of her brother,' Feluda mused. 'Feelings and emotions are a complex business, Lalmohan Babu. I think what Mrs Munshi feels for her brother is more than just sympathy and compassion. She is protective, like a mother. Don't forget she has not got children of her own, nor is she close to her stepson. Her brother has probably always been like a child to her.'

'Besides, they are twins. So naturally they are close.'

'Right.'

'Do you think she did not get on very well with her husband?'

'I couldn't say, Lalmohan Babu, without a degree of intimacy with the Munshi family. In my job, I have to make my deductions solely from what my eyes and ears tell me.'

'What did your ears tell you in this case?'

'Something struck me as odd.'

'What did?'

'You should have realized it too. I am surprised you didn't.'

Now I felt I had to tell him what was bothering me.

'Could it be that she has read Dr Munshi's diary? Is that what you mean, Feluda?'

'Well done, Topshe! That's the impression I got from what she said.'

'Why, Felu Babu, Dr Munshi could simply have told her what he had written in his diary. How do you know she read it?'

'Maybe she didn't. But it's the same thing, isn't it? The point is that she knows what that diary contained.'

'I realized something when I read that manuscript, Felu Babu. Dr Munshi clearly had a lot of affection for his wife. The very first page proved that. I mean, if he was indifferent to her, why should he have dedicated his book to his wife?'

'Yes, that's a good point.'

'I picked up something else. I use my ears, too, you know. Dr Munshi's son may feel his father ignored him and was uncaring. But he was kind and generous to his secretary. So he could not have been a totally uncaring man, could he?'

'Good, good!' said Feluda somewhat absently and began pacing up and down.

A minute later, Lalmohan Babu asked, 'What's bothering you now?'

'Just this: there is only one name among the three that we don't know. Who is R? My enquiries would never be complete unless I can find out who he is. But I suppose I'll just have to . . .'

Feluda was interrupted by the telephone. It was a new instrument. Its ring was louder and sharper than the old one. Feluda answered it.

It was an incredible call, a perfect example of what Feluda refers to as telepathy. The conversation went like this:

'Hello.'

'Mr Mitter?'

'Speaking.'

'This is R. The R in Munshi's diary.'

'What!'

'Yes.'

'Oh. Oh, I see. But why are you calling me? How do you know about my connection with Dr Munshi?'

'You went to his house this morning, didn't you?'

'Yes, I certainly did. He was killed early this morning. That's why I was there.'

'You are a pretty well-known figure, Mr Mitter. A neighbour of Munshi's saw you go into the house and recognized you. This neighbour happens to be one of my patients. Oh, didn't you know I was a doctor too? Yes, I am; and I visited this patient only about an hour ago. When he mentioned having seen you, I put two and two together and deduced that you must have been employed by Munshi.'

'Will you tell me your real name, please?'

'No. That must remain a secret. But I want to know what Munshi said about me.'

'He said he knew you well, and had told you about the publication of his diary. He said you had no objection to his mentioning your case and referring to you as R.'

'Nonsense! That's a complete lie. How could he have spoken to me? I wasn't even here! I got back to Calcutta only the day before yesterday after a long absence. While going through old copies of the *Telegraph,* I came across a report that said Penguin was going to publish his diary. This worried me. I knew how well-informed he was about the intimate details of his patients' lives, including my own. So I rang him and asked him straightaway if he had mentioned my case. He tried to reassure me by saying it did not matter since he had only used the first letter of my name. But that wasn't good enough. I was a doctor twenty-four years ago, when I had to consult Munshi. The patients I used to treat then still come to me. Where is the guarantee that they will not recognize me if they read Munshi's book?'

'I have read the book,' Feluda interrupted, 'and I do not think you have anything to fear.'

'I would never take anyone's word for it, Mr Mitter. I told Munshi I wanted to read his manuscript and judge for myself whether I stood in any danger or not. I said if he did not hand it over to me, I would reveal everything about his murky past.'

'What! What are you talking about?'

'Yes, sir. Munshi and I went to London together to study medicine. Our subjects were different, but we were good friends. I have seen a side to Munshi's character that no one here has ever seen. He began to drink, fell into bad company, and would have ruined both himself and his career; but I made him see sense. Eventually, after coming back to Calcutta and starting his practice, he got back on the right track.'

'You went to Dr Munshi's house to get the manuscript?'

'Yes, sir. Last night, at eleven o' clock. I told him I would return it in two days. But now I can see that would not be necessary.'

'Why not? What do you mean? That manuscript will be published the instant it is handed to the publishers. Haven't you heard of posthumous publications?'

'Of course I have. But in this case, that will not happen. I have read the whole thing Mr Mitter. I do not want it to be printed, and it will stay with me. Goodbye.'

Feluda put the receiver down slowly. His face looked grim.

'That . . . that was a total knock-out, wasn't it? I don't believe this! That man's got the manuscript, and I can't do anything about it. Apart from anything else, it was such a well-written book. Now it'll never see the light of day.'

'Never mind about the book Felu Babu,' Lalmohan Babu said a little crossly. 'Surely the murder is more important?'

'But you have read the book, you ought to know . . .'

'Yes, yes, I know you are right. But where a murder has been committed, nothing else should matter.'

Srinath arrived to announce that lunch had been served. Lalmohan Babu ate his meal with great relish. 'Your cook is a marvel!' he said, taking a second helping of the prawn curry. Feluda remained silent throughout the meal.

Afterwards, we helped ourselves to paan and returned to the living room. The phone began ringing again. It was Inspector Shome. I handed the receiver to Feluda. Before replacing the receiver, he said only two things: 'In that case, it appears to be an inside job!' and 'Very interesting, I'll be there shortly'.

'Where are you off to?' I asked him as he put the phone down and picked up his packet of Charminar and his lighter.

'Munshi Palace,' he replied.

'Why did you say it's an inside job?' Lalmohan Babu asked.

'Because a maid has discovered that the heavy iron rod of their hand-grinder is missing. A perfect weapon for murder.'

'And what's so interesting?'

'The police have found another diary. It began on 1 January this year, and the last entry was made the day before Dr Munshi died. Come on, let's go!'

EIGHT

The diary Penguin was going to publish ended in December 1989. The one the police had just discovered in Dr Munshi's bedroom ran from 1 January 1990 to 13 September, which meant that he had made the last entry a few hours before he was killed. The diary was probably kept on a bedside table, and had somehow slipped between the bed and the table. A constable had found it lying on the floor.

Feluda took it from the inspector, opened it and found something on the very first page that seemed to intrigue him greatly. He frowned, staring at the page, then shut it and turned to Shankar Munshi. 'Did you know your father had continued to maintain a diary?'

'No, but it does not surprise me. After all, he had made entries in his diary every day for forty years. There was no reason for him to have stopped.'

'Did Mr Chakravarty know about this diary?'

'I don't know. Why don't you ask him?'

We were all sitting in the living room. Mr Chakravarty arrived a minute later. On being asked about the new diary, he said, 'Dr Munshi used to write in his diary each night just before going to bed. That explains why it was found in his bedroom. No, I had never seen it before.'

'Please sit down, Mr Chakravarty.'

Sukhamoy Chakravarty sat down, looking faintly taken aback. Feluda obviously had more questions for him.

'Mr Chakravarty,' said Feluda, 'you do want Dr Munshi's murderer to be caught and punished, don't you? My duty is to find that culprit. I now have reason to believe that the killer is present in this house. I have already spoken to all of you. But that did not tell me everything I needed to know. Perhaps I didn't ask the right questions, or perhaps not all of you told me the truth. I did not ask you something before. I would like to do so now.'

'Yes?'

'Something has struck us all as rather strange.'

'What?'

'According to Shankar Munshi, all his father cared about was his patients and his writing. You are not his patient; but he had always been extremely kind to you. I read in his manuscript that five years ago, you had appendicitis and had to have surgery. Then you went to Puri for ten days to convalesce. Dr Munshi paid your medical bills, as well as costs for your stay in Puri. Why? Why should he have been so partial to you?'

'I don't know.'

There was a second's pause before Mr Chakravarty's reply came. Feluda did not fail to notice it. 'Please, Mr Chakravarty, if you tell me the truth, or at least stop hiding it from me, my work will become a lot easier,' he repeated.

This time, Mr Chakravarty's reply came at once. 'I am telling you the truth, Mr Mitter,' he said.

Feluda had no more questions. Lalmohan Babu dropped us home, and left with a wave and a brief 'Tomorrow morning!'

Feluda went straight into his room and shut the door. He was now going to read the new diary and was not to be disturbed. It was half past three. I spent the next hour in the living room, lying under the fan which was rotating at full speed, and going through a very interesting article on the Antarctic in the *National Geographic*. It had some lovely photos.

At four-thirty, Srinath came in with two cups of tea. He gave me one, and took the other to Feluda. But Feluda came out as soon as Srinath knocked on his door, saying, 'It's all right, Srinath, I'll have my tea in the living room.'

He had obviously finished reading the diary. 'Did you find anything useful?' I asked. Feluda sat down on a couch, took out the diary and his packet of cigarettes from his pocket, and then took a sip from his cup.

'Listen to these sections,' he said. 'It might give you food for thought.'

I noticed that he had marked some of the pages. With unhurried movements, Feluda lit a cigarette, inhaled deeply and opened the diary.

'Listen to this. This entry was made three weeks ago:

> A new patient arrived today. Radhakanta Mallik. The first thing he did on entering my room was to take out a piece of paper from his pocket, stare alternately at my face and that paper a few times, then crumple it and throw it away into a wastepaper basket. When I asked him what it was, he said it was a report on me, including my photograph, published in the Telegraph. I said, "Was it to make sure you had come to the right person?" Mallik nearly exploded. "I don't trust anyone. No one at all. Of course I had to make sure. I must make sure each time, all the time!" he said. I think it is a case of persecution mania.

The second entry had been made four days later:

> Radhakanta Mallik has become a problem. He cannot live in his own house. He is terrified of his father, his brother, his neighbours, practically everyone he knows. It's a difficult case. I have told him to come and stay here until he's better. There are two spare rooms on the first floor. He can stay in one of them.

The third entry, made a few days later, said:

> RM continues to cause problems. He came into my office this morning before our session. I was reading an important letter at the time, so at first I paid no attention. But when I happened to look up, I found him holding a heavy paperweight in his hand and staring at me with a strange look in his eyes. If he starts to think of me also as his enemy, how am I going to treat him?

The fourth entry said:

> I had left my bottle of pills in my office. When I went to fetch it before going to bed tonight, I saw that the light was on. At first, I thought Sukhamoy was working late. But it turned out to be Shankar. When I entered the room, I found him bending low in order to close the bottom drawer of my table. He seemed very

embarrassed when he saw me, and said he had been looking for airmail envelopes. I gave him a couple of envelopes . . . I keep my manuscript in the same drawer.'

The fifth entry Feluda read out was the last one. It did not mention Radhakanta Mallik, but it was quite mysterious:

How utterly mistaken I was! Thank goodness I know the truth now. But is this business with R going to continue forever? Or am I worrying unnecessarily?

Feluda closed the diary and sighed. 'What a strange case!' he exclaimed.

'Does that mean you haven't been able to unravel the mystery?'

'Yes, that's what it means. But now I think I know how to proceed. Well, I must get moving and make some routine enquiries. Ring Jatayu and tell him to come tomorrow evening. I am not going to be home in the morning.'

NINE

Feluda left at eight o'clock the following day and returned at half past two. I didn't dare ask him whether his mission had been successful, but I did notice a suppressed excitement in his movements. Was it a sign of success, or failure?

'Yes, I've had my lunch,' he said in reply to my question, 'and now I must make a couple of phone calls.' He rang Shankar Munshi first, and then Inspector Shome. Both were given the same message: everyone concerned in this case should gather in the living room of Dr Munshi's house at ten o'clock tomorrow morning.

Feluda rang off, lit a Charminar and stretched his legs. 'Like Munshi, I feel like saying: how utterly mistaken I had been! Every key to the mystery was staring me in the face, and yet I couldn't see anything.'

'Is . . . is the culprit someone we know?' I asked a little hesitantly.

'Sure,' Feluda replied. 'Since you are clearly feeling very curious, let me ask you a few questions. If you can answer them correctly, maybe you can solve the mystery yourself.

'Question one: what did you think of the entries I read out to you?

Was there anything special?'

'Well, I found it a little odd that he wrote in his diary until the night before he died, but there was no mention of R's phone call, or his arrival.'

'Excellent. Question two: what does the word "immersion" suggest to you?'

'Water. Something thrown into water?'

'Good. Three: what is nemesis?'

'Nemesis?'

'Yes. It's a Greek word.'

'How should I know Greek?'

'You'll find it in any English dictionary. Nemesis is retribution. One may commit a crime and avoid punishment somehow, for the time being, or even a few years . . . but one day, the criminal gets what he deserves. That is called nemesis. It was this nemesis that A, G and R were afraid of.'

I found the idea very interesting, so when Feluda asked nothing further, I prompted him: 'Is there anything else?'

'I will tell you only one more thing. If I say any more, you won't enjoy the drama I've planned for tomorrow.'

'All right.'

'Have you heard the saying, "physician, heal thyself"?'

'Yes.'

'Then that's all you need to know.'

This made no sense, but before I could ask anything, Jatayu turned up.

'What stage have we reached, Felu Babu?' he asked.

'The penultimate.'

'Penalty—what?'

'Oh, is that word too big for you? Penultimate means last but one.'

'I see. When are we going to reach the final stage?'

'Tomorrow morning. The curtain rises at ten o'clock at Munshi Palace.'

'And when does it come down?'

'Say, half an hour later.'

'We've got four suspects, right?'

'Yes—eeni, meeni, meini, mo.'

'Be serious, Felu Babu. There's Shankar, Sukhamoy, Radha—'

Feluda raised a hand. 'Stop, Lalmohan Babu. Say no more. All further discussion on this subject is closed.'

'Really? Well, let me just say this, Felu Babu. I am going to provide the climax to the drama tomorrow. It cannot be you.'

'Now you've got me intrigued; even a little apprehensive.'

'No, there's nothing to feel apprehensive about. You will still get most of the applause, I assure you. You will certainly be the star attraction. But I am going to be a mini-star and claim a mini-applause for myself. That's a promise!'

A heavy shower in the morning left our street partially waterlogged, but even so, Lalmohan Babu arrived at half past nine with an umbrella under his arm, a bag hanging from his shoulder and a grin on his face. 'Tapesh bhai,' he said to me upon coming in, 'do tell your cook to make khichuri this afternoon. I think I'll eat with you again, once this morning's drama is over.'

'Certainly, you'd be most welcome,' I said and went off to tell Srinath.

We left after a quick cup of tea, and reached Swinhoe Street at five to ten. The police were already there. Inspector Shome greeted us with a smile. 'Good morning!' he said. 'I know your style, Mr Mitter. So I told everyone to go straight to the living room. The only thing I was not sure of is whether you'd like Mrs Munshi to be included in your audience.'

'No. In fact, I'd much rather she remained absent.'

A big wall clock on the ground floor announced it was ten o'clock as soon as everyone was seated. Feluda rose, glanced around the room, waited until the last chime died away. Then he began speaking.

'First of all, I'd like to ask Shankar Munshi a question.'

Mr Munshi was sitting on the other side of the room. He turned his eyes on Feluda without saying anything.

'The other day,' Feluda went on, 'when I said your father had mentioned you in his diary, you seemed surprised. And when I said he must have written what he felt to be true where you were concerned, you got irritated and said, "I cannot see how my father got to know me when all he ever thought of was his patients!" Tell me now, Mr Munshi, why did you assume your father had written only unpleasant things about you? I didn't say anything.'

'My father never ever praised me, or spoke a good word about me, in my presence.'

'Did he openly criticize you? Find fault with whatever you did?'

'No. He did not do that, either.'

'Then how can you be so sure about what he really thought of you?'

'Because it is not difficult for a son to realize how his father feels about him. I could guess, easily enough.'

'Very well. Let me now speak of something else. I came here alone yesterday afternoon, and spoke to some of your servants. Among them was your mali, Giridhari. I asked him if he had seen you leave the house early in the morning before Dr Munshi's body was discovered. Giridhari told me that he had. Then I asked him if your hands were empty, or whether he had seen you carrying anything. Giridhari said you had a briefcase in your hand. A black leather briefcase. What was in it, Mr Munshi?'

Shankar Munshi did not reply. His breath came faster.

'Shall I tell everyone what it contained?'

Still Mr Munshi did not reply. Feluda continued, 'It was your father's manuscript, wasn't it? It is true that you were going to look for your doctor by the lake. But either before or after you saw him, you threw that manuscript into the lake. And the reason for doing so was that your father had not written a single word of praise for you. He—'

Shankar Munshi spoke this time. His voice rose above Feluda's: 'Yes, yes!' he cried. 'If that book was published, I could never have shown my face anywhere. It would have affected my job, my whole life. He called me a fool, irresponsible, unenterprising, devoid of initiative and imagination . . .'

'Right. Since you have admitted all that, please be good enough to confirm this: was it you who rang me at home and pretended to be R? You changed your voice and told me a pack of lies, simply so that no suspicion could ever fall on yourself. Is that right?'

Shankar Munshi had risen to his feet. At Feluda's words, his face went blank and he flopped down on his chair once more. No answer was really needed from him.

'All right. While on the subject of R, let us consider it for a moment longer.' Feluda turned to Sukhamoy Chakravarty.

'My next question is for you.'

'Yes?'

'A strange hunch made me visit 37 Beltola Road yesterday. You had told me your mother and your aunt lived at this address. I wanted to talk to your family because I felt you were trying to hide something from me. Well, I did speak to your mother. She told me that your father had died twenty-four years ago. He was run over by a motorist. Did Dr Munshi know this fact?'

Mr Chakravarty was gazing at the floor. He replied without raising his eyes, 'Yes, he did. When he interviewed me for this job, he asked me when and how I had lost my father. I told him.'

'Very well. Now let me tell you something else. This is an example of how even the most alert and meticulous of men can overlook certain things. When Shankar Munshi first came to my house, he told me he was Dr Rajen Munshi's son. Now, the name "Rajen" disappeared totally from my memory. I kept thinking of the deceased only as Dr Munshi. The day before yesterday, when I began reading his latest diary that the police had found, I saw his full name on the first page. It was only then that it suddenly dawned on me that the R in his manuscript could well have been himself. Rajen Munshi had run over a man twenty-four years go, but had not been caught and punished. It was the dead man's son who had come to him for a job, so many years later.'

'No, no, no!' Mr Chakravarty cried. 'You are wrong, utterly wrong! The man who killed my father was arrested and punished. It was not Rajen Munshi.'

'No? Did Dr Munshi know that?'

'No. Not until . . . not until the night before he died. Until that night, he had held himself responsible for my father's death.'

'How did he learn the truth?'

'He called me to his office, and said that he had a confession to make. He could no longer carry his load of guilt. Imagine his surprise when I told him my father's killer was someone else. Dr Munshi's assumption was quite wrong, and he had suffered for years, perfectly unnecessarily. But that explained why he had been so kind to me.'

Someone laughed dryly from the other side of the room. It was Shankar Munshi.

'Would you like to say something?' Feluda asked.

'If I don't, Mr Mitter, you'll keep going down the wrong track.'

'What does that mean?'

'My father never drove in his life.'

'I am aware of that, Mr Munshi. I spoke to your driver as well as your mali.'

'What did the driver say?'

'He has worked for your family for thirty years. In all that time, he's been involved in just one accident. That occurred only because Dr Munshi was in a hurry. So he told the driver to drive fast even though there were a lot of people on the road. When a man was run over—by the driver, not your father—Dr Munshi couldn't help feeling he was partly to blame. So he did everything he could to save his driver. However, although the law didn't get him, the poor driver's conscience troubled him so much that he nearly had a breakdown. He couldn't live with a constant regret for what he had done, and fear for himself. Dr Munshi treated him, and eventually he recovered and went back to his old job. What your father wrote in his diary was a most accurate account of what had happened. The R stood not for Rajen, but Raghunandan. Isn't that what your driver is called? Raghunandan Tiwari?'

'Yes, but who killed my father?' shouted Mr Munshi impatiently.

'I am coming to that, Mr Munshi. One thing at a time.' Now Feluda's eyes moved from Shankar Munshi to another man.

'There is someone in this room,' he said, 'who is supposed to be a psychiatric patient. We have met him twice before; and each time he has tried to convince us that he is unwell. Today, however, I can see that there is no abnormality in his behaviour. Why, Mr Mallik, did your mania vanish, just like that?'

Radhakanta Mallik gave a violent start, as if he had received an electric shock. 'What . . . what are you trying to say?'

'What I am saying, Mr Mallik, is that nearly everyone I questioned either told lies, or only half-truths. You take the cake in this matter.'

Mr Mallik stared at Feluda, his face impassive. Feluda went on, 'You told me you worked for Popular Insurance. I went there to check, but they said you had left four months ago. Were you working anywhere else? No one there seemed to know, but they gave me your address. Satish Mukherjee Road, isn't that right?'

Mr Mallik was still silent, staring straight ahead.

'This case was full of surprises,' Feluda continued. 'You had told Dr Munshi that you were afraid of everyone, including your father and brother. But when I went to your house, the only person I found was your mother. She told me your father had died nearly twenty-five years ago, and you never had a brother. She seemed to think you had joined the theatre and were currently on a tour with your group!'

Now Mr Mallik opened his mouth. 'I never claimed to have spoken the truth at all times. But what are you trying to imply? That I am the murderer?'

'Mr Mallik, I tend to walk step by step, not by leaps and bounds. Whether you are the killer or not is something we can discuss later. Right now, we know you are a cheat and a liar. You only pretended to have an ailment and came to Dr Munshi for treatment. You—'

'Do you know why I came here?' Mr Mallik interrupted in a loud voice.

'I learnt something from your mother. She said your father had been killed in an accident. The man under whose car he was crushed got away with it. All he did was offer her five thousand rupees as compensation. He was never arrested.'

'No, he wasn't!' shouted Radhakanta Mallik. 'I saw his face clearly then, and after almost twenty-five years, I saw it again in the *Telegraph*. That's when I decided he had to die. Can you imagine what I have had to go through? I was only twelve when my father died. A twelve year old child climbs down from a tram, only a few paces behind his father, and . . . and . . . before his eyes, his father disappears under the wheels of a car. It was such a horrible sight! Even now, when I think about it, I can feel my flesh creep. Day after day, I asked my mother, "Ma, what about the man who did it? Isn't he going to be punished?" And my mother said, "No, son, the rich don't ever get punished." . . . Then, after so many years, there he was. It took me only a second to make up my mind. This man was going to get what he deserved, and I was going to give it to him.'

'Is that why you came here pretending to be suffering from persecution mania?'

'Yes, but who knew killing a man could be so difficult? I realized I needed to prepare myself, to steel my heart. At long last, after many weeks, I felt I could do it. I even found the right weapon. It was a sharp paper knife which was kept in Munshi's office. I had seen my father's body covered in blood. I wanted to see Munshi in exactly the same way. Or it wouldn't be a just punishment, I thought. But. . .'

'But what, Mr Mallik?'

'It was amazing, absolutely incredible! I crept into his room, clutching the knife. Moonlight came in through an open window and fell on his face. His mouth was open, his eyes half closed. His body was still. How could I kill him? He was already dead, dead, dead!'

Something fell with a thud even before Mr Mallik could finish speaking. It was Dr Munshi's brother-in-law, Chandranath Basu. He had fainted and slipped from his chair onto the floor. Inspector Shome rushed forward to attend to him.

Feluda spoke quietly. 'Mr Munshi, look carefully at that man lying on the ground. He is your father's killer. Yes, the murderer is none other than your stepmother's twin.'

This remark was greeted by an amazed silence. It was Lalmohan Babu who broke it by saying, 'What do you mean? What possible motive could he have had?'

Feluda glanced at Shankar Munshi. 'Couldn't you tell us, Mr Munshi?' he asked. 'You read the diary, didn't you?'

Shankar Munshi nodded slowly.

'It isn't easy to get to know a person, Mr Munshi,' Feluda went on. 'The real difference between a man and an animal is that an animal does not know how to hide its feelings, or put on an act . . . Dr Munshi was not indifferent towards your stepmother at all. If he was, he would never have allowed her to read his diary, or dedicate his book to her. The truth is just the opposite. It was Dr Munshi's wife who did not care for him. In fact, she did not care for anyone except her useless, good-for-nothing brother, on whom she chose to shower all her love and affection. Her thoughts were only for him, her concern only for his future . . . now can you tell us what the motive behind the murder was?'

Shankar Munshi's voice sounded flat and lifeless. He spoke like a robot, 'It was my father's will. He spoke about it in his diary. One-fourth of his assets was to go to institutions involved in psychological research, one-fourth was to come to me, and . . . and my stepmother was to get the rest.'

Mr Basu had regained consciousness in the meantime. Feluda looked straight at him.

'Was the murder your own idea?' he asked.

Mr Basu shook his head and sighed. He could not raise his eyes. When he spoke after a short pause, his voice sounded so faint that I had to strain my ears to hear his words.

'No,' he said, 'the idea was Dolly's. That's . . . that's my sister. It was she who got that iron rod and handed it to me.'

'I see.'

Feluda sat down at last, suddenly looking tired. 'That clears up the murder,' he said, almost to himself. 'I have only one regret. A very deep regret. If that diary got published, Dr Munshi's name would have become well-known in literary circles. He had a wonderful style. But that diary is now immersed in the lake, lost for ever.'

'Attention! Spotlight!'

Jatayu's voice rang out, startling everyone considerably. Finding every eye fixed on him, he smiled triumphantly and pulled out a folder from his shoulder bag. Then he held it over his head like a trophy and shouted, 'Not lost, sir! Not immersed, either. Here it is!'

'Dr Munshi's manuscript?' Feluda sounded openly astonished. 'How can that be?'

'Yes, sir. Thanks to the recent advances made by modern technology. I knew I could not finish reading the whole thing in just a day, so I had it photocopied. That's right, X-E-R-O-X! Here you are, Mr Chakravarty, you can start typing it straightaway, and then send it to the North Pole.'

Here he made a typical Jatayu-like mistake. But looking at his jubilant face, none of us had the heart to point out that penguins are to be found at the South Pole, not the North.

The Mystery of Nayan

ONE

Feluda had been quiet and withdrawn for many days. Well, I say he was withdrawn. Lalmohan Babu had used at least ten different adjectives for him, including distressed, depressed, lifeless, listless, dull, morose and apathetic. One day he even called him moribund. Needless to say, he didn't dare address his remarks directly to Feluda. He confided in me, but like him, I had no idea why Feluda was behaving so strangely.

Today, quite unable to take it any longer, Lalmohan Babu looked straight at Feluda and asked, 'Why do you seem so preoccupied, Felu Babu? What's wrong?'

Feluda was leaning against a sofa, his feet resting on a small coffee table. He was staring at the floor, his face grim. He said nothing in reply to Lalmohan Babu's question.

'This is most unfair!' Lalmohan Babu complained, a trifle loudly. 'I come here only to have a good chat, to laugh and to spend a few pleasant moments with you both. If you keep behaving like this, I'll have to stop coming. Do give us at least a hint of what's on your mind. Who knows, maybe I can help find a remedy? You used to look pleased to see me every day. Now you just look away each time I enter your house.'

'Sorry,' said Feluda softly, still staring at the floor.

'No, no, there's no need to apologize. I am concerned about you, that's all. I really want to know why you're so upset. Will you tell me, please?'

'Letters,' said Feluda, at last.

'Letters?'

'Yes, letters.'

'What letters? What was written in them that made you so unhappy? Who wrote them?'

'Readers.'

'Whose readers?'

'Topshe's. Readers who read the stories Topshe writes, all based on the cases I handle. There were fifty-six letters. Each one said more or less the same thing.'

'And what was that?'

'Feluda's stories do not sound as interesting as before, they said. Jatayu can no longer make people laugh. Topshe's narrative has lost its appeal, etc. etc.'

I knew nothing about this. Feluda received at least six letters every day. But I had never bothered to ask what they said. His words surprised me. Lalmohan Babu got extremely cross.

'What do they mean? I can't make people laugh? Why, am I a clown or what?'

'No, no. That's not what they mean. No one tried to insult you. They just . . .'

Lalmohan Babu refused to be pacified. 'Shame on you, Felu Babu!' he said, standing with his back to Feluda. 'I am really disappointed. You read all these stupid letters, you stored them away, and you let them disturb you so profoundly. Why? Why didn't you just throw them away?'

'Because,' Feluda replied slowly, 'these readers have given us their support in the past. Now if they tell me the Three Musketeers have grown old much before their time, I cannot ignore their words.'

'Grown old?' Lalmohan Babu wheeled around, his eyes wide with anger and amazement. 'Tapesh is only a young boy, you are as fit as ever. I know you both do yoga regularly. And I . . . why, I managed to defeat my neighbour in an arm wrestle only the other day! He is seventeen years my junior. Now is that a sign of old age? Doesn't everyone grow older with time? And doesn't age add to one's experience, improve one's judgement, sharpen one's intelligence, and . . . and . . . things like that?'

'Yes, Lalmohan Babu, but obviously the readers haven't found any evidence of all this in the recent stories.'

'Then that itself is a mystery, isn't it? Do you think you can find an answer to that?'

Feluda put his feet down on the floor and sat up straight.

'It's a wonderful thing to be popular among readers. But such popularity and fame often demand a price. You know that, don't you? Don't your publishers put pressure on you?'

'Oh, yes. Tremendous pressure.'

'Then you should understand. But at least your stories and your characters are entirely fictitious. You can create events and people to satisfy your readers. Topshe cannot do that. He has to rely on what really happens in a case. Now, although I admit truth can sometimes be stranger than fiction, where is the guarantee that all my cases would make good stories? Besides, you mustn't forget that Topshe's readers are mainly children between ten and fifteen. I have handled so many cases that may well have had the necessary ingredients for a spicy novel, but in no way were they suitable for children of that age.'

'You mean something like that double murder?'

'Yes. That one was so messy that I didn't let Topshe anywhere near it, although he is no longer a small child and is, in fact, quite mature for his age.'

'Does that mean Tapesh hasn't been choosing the right and relevant cases to write about?'

'Perhaps, but he is not to be blamed at all. The poor boy has to deal with impatient and unreasonable publishers. He doesn't get time to think. But even that is not the real problem. The real problem is that it is not just children who read his stories. What he writes is read by parents, uncles, aunts, grandparents, and dozens of other adults in a child's family. Each one of them has a particular taste, and a particular requirement. How on earth can all of them be satisfied?'

'Then why don't you give Tapesh a little guidance? Tell him which cases he should write about?'

'Yes, I will. But before I do that, I'll have to have a word with the publishers. They ought to be told that a Feluda story will be ready for publication only if a suitable case comes my way. If it doesn't, too bad. They'll just have to give the whole thing a miss occasionally, and hold their horses. They're hardcore businessmen, Lalmohan Babu. Their only concern is sales figures. Why should they worry about my own image and reputation? I myself will have to take care of that.'

'And your readers? All those who wrote those awful letters to you? Shouldn't you have a word with them as well?'

'No. They're not fools, Lalmohan Babu. What they have said is neither unfair nor incorrect. Now, if Topshe can provide what they expect from him, they'll stop feeling disappointed in me.'

'Hey, what about me?'

'And you, my dear friend. We complement each other, don't we? You've been with us throughout, ever since our visit to Jaisalmer. Why, I don't suppose any of our readers could think of me without thinking of you, and vice versa!'

This finally seemed to mollify Lalmohan Babu. He turned to me and said seriously, 'Be very careful in choosing your stories, Tapesh.'

'It's going to be quite simple, really,' Feluda said to me. 'Don't start writing at all until I give you the go-ahead. All right?'

'All right,' I replied, smiling.

TWO

I made this long preamble to show my readers that I am going to write about the mystery of Nayan with full approval from Feluda. In fact, even Lalmohan Babu seemed to agree wholeheartedly.

'Splendid! Splendid!' he said, clapping enthusiastically. 'What a good idea to write about Nayan! Er . . . I hope my role in it is going to remain the same? I mean, you do remember all the details, don't you?'

'Don't worry, Lalmohan Babu. I noted everything down.

But where should I start?

'Start with Tarafdar's show. That really was the beginning, wasn't it?' Feluda said.

Mr Sunil Tarafdar was a magician. His show was called 'Chamakdar Tarafdar'. Magicians were growing like mushrooms nowadays. Some of them were serious about their art, but the stiff competition made many of them fade into oblivion. Those who stayed on had to maintain a certain standard. Feluda had once been interested in magic. In fact, it was I who had revealed this a long time ago. As a result, many up and coming magicians often invited Feluda to their shows. I accompanied Feluda to some of these, and was seldom disappointed.

Sunil Tarafdar was one of these young magicians on the way up. His name had started to feature in newspapers and journals a year ago. Most reports spoke favourably about him. Last December, he turned up in our house one morning and greeted Feluda by touching his feet. Feluda gets terribly embarrassed if anyone does this, so he jumped up, saying, 'No, no, please don't do that . . . there's no need . . .' Mr Tarafdar only smiled. He was a young man in his early thirties, tall and slim. He sported a thin, carefully trimmed moustache.

'Sir,' he said, straightening himself, 'I am a great fan of yours. I know you are interested in magic. I am going to hold my next show in Mahajati Sadan on Sunday. I have had three tickets reserved for you in the front row. The show begins at 6.30 p.m. I'll be delighted if you come.'

Feluda did not say anything immediately. 'I am inviting you, sir,' Mr Tarafdar continued, 'because the last item in my show is going to be absolutely unique. I am very sure no one has ever shown anything like this on stage before.'

Feluda agreed to go. Lalmohan Babu arrived at 5.30 in his green Ambassador the following Sunday. We chatted for a while over a cup of tea, and left for Mahajati Sadan at six. We got there just five minutes before the show was to start. The hall was packed. Obviously, the large advertisement that had appeared in the press recently had worked. We found our seats in the front row. 'Did you see the ad in the paper?' asked Lalmohan Babu.

'Yes,' Feluda replied.

'It said something about a totally new attraction . . . something called "Jyotishka". What could it be?'

'I don't know, Lalmohan Babu. Just be patient, all will be revealed shortly.'

The show began on the dot of six-thirty. I saw Feluda glance at his watch as the curtain went up, raise his eyebrows and smile approvingly. Punctuality was something he felt very strongly about. He had obviously given Mr Tarafdar a bonus point for starting on time.

The few items we saw in the first half of the programme were, sadly, nothing out of the ordinary. It also became obvious that apart from a costume made of brocade, Sunil Tarafdar had not been able to pay much attention to glamour and glitter in his show, which was unusual for a modern magician.

The show took a different turn after the interval. Mr Tarafdar came back on the stage and began to hypnotize people from the audience. Very soon, it was established beyond any possible doubt that hypnotism was indeed his forte. Certainly, I had never seen anyone with such skill. The applause he got was defeaning.

But then, Mr Tarafdar made a sudden false move. He turned towards Feluda and said, 'I would now request the famous sleuth, Mr Pradosh Mitter, to join me on stage.'

Feluda rose, pointed at Lalmohan Babu and said politely, 'I think it would be a better idea to have my friend join you instead of me, Mr Tarafdar. Having me on the stage might lead to difficulties.'

But Mr Tarafdar paid no attention. He smiled with supreme confidence and insisted on Feluda going up on the stage. Feluda obeyed, and it became clear in a matter of minutes why he had warned about difficulties. The magician tried his utmost to hypnotize Feluda and turn him into a puppet in his hands, but failed miserably. Feluda remained awake, alert and in full control of his senses. In the end, Mr Tarafdar turned to the audience and said the only thing he could possibly say to save the situation.

'Ladies and gentlemen,' he declared, 'you have just witnessed what tremendous powers Mr Mitter is in possession of. I have no regret at all in admitting defeat before him!'

The audience burst into applause again. Feluda came back to his seat. 'Felu Babu,' Lalmohan Babu remarked, 'your entire physiology is different from other men, isn't it?' Before Feluda could respond to this profound observation, Mr Tarafdar announced his last item. The unique, hitherto unseen and unheard of 'Jyotishka' turned out to be a good-looking boy of about eight. What he performed a few minutes later took my breath away.

Mr Tarafdar placed a chair in the middle of the stage and invited the boy to sit down. Then he took the microphone in his hand. 'Ladies and gentlemen,' he said, 'this child is called Jyotishka. He, too, is in possession of a highly remarkable gift. I admit I have nothing to do with his power, it is entirely his own. But I am proud to be able to present him before you.' Then he turned to the boy. 'Jyotishka, please look at the audience.'

Jyotishka fixed his gaze in front of him.

'All right. Now look at that gentleman on the right . . . the one over there, wearing a red sweater and black trousers. Do you think he's got any money in his wallet?'

'Yes, he has,' the boy replied in a sweet, childish voice.

'How much?'

'Twenty rupees and thirty paise.'

The gentleman slowly took out his wallet and brought out its contents.

'My God, he's absolutely right!' he exclaimed.

'Well, Jyotishka,' Mr Taradfar went on, 'he has got two ten-rupee notes. Can you tell us the numbers printed on them?'

'11 E 111302; and the other is 14 C 286025.'

'Oh my goodness, he's right again!' the gentleman stood with his mouth hanging open. The hall began to boom with the sound of clapping.

'Any one of you can ask him a question,' said Mr Tarafdar when the noise subsided a little. 'All you have to remember is that the answer to your question must be in numbers. But I must warn you that Jyotishka finds this exercise quite strenuous, so I will allow only two more questions this evening.'

A young man stood up. 'I came here in a car. Can you tell me its number?'

Jyotishka answered this correctly and added, 'But you have another car. And the number of that one is WMF 6232.'

Mr Tarafdar picked out another boy from the audience.

'Did you sit for an exam this year?' he asked.

'Yes, sir. Class X,' the boy replied.

'Jyotishka, can you tell us how much he got in Bengali?'

'Yes. He got eighty-one. In fact, he got the highest marks in Bengali this year.'

'Yes, that's right! But how did you guess? Who told you—?'

The boy's remaining words were drowned in thunderous applause.

'We must go backstage and thank Tarafdar,' Feluda said.

Mr Tarafdar was sitting in front of a mirror, removing his make-up when we found him. He beamed as he saw us.

'How did you like my show? Tell me frankly, sir.'

'Two of your items were truly remarkable. One was your hypnotism, and the other was this child. Where did you find him?'

'He used to live in Nikunjabihari Lane, near Kalighat. His real name is Nayan. I found the name Jyotishka for him. Please don't tell anyone else.'

'No, of course not,' said Feluda. 'But how exactly did you come to know about him?'

'His father brought him to me, in the hope that Nayan's power with numbers might help add to their family income. They're not very well off, as you can imagine.'

'Oh, I'm sure Nayan would have no problem at all in making money. Does he not live with his father any more?'

'No. I have kept him in my own house. A private tutor has been arranged for him, and I've had a doctor work out his diet. He is going to be well looked after, I assure you.'

'Yes, but that would mean spending a lot of money on him, wouldn't it?'

'Yes, I am aware of that. But I also realize Nayan is a gold mine. If initially I have to borrow from friends to raise enough funds, I wouldn't mind doing that because I know I can recover whatever they lend me, in no time.'

'Hmm . . . but ideally, you ought to look for a sponsor.'

'You're right. I will contact the right people, in due course . . . just give it a little time.'

'All right. There are only two things I'd like to say, and then we'll leave you in peace. One—make sure you do not lose this gold mine. You really must keep an eye on that boy, at all times. And second, did I see journalists sitting in the second row during your show?'

'Yes. Eleven journalists and reporters came to see the show this evening. They're all going to write about it next Friday. I don't think there's any cause for concern there, at least not until the full story gets printed.'

'Very well. But please remember that if there are any enquiries made regarding Nayan, or if someone wants to meet him, or anything suspicious happens, I am here to help you.'

'Thank you very much, sir. And . . . er . . .'

'Yes?'

'Please call me Sunil, Mr Mitter.'

THREE

To my surprise, Sunil Tarafdar rang us on Tuesday. Surely the press reporters were not going to report anything for another couple of days?

Feluda spoke briefly on the phone, then told me what had happened.

'The news has spread, you see, Topshe,' he said. 'After all, eight hundred people saw his show on Sunday. A lot of them must have talked about Nayan. Anyway, the upshot was that Tarafdar got four telephone calls. Each one of these four people are wealthy and important, and they all want to talk to Nayan. Tarafdar asked them to come after nine tomorrow morning. Each one will be given fifteen minutes, and they've been told three other people will be present at the interview—that's you, me and Lalmohan Babu. Ring him now and tell him.'

'I will, but who are these four people?'

'An American, a businessman from north India, an Anglo-Indian and a Bengali. The American is supposed to be an impresario. Tarafdar wants us to be around because he's not sure he can handle the situation alone.'

When I rang Lalmohan Babu, he decided to come over at once.

'Srinath!' he yelled as he came in and sat down in his favourite couch. Srinath was our cook. He appeared with fresh tea in just a few minutes.

'What's cooking, Felu Babu?' Lalmohan Babu asked with a grin. 'Do I smell something familiar?'

'You are imagining things, my friend. Nothing's happened yet for anything to start cooking.'

'I've been thinking about that boy constantly. What an amazing power he's got, hasn't he?'

'Yes. But these things are entirely unpredictable. One day, without any apparent reason, he may lose this power. If that happens, there won't be any difference left between Nayan and other ordinary boys of his age.'

'Yes, I know. Anyway, we're going to Tarafdar's house tomorrow morning, right?'

'Yes, but let me tell you something. I am not going in my professional capacity.'

'No?'

'No. I will simply be a silent spectator. If anyone has to talk, it will be you.'

'Hey, you really mean that?'

'Of course.'

'Very well, Felu Babu. I shall do my best.'

Mr Tarafdar lived in Ekdalia Road. His house must have been built over fifty years ago. It had two storeys and a small strip of a garden near the front gate. An armed guard stood at the gate. Mr Tarafdar had clearly taken Feluda's advice. The guard opened the gate on being given Feluda's name. As we made our way to the main door, Feluda said under his breath, 'Within two years, Tarafdar will leave this house and move elsewhere, you mark my words.'

A bearer opened the door and invited us in. We followed him into the drawing room. The room wasn't large, but was tastefully furnished. Sunil Tarafdar arrived a minute later, accompanied by a huge Alsatian. Feluda, I knew, loved dogs. No matter how large or ferocious a dog might be, Feluda simply couldn't resist the temptation to stroke its back. He did the same with this Alsatian.

'He's called Badshah,' Mr Tarafdar informed us. 'He's twelve years old and a very good watchdog.'

'Excellent. I am please to see your house so well-protected. Well, here we are, fifteen minutes before the others, just as you had asked.'

'Thank you, Mr Mitter. I knew you'd be punctual.'

'Did you take this house on rent?'

'No, sir. My father built it. He was a well-known attorney. I grew up in this house.'

'Aren't you married?'

'No.' Mr Tarafdar smiled. 'I am in no hurry to get married. I must get my show established first.'

The same bearer came in with tea and samosas. Feluda picked up a samosa and said, 'I am not going to utter a single word today. This gentleman will do the talking. You do know who he is, don't you?'

'Certainly!' Mr Tarafdar exclaimed, raising his eyebrows. 'Who doesn't know the famous writer of crime thrillers, Lalmohan Ganguli?'

Lalmohan Babu acknowledged this compliment with a small salute, thereby indicating openly that he thought modesty was a waste of time.

Feluda finished his samosa and lit a Charminar.

'I'd like to tell you something quite frankly, Sunil,' he began. 'I noticed an absence of showmanship in your performance. A modern magician like you mustn't neglect that particular aspect. Your hypnotism and Nayan are both remarkable, no doubt, but today's audience expects a bit of glamour.'

'I know that, sir. I did not have enough resources to add glamour to my show. But now I think that lapse is going to be remedied.'

'How?'

'I have found a sponsor.'

'What! Already?'

'Yes. I was about to tell you myself. I don't think I need worry any more about money—at least, not for the moment.'

'May I ask who this sponsor is?'

'Excuse me, sir, but he wants to keep his identity a secret.'

'But how did it happen? Are you allowed to tell me that?'

'Why, yes, by all means, sir. What happened is that a relative of this sponsor saw Nayan on the stage on Sunday, and told him about it. My sponsor rang me the same evening and said he'd like to see Nayan immediately. I told him to come at 10 a.m. the following morning. He arrived right on time, and met Nayan. He then asked him a few questions, which, of course, Nayan answered correctly. The gentleman stared at him for a few seconds, quite dumbfounded. Then he seemed to pull himself together and gave me a fantastic proposal.'

'What was it?'

'He said he'd bear all the expenses related to my show. In fact, he's going to form a company called "Miracles Unlimited". I am going to perform on behalf of this company, although no one is going to be told who its owner is. I will get all the credit if my shows are successful. My sponsor will keep the profit. Nayan and I will both be paid a monthly salary. The figure he quoted was really quite generous. I accepted all these terms for the simple reason that it removed a major worry at once—money!'

'But didn't you ask him why he was so interested?'

'Oh yes. He told me rather a strange story. Apparently, this man has been passionately interested in magic since his childhood. He had taught himself a few tricks and had even bought the necessary equipment. But before he could take it up seriously, his father found out what he was doing, and was furious. My sponsor was afraid of his father for he had always been very stern with him. So, in order to please his father, he gave up magic and began to do something else to earn his living. In time, he became quite wealthy, but he couldn't forget his old passion. "I have earned a lot of money," he said to me, "but that has not satisfied my soul. Something tells me this young child will bring me the fulfilment I have craved all my life." That was all, Mr Mitter.'

'Have you actually signed a contract?'

'Yes. I feel so much more relieved now. He's paying for Nayan's tutor, his doctor, his clothes and everything else. Why, he's even promised to pay for me to go and have a show in Madras!'

'Really?'

'Yes. You see, I got a call from a Mr Reddy from Madras, just a few minutes before my sponsor arrived. A South Indian gentleman who lives in Calcutta had seen my show on Sunday and rung Mr Reddy to tell him about it. Mr Reddy owns a theatre. He invited me to go to Madras and perform in his theatre. I said I needed time to think about it. But in just a few minutes my sponsor arrived. When he heard about Mr Reddy's invitation, he told me I shouldn't waste time thinking, and should cable Mr Reddy at once, accepting his offer. All expenses would be paid.'

'But surely you'll have to account for what you spend?'

'Of course. I have a close friend called Shankar who acts as my manager. He'll take care of my accounts. He's a most efficient man.'

A bearer turned up and announced that a foreigner had arrived with a Bengali gentleman. I glanced at my watch. It was only a few seconds past 9 a.m.

'Show them in,' said Mr Tarafdar.

Lalmohan Babu took a deep breath. Feluda remained silent.

The American who entered the room had white hair, but the smoothness of his skin told me he wasn't very old. Mr Tarafdar rose to greet him, and invited him to sit down.

'I am Sam Kellerman,' said the American, 'and with me is Mr Basak, our Indian representative.' Mr Basak, too, was offered a seat.

Lalmohan Babu began his task.

'You are an impresoria—I mean, impresario?'

'That's right. People in America are very interested in India these days. The *Mahabharat* has been performed as a play, and has also been made into a movie, as I'm sure you know. That has opened new avenues for your heritage.'

'So you are interested in our culture?'

'I am interested in that kid.'

'Eh? You take an interest in young goats?'

I had been afraid that this might happen. Lalmohan Babu obviously didn't know Americans referred to children as 'kids'.

Mr Basak came to the rescue. 'He is talking of Jyotishka, the boy who appears in Mr Tarafdar's show,' he explained quickly.

'What exactly do you want to know about him?' Mr Tarafdar asked.

'I want,' Mr Kellerman said slowly and clearly, 'to present this boy before the American people. Only in a country like India could someone be born with such an amazing power. But before I make any final decision, I'd like to see him and test him for myself.'

'Mr Kellerman is one of the three most renowned impresarios in the world,' Mr Basak put in. 'He's been doing this work for more than twenty years. He's prepared to pay handsomely for this young boy. Besides, the boy will get his own share regularly from the proceeds of every show. All that will be mentioned in the contract.'

Mr Tarafdar smiled. 'Mr Kellerman,' he said gently, 'that wonder boy is a part of my own show. The question of his leaving me does not arise. I am shortly going to leave for a tour of south India, starting with Madras. People there have heard of Jyotishka and are eagerly looking forward to his arrival. I am sorry, but I must refuse your offer, Mr Kellerman.'

Kellerman's face turned red. After a brief pause, he said a little hoarsely, 'Is it possible to see the child at all? And to ask him a few questions?'

'That's no problem,' said Mr Tarafdar and told a bearer to fetch Nayan.

Nayan arrived a few seconds later, and went and stood by Mr Tarafdar's chair. He looked no different from other ordinary boys, except that his eyes held a quiet intelligence. Mr Kellerman simply stared at him for a few moments.

Then he said, without removing his eyes from the boy, 'Can he tell me the number of my bank account?'

'Go on, Nayan, tell him,' Mr Tarafdar said encouragingly.

'But which account is he talking about?' Nayan sounded puzzled. 'He's got three accounts in three different banks!'

Kellerman's face quickly lost its colour. He swallowed hard before saying, in the same hoarse voice, 'City Bank of New York.'

'12128-74,' said Nayan promptly.

'Jesus Christ!' Kellerman's eyes looked as though they would pop out of their sockets any minute. 'I am offering you twenty thousand dollars right now,' he said, turning to Mr Tarafdar. 'He could never earn that much from your magic shows, could he?'

'I've only just started, Mr Kellerman. I shall travel with Nayan all over my country. Then there's the rest of the world to be seen. People anywhere in the world would love a magic show, and you've just seen what Nayan is capable of doing. How can you be so sure we'll never earn the kind of money you're talking about on our own merit?'

'Does he have a father?'

'Does that matter? Nayan is in my care, officially I am his guardian.'

'Sir,' Lalmohan Babu piped up unexpectedly, 'in our philosophy, sir, to make a sacrifice is more important than to acquire a possession!'

Mr Basak rose to his feet. 'You are letting a golden opportunity slip through your fingers, Mr Tarafdar,' he said. 'Please think very carefully.'

'I have.'

Mr Kellerman was now obliged to take his leave. He glanced once at Mr Basak, who took out his visiting card from his pocket and handed it to Mr Tarafdar. 'It's got my address and telephone number. Let me know if you change your mind.'

'Thank you, I will.'

Mr Tarafdar went to see them off. Nayan went back with the same bearer.

'Basak is a clever man,' Feluda remarked, 'or he wouldn't be an American impresario's agent. And he must be wealthy, too. He was reeking of French aftershave, did you notice? But there was a trace of shaving cream under his chin. I don't think he's an early riser. He probably had to shave in a hurry this morning simply to keep his appointment with us.'

FOUR

'Well, that's one down. Let's see how long the second one takes. He should be here any minute now.' Mr Tarafdar said. The doorbell rang in a couple of minutes. A man in a dark suit was ushered in. 'Good morning,' greeted Mr Tarafdar, rising. 'I'm afraid I didn't quite catch your name on the telephone. You must be . . . ?'

'Tiwari. Devkinandan Tiwari.'

'I see. Please have a seat.'

'Thank you. Have you heard of T H Syndicate?'

Lalmohan Babu and Mr Tarafdar looked at each other in silence. Clearly, they had not. Feluda was obliged to open his mouth.

'Your business has something to do with imports and exports, right? You have an office in Pollock Street?"

'Yes, that's right,' Mr Tiwari said, looking a little suspiciously at Feluda.

'These three people are my friends. I hope you won't mind talking to me in their presence?' Mr Tarafdar asked.

'Oh no, not in the least. All I want to do, Mr Tarafdar, is ask that young chap a question. If he can give me the correct answer, I shall be eternally grateful.'

Nayan was brought back into the room. Mr Tarafdar laid a hand on his back and said kindly, 'I'm sorry, Nayan, but you have to answer another question. All right?' Nayan nodded. Mr Tarafdar turned to Mr Tiwari. 'Go ahead, sir. But please remember the answer to your question must be in numbers.'

'Yes, I know. That is precisely why I've come.' Mr Tiwari fixed his eyes on Nayan. 'Can you tell me the combination of my chest?'

Nayan stared back, looking profoundly puzzled.

'Listen, Jyotishka,' said Feluda quickly, before anyone else could speak, 'perhaps you don't understand what Mr Tiwari means by a combination. Let me explain. You see, some chests and cupboards don't have ordinary locks and keys. What they have is a disc attached to the lid or on the door that can be rotated. An arrow is marked on the disc, and around it are written numbers from one to zero. A combination is a series of special numbers meant for a particular chest or a cupboard. If you move the disc and bring the arrow to rest against the right numbers, the chest opens automatically.'

'Oh, I see,' Nayan said, nodding vigorously.

Lalmohan Babu suddenly asked a pertinent question.

'How come you don't know the combination of your own chest?'

'I knew it . . . in fact, I had known it and used it to open my chest a million times over the last twenty-three years. But,' Mr Tiwari shook his head regretfully, 'I am getting old, Mr Tarafdar. My memory is no longer what it used to be. For the life of me, I cannot remember the right numbers for that combination. I had written it down in an old diary and I have spent the last four days looking for it everywhere, but I couldn't find it. It's gone . . . vanished.'

'Didn't you ever tell anyone else what the number was?'

'I seem to remember having told my partner—a long time ago—but he denies it. Maybe it's my own memory playing tricks again. After all, one doesn't go about giving people the details of a combination, does one? Besides, this chest is my personal property, although it's kept in my office. I don't keep any money or papers related to our business in it. It only has the money—my own personal money, you understand—that I don't keep in my bank . . . I tell you, Mr Tarafdar, I was getting absolutely desperate. Then I heard about this wonder boy. So I thought I'd try my luck here!' He brought his gaze back on Nayan.

'It's 6438961,' Nayan said calmly.

'Right! Right! Right!' Mr Tiwari jumped up in excitement and quickly took out a pocket diary to note the number down.

'Do you know how much money there is in that chest?' asked Mr Tarafdar.

'No, I couldn't tell you the exact figure, but I think what I have is in excess of five lakhs,' Mr Tiwari said with a slight smile.

'This little boy could tell you. Would you like to know?'

'Why, yes! I am curious, naturally. Let's see how far his power can go.'

Mr Tarafdar looked at Nayan again. But, this time, Nayan's reply did not come in numbers.

'There's no money in that chest. None at all,' he said.

'What!' Mr Tiwari nearly fell off his chair. But then he began to look annoyed. 'Obviously, Mr Tarafdar, this prodigy is as capable of making mistakes as anyone else. However, I'm grateful he could give me the number I really needed. Here you are, my boy, this is for you.' Mr Tiwari offered a slim package to Nayan.

'Thank you, sir,' said Nayan shyly, as he took it.

Mr Tiwari left.

'Open it and see what's inside,' Feluda said to Nayan. Nayan took the wrapper off, revealing a small wrist watch.

'Hey, that's very nice of Mr Tiwari!' Lalmohan Babu exclaimed. 'Wear it, Nayan, wear it!'

Nayan put it round his wrist, looking delighted, and left the room.

'I think Mr Tiwari is in for a rude shock,' Feluda remarked when Nayan had gone.

'I bet he'll suspect his partner when he discovers the money's missing—unless, of course, Nayan really made a mistake this time?' Lalmohan Babu said. With a shrug, Feluda changed the subject.

'How are you travelling to Madras? By train or by air?' he asked Sunil Tarafdar.

'It'll have to be by train. I have far too much luggage to go by air.'

'What about security for Nayan?'

'Well, I am going to be with him throughout our journey, so I don't think that's a problem. When we get to Madras, I will be joined by my friend, Shankar. We'll both look after Nayan.'

Feluda started to speak, but was interrupted by the arrival of another gentleman, also attired in a formal suit and tie.

'Good morning. I am Hodgson. Henry Hodgson. I made an appointment with—'

'Me. I am Sunil Tarafdar. Please sit down.'

Mr Hodgson sat down frowning and casting looks of grave suspicion at us. He was obviously a Christian, but I couldn't make out which part of India he came from. Perhaps he had lived in Calcutta for a long time.

'May I ask who all these other people are?' he asked irritably.

'They are very close to me. You may speak freely in front of them. I did tell you they would be present,' Mr Tarafdar said reassuringly.

'Hmm.' Mr Hodgson continued to frown. Why was he in such a bad mood?

'A friend of mine happened to see your show last Sunday,' he said at last. 'He told me about your wonder boy. I didn't believe him. I don't even believe in God. Therefore I have no faith in the so-called supernatural powers some people are supposed to possess. But if you bring that boy here, I'd like to talk to him.'

Mr Tarafdar hesitated for a few seconds before asking his bearer to call Nayan once more. Nayan reappeared in a minute.

'So this is the boy?' Mr Hodgson looked steadily at Nayan. Then he said, 'We have horse races every Saturday. Did you know that?'

'Yes.'

'Well, can you tell me which horse won the third race last Saturday? What was its number?'

'Five,' replied Nayan instantly.

Mr Hodgson's demeanour changed at once. He stood up and began pacing restlessly, his hands thrust in his pockets.

'Very strange! Oh, how very strange!' he muttered. Then he stopped abruptly and faced Mr Tarafdar. 'All I want is this,' he said, 'I will come here once a week to learn the number of the horse that will win the following Saturday. I shall be frank with you, Mr Tarafdar. Horse races are a passion with me. I've lost a great deal already, but that cannot stop me. If I lose some more, however, my creditors will have me sent to prison. So I want to be absolutely definite that I back only the winning horse. This boy will help me.'

'How can you be so sure? What makes you think that he will?' Mr Tarafdar asked coldly.

'He must, he must, he must!' cried Mr Hodgson.

'No, he must not!' Mr Tarafdar returned firmly. 'This boy's powers must not be misused. There's no use arguing with me, Mr Hodgson. I am not going to change my mind.'

Mr Hodgson's face seemed to crumple. When he spoke, his voice shook.

'Please,' he begged, folding his hands, 'let him at least tell me the numbers for the next race. Just this once.'

'No help for gamblers, no help for gamblers!' said Lalmohan Babu, speaking for the first time since Mr Hodgson's arrival.

Mr Hodgson turned to go. His face was purple with rage.

'I have never seen such stupid and stubborn people, damn it!' he exclaimed and strode out.

'What a horrible man!' Lalmohan Babu wrinkled his nose.

'We've certainly met some weird characters today,' Feluda remarked. 'Mr Hodgson was smelling of alcohol. I caught the smell, I suppose, because I was sitting close to him. His financial resources have clearly hit rock bottom. I noticed patches on his jacket—the sleeves, in particular. And he travelled this morning by bus, not by taxi or the metro rail.'

'How do you know that?'

'Someone trod on his foot and left a partial impression of his own shoe on his. This can happen only in a crowded bus or a tram.'

Feluda's powers of observation bordered on the supernatural, too, I thought.

A car came and stopped outside the main gate. All of us automatically looked at the door.

'Number four,' said Feluda.

FIVE

A minute later, a strange creature was shown in: a smallish man in his mid-sixties, clad in a loose and ill-fitting yellow suit, a green tie wound rather horrifically round his throat, a beard that stood out like the bristles of an old brush and a moustache that reminded me of a fat and well-fed caterpillar. His eyes were abnormally bright, and he carried a stout walking-stick.

He looked around as he entered the room and asked in a gruff voice, 'Tarafdar? Which one of you is Tarafdar?'

'I am. Please sit down,' Mr Tarafdar invited.

'And these three?' The man's eyes swept over us imperiously.

'Three very close friends.'

'Names? Names?'

'This is Pradosh Mitter, and this is his cousin, Tapesh. And over there is Lalmohan Ganguli.'

'All right. Now let's get to work, to work.'

'Yes, what can I do for you?'

'Do you know who I am?'

'You only mentioned your surname on the phone, Mr Thakur. That's all I know.'

'I am Tarak Nath Thakur. TNT. Trinitrotolvene—ha ha ha!'

Mr Thakur roared with laughter, startling everyone in the room. I knew TNT was used in making powerful explosives. But what was so funny about it?

Mr Thakur did not enlighten us. Feluda asked him a question instead.

'Does an exceptionally small dwarf live in your house?'

'Kichomo. A Korean. Eighty-two centimetres. The smallest adult in the entire world.'

'I read about him in the papers a few months ago.'

'Now the Guinness Book of Records will include his name.'

'Where did you find him?' Lalmohan Babu asked.

'I travel all over the world. I have plenty of money. I got it all from my father, I've never had to earn a penny in my life. Do you know how he made his money? Perfumes, he ran a thriving business in perfumes. Now a nephew of mine looks after it. I am a collector.'

'Oh? What do you collect?'

'People and animals. People from different countries and different continents. People who have some unique trait in them. I've just told you about Kichomo. Besides him, I have a Maori secretary who can write simultaneously with both hands. He's called Tokobahani. I have a black parrot that speaks three different languages, a Pomeranian with two heads, a sadhu from Laxmanjhoola who sits in the air—quite literally, six feet from the ground, and . . .'

'Just a minute, sir,' Lalmohan Babu interrupted. Tarak Nath Thakur reacted instantly. He raised his stick over his head and shouted, 'You dare interrupt me? Me? Why, I—'

'Sorry, sorry, sorry,' Lalmohan Babu offered abject apologies. 'What I wanted to know was whether all these people in your collection stay in your house totally voluntarily?'

'Why shouldn't they? They're well-fed, well-paid and kept in comfort, so they're quite happy to live where I keep them. You may not have heard of me or my collection, but hundreds of people elsewhere in the world have. Why, only the other day, an American journalist interviewed me and published an article in the New York

Times called "The House of Tarak".'

'That's all very well, Mr Thakur,' put in Mr Tarafdar, 'but you still haven't told me why you're here.'

'You mean I must spell it out? Isn't it obvious? I want that boy of yours for my collection . . . what's his name? Jyotishka? Yes, I want Jyotishka.'

'Why? He's being very well looked after here, he's happy and content. Why should he leave me and go and live in your queer household?'

Mr Thakur stared at Sunil Tarafdar for nearly a minute. Then he said slowly, 'You wouldn't speak quite so recklessly if you saw Gawangi.'

'What is Gawangi?' asked Lalmohan Babu.

'Not what, but who,' Mr Thakur replied. 'He's not a thing, but a man. He comes from Uganda. Nearly eight feet tall, his chest measures fifty-four inches and his weight is 350 kg. He could beat the best of Olympic heavyweight champions hollow, any day. Once he spotted a tiger in the jungles of Terai that had both stripes and spots. A perfectly unique specimen. He managed to knock it unconscious with a shot of a tranquillizer. Then he carried that huge animal for three-and-a-half miles. That same Gawangi is now my personal companion.'

'Have you,' asked Lalmohan Babu, with considerable courage, 'reintroduced the old system of slavery?'

'Slavery?' Mr Thakur almost spat the word out. 'No, sir! When I first saw Gawangi, he was facing a totally bleak future. He came from a good family in Kampala, Uganda's capital. His father was a doctor. It was he who told me that Gawangi had reached the height of seven-and-a-half feet even before he had turned fifteen. He couldn't go out anywhere for little urchins threw stones at him. He had had to leave school because his classmates teased and taunted him endlessly. His height and his size were a constant source of embarrassment to him. When I met him, he was twenty-one, spending his days quietly at home, worrying about his future. He would have died like that, had I not rescued him from that situation and brought him with me. He found a new life with me. Why should he be my slave? I look upon him like a son.'

'All right, Mr Thakur, we believe you. But even so, I cannot allow Jyotishka to go and join your zoo.'

'You say that even after being told about Gawangi?'

'Yes. Your Gawangi has nothing to do with my decision.'

For the first time, Mr Thakur seemed to lose a little bit of his self-assurance. I heard him sigh. 'Very well,' he said, 'but can I at least see the boy?'

'Yes, that can be easily arranged.'

Nayan returned to the room. Mr Thakur looked him over, scowling.

'How many rooms does my house have?' he asked abruptly.

'Sixty-six.'

'Hm . . .'

Mr Thakur slowly rose to his feet, gripping the silver handle of his walking-stick firmly with his right hand.

'Remember, Tarafdar, TNT does not give up easily. Goodbye!'

None of us spoke for a long time after he left. At last, Lalmohan Babu broke the silence by saying, 'Felu Babu, number four is quite an important number, isn't it? I mean, there are the four seasons, and four directions, most of our gods and goddesses have four arms, then there are the four Vedas . . . I wonder what these four characters might be called?'

'Just call them FGP—Four Greedy People. Each was as greedy as the other. But none of them got what they wanted. I must praise Sunil for that.'

'No, sir, there's no need for praise. I only did what struck me as very simple. Nayan is my responsibility. He lives in my house, he knows me and I know him. There's no question of passing him on to someone else.'

'Good. All right, then. It's time for us to leave, I think.'

We stood up.

'There's just one thing I'd like to tell you before I go,' Feluda added. 'No more appointments with strange people.'

'Oh no, sir. I've learnt my lesson! This morning's experience was quite enough for me.'

'And please remember, if Nayan needs my protection, I am always there to do what I can. I've already grown rather fond of that boy.'

'Thank you, sir, thank you so much. I'll certainly let you know if we need your help.'

SIX

It was Thursday. We had spent the previous morning with the Four Greedy People. Things were now getting exciting, which was probably why Lalmohan Babu had turned up at 8.30 today instead of 9 a.m.

'Have you seen today's papers?' Feluda asked him as soon as he came in.

'I'm afraid not. A Kashmiri shawl-walla arrived early this morning and took such a lot of time that I never got the chance. Why, what do the papers say?'

'Tiwari opened his chest, and discovered it was empty.'

'Wha-at! You mean young Nayan was right, after all? When was the money stolen?'

'Between two-thirty and three one afternoon. At least, that's what Mr Tiwari thinks. He was in his dentist's chamber during that time. His memory is now working perfectly. Apparently, he had opened the chest two days before the theft and found everything intact. The money was indeed in excess of five lakhs. Tiwari suspects his partner, naturally, since no one else knew the combination.'

'Who is his partner?'

'A man called Hingorani. The "H" in T H Syndicate stands for Hingorani.'

'I see. But to tell you the truth, I'm not in the least interested in Tiwari or his partner. What amazes me is the power that little boy has got.'

'I have been thinking about that myself. I'd love to find out how it all started. Topshe, do you remember where Nayan's father lives?'

'Nikunjabihari Lane. Kalighat.'

'Good.'

'Would you like to go there? We might give it a try—my driver is familiar with most alleyways of Calcutta.'

As it turned out, Lalmohan Babu's driver did know where Nikunjabihari Lane was. We reached there in ten minutes. A local paanwalla showed us Nayan's house. A rather thin gentleman opened the door. Judging by the towel he was still clutching in his hand, he had just finished shaving.

'We are sorry to disturb you so early,' Feluda said pleasantly. 'Were you about to leave for your office? May we talk to you for a minute?'

'Yes, of course. I don't have to leave for another half an hour. Please come in.'

We walked into a room that acted as both a living room and a bedroom. There was no furniture except two chairs and a narrow bed. A rolled-up mattress lay on it.

'Let me introduce myself. I am Pradosh Mitter, and this is my cousin, Tapesh, and my friend Lalmohan Ganguli. We came to find out more about Nayan. You see, we've come to know him and Tarafdar recently. What a remarkable gift your child has been blessed with!'

Nayan's father stared at Feluda, open awe in his eyes. 'You mean you are *the* Pradosh Mitter, the investigator? Your pet name is Felu?'

'Yes.'

'Oh, it is such a privilege to meet you, sir! I am Ashim Sarkar. What would you like to know about Nayan?'

'I am curious about one thing. Was it Tarafdar's idea that Nayan should stay with him, or was it yours?'

'I shall be honest with you, Mr Mitter. The suggestion was first made by Mr Tarafdar, but only after he had seen Nayan. I had taken my son to see him.'

'When was that?'

'The day after I came to know about his power with numbers. It was the second of December.'

'Why did you decide to take him to Tarafdar in the first place?'

'There was only one reason for that, Mr Mitter. As you can see, I am not a rich man. I have four children, and only a small job in a post office. My salary gets wiped out long before a month gets over. I have no savings. In fact, I haven't been able to put Nayan in a school at all. When I think of the future of my family, it terrifies me. So when I realized Nayan had a special power, I thought that might be put to good use. It may sound awful, but in my situation, anyone would welcome the chance to earn something extra.'

'Yes, I understand. There's nothing wrong with what you did. So you took Nayan to see Tarafdar. What happened next?'

'Mr Tarafdar wanted to test Nayan himself. So I told him to ask him any question that might be answered in numbers. Tarafdar said to Nayan, "Can you tell me how old I am?" Nayan said, "Thirty-three years, three months and three days." Tarafdar asked two more questions. Then he made me an offer. If I allowed him to take Nayan on the stage with him, he'd pay me a certain amount of money regularly. I agreed. Then he asked me how much I expected to be paid. With a lot of hesitation, I said, "A thousand rupees." Tarafdar laughed at this and said, "Wrong, you're quite wrong. Nayan, can you give us the figure that's in my head?" And Nayan said immediately, "Three zero zero zero." Mr Tarafdar kept his word. He's already paid me an advance of three thousand rupees. So when he suggested that Nayan should stay in his house, I couldn't refuse him.'

'Was Nayan happy about going and living with a virtual stranger?'

'Yes, surprisingly enough. He agreed quite happily, and now seems to be perfectly content.'

'One more question, Mr Sarkar.'

'Yes?'

'How did you first learn about his power?'

'It happened purely out of the blue. One fine morning he just woke up and said to me, "Baba, I can see lots of things . . . they're running helter-skelter, and some are jumping up and down. Can you see them, too?" I said, "No, I can see nothing. What are these things, anyway?" He said, "Numbers. They're all numbers, from nine to zero. I've a feeling if you asked me something that had anything to do with numbers, these crazy ones would stop dancing around." I didn't believe him, of course, but thought a child ought to be humoured. So I said, "All right. What is that big fat book lying in that corner?" Nayan said, "That's the *Mahabharat*." I said, "Yes. Now can you tell me how many pages it's got?" Nayan smiled at this and said, "I was right, Baba. All the numbers have gone away. I can see only three, standing still. They are nine, three and four." I picked up the *Mahabharat* and looked at the last page. It said 934.'

'I see. Thank you very much, Mr Sarkar. I haven't got any more questions. We're all very grateful to you for giving us your time.'

We said namaskar, came out of the house and got into our car.

We returned home to find two visitors waiting for us. One of them was Sunil Tarafdar. I did not know the other.

'Sorry,' said Feluda hurriedly. 'Have you been waiting long?'

'No, only five minutes,' said Mr Tarafdar. 'This is my manager, Shankar Hublikar.'

The other gentleman rose and greeted us. He seemed to be of the same age as his friend. His appearance was neat and smart. 'Namaskar,' said Feluda, returning his greeting. 'You are from

Maharashtra, aren't you?'

'Yes, that's right. But I was born and brought up here in Calcutta.'

'I see. Please sit down.' We all did. 'What brings you here this morning?' Feluda asked Mr Tarafdar.

'It's something rather serious, I'm afraid.'

'What do you mean?'

'We were attacked last night by a giant.'

My heart skipped a beat. Was he talking about Gawangi?

'Tell us what happened.'

'I got up this morning as usual at 5.30 to take my dog Badshah for a walk. I came downstairs to collect him, but had to stop when I reached the bottom of the stairs.'

'Why?'

'The floor was covered with blood, and someone's footprints went from there right up to the front door. I measured these later. Each was sixteen inches long.'

'Sixt . . .?' Lalmohan Babu choked.

'And then?'

'There is a collapsible gate at my front door, which stays locked at night. That gate was half open, the lock was broken, and outside that gate was lying my chowkidar, Bhagirath. The bloody footprints went past him up to the main compound wall. Well, I washed Bhagirath's head with cold water and brought him round. He began screaming, "Demon! Demon!" the minute he opened his eyes and nearly fainted again. Anyway, what he then told me was this: in the middle of the night, he happened to be standing just outside the collapsible gate, under a low power bulb that's left on all night. Bhagirath looked up at a sudden noise and, in the semi-darkness, saw a huge creature walking towards him. It had obviously jumped over the wall, for outside the main gate was my armed guard, who had not seen it. Bhagirath told me he had once been to the zoo and seen an animal called a "goraila". This creature, he said, looked very much like a "goraila", except that it was larger and more dangerous. I couldn't learn anything more from Bhagirath because one look at this "demon" made him lose consciousness.'

'I see,' said Feluda, 'the demon then presumably broke open the collapsible gate and got inside. Your Badshah must have attacked him after that and bitten his leg, which forced him to run away.'

'Yes, but he didn't spare my Badshah, either. Badshah's body was found about thirty feet from the main gate. This horrible creature had wrung his neck.'

The only good thing about this whole gruesome story, I thought, was that TNT had failed in his attempt. Nayan, thank God, was still safe.

Feluda fell silent when Mr Tarafdar finished his tale. He simply sat staring into space, frowning deeply.

'What's the matter, Mr Mitter?' Mr Tarafdar said impatiently. 'Please say something.'

'The time has come to act, Sunil. I can no longer sit around just talking.'

'What're you thinking of doing?'

'I have decided to accompany you and Nayan—all over south India, wherever you go, starting with Madras. He's in grave danger, and neither you nor your friend here could really give him the protection he needs. I must do my bit.' Mr Tarafdar smiled for the first time.

'I can't tell you how relieved I feel, Mr Mitter. If you now start working in your professional capacity, I will naturally pay your fee and all expenses for the three of you to travel together. I mean, my sponsor will meet all costs.'

'We'll talk about costs later. Which train are you taking to Madras?'

'Coromandel Express, on 19 December.'

'And which hotel are you booked at?'

'The Taj Coromandel. You'll travel by first class AC. Just let me have your names and ages. Shankar will make the reservations.'

'Good,' said Feluda. 'If you have any problems, let me know. I know a lot of people in the railway booking office.'

SEVEN

Mr Tarafdar and his friend left at a quarter to ten. Just five minutes after they had gone, Feluda received a phone call that came as a complete surprise. He took it himself, so at first we had no idea who it was from. He spoke briefly, and came back to join us for a cup of tea.

'I checked in the directory,' he said, raising a cup to his lips, 'there are only two such names listed.'

'Look, Felu Babu,' Lalmohan Babu said, a little irritably, 'I totally fail to see why you must create a mystery out of every little thing. Who rang you just now? Do you mind telling us simply, without making cryptic remarks?'

'Hingorani.'

'The same Hingorani we read about this morning?'

'Yes, sir. Tiwari's partner.'

'What did he want?'

'We'll find that out when we visit him in his house. He lives in Alipore Park Road.'

'Have you made an appointment?'

'Yes, you ought to have realized it while I was speaking to him. Obviously, you were not paying enough attention.'

'I heard you say, "Five o' clock this evening",' I couldn't help saying. This annoyed Lalmohan Babu even more. 'I don't listen in on other people's telephone conversations, as a matter of principle,' he declared righteously. But he was much mollified afterwards when Feluda asked him to stay to lunch, and then spent the whole afternoon teaching him to play scrabble. This did not prove too easy, since it turned out that Lalmohan Babu had never done a crossword puzzle in his life, while Feluda was a wizard at all word games, and a master at unravelling puzzles and ciphers. But Lalmohan Babu's good humour had been fully restored; he didn't seem to mind.

We reached Mr Hingorani's house five minutes before the appointed time.

There was a garage on one side of his compound in which stood a large white car. 'A foreign car?' asked Lalmohan Babu.

'No, it's Indian. A Contessa,' Feluda replied.

A bearer stood at the front door. He looked at Lalmohan Babu and asked, 'Mitter sahib?'

'No, no, not me. This is Mr Mitter.'

'Please come with me.'

We followed him to the drawing room. 'Please sit down,' said the bearer and disappeared. Lalmohan Babu and I found two chairs. Feluda began inspecting the contents of a book case.

A grandfather clock stood on the landing outside. Mr Hingorani entered the room as the clock struck five, making a deep yet melodious sound. Mr Hingorani was middle-aged, thin and perhaps ailing, for there were deep, dark circles under his eyes. We rose as he came in. 'Please, please be seated,' he said hurriedly. We sat down again.

Mr Hingorani began talking. I noticed that the strap of his watch was slightly loose, as it kept slipping forward when he moved his arm.

'Have you read what's been published in the press about T H Syndicate?' he asked.

'Yes indeed.'

'My partner's gone totally senile. At least, I can't think of any other explanation. Nobody in his right mind would behave like this.'

'We happen to know your partner.'

'How?'

Feluda explained quickly about Tarafdar and Nayan. 'Mr Tiwari went to Sunil Tarafdar's house to meet Jyotishka,' he added, 'and we happened to be present. That little wonder boy told him the right numbers for the combination and said there was no money in the chest.'

'I see . . .'

'You told me on the phone you were being harassed. What exactly has happened?'

'Well, you see, for well over a year Tiwari and I hadn't been getting on well, although once we were good friends. In fact, we were classmates in St Xavier's College. We formed T H Syndicate in 1973, and for a few years things worked out quite well. But then . . . our relationship started to change.'

'Why?'

'The chief reason for that was Tiwari's memory. It began to fail pretty rapidly. At times, he couldn't even remember the simplest of things, and it became very difficult to have him present during meetings with clients. Last year, I told him I knew of a very good doctor who I thought he should see. But Tiwari was most offended at my suggestion. That was when our old friendship began to disintegrate. I was tempted to dissolve the partnership, but stayed on because if I hadn't, the whole company would have had to close down. Still, things might have improved, but . . . but Tiwari's recent behaviour really shook me. He came straight to me when he found his chest empty and said, "Give me back my money, this minute!"'

'Is it true that he had once told you what numbers made up the combination?'

'No, no, it's a stinking lie! He kept his own money and personal papers in that chest. There was no reason for him to have told me the combination. Besides, he seems to think that I stole his money while he was at his dentist's. Yet, I can prove that I was miles away during that time. As a matter of fact, I had gone to visit a cousin who had had a heart attack, in the Belle Vue clinic at 11 a.m. and I returned at half past three. Tiwari, however, doesn't believe me and has even threatened to set goondas on me if I don't return his money. He's lost his mind completely.'

'Do you have any idea as to who might have stolen the money?'

'To start with, Mr Mitter, I don't believe there's been a theft at all. Tiwari himself must have kept it elsewhere or spent it on something that he's now forgotten. I wouldn't put it past him, really. Have you ever heard of anyone who forgets the numbers of his own combination lock, having used it for over twenty years?'

'I see what you mean. Let's now come to the point, Mr Hingorani.'

'Yes, you wish to know why I called you here, don't you?'

'That's right.'

'Look, Mr Mitter, I need protection. Tiwari himself might be forgetful, but I'm sure his hired hooligans would never forget their task. They'd be cunning, clever and ruthless. Now, protecting a client from criminals does form a part of a private detective's job, does it not?'

'Yes, it does. But I have a problem. You see, I am going to be away for about five weeks. So I cannot start my job right away. Do you think you can afford to wait until I get back?'

'Where are you going?'

'South India, starting with Madras.'

Hingorani's eyes began shining. 'Excellent!' he said, slapping his thigh. 'I was going to go to Madras, in any case. Someone told me of a new business opportunity there. I've stopped going to our local office here, you see. After the way Tiwari insulted me, I just couldn't face going back there. But obviously, I can't stay at home all my life. So I thought I'd try and find out more about the offer in Madras. Are you going by air? We could all go together, couldn't we?'

'We are travelling by train, Mr Hingorani. In fact, I am going simply in order to protect somebody else—a little boy of eight. He's the child called Jyotishka who helped Tiwari. Three different men want to use him for their own purpose. Mr Tarafdar and I must ensure no one gets near him and puts his power to misuse.'

'Of course. But why don't you kill two birds with one stone?'

'How do you mean?'

'If you start working for me, I'll pay you your fee as well. So you can keep an eye both on me and Jyotishka.'

Feluda accepted this offer. But he gave a word of warning to Mr Hingorani. 'I'll do my best, of course, but please remember that may not be sufficient. You yourself must be very careful indeed in what you do and where you go.'

'Yes, naturally. Where will you be staying in Madras?'

'Hotel Coromandel. We'll reach there on the 21st.'

'Very well. I'll see you in Madras.'

We left soon after this. On our way back, I said to Feluda, 'I noticed two empty spaces on the wall in the drawing room, rectangular in shape. It seemed as though a couple of paintings had once hung there.'

'Good observation. They had probably been oil paintings.'

'And now they are missing,' Lalmohan Babu remarked. 'Could that have any special significance, do you think?'

'It's obvious that Mr Hingorani got rid of them.'

'Yes, but why? What does it imply?'

'It can have a thousand different implications, Lalmohan Babu. Would you like a list?'

'I see. You are not treating this matter very seriously, are you?'

'I see no reason to. I've noted the fact and stored it away in my memory. It will be retrieved, if need be.'

'And what about this second case you have just taken on? Will you be able to manage both?'

Feluda did not reply. He looked out of the window of our car with unseeing eyes and began muttering under his breath.

'Doubts . . .' I heard him say, 'Doubts . . . doubts . . .'

EIGHT

Many of the leading papers next morning carried reports of Tarafdar's forthcoming visit to Madras. His first show there would be held on 25 December, they said.

Feluda had gone to have a haircut. When he returned, I showed him the reports. 'Yes, I've already seen them,' he said, frowning. 'Clearly, Sunil Tarafdar couldn't resist a bit of publicity. I rang him before I left to give him a piece of my mind, but he refused to pay any attention to what I said. He told me instead how important it was for him to make sure the media took notice of what he was doing. When I pointed out that those three people would now come to know about Nayan's movements and that wasn't desirable at all, he said quite airily that they wouldn't dare do anything now, not after the way he had handled them the other day. I put the phone down after this since he obviously wasn't gone to change his mind. But this means my job is going to get a lot more difficult and I have to be ten times more alert. After all, I know Nayan is still in danger.'

A car stopped outside and, a few seconds later, someone rang the bell twice. This had to be Lalmohan Babu. He was late today. It was almost ten-thirty.

'Have I got news for you!' he said as he walked in, his eyes wide with excitement.

'Wait!' Feluda said, smiling a little. 'Let me guess. You went to New Market this morning, right?'

'How do you know?'

'A cash memo of Ideal Stores in New Market is peeping out of the front pocket of your jacket. Besides, that big lump in your side pocket clearly means that you bought a large tube of your favourite toothpaste.'

'All right. Next?'

'You went to a restaurant and had strawberry ice cream—there are two tiny pink drops on your shirt.'

'Shabash! Next?'

'Naturally, you didn't go into a restaurant all alone. You must have run into someone you knew. You didn't invite him to have an ice cream. He did. I am aware that you don't have a single close friend—barring ourselves—with whom you'd want to go to a restaurant. So presumably, this person was someone you met recently. Now, who could it be? Not Tarafdar, for he's far too busy. Could it be one of the four greedy people? Well, I don't think it was Hodgson. He hasn't got money to waste. TNT? No, he wouldn't travel all the way to New Market to do his shopping. That leaves us with—'

'Brilliant, Felu Babu, absolutely brilliant! After a long time, you've shown me today that your old power of deduction is still intact.'

'Was it Basak?'

'Oh yes. Nandalal Basak. He told me his full name today.'

'What else did he tell you?'

'Something rather unpleasant, I'm afraid. Apparently, Basak added ten thousand dollars to their original offer. But even so, Tarafdar refused. That naturally annoyed Basak very much. He said to me, "Go tell your snoopy friend, Mr Ganguli, Nandalal Basak has never been defeated in his life. If Tarafdar does a show in Madras, he'll have to drop the special item by that wonder boy. We'll see to it!"'

My hands suddenly turned cold not because Basak's words meant that he had recognized Feluda, but because there was a hidden menace behind his words that I didn't like at all.

'That accounts for Basak,' said Feluda coolly. 'Tiwari is out of the picture. So we now have to watch out for Tarak Nath Thakur and Hodgson.'

'Tarak Nath cannot do anything by himself. It's Gawangi we have to deal with.'

Feluda started to speak, but was interrupted by the door bell. I could hardly believe my eyes when I opened the door. Never before had I seen telepathy work so quickly. TNT himself stood outside.

'Is Mr Mitter in?'

'Come in, Mr Thakur,' Feluda called. 'So you've worked out who I really am?'

'Of course. And I also know who this satellite of yours is,' TNT said, turning to Lalmohan Babu. 'You are Jatayu, aren't you?'

Yes.'

'I had once thought of keeping you in my zoo, do you know that? After all, in the matter of writing absolute trash, you're quite matchless, I think. *Hullabaloo in Honolulu* . . . ha ha ha!'

The sound of his loud laughter boomed out in our living room. Then he looked at Feluda again. 'So we're meeting once more in Madras, I think?'

'Have you made up your mind about going there?'

'Oh yes. And I won't be alone. My Ugly from Uganda will accompany me, of course. Isn't that marvellous? Sounds just like the title of one of your books, doesn't it, Mr Jatayu?'

'Are you going by train?' Feluda asked.

'I have to. Gawangi couldn't fit into a seat in an aircraft.'

Mr Thakur burst into a guffaw again. Then he rose and began walking towards the front door. 'There's only one thing I'd like to tell you, Mr Mitter,' he threw over his shoulder. 'In some situations, brain power can't possibly be a match for muscle power. Your intelligence may be thousand times stronger than Gawangi's, but if it came to a physical combat, he'd win with both his hands tied behind his back. Goodbye!'

Mr Thakur disappeared as suddenly as he had appeared. I'd love to see this Gawangi in person, I thought.

NINE

There was no sign of either Gawangi or TNT on the train. Our journey to Madras proved to be totally eventless.

'I fail to see,' Lalmohan Babu remarked on our way to the hotel, 'why Madras is clubbed together with cities like Delhi, Bombay and Calcutta. Why, any small town in Bengal is more lively than this!'

In a way, he was right. The roads were so much more quiet than the streets of Calcutta. But they were wide, smooth and devoid of potholes. There weren't many skyscrapers, either; nor were there any traffic jams. I began to like the city of Madras. Heaven knew why Lalmohan Babu was still looking morose. However, he cheered up as we entered the brightly-lit lobby of our hotel. He looked around a few times, then nodded approvingly and said, 'Beautiful. Hey, this is quite something, isn't it?'

We had already decided that we'd spend the first three days just seeing the sights. Nayan and Mr Tarafdar would, of course, accompany us. 'We've seen the Elephanta caves, Ellora and the temples of Orissa,' said Feluda. 'Now we ought to visit Mahabalipuram. That'll show us a different aspect of architecture in India. Have a look at the guide book, Topshe. You'll enjoy things much better if you're already aware of certain points of interest.'

Since it was already dark, we did not venture out in the evening. In fact, each one of us felt like an early night, so we had dinner by 9 p.m. and went to bed soon after that. The next morning, Feluda said as soon as we were ready, 'Let's go and find out what Sunil and Nayan are doing.'

Unfortunately, we had been unable to get rooms on the same floor. Ours was on the fourth, while Nayan's was on the third. We climbed down a flight of stairs and pressed the bell outside room 382. Mr Tarafdar opened the door. We found Shankar Hublikar in the room, and another gentleman. But there was no sign of Nayan.

'Good morning, Mr Mitter,' said Tarafdar with a big smile, 'meet

Mr Reddy. He is the owner of the Rohini Theatre, where I am going to have my first show in Madras. He says there's a tremendous interest among the local public. There have been a lot of enquiries and he thinks the tickets will sell like . . .'

'Where's Nayan?' Feluda interrupted a little rudely.

'Being interviewed. A reporter from the *Hindu* arrived a little while ago to take his interview. This will mean more publicity for my show.'

'Yes, but where is this interview taking place?'

'The manager himself made arrangements. There's a conference room on the ground floor . . .'

Feluda darted out of the room even before Tarafdar had finished speaking, I followed Feluda quickly, Tarafdar's last words barely reaching my ears, ' . . . told him no one should go in . . .'

We rushed down the stairs without waiting for the lift. Feluda kept muttering under his breath. I caught the words 'fool' and 'imbecile', which I realized were meant for our magician.

A passing waiter showed us where the conference room was. Feluda pushed open the door and marched in. There was a long table, with rows of chairs around it. Nayan was sitting in one of them. A bearded man sat next to him, jotting something down in a notebook. Feluda took this in and, a second later, strode forward to grab the reporter and pull at his beard. It came off quite easily. Henry Hodgson stood staring at us.

'Good morning,' he grinned, without the slightest trace of embarrassment.

'What was he asking you?' Feluda asked Nayan.

'About horses.'

'All right, Mr Mitter, have me thrown out,' said Hodgson, still grinning. 'I have already got the numbers of all the winning horses in every race for the next three days. I shouldn't have a care in the world for many years to come. Good day, sir!'

Mr Hodgson slipped out. Feluda flopped down on a chair, clutching his head between his hands. Then he raised his face and looked straight at Nayan. 'Look, Nayan,' he said somewhat impatiently, 'if anyone else tries talking to you, from now on, just tell them you're not going to utter a word unless I am present. Is that understood?'

Nayan nodded sagely.

'There is one consolation, Feluda,' I ventured to say. 'At least

Hodgson's not going to bother us again. He'll now go back to Calcutta and put his last few pennies on horses.'

'Yes, that's true, but I am concerned at Tarafdar's totally irresponsible behaviour. A magician really ought to know better.'

We took Nayan back to Tarafdar's room. 'Did you want publicity, Sunil?' Feluda said sarcastically. 'You'll get it in full measure, but not in the way you had imagined. Do you know who was taking Nayan's interview?'

'Who?'

'Mr Henry Hodgson.'

'What! That bearded—?

'Yes, it was that bearded fellow. He's got what he wanted. Didn't I tell you Nayan wasn't out of danger? If Hodgson could follow us to Madras, why shouldn't the others? Now, look, if you want Nayan to remain safe, you've got to do as I tell you. Or else don't expect any help from me.'

'Y-yes, sir!' Mr Tarafdar muttered, scratching his neck and looking somewhat shamefaced.

'Leave the publicity to Mr Reddy,' Feluda continued. 'Neither you nor your friend Shankar should go anywhere near reporters from the press. Many genuine reporters will want interviews and information. You must learn to stay away from them. Your main priority should be Nayan's safety because—remember—if your show is successful, it will be because of his power and what he does on stage, not because of any publicity you might arrange for yourself. Do I make myself clear?'

'Yes, sir. I understand.'

Over breakfast, we told Lalmohan Babu about Hodgson's visit. 'Good, good!' he exclaimed, attacking an omelette. 'I was afraid things would go quiet in Madras. I'm glad something like this has happened. It all adds to the excitement, don't you think?'

We returned to our room to get ready to go out. It had been decided that we'd go to the snake park today. An American called Whitaker had created it and, by all accounts, it was certainly worth a visit. Just as we were about to leave, the doorbell rang. Lalmohan Babu had already joined us in our room. Who could it be?

I opened the door to find Mr Hingorani. 'May I come in?' he asked.

'Of course, please do,' Feluda invited.

Mr Hingorani came in and took a chair. 'So far, so good!' he said with a sigh of relief. 'I don't think Tiwari knows I'm here. I left without a word to anyone.'

'Good. But I hope you're being careful. There's something I really must stress, Mr Hingorani. If anyone rings your doorbell, you must always ask who it is, and open the door only if the person who answers is known to you.' Before Mr Hingorani could say anything, our own doorbell rang again. This time, it was Tarafdar and Nayan.

'Come in,' said Feluda.

'Is this that famous wonder boy?' Mr Hingorani asked.

Feluda smiled. 'Is there any need to introduce these two people to you?'

'What do you mean?'

'Mr Hingorani, you have appointed me for your protection. You ought to have realized that if a client doesn't come clean with his protector, the protector's job becomes much more difficult.'

'What are you trying to say?'

'You know that very well, but you're pretending you don't. But then, you're not the only one who did not tell me the whole truth.'

Feluda looked at Mr Tarafdar, who stared blankly. 'Very well, since neither of you will open your mouth, allow me to do the talking.' Feluda was still looking at Mr Tarafdar. 'Sunil, you said you had got a sponsor from somewhere. My guess is that your sponsor is none other than Mr Hingorani here.'

At this, Mr Hingorani jumped up in sheer amazement. 'But how did you guess?' he cried. 'Are you a magician, too?'

'No, my guess had nothing to do with magic. It was simply the result of keeping my eyes and ears open.'

'How?'

'When we had gone to see Sunil's show, Nayan had told someone from the audience the number of his car. It was WMF 6232. I saw the same number on your white Contessa. It wasn't too difficult to guess that the young man in the audience was someone from your family, and that he had told you about Jyotishka.'

'Yes, yes. It was Mohan, my nephew.' Mr Hingorani still seemed bemused.

'Besides,' Feluda went on, 'when we went to your house the other day, I noticed quite a few books on magic in your book case. This could only mean—'

'Yes, yes, yes!' Mr Hingorani interrupted. 'When my father found out about my interest in magic, he destroyed all my equipment, but not my books. I managed to save those, and have still got them.'

I glanced at Mr Tarafdar. He was looking extremely uncomfortable. 'Don't blame Sunil,' Mr Hingorani added. 'It was I who asked him to keep my name a secret.'

'But why?'

'There is an important reason. You see, my father is still alive. He's eighty-two, but quite strong and alert for his age. He lives in Faizabad in our old ancestral home. If he finds out that I've got involved with magic and magicians, then even at this age, he's very likely to cut me out of his will.'

'I see.'

'When Mohan told me about Jyotishka, I decided almost immediately to finance his show. By then it was pretty obvious to me that Tiwari and I would soon have to part company, and I'd have to find a new source of income. So I met Tarafdar the next day and made a proposal, which he accepted. Two days later, Tiwari came to me to accuse me of stealing. I just couldn't take it any more. I wrote to Tiwari the following morning, and told him that I was unwell, and that my doctor had advised me a month's rest. I stopped going to my office from the next day.'

'That means you were going to travel to Madras, in any case, to see Tarafdar's show?'

'Yes, but what I told you about my life being in danger is absolutely true, Mr Mitter. I would have had to seek your help, anyway.'

'What about the new business opportunity in Madras you mentioned?'

'No, that was something I just made up. It isn't true.'

'I see. So I've been appointed to protect you from Tiwari's hoodlums, and to save Nayan from three unscrupulous men. We can arrange for one of us to be present with Nayan at all times. But you must tell me what you're going to do to make my job a little easier.'

'Well, I promise to do as I'm told. I have visited Madras many times before. So I don't have to go sightseeing. Tarafdar's manager can keep me posted about sales figures, once the show starts. In other words, there's no need for me to step out of my room; and most certainly I'm not going to open the door to anyone I don't know.'

'Very well. All right then, Mr Hingorani, I suggest you go back to your room and stay in it. It's time for us to leave.'

All of us rose. 'Come along, Nayan Babu,' said Jatayu, offering his hand. Nayan took it eagerly. He and Jatayu had clearly struck up a friendship.

TEN

We didn't spend very long in the snake park, but even a short visit showed us what a unique place it was. It seemed incredible that a single individual had planned the whole thing. I saw every species of snake that I had read about, and many that I didn't know existed. The park itself was beautifully designed, so walking in it was a pleasure.

No untoward incident took place during our outing on the first day. The only thing I noticed was that Lalmohan Babu tightened his hold on Nayan's hand each time he saw a man with a beard. 'Hodgson has gone back to Calcutta, I'm sure,' I said to him.

'So what?' he shot back. 'How can you tell Basak won't try to appear in a disguise?'

We were strolling along a path that led to an open marshy area. To our surprise, we discovered that this area was surrounded by a sturdy iron railing, behind which lay five alligators, sleeping in the sun. We were watching them closely and Lalmohan Babu had just started to tell Nayan, 'When you're a bit older, my boy, I'll give you a copy of my book *The Crocodile's Crunch,'* when a man wearing a sleeveless vest and shorts turned up, carrying a bucket in one hand. He stood about twenty yards away from the railing and began taking out frogs from the bucket. He threw these at the alligators one by one, which they caught very neatly between their jaws. I watched this scene, quite fascinated, for I had never seen anything like it before.

We returned to our hotel in the evening, all safe and sound. None of us knew what lay in store the next day. Even now, as I write about it, a strange mixture of amazement, fear and disbelief gives me goose-pimples.

The guidebook had told me Mahabalipuram was eighty miles from Madras. The roads were good, so we expected to get there in two hours. Shankar Babu had arranged two taxis for us. Nayan insisted on joining us instead of Mr Tarafdar as Jatayu had started telling him the story of his latest book. *The Astounding Atlantic*. I sat in the front seat of the car, Nayan sat between Jatayu and Feluda in the back.

It soon became clear that we were travelling towards the sea. Although the city of Madras stood by the sea, we hadn't yet seen it. Two hours and fifteen minutes later, the sea came into view. A wide empty expanse stretched before us, and on the horizon shimmered the dark blue ocean. The tall structures that stood out on the sand were temples.

Our taxi stopped next to a huge van and a luxury coach. A large number of tourists—most of them Americans—were getting into the coach, clad in an interesting assortment of clothes, wearing different caps, sporting sunglasses in different designs, and carrying bags of every possible shape and size. We stopped and stared at them for a minute. 'Big business, tourism!' proclaimed Lalmohan Babu and got out of the car with Nayan.

Feluda had never visited Mahabalipuram before, but knew what there was to see. He had already told me everything was spread over a vast area. 'We cannot see it all in a day, at least not when there's a small child with us. But you, Topshe, must see four things—the shore temple, Gangavataran, the Mahishasurmardini Mandap and the Pancha Pandava caves. Lalmohan Babu and Nayan can go where they like. I have no idea what Shankar and Sunil wish to do. They don't seem at all interested in temples or sculpture.'

We began walking together.

'All this was built by the Ballabhas, wasn't it?' asked Lalmohan Babu.

'Not Ballabhas, Mr Ganguli,' Feluda replied solemnly. 'They were Pallavas.'

'Which century would that be?'

'Ask your young friend. He'll tell you.'

Lalmohan Babu looked faintly annoyed at this, but did not say anything. I knew Mahabalipuram had been built in the seventh century.

We went to take a look at the shore temple first. Noisy waves lashed against its rear walls. 'They certainly knew how to select a good spot,' Lalmohan Babu remarked, raising his voice to make himself heard. On our right was a statue of an elephant and a bull. Next to these were what looked like small temples. 'Those are the Pandava's chariots,' Feluda said. 'You'll find one that looks a bit like a hut from a village in Bengal. That's Draupadi's chariot.'

Gangavataran made my head reel. Carved in relief on the face of a huge rock was the story of the emergence of Ganges from the Himalayas. There were animals and scores of human figures, exquisite in every detail.

'All this was done by hand, simply with a chisel and hammer, wasn't it?' Lalmohan Babu asked in wonder.

'Yes. Just think, Lalmohan Babu. There are millions of carved figures like these, to be found in temples all over our country. It took hundreds of years to finish building these temples; dozens and dozens of craftsmen worked on them. Yet, nowhere will you find a single stroke of the hammer that's out of place, or a mark made by the chisel that doesn't fit in. If something goes wrong with a figure of clay, the artist may be able to correct his mistake. But a single mark on a piece of rock would be permanent, absolutely indelible. That is why it always takes my breath away when I think of how totally perfect these ancient artists' skill had been. God knows why modern artists have lost that sense of perfection.'

Mr Tarafdar and Shankar Babu had gone ahead. 'You may as well go and see the two caves I told you about,' Feluda said to me. 'I am going to look at these carvings more closely, so I'm going to take a while.'

I took the guidebook from Feluda and looked at the map to see where the caves were located. 'Look, Lalmohan Babu,' I said, pointing at two dots on the map, 'this is where we have to go.' But it was not clear whether Lalmohan Babu heard me, for he had already resumed his story about the Atlantic and started to walk away. I followed him, and soon found a path that went up a small hill. According to the plan, I was supposed to go up this path. The noise of the waves was a lot less here. I could hear Lalmohan Babu's voice quite clearly. Perhaps his story was reaching its climax.

I found the Pancha Pandava cave. Before I could go in, I saw Lalmohan Babu and Nayan come out and walk further up the same path. Neither seemed even remotely interested in the astounding specimens of sculpture all around.

I took a little time to inspect the carvings. The figures of animals were surprisingly lifelike. Even in thirteen hundred years, their appearance hadn't changed. When I stepped out of the cave, two things struck me immediately. The sky had turned grey, and the breeze from the sea was stronger. There was no noise except the steady roar of the waves and an occasional rumble in the sky.

The Mahishasurmardini Mandap stood in front of me. Since Lalmohan Babu had come in the same direction, he should have been in there, but there was no sign of either him or Nayan. Could he have walked on without going into the mandap at all? But why would he do that? There was nothing worth seeing on the other side. Suddenly, I felt afraid. Something must have happened. I came out quickly and began running, almost without realizing it. Only a few seconds later, a new noise reached my ears—and froze my blood.

'Ha ha ha ha ha ha!'

There could be no mistake. It was TNT's laughter.

I turned a corner sharply, and my eyes fell on a horrible sight. A colossal black figure, clad in a red and white striped shirt and black trousers, was walking rapidly away, carrying Lalmohan Babu and Nayan, one under each arm. I could now see for myself why Mr Tarafdar's chowkidar had called him a demon.

Under any other circumstances, I would have been petrified. But now there was no time to lose. 'Feluda!' I yelled and began sprinting after the black giant. If I could attach myself to one of his legs, perhaps that would slow him down?

I managed to catch up with him eventually and lunged forward to grab his leg. He let out a sharp yelp of pain, which could only mean that my hands had landed on the same spot where Badshah had bitten him. But in the next instant, I found myself being kicked away. Two seconds later, I was lifted off the ground and placed under the same arm which held Nayan. My own legs swung in the air like a pendulum. I was held so tightly that, very soon, I began to feel as though I'd choke to death. Lalmohan Babu, too, was crying out in pain.

But TNT was still laughing. Out of the corner of my eye, I saw him raise his stick in the air, making circular movements, and heard him shout like a maniac, 'Now do you see what I meant? How do you find Gawangi, eh?'

I would have told him, but at this moment, events took a dramatic turn. Two men emerged from behind TNT. One of them was leaning forward and walking strangely, taking long, measured steps. He was also swaying his arms from side to side.

Mr Tarafdar! And his friend, Shankar Hublikar.

I knew what Mr Tarafdar was trying to do. I had seen him make the same gestures on stage, when he hypnotized people. He continued to move forward, his eyes fixed on our captor. By this time, TNT had seen both men. He charged at Tarafdar, his stick still raised high. Shankar Hublikar snatched it from his hand.

Gawangi slowed down. He suddenly seemed unsure of himself. I saw TNT tear at his hair and shout at him; but I couldn't understand a word of the language he spoke.

Mr Tarafdar and Gawangi were now facing each other. With an effort, I managed to turn my head and look up at Gawangi's face. What I saw took me by surprise again. His eyes were bulging, his jaw sagged and I could see all his teeth. I had never seen a human face like that.

Then, slowly, the huge arms that were carrying us began to lower themselves. A few moments later, I felt solid ground under my feet, and realized that Lalmohan Babu and Nayan had also landed safely.

'Go back to your car,' Mr Tarafdar spoke through clenched teeth. 'Let me deal with this, then we'll find ours.'

The three of us turned and began running back towards the caves. I saw TNT sit down on the sand, his face between his hands.

We found Feluda still looking at Gangavataran. The sight of three figures rushing forward madly made him guess instantly what had happened. He ran quicker than us and opened the doors of our taxi. Luckily, the driver had not left his seat.

All of us jumped in.

'Turn back!' shouted Feluda. 'Go back to Madras, fast!'

Only one of us spoke as our car started to speed towards the city. It was Nayan.

'That giant has forty-two teeth!' he said.

ELEVEN

We were having a most enjoyable lunch in the dining room called Mysore in our hotel. It specialized in Moghlai cuisine. Lalmohan Babu had offered to pay for this meal, as a token of thanks to Mr Tarafdar for having saved his life. Tarafdar and Shankar Babu had rejoined us in the hotel.

'But how did Gawangi find you in the first place?' Feluda asked Lalmohan Babu.

'Don't ask me, Felu Babu! What happened was this: I was totally engrossed in telling my story, and Nayan was hanging on to every word. We kept going into and coming out of caves and mandaps, without really taking anything in. In one of these, suddenly I saw a statue of Mahishasur. I was about to come out after just one glance, when my eyes fell on another statue, painted black from head to toe, except that its torso was covered with red and white stripes. It was massive, and it was horrible. I was staring at it, quite puzzled by this deviation from all the other sculptures in the complex and wondering if it might perhaps be a statue of Ghatotkach—I mean, there were characters from the *Mahabharata* strewn about, weren't there?—when the statue suddenly opened its eyes. Can you imagine that? The monster had actually been sleeping while standing up! Anyway, he lost not a second when he opened his eyes and saw us. Before either of us could get over the shock, he had picked us up and was striding ahead. Well, I think you know the rest.'

'Hm. Gawangi might be physically exceptionally strong, but I'm sure he's actually quite simple. Thank Heavens for that, or Sunil would have found it a lot more difficult to hypnotize him.'

'Yes, you're right,' Mr Tarafdar said. 'We had no idea, of course, that we had been followed. You see, Shankar is interested in ayurveda. He'd heard somewhere that a herb called Sarpagandha could be found in Mahabalipuram. So we had gone to look for it. In fact, we even found it and were returning feeling quite jubilant, when we saw Gawangi and Thakur.'

'Sarpagandha? Isn't that given to people with high blood pressure?' Feluda asked.

'Yes,' Shankar Babu replied. 'Sunil's pressure tends to climb up occasionally. I wanted the herb for him.'

Lalmohan Babu threw a chicken tikka into his mouth. 'Felu Babu,' he said, munching happily, 'we managed without your help today. Perhaps you're not going to be needed any more!'

Feluda ignored the jibe and said, 'What is more important is that Gawangi and Thakur's efforts failed.'

'Yes. We're now left with only Basak.'

Mr Reddy, who had arrived just before lunch and had been persuaded to join us (although he ate only vegetarian food), spoke for the first time. 'Tell you what, Mr Tarafdar,' he said gently. 'I suggest you don't go out anywhere else today. In fact, you should rest in the hotel tomorrow as well. After today's events, I really don't think you should run any more risks with that boy. After all, your show begins the day after tomorrow and we're sold out completely for the first couple of days. If anything happened to Nayan, every single person would want his money back. Where do you think we'd stand then?'

'What about security during the shows?'

'I have informed the police. Don't worry, that's been taken care of.'

Mr Reddy had indeed worked very hard to arrange good publicity for the show. We had seen large posters and hoardings on our way back from Mahabalipuram which showed Mr Tarafdar in his golden costume and introduced Nayan as 'Jyotishkam—the Wonder Boy'.

'We've all got to be a lot more vigilant,' Feluda said. 'I must apologize both to you, Mr Reddy, and to Sunil for not taking better care of Nayan. Those statues and carvings in Mahabalipuram simply turned my head, you see, or else I wouldn't have allowed Nayan to get out of my sight.'

We finished our meal and left the dining room. Nayan went back with Mr Tarafdar since Jatayu had finished his story. Feluda, Lalmohan Babu and I returned to our room, and barely five minutes later, came the second surprise of the day.'

Feluda was in the middle of telling Jatayu, 'I must now think of retirement, mustn't I? I ought to put you in charge, I think. I'm sure you'll make a very worthy successor—' and Lalmohan Babu was grinning broadly, thoroughly enjoying being teased, when the telephone rang. Feluda broke off, spoke briefly on the phone, then put it down.

'I have no idea who he is. But he wants to come up and see us. He rang from the lobby. So I told him to come. Mr Jatayu, please take over.'

'What!' Lalmohan Babu gasped. 'What do you mean?'

'You said my days were over. Let's see how well you can manage on your own.' The bell rang before Lalmohan Babu could utter another word. I opened the door to find a middle-aged gentleman, of medium height, sporting a thick black moustache, although his hair was thin and grey. He walked into the room, glanced first at Feluda and then at Lalmohan Babu, and said, 'Er . . . which one of you is Mr Mitter?'

Feluda pointed at Lalmohan Babu and said coolly, 'He is.'

The man turned to face Lalmohan Babu, with an outstretched hand. Lalmohan Babu pulled himself together, and gave him a manly handshake. I remembered Feluda had once said to him, 'A handshake is a Western concept. Therefore, if you must shake hands with someone, do so as a Westerner would—a firm grip, and a smart shake.' Perhaps, like me, he had recalled these words for I saw him clutch the other gentleman's hand tightly and give it a vigorous shake. Then he withdrew his hand and said, 'Please sit down, Mr—?'

The man sat down on a sofa. 'I could tell you my name, but that wouldn't mean anything to you,' he said. 'I have been sent here by Mr Tiwari. I have known him for many years. But that isn't all. You see, I am a private detective, like yourself. The company called Detecnique, for which I work, moved from Calcutta to Bombay more than twenty years ago. That is why I never got round to meeting you before, although I did hear your name. Pardon me, Mr Mitter, but I am a little surprised. I mean, you don't look like an investigator . . . in fact, this gentleman here is more . . .' He glanced at Feluda.

'He is my friend, Lalmohan Ganguli, a powerfully outstanding writer,' Lalmohan Babu announced solemnly.

'I see. Anyway, let me tell you why I'm here.' He took out a photograph from his pocket. I could see from where I was standing that it was a photo of Mr Hingorani.

'You are working for this man, aren't you?'

Feluda's face remained impassive. Lalmohan Babu's eyebrows rose for a fleeting second, but he said nothing. We were under the impression that no one knew about Mr Hingorani and us. How had this man found out?

'If that is the case, Mr Mitter,' continued our visitor, 'then I am your rival, for I am representing Tiwari. I contacted him when I read about his case in a newspaper. He was delighted, and said he needed my help. I agreed, and left for Calcutta immediately. The first thing I did on reaching Calcutta was ring Hingorani. His nephew answered the phone and said no one knew where his uncle had gone. Then I checked with Indian Airlines and found his name on the passenger list of a Calcutta-Madras flight. It became clear that he had fled after Tiwari's threats. So I went to his house, and met his bearer. He told me that three days ago, three visitors had been to the house. One of them was called Mr Mitter. This made me suspicious, and I looked up your number in the telephone directory. When I rang you, I learnt that you, too, had left for Madras. I put two and two together and decided to discover where you were staying. So here I am, simply to tell you what the latest situation is. You do admit, don't you, that Hingorani appointed you to protect him?'

'Any objections?'

'Many.'

Nobody spoke for a few seconds. Feluda kept smoking, blowing out smoke rings from time to time, his face still expressionless.

'Do you know what developments have taken place regarding Tiwari's case?' our visitor asked.

'Why, has anything been reported in the press?'

'Yes. Some new facts have come to light, that open up a totally different dimension. Are you aware what kind of a man you're protecting? He is a thief, a liar and a scoundrel of the first order.' The man raised his voice and almost shouted the last few words. Lalmohan Babu gulped twice and, despite a heroic effort, failed to hide the anxiety in his voice.

'H-how do you kn-know?'

'Tiwari found irrefutable evidence. Hingorani's ring—a red coral set in gold—was found under the chest. It had rolled to the far end, which was why no one saw it at first. A sweeper found it eventually. Everyone in the office recognized the ring. Hingorani had worn it for years. This is my trump card, Mr Mitter. This will finish your client.'

'But when the theft took place, Mr Hingoraj—no, I mean Hingorani, was visiting his cousin in a hospital.'

'Nonsense. He stole into the office at two in the morning to remove the money. He had to bribe the chowkidar to get in. How do I know? I know because the chowkidar made a full confession to the police. Hingorani paid him five hundred rupees. Tiwari told me he could now remember perfectly when and how he had told his partner about the combination. It was nearly fifteen years ago. Tiwari had suffered a serious attack of hepatitis. He thought he'd die, so he called Hingorani and gave him the number.'

'But why should Hingorani steal his partner's personal money?'

'Because he was nearly bankrupt, that's why!' our visitor raised his voice again. 'He had started to gamble very heavily. He used to travel to Kathmandu pretty frequently and visit all the casinos. He lost thousands of rupees at roulette, but that did nothing to make him stop. Tiwari tried to warn him. He paid no attention. In the end, he had begun to sell his furniture and paintings. When even that didn't bring him enough, he thought of stealing Tiwari's money.'

'Well, what do you intend to do now?'

'I will go straight to his room from here. It is my belief that he's brought the stolen money with him. Tiwari is such a kind man that he's offered not to take any action against Hingorani as long as he gets his money back. I am going to pass his message to Hingorani, and hope that he will then come to his senses and return the money.'

'What if he doesn't?'

Our visitor's lips spread in a slow, cruel smile. 'If he doesn't,' he said with relish, 'we'll have to think of a different course of action.'

'You mean you'll use force? But that's wrong, that's unlawful! Why, you are a detective, aren't you? Your job is to expose criminals, not to break the law yourself!'

'Yes, Mr Mitter. But there are detectives, and detectives. I believe in playing things by ear. Surely you know that the dividing line between a criminal and a good sleuth is very, very thin?' He rose. 'Glad to have met you, sir. Good day!' he said, shaking Lalmohan Babu's hand again. Then he swiftly went out.

The three of us sat in silence after he had gone. Then Feluda spoke. 'Thank you, Lalmohan Babu. The advantage in staying silent is that one gets more time to think. I now realize that Mr Hingorani has recently lost a lot of weight. He's been ailing for some time, perhaps with diabetes, I don't know. Anyway, the point is that that's why the strap of his watch became loose, and so did his ring. When it slipped off his finger and rolled under the chest, he didn't even notice it.'

'What! You mean what that man just said was true? You're prepared to believe him?'

'Yes, I am. A lot of things that were unclear to me before have now become crystal clear. But that man was wrong about one thing. Hingorani did not steal Tiwari's money to settle his gambling debts. One look at Nayan had told him his financial worries were over. He took the money simply to create the Miracles Unlimited Company, and to support Tarafdar.'

'Won't you go and talk to Hingorani now?'

'No, there's no need. That man from Detecnique will do all the talking. And Hingorani will return Tiwari's money, if only to save his own life. He has no future left as Tarafdar's sponsor.'

'But that means—?'

'Stop it right there, Lalmohan Babu. I do not know what that means, or what all the future implications are. Give me time to think.'

TWELVE

Lalmohan Babu and I went for a walk in the evening by the sea. Heaven knew what lay in store for Mr Hingorani, but perhaps Nayan was safe for the moment. As a matter of fact, I thought, if Hingorani managed to produce just enough money to pay for his first show—that is, after he had paid Tiwari back—then everything would be all right. Once people had actually seen what Nayan was capable of, the money would come rolling in and Mr Hingorani would be able to manage quite well.

However, Lalmohan Babu was most annoyed when I told him my theory. 'Tapesh, I am shocked!' he said sternly. 'That man is a criminal. He's stolen a lot of money from his partner. How can you feel happy about the same man making use of Nayan?'

'I am not happy about it, Lalmohan Babu. There is enough evidence against Hingorani to put him in prison right away. But if Tiwari is willing to forgive him, why should either you or I mind if he just gets on with his life?'

'I mind because that man's a gambler. I have no sympathy for gamblers.'

I said nothing more. A little later, Lalmohan Babu seemed to calm down and suggested we stop somewhere for a quick coffee. I was feeling thirsty, too; so we found a café near the beach and went in. It was fairly crowded, but we managed to find a table. 'Two cold coffees, please,' I said to the waiter. A minute later, two tall glasses with straws landed in front of us. Both of us bent our heads slightly to take a sip through the straw.

'Did you speak to your snoopy friend?' asked a voice. Lalmohan Babu choked. I raised my eyes quickly to find Mr Nandalal Basak standing by our table, dressed in a garish shirt. 'Tell your friend, and Tarafdar,' he added, when Lalmohan Babu stopped spluttering, 'that Basak doesn't let grass grow under his feet. He may well have his show on the 25th, but that wonder boy will never get the chance to appear on stage. I can guarantee that.'

Without waiting for a reply, Mr Basak walked out of the café and disappeared from sight. It was already dark outside, so I couldn't see where he went. We paid for our coffee and took a taxi back to the hotel. We reached it in half an hour, to find the lobby absolutely packed with people. Right in the middle of the lobby was a huge pile of luggage. Obviously, several large groups of tourists had arrived had arrived together.

We made our way to the lift as quickly as we could and pressed number 4. When we reached our room, we realized someone else was in the room already, for Feluda was speaking to him with a raised voice, sounding extremely cross.

He opened the door a few seconds after I rang the bell, and began shouting at us. 'Where the hell have you two been? What's the point in having you here, when I can't ever find you when you're needed?'

Rather embarrassed, we went into the room and found Mr Tarafdar sitting on the sofa, looking as though the world had come to an end.

'What . . . what happened?' Lalmohan Babu faltered.

'Ask your magician.'

'What is it, Sunil?'

Mr Tarafdar did not reply.

'He's bereft of speech,' Feluda said, his voice sounding cold and hard, 'so perhaps I should tell you what happened.'

He lit a Charminar and inhaled deeply. 'Nayan's gone. Been kidnapped. Can you believe that? How will anyone ever be able to trust me again? Didn't I tell you he mustn't step out of your room? Didn't I say so a thousand times? But no, he had to go out with Shankar to the hotel bookshop, when the whole place is crawling with strangers.'

'And then?' I could hear my own heartbeats.

'Go on, Tarafdar, tell them the rest. Or do I have to spend my life speaking on your behalf?' I had very seldom seen Feluda so totally livid with rage.

Mr Tarafdar finally raised his face and spoke in a whisper. 'Nayan was getting fed up of being couped up in the room. He kept badgering Shankar all day to take him out to buy a book. So Shankar went out with him in the evening, only as far as the hotel shopping arcade, and found the bookshop. Nayan chose two books, and passed them to the lady at the cash till. Shankar was watching her make the bill and wrap the books up, when she suddenly said, "That boy . . . where is that boy?" Shankar wheeled around to find Nayan had vanished. He looked for him everywhere. But . . . but there was no sign of him. There were so many people there, such a lot of pushing and jostling . . . who would have noticed a little boy of eight?'

'When did this happen?'

'That's the beauty of it!' Feluda shouted again. 'All this happened an hour and a half ago. But Sunil decided to inform me barely ten minutes before you arrived.'

'Basak,' Lalmohan Babu said firmly. 'Nandalal Basak did this. No doubt about it, Felu Babu. Absolutely none.'

'How can you be so sure?'

I explained about our encounter with Mr Basak. Feluda's frown deepened.

'I see. This is what I had been afraid of. He must have spotted you in that café, soon after he had had Nayan removed from this hotel.'

'Where is Shankar?' Lalmohan Babu asked.

'He's gone to the police station,' Mr Tarafdar replied.

'But informing the police alone isn't going to solve your problem, is it? You'll have to tell your sponsor and Mr Reddy. Do you think they'll still be prepared to go ahead with your show, even without Nayan? I doubt it!'

'Well, then . . . who's going to tell Hingorani?' Lalmohan Babu asked.

'Not our hypnotist here,' Feluda said. 'He hasn't got the nerve. He's already asked me to do it, since he's afraid Hingorani will throttle him to death, on the spot.'

'All right,' Lalmohan Babu held up a hand, 'neither of you need tell Hingorani. We will. Tapesh, are you ready?'

'Yes, of course.'

'Very well,' Feluda said slowly, 'You two can go and give him the bad news. Go at once. He's in room 288.'

We took the staircase to go down to his room and rang the bell. Nothing happened. 'These bells don't work sometimes,' Lalmohan Babu told me. 'Press it hard.' I did, three times in a row. No one opened the door. So we went down to the lobby once more and rang room 288 from a house telephone. The phone rang several times, but there was no answer. Puzzled, we went to the reception.

'Mr Hingorani must be in the room for his key isn't here,' said the receptionist.

'But . . .' Lalmohan Babu grew agitated, 'he may be sleeping, right? We need to check, see? Very important for us to see him. Now! No duplicate key?' Something in the way he spoke must have impressed the receptionist. Without another word to us, he asked a bell-boy to take a duplicate key and come with us. This time, we took the lift to go up to the second floor. The bell-boy unlocked the door and motioned us to go in.

'Thank you,' said Lalmohan Babu and pushed the door open. Then he took a few steps forward, only to spring back again and run straight into me.

'H-h-h-ing!' he cried, looking ashen.

By this time, I, too, had seen it. It made my heart jump into my mouth, and my limbs began to go numb.

Mr Hingorani was lying on his back, although his legs stretched out of the bed and touched the floor. His jacket was unbuttoned and, through the gap, I could see a red patch on his white shirt, from the middle of which rose the handle of a dagger.

Someone had left the TV on, but the sound had been switched off. People talked, laughed, cried, moved and jumped on the screen, in absolute silence. Strange bluish shadows, reflected from the TV screen, danced endlessly on Mr Hingorani's dead face.

THIRTEEN

There seemed little doubt that Mr Hingorani had been killed by the man from Detecnique. The police surgeon put the time of death between 2.30 and 3.30 p.m. Our visitor had left our room at 2.45 and had told us that he would go straight to see Hingorani. It was obvious that Mr Hingorani had refused to return Tiwari's money, and so Mr Detecnique had decided to kill him. The police found only sixty-five rupees in a drawer and a handful of coins. The only luggage in the room was a suitcase, partly filled with clothes. If indeed Mr Hingorani had carried lakhs of rupees with him, he'd have put it in a briefcase. There was no sign of a briefcase anywhere.

Feluda spoke to the police and gave them a description of the man from Detecnique. 'I couldn't tell you his name,' he said, 'but if he's taken the money, he'll pass it on to Devkinandan Tiwari of T H Syndicate in Calcutta. I think your colleagues there ought to be informed.'

Mr Reddy had heard of the double tragedy, and was now sitting in our room. I had expected him either to throw a fit, or have a heart attack. To my amazement, he remained quite calm and began to discuss how the magic show might still go ahead, even without Nayan.

'Suppose you concentrate more on your hypnotism?' he said to

Tarafdar. 'I will get leading personalities—politicians, film stars, sportsmen—on the opening night. You can hypnotize each one of them. How about that?'

Mr Tarafdar shook his head sadly. 'It's very kind of you, Mr Reddy. But I can't spend the rest of my life performing on your stage. I have to move on, but who will treat me with such kindness in other cities? The word has spread, everyone will expect Nayan on my show. Most theatre managers are ruthless businessmen. They wouldn't dream of giving me a chance. I am finished, Mr Reddy.'

'Did Hingorani pay you anything at all?' Feluda asked.

'Yes, he paid me a certain sum before I left Calcutta. It was enough to cover our travel and stay here. Tomorrow, he was supposed to pay me another instalment. You see, he believed in astrology. Tomorrow, he had told me, was an auspicious day.'

Mr Reddy looked sympathetically at Mr Tarafdar.

'I can see what you're going through. You can't possibly perform in your present state of mind.'

'It isn't just me, Mr Reddy. My manager, Shankar, is so upset that he's taken to his bed. I can't manage without him, either.'

The police had left half an hour ago. A murder enquiry had been started. Every hotel and guest-house in the city was going to be asked if they had had a visitor in the recent past who fitted the description Feluda had given. Hingorani's nephew, Mohan, had been contacted. He was expected to arrive the next day. The police had removed the body.

Feluda himself was going to make enquiries about Nayan and try to find him. 'I am relying solely on you, Mr Mitter,' Mr Reddy said, rising. 'I can postpone the show for a couple of days. Find our Jyotishkam in these two days. Please!'

Mr Reddy left. A minute later, Mr Tarafdar said, 'I think I'll go back to my room. I'll wait for two more days, as Mr Reddy suggested. If Nayan can't be found, I'll just pack my bags and go back to Calcutta. What else can I do? Will you stay on in Madras?'

'Well, obviously I cannot stay here indefinitely. But I'm not going to go back without getting to the bottom of this business. Why should anyone pull the wool over our eyes and be allowed to get away with it?'

'Very well,' said Mr Tarafdar and went out. Feluda took a long puff at his Charminar, and then muttered a word I had heard him use before: 'Doubts . . . doubts . . . doubts . . .'

'What are you feeling doubtful about?' Lalmohan Babu asked.

'To start with, Hingorani had been told not to open his door to a stranger. How did Mr Detecnique manage to get in? Did Hingorani know him?'

'He may have. Is that so surprising?'

'Besides, Feluda, why are you thinking only of Hingorani's murder? Isn't finding Nayan more important?'

'Yes, Topshe. I am trying to think of both Hingorani and Nayan . . . but somehow the two are getting entangled with each other in my mind.'

'But that's pure nonsense, Felu Babu! The two are totally separate incidents. Why are you allowing one to merge with the other?'

Feluda paid no attention to Lalmohan Babu. He shook his head a couple of times, and said softly, 'No signs of struggle . . . absolutely no signs of struggle . . .'

'Yes, that's what the police said, didn't they?'

'Yet, it wasn't as though the man had been murdered in his sleep.'

'No, of course not. Have you ever heard of anyone going to bed fully dressed, without even taking off his socks and shoes?'

'People do sometimes, if they are totally drunk.'

'But this man hadn't been drinking. At least, not in his room. He might have gone out, of course, and returned quite sozzled.'

'No.'

'Why not?'

'Because the TV had been left on. And there was a half-finished cigarette in the ash-tray, which means someone had rung the bell while he was in the room, smoking and watching television. He stubbed his cigarette out, switched off the sound of his TV, and opened the door.'

'But surely he'd have wanted to know who it was before opening the door?'

'Yes, but if it was someone he knew, he would naturally have let him in.'

'Then you must assume he knew this man from Detecnique. What he probably didn't know was that Mr Detecnique was a merciless killer.'

'That still doesn't make sense. Why didn't Hingorani resist him when he took out a large knife and attacked him?'

'I don't know, Felu Babu! You must find out the reason, mustn't you? If you can't, we'll have to admit you've lost your touch and

Tapesh's readers have every right to complain. Where is your earlier brilliance, sir? Where is that razor sharp—?'

'Quiet.'

Lalmohan Babu had to stop in mid-sentence. Feluda was no longer looking at us. His eyes were fixed on the blank wall, his brows creased in a deep frown. Lalmohan Babu and I stared at him for a whole minute without uttering a single word. Then we heard him whisper, 'Yes . . . yes . . . I see . . . I see. But why? Why? Why?'

'Would you like to be left alone for a few minutes, Felu Babu?' Lalmohan Babu asked gently.

'Yes. Thank you, Mr Jatayu. Half an hour. Just leave me alone for half an hour.'

We came away quietly.

FOURTEEN

'Shall we go down to the coffee shop?' I suggested tentatively.

'Hey, that's exactly what I was going to suggest myself,' Lalmohan Babu replied, looking pleased.

We found an empty table in the coffee shop. 'We could have some sandwiches with a cup of tea,' Lalmohan Babu observed. 'That'll help us kill more time.'

'Two teas and two plates of chicken sandwiches, please,' I told the waiter. I was hungry, but food didn't seem all that important just now. Feluda had obviously seen the light. Whether it was only a glimmer, or whether he had solved the whole mystery, I didn't know. But I began to feel elated.

Lalmohan Babu found another way of killing time. He started to tell me the story of his next book. As always, he had already decided on the name. 'I am going to call it *The Manchurian Menace*. It will mean reading up on China and the Chinese way of life, although my book will have nothing to do with modern China. It will be set during the time of the Mandarins.'

Soon, we finished our tea and sandwiches. Lalmohan Babu finished his story, but even so we had about ten minutes to spare.

'What should we do now?' he asked as we came out in the lobby.

'Let's go to that bookshop,' I said. 'After all, it's become a sort of historic place, hasn't it, since that's where Nayan was seen last?'

'Yes, you're right. Let's go and have a look. Who knows, they might even have displayed copies of my books!'

'Er . . . I don't think so, Lalmohan Babu.'

'Well, no harm in asking, is there?'

There was only one lady in the shop, sitting behind a counter. She was both young and attractive.

'Excuse me,' said Lalmohan Babu, walking straight up to her.

'Yes, sir?'

'Do you have crime novels for . . . for . . . youngsters?'

'In which language?'

'Bengali.'

'No, sir, I'm afraid we don't keep books written in Bengali. But we have lots of books for children in English.'

'I know. Today—in fact, this afternoon—a friend of mine bought two books from this shop for a young boy.'

The lady gave him a puzzled glance. 'No, sir,' she said.

'Eh? What do you mean?'

'I would have remembered, sir, if someone had bought two children's books today. I haven't sold a single one over the last four days.'

'What! But he said . . . maybe some other lady . . . ?'

'No, sir. I handle the sales alone.'

Lalmohan Babu and I looked at each other. I looked at my watch and said, 'Half-an-hour's up!' Lalmohan Babu grabbed my hand. 'Let's go,' he said, dragging me out with him. He paused for a second at the doorway, turned his head and threw a 'Thank you, Miss!' at the lady, then broke into a run to catch a lift.

'How very odd!' he exclaimed, pressing a button. I said nothing. for I simply didn't feel like talking.

The few seconds it took us to reach our room seemed an eternity.

'Feluda!' I said, as we burst in.

'Felu Babu!' said Jatayu, simultaneously.

'One at a time,' Feluda replied sternly.

'Let me speak,' I went on breathlessly. 'Shankar Babu did not go to the bookshop!'

'That's stale news, my boy. Do you have anything fresh to deliver?'

'You mean you knew?'

'I did not sit around doing nothing. I went to the bookshop nearly twenty minutes ago. I spoke to Miss Swaminathan there, and then went to find you to give you the news. But when I saw you were busy gobbling sandwiches, I came away.'

'But in that case—?' I began. Feluda raised a hand to stop me. 'Later, Topshe,' he said, 'I'll hear you out later. Tarafdar rang me from his room just now. He sounded pretty agitated, so I told him to come straight here. Let's see what he has to say.'

The bell rang. I let Mr Tarafdar in.

'Mr Mitter!' he gave an agonized cry. 'Save me. Oh God, please save me!'

'What's happened now?'

'Shankar. Now it's Shankar! I went to his room a few minutes ago, and found him lying unconscious on the floor. I can't believe any of this any more . . . is there going to be no end to my problems?'

The reply that came from Feluda was most unexpected. 'No, Sunil,' he said casually, 'this is just the beginning.'

'What is that supposed to mean?' Mr Tarafdar croaked.

'My meaning is simple enough, I think. You're still pretending to be totally innocent. You should stop the act now, Sunil. The game's up.'

'I do not understand you at all, Mr Mitter. You are insulting me!'

'Insulting you? No, Sunil. All I'm doing is speaking the truth. In five minutes, I'm going to hand you over to the police. They're on their way.'

'But what did I do?'

'I'll tell you gladly. You are a murderer and a thief. That's what I told the police.'

'You have gone mad. You don't know what you're saying.'

'I am perfectly aware of what I'm saying. Mr Hingorani would never have opened his door to a stranger. He did not know that man from Detecnique; and that man didn't know him, either, which was the reason why he had brought a photo of Hingorani with him, just to make sure he spoke to the right man. So we can safely assume that Hingorani did not let him get inside his room. But you, Sunil? He knew you well enough. There was no reason for him to keep you out, was there?'

'You are forgetting one thing, Mr Mitter. Remember what the police said? There were no signs of struggle. If I took out a knife and tried to kill him, do you think he would have let me, without putting up a fight?'

'Yes, he would, under a special circumstance.'

'What might that be?'

'It is your own area of specialization, Sunil Tarafdar. Hypnotism. You hypnotized Hingorani before you killed him.'

'Do stop talking nonsense, Mr Mitter. Hingorani was my sponsor. Why should I bite the hand that fed me? Why should I destroy the only man who was prepared to support me? You . . . you make me laugh!'

'All right then, Mr Tarafdar. Laugh while you can, for you'll never get the chance to laugh again.'

'Are you trying to imply that I lost my mind after Nayan was kidnapped? That a sudden attack of insanity made me—'

'No. According to your own story, Nayan went missing in the evening. And Hingorani was killed between 2.30 and 3.30 p.m.'

'You are still talking pure drivel. Try to calm down, Mr Mitter.'

'I can assure you, Sunil Tarafdar, I have seldom felt more calm. Allow me now to give you a piece of news. I went to the hotel bookshop, and spoke to the lady there. She told me no one bought children's books in the last four days, and most certainly no small boy was seen in the shop today.'

'She . . . she lied to you!'

'No, she didn't—but you clearly did. You have been telling lies all day, as has your friend, Shankar Hublikar. He might come to his senses after being hit with a heavy porcelain ash-tray, but you . . .'

'What! You hit Shankar with an ash-tray? Is that what knocked him unconscious?'

'Yes.'

'But why?'

'He conspired with you. He helped you to hide your motive for murder.'

The bell rang again.

'That will be Inspector Ramachandran. Bring him in, Topshe.'

Inspector Ramachandran walked in and looked enquiringly at Feluda. Mr Tarafdar turned to him before Feluda could open his mouth. 'This man here says I killed Hingorani,' shouted Mr Tarafdar, 'but he cannot show a motive.'

'It isn't just murder,' Feluda said icily, 'you are also being accused of stealing. The five lakhs that Hingorani had brought with him is now in your own possession. You were going to support yourself with that money, weren't you?'

'Why? Why would I do that?'

'Because,' Feluda spoke slowly, 'Hingorani refused to pay you another paisa. There was no reason for him to continue to support you; not after he learnt what had happened to Nayan.'

'Wh-what happened to Nayan?'

Feluda turned to me. 'Topshe, open the bathroom door. Someone's hiding in there.'

I opened the door, and to my complete bewilderment, found Nayan standing there. He came out slowly and stood by Feluda's chair.

'Shankar had had him locked in his bathroom. He wasn't kidnapped at all. I went to Shankar's room the minute I got the whole picture. He denied my allegations, of course, so I had to knock him out in order to rescue Nayan. Are you still going to harp on the motive for murder, Mr Tarafdar? Very well then, Nayan will tell you.'

Mr Tarafdar opened his mouth, but no words came. His hands trembled.

'Nayan,' said Feluda, 'how many years do you think Mr Tarafdar will have to spend in prison?'

'I don't know.'

'Why not? Why can't you tell?'

'I cannot see numbers any more.'

'Not at all?'

'No. I told you, didn't I? Every single number disappeared this morning, when I woke up. They just didn't come back again. So I told Mr Tarafdar and Shankar Babu, and then . . . then they locked me up.'

Mr Tarafdar sat very still. No one spoke. Only the inspector moved forward swiftly.

Robertson's Ruby

ONE

'DO the words "Mama-Bhagney" mean anything to you?' Feluda asked Jatayu.

I knew what he meant, hut looked curiously at Lalmohan Babu to hear his reply.

'Uncle and nephew?' he asked.

'No, a mere translation of the words won't do. We all know "mama" means uncle and "bhagney" is nephew. What do the words remind you of?'

'To be honest, Felu Babu I haven't the slightest idea what you're talking about. Your questions always startle me. You tell me what you mean.'

'Have you seen the film *Abhijaan*?'

'Yes, but that was years ago. Why does that—oh, yes, yes!' Jatayu's eyes lit up. 'Now I do remember. Rocks, aren't they? There is a small, flat rock balanced on top of a bigger rock. It seems as though one little push would make the smaller one jiggle and dance. It's Uncle giving his nephew a piggy-back, isn't it?'

'Right. That's what the locals say. But can you remember which district it's in?'

'No.'

'It's in Birbhum. I have never been there. Have you?'

'No, sir.'

'Shameful, isn't it? You are a writer, Lalmohan Babu. Never mind what you write, or who reads your books. You ought to have visited the area in which Tagore spent so many years of his life.'

'The thing is, you see, I have often wanted to go there, but somehow couldn't manage it. Besides, how can Tagore possibly provide any inspiration to someone who writes stuff like *The Sahara Shivers*?'

'Yes, but Birbhum isn't famous only because of Santiniketan. There are the hot springs of Bakreshwar, there's Kenduli where the poet Jaydev was born, there's Tarapeeth where the famous tantrik Bama Khepa used to live, there's Dubrajpur which has those funny rocks we were just talking about, apart from endless temples made of terracotta.'

'Terracotta? What's that?'

Feluda frowned. Lalmohan Babu's ignorance often turned Feluda into a schoolteacher. 'It's a mixture of Latin and Italian,' he said.

'Terra is a word meaning soil, and cotta is burnt. It refers to statues and figures made with clay and sand, and baked in fire, like bricks. There are many temples in Bengal that have work done in terracotta, but the best and the most beautiful are in Birbhum. If you didn't know about these, Lalmohan Babu, I'm afraid there's very little that you've learnt about your own state.'

'Yes, I see that now. Forgive me, Felu Babu. Kindly excuse my ignorance.'

'And yet, a European professor has done such a lot of research in this subject. It's really most impressive. I assume you don't read anything but the headlines in newspapers, so obviously you've missed the article published in today's *Statesman*. The name of this professor has been mentioned in this article. He was called David McCutcheon.'

'Which article do you mean?'

'"Robertson's Ruby".'

'Right, right! I did see it, and the colour photograph of the ruby, too. But just as I had begun to read it, you see, my dhobi turned up, and then I forgot all about it.'

'The writer of that article, Peter Robertson, is visiting India at present. He appears to be very interested in India and Indians. McCutcheon's work and what he wrote about the temples of Birbhum made Robertson want to see them. He wants to go to Santiniketan, too.'

'I see. But what's this about a ruby?'

'There's a story behind it An ancestor of Peter Robertson called Patrick had fought in the mutiny against the sepoys. Although he was in the Bengal regiment, he happened to be in Lucknow when the mutiny ended and the British won. He was only twenty-six at the time. He joined some of the other British officers who barged into the palace of a nawab and looted whatever they could lay their hands on. Robertson found a huge ruby which he brought back to England with him. In time, it became a family heirloom for the Robertsons, and people began to refer to it as "Robertson's Ruby". Only recently, someone found a diary Patrick Robertson had kept in his old age. No one had been aware of its existence so far. In it, he apparently expressed deep regret at what he had done as a young man, and said that his soul would find ultimate peace only if someone from his family went back to India and returned the ruby to where it had come from. Peter Robertson has brought it with him.

He'll give it to an Indian museum before he returns to England.'

Lalmohan Babu remained silent for a few minutes when Feluda finished his story. Then he said, 'Kenduli has a big mela every winter, doesn't it?'

'Yes. A large number of hauls come to it.'

'When does it start?'

'As a matter of fact, it has started already this year.'

'I see. Which is the best way to go?'

'Do you really want to go to Birbhum?

'Very much so.'

'Well, then, I suggest you ask your driver to take your car straight to Bolpur. We'll go the same day by the Santiniketan Express. We should reach Bolpur in less than three hours. This train stops only at Burdwan. We need to book rooms for ourselves at the tourist lodge.'

'Why should we go by train?'

'Because this train is different from all the others. It has a first class compartment called the Lounge Car. It's huge, like the ones they had years and years ago, furnished with settees, tables and chairs. Travelling in it will be an experience none of us should miss.'

'Oh, I quite agree. Perhaps I ought to inform Shatadal.'

'Who is Shatadal?'

'Shatadal Sen. We were together in school. Now he lives in Santiniketan, a professor of history in Vishwa Bharati. He was a brilliant student. I could never beat him.'

'You mean you were a brilliant student yourself?'

'Why, is that so difficult to believe about a man who is the most popular writer of thrillers in Bengal?'

'Well, your present IQ—' Feluda broke off, adding, 'Yes, by all means inform your friend.'

It took us a few days to make all the arrangements. A double and a single room were booked in the Bolpur Tourist Lodge. We packed our woollens carefully, since we knew Santiniketan would be a lot cooler than Calcutta. I found the book by David McCutcheon and quickly leafed through it before we left. It was amazing how a foreigner had collected such detailed information about something my own country possessed, but of which I knew virtually nothing.

The following Saturday, Lalmohan Babu's driver left early with his green Ambassador. We reached Howrah at 9.30 a.m.

'My right eye has been twitching for the last two days. Is that a good sign?' asked Lalmohan Babu.

'I wouldn't know. You know very well I don't believe in such superstitions,' Feluda retorted.

'I had begun to think this might be an indication that we're heading for another mystery, another case,' Lalmohan Babu confided, 'but then I thought Tagore couldn't possibly have any connection with crime, could he? You're right, Felu Babu. If we're going to visit Bolpur, there's no chance of getting mixed up in funny business.'

TWO

Lalmohan Babu claimed afterwards that what happened later was related directly to his twitching eye. 'A coincidence, Lalmohan Babu, that's all it was,' Feluda told him firmly.

The Lounge Car of the Santiniketan Express was large enough to hold twenty-five people. But when we boarded the train, we discovered there were only seven others including two foreigners. Both were white. One was clean shaven with blond hair; the other had a thick beard. Long, dark hair rippled down to his shoulders. Something told me one of them was Peter Robertson. Ten minutes after the train started, I found that I was right.

The three of us were sitting together on a sofa. I had never travelled in such a comfortable carriage. Feluda leant back and lit a Charminar. At this moment, the man with the blond hair, who happened to be sitting close by, stretched out a hand and said, 'May I—?'

Feluda passed him his lighter and said, 'Are you going to Bolpur?'

The man lit his own cigarette and returned the lighter to Feluda. Then he said, smiling and proffering his hand, 'Yes. My name is Peter Robertson and this is my friend, Tom Maxwell.'

Feluda shook his hand, and then introduced us. 'Was it your article that I read the other day?' he asked.

'Yes. Did you like it?'

'Oh yes. It was a very interesting article. Have you already handed that ruby to a museum?'

'No, it's still with us. But we've spoken to the curator of the Calcutta Museum. He said he'd be very pleased to accept it if he gets the go-ahead from Delhi. Once that is confirmed, we'll hand it over to him officially.'

'You have an Indian connection, I know. Does your friend?'

'Yes. Tom's great-great-grandfather was the owner of an indigo factory in Birbhum. The British stopped growing indigo in India when the Germans found a way of producing it artificially and began selling it cheap. That was when Tom's ancestor, Reginald Maxwell, returned to Britain. Tom and I were both bitten by the travel bug. We've travelled together quite often. He's a professional photographer. I teach in a school.'

Tom was sitting with a leather bag resting at his feet. That must contain his camera and other equipment, I thought.

'How long will you be in Birbhum?'

'About a week. Our main work is in Calcutta, but we'd like to see as many temples as we can in Birbhum.'

'There are many other things in Birbhum besides temples that are worth seeing. Maybe we could see them together? Anyway, going back to your article, hasn't there been any feedback from your readers?'

'Oh my God, yes! The *Statesman* began receiving dozens of letters within a couple of days. Some of them were from old maharajas, some from wealthy businessmen, or collectors of rare jewels. But I had made it quite plain in my article that I wasn't prepared to sell it. You know, I had it valued in England before I came here. I could have sold it there, had I so wished. I was offered up to twenty thousand pounds.'

'You have the stone with you right here?'

'Tom's got it. He's a lot more careful than I am. Besides, he's got a revolver that he can use, if need be.'

'May we see the ruby, please?'

'Of course.'

Peter looked at Tom. Tom picked up his leather bag and took out a small blue velvet box from it. He passed it to Feluda. Feluda opened it slowly, and all three of us gave an involuntary gasp. Not only was the stone large and beautifully cut, but its colour was such a deep red that it was really remarkable. Feluda held the ruby in his hand for a few seconds, turning it around and looking at it closely. Then he returned it to Tom, saying, 'It's amazing! But there's something else I'd like to see, if I may. Will you show me your revolver, please? You see, I know something about firearms.' He handed one of his visiting cards to Peter.

'Good heavens!' Peter exclaimed. 'You're a private investigator, are you? I'm glad we've met. If we have problems we might have to seek your help.'

'I hope it won't come to that, but a lot depends on you, Mr Maxwell, for the ruby is with you for safe-keeping.'

Tom Maxwell said nothing in reply. He just took out his revolver and showed it to Feluda. It was not a Colt like Feluda's.

'Webley Scott,' Feluda said, looking at it. Then he added, 'May I ask you something?'

'Of course,' said Tom, speaking for the first time.

'Why do you need to keep a revolver with you?'

'My work takes me to all kinds of places, some of which are remote and dangerous. I've taken photographs of tribal people in jungles. Not all tribes are friendly, I can tell you. Having a revolver makes my job a lot easier. I once killed a black Mamba snake in Africa with this very revolver.'

'Have you been to India before?'

'No, this is my first visit.'

'Have you started taking photos?'

'Yes, I've taken some of a poor and congested area of Calcutta.'

'You mean a slum?'

'Yes, that's right. I like taking pictures of people and places that are totally different from anything I've known or anything I'm familiar with. The stranger or more alien the subject, the better I find it to photograph. Poverty is, for instance, I think, far more photogenic than prosperity.'

'Photo—what?' Lalmohan Babu whispered.

'Photogenic. Something which looks good when photographed,' Feluda explained.

Lalmohan Babu gave me a sidelong glance and muttered softly, 'Does he mean to say that a hungry, starving man is more photogenic than a well-fed one?'

Tom didn't hear him. 'I will take photographs here in India with the same idea in my mind,' he added. I found his words and his attitude rather peculiar. Peter was undoubtedly a lover of India, but his friend's views appeared to be devoid of any feelings or sympathy. How long would they remain friends, I wondered.

The train stopped at Burdwan. We called a chaiwalla to have tea from small earthen pots. Tom Maxwell took photos of the chaiwalla.

Soon, the train pulled in to Bolpur station. The sight of dozens of rickshaws outside the main gate made Tom want to stop for photos again, but this time Peter was firm and said they mustn't waste time.

We had to hire four rickshaws for ourselves and our luggage. Peter and Tom were also booked at the tourist lodge. By the time we reached it, it was ten minutes past one.

THREE

Lalmohan Babu's friend, Shatadal Sen, had come to the station to meet us. He accompanied us back to the lodge. A man of about the same age as Lalmohan Babu, he seemed to know him pretty well. After a long time, I heard someone call him 'Lalu'.

We sat chatting in the lobby before going to our rooms.

'You're expecting your car at three, did you say?' Mr Sen asked. 'You can come to my house when your car gets here. Anybody in Pearson Palli will show you my house. I'll take you to see the complex at Uttarayan.'

'Thank you. May we bring two foreign visitors with us?' Feluda asked.

'Yes, of course. They'd be most welcome.'

Mr Sen left. We moved into our rooms. I was struck immediately by the peace and quiet of our surroundings. This should do Feluda a lot of good. He had just finished solving two complex cases of murder and fraud. He needed a break.

A little later, we found Peter and Tom in the dining hall. Feluda told them of our plans for the evening. Peter seemed delighted, but Tom didn't say anything. 'By the way,' said Peter, 'I received a call from a businessman in Dubrajpur. That's not far from here, I gather. He got his son to call me since his spoken English, his son said, isn't all that good. Anyway, he said he had heard about my ruby and wanted to buy it. When I told him I would never sell it, he said that was fine, but he'd like to see it once, so would I be kind enough to visit his house? I agreed.'

'What is this man called?'

'G.L. Dandania.'

'I see. When do you have to meet him?'

'At ten tomorrow morning.'

'May we go with you?'

'Certainly. In fact, I'd be quite grateful for your company. You could act as an interpreter, couldn't you? After we finish our business with Dandania, we could go and have a look at the terracotta temples in Dubrajpur and Hetampur. McCutcheon wrote about those.'

'There are many other things in Dubrajpur worth seeing. We could look at those, too, if we have the time,' Feluda told him.

Lalmohan Babu's driver arrived with the car at 3.45 p.m. 'I stopped for lunch in Burdwan,' he said, 'and I don't think I need a rest. If you want to go out, sir, I can take you any time.'

We left for Mr Sen's house almost immediately. Only a few minutes later, we found ourselves in Uttarayan. Peter said he had never seen a building like it. 'It looks like a palace out of a fairy tale!' he exclaimed. Then we went to Udichi and Shyamali, which were as beautiful. Tom, I noticed, did not take out his camera even once, possibly because there was no evidence of poverty anywhere.

Lalmohan Babu looked at everything with great interest. In the end, however, he shook his head sadly and said, 'No, sir, in a serene atmosphere like this, I could never think up a plot for a thriller. I'd need to go back to Calcutta to do so.'

On our way back, Peter and Tom got into a rickshaw. 'Someone told us there's a tribal village near here. Tom would like to take some pictures,' Peter said. They were obviously off to a Santhal village. We waved them off and returned to the lodge, where we spent the rest of the evening playing antakshari.

'Look, I nearly forgot!' said Mr Sen before taking his leave. 'Lalu, I brought this book for you—*Life and Work in Birbhum*. It was written by a priest a hundred years ago. He was called Reverend Pritchard. It's full of interesting information. You must read it.'

'I certainly will, even if your friend doesn't. Thank you, Mr Sen,' said Feluda.

We finished breakfast by eight-thirty the next day. Dubrajpur was only twenty-five kilometres away. Mr Dandania's son had given us excellent directions, and told us that theirs was the largest house in the area.

We arrived a little before ten o'clock at a large house with a very high boundary wall. The name plate on the tall iron gate said

'G L Dandania'. A chowkidar quickly opened the gate for us. He had clearly been warned about our visit. Our car passed through the gate and the long driveway, before coming to a halt at the front door.

A young man in his mid-twenties was tinkering with a scooter just outside the door. He left the scooter and came forward to greet us as we got out of our car. 'My name is Peter Robertson,' said Peter, shaking his hand. 'You must be Kishorilal.'

'Yes, I am Kishorilal Dandania. My father would like to see you. Please come with me.'

'Can my other friends come, too'

'Of course.'

We followed Kishorilal through a courtyard, up a flight of stairs, past a couple of rooms before he finally stopped outside the open door of their drawing room.

'Should we take off our shoes?' asked Feluda.

'No, no, there's no need.'

The drawing room was large, furnished partly with sofas and chairs. One end was covered by a thick mattress. Mr G.L. Dandania sat in one corner of the mattress, leaning on a bolster. He was a pale, thin man with a huge moustache that looked quite incongruous. Besides him in the room was another man of about fifty, wearing grey trousers and a brown jacket. He stood up as we entered. Peter looked at the thin man with the moustache and folded his hands.

'Namaste,' he said. 'Mr Dandania, I presume?'

'Yes, and this is my friend, Inspector Chaubey,' replied Mr Dandania.

'How do you do? Meet my friend, Tom Maxwell. And here are my other friends, Mr Pradosh Mitter, Lalmohan Ganguli and Tapesh.'

'Glad to meet you all. Please be seated. Kishori, *inke liye mithai aur sharbat mangwao* (send for sweets and sherbet for them).'

Kishori disappeared and returned in a few moments. 'I realize you made an appointment to see Mr Robertson,' Feluda said when we were all seated. 'If you have any objection to our presence, we shall leave the room.'

'No, no, please don't worry. All I want to do is take a look at that ruby. Your presence makes no difference to me.'

Tom spoke unexpectedly. 'May I take some pictures?'

'What pictures?'

'Of this room.'

I noticed for the first time that there were innumerable pictures of Hindu gods and goddesses hanging on the walls. It reminded me of Maganlal Meghraj's room in Benaras.

'Theek hai.'

'He says you may,' Feluda translated.

'Lekin pehle woh cheez to dikhaiye.'

'He wants to see the ruby first.'

'I see.'

Tom Maxwell brought out the blue velvet box from his leather bag. Then he opened the lid and passed it to Mr Dandania. For some strange reason, my heart suddenly started to flutter.

Mr Dandania held the ruby in his hand and stared at it for a few seconds, his face impassive, before passing it to his friend, Inspector Chaubey. Chaubey glanced at it with open admiration in his eyes, then handed it back to Dandania.

'What price in England?' Mr Dandania asked.

'Twenty thousand pounds,' Peter replied.

'Hm. *Dus lakh rupaye . . .*' He put the ruby back in its box and returned it to Maxwell. *'Hum denge dus lakh,'* he added.

'He says he'll pay you a million rupees for it,' Feluda said obligingly.

'But surely he knows that's out of the question? I'm not here to sell it.'

Mr Dandania switched to English again, thereby revealing that he could understand and speak it well enough.

'Why not?' he asked.

'Because my ancestor wanted it to return to India. I came simply to fulfil his wish. The last thing I want to do is set a price on it and give it to someone else for money. It will go to the Calcutta Museum, and that's that!'

'You are being foolish, Mr Robertson. In a large museum like that it will simply lie in a corner gathering dust. People will forget all about it.'

'And if I sold it to you? Would it not lie hidden in a chest somewhere, totally out of sight?'

'Nonsense! Why should I allow that to happen? I'd open a private museum of my own, like the Salar Jung in Hyderabad. Ganesh Dandania Museum. Your ruby will get special attention. Everyone will see it. I will put up a plaque outside its case, explaining its history. It will include your own name.'

Before Peter could reply, a bearer came in with sweets on a large plate and glasses of sherbet. We began helping ourselves. Only Tom Maxwell dropped a tablet in his glass before drinking from it.

'*Inko kahiye yehan ke paani ko shudh karne ki zaroorat nahin hai,*' said Mr Dandania, glaring. I looked at Feluda with interest, to see how he might tell Tom there was no need to purify the water; but Feluda only smiled and said nothing.

It took us only a few minutes to finish the sweets.

'Well?' Mr Dandania said in his deep voice. Like his moustache, his voice came as a surprise.

'Very sorry, Mr Dandania,' said Peter. 'I told you before I wouldn't sell it under any circumstances. I showed it to you only because you had made a special request.'

Inspector Chaubey spoke suddenly. 'Look, Mr Robertson,' he said, 'whether or not you wish to sell the ruby is your business. What concerns me is that your friend is roaming around with that ruby in his bag. I don't like this at all. If you like, I can arrange to send a constable with you wherever you go. He'll be in plain clothes, you won't even realize he's with you. But he'll be able to ensure your safety.'

'No,' Tom Maxwell said firmly. 'I am quite capable of taking care of it, thank you. Should anyone try to steal it, I'd know how to deal with him. I can use a gun myself, and I can do without any help from the police.'

Inspector Chaubey gave up. 'Very well. If you are so utterly confident of yourself, there is nothing more to be said.'

'How long are you here for?' Mr Dandania asked.

'Another five days, I should think.'

'All right. Please think this over, Mr Robertson. Think carefully, and come to me again in two days.'

'OK. Thinking can't hurt, can it? I'll consider your proposal very seriously, and let you know what I decide.'

'Good,' Mr Dandania replied, looking grave. 'And goodbye.'

FOUR

'Unbelievable! This is really incredible, isn't it?' Lalmohan Babu whispered. I found myself in full agreement. All that stretched before our eyes was an ocean of rocks. Stones and boulders of various shapes and sizes lay scattered on the ground, covering a total area of at least one square mile. Some lay flat, others on their side. Some were huge—as high as three-storeyed buildings—but others were relatively small. A few had large cracks running right across, possibly the result of an earthquake hundreds of years ago. It might have been a scene from prehistoric times. If a dinosaur had peeped out from behind a boulder, I would not have been surprised.

This was one of the sights Dubrajpur was famous for. We had already seen the well-known pair called 'Mama-Bhagney'. Soon after leaving Ganesh Dandania's house, Feluda had suggested we saw these famous rocks. Inspector Chaubey, who had accompanied us, agreed that it was a good idea. Peter seemed absolutely overwhelmed. 'Fantastic! Fantastic!' I heard him mutter more than once. Tom, too, seemed a lot happier. I saw him smile for the first time, possibly because he had found a new subject for photography. Right now, he was sitting atop a huge rock, running a fine comb through his beard. How he had got there, I could not tell.

'Tell me,' said Peter, 'how come there are so many stones lying around at this particular spot, when there are no mountains or hills nearby? Isn't there a story or a legend behind this?'

Before Feluda could say anything, Lalmohan Babu piped up most unexpectedly. 'Do you know of the god Hanuman?' he asked.

'I have heard of him,' Peter said, smiling.

'Well, when Hanuman was flying through the air with Mount Gandhamadan on his head, some rocks from the mountain fell here in Dubrajpur.'

'How interesting!' Peter nodded.

Feluda gave Jatayu a sidelong glance and said under his breath, 'You just made that up, didn't you?'

'No, sir!' Jatayu protested loudly. 'I heard that story from the manager of the lodge this morning. Everyone in this region believes in it. Why should I have made it up?'

'Because, my friend, the story I read in my guide book is different. According to it, it was Ram who had dropped these stones here accidentally, when he was gathering stones to build a bridge across the ocean.'

'I don't care what you've read, Felu Babu! I think my story is much better.' Lalmohan Babu walked away in a huff.

By this time, Tom had climbed down from his rock and joined us.

Now he was looking a little bored. Perhaps the stones and rocks weren't photogenic enough for him. His real chance came a few minutes later when we made our way to an old and well-known Kali temple. This was probably the first time he was seeing Hindu devotees having a puja in a temple. His camera didn't stop clicking.

This seemed to upset Inspector Chaubey. 'Look, Mr Maxwell,' he said, 'people here don't like to see photographs taken of religious rituals. You'll have to be a little more discreet.'

'Why?' Tom shot back angrily. 'I am not doing anything illegal or unethical. I am merely taking photos of a public event, openly in front of everyone.'

'Yes, but people can sometimes be extremely sensitive. A foreigner may well find our customs and traditions strange and difficult to accept. Some may object to his taking these photos back home, misrepresenting our values and ideas.' Maxwell started to protest again, but this time Peter looked at him sternly, which made him shut up.

By the time we finished seeing all the sights of Dubrajpur, we were all quite thirsty. So we found a roadside tea stall and sat down at two of the long benches that were placed outside.

Inspector Chaubey sat between Feluda and me. 'I realized who you were the minute I heard your name,' I heard him say to Feluda, 'but I didn't say anything since I thought you might not wish to reveal your profession to all and sundry.'

'You were absolutely right.'

'Are you here on holiday?'

'Yes, purely.'

'I see.'

'You are from Bihar, aren't you?'

'Yes. But the last five generations of my family had lived here in Birbhum. By the way, has that boy called Maxwell got an Indian connection?'

'Yes. His great-great-grandfather used to own an indigo factory here. I think his name was Reginald Maxwell.'

'I see. My own grandfather used to talk about a Mr Maxwell, who was also a factory owner. Although he had lived many years ago, his name had not been forgotten. From what little I have seen of Tom Maxwell, it is obvious that this other Maxwell was his ancestor.'

'How is it obvious?'

'Reginald Maxwell hated Indians. He was unbelievably cruel to his workers. Tom Maxwell seems to have inherited his arrogance. But Mr Robertson seems just the opposite. He's clearly genuinely fond of this country.'

Feluda made no reply. We had finished our tea. Peter and Tom joined us, and we set off for Hetampur, which was famous for its terracotta temples. The carvings on these enthralled Peter, particularly that of a European lady on a temple wall. It was two hundred years old, we were told. Tom wasn't interested in temples or carvings. He began taking photos of a child being given a bath by its mother at a tubewell.

Just before getting back into our car to return to the tourist lodge, Feluda turned to Inspector Chaubey to bid him goodbye. 'You seemed to know Dandania pretty well,' he said. 'What sort of a man is he?'

'Very clever. I know him, but I certainly do not regard him as a friend. He tries to keep himself in my good books. He's involved in a lot of shady dealings, so he thinks if he knows someone in the police it might help. I go to his house occasionally, but I keep my eyes and ears open. If I catch him doing anything wrong, I shall not spare him. But he is extremely wealthy. He could quite easily buy that ruby for ten lakhs.'

'Does his son look after his father's business?'

'Kishori? No, he doesn't really want to. He wants to start something of his own. Ganesh is fond of his son. I think he'll agree in the end and let Kishori go his own way.'

'I see.'

'Oh, by the way, what are your plans for tomorrow?'

'We might go to see the mela in Kenduli.'

'Are you all planning to go together? I mean, would Robertson and Maxwell go with you?'

'Yes, why?'

'I would like you to keep an eye on Maxwell, Mr Mitter. His behaviour worries me.'

'Very well, Inspector. I'll do my best.'

We returned to the lodge in Bolpur a little before 2 p.m. Soon after our return, two men turned up to meet Peter and Tom. One of them was Aradhendu Naskar, a well-known businessman from Calcutta. The other was called Jagannath Chatterjee, a historian who had specialized knowledge of the temples in Birbhum. Both had read Peter's article in the *Statesman* and decided to meet him. Peter said he'd be very grateful for Mr Chatterjee's help, and asked him to stay in touch. Mr Chatterjee agreed happily.

Mr Naskar took much longer. 'What can I do for you?' Peter asked politely, shaking his hand.

Mr Naskar pulled up a chair and sat down, facing Peter.

'First of all, I want you to confirm one thing.'

'Yes?'

'Is it really true that you have come here to fulfil the wish of your ancestor? I mean, are you visiting because of what he wrote in his diary more than a hundred years ago?'

'Absolutely.'

'You mean you really and truly believe that his soul will find ultimate peace if you return that ruby to India?'

'I don't think what I believe is of any relevance,' Peter replied dryly. 'You sound as though you're interested in buying the ruby. I am not going to sell it, Mr Naskar.'

'Have you had it assessed in your country?'

'Yes, it's worth twenty thousand pounds.'

'I see. May I see it, please?'

Tom took it out of his bag without a word and passed it to Mr Naskar. Mr Naskar held it between his thumb and forefinger and turned it to catch the light. Then he turned to Peter and said, rather unexpectedly, 'Neither of you appears to be well off.'

'We're not, Mr Naskar; nor are we greedy.'

'However,' Tom spoke suddenly, 'we don't always think alike.'

'What do you mean?' Mr Naskar raised his eyebrows. Peter answered before Tom could say anything. 'What he means is that we've had a difference of opinion in this matter. Tom doesn't mind selling the ruby, but I do. It is, after all, my property, not his. So you needn't pay any attention to him at all.' I looked at Tom. He scowled in silence.

'Anyway,' said Mr Naskar, 'I am going to be here in Santiniketan for the next three days. I'll stay in touch with you. You can't get rid of me that easily, Mr Robertson. I'm prepared to give you twelve lakhs. My collection of precious stones is well-known, all over the country. I can't see why you're refusing such a splendid chance to earn good money. I hope you'll change your mind in due course.'

'Perhaps I should tell you something, Mr Naskar. I've already had an offer for this ruby.'

'Who made it?'

'A businessman in Dubrajpur.'

'Dandania?'

'Yes.'

'How much did he offer you?'

'Ten lakhs. But who's to tell his offer won't go up?'

'All right. I know Dandania quite well. I'll manage him.'

'Very well, Mr Naskar. Goodbye!'

'Goodbye!'

Mr Naskar left at last. We rose and went into the dining hall. I was starving.

FIVE

The fair at Kenduli was being held at a temple built two hundred and fifty years ago, by the Maharani of Burdwan.

We had arrived together in Lalmohan Babu's car. His driver was given the day off. Feluda drove. Lalmohan Babu and I sat next to him. Peter, Tom and Jagannath Chatterjee sat at the back.

A large group of hauls had gathered under a huge banyan tree. One of them was playing his ektara and singing. Mr Chatterjee began explaining the history of the place and the details of the carvings. I noticed, to my surprise, that many of the figures carved on the walls and pillars of the temple were figures from the *Ramayana* and *Mahabharata*. Peter was listening to Mr Chatterjee with rapt attention. Tom had disappeared. Mr Chatterjee stopped after a while and ambled off in a different direction. Feluda seized this opportunity to ask Peter the question that had been bothering me since yesterday. 'Is everything all right between Tom and you? He's been behaving rather oddly, hasn't he? I don't like it, Peter. Can you really trust him?'

'Yes, I think so. I've known him for twenty-two years. We went to the same school and college. He was fine back home but I've noticed a few changes in him since our arrival in India. Sometimes he behaves as though the British are still the rulers here. Besides, back in England he didn't seem interested in selling the ruby at all. Now, he's not averse to the idea of filling his pockets.'

'Is he in need of money?'

'In a way, yes. You see, he wants to travel all over the world, taking photos everywhere, particularly where he can see stark poverty. At this moment, neither of us has the kind of money we'd need to travel so widely. But if we sold that ruby, then there would be no problem.'

'What if he sold it without telling you?'

'No, I'm sure he would not betray my trust completely. I've been speaking to him sternly and seriously since yesterday, trying to make him see reason. I think he'll come round before long.'

Feluda looked around for Tom. But still there was no sign of him.

'Do you know where he's gone?'

'No, I'm afraid not. He didn't tell me.'

'I am beginning to get a nasty suspicion.'

'What do you mean?'

'Look over there. Can you see smoke rising from the riverside? That means there's a cremation ground. Could he have gone there to take photos? We ought to go and find out.'

We left at once, making our way through groups of bauls. The river bank lay just beyond, sloping gradually to lead to the water.

Here was the cremation ground. A corpse lay on a burning pyre.

'Look, there's Tom!' cried Peter.

Tom was standing a few yards away from the pyre, getting his camera and various lenses out of his bag.

'He is doing something utterly foolish,' Feluda said. Almost instantly, his words were proved right. Four young men were sitting near the pyre. One of them saw what Tom was about to do. He ran forward, snatched the camera from Tom's hands and threw it on the sand.

And Tom? Tom took a step forward, curling his right hand into a fist. It landed on the young man's nose a second later. He fell on the ground, clutching his nose. When he removed his hand, we could all see it was smeared with blood.

Feluda did not waste another moment. Before either the first young man or his friends could move, he strode across and placed himself between Tom and the others. 'Please,' he said, raising his hands placatingly, 'please forgive my friend. He is new to our country, and he hasn't yet learnt what he should or shouldn't do. It was very wrong of him to have tried to take a photo of a pyre. I'll explain everything to him, and he won't repeat this mistake, I promise you. But please let him go now.'

To my surprise, one of the young men came forward and quickly touched Feluda's feet.

'What . . . what are you doing?'

'You are Felu Mitter, aren't you? *The* Pradosh Mitter? The famous—?'

'Yes, yes,' Feluda said hurriedly. 'I am Felu Mitter, I am an investigator and this gentleman here is my friend. Please will you forgive him and let him go?'

'All right, sir, never mind. No problem,' said the three men, staring at Feluda with a mixture of awe and admiration. Getting recognized, I thought, was no bad thing, after all.

But the injured man, who had by now risen to his feet, was not so easily impressed. 'I shall pay you back, sahib,' he spoke clearly. 'I'll settle scores with you before you go back. Just remember that. No one lays a hand on Chandu Mallik and gets away with it!'

None of us said anything to him. We turned around to go back. Tom's camera appeared undamaged. But he himself seemed totally taken aback by this sudden development. Perhaps this would teach him to be more careful, I told myself.

We had lunch back in the tourist lodge, and were sitting in the lounge when Inspector Chaubey turned up. 'I came to find out how you were doing,' he said, 'and I can tell there's something wrong.'

'You're quite right, Inspector,' Feluda replied, and briefly explained what had happened. 'Does the name Chandu Mallik mean anything to you?' he asked.

'Oh yes. He's a notorious goonda. He's been to prison at least three times. If he has threatened to settle scores, we cannot just laugh it off.'

Tom had gone back to his room. Peter was sitting with us.

'Mr Robertson,' the inspector said, 'only you can do something to help.'

'How?'

'Talk to your friend. Tell him he must learn to control his temper. India became independent forty-five years ago. No Indian today would accept from a Britisher the kind of behaviour Mr Maxwell has shown.'

'I suggest you tell him that,' Peter said a little sadly. 'I can't think straight. Tom is behaving so strangely I feel I don't know him at all. He's just not listening to me any more. If you talk to him, maybe that'll work?'

'Very well, I'll do as you say. But must you let him keep you ruby? Why don't you take it back?'

'I have a problem, Inspector. I am extremely forgetful and absentminded. Tom isn't. The ruby is really much safer in his custody. Besides, despite everything, I'm convinced he won't sell it without telling me.'

We rose and went to find Tom in his room. Peter did not come with us.

He was sitting in a chair, deep in thought, a half-finished cigarette dangling from his lips. The door was open. He looked up as we arrived, but did not rise to greet us. Inspector Chaubey took the second chair. Feluda, Lalmohan Babu and I sat on the bed.

'Are you trying to put pressure on me?' asked Tom.

'No. We have come to plead with you,' said the inspector very politely.

'What for?'

'Mr Maxwell, you are free to think what you like about the country you're visiting and its people. But please do not show your feelings so openly.'

'Who are you to tell me how I should behave? I will do exactly as I please. I have seen in the last couple of days just how backward your country is. You haven't moved an inch in forty-five years. Your farmers are still using animals to till the land. I have seen dozens of men in Calcutta pulling rickshaws. Millions sleep on footpaths. And you dare call yourselves civilized? I know you wish to hide these disgraceful facts from the rest of the world, but I won't let you. I will take photographs of the real India and expose the depths of your hypocrisy to the whole world.'

'You are making a grave error, Mr Maxwell. You can't just talk of India's poverty and harp on our shortcomings. Why, haven't you seen the progress we have made? We've explored outer space, we've started producing everything one might need to live in comfort, from clothes to cars to electronics—just name it! Why should you let your eyes stay focused on only one single negative aspect of our culture? Nobody's denying there's poverty in our country, and there's exploitation. But is everything in your own country totally above reproach, Mr Maxwell?'

'Don't compare your country with mine, Mr Chaubey! You talk of India's independence? That whole business is a bloody farce. I'll get my camera to prove it. You need someone to rule over you, just as my ancestors did all those years ago. That's what you deserve. My great-great-grandfather was absolutely justified in doing what he did.'

'What do you mean?'

'He owned an indigo factory. Once he kicked one of his servants to death.'

'What!'

'Yes. It was his punkha-puller. I have heard how terribly hot and stuffy this place can get in the summer. Well, one night in the summer, my ancestor, Reginald Maxwell, was sleeping in his bungalow. The punkha-puller was doing his job. But a little later he fell asleep. Reginald Maxwell woke in the middle of the night, feeling hot and sticky and covered with mosquito bites. He came out of his room and found the punkha-puller fast asleep. Wild with rage, he kicked him hard in the stomach. As it happened, he was wearing heavy boots. The punkha-puller never woke up after that. His body was removed in the morning. That, sir, was the right treatment. Today I wanted to take photos of your awful system of burning corpses. I wanted to show the people of my country how you treat your dead. But a local hoodlum came to threaten me. Yes, I punched his nose because he asked for it. I have no regrets. None at all.'

After a few moments of silence, Inspector Chaubey said slowly, 'Mr Maxwell, there is only one thing I'd like to say. The sooner you leave this country, the better. Your staying here will simply mean more trouble, not just for our poor country, but also for yourself. Surely you realize that?'

'I have come here to take photos. I will not leave until I have finished my job.'

'But that's not the real reason why you're here, is it? You came chiefly to return the ruby to India, didn't you?'

'No. That was Peter's wish. I think he is being very stupid about the whole thing. I'd be a lot happier if he sold it.'

SIX

We were back in our room after dinner, chatting idly, when Lalmohan Babu suddenly announced that he must return to his room.

'Why? What's the hurry?' Feluda asked.

'It's that book Shatadal gave me. You know, the one written by Rev. Pritchard called *Life and Work in Birbhum*. It's absolutely gripping. In fact, there's mention of the story we just heard from Maxwell about a punkha-puller being kicked to death.'

'Really?'

'Yes. This happened towards the end of the nineteenth century. Reginald Maxwell killed his servant, but no one punished him for doing so . . . The punkha-puller was called Hiralal. His wife had died, but he had a little boy. When Rev. Pritchard heard about the murder, he rushed to Maxwell's house, and found the orphan boy. He brought the child back with him and began looking after him as though he was his own. The child was called Anant Narayan. Eventually, he became a Christian and was put in a missionary school. Now I am dying to find out what happened next. So if you'll excuse . . .'

Someone knocked on the door. I found Peter standing outside.

'May I come in?'

'Of course.'

Feluda rose. Lalmohan Babu, who was about to leave, changed his mind and sat down again. Peter looked extremely unhappy. Something serious must have happened.

'What's the matter, Peter?' Feluda asked.

'I have decided to sell the ruby.'

'What! Why? Oh, do sit down, Peter. Tell us what happened.'

Peter sat down. 'I don't want to lose an old friend. Tom is totally obsessed with the idea of selling that ruby. His dream is to travel all over the world, and that dream can come true if the ruby is sold. I thought things over, and felt there was no point in giving it away to a museum. After all, how many people would really get to see it, tell me? So I thought . . .' his voice trailed away.

Feluda frowned. After a short pause, he said, 'Well, it's your decision. Who am I to say anything? I am disappointed, but it's really none of my business, is it?'

'When do you want to sell it?' Lalmohan Babu asked.

'I've just spoken to Dandania. He made the first offer, so I think I should go back to him. He told me to meet him the day after tomorrow at ten.'

'I thought your return to India would result in a historic event,' Feluda said sadly, 'but now all one would get to see would be a simple commercial transaction.'

'I am very sorry,' said Peter, and left.

We sat in silence, feeling terribly deflated and let down.

We had planned to visit Bakreshwar the following morning. We had just finished our breakfast and reached the lounge, when Mr Naskar arrived in his car.

'Good morning,' he said, coming in to the reception area.

'Good morning.'

'Would you like to see a Santhal dance this evening? A dance has been arranged in the Phulberey village. It should be worth seeing, especially as there's going to be a full moon tonight.'

'Who has arranged it?'

'The local people, for a group of Japanese tourists. I've come to invite all of you to dinner at my place this evening. If you're interested in seeing the dance, I can take you there myself, after dinner. The village is only two miles from my house.'

'Does your invitation include Peter and Tom?' Feluda asked.

'Yes, yes, of course. All five of you are invited.'

'Thank you very much. When would you like us to arrive?'

'About eight, if that's all right. Should I send my car?'

'There's no need. We can quite easily go in ours. There shouldn't be any problem.'

'Very well. I shall look forward to seeing you later. Good day!'

Bakreshwar turned out to be a place that hadn't bothered to step out of primitive times. There were rows of old temples behind which stood several large trees. Most of these were banyan trees. Huge roots hung down from these and clung to the temple walls. Nearly every temple had its own pond. Jagannath Chatterjee, who had accompanied us again, told us what each pond was called. Peter stopped at one called 'Soubhagya Kunda', and went in for a swim. Someone had told him what 'soubhagya' meant. So he laughed as he came up and said, 'This should bring me good luck!'

There were scores of beggars near the temples. Tom took out his camera and soon found several people with special photogenic-features.

Half an hour after our return to the tourist lodge, Inspector

Chaubey rang Feluda. 'Did you know there's going to be a Santhal dance later today?' he asked.

'Yes, Mr Naskar told us. In fact, we're going to have dinner at his place this evening. He's offered to take us to the dance afterwards. We should reach there by 10 p.m.'

'Good. I hope to get there by half past ten, so I guess that's where we shall meet tonight.'

Mr Naskar had given us very good directions. We found his house without any problem. It was a fairly large house with two storeys and a carefully maintained garden. Mr. Naskar came out to greet us as we got out of our car, and then took us straight to his drawing room. A bearer came in with drinks almost immediately.

'You stay here alone, don't you?' Feluda asked, picking up a cold drink from a tray.

'Yes, but I have a lot of friends. We normally arrive in groups to spend a few days here. This time, I came alone.' Mr Naskar suddenly turned to Lalmohan Babu. 'I had heard of Mr Mitter, but I don't think I got your name—?'

'Most people don't know his real name,' Feluda answered. 'He writes crime thrillers under a pseudonym. Millions know him simply as Jatayu. His books are immensely popular.'

'Yes, yes, now that you mention . . . why, I've read some of your books, too! *Shaken in Shanghai* was one, wasn't it?' Lalmohan Babu smiled politely. 'I don't like serious books at all,' Mr Naskar continued. 'All I ever read are thrillers. What are you writing now?'

'Nothing at this moment. I'm here simply on a holiday. My latest book was published only a couple of months ago. *Dumbstruck in Damascus* it was called.'

'Another best-seller?'

'Well . . . four thousand copies have been sold already, heh heh.'

Mr Naskar smiled and turned to Peter. 'Have you thought any more about my proposal?' he asked, coming straight to the point.

'I've decided to sell the ruby.'

'That's excellent.'

'But not to you.'

'Are you selling it to Dandania?'

'Yes, since his was the first offer I received.'

'No, Mr Robertson. You will sell your ruby to me.'

'How is that possible, Mr Naskar? I've told Dandania already. My mind is made up.'

'I'll tell you how it's going to be possible. You don't believe me, do you? All right, let's get someone totally impartial to explain things. Mr Ganguli!'

'Y-yes?' Lalmohan Babu looked up, startled.

'Do you mind stepping forward and standing here on this rug?'

'M-me?'

'Yes. I want you as you have no interest in the ruby, and you've got a pleasant, amiable nature.'

'What has that to do with anything?'

'Don't be afraid, Mr Ganguli. You'll come to no harm, I promise you. The thing is, you see, I haven't yet told you of a special skill that I acquired years ago. I can hypnotize people, and get them to give me correct answers to vexing questions. The reason for this is that when a person's been hypnotized, he temporarily loses the ability to make things up and tell lies. This ability, that comes naturally to most people, is replaced by an extraordinary power. A hypnotized person always tells the truth. I'll soon prove this to you.'

Before Lalmohan Babu got a chance to protest, Mr Naskar caught him by his shoulders and dragged him to stand on a rug in the middle of the room. Then he switched off all the lights and took out a small red torch from his pocket. I glanced at Feluda, but found him watching the scene with an impassive face. I knew he sometimes quite enjoyed it if anyone involved Lalmohan Babu in a bit of harmless fun.

Mr Naskar switched on the torch and shone it on Lalmohan Babu's face, moving it slowly. 'Look at this carefully, Mr Ganguli,' he whispered, 'and forget everything else. You are about to become a totally different person . . . a new man with a special magical power to tell the truth . . . that no one knows but you . . . just you . . . yes, yes, yes, yes . . .'

Lalmohan Babu's eyes soon began to look glazed. He stared into space unseeingly. His mouth fell open. Mr Naskar stopped moving the torch, but did not switch it off. After a few seconds of silence, he asked his first question.

'What is your name?'

'Mr Know All, alias Lalmohan Ganguli, alias Jatayu.'

Mr Know All? I had never heard anyone call him that!

'How many people are present in this room?'

'Six.'

'Are they all Indian?'

'No, there are two Englishmen among them.'

'What are their names?'

'Peter Robertson and Tom Maxwell.'

'Where in England do they come from?'

'Lancashire.'

'How old are they?'

'Peter is thirty-four years and three months. Tom's age is thirty-three years and nine months.'

'Why are they visiting India?'

'Peter wants to return Robertson's Ruby to India.'

'Who has actually got the ruby?'

'Tom Maxwell.'

'What is the future of this ruby?

'It will be sold.'

'To Ganesh Dandania?'

'No.'

'But he's already made an offer, hasn't he?

'Yes, but he'll go back on his word. He'll now offer only seven lakhs for it.'

'And Peter won't sell his ruby to him. Is that what you're saying?'

'Yes.'

'Then who will he sell it to?'

'Ardhendu Naskar.'

'For how much?'

'Twelve lakhs.'

'Thank you, sir.'

Mr Naskar switched the torch off and shook Lalmohan Babu gently. I saw him give a start. By the time Mr Naskar came back to his chair after turning the lights back on again, Lalmohan Babu was once more his normal self.

'Well, Mr Robertson?' Mr Naskar asked.

'That was most impressive,' Peter replied.

'Now do you believe me?'

'I don't know what to think.'

'You needn't think at all. I am in no great hurry. Go and see Dandania tomorrow. Sell your ruby for seven lakhs, if you so wish. However, should you change your mind, my own offer of twelve lakhs still stands.'

Peter was spared the necessity of making a reply by the arrival of Mr Naskar's cook. 'Dinner has been served,' he announced.

We rose and made our way to the dining room.

SEVEN

We left for Phulberey after a most sumptuous meal. By the time we got there, it was a quarter past ten. A crowd had gathered in a large open field. Not many of them were Santhals; obviously, people from towns nearby had arrived to see the dance. The full moon and torches that burnt here and there made it possible to see everything clearly.

Inspector Chaubey emerged from the crowd. 'You'll find many other familiar figures here,' he informed us.

'Why, who else has turned up?'

'I saw Kishorilal and Chandu Mallik. And that gentleman who's an expert on Birbhum.'

'Jagannath Chatterjee. Well, that's good news. When is the dance going to start?'

'Any minute now. Look, the dancers are all standing together.'

Feluda spotted Peter. 'Don't get lost, Peter,' he called. 'If we don't stay relatively close to each other, going back together won't be easy.'

I saw Tom getting his camera ready with a flash gun. Mr Naskar, too, was holding a small camera in his hand. 'Do you have a studio of your own?' he asked Tom.

'No. I am not a studio photographer. I take photographs while I travel. I only do freelance work. My photos have been printed in several magazines and journals. In fact, this assignment in India is being paid for by the *National Geographic*.'

The drums began to roll. All of us moved forward to get a better view. About thirty women, dressed in their traditional costume and jewellery, were standing in a semicircle, holding hands and swaying gently to the rhythm of the music. Two men playing flutes sat with the drummers. The drummers wore bells around their ankles.

Lalmohan Babu came and stood by my side. 'Now my left eye is twitching. Heaven knows what's in store,' he muttered.

'Getting hypnotized didn't have any adverse effects on you, I hope?' I asked.

'No, no. It's been an amazing experience, you know. I can't remember even a single word that I spoke.'

In the light of a torch, I saw Chandu Mallik smoking a beedi and moving slowly in the direction of the dancers. But no. It was not the dancers he was interested in. He had seen Tom, and was sneaking up to him.

'We must keep an eye on him, Lalmohan Babu,' I whispered.

'Yes, you're quite right.'

But Tom had moved from where he had been standing to a different spot, possibly to get a better angle. Were all photographers restless like him?

Chandu Mallik came and stood in front of us. He was frowning. His hands were stuffed into his pockets. Then he moved on in a different direction. Our group dispersed gradually. Lalmohan Babu and I stayed together, trying to spot the others for we were all supposed to regroup once the dance was over. There was Feluda in the distance. Chaubey had been standing next to him even a moment ago, but now I couldn't see him. Mr Naskar was busy clicking; I saw his camera flash more than once. The dancers were still swaying with a slow and easy grace.

Suddenly, I saw Kishorilal approaching Peter. What was he going to tell him? Curious, I left Lalmohan Babu and moved forward to hear their conversation.

'Good evening,' Peter said to Kishorilal. 'Our appointment tomorrow still stands, I hope?'

'Oh yes.'

'Your father's not likely to change his mind, is he?'

'No, sir. His mind is made up.'

'Good.'

Kishorilal left. Jagannath Chatterjee took his place.

'Hello, Mr Chatterjee,' greeted Peter. 'I'm glad I've run into you. Will you please explain to me the purpose of this dance? I mean, does this signify anything?'

'Why, certainly,' Mr Chatterjee came closer and began explaining various aspects of tribal culture. I returned to rejoin Lalmohan Babu.

Feluda was now standing near a burning torch. I saw him light a cigarette. The first dance came to an end, and the second one began. The rhythm of this one was much faster, and a group of singers joined the drummers. The dancers increased their pace to match the rhythm, bending and straightening their bodies, their feet rising and falling in a uniform pattern.

'Very exciting,' remarked Lalmohan Babu.

Mr Naskar passed us by, camera in hand. 'How do you like it?' he asked, but moved on without waiting for an answer.

Feldua saw us and walked across.

'Why, Felu Babu,' Lalmohan Babu asked, 'why are you frowning even on a joyous occasion like this? Those drummers are really playing well, aren't they?'

'Yes, but there's something not quite right over here. I feel distinctly uneasy. Have you seen Tom Maxwell?'

'I saw him a few minutes ago. But I don't know where he went.'

'We must find him,' said Feluda and moved to the left.

'Your cousin needs our help, I think,' Lalmohan Babu said to me and leapt forward to follow Feluda, dragging me with him. In a few seconds, we found ourselves behind the dancers. The crowd was thinner here. I could see Chandu Mallik and Kishorilal roaming about. Where was Tom?

There was Peter, standing alone and looking around. 'Have you seen Tom?' he asked Feluda.

'No, we've been looking for him, too.'

'I don't like this at all.'

Peter moved off in one direction to look for Tom. We went to the other side. Feluda soon got lost in the crowd. The music and the dancing were getting faster every minute, but there was no time to stop and enjoy it. Feluda reappeared suddenly. 'Chaubey? Have you seen him?' he asked anxiously.

'No. Why, Feluda, what's—?'

But he was already a few steps ahead of us, calling, 'Inspector Chaubey! Inspector Chaubey!'

Chaubey must have been standing somewhere close by, for only a minute later, he and Feluda came out of the crowd and began hurrying away.

'What's the matter?' Lalmohan Babu asked, struggling to keep pace with them.

'Maxwell,' Feluda replied briefly.

We broke into a run. Feluda stopped abruptly near a tree. A torch was burning about ten feet away. In its light, we saw Tom Maxwell lying on the ground. His camera and his bag containing other equipment were lying on the grass beside him.

'Is he . . . is he dead?' Chaubey asked, breathing hard.

'No,' Feluda replied, bending over Tom and taking one of his wrists between his fingers, 'I can feel his pulse. He is not dead . . . at least, not yet.'

Chaubey took out a small torch from his pocket and shone it on Tom's face. His eyes seemed to flicker for a second. Feluda shook him by his shoulders.

'Tom! Maxwell!'

At this moment, another figure tore through the crowd and came up panting. It was Peter. 'What's the matter with Tom? My God, is he . . . he's not . . . ?'

'No, he's just unconscious. But I think he's coming round.'

Tom had begun to stir. Now he opened his eyes, wincing. 'Where does it hurt?' Feluda asked urgently. With an effort, Tom raised a hand to indicate a spot at the back of his head.

In the meantime, Peter had picked up his bag and looked inside. He glanced up, the pallor on his face clearly visible even in the semi-darkness.

'The ruby is gone!' he cried hoarsely.

We returned to Mr Naskar's house with Tom. When told about the theft, Mr Naskar's face became a study in fury and disappointment.

'You should be happy!' he snapped. 'You got what you wanted, didn't you? Robertson's Ruby came back to India all right, though now you'll never be able to go on that world tour.'

One Dr Sinha from the neighbourhood was called to examine Tom.

'There is a swelling on his head where he was struck. Someone attacked him with a heavy object,' Dr Sinha said.

'Could this blow have killed him?' Peter wanted to know.

'Yes, if his attacker had hit him harder, your friend might well have been killed. But that did not happen, so please don't dwell on it. Give him an ice-pack which will help the swelling to subside. If the pain gets very bad, take a pain-killer, Mr Maxwell. There's nothing else to be done at this moment. Don't worry though. You'll recover soon enough.'

Chaubey opened his mouth when Dr Sinha had gone.

'Mr Maxwell,' he said, 'you didn't actually get to see who attacked you, did you?'

'No, I didn't.'

'I wonder what his motive was. To steal the ruby? But not too many people knew the ruby was with Tom Maxwell, and not Peter

Robertson. In fact, the only people who knew this fact were Mr Mitter, Mr Ganguli, Tapesh, Kishorilal, Jagannath Chatterjee, Mr Naskar and myself.'

'What are you saying, Inspector?' Mr Naskar protested. 'I would have got that stone, anyway. Why should I do something absurd like this? Why, for heaven's sake, Tom might have been killed! Would I risk being charged with murder when all I had to do was just wait for another day?'

'It's no use arguing, Mr Naskar. You are a prime suspect. What Mr Ganguli said when he was supposedly hypnotized is of no consequence. After all, there was no guarantee that his words would come true, was there? There was every chance of that ruby being sold to someone else. We all know it was no ordinary ruby, and you are no ordinary collector. So why shouldn't I assume that you tried to get there first, without paying a paisa for it?'

'Nonsense! Nonsense!' said Mr Naskar, just a little feebly.

'Apart from yourself, there's Kishorilal to be considered,' Chaubey went on. 'His father was going to buy it, but that would not have been of any use to Kishori. He knew its value, and he knew where to find it. So if he found Maxwell alone, he might simply have given in to temptation, who knows? . . . A third suspect is Chandu Mallik. He had already threatened to settle scores with Tom. But did he know about the ruby? I don't think so. If he did find it, it must have been by accident. After knocking Tom down, he might have slipped his hand into his bag to look for money, and come across the ruby. This possibility cannot be ruled out . . . Then there is Jagannath Chatterjee. He knew about the ruby and where it was kept. Pure greed might have prompted him to remove it.'

'You have left out one important suspect, Inspector,' Feluda said.

'Who?'

'Peter Robertson.'

'What!' Peter jumped to his feet.

'Yes, Peter. You had wanted to hand over the ruby to the museum in Calcutta. Your friend opposed the idea. You agreed to sell it because you didn't want to lose your friend. But who's to say you didn't change your mind? What if you went back to your original decision and found a way of getting the ruby back without risking your friendship with Tom?'

Peter stared at Feluda, rendered speechless for the moment. Then he raised his arms over his head and said slowly, 'There is a very simple way to find out if I'm the culprit. If I did indeed take the ruby back, I would still have it with me, wouldn't I? I mean, I have been with all of your throughout since we found Tom. So search me, Inspector Chaubey. Come on, search me!'

'Very well,' said Chaubey and searched Peter thoroughly. He found nothing.

'All right, Inspector,' Feluda said. 'Since you took the trouble to search Peter, I think you should do the same for each one of us.' Chaubey seemed to hesitate. 'Come along now, Inspector, there is no reason to leave us out,' Feluda said again. This time, Chaubey stepped forward and searched everyone in the room, including me. Still he didn't find the ruby.

'Mr Robertson,' he asked, 'would you like me to carry out an official investigation?'

'Of course!' Peter said firmly. 'I want that ruby back at any cost.'

EIGHT

Tom seemed a lot better in the morning. He was still in pain, but the swelling had gone down and, hopefully, in a couple of days he'd recover completely.

But he couldn't get over the shock of having lost the precious ruby. 'I never thought I'd have to leave that stone here with an unknown criminal,' Peter kept saying.

'Oh, why didn't we sell it to Dandania the first day?' moaned Tom time and again. It was difficult to tell who was more sorry at the loss.

Inspector Chaubey came to our room around 11 a.m.

'I've just been to see Tom,' he said.

'Tom's doing fine. Have you made any progress?' Feluda asked.

'One of the suspects has had to be eliminated from my list.'

'Really?' Who?'

'Kishorilal.'

'Why?'

'Well, I happen to know Kishori pretty well. It's not like him to do anything so reckless. Besides, his father has recently bought him a plastics factory. Kishori has been going there regularly. Dandania, I know, keeps a careful eye on his son. If Kishori stole that ruby simply to sell it and make a packet for himself, his father would most certainly come to know, and then there would be hell to pay. So

Kishori is out.'

'I see. What about Chandu Malik?'

'As far as I can make out, Maxwell was attacked at around a quarter to eleven last night. Chandu had left the dance before that and was sitting with friends having a drink in a small shop. There are several witnesses who'd vouch for him. I've already spoken to most of them. That rules out Chandu, too.'

'And the others?'

'I searched Naskar's house this morning. I didn't find the ruby, of course, but that doesn't mean a thing. He could easily have hidden it somewhere else. But I have started to think Jagannath Chatterjee is our best bet.'

'Why do you say that?'

'He claims to be an authority on Birbhum. But he's lived here only for the last three years. My guess is that he's no expert at all. All his information probably comes from a guide book for tourists. Besides, I discovered he'd been arrested for fraud in Burdwan where he used to live before. He's a criminal, Mr Mitter. I'm convinced he's our man. Did you know he was charging a fee for his services? Yes, sir. Mr Robertson paid him a hundred rupees each time he met him!'

'No, I did not know that. Have you searched his house?'

'No, but I will this afternoon, though I don't think a search will yield anything. What I have to do is speak to him sternly and put the fear of God in him. Anyway, aren't you going to do anything?'

'No. Any action you as a police officer may take will have a lot more effect, I think. But I'll keep my eyes and ears open, naturally, and will let you know if I notice anything suspicious. Oh, by the way, what about the fifth suspect I mentioned?'

'You mean Peter Robertson?'

'Yes. I have a feeling Peter would now accept the loss of an old friendship, if need be. What is important to him is that his ancestor's wish be fulfilled. He's changed his mind about selling that ruby. I know he has.'

'Yes, you said so last night, didn't you? I remembered your words, Mr Mitter, and I searched Peter Robertson's room only a few minutes before I came here. Need I tell you there was no sign of the ruby?'

Feluda made no reply. Inspector Chaubey rose. 'I'll come and see you again in the evening,' he said and left.

'A most complicated case,' Feluda sighed. 'Five suspects . . . all strewn in five different places. What can I do from here? The police have certainly got the upper hand this time.'

'Come on, Felu Babu, you're not even trying. Tell us who you really suspect,' said Lalmohan Babu.

'Out of these five?'

'Yes.'

'I had ruled out Kishorilal for the simple reason that he didn't strike me as the type who'd resort to violence to get what he wanted. He hasn't got the courage it would take to knock someone out, steal something from his bag and run away, especially when there were so many people about.'

'What about Chandu Mallik?'

'Chandu might have hit Maxwell—he's quite capable of having done that—but how could he have known that the ruby was in his bag? No, Chandu did not do it. Mr Naskar? It's difficult to imagine him getting into a messy business like this. There was absolutely no need for him to go to such lengths; not with the kind of money he's got.'

'There's something I don't understand at all,' Lalmohan Babu confessed.

'What is it?'

'Do people always speak the truth when they're hypnotized?'

'What is the truth you're supposed to have spoken?'

'Why, didn't I tell you all how old Peter and Tom were, and that they came from Lancashire? They never mentioned it to me, so how did I know? Mind you, I don't remember having said it, but Tapesh says I did.'

'Both those facts had been mentioned in that article in the *Statesman*. Even if you didn't read the whole thing, Lalmohan Babu, your memory had somehow absorbed those details, and it came out when you were asked a specific question. Everything else you said has already been proved to be quite incorrect. So please don't go around thinking you had acquired any extraordinary powers at any time.'

'All right, Felu Babu, point taken. But do you agree with Inspector Chaubey? Was it Jagannath Chatterjee?'

'Who else could it be? It's such a pity the whole thing had to end so tamely, but . . .' Feluda couldn't finish his sentence. Someone knocked on the door.

It turned out to be Tom Maxwell, looking rather grim. Feluda offered him a chair, but he shook his head.

'I haven't come to sit down and chat with you,' he said.

'I see.'

'I am here to search your room and your friend's.'

'But we were all searched yesterday. Wasn't that good enough for you?'

'No. You were searched by an Indian policeman. I have no faith in him.'

'Do you have a warrant? Surely you're aware that you cannot search anyone's room without a proper warrant?'

'You mean you won't let me—?'

'No, Mr Maxwell. Neither my friend nor I will let you go through our things. Inspector Chaubey searched each one of us yesterday, in your presence. You'll have to be satisfied with that.'

Tom made an about-turn without another word and strode out of the room.

'Just imagine!' Lalmohan Babu exclaimed. 'I have been on so many cases with you, Felu Babu, but I've never ended up as one of the suspects!'

'Put it down to experience, Mr Ganguli. It's good to have all sorts of experiences, isn't it?'

'Yes, that's true. But are you going to spend all your time indoors?'

'I'll go out if I feel like it. Right now all I want to do is think, and I can do that very well without stirring out of my room. But that's no reason why you and Topshe shouldn't go out. There's a lot still left to be seen.'

'Very well. Let's go and get hold of Shatadal. He may be able to make some useful suggestions. Tell you what, Felu Babu. I'll leave that book with you, the one that Shatadal lent me. Read it. You'll get a lot of information about Tom Maxwell's ancestor. And if you wish to learn about how indigo was grown and what the British did with it, this book will tell you that, too.'

'Thank you, Lalmohan Babu. I should love to read your book.'

We left soon after this, leaving Feluda to go through what Rev Pritchard had written. Shatadal Sen happened to be free, and offered to take us to see a village by the river Kopai, which Tagore used to watch and admire. I had seen villages and rivers before, but there was something about Kopai and the village called Goalpara that touched my heart and lifted my spirits instantly.

Lalmohan Babu went a step further and began reciting poetry.

'My favourite poet, Baikuntha Mallik, visited Santikiniketan, you see, and wrote quite a few poems on its natural beauty,' he told me. 'Listen to this:

O Kopai, thin you might be,
but you're fast.
May your beauty forever last,
you are a pleasure to see.

Rice fields lie by your sides,
nature's bounty in them hides,
etching pictures in my memory.
Kopai, you are a pleasure to see.'

NINE

Inspector Chaubey returned to our room at 5 p.m. The announcement he made wasn't altogether unexpected, but nevertheless we were all somewhat taken aback.

'The mystery is cleared up,' he said. 'I was right. Jagannath Chatterjee took the stone. When I searched his house, I didn't find it at first; but a few threats from the police can often work wonders, as they did in this case. Chatterjee broke down and confessed in the end. He even returned the stone to me. Do you know where he had hidden it? In a flower-pot!'

'Have you brought it here?'

'Yes, naturally.'

Chaubey took it out of his pocket. It lay on his palm, glowing softly under the light. It felt strange to look at it.

'How very odd!' Feluda exclaimed.

'What's odd?'

'Chatterjee might well be a thief, but somehow I can't see him lifting a heavy object and striking someone with it. He wouldn't have the nerve, Inspector. He doesn't look the type.'

'Don't judge anyone by his looks, Mr Mitter.'

'Yes, you're right. My own experience has taught me just that. And yet . . .' Feluda broke off, frowning.

'Shall we go now and return this stone to its owner?' Chaubey asked.

'Yes, let's do that.'

We left our room and made our way to Peter's. Peter himself opened the door. Tom was with him.

'Well, Mr Robertson,' said Chaubey, 'I have a little gift for you.'

'A gift?'

Silently, Chaubey handed the ruby back to Peter. Peter's mouth fell open.

'I don't believe this! Where—how—?'

'Never mind all that, Mr Robertson. Just be happy that you've got it back. Mr Maxwell,' I hope you'll now agree that the Indian police isn't altogether stupid and incompetent. Anyway, now you must decide what you want to do with it.'

Peter and Tom had both risen to their feet. Now they sank back into their chairs. Peter said softly, 'Good show, Inspector. Congratulations!'

'Thanks. May I now take your leave?' asked Chaubey.

'I . . . I don't know how to thank you!' Tom spoke unexpectedly.

'You don't have to. That the thought of saying thanks crossed your mind is good enough for me. Goodbye!'

'What are you thinking, Felu Babu?' Lalmohan Babu asked over breakfast the next day.

'There is something wrong . . . somewhere . . .' muttered Feluda absent-mindedly.

'I'll tell you what's wrong. For the first time, the police caught the criminal before you. The inspector won, Felu Babu, and you lost. That's what's wrong.'

'No. The thing is, you see, I cannot believe that the case is over, and there's nothing for me to do.'

Feluda grew preoccupied again. Then he said, 'Topshe, why don't you and Lalmohan Babu go for a walk? I need to be alone. I need to think again.'

'We can sit in my room. Come on, Tapesh.'

'I don't like this, Tapesh, my boy,' Lalmohan Babu said, offering me a chair in his room. 'We got such a good opportunity to solve a mystery, and yet it just slipped through our fingers. Maybe it's because my left eye was twitching? No, I mean seriously, is your cousin all right? He looked tired, as though he hadn't slept very well.'

'He sat up late reading the book you gave him. I don't know what time he went to bed, but he was up at five this morning to do his yoga.'

'Topshe!' called Feluda from outside. His voice sounded urgent. Why had he followed us? Was anything wrong?

I opened the door quickly. Feluda rushed in and said, 'We have to go and see Chaubey, immediately.'

'What happened?'

'I'll tell you later.'

'OK.'

We were both ready to go out in just a few seconds.

'To Dubrajpur,' said Feluda to the driver. 'We need to find the police station there.'

This was not difficult. Our car went straight to the police station and stopped before the main gate. The constable on duty looked up enquiringly as we got out. 'May we see Inspector Chaubey?' Feluda asked.

'Yes, please come this way.'

Chaubey was in his room, going through some files. He looked up with a mixture of pleasure and surprise.

'Oh, what brings you here?'

'There is something we need to talk about.'

'Very well. Please sit down. Would you like a cup of tea?'

'No, thanks. We've just had breakfast.'

'I see. So what can I do for you?'

'There's just one thing I'd like you to tell me.'

'Yes?'

'Are you a Christian?'

Chaubey raised his eyebrows. Then he smiled and said, 'Why do you suddenly need to know that, Mr Mitter?'

'There's a reason. Are you?'

'Yes, I am a Christian. But how did you guess?'

'Well, I saw you eat with your left hand, more than once. At first I paid no attention, but later it struck me as odd since Hindus—unless they're left-handed—prefer using their right hands to eat. I wondered if you were a Christian, but didn't ask at the time for I didn't realize it might have a special significance. I think I now know what it means.'

'Really? So what does it signify, Mr Mitter? You didn't come all this way just to tell me you'd guessed my religion, did you?'

'No. Allow me to ask you another question.'

'Go ahead.'

'Who was the first in your family to become a Christian?'

'My grandfather.'

'What was his name?'

'Anant Narayan.'

'What was his son called?'

'Charles Premchand.'

'And his son?'

'Richard Shankar Prasad.'

'That's you, isn't it?'

'Yes.'

'Was your great-grandfather called Hiralal?'

'Yes, but how did you—?'

Chaubey had stopped smiling. He only looked amazed and bewildered.

'It was the same Hiralal who used to pull the *punkha* for Reginald Maxwell. Am I right?'

'Yes, but you have to tell me how you learnt all this.'

'From a book written by a Rev. Pritchard. He took charge of Anant Narayan after Hiralal's death, made him a Christian and helped him build a new life and find new happiness.'

'I didn't know there was such a book!'

'Indeed there is, though it's not easily available.'

'But if you know all that, you must have . . .'

'What?'

'You must know . . .'

'What, Inspector? What should I know?'

'Why don't you tell me yourself, Mr Mitter? I would find it extremely awkward to say anything myself.'

'All right,' said Feluda slowly, 'I'll tell you what happened. You grew up hearing tales of Reginald Maxwell's cruelty. You could never forget that he was responsible for your great-grandfather's death. But there was nothing you could do about it. However, when you heard Reginald's great-great-grandson Tom was here and saw that Tom had inherited Reginald's arrogance and hatred for Indians in full measure, you . . .'

'Stop, Mr Mitter! Please say no more.'

'Does that mean I am right in thinking that it was you who struck

Tom at the dance, just because you felt like settling old scores? And then you took the stone so that the suspicion fell on the others?'

'Yes, Mr Mitter, you are absolutely right. Now you must decide how I ought to be punished. If you wish to report the matter—'

'Inspector Chaubey,' Feluda suddenly smiled. 'I wish to do no such thing. That is what I came to tell you.'

'What!'

'Yes, sir. I thought the whole thing over and realized that had I been in your shoes, I'd have done exactly the same. In fact, I think Tom's behaviour called for something much worse than what you did to him. Relax, Inspector. Nobody's going to punish you.'

'Thank you, Mr Mitter, thank you!'

'Which one of your eyes is twitching now, Mr Know-All Ganguli?'

'Both, Felu Babu, both. They're dancing with joy. But we mustn't forget one thing.'

'I know what you mean.'

'What do I mean?'

'We mustn't forget to thank your friend Shatadal Sen.'

'Correct. If he hadn't lent us that book—'

'—We couldn't have solved this case—'

'—And Jagannath Chatterjee would have remained a criminal'

'At least in our minds.'

'Yes. To Mr Sen's house, please driver, before you take us back to the lodge.'

Robertson's Ruby eventually went to the Calcutta Museum. Needless to say, Feluda played an important role in the actual transfer. He pointed out to Peter that Tom was simply being greedy. If he could get sponsorship from a famous journal like the *National Geographic,* he couldn't, by any means, be lacking in funds.

Tom Maxwell did his best to influence his friend's decision again, but this time Peter was adamant.

Patrick Robertson's last wish was finally fulfilled.